THE

FOURTH REICH

ROBERT VAN KAMPEN

A DELL BOOK

Published by
Dell Publishing
a division of
Random House, Inc.
1540 Broadway
New York, New York 10036

Scripture quotations are from the New American Standard Version.

Cover photo copyright © 2000 by Archive Photos/PNI

Dell® is a registered trademark of Random House, Inc., and the colophon is a trademark of Random House, Inc.

ISBN-13: 978-0-440-23607-8

ISBN-10: 0-440-23607-X

Reprinted by arrangement with Baker Book House Company

Printed in the United States of America

Published simultaneously in Canada

January 2000

10 9 8 7 6 5 4 3 2 1

OPM

"I AM ALIVE!" HITLER SHOUTED. "I AM RISEN FROM THE DEAD!"

The delegates erupted in wild confusion, but the man on the platform held his salute while he waited for silence.

"In 1945 my last words were 'Wait for the coming man.' Today I have arrived. I have come again to save the world. By my death, you shall be forgiven. By my life, you shall be delivered. The All-Powerful One has sent me to give you peace and prosperity! Upon his authority, *I* will rule the world."

He stopped speaking. A hush fell over the auditorium. Then he whispered into the microphone. "But never forget this one thing: The All-Powerful One, father of all, has also sent me to cleanse the world of all unrighteousness! To rid the world of rebels who prefer their God to my god, their leaders over my leadership. These are the blemishes of evolution! They must be eliminated! What I failed to accomplish at my first coming, I *will* accomplish this time!"

With that, the number "666" suddenly appeared in an iridescent red, hanging as it were, without support, in space above the Nazi flag for all to see.

To my wife, Judy
For her love for me, our family, and for Christ.

I wish to thank my wife, Judy, and my three daughters, Kristen Wisen, Karla Van Kampen-Pierre, and Kim Van Kampen, for all the help they were in writing *The Fourth Reich*. All four have sat patiently through many of my prophecy classes, and their thorough knowledge of the sequence and timing of endtime events was critical in plotting this novel, as their gifted, creative minds helped me develop the characters and storyline.

In addition, my wife, bless her heart, had to put up with a husband who has been consumed with this project for over a year and a half. She covered for me when I was writing, and must have read the manuscript through ten times before letting me send it off to the professional editors.

And last, but certainly not least, I must thank Frank Simon and Judith Markham; Frank for his incredible, creative flair and Judith for her rewrite skills that let me say the same thing in 30 percent fewer words! Without their giftedness, this novel would probably sound more like an instruction manual for the military! For being so patient with me, and for your creative writing and rewriting, thank you!

PROLOGUE

The weak red orb of the sun hovered low over the eastern horizon, as if it hadn't the strength to rise any higher. A wintry blast of arctic wind rocked the black limousine as the driver skidded the vehicle onto the road leading to a delivery gate at Moscow's Sheremetyevo I Airport.

In the broad back seat, separated from the driver by a glass panel, a woman sat huddled beside her husband. Feeling her shiver, Georgi Belov patted his wife's hand.

"Your hands are freezing, my dear."

"I am worried, Georgi. Are we doing the right thing?"

Belov closed his eyes momentarily, struggling to hide his irritation. "We've been through this many times, Olga. We both want children, but the doctors tell us you cannot conceive. Fortunately, there are things that can be done."

"Yes, I know. I only wish I didn't have to leave Russia. What if something goes wrong?"

"This is the only way, Olga. This particular in-vitro process is new. None of our Russian doctors do it yet." He did not add that the DNA fertilization procedure was also still experimental in Germany.

"I wish you were coming with me."

"If I could, I would, darling, but you know my duties will not permit it. I will be along in two weeks." He patted her knee. "Although the procedure is new, the father must still provide his contribution." His attempt at humor brought no smile to her face. "Olga, you must be brave. Will you—for me?"

She nodded, but continued to look down at her hands, clasped tightly together in black leather gloves.

"Now cheer up, Olga. Think of our future son—or daughter."

The driver pulled up at the gate and rolled down his window. Belov watched through the glass partition as the man held out the security papers to the Federal Security Bureau guard. The guard examined them under the feeble glow of the single light bulb over his tiny shack, then glanced quickly toward the passengers. As he shoved the papers back through the window, the guard stiffened into the stance of a salute. Belov gave him a stern nod as they drove through the gate and onto the tarmac.

Mechanics and other personnel moved among the parked aircraft, service vehicles, and refueling trucks as the busy airport prepared for the day's flights to domestic destinations. The driver stopped the limousine at the stairs leading up to the Antonov 24V's doors and stepped out to open the rear door for his passengers.

"Time for you to go, my dear," Belov said. He kissed Olga lightly on the lips.

"I will miss you."

"I will miss you, too, but you have nothing to worry about. I have arranged for everything."

"Yes, I know. Thank you, Georgi."

He squeezed her hand, then stepped out onto the tarmac. He helped her from the limousine and escorted her to the bottom of the stairs that led up to the aircraft door. Above, in the doorway of the plane, a uniformed flight attendant waited, a bored expression on his face.

Belov watched as his wife made her way up the stairs, clutching her black cloth coat around her against the cold. As soon as she entered the cabin, the ground crew pulled the stairs away while the flight attendant closed the door of the aircraft. Belov settled himself once more in the limousine and leaned into the leather comfort of the seat as his driver turned the vehicle and headed back to the city.

Dr. Karl Fischer pushed his black-rimmed glasses back up the bridge of his nose and nervously checked the microscope once more. Then he straightened up, rubbed the back of his tired neck, and exhaled an impatient breath into the sterile surgical mask. It was well past midnight and he had not moved from this spot in several hours.

Fischer had been introduced to the project the preceding year. The research project had been interesting when it began, but it soon took on the distinctly unpleasant odor of political intrigue when a Dr. Otto Heine arrived at Fischer's genetics lab, bearing frozen samples of skull fragments in a box with Russian lettering. Inside, he found a small tag attached to the lip of the sample bags; it read, "Berlin, 4 May 1945."

Much about Dr. Heine disturbed Fischer, but the man's offer proved irresistible: In exchange for the successful extraction of viable cell nuclei from the bone fragments, Fischer would be provided with a significant stipend, a blank check for equipment as well as personnel. Fischer's only restriction was an absolute prohibition of any discussion of the experiment, including publication of the results. The project had been classified as high-security government research. Still, Karl figured that what he learned he would remember.

Weary, but not ready to go home for the day, he again leaned over his microscope. His concentration was interrupted, however, when the lab door suddenly swung open. A small, intense figure entered with an air of authority. Dr. Otto Heine was a man totally devoid of patience or tact.

"Are we alone?" Heine barked.

"We are." Fischer barely refrained from rolling his eyes at the man's paranoia.

"Good. You have something to report, I understand."

"Yes. The extraction from the skull fragment was successful. I have examined the nuclei myself. They are viable." Fischer nodded at the microscope.

"Good," Heine said and leaned over to peer through the lens.

"Very good," he said a few moments later. "Stay here." Heine turned abruptly and, without formalities, made his exit.

Dr. Karl Fischer fumed. Blank-check grants or not, there were some things a research scientist should not have to endure from a glorified government worker. Heine's arrogance was beyond belief, even in these heady circles. Within min-utes, Heine returned. In his hand he carried a petri dish, which he gingerly placed beside the microscope. Fischer no-ticed the label attached beneath the clear laboratory dish.

"What is that?" Fischer asked. "Is it from the in-vitro lab? Why are *my* samples going to the in-vitro lab?" he asked.

Almost before the words left his lips, Heine whirled on him. Fischer made an involuntary step back when he saw the cold black eyes above the white surgical mask.

"I can see that you never leave this building," Heine said, threateningly. "Remember the papers you signed when the project began? You are to ask no questions—nothing! Do I make myself clear?"

Karl nodded.

"Very well. I will not warn you again!"

With that, Heine turned back to the table and as Fischer watched, initially in astonishment and then in chilling fear, the dark room began to be illuminated as an eerie purple glow surrounded the man standing in front of him. As the hue grew in intensity, Heine's features seemed to bulge and melt. His lab coat and mask disappeared, revealing a figure that only re-motely resembled a human being.

Karl backed farther and farther away toward the corner of the lab, wide-eyed and shaking, as the darkness revealed a hu-manoid face, with only the cruel eyes recognizable as those of the former man. The being seemed to tower over the petri dish. Suddenly, the glass dish containing the fertilized egg drifted upward into midair. Then the dish dropped away, leaving suspended in air a clear, mucus-like substance with a pinpoint in the center, growing before his very eyes. Soon the egg's details were clearly visible, with the nucleus in the center of it.

Responding to a simple hand motion by the dark being that moments before had been Dr. Heine, the single test tube that contained the DNA particles, extracted from the skull frag-ment, rocketed out of its rack and dumped its contents onto the magnified egg. The mass of DNA resolved itself into thou-sands of individual particles, which seemed to swarm around the egg beneath.

"Now!" the being rumbled.

The egg's nucleus quivered and shrank, turning black as it died inside its membrane. Then a single particle broke free of the DNA mass and penetrated the egg, replacing the egg's black nucleus that had been killed only seconds earlier. Suddenly the egg seemed to implode as it diminished rapidly in size.

Again, with only the slightest movement of the being's hand, the petri dish rose to catch the egg and surrounding liquid, after which the dish and test tube returned to their places.

At the same time, the dark being shrank and once again became the figure of Dr. Otto Heine. As if nothing unusual had happened, he turned to Karl and smiled. The rich voice boomed in the empty room. "You will, of course, remember the terms of our agreement."

It was a statement, not a question. Karl shivered and nodded, numbly wondering if he had been hallucinating in the lateness of the hour.

"Good."

Heine took the petri dish with him, leaving Dr. Karl Fischer alone with his thoughts.

Dr. Helmut Hauptmann looked toward the surgical suite's double doors. As if on cue, Dr. Otto Heine pushed through the doors, followed by a large young man whose brooding eyes peered above the surgical mask that covered his mouth and nose. The lights flickered once as the Bonn power grid struggled to keep up with the electricity demand on this frigid January morning.

"Who is this?" Hauptmann asked.

"Gerhardt Otterbein, my associate. He is here to observe this procedure," said Heine with finality. "Is everything ready, doctor?"

"The lab called a moment ago. They are loading the cannula now. The technician should be here shortly." He paused.

"Is something wrong?" Heine asked.

"I don't know. The lab reported only one viable egg. They were positive that four had been fertilized and were puzzled why the other three failed."

"We go with one. The others are of no importance."

"You realize, of course, this lessens the chances of success."

"Everything will go well," Heine said with a smile.

Hauptmann shrugged. He glanced down at his patient. The woman's chart identified her as thirty-five-year-old Gretchen Schluter. A sheet covered all but her face, but the doctor's first glance had told him this was no German frau. The high cheekbones and broad Slavic face probably belonged to a Russian.

So, Hauptmann thought, some important Russian official and his wife were having trouble conceiving. They must have high connections with the German government to get such priority treatment. Interesting and unusual, but not unheard of. Money or power, or both, can accomplish great things. It can get a woman in the family way if her husband cannot, Hauptmann mused, smiling to himself.

The double doors opened, and a young female technician came in bearing a sterile tray supporting a cannula attached to a syringe.

Hauptmann nodded to the surgical nurse, who lifted the sheet as he picked up the cannula and syringe and carefully inserted the tube into the woman's body.

When the procedure was completed, Hauptmann removed the tube.

"Take her to her room," he said to the nurse.

"Very good, doctor," Dr. Otto Heine observed as the doors swung closed behind the departing gurney.

"We will know soon. However, I fear our chances with this one are not as good, with only one viable egg."

"You have done better than you know," Heine said as he and his young associate turned and left the operating room.

That evening, Hauptmann thought briefly about Heine's enigmatic comment as he settled down before dinner with his whiskey and the evening paper. But his attention was diverted by the sight of a familiar face on the back page. Dr. Karl Fischer, from the research institute, had been found dead in his laboratory. The autopsy had identified the cause as a massive heart attack. Hauptmann put down the newspaper with a sigh and lifted his drink, pondering the brevity of human life.

Olga Belov screamed in the face of blinding pain.

"One more time," the nurse encouraged. "The head is out."

Olga summoned her remaining strength and pushed one more time.

The doctor said, "You have a son," as he pulled the child from her body.

Olga lay back in exhaustion, listening to her baby test his lungs.

The umbilical cord was tied off and cut and the infant wiped and wrapped.

"Can I see him?" Olga asked.

The nurse brought the baby around and placed him in the mother's arms. His pinched red face was squalling and his tiny fists were clenched, but Olga sighed with pleasure as she held her son.

"Only a few minutes," the doctor said, as another nurse entered the room. "Then he is off to the nursery. We want to check your new son carefully." He saw her worried expression. "Nothing to worry about. Just our usual procedure."

"Is Georgi here yet?"

"He got here a few minutes ago," said the nurse who had just arrived. "Now let me take this little guy to the nursery, and we'll get you cleaned up for your husband."

The following morning Olga awoke to a nightmare. The doctor who had delivered their child sadly informed the Belovs that their son had died during the night. They had tried everything to revive him, but to no avail. He took a long time to explain how these things can happen. Then he gave Olga a sedative and left the couple alone to share their grief.

Belov waited until his wife's sobs had subsided into fitful slumber. Then he tiptoed out and walked quickly to the waiting room. The large young man with dark brooding eyes who had been with his wife in the surgical room in Bonn, now watched him approach.

"Is it all arranged?" Belov asked with a sigh.

"It is. An appropriate substitute has been found. You did ask for cremation, did you not?"

Belov bristled. "I don't care what you do, but leave my wife out of it. She can't take any more."

"Very good," the man said. The cold eyes seemed to drill right through him. "You have served your country well."

"What will become of the boy?" Belov asked.

"That is something you will never know."

At that, the man turned and left the room. Belov never saw him again.

PART 1

THE BEGINNING OF THE END

And as He was sitting on the Mount of Olives,
the disciples came to Him privately, saying,
"Tell us, when will these things be,
and what will be the sign of Your coming,
and of the end of the age?"

—*Matthew 24:3*

ONE

Sonya Petrov stood in the center of the empty flat on the sixth floor of the Moscow tenement. Their new home consisted of three small bedrooms, a tiny living room separated from the cramped kitchen area by a table, and a small cubicle that was only a bit larger than the average closet, entirely taken up by a toilet and a tub.

Inside, their flat looked like every other one in the building. Outside, their building looked exactly like the other twenty gray concrete monoliths in the complex. Surrounding these stood hundreds of other architectural eyesores that were supposed to relieve the housing shortage in Moscow.

Potholed streets, dreary blocks of tenements with trashy common areas, horrible traffic jams in the city center—yes, Moscow remained much as Sonya remembered it, even after her nine-year absence. She looked at the depressing dark green wallpaper, noting one more thing she wanted changed. She knew she should be grateful that the state had permitted her three bedrooms, even though, put together, they didn't equal the size of a one-bedroom flat in Israel.

She ran a hand through her short auburn hair, then pressed both hands against the small of her back. As usual, the elevators were not working. Helping Yacov haul their furniture and other belongings up five flights from the street had strained even her well-toned muscles.

Though it was spring in Moscow, the weather was cold and

rainy. Sonya thought longingly of the hot sun and blue seas of the Mediterranean and the golden air of Jerusalem, which was unlike that of any other city. She and Yacov might still be in Israel if their father's health had not broken down completely. Vitali Petrov had been partially paralyzed for years, the result of a military accident when the loading carousel in a T–72 tank had snagged his uniform and bashed him around the turret. Miraculously he had survived, only to face several operations followed by ineffective rehabilitation treatments. Still, their indomitable and courageous father had managed to take care of himself until recently, when excruciating pain and weakness made it impossible for him to live alone. Though he was only in his late fifties, the years of pain and paralysis had taken their toll. Sonya and her brother loved their father too much to leave him in the hands of the uncaring state system. Bound by the promise to their father that they would not take him away from Mother Russia if he could not care for himself, Sonya and Yacov sacrificed the comforts of Israel for the care of their father.

Sonya and Yacov had made *aliya* to Israel almost nine years earlier, intending that this return to the land of their ancestors would be permanent. Each had completed degrees at Hebrew University in Jerusalem, Sonya in international relations and Yacov in computer science. Both had served in the Israel Defense Forces, although Sonya's military career had been the more visible and distinguished. Her leadership and daring had been quickly recognized, and by the end of her four years in the IDF, she had become a respected leader. On the basis of the highest recommendations possible, she had been recruited by the Shabak—the intelligence unit of the Israeli Police Force. Her outstanding work for the Shabak had again, as before, received the highest notice. When she left Israel to return to Russia, she was reporting directly to Prime Minister Shefi himself.

Yacov, although four years older, had always seemed to stand in Sonya's shadow, yet without resentment. Since the day she was born and their mother died giving birth, he had looked after his little sister. He loved her dearly and was prouder of her success than was Sonya herself. Wherever

Sonya was, Yacov was always close by. So much so, that he had spent the past three years putting his computer skills to use in the code encryption division of military intelligence, enabling him to work in the same building as Sonya.

She smiled now, remembering the headiness of reporting directly to the prime minister. She had always had remarkable success in her career, despite her youth—and loved every minute of it. Indeed, without her personal relationship with the prime minister, she and Yacov would never have been allowed to return to Russia. She owed Prime Minister Shefi, and she would not forget her debt.

"You ready for me to bring Papa up?" Yacov asked, as he stacked two more boxes inside the door, snapping her out of her reverie.

"I think so," she said. "He can rest on the couch until I make his bed. How are you doing?"

Yacov's brown eyes twinkled beneath his mop of curly brown hair. "I am hot and smell like a Moscow public toilet, but I will survive. And you, little sister?"

"I wish I could say it is nice to be here."

"I know. But this is still our home."

"Israel is our home," she said, her brown eyes flashing.

"But there is Papa," he said.

"Yes, there is Papa." Her mouth softened into a smile.

Yacov grinned and disappeared, his long strides taking him to the closest stairwell, cluttered with trash since no one assumed responsibility to clean it up. Fifteen minutes later he returned, carrying the slight form of Vitali Petrov.

"Here we go, Papa," he gasped, as he lowered his father to the couch and tried to catch his breath. "Sonya is preparing your bed."

"Thank you, Yacov," Vitali said, trying not to show his pain.

"The bed's ready," Sonya called.

Yacov hoisted his father in his arms once more and carried him into the small bedroom where there was barely enough space for the single bed and wooden bureau. Yacov settled his father on the bed and straightened his soft gray sweatsuit while Sonya pulled the well-worn quilt over Vitali and kissed him on the forehead as he smiled up at her.

"Get some rest, Papa," she whispered.

Vitali nodded and closed his eyes.

Sonya and Yacov closed the door behind them, then stood there surveying the chaos and clutter of moving. Boxes covered the floor and furniture, crammed in wherever there was space.

Sonya sighed. "We are never going to fit everything into this place."

"Do you regret coming back?" Yacov asked.

"We had to, for Papa's sake."

"That's not exactly what I asked."

Sonya exhaled sharply, then shrugged her shoulders as an irritated scowl wrinkled her forehead. With Yacov, there was no need to hide her frustration and disappointment.

"I will miss it too," Yacov admitted. "*Aliya* was the right thing to do. But . . ."

"Family comes first," Sonya finished for him. "And it does. I know that. We're the only ones who care about Papa. If we don't take care of him . . ."

Yacov nodded and slumped down on the couch to rest for a few minutes, while Sonya started pacing the narrow trails between the untidy towers of boxes. She examined a few of the labels and looked around the room, mentally unpacking.

A sharp knock broke the silence. Yacov jumped up in surprise. "Who could that be?" he said. "Hopefully not another security check!"

He wended his way to the door, unlocked it, and pulled it open just wide enough to peer cautiously into the corridor. A tall man stood in the dim hallway.

Yacov beamed as he recognized the ruggedly handsome, tanned face. "Anatoly! Come in."

As Anatoly Altshuler stepped into the flat, Yacov embraced him in a customary Russian bear hug and thumped him on the back. "How are you? How did you know where we'd be living?"

"How do you think?" Anatoly laughed.

"The good old *Pravda* network, right? Since we now work for the Federal Security Bureau, we are worth cultivating, am

I right? Is that what brings you here?" Yacov kidded, happy to see their old friend.

"How could you think such a thing?" Anatoly asked, shaking his head. "*Pravda* no longer exists and *Isvestia* is certainly not the official voice of the government as *Pravda* once was! Besides, who are you to speak? Painting out the spots on a leopard doesn't turn it into a house cat. With the KGB you always knew where you stood. Now that it's called the Federal Security Bureau, *you* want respect?"

As Yacov laughed, Anatoly looked past him, and his hazel eyes warmed as they locked with Sonya's. In that fleeting moment, the years disappeared and memories came alive as they studied each other. Whether looking for changes or similarities, who could say.

"How long has it been?" Anatoly asked.

Sonya touched the cropped neckline at the back of her head, as though unconsciously seeking the shoulder-length hair she'd had when last she had seen him. "Almost nine years," she answered softly.

"Nine years," he repeated slowly.

"Ah, you did not really come to see me," Yacov chided.

"Then you may leave!" Anatoly said with a wry smile. "There was only one Petrov ever worth looking at."

Yacov laughed and waved his hand toward the couch. "Sit down. Sit down." Sonya pushed more boxes away and sat at one end of the couch. Anatoly sat next to her, while Yacov perched on a box of books.

"It's great to have you back home," Anatoly said with enthusiasm.

"This is not home," Sonya began before Yacov's look cut her off.

"I understand, really, I do," Anatoly continued, not wishing Sonya to be embarrassed. "I remember the last time we were together like this, when you were both telling me that *aliya* was what every Jew should do. Even then I remember arguing that I wasn't a Zionist—which didn't go over very well, as I recall. Now, I come across this press release about these two ex-Israeli-military-intelligence, Russian-born Jews returning to Moscow to take care of their father, who just happened to be injured in a tank accident. That narrows it down a bit! Thanks for letting your old friend know you were back in town!"

"It all happened very quickly," Sonya said. "We had little time to tell anyone. Through connections that I had in intelligence, we were able to pack up and leave in less than two weeks. Papa needed immediate attention."

"We should have e-mailed you, but frankly we were so busy tying up loose ends in Israel, it completely slipped our minds," Yacov added quickly.

"Vitali is here, now?"

Yacov nodded toward the closed bedroom door. "Yes. He can't take care of himself anymore, and we weren't about to let the state do it."

The smile left Anatoly's face. "I understand. I love Mother Russia as much as anyone, but I wouldn't want someone I cared about in one of our state institutions."

"In the old days, that would have been dangerous talk," said Yacov.

"It's not entirely safe today. You don't suppose . . ." Anatoly glanced around the room.

"I doubt it. We're not that important, as you can see from our surroundings."

"You might be surprised. You may not think much of this flat, but with three bedrooms it's definitely above average and well situated, with the Metro practically at your door to whisk you to Federal Security Bureau headquarters. No doubt a perk, thanks to your new employer."

"Yes," Sonya admitted "I guess living in Israel makes us forget."

"And what have you been doing since we saw you last, Anatoly?" Yacov asked, out of both curiosity and a desire to keep his sister from dwelling too longingly on the land they had left behind.

Anatoly cleared his throat in mocking self-consciousness. "Well, as you may recall, I was a relatively junior reporter with *Isvestia* when you left. Now, after almost nine years' hard work, I have arrived at the lofty position of senior reporter.

Which means my cubicle is about a centimeter wider and the assignments are a little nicer, though not much. However, I do have a lot more contacts now, and that makes my job quite interesting. In fact, one of those contacts has become a good friend. Yuri Kagan, a CNN reporter in their Moscow bureau. If you watch the news on CNN, you'll find his name is a household word here in the big city. He does a lot of TV specials as well as reporting. I want you to meet him, and he wants to meet you. He's heard me talk about my two friends doing their thing down in Israel, and he thinks there could be a story in you two, now that you've returned. You know how we reporters are—always looking for the angle, the next good lead."

"Kagan. That's a Jewish name, isn't it? Either with a 'k' or a 'c' it comes out Cohen to me."

"Interesting observation. I happen to agree with you, but he won't own up to it. In fact, he's extremely sensitive about it. It's about the only thing you don't tease him about, and it won't do any good, anyway, because he adamantly denies it! He claims his real name is Klagman but somehow ended up Kagan when his great-grandparents immigrated to Russia! They came from Germany originally, and we've had some heated debates about World War II. In fact, we disagree about almost everything. He's terribly Aryan but not, on the other hand, anti-Semitic, if you know what I mean."

"Probably because he's afraid of what his own lineage might be," Sonya interjected.

"Well, whatever, we'll probably never know for sure. One thing though: he's got a great sense of humor. You'll like him."

"There's so much we need to catch up on," said Yacov. "Stay for dinner?"

"Yes," Sonya agreed quickly, her eyes shining.

"I'd love to," Anatoly replied.

"Good," Yacov said. "You can help us stand in lines at the markets. Our shelves are bare. Nine years made me forget what it was like. Nothing much has changed, has it?"

"Well," Anatoly answered, trying to sound cheerful, "the lines are shorter now than when you left!"

Anatoly smiled at the look of resignation Sonya flashed Yacov. She walked over and opened the bedroom door to check on her father, who was sleeping soundly. Then the three left for the necessary but aggravating chore of stocking the pantry.

They spent hours looking for things that were so readily accessible in Israel. Even then, they had not found everything she wanted, Sonya thought. The tiny electric stove proved to be as unreliable as it looked, and the stewing hen was as tough as leather. Her only consolation was that by the time they sat down to eat, they were too hungry to care what was on the table.

After dinner they were settled in the narrow living room with their little cups of instant coffee. Anatoly and Yacov had cleared the boxes off the two old upholstered chairs, the only places to sit beside the couch. They had each taken a chair, and Sonya sat at one end of the couch, slipped off her loafers, and curled her legs up beneath her. Anatoly seemed to be watching every movement she made, in a way he had never done in the old days, when he was more Yacov's friend than hers. In some ways, those days seemed like yesterday. In other ways, it seemed like an eternity ago.

"That was an excellent supper, Sonya," Yacov said, trying to sound sincere.

"It was the best I could do with what we have," she grumbled.

"You couldn't have done better," Anatoly comforted, coming to her defense.

"Well, thank you . . . I guess."

"This isn't Israel, Sonya," Anatoly reminded her. "You will get used to it—again."

Sonya wondered if he was criticizing her attitude, and was surprised to find that what he thought mattered to her. But glancing at his face, she realized that ideology was not uppermost in his mind at the moment. She felt her face grow warm as he continued to gaze at her, apparently unaware he was doing it. She looked down, pretending to be interested in a tower of books that had been stacked temporarily next to the couch.

"Neither one of you was a sterling letter writer during your sojourn in the promised land," Anatoly said as he settled into the sagging cushions of the chair whose original plaid had long ago faded into blotchy browns. "Thank goodness for the occasional e-mail. By the way, Yacov, the last I knew you sounded pretty serious about an Israeli girl. How's that going, especially now that you've moved back here to Moscow?"

Yacov shifted uncomfortably. "If you had asked me that two months ago, I would have said wonderful."

"I'm sorry," Anatoly said. "I didn't mean to . . ."

"No, I don't mind talking about it," Yacov continued. "I did mention her to you. Her name's Mira. She's a *sabra*—you know, someone born and raised in Israel." Anatoly nodded. "And you're right, we were serious. Or at least I thought we were. We were talking about marriage. We even began talking about where we would live. I loved her and I thought she loved me. Maybe she did, but not enough to immigrate to Russia."

"I don't know, Yacov, maybe she couldn't get used to the idea of living with both you and Sonya," Anatoly added, jokingly.

"Yacov, I told you to stay," Sonya said, looking at her brother with compassion. "I am perfectly capable of taking care of Papa. You can still go back."

"We've already been through this, Sonya," Yacov said in irritation. "My place is here, with you and Papa. Mira has made her choice."

"Tell me, where did you learn your Hebrew?" Anatoly asked, deciding it was time to change the topic. Hebrew had been a subject he had excelled in back in his university days, but he was well aware that it was a language that didn't come easily to everyone.

Sonya sighed. "The Shabak provided me with Hebrew and English classes at the university. It was wonderful. In fact, I even got to take some classes with Yacov. We had world-class profs, and you couldn't ask for a more intellectual climate."

"Which did you find harder—Hebrew or English?"

"Difficult question. English, I would say. I still remember how hard I struggled with it in my classes here, and it didn't seem to get any easier when I studied it there. It's such an inconsistent conglomeration of grammatical structures and rules."

"Sonya used to tell her English professor that," Yacov laughed. "She made a very good case against it! You know Sonya. You want her on your side in any argument."

Anatoly laughed. "I can imagine. After you left, I continued my English studies at the state university and I remember how difficult it was—far more than Hebrew, at least for me. But, like it or not, a lot of my sources speak English, which is one of the reasons I've done well at *Isvestia*, I'm sure."

"Perhaps the best thing about Hebrew University is that it's in Jerusalem," Sonya said, returning to the original subject. "I can't tell you what it meant to be there, Anatoly. It was as though I was at home at last. At home in Israel, among Jews in our own land."

"It's still hard to believe that you both ended up in intelligence," said Anatoly, "even though you were in separate areas."

"We saw a lot there, I can tell you," said Sonya. She glanced at her brother. "Actually, I can't tell you."

Yacov laughed. "Sonya was the super-spy, not me. I was the computer nerd who tried to break the enemy codes. Sonya became the intelligence expert only after giving up her exciting commando life in the IDF. She was actually briefing the prime minister and his personal staff on military matters—the head guy himself! Now, that's what I call pretty heady stuff!" Though he said it jokingly, it was obvious that Yacov took great pride in his sister's accomplishments.

Sonya smiled self-consciously. "Being as strategically informed as we both were, it took Prime Minister Shefi to get us permission to leave Israel and return to Russia. We owe much to him. Which reminds me, Anatoly—even the little we've told you can't leave this room, ever. Especially my personal relationship with the PM. He'd never have let me return to Russia if he'd thought my relationship to him might become public knowledge."

"Better listen to her, old buddy." Yacov leaned toward his friend conspiratorially. "With all that commando training under her belt, you wouldn't be the first person she's eliminated!"

Anatoly wondered whether Yacov's joking had an element of truth to it. Sonya's blush of embarrassment told him she had read his thoughts. "I'm just glad to have my good friends back home again," he said. "And I assure you, whatever has been said tonight will not leave this room. I can't tell you how much I have missed both of you," he added, noting the warm smile that touched Sonya's lips.

Anatoly glanced at his watch. "Look at the time! I have got to go. My deadline is in less than two hours. It's either my column or my head. I'd rather it be my column."

"Me too," Sonya said.

Anatoly smiled as he stood to his feet and stretched. "I will call," he said as he made his way to the door. "Oh, I almost forgot. Yuri Kagan—my friend at CNN. He really does want to do a local interest piece on you—you know, the fact that you've spent almost nine years in Israel and have returned to care for your father, and all that. Probably his Jewish subconscious getting the better of him. Can I tell him it's all right to call you?"

Sonya hesitated briefly, then said, "That will be fine. This could be a way of letting our people here in Russia know more about Israel."

"We will look forward to meeting him," Yacov added.

Two

Sergei Lomonosov crossed his arms over his ample middle as he waited impatiently in an overstuffed chair. His close-set gray eyes brooded under heavy black eyebrows as he looked through the plate glass window at the magnificent view of the Black Sea coast. Sailboats with bright sails pirouetted in the distance as they caught the fresh breeze charging over the choppy water under the fluffy white clouds of late spring. As usual, Sergei was unmoved by the beautiful view from the *dacha*. There were more important things on his mind.

The door to Anna Makarova's suite swung open and Nikolai Bulgakov came through, closing the door behind him. His smile made it obvious that Anna had been entirely satisfactory. Sergei's scowl grew deeper as he mentally evaluated the man's priorities.

Nikolai caught the expression before Sergei could erase it. "You still do not understand, do you, Sergei, how it is with men and women?" he asked with amused cynicism.

"It is not that," Sergei replied. "We have much work to do—important work."

In an instant, amusement faded into cold distance. "You would reprimand me, my dear friend?"

Sergei looked at the man whose magnetism was captivating millions all over Russia. Sometimes he was amazed at the loyalty the name Nikolai Bulgakov could command. Examined critically, Nikolai did not cut a particularly imposing figure. He was of medium height, trim but not muscular. A full beard framed his face, and his dark brown hair was worn almost unfashionably in a side-parted nondescript style. It was those strange, penetrating blue-gray eyes, the commanding voice, and his electricity-charged rhetoric that riveted people.

"You know my loyalty, Nikolai," Sergei answered defensively. "It's this waiting. Why can't we do whatever you're going to do and get it over with?"

Sergei knew a little about what Nikolai Bulgakov had been chosen to accomplish—sparse details that Nikolai had been willing to tell him, plus what he had observed for himself. But he never had fully understood why the process had to take so long. How many years now? Forty-some? A chill went down his spine as he remembered the one time he had voiced those questions. Nikolai had exploded. "Thirty years! Forty years! What is that compared to thousands?" Sergei never again questioned him about timing. Still, the waiting without knowing drove him crazy.

"Destiny," Bulgakov said with a short laugh as he sat down in the chair opposite his advisor. "You have seen enough. You know what I say is true. And other than our old friend from Germany, you alone know of my Prince, the All-Powerful One."

"Yes. You have told me of him often enough, yet I have still to see him with my own eyes," Sergei complained.

"Then you already know the answer to your question, my forgetful one," Nikolai answered, impatience in his voice. "He will tell us when it is time. Until then, we do what we are told to do. Do you understand?"

Sergei nodded in agreement because that's what his master expected, but the truth was, he didn't understand and perhaps never would.

"Be assured," Nikolai Bulgakov continued in his instructional voice, "it will be soon enough. But remember, Sergei, you belong only to me. Only not in the same sense that Anna does." Breaking the tension, he laughed, enjoying the other man's discomfort. "Now, let's get to work."

Nikolai stood suddenly and started pacing, an impatient scowl erasing the smile of only a few seconds earlier. Sergei had seen this instant transformation often. The fact was, Sergei preferred his master in the role of leader, focused on one mission. "What shall we plan for St. Petersburg, Sergei? What can we do to make life more miserable for our dear President Katanov? Many chafe under Vladimir Katanov's rule, but he is still president of all Russia, is he not? For now, he is our primary concern. Tell me, how are we doing with the people? What do your latest polls reveal?"

"Your followers are increasing," Sergei began. "Katanov knows this, and he also knows our next stop is St. Petersburg. The polls speak loudly of your ability to captivate the people. Your speeches cut completely across ethnic and religious boundaries. You appeal to all of Russia—to the secularists, the Orthodox, the Muslims, even the Jews. All of them!" He paused. "At last the people of Russia are hearing what they want to hear: that we need a strong military for the *rodina*; that we need economic reform while staying true to socialism; that we need to protect the rights of the people—all the people! When you say 'All the people,' they believe you! When you speak, the words do not matter. Do whatever it is that you do and you will have the people shouting before it is over."

"Yes, I know. My gift of oratory. I have been told that we would win the popular vote if an election were held today."

"That's true," Sergei agreed. "Only Katanov won't allow an election. He thinks he can stop the inevitable by evoking his stupid, temporary emergency laws."

Bulgakov's smile turned sinister, the intensity over his mission now commanding his entire attention. "If I could aggravate him enough, just once, so that he would lash out with force against me in a public forum, perhaps it would bring about a civil war. If it did, we would accomplish what we want, right now, rather than having to wait for the emergency laws to be lifted. In St. Petersburg, I must use rhetoric that not only excites the people, but also ignites President Katanov to react without thinking."

"And if he does, you will be president in less than a week," agreed Sergei. "But Katanov knows that. He may be dumb, but he certainly is not that stupid!"

"Old habits die hard, Sergei. His first instinct will be to end the threat by force, if he thinks it's real enough. I want you to be prepared for the worst at the St. Petersburg rally. From now on, my job is to so intimidate him with words that he—purely out of instinct—does what we want him to do—react against us with force."

"And if he doesn't?" said Sergei.

"If he doesn't," Nikolai snapped, momentarily showing his own impatience with destiny, "we keep on with what we're doing. We are still making progress. Either way, it is only a matter of time."

"You know better than I whom we serve, and what it is that he has destined for us to do," Sergei said. "Is it possible that we could lose?"

Nikolai's thin lips softened into a smile. "No, it is not! My Prince has assured me I cannot lose as long as things are done his way."

"In the meantime," Sergei added cautiously, "there is one other possibility we must consider."

"And what is that?" Nikolai asked with genuine interest.

"If Katanov cannot stop you by legitimate means, the old fool may invite you into the government instead."

"Why would he do that?"

"To take advantage of your popularity. That, and the mistaken idea that he could control you if he did."

Nikolai Bulgakov put his fingertips together, propping his chin on them. "Yes, I think you're right. And if he does, do you think I should accept?"

"Absolutely," Sergei laughed.

Nikolai shifted in his chair and looked out over the choppy waters of the Black Sea, the wisdom of Sergei's advice beginning to take form in his mind. When he spoke again, his voice was low. "Sergei, you are not only my advisor. You have been my dearest friend since we were boys. I, better than you, know what I have been called to do. But I tell you in all honesty, that while I know the master plan, I don't know all the details. In my heart, I am as impatient as you. But Sergei"—he gripped the armrests with white knuckles—"I can never go back! I can never return! It is not an option. Ever! Do you understand me?"

Sergei had seen this frantic mood dominate his master before, although he had never fully understood the unnamed fear that so haunted him. Sergei weighed his words before answering. "We are proceeding well. I agree with your strategy for St. Petersburg. We should also be ready to accept an invitation into government circles if our popularity continues to soar and Katanov refuses to do something stupid at one of our public rallies. So, what would you have me do that we are not already doing?"

"For now, only one other thing. Ultimately, everything hinges on my relationship with the Jews," Nikolai continued. "I need better information on the state of Israel if I am to be ready to do what I must do when the time finally comes."

"We already have our sources."

"They are not immediate enough or good enough for our purposes. I must have better information. Now! This is absolutely vital to all our plans for the future—you know that!"

"Yes, that much I understand. What do you have in mind?"

Nikolai turned steel-hard eyes on Sergei. "I saw a special report on CNN—a rather sentimental story of a brother and sister who have returned to Russia from Israel to take care of their invalid father. My people have checked them out. Both were involved in the IDF—Israel Defense Forces—the brother eventually winding up in military intelligence, the sister working for the Shabak. Both are Russian-born but speak Hebrew fluently. The sister is the one I really want. She spent her last five years working for the Shabak. That's a police agency that provides internal intelligence to the prime minister's office. She's perfect for what I want. But the brother would also be useful as well, especially with his code encryption background. It seems they do everything together. Offer them a joint deal that promises something for their Jewish brothers and sisters, and they'll find the offer irresistible!"

"Their name?"

"Petrov."

"What are they doing now?"

"Medium-level jobs with the Federal Security Bureau. A natural choice, considering their Israeli-intelligence training. They're probably just marking time until their father dies and they can return to Israel—which could also work to our advantage later."

Sergei whistled. "An interesting challenge," he said. "So, how much can I tell them?"

"Whatever it takes—within reason. Just do it smart."

Yacov scowled as he fished in his pockets for change. What possible reason could there be for an FSB computer specialist to cover a political rally in St. Petersburg? Were no other agents available? Of course, he could understand President Katanov's desire to keep tabs on his opponent. Nikolai Bulgakov was running high in the polls and had been drawing unprecedented crowds all over Russia. But why me? he wondered. This is not my field of expertise.

Still, he had to admit, he wanted to hear this political firebrand himself. So why gripe about the opportunity that had been dropped in his lap? Besides, he and Sonya had never trusted Katanov, even while they were living in Israel. Katanov hated Jews and did nothing to conceal the fact. If it hadn't been for Russia's need for better Arab intelligence in the Middle East—Sonya's specialty—or the latest computer technology his background and training provided, there was no way on earth that the present government would have shown any interest in a Jewish brother and sister just returned from Israel.

Yacov punched in the number and waited while the phone rang.

"Hello."

"Sonya. I'm in St. Petersburg."

"Why are you yelling?"

"Sorry," he said, lowering his voice slightly. "I'm near the square and you wouldn't believe the crowd. It's difficult to hear."

"What does the place look like after all these years?"

"The city has lost nothing of her elegance in the years we've been gone. Bulgakov is going to deliver his speech on the Palace Square with the Winter Palace in the background. I don't know why I was sent, but at least I'm getting to see St.

Petersburg again. And to hear Bulgakov firsthand instead of a bunch of out-of-context sound-bytes."

"I'm eager to hear your reaction, since he's gaining such a strong following."

"You should see the crowd. They completely cover the square, and they're around the palace and down the surrounding streets. I wouldn't be surprised if there's more than half a million people here."

Yacov stuck a finger in his other ear so he could hear Sonya's reply. "You don't suppose there is any significance to the speech site, do you?"

Yacov laughed. "Why, my dear sister, you couldn't possibly be referring to the storming of the Winter Palace, could you? Perhaps another Red October? Mr. Bulgakov would never so subtly suggest that the people have legitimate complaints against the present government, would he?"

"The thought never entered my mind."

"Historically significant or not, it is an excellent place for a rally. So far everything is peaceful, although the city police are out in force. Even the mounted guards."

"When will you be home?"

"I'm booked on a flight into Sheremetyevo II a little after one in the morning."

"I'll meet you."

"No. I'll take the Metro home. Don't stay up. No point in both of us losing sleep over this."

"All right. Just be careful."

"Thank you, Mother. See you in the morning."

Yacov hung up the phone and began pushing his way through the crowd.

In the short time he'd been back in Russia, Yacov had seen clips of Bulgakov's speeches, but he had never seen or heard the man in person. Now he watched in fascination as the bearded politician struck the air with his fists and hurled his rhetoric at the audience, as if wielding a weapon. The sound system carried Bulgakov's strident voice across the crowd, his words and accusations ringing with sincerity. The masses mobbing the Palace Square exploded their agreement in wild shouts, waving hands, and homemade signs and flags.

Despite his own training and knowledge, Yacov found himself getting caught up in the speech too. Slowly, masterfully, the brilliant orator worked the audience up into a frenzy. Yacov sensed that the political rally was rapidly becoming a potential riot, a bomb, ready to explode at the slightest suggestion of Nikolai Bulgakov. Even Yacov felt a compelling urge to do something.

Suddenly, he heard the roar of engines and turned toward the sound. Unable to see over those behind him, he climbed up on a crowd barrier, then swore as he watched a dozen water tankers turn onto Nevsky Prospekt, coming straight for Palace Square. He was not the only one who sensed the imminent danger of riot. The police had decided to make their move before it was too late.

"My friends!" Bulgakov thundered. "Look down Nevsky! See for yourselves that President Katanov does not trust you! Do not let him get away with this! Strike now! Claim what is rightfully yours!"

An angry murmur ran through the crowd. Seizing the moment, Bulgakov roared into the microphone. "Katanov does not want a strong Russia! Katanov does not care what happens to you! Will you put up with this? Will you? Or will you rise up and demand change!?"

Palace Square exploded into action. Yacov whirled around, hoping to escape before the worst began, but the wall of people surrounded him, propelling him toward the water cannons. He tried to push his way to the sidewalk but was unable to break free. He struggled to stay on his feet, knowing a fall meant certain death.

The crowd-control vehicles loomed, now spread out in attack formation, as the mob swept Yacov along toward the platform. A man directly in front of him went down. Yacov leaped over him, almost falling. The man screamed in agony as countless feet ground him into the pavement.

The turret on the nearest cannon swiveled and a white gush of water erupted from the nozzle. The water stream jetted against the ground, short of its target. It glanced off the pavement and washed across the vanguard of the mob. The cannon began sweeping from side to side like a scythe, mowing down increasing numbers as the mob approached. The truck went into reverse and backed up about 30 meters, then it resumed spraying the people with high-pressure water.

The crowd surged forward in mass rage. Yacov screamed as a heavy boot caught his heel and he started falling. From out of nowhere an open hand flashed down and grabbed a handful of his shirt, jerking him up again. Stumbling and shoving, Yacov managed to reach the sidewalk, but he still could not escape the crowd's momentum.

Yacov saw the light pole just before he hit it, crying out in pain as he struck the standard dead-center with his head. His broken glasses fell away, and warm blood ran down his face as he struggled to stay on his feet. He pried his head away from the pole and stared at the red smear on it through unfocused eyes.

Anna Makarova stood at the side, below the speaker's platform, looking across the riot-torn square. Nikolai and Sergei were still standing behind the bank of microphones, watching the scene unfold before them. She moved to her left, where the view was better, and looked down Nevsky Prospekt, trying to see for herself what was happening. Suddenly the tankers stopped, at precisely the same time, and their water cannons swiveled to the rear. Once again the jets of water shot out, but now they were being used to clear the way behind the tankers as they reversed into a hasty retreat, leaving scattered human debris in their wake. Anna clutched helplessly at her chest as she saw the still forms appear where seconds before the mobs had surged.

"They're retreating," she screamed over the din that surrounded her.

She ran up the platform to Nikolai's side and clasped his arm. He glared at her in irritation, frustrated by the sudden turn of events. The people, sensing the worst was now over, began to search for friends and loved ones lost in the confusion of the adrenaline-driven uprising.

"What happened?" she said. "Why are they leaving?"

"Katanov called them off," he said angrily. "If he had only

kept pushing, the people would have swept us clear into Moscow."

"They will anyway," Sergei interrupted impatiently. "The people are with you, Nikolai. But there is something you need to do now. See all the injured? Does Katanov care about them?" he asked. "The media are here. Help the people! Do what Katanov refuses to do," he instructed his master. "This is why the cameras are here—to show the world *you* care about people."

Bulgakov turned to look at the scores of wounded lying on the street where, only moments ago, the masses had stood, hanging on his every word. He glanced at Sergei, who nodded. "You warned me to be prepared for the worst, and we are."

"Come with us, Anna," Bulgakov ordered.

As the three left the platform, Sergei shouted for an aide to send for the private ambulances that had been arranged for in advance. Bulgakov led the way down Nevsky, careful not to acknowledge the presence of the television cameras whose all-seeing eyes missed nothing. A siren signaled the arrival of the first ambulance.

Bulgakov bent over an old woman sitting on the ground, dazed and crying. Blood ran freely from a cut on her forehead and her right arm hung at an awkward angle. He waved for the ambulance attendants.

"These kind men will take care of you," Bulgakov assured her. He watched as the paramedics lifted her onto a stretcher and carried her away.

More ambulances screeched onto Nevsky, their blue lights flashing. The crowd slowly drifted away, although a few stayed to help wherever they could. Bulgakov and his two companions proceeded across the square, stopping to speak words of comfort to the injured.

Sergei knelt beside a young man who was slumped on the ground, his back against a light pole. A wide streak of oozing red bisected his forehead and he stared at Sergei with dazed eyes. Sergei leaned over and picked up a half-open wallet that had fallen beside him, intending to place it back in his coat pocket, when he noticed the Federal Security Bureau identification card with the man's name printed next to his photograph. Sergei gasped as he recognized the opportunity fate had laid in their laps.

"Nikolai!" he shouted. "Come over here!"

Bulgakov quickly came over to his side. "What?" he asked.

He stood and whispered in his ear, "This is Yacov Petrov."

Nikolai grabbed the card, comparing the photograph with the man who sat in front of him. The curly brown hair, brown eyes, and lean, handsome face matched the man he remembered from the CNN interview. The horn-rimmed glasses were gone, but Anna spotted the smashed spectacles nearby. Bulgakov looked up into Sergei's face and their eyes met in silent agreement.

"Sergei, order the attendants to take him to the Pushkin Cooperative Clinic. Anna, you ride in the ambulance and we'll join you later. I should stay around here until all the injured are taken care of."

As Sergei called for a stretcher and instructed the attendants where to take the man, Bulgakov made his way to another victim of Katanov's brutality. The cameras continued to record the scene. None had caught the significance of the brief exchange beside the light pole.

"How is he?" Anna asked the doctor, smoothing the ends of her silky blond hair behind her ears. She had been sitting in the waiting room for about an hour, an unbelievably short wait given the inefficiency of the socialized health care system. The name of Nikolai Bulgakov commands some respect, Anna thought with a secret sense of pride.

"Mr. Petrov has a slight concussion, and he will undoubtedly have a terrible headache. He needs to take two or three of these capsules every four hours, if needed," the doctor said, handing her a medicine packet. "Watch for dizziness, disorientation, and fainting spells. If anything like this happens, he should be seen by a doctor at once."

"Can he leave the hospital?"

"Yes, as long as someone keeps an eye on him. He could probably use a little more rest here, but he may leave when he is ready. There is nothing to sign. All has been taken care of in advance."

"Very well, doctor. You will be available if I need you?"

"Of course. Ring the buzzer and I will come immediately."

Anna produced the smile that was her business card, then went to the nearby phone and called the Federal Security Bureau in Moscow.

Fifteen minutes later, she opened the door to the VIP suite. Yacov Petrov looked lost in the hospital bed that stood in the exact center of the huge room. Everything was immaculate, from the mirror shine on the tile floor to the large-screen TV set that stood by itself, to the left of the bed. A door to the right opened into an adjoining suite of rooms.

Anna looked down at the man, who was now conscious and regarding her curiously.

"You know who I am?" she asked.

"Everyone in Russia knows who you are, Ms. Makarova." The face of the Bolshoi's prima ballerina had appeared in every publication, and she had become a source of endless gossip when she retired suddenly from a brilliant career. She was often seen at Nikolai Bulgakov's side at public rallies, and for this reason it had been rumored that she was his mistress.

"Please, call me Anna."

She could see his discomfort and confusion.

"Thank you, Anna," he said finally. "If I may ask—what am I doing here?"

She laughed. "You may, Mr. Petrov. You are in the VIP suite of Pushkin Cooperative Clinic by the order of Nikolai Bulgakov. President Katanov may not care for the Russian people, but Nikolai does. He ordered that all those injured at the rally today be given the best medical care available."

Yacov Petrov smiled briefly, but a sudden pain turned it into a wince. "You know who I am?"

"We found your wallet on the ground next to you. Apparently it fell out of your pocket when you collided with the light pole, so we looked for your identification card. You are Yacov Petrov, agent for the Federal Security Bureau."

Yacov nodded.

"Relax," she said with a smile. "I understand you can say nothing about your reasons for being in St. Petersburg. We are not interested in those reasons. We are only interested in your well-being. I am here to see that you are taken care of."

"Am I free to go?"

"The doctor has released you. You can go whenever you feel rested enough to leave."

"That's it?"

The smile left her face. "The doctor says you have a slight concussion, so it could be dangerous for you to travel alone. You must get as much rest as possible and be watched for the next couple days."

"But I must get home. How do I call my family from here?"

"I called the FSB office after the doctor examined you. They put me in touch with your sister and I told her about your condition."

"Thank you," he said, wondering if all the injured had received the same personal touch. "I'm booked on an Aeroflot flight this evening."

"Yes, I know. I am booked on the same flight. I will accompany you in case you have any problems. Your sister will meet you at the airport."

"I don't know what to say. I am grateful for your help." Despite his obvious relief, he still looked concerned.

"Don't worry," said Anna. "There will be no record of your treatment here, in case you are afraid someone will associate you with Nikolai."

"Again, thank you," he said. "You seem to have anticipated my every need. There is probably no reason for concern, but one never knows."

"You are welcome." Anna paused before continuing. "Mr. Petrov, may I ask you a personal question?"

He hesitated. "I guess so." Then he chuckled. "With your connections, you can find out whatever you want."

Anna smiled briefly, then said, "From your name, I assume you are Jewish. Am I right?"

Yacov gave a short laugh. "That's not hard to figure out. Yes, I am."

"In that case, I think there is something you should know

about Nikolai. He is against the anti-Semitism that exists today in Russia. But for change to come, it must start at the top. If anti-Semitism is to be stamped out, it must begin with our country's leaders and their view of the Jewish people. Nikolai is committed to loyal Russian Jews, like yourself, and to peaceful and friendly relations between Russia and Israel."

Yacov started to speak, but Anna held a finger to her lips. "Don't say anything, Mr. Petrov. We understand the delicate position you are in, being with the Federal Security Bureau. Nikolai just wanted you to know where he stands. Now, rest until it is time to go to the airport."

THREE

Vladimir Katanov stood alone in his Kremlin office, staring out across the massive stone and brick structure with its high towers and crenelated walls, the jewel for which Red Square was the setting. The tall, beefy, 63-year-old president of Russia — with a belly that betrayed his love for vodka — inventoried what he saw in minute detail, as if to reassure himself that in spite of what had happened yesterday in St. Petersburg Square, he still controlled all he surveyed. His reverie was broken by a knock at the door. He ignored it until it came again, then sighed and sank into the executive swivel chair behind his immense desk.

"Come in."

The door opened slightly and the weathered face of Aleksandr Dmitrovich Pavlichenko poked around it. Katanov gestured his prime minister in impatiently. The door opened wider to admit the short, bulky figure in the ill-fitting gray suit that most Eastern Europeans assumed to be some sort of unspoken uniform of office. The man stood a respectful distance from the desk. When Katanov waved him toward a chair, Pavlichenko sat on the edge, knowing full well that this would be no comfortable little chat between two old war heroes who had fought many battles together long ago, in the days of their youth.

"Mr. President, I have reviewed the latest reports from St. Petersburg."

The president ran a hand through his thinning white hair.

He glared at his prime minister, as if seriously thinking of killing the messenger.

"I assure you, everything is under control," Pavlichenko continued, patronizingly. "Order has been restored."

Katanov threw his copy of *Isvestia* across the room. It fell to the floor like a wounded bird.

"Under control?" he roared. "That idiot's rhetoric incites a riot the police cannot put down, and you say everything is under control? If I hadn't called them off, we'd have a civil war on our hands. And yet I am the one blamed for the riot, not Bulgakov. You have read the papers, yes? You have seen the polls, yes? Bulgakov is leading in all of them."

"I've seen them, Mr. President," Pavlichenko answered, unconsciously shrinking back into his chair. "The numbers will do him no good. There can be no national elections while the state of emergency exists."

"I am to rejoice at that?" snapped Katanov. "We must get rid of him, once and for all."

"A martyr might truly start a civil war."

Katanov leaned forward angrily, then took a deep breath and sat back, drumming his fingers on the arms of his chair. He knew what his prime minister said was true. This was not new thinking; it had been gone over before, many times. "So, what are we to do?" It occurred to him, even as he spoke, that he had asked this same question as well, many times in the past.

"Nothing, at least for now."

Katanov gave no response, but his body language made it clear that he was tired of doing nothing while his opponent continued to gain the support of the people.

"In fact," Pavlichenko continued, "we must avoid trying to suppress future rallies. That ploy can only backfire. Wait until Bulgakov makes a mistake, then nail him. As long as he is outside the corridors of power, he cannot overcome us. We must . . ."

Katanov waved him to silence as he suddenly rose to his feet. The big man paced before the two narrow office windows that stretched from floor to ceiling. Finally he flopped down in his chair again. He played with his gold pen as he considered the thought his prime minister had triggered.

"My dear Aleksandr Dmitrovich, you have it exactly backward. My problem is that Bulgakov *is* outside the government. Bringing him into the government might well be our solution."

"I do not understand, Mr. President."

"I did not think you would," Katanov said, knowing clearly at that instant what he must do. But to make it work, he had to take advantage of the opportunity while it existed, creating a positive out of the mess that had occurred yesterday in St. Petersburg. "He is popular? Then I will bring him into the government as my prime minister."

"What do you mean?" the second-in-command challenged.

"What I mean, Aleksandr Dmitrovich, is that he will replace you. We must all serve the *rodina*, however we are called to serve. I know you believe this."

"But why? How?"

"I will announce that I have lost confidence in you and am looking for your replacement. I will convince the Central Committee that you alone were responsible for what happened yesterday in Palace Square and you will agree, because you will do what is best for the *rodina*, even at the expense of your political career. Publicly, you will be blamed for the riot in St. Petersburg because you ordered the police to intervene—strictly *without* my permission."

"But, Mr. President, you know that's not . . ." Pavlichenko blurted out.

Katanov cut him off. "We will tell the people that I called off the police as soon as I realized what you had done. Under the circumstances, the Politburo will have no choice but to remove you as prime minister," he continued. "Then I will invite Bulgakov in and ask him to serve in your place. I have the votes on the Central Committee to back me up on this," he added, totaling in his mind the men he could count on in a crisis. "He makes all of us uncomfortable because of his popularity with the people and his talk of reform. But inside the system, his platform is removed and he can be controlled."

"But he would never consider playing second fiddle to you," Pavlichenko pleaded.

"How can he refuse? While the state of emergency exists, all he can do is make empty talk about what he would like to do, if elected. But, serving at my side, he will think that he can do something about those things he campaigns against. If he says no, then the people will see him as a self-serving politician who talks big but rejects a golden opportunity to take action. If he agrees, we have him where we want him. Either way, I win!"

"But I have served you faithfully, Vladimir." Sweat beaded Pavlichenko's brow as he struggled to change his leader's mind. "Why *my* job? For old times' sake, couldn't you offer him a less sensitive position?"

Katanov frowned. "Yes, yes, I know you have served the *rodina* faithfully, Aleksandr, but when times are difficult, the opportunities must be taken no matter who gets hurt—for the greater cause. If I can get the Central Committee to move quickly, it will get me—all of us—out of disgrace with the public, and give me the control over Bulgakov I need to keep him under my thumb. Any other position in this government would never appeal to him. If he is to take the bait, the opportunity must equal the man's assessment of himself. You have served your country and me well in the past, Aleksandr, and you will serve us both again in this, is that not true?"

"He will turn it against you," his prime minister warned.

A knowing smile replaced the frown on Katanov's face. "The naïve upstart probably thinks he can, but I hold all the cards. As long as he is working for the government, between the Central Committee and myself we shall control all his activities."

"But he has a power over the people. They love him as they have never loved you." Aleksandr felt a sudden boldness.

"Indeed, and I shall put it to good use. Do not worry for me, my friend." Katanov's smile was cruel, never reaching his eyes. "This will neutralize Bulgakov once and for all. But the one who actually advises me is my business—and it certainly will *not* be the *new* prime minister. If you act responsibly now, you will continue to be useful to me in the future, behind the scenes. In time, once the Bulgakov threat is behind us, your actions in St. Petersburg will be viewed as heroic. Then you will be restored to your previous position, with great honor. You will do this for me, for your country, will you not, Aleksandr?" he stated rather than asked.

Pavlichenko cleared his throat noisily. "Of course, Mr. President."

Vladimir Katanov stood behind his imposing desk as his rival was ushered through the door. "Ah, Mr. Bulgakov," he said, his blue eyes flashing a cordial greeting. "Come in. I am so glad you could come right away. Please, have a seat."

"Thank you, Mr. President."

"Please, call me Vladimir. May I call you Nikolai?"

"Of course." Bulgakov took the offered chair with cool confidence as the president seated himself.

"How was your trip from the Black Sea?"

"Very pleasant, thank you. The weather there is so much better than in Moscow."

"You get no argument from me on that. Though I must spend most of my time here, I much prefer my Black Sea *dacha*, when I can get away. After all, what are summer homes for?"

Bulgakov's blue-gray eyes glinted, though no smile crossed the thin lips framed by his well-trimmed dark brown beard. "We think alike on some things, I see."

A short rap sounded on the door, and a maid opened it without waiting for an answer. She advanced to the desk and carefully placed a silver tea service on the left-hand corner. She glanced over the tray's contents quickly, bowed, and left the room.

Katanov rose to his feet and busied himself pouring tea into two tea glasses with silver holders. "Something to sweeten it with?" he asked, as he reached for the silver dish containing the coarse brown cubes of natural sugar.

"If you please, Vladimir."

Bulgakov watched as the president dropped sugar cubes into both cups and placed generous slices of lemon on the saucers. He was carefully handed the saucer, along with an embroidered linen napkin.

The president returned to his chair, squeezed a slice of lemon into his own tea, stirred, and sampled it. Satisfied, he settled back and once again made steady eye contact with his guest.

"I called for you, Nikolai, because I wish to apologize personally for the riot my policemen caused at your rally in St. Petersburg last month. It was a terrible mistake on the part of my prime minister, but the Central Committee is dealing with the problem. Aleksandr Pavlichenko wishes to rejoin the faculty of Moscow State University, and the Politburo has accepted his resignation."

Bulgakov nodded. "Yes, I read the report in *Isvestia*. An unfortunate lapse in good judgment. So you have invited me here to tell me this?"

"Yes, but that is not all. I have a more serious matter to discuss with you." Katanov's eyes narrowed. "You tell the people you want to help Russia," he said. "What if I—your government—can give you that chance now?"

Bulgakov looked down to stir his tea so that his eyes would reveal nothing. He knew what was coming next, but it was important to make Katanov believe that his proposal came as a complete surprise. "Please, go on," he said evenly.

"This may take a while. Are you comfortable? I could ring for some *krendel* if you are hungry."

"I am fine, thank you. Please continue." Come on, you idiot! Forget all this hospitality nonsense and say what you want to say! His impatience was beginning to well up on the inside, but his warm demeanor on the outside continued to keep the president convinced he was in charge of this meeting.

The president's eyes bored into his guest. "Nikolai, I want to offer you a real chance to serve the *rodina* rather than merely talking about it. The Central Committee has given me permission to invite you to replace Pavlichenko as prime minister of Russia!"

Bulgakov purposely returned his cup to its saucer with a clatter and looked at Katanov with sharp surprise, as if this thought had never occurred to him. "You cannot mean this! You will forgive me, Mr. President—Vladimir—but we do have serious differences."

Katanov waved aside the objection. "Please, hear me out. I know this comes without warning, but I am willing to take the chance of being misunderstood for the sake of the *rodina*. I am committed to serving Russia the best way I know how. So are you. It's just that we can't agree on methodology, is that not so?"

Bulgakov nodded as if he was speechless by what was being offered. The heavy, brass mantel clock bearing the Imperial Arms of the Romanovs beat steadily in the background. If you use the *rodina* excuse one more time, I just might vomit all over your nice presidential carpet here in your nice private office, Nikolai thought to himself, the expression on his face giving no indication of what he was thinking.

"As prime minister," Katanov continued, "you would have the ear of the Central Committee. As prime minister, you would be given the opportunity to right the wrongs you campaign against." Katanov laughed. "You get to help the *rodina*, and we get the benefit of your wisdom and . . . ," the two men stared knowingly at each other, "your love for the people. Fair enough?"

Bulgakov picked up his cup and took a small sip. By now his tea had become lukewarm but he didn't notice. Now he must respond, convincingly. He must play his part in this little game Katanov was playing. He must accept, but he must not appear too anxious; he must hesitate just long enough, and then answer in a believable manner.

He sat for a few moments with his head bowed. Then he looked up, directly into Katanov's eyes, and spoke slowly and soberly. "You leave me no choice, Mr. President. For the *rodina* I cannot do otherwise. If this is what you and the Committee want, I can only agree to serve the *rodina* with whatever humble means are at my disposal." Well, why not? Two can play that silly *rodina* game.

"Good," said Katanov, rubbing his hands together briskly, then leaning back expansively. "We will work well together, as long as you remember that we need each other. I think all will go well as long as we understand each other." Only verging on a threatening tone, Katanov quickly changed gears. "There is much to do. The Politburo will be pleased with your decision. I think the vote can occur when the Central Committee convenes tomorrow at noon. After that, I want you here, as soon as possible. My staff will help you get oriented. You will want your own special advisors and assistants—with my approval, of course. For this, you have immediate access to anyone on the government's payroll. Outsiders may take a few days more, because security will have to check them out."

Bulgakov paused, as though deliberating. "Other than the small staff I already have, headed by my personal friend and advisor, Sergei Lomonosov, I have had my eye on only two other candidates. They came to my attention during a special CNN report on them several months ago when they returned here from Israel."

"Israel? Who are they?"

"Yacov and Sonya Petrov. They are with the Federal Security Bureau."

"Ah, then they have already been cleared by security. You can have them immediately." Katanov paused, frowning slightly. "If they were in Israel, they must be Jewish?"

"I don't know. I suppose they are. Does it make a difference, Mr. President?"

"No, no, of course not. Having some Jews working directly for the prime minister might be good for our image."

There was only a hint of sunset when Nikolai Bulgakov finally boarded a private government jet for the flight back to his *dacha*. The perks provided by the State were definitely to his liking.

Sergei and Anna were nowhere in sight when he arrived at the *dacha*, but they would have to wait to hear the startling news. Instead, he bounded up the stairs to his second-floor suite.

Once there, Bulgakov took out a key and inserted it into a door that looked like it led to a closet. The lock gave a loud click and he pulled the heavy wooden door open. Inside, he flipped on the light with one hand and closed the door with the other, then quickly shoved home the inside bolt. The small square room was windowless and completely bare, except for two objects. An ancient framed tapestry hung on the wall opposite the door, its woolen threads ravaged by time. Rust-colored threads, the color of old blood, formed a pentagram on the drab gray background. In the very center of the room, on a low altar, a tall black candle protruded from the skull of a goat.

Bulgakov knelt and lit the candle. Then he closed his eyes and waited.

Nothing happened for several minutes. Then he sensed an approaching presence, as the atmosphere became heavy and oppressive. The pentagram shimmered as a purple glow formed and began to take substance before it. Gradually, the familiar black shape, large and indistinct at first, came into focus. As the glow faded, Bulgakov lowered his head, aware that the being stood before him, filling the tiny room. He could not see the two burning eyes which glared down at him, but he heard the monstrous voice.

"You have done well, my son," the being rumbled, rattling the tapestry frame. "Soon your destiny will be proclaimed for all the world to know."

A great sense of oppression weighed down and froze every muscle in Bulgakov's body. He could not force himself to meet those hollow eyes. "I have done as you told me, my Prince. And all is beginning to happen, just as you said."

"Did you doubt me?"

Bulgakov shivered as if caught in an arctic blast. A force stronger than any human prostrated him before the being. "No, my Prince. I trust you completely, only . . ."

"Only what, my son?" Bulgakov's All-Powerful One demanded. "Stand up and talk to me like a man."

"Don't send me back!" Bulgakov cried, the agony of his soul giving emphasis to the words he was speaking.

"You fool! Do as you are told, and you will never go back. Do you understand me?"

"Yes. But how do I forget? The pain! The fire! The hopelessness. I can't go back. Ever!"

"You will not return if you do as you have been instructed,

by my power. Destroy our enemies, all Jews and all Christians who refuse to bow down to me. Then I will have the power to destroy their leader, Iesus, the same Jewish Yeshua I killed over two thousand years ago, only this time, forever! Then will you become the true god of this world, my son, and the flames of hell can be forgotten," the All-Powerful One rumbled.

"But what of their so-called Almighty God? How do we defeat Him?"

"Destroy His people and destroy His Son, and you destroy the very purposes of Almighty God. Then I, the true, All-Powerful One, your Prince, will rule the universe, and you, my son, will rule the Earth. On that day, Almighty God will serve me! Do you understand me?"

"Yes, yes! But what if we can't? What if we don't succeed?"

"We *will* succeed!" he thundered. "It is our destiny. Only if you choose to disobey your Prince, will you be thrown back into the pit from where you have come! You may ask, but you must never question! Remember, there are others who cry out to me—others, who like you, will do anything to escape the abyss. Either way, by you or by them, my purposes will be established. I will accomplish all my good pleasure! In my time, on my terms! Do you understand me?"

Suddenly, intense pain seared through Bulgakov's head. He grabbed his head, fighting insanity. Then, just as quickly, it was over.

The glow faded, the candle flickered and went out, and Nikolai Bulgakov was left alone in the darkness, his face to the floor.

FOUR

The flight from Moscow on Nikolai Bulgakov's private jet had been smooth. Sonya Petrov watched the ground rush past below them as the plane landed at the small terminal at the restricted airport on the eastern end of the Black Sea. For the umpteenth time, she wondered why she and Yacov had been ordered so summarily to the new prime minister's *dacha*.

His appointment by majority vote of the Politburo had been shocking enough. But then yesterday, she and her brother had been assigned to his office and then ordered to meet with him personally at his summer home. The prime minister's office had even assigned a full-time nurse to care for their father while they were gone.

"I must have made a great impression on him in St. Petersburg, lying there bleeding on the street and all," Yacov had said lightly.

"Or his girlfriend has her eye on you," Sonya added with a barb.

"Well, that takes care of me," he grinned, "but what's your excuse?"

"I don't have the faintest clue."

Now, as their plane rolled to a stop beside the terminal, the early afternoon sun bathed the ground crew in cheerful light. At the foot of the boarding stairs, a black limousine waited for them, the driver already standing by the rear door.

Sonya allowed the driver to help her into the limousine, and Yacov climbed in beside her. While the driver walked around to the front, one of the ground crew placed their baggage in the trunk.

On reaching the coastal highway, the driver turned left, following the road that paralleled the Black Sea. Twenty kilometers later, he slowed and turned right onto a steep, paved drive. The limousine roared over the crest of a hill and pulled up at a heavy steel gate with coiled razor wire along the top. Two armed guards in dark-olive military uniforms peered in at Sonya and Yacov before one of them punched in the code to open the gate. From there, the road twisted and turned as it wound its way through a heavy stand of trees that sheltered the gently rising slope.

"Can you see the house yet?" Sonya asked.

Yacov scanned the windows. "Not yet. Must be beyond that rise ahead."

They caught a glimpse of the second story as the limousine made a turn. Then the car topped the rise and pulled in under a broad porte cochere. The door opened and Anna Makarova came out with two servants.

"Welcome," she said as the driver helped Sonya out. "I hope your trip was pleasant."

"Anna!" Yacov blurted out in surprise. "So nice to see you again."

The two women smiled and exchanged greetings as Anna led them through the front door. A fleeting thought crossed Sonya's mind: Maybe I shouldn't joke about it. Maybe she really is attracted to my brother!

"You look better than the last time I saw you, Yacov," Anna said, ushering them into a large room overlooking the seashore.

"I feel a lot better," he laughed. "Thank you again for your kindness to me and for getting me home safely."

"You are most welcome." Anna turned to his sister. "And Sonya—it is good to see you in a more pleasant setting. Sheremetyevo Airport at two in the morning is not the nicest place in the world. Unfortunately, our national airline is not a good way to travel even under the best of circumstances."

"Certainly not like our trip today."

Anna laughed. "Nikolai insists on taking care of his own."

She waved toward a couch that faced the long plate glass window. "Please, sit down. Nikolai will be out in a moment."

Yacov and Sonya sat on the couch while the petite blonde took a wingback chair across from them. Sonya watched a ferry out on the Black Sea which seemed almost motionless as it made its way toward Sochi.

"Lovely, isn't it?" Anna asked.

"I've never seen a more beautiful view," Sonya replied.

"I never tire of it myself."

A door opened behind them, and Yacov stood as Nikolai Bulgakov strode into the room briskly, a warm smile on his bearded face. "Welcome, welcome. Yacov—I'm glad to see you have recovered from your St. Petersburg adventure." The men shook hands. "Please, sit down. And you, of course, are Sonya," he said, turning to her. "What a lovely addition to my staff! I am so glad you could join us this weekend. I'm afraid we have a lot of work to do, but I think we can make it pleasant."

As the prime minister settled into the armchair opposite Anna's, the ex-ballerina rose gracefully and excused herself.

"We are honored to be here, sir," Sonya replied. "And eager to know what is expected of us."

"Please, call me Nikolai," he said. "Your luggage has been taken to your rooms, and I'm sure you will want to freshen up before dinner. Let me show you where everything is. Then you can rest a bit. We will dine at eight, but join me here earlier for cocktails."

After dinner that evening, Bulgakov ushered his two guests back into the living room. Anna excused herself and again made an exit, leaving the three of them alone. This time they gathered around the fireplace that was opposite the large window, now filled with the inky blackness of night.

After helping themselves from the coffee service that had been set out on a side table, they settled into the large comfortable chairs facing the blazing fire. Summer evenings beside the sea were still cool.

"We start our real work tomorrow when the rest of my staff arrives," Bulgakov said, setting his china cup and saucer on the small ornately carved table beside his chair. "But, before we begin, I wanted to meet with you both privately so we could get to know each other. I have studied your files, so I know the excellent work you have done. I am looking forward to working with you."

"We are honored to have been chosen," said Yacov.

Sonya smiled and nodded in agreement.

"You already know that I want to strengthen Russia and maintain a fair government—for all the people in Russia, not just those in the West," Bulgakov continued. "And that definitely includes my Jewish countrymen. President Katanov has promised me that I can work on those issues that are important to me, and because of your own unique experience, I believe you can be of invaluable service to me, helping to accomplish these things."

"Do you have something specific in mind, Nikolai?" Sonya asked. She took a sip of coffee.

He pursed his lips and frowned. "Anti-Semitism has reigned long in Russia, and our leaders have traditionally sided with the Arab states against Israel. I want this to change—not only in perception, but in fact. This isn't high-sounding rhetoric. I want to make a statement to every Jew—and Gentile, for that matter—in Russia. And that statement begins with putting two of our country's brightest young Jewish minds on my personal staff."

Sonya looked at him intensely, wondering whether to believe him. "I must admit, other than playing the role of 'token Jews,' I can't find any believable reason why you'd add two low-level, nonpolitical, inexperienced Jews to your small, elite staff," she said. "In fact, are you sure you have the right people?"

Bulgakov threw back his head and laughed. "I like that! Honesty! You are exactly the two people I want on my staff, the downpayment of my commitment to every Jew living in Russia. And you will be anything but 'token Jews'! What I need is your help. I need your loyalty. I need your keen, committed minds to help make these things happen. But never forget this: what we do together for Russia today will help Israel in her quest for peace tomorrow. You have my word on that."

He turned to Yacov. "What do you think?"

"I thought I would never hear this from a Russian leader."

"Sonya?"

"Nor did I." A thought played in the back of her mind. *Should I mention my connection with Prime Minister Shefi?* As quickly as the question flickered, her natural caution asserted itself. She knew and trusted Anatoly, so she'd had no reservations about telling him of her relationship to the Israeli prime minister. She did not know Nikolai Bulgakov, however. If he was genuine, the right time would present itself. For now, she would wait and see.

"I look forward to working for you," she added simply.

"Not *for* me, Sonya. *With* me," he said, gesturing expansively. "Trust me. Give me your loyalty. Together we will accomplish things beyond anything you ever dared to imagine. You will see."

Sonya nodded, knowing that in reality she would reserve judgment. All her training told her not to be gullible. Only time would tell. If indeed Nikolai Bulgakov deserved her loyalty, he would have it—all of it.

"Tomorrow we roll up our sleeves and get to work. You will meet the others on my personal staff. Then we will start planning on how to best administer government policy assigned to me."

Nikolai Bulgakov stood abruptly. "I would like to spend more time with you tonight, but there are still several more matters I need to work through before tomorrow morning's meeting. Let the staff here know if there is anything you need. You will find them most attentive. Now, excuse me."

He gave a courtly bow and left the room.

"What do you think?" Yacov asked with a shake of his head, still overcome by the events of the past twenty-four hours, to say nothing of the conversation they had just had with Nikolai Bulgakov.

"Well, first of all, it looks like I won't have to protect my older brother from the fallout of a torrid love-triangle with the prime minister and his mistress!" Sonya kidded, then turned serious.

"Come on, Sonya, give me a break. I'm still mourning Mira!"

"I know I'm just kidding," she laughed. "I'm not sure I heard our new boss correctly. In fact, I'm not sure *he* knows what he said," she continued. "On the other hand, if he means what he says and his actions match his words, when he becomes president—and believe me, there's no doubt in my mind that's his real intention—it could be the best thing that has ever happened for Jews living in Russia. Our people need someone like him in power, here in Russia—and so does Israel." She looked at her brother intently. "How do you size it up?"

"I'm not as analytical as you, but I have to agree with your assessment. I'm not superstitious either, but I'm beginning to think that perhaps we were brought back to Russia for reasons other than Papa. We should talk to Anatoly as soon as we get back to Moscow and get his perspective. He's more informed about Bulgakov than we are. With his connections at *Isvestia*, he could be a great help to Nikolai. Wouldn't it be great to work together, after all these years?"

"Yes, it would be." Her face suddenly felt very warm. "Anatoly could be helpful," she added quickly, attempting to hide her feelings.

Yacov cocked an eyebrow at her. "Do I hear a heart beating rapidly, or is it only the waves against the shore?"

"A little tit for tat, huh?" Sonya countered as she leaned across the space between their chairs and yanked his ear lobe.

"Take it easy! Your secret is safe with me," he said. "Anatoly is a fine man, Sonya. For what it's worth, I think you two make a handsome couple."

She looked to see if he was making fun of her. He wasn't.

Several months later, on a mild October evening, Sonya and Anatoly climbed the five flights of stairs to the Petrov flat.

"So, how was the Bolshoi?" Yacov asked from the couch as soon as they walked in the door. He threw down the papers he'd been working on.

"Wonderful!" Sonya replied, her face glowing. Anatoly helped her out of her coat, then hung it, along with his trench coat, in the small curtained closet near the door.

"Papa and I had a good evening, too," said Yacov. "We had a rousing game of chess. He's asleep now."

Sonya walked into the kitchen to put on the teakettle, while Anatoly joined Yacov on the couch.

"I don't know how I feel about seeing a Wagner opera," Anatoly said.

"He's in one of his sensitive moods," Sonya said over her shoulder. "I found *Die Walküre* very stimulating."

"She thought Brunhild was great," said Anatoly, nudging his friend with his elbow. "Think that has any deep significance?"

"Hmmm," Yacov replied. "The head Valkyrie is rather robust, as I recall. Handy to have around in a street brawl. With that headgear and spear, who would mess with her?"

"You two are hopeless," Sonya said. "No artistic sense."

Their conversation continued in this light vein until Sonya brought in three mugs of coffee and a plate of sugar cookies. She and Yacov had gotten hooked on coffee and the capacity of coffee mugs while living in Israel. Now she was trying to educate her friends here in Moscow.

"Have you recruited him yet, Sonya?" asked Yacov, gesturing toward Anatoly with his coffee mug.

"As a matter of fact, we've discussed Nikolai a number of times," she said, thinking of the many pleasant evenings she and Anatoly had shared together since the weekend at Bulgakov's *dacha*.

"I'm not plugged in like you two," Anatoly said. "You've had almost four months on the inside to see what's going on. I'm still on the outside. Besides, I'm paid to be the skeptic—especially when it comes to anything or anyone political."

"You're ducking the question, Anatoly," said Sonya lightly. "Which means he still doesn't want to discuss it, Yacov. I'm used to his tactics by now," she laughed.

"Come on, Anatoly. What do you really think?" Yacov asked. "You've had time to size him up, even if it's been from a distance."

"Okay, okay," Anatoly said, setting his mug on the lamp table beside the couch. "You know that I've always thought Bulgakov's speeches were too idealistic to get him the presidency. It's not that he doesn't say the things I—the people of Russia—want to hear. It's just that I never thought of him as anything other than another politician making shallow promises to gain the approval of the people. I respect his ability to sway an audience but I've always suspected his concern for the people was about as sincere as Stalin's."

"Stalin? I agree with you concerning his gift for oratory," Yacov said, "but I think the rest of your statement may be a little strong."

"Maybe. But the Politburo—which we all know is nothing but a bunch of old, far-right, hard-line, Stalinist cronies—doesn't seem to take his words that seriously, or else he would never have been made prime minister," Anatoly shot back.

"We've been over this, again and again," Sonya broke in. "He's told me personally they had to include him on the inside in order to get him off their case, publicly—vis-à-vis the St. Petersburg riot."

"Well, after hearing your firsthand observations these past months, I am willing to go so far as to say that I may have been wrong. But you must admit, you do have an advantage I don't have. If he does prove to you the integrity you say he has, then you two have been offered a rare opportunity to really help our people. And, yes, Sonya is probably right—as she has reminded me numerous times—perhaps that opportunity is mine as well. So," he paused before continuing, "officially I want you both to know that as of this moment, I have decided to do whatever I can to help this man and his cause."

"Hey, hey," Sonya cheered.

"Atta boy," Yacov added, "but what will *Isvestia* think?"

"*Isvestia* will always be happy with anything I come up with on the new prime minister. More important, I can be sure that whatever is written gets the right emphasis, the right spin so to speak! But know this: I trust your instincts and judgment far more than anything Nikolai Bulgakov himself could ever say or promise."

"Thank you," Sonya said, her voice betraying the emotion she felt.

"Don't thank me," he said. "If Bulgakov is what he claims to be, he is what we desperately need. It will be a privilege to play a small part in such a worthy cause." His gaze lingered on Sonya. "And, truthfully speaking, I am looking forward to working hand in hand with my dearest friends."

Sonya smiled self-consciously, then looked down at her hands. Yacov reached across the sofa to clasp Anatoly's shoulders in a bear hug.

"When can I meet him?" Anatoly asked, pushing his friend away good-naturedly.

Nikolai Bulgakov beamed at the three young people and waved them toward the chairs around the large circular table in his conference room. An amused smile played across Sonya's face as she watched Anatoly try and figure out where he should sit.

"Sit anywhere, except in Nikolai's place," Sonya whispered, adding to Anatoly's confusion.

A booming laugh sounded behind them. "Shame on you, Sonya," Bulgakov said as he closed the door. "How unkind you are to our guest. Sit anywhere you please, Anatoly, and pay no attention to Sonya. I don't have any particular place and she knows it."

Anatoly laughed, while Sonya pointedly ignored him. Bulgakov placed a tray of *krendel* on the table, and then asked Sonya if she would serve the tea. When everyone was taken care of, he looked across the large conference table, directly at Anatoly, his mood suddenly all business.

"Yacov and Sonya have told me a lot about you. They say, and others confirm, that you are one of the brighter lights at *Isvestia*. You serve Russia well, Anatoly—and I do mean Russia, not the present government. More important, Yacov and Sonya tell me that our cause is your cause and that I can trust you as I trust them. That, my friend, says a lot about you!"

"Thank you, sir."

Bulgakov glanced at Sonya. "We are off the record, are we not?"

"Yes, Nikolai. We discussed this beforehand. Anatoly knows that you want to discuss highly sensitive information with us—information that can never leave this room."

Anatoly nodded in agreement. "Strictly off the record, if that is your desire, Mr. Prime Minister."

"It is, Anatoly, and my name is Nikolai. I keep no secrets from my trusted staff, even though I must choose the appropriate moment to bring them into the loop on some things. Today is the day that Yacov and Sonya learn more of my plans for Russia . . . and for Israel," Bulgakov explained. "I am including you because they trust you and I need your help." He paused briefly, looking around the table at each of them. "What I am going to tell you will someday headline every newspaper in the world, but for now, for reasons that will become obvious to you, what I tell you must be kept in strictest confidence." The new prime minister's magnetic blue-gray eyes seemed to hold them all in place, like some invisible force.

"I have developed a master plan for Russia," Bulgakov continued briskly, "which will include all her peoples: the Russian Orthodox in the west, the Muslim people in the east, and the millions of Jews scattered throughout our great land. This is the only way to truly unite Russia, to bring all of her people together.

"As worthy as that goal may seem, however, that is not the true goal of our president or the Politburo he serves. The majority of these men are right-wing hard-liners, who want to take our great nation back to the days of Stalin. To them, the needs of the people are only to satisfy the needs of the state over which they—and they alone—rule."

Anatoly listened carefully, hearing Bulgakov voice the very same concerns Sonya and Yacov had discussed with him many times. "So how do you plan to accomplish your master plan in light of the thinking of those who not only sit in high places, but hold all the cards as well?" he asked.

"I will need the help of others. Others such as yourselves, committed to the same principles and goals. With your help there is no question that I will accomplish the things we are speaking about today. But you must understand this: my ultimate goal is for genuine *worldwide* peace, not just peace in our own land. And be assured of one more thing: I *will* succeed!"

Bulgakov waited a moment before continuing, giving them time to absorb what he had just said to them. "To accomplish my goals for the world, however, I must first demonstrate that I can accomplish them here in Russia. When I become president, all Russians will be treated fairly and will be respected for their individual origins and beliefs: something that has never occurred before in Russian history."

"You are right, Nikolai," Sonya agreed, enthusiastically. "This has never happened in our history—unless you want to count what Lenin tried to do."

"The people are the focal point of all that I intend to do. You already know how I feel about the Jewish men and women of our great land, and what I have promised to do for them. But to accomplish my goals for your people, I must start by truly unifying all of Russia into one country. This can never happen until I gain the complete confidence of the Muslim people in eastern Russia, and that of their leader, Assam. The day will soon come when he will willingly bring his people under my leadership. But that will only be the beginning. My plans go far beyond the motherland. I will share them with you, but what I tell you now must never leave this room. Do I make myself clear?"

The soft whisper of a heating vent was all that could be heard in the pause that followed. The three listeners were spellbound by the prime minister's words.

When he continued, his voice was low and intense. "When I unite the peoples of our great nation, something else— totally unexpected—will occur. *A powerful Western nation will unite with us, under my leadership, bringing us one step closer to my ultimate goal of a one-world government, united for the cause of world peace.*"

"Who?" the three asked in unison.

"Germany!"

The stunned expressions on their faces spoke louder than words.

Sonya finally broke the silence. "What possible incentive could ever entice Germany to unite with Russia? That's like telling me the Arabs are going to unite with Israel, under Israeli leadership! I can't believe they would even consider yielding their fierce independence to a nation they have opposed for centuries."

Bulgakov nodded in satisfaction, knowing the questions and the answers long before they ever crossed Sonya's mind.

"Two good points, Sonya—points I am not at liberty to address right now. All I can tell you is this: negotiations are *already* under way with Chancellor Otterbein of Germany, as well as with Assam, the leader of the Muslims here in Russia. Be assured, what I have told you *will* happen exactly as you have heard it from me today."

"Why are you telling us this?" interrupted Anatoly, unable to hide the disbelief behind his question.

"For several very good reasons, Anatoly. First, to accomplish the things I have just outlined, I am going to need your help. And for you to help me, you must understand me. To do that, it is imperative that you know my ultimate goals. As evidence of my trust in you, I have been completely honest with you concerning my master plan. No secrets, no surprises. Do you understand?"

The three nodded, still too stunned by what they were hearing to respond intelligently.

"The second reason is to test *your loyalty* to me. I will be open and honest with you, but I must be able to trust each of you completely, as you must trust me completely. What better way to show our loyalty to one another than to tell you openly of my plans and expect each of you to keep my confidence? Are you still with me?"

After their verbal assents, he continued. "The third reason is that I wanted to predict something so implausible that when it does come to pass, you will realize that I have the power to do everything I claim I will do. When you see these things begin to happen—and believe me, they *will* happen—then know that it is the beginning of the New United Empire, an alliance of nations which will usher in peace and prosperity to the entire world under my—*our*—rule! That includes the genuine, peaceful coexistence of your people, not only here in Russia, but also in Israel as well as the rest of the world!"

Anatoly tilted his head to one side, wondering if he had heard Bulgakov correctly. *This man proposes to unite Russia, ally with Germany, and then rule the world?*

"How do you expect to accomplish all of this?" he asked cautiously, skepticism seeping out of each word.

"Anatoly, I understand your disbelief, but know that my plan is fool-proof! All of these things will come to pass when the time is right," Bulgakov answered patiently. "You will be told what you need to know as the time approaches. But for now, you need to trust me. I have already told you more than you ever expected to hear, is that not true? Just remember, when you see Germany uniting with the Muslim people of Russia in the east and the Orthodox people of Russia in the west, under my leadership, the future of the entire world is about to change—forever!"

He paused for a moment. "Now, let me add one more thing that will be of vital interest to the three of you. After the nation of Germany joins a new, united Russia, *my first priority will be to ensure a meaningful, lasting peace for Israel*. With your help, I will guarantee Israel's right to a genuine, peaceful existence. With your help, I will make a covenant with your people, Israel, guaranteeing her rights as a sovereign nation, and I will back it up with the entire might of the New United Empire. Trust me: it *will* happen."

Again, dead silence. The new prime minister continued.

"Let me explain: To reach my ultimate goal of world peace, I need Israel. *When the world sees that I alone can bring peace to the most beleaguered nation in the world, then they will know that I alone can bring genuine peace to the entire world*. To guarantee a genuine peaceful existence for Israel, I need the New United Empire. To bring in the New United Empire, I need your help. You are either with me or against me."

Sonya sat upright in her chair. Suddenly she felt the chilling conviction that Nikolai Bulgakov would accomplish exactly what he claimed. For the first time since returning to Russia, she felt the thrill of expectation, knowing she was once again working for someone she could completely trust, someone whose goals were her goals. She wanted a challenge, and the challenge had just been presented to her, on a silver platter.

"That is all I am at liberty to tell you at this time," Bulgakov continued. "I have given you enough to think about for one night."

He glanced at his watch. "Now, I have an important meeting with the president that I must attend." He picked up a slender attaché case from the table near the door, then turned toward them again. "I have taken the liberty of arranging dinner at the Hotel Savoy and box seats at the Bolshoi for you tonight. Duties prevent me from joining you, but Anna will.

"Yacov, my secretary has everything you need for our status meeting tomorrow. Sonya, I'm looking forward to your report on the new tensions that appear to be escalating between Israel and her Arab neighbors. Now if you will excuse me . . ." He nodded and left the conference room.

No one said anything for a while. Yacov finally broke the silence.

"Unbelievable! If he can pull all that off, he'll be the greatest man to ever live!"

"If he can deliver," Sonya said pensively, the enthusiasm of the moment beginning to be dampened by the reality of her logical mind. "A united Russia, together with Germany, forming a New United Empire? Guaranteeing the peace and safety of Israel? In our lifetime?"

"Not quite," said Anatoly, a strange icy coldness suddenly gripping his stomach. "What he said was this: *his* New United Empire was going to someday *rule the world!*"

"What got my attention was the assurance with which he spoke," Yacov continued, apparently ignoring the skepticism that accented Anatoly's assessment of the conversation. "Almost as though he could foresee the future."

Anatoly leaned back in his chair, whistling softly through his teeth. "Do you realize that I've just been handed the story of the century, and I can't tell a soul about it? I can't take any more of this! Let's get out of here! Dinner sure sounds great. What's at the Bolshoi?"

Yacov glanced down at his digital assistant, then looked up at his friend with a wide grin. "Wagner! What else?"

FIVE

Anatoly yawned and stretched, trying to settle himself more comfortably before the large-screen monitor in his cubicle at *Isvestia*. He thought about getting a cup of coffee, but his stomach was already sour from the quantity he'd consumed. He'd been doing research for several hours and still had not finished. A fierce December storm raged outside, but thankfully, at least so far, it had not affected the Moscow power grid.

He glanced at his watch — 11:30 P.M. — then sighed, clicked the mouse, and started his Internet gopher program on its electronic odyssey through the vast interconnection of worldwide networks. He needed information on Messianic Judaism for his latest assignment. When the general editor suggested that he would be perfect for the piece, Anatoly did not bother trying to explain that he had no idea what the differences were between an observant Jew and a Messianic one. The truth was, whatever they were, he was neither. So now, here he sat in the middle of the night, trying to find out specifically where one found a Messianic Jew.

The progress bar crept slowly to the right until the sound card played a short clip from the "1812 Overture" to indicate the gopher's successful mission. A world map flashed onto the screen with the countries in colors ranging from blue to red. The more red, the higher the number of hits. The United States glowed cherry red.

"That figures," Anatoly grumbled as he moved the pointer to the center of the North American continent and clicked.

The globe rotated, the United States block expanded, and lines outlined the individual states. Again the color histogram showed the locations of the most hits. The Midwest and Southeast were the hottest areas, and a sea of red washed over certain states in those areas.

Flipping a mental coin, Anatoly clicked on Florida. The state separated from the others and grew until it filled the screen. Tiny ruby dots marked each Internet site. Anatoly swept the pointer over the sites, finally selecting one in the middle of the state.

"Forty-nine entries," he muttered absentmindedly. He looked closer. It was a site in Orlando. "I'm going to Disney World?" he asked himself with a chuckle.

He clicked on the site and brought up a series of graphics in the main window. Some were keywords while others were e-mail or worldwide web addresses. He randomly clicked on a worldwide web address.

"That home page is certainly graphic enough," Anatoly said to himself, as a large picture of a skull with miniature Earths in the eye sockets filled the screen. The words "The Covenant with Death" leapt off the screen immediately under the owner of the page, "Mount Zion Ministries." Catchy little name! he thought. Intrigued, he pushed the page-down key and came to an electronic sidebar titled "The Antichrist and Israel." On the screen he read

OVERVIEW: *The Covenant with Death* is a book about a man that the Scriptures refer to as "The Antichrist," a man who will precipitate the worst Holocaust known to Israel since the beginning of time, making the Nazi Holocaust of World War II pale in comparison.

If ever there was a grabber lead-in, this one is right up there, Anatoly thought. He continued reading.

SUMMARY: In the last days, the nation of Israel will make a "covenant with death"—a peace treaty of some sort—with a world leader whose real agenda will be Israel's total destruction. Called the Antichrist (or the

Beast) in the sacred Judeo-Christian writings, this man—seemingly a peacemaker in all outward appearances—will begin his worldwide conquest by gaining control of three strong northern European nations or ethnic groups and forming a singular alliance. This new alliance, led by the Antichrist, will then enter into a seven-year treaty with Israel, supposedly guaranteeing Israel her national security. After this treaty is signed, seven more nations—most of which have historically been enemies of Israel—will pledge their allegiance to Antichrist, making him the sovereign of ten powerful nations secretly bent on worldwide dominion and the destruction of Israel.

At the midpoint of his seven-year covenant, Antichrist will break his treaty with Israel and assume the role of dictator over a one-world government—under the guise of world peace. He will rule the world from a throneroom that will be established in the holiest part of Israel's rebuilt temple in Jerusalem. In addition, this man will claim divinity, demanding the worship of all people, beginning with every Jew in Israel. He will enforce his edicts by unleashing the worst persecution known to mankind on those who refuse either his leadership or his lordship. Many Jews will resist and die. Others will resist and go into hiding before they can be caught and killed. Still others will choose to publicly identify with this false Messiah. Eventually, two out of three Jews living in Israel will die at this man's hands.

The persecution at the hands of Antichrist will come to an abrupt end when the true God of Abraham, Isaac, and Jacob displays His long-awaited sign in the sun, moon, and stars, announcing to the world the coming of the true Messiah of Israel, Jesus Christ. When the sign appears in the heavens, He will *rescue* those who have remained true to Him, *protect* those Jews who have resisted this false Messiah, and *initiate* the wrath of God—called "the Day of the Lord"—on the followers of Antichrist, destroying them all in preparation for an everlasting kingdom that the true Messiah will then establish on Earth. The remnant of Israel that survives the Holocaust of Antichrist will all receive Jesus as their Messiah and will become the citizens of this earthly kingdom of God, experiencing genuine peace and safety for the first time in their nation's existence.

Anatoly skimmed through the paragraphs quickly, then read them again more slowly. Was this some kind of science fiction? If so, why did certain phrases sound so familiar? He read it through a third time, then clicked the icon to pull up the entire book and began skimming through it, chapter by chapter, to see what other information he could find. When he came to a chapter titled "The Antichrist Comes to Power," he slowed down and read it all the way through — twice. When he finished, he leaned back in his swivel chair, a cold chill running up his spine.

The author was predicting that this Antichrist would unite two major ethnic groups in Russia, the Orthodox and the Muslim peoples, and, at the same time, *bring a Germanic people under his leadership!* Didn't all of that sound like Nikolai Bulgakov's master plan for his New United Empire? So how did Bulgakov's big secret get into this book?

Could this be a mere coincidence? Anatoly scrolled to the beginning of the document and checked the copyright date. There was no way the writer could have known Bulgakov's plans. The book had been written years before Bulgakov ever came on the scene in Russia. Did that mean he had read the book himself and decided to use its premises as a pattern for his own political schemes? Could mere coincidence account for the similarity of details, at least those Bulgakov had shared with him?

Anatoly considered calling Yacov, but it was too late and anyway, there was more he needed to know before he could determine whether it was worth discussing. He jumped to the bottom of the home page, where he found an e-mail address for those wanting more information. The "who" part of the address was "mteasdale." He paused, then clicked on the address. The gopher obligingly popped open a message window with the address information already filled in. Anatoly tapped out a quick message, added his office phone number, clicked the "send" button, and saw the "message sent" confirmation a few seconds later. He checked his watch. It was close to midnight, which meant it was mid-afternoon in Florida. He wondered how long it would be before he got an answer.

The next day, returning to his office from lunch, Anatoly saw the message light blinking on his phone. He pressed the play button.

"This is Michael Teasdale," said a voice, speaking Russian with a heavy American accent. "I read your e-mail this morning. When I noticed the *Isvestia* extension, I decided to call instead of message you, since I'm here in Moscow. Your e-mail was in English, so I assume you speak it, too. I certainly hope your English is better than my Russian!

"I'll be in the vicinity of *Isvestia*'s building sometime after lunch. If I can find it, I'll stop and see if you are in. Hope to see you soon."

The recorded message had just clicked off when his phone chirped. It was the receptionist, telling him he had a guest in the lobby. In the light of day, he began to wonder if sending the message had been such a good idea.

When Anatoly turned the corner into the lobby, he saw a middle-aged man in a heavy topcoat, sitting in a chair next to the receptionist's desk, busily polishing his glasses with a handkerchief. He was dressed like everyone else in Moscow except for his footwear—cowboy boots. After giving his wire-rimmed glasses a final inspection, he put them on.

"Are you Michael Teasdale?" asked Anatoly.

"I am," the man said in fairly decent Russian as he stood and offered his hand. Anatoly noticed he had a pleasant face.

Anatoly shook his hand. "I am Anatoly Altshuler, Mr. Teasdale."

"Pleased to meet you," the man said with a warm smile in his hazel eyes. "And my friends call me Mike."

"Mike it is," said Anatoly in English. "If it is all right with you, I would like to speak English. I need the practice."

The American smiled in relief as he switched languages.

"I'm glad your English is better than my Russian. I was worried about how we were going to communicate."

"Speaking of communication," said Anatoly, "this is the first time I've ever had an Internet message answered in person."

Mike laughed, shrugging out of his overcoat and folding it over his arm. "I don't usually do this. But, then, I don't usually get messages from *Isvestia* reporters. Your e-mail to our Orlando site was relayed to my Moscow Internet provider. My wife and I just moved into an apartment—ah, I mean a flat—not more than a mile from here! That's a coincidence I had to check out."

"Fair enough." As Anatoly led his visitor up the flight of stairs to his second-floor office, he said, "Let's see if we can find a conference room that's not in use. My cubicle is too cramped and not very private."

Anatoly chose a small room near his office. The room was seldom used because of its size, so he knew they would not be disturbed. He waved Mike Teasdale to one of the three mismatched chairs around the square wooden table, scarred with cigarette burns and white ring patterns left from tea and coffee cups.

"Can I get you something to drink?"

"No, thank you. I just finished lunch."

Teasdale draped his coat over the back of one of the chairs and sat down in another, stretching out his legs.

"I like your cowboy boots," said Anatoly, pointing toward them. "I didn't know there were ranches in Orlando, Florida. I thought that was the home of Mickey Mouse."

Mike laughed. "Mount Zion Ministries is headquartered in Orlando, but I'm from San Antonio, Texas, myself. In this cyberspace world, e-mail is as close as the nearest phone jack."

Anatoly nodded. "I certainly didn't anticipate a personal visit, but I'm delighted you stopped by. So let me come directly to the point: I accidentally picked up your web site while I was researching an article on Messianic Judaism. And something about that book—*The Covenant with Death*—intrigued me. It was . . . disturbing, I guess you would say. I don't know how else to describe it."

"The message is a strong one," Mike agreed.

"Ordinarily I wouldn't have given it a second thought. You see a lot of crazy stuff in life, and as a reporter I see more than most. I'm curious. Is the book fiction or what?"

"Actually, it's a compilation of biblical prophecy, *anything but fiction*. Why do you ask?"

"Well, there was one thing in that book that hit close to home."

"What was that?" Mike asked, leaning forward in obvious curiosity.

Anatoly regarded him for a long moment before answering. He had no idea who this man was, so he had to proceed with caution. "I would like to talk with you about certain issues raised in this book, but I would prefer that anything we discuss be confidential, what you Americans refer to as 'off the record.' " He looked deeply into the American's eyes.

"I don't betray confidences. Whatever we say will be strictly between the two of us."

"Good," said Anatoly, pulling his chair closer to the table. "I'm not sure how to begin." He paused. "What if I spoke to you hypothetically?"

"Fine," said Mike.

"Okay. As far as I'm concerned, the book you promote reads like the typical religious myth—until it gets to the part where this man, the Antichrist I believe you call him, unites three nations into one, and then makes a false treaty with Israel, which, if I understand properly, is what the title of this book is referring to as the 'covenant with death.' "

"Actually," said Mike, "it will more likely be three 'diverse' ethnic groups rather than specific countries, but the rest you have right. Go on."

"Okay, now, hypothetically speaking of course, suppose that someone heard of a scenario, now in the planning stages, that parallels some of what is in this book."

Anatoly noticed Mike's hands tighten around the armrests of his chair. "How close to the book does your hypothetical scenario come?"

"For the sake of our discussion, what would you say if I

told you . . . ," Anatoly paused, and then decided to go for broke, ". . . exactly."

He was watching the American closely and could see that his words deeply affected the man. Any good reporter had to know how to size up the person he was interviewing. *Isvestia* had given him years of experience! Surprise he had expected, but not the guarded shock that now registered all over the man's face. His reaction left little doubt in Anatoly's mind: Teasdale did not view the book as fiction. He took it seriously. Very seriously!

"Well, what do you think?" asked Anatoly.

"Without knowing specifics, I wouldn't want to say for sure, but believe me, I'd be asking some awfully important questions," Mike said. The American's mind was spinning with the implications of what he was hearing. He needed to know more—as much as this young man, sitting on the other side of the table, was willing to tell him. "What else can you tell me, hypothetically speaking of course?"

"I've told you all I can."

Mike looked directly into Anatoly's eyes before he spoke, but when he finally did, Anatoly could not miss the seriousness of his tone of voice. "Could I make a suggestion?"

"Please do."

"If you truly are on to something real, not hypothetical, you need to check this thing out, and the *sooner* the better," Mike said. "If you are willing to take a little direction from me, you can use the investigative skills you practice in your vocation and find out for yourself. This is too important to dismiss simply as religious myth! But before you start, you need some vital information against which you can check the details."

"What do you suggest?"

"I think it would be better to discuss this privately. Could you come to our apartment, tonight?"

Anatoly's reporter's instinct would not let him refuse.

SIX

At seven o'clock that evening, Anatoly punched the elevator button in the Teasdales' apartment building. As he waited for the car to descend, a nagging fear sat in his stomach like a lead weight. Was he doing something foolish—perhaps even dangerous? Could he really trust this American? Were his suspicions about Bulgakov totally unfounded? He had never completely trusted the man and his glib charisma, but was he just being paranoid? Sonya and Yacov certainly thought the prime minister was genuine! Was he reading too much into a bizarre religious book that might simply be fabricated coincidence?

Even as this thought flashed, reason dampened it. No, Bulgakov's plans—at least the few he knew about—were too close to what he had read in *The Covenant with Death* to be mere coincidence. Perhaps Mike Teasdale could answer the questions that were haunting him so. After their brief meeting earlier that day, he felt comfortable with the American. Interviewing as many people as he did for *Isvestia*, he had learned to trust his instincts. Still, he must be careful.

The elevator door opened on the ground floor, and a family of six pushed past him into the lobby. Anatoly got in the car, pushed the button for the eighth floor, and the ancient machine began its sluggish ascent. Once again, conflicting thoughts and emotions raced through his mind.

He was a reporter doing research on a wild scenario in which Russia played a critical part. He had every right to delve further into the matter—not out of disloyalty to Nikolai Bulgakov or his friends, Sonya and Yacov, but out of loyalty to his country. And if push came to shove—if Teasdale should try to use anything against him—a senior reporter from *Isvestia* would be believed before some unknown American promoting religious propaganda.

Anatoly began to relax a bit as the elevator stopped and the door finally opened. He got off into a shadowy hallway lit only by a single naked bulb in the ceiling. He turned to his right, as Teasdale had instructed, found the flat, and knocked.

When the door opened, the brightness of the room inside momentarily caught him by surprise after the dark hallway.

"Come in, Anatoly," Mike Teasdale said cheerfully, ushering him into the tiny, sparsely furnished living room. "Let me take your coat."

A middle-aged woman with medium-length brown hair came into the room, and Mike turned away from the small closet where he had hung Anatoly's topcoat.

"Marlee, this is the man I was telling you about," he said, the tone of his voice betraying the pleasure he took in having Anatoly in his flat. "Anatoly, this is my wife, Marlee."

As the introduction was completed and pleasantries exchanged, Anatoly was struck by Marlee Teasdale's loveliness. She was of average height and build, and probably looked younger than she actually was. Soft brown eyebrows arched gracefully over clear green eyes, and a deep rose flushed her cheekbones. Her sweet smile revealed the even white teeth so common among Americans.

"Marlee is an unusual name," Anatoly found himself saying.

"Well, that's a long story," Mike laughed. "Seems there was a Kentucky Derby winner by that name back in the 1930s, and, well, . . ."

"And, well, he's just thankful," Marlee interrupted, "that I didn't become the namesake of Man O' War!"

Their laughter bridged any awkwardness Annatoly might have felt, and within a few minutes the three of them were crowded around a small table in the kitchen. After Mike bowed his head and thanked God for the food they were about to eat, Marlee began passing them sliced beef in a dark reddish brown sauce, baked potatoes, and creamed corn. Taken aback by Mike's public prayer in front of a complete stranger, Anatoly had respectfully bowed his head. It brought to mind scenes from his childhood, when it was expected that he attend the synagogue. At least on the holidays!

"Mike tells me you two met through the Internet," Marlee said as they filled their plates.

"Yes. I sent him an e-mail after I saw your home page," replied Anatoly. He took a bite of the beef. "The sauce on this meat is delicious. What is it?"

"Homemade barbecue sauce," said Marlee. She smiled. "We Texans are big on barbecue."

"What made you leave Texas and come to our country?" he asked.

"Marlee and I have a deep concern for your country," Mike began. "As Christians, we felt we were needed here, so here we are."

"One thing that has certainly helped us is that we both studied Russian in college," added Marlee, "although we are far from fluent."

"Your Russian is better than most Russians' English," Anatoly replied with a laugh. Then he said seriously, "But are you saying that your being here has something to do with your Christian faith? Did a church send you? Are you Christian missionaries—I think that is the term you use, if my English hasn't failed me?"

"Your English is perfect, but, no, we have not been sent here by a mission organization. I had a good job for many years, and we made some wise investments. Our kids have been out on their own for some time now, and earlier this year I was able to take early retirement. So, as I said, here we are."

"But I still don't understand why you are here in Moscow, when you could enjoy your retirement in the United States."

"We are convinced God wants us here, Anatoly," said Marlee. "It's as simple as that. We call it living by faith—trusting that what we are doing is what God wants us to do, even when we don't find out the reasons until later."

"But why Russia? Why not somewhere else?"

"Until today, we weren't sure," said Mike. He paused for a moment. "Anatoly, I genuinely believe that God may have sent us here for the sole purpose of meeting you."

Anatoly shifted uncomfortably. "I almost didn't come. In fact, I was even a bit hesitant when you showed up at the office today. But I can't get what I read in *The Covenant with Death* out of my mind. I have to tell you, though, that I am coming from a very different perspective than you are. I am Jewish, and I know little about your Christianity."

At these words, Mike sat back in his chair. Some unspoken message seemed to pass between him and his wife.

"Why don't we have our dessert in the living room where it's more comfortable?" suggested Marlee.

As Mike led Anatoly into the living room, they chatted about places to see in the Moscow area. Anatoly made a number of suggestions and also recommended that they visit St. Petersburg. Marlee called for Mike to help her, and in a minute the two returned with cups of coffee and plates of something Marlee called "pineapple upside-down cake." The coffee was fixed American-style—too sweet, but good—and the cake, still warm from the oven, was delicious.

When the three were settled once more, Mike returned to the subject that was Anatoly's reason for being there.

"You dropped the proverbial bombshell on me this afternoon when you suggested that certain events described in *The Covenant with Death* could—hypothetically of course—be in the planning stages today."

"I think I figured that out from your reaction," said Anatoly. "That's one of the reasons I felt I had to follow up on it."

"Learning that you are Jewish only heightens my belief that God has brought us together for a reason," said Mike.

"May I ask what my ethnic background has to do with anything?" Anatoly asked coolly, wondering if he was once again going to come up against the kind of prejudice that always seemed to be waiting for anyone of Jewish descent.

"Because, Anatoly, the information found in *The Covenant with Death* is not solely a Christian perspective. Your own prophet Zechariah predicted that when the Antichrist takes control of the world, two out of three Jews will die! Even Hitler didn't come close to the kind of massacre this man will bring down on your Jewish brothers and sisters, when the day comes!"

"Do you really believe this?"

"Absolutely," said Mike. "But it reaches far beyond that, as horrible as it sounds. When a relatively unknown man comes along and begins to articulate plans paralleling the scenario you read about, and the things described in *The Covenant with Death* begin to happen, everyone—and I mean *everyone!*—who opposes him is in for the most horrific persecution and death known to man. Hitler, Stalin, anyone you can mention, pales in comparison to what this man will do to those who oppose him, especially in Israel!"

For a moment Anatoly wondered what he had gotten himself into. Were these people some kind of cult members, some end-of-the-world lunatics so prevalent in the United States? Even as his mind raised the question, the demeanor of Mike and Marlee told him this was not the case.

"Okay, then," he said, "let's just assume I'm working on an article that requires me to do an investigative report on what role Christians think Russia will play in these endtime events you're talking about—hypothetically speaking, of course."

"I understand your need for caution, Anatoly. We will discuss this issue from any perspective you choose. But I assure you, what will happen is not hypothetical. And for this reason, and others as well, you can trust Marlee and me—completely," Mike said. Marlee nodded her own punctuation to each of the statements her husband was making. "Anything you say will go no farther than this room. You have our word on that."

Instinctively, Anatoly felt he could trust the Teasdales. Besides that, he had inadvertently come across information that, if true, had great significance for both the Russian people and his own Jewish brethren, and he had a responsibility, not only as a reporter but as a Russian citizen with Jewish ancestry, to check this information out carefully.

"I want to know whatever you can tell me," he said finally.

"Good," said Mike. "To begin, let's go back to what I said earlier today when I told you that you needed to check some things out for yourself. What I meant was, you need to understand the sources behind what is written in *The Covenant with Death*. Too much is at stake for you to blindly trust one author of one book."

"I couldn't agree more," said Anatoly.

"In that case, it may surprise you to learn that almost all the original sources are Jewish, and that their writings are found in the Bible. In fact, they are some of Israel's most revered prophets." Mike smiled. "So if you don't like what you hear, your argument is with your Jewish prophets, not with me!"

Anatoly laughed, then said, "Since you are obviously using the Bible as your proof text, you should know that observant Jews accept only the *Tanach*—what you call the Old Testament—as holy. They do not accept the *Brith Hadasha*—what you call your New Testament."

Mike nodded. "*The Covenant with Death* is based on the *Tanach*, the Old Testament, Anatoly. The New Testament only fills in the gaps. But the two Testaments, the Old and the New, fit together perfectly. Also, *The Covenant with Death* contains over five hundred pages of prophetic theology. What I can give you tonight is only the tip of the iceberg."

"But how can I understand these things? I am not a rabbi."

"That doesn't make any difference," said Marlee. She had cleared away the cake plates and poured more coffee, then settled into her chair and picked up a knitting project from a basket beside her, all the while listening intently to both of them. "Anatoly, the Scriptures were written for the common people in their everyday language. The Word of God has never been reserved only for scholars. Read it for yourself. You can understand it."

"That's right," said Mike. "And for now, don't worry about what the New Testament—the *Brith Hadasha*—says. As I mentioned, it only adds more detail and clarity to what the *Tanach* already teaches. The whole argument outlined in *The Covenant with Death* originates in your *Tanach*."

"Okay," said Anatoly, then added with a laugh, "fire away."

"A world leader that the Scriptures call 'the Antichrist'—the prophet Daniel refers to him as 'the Beast,' which in Hebrew is appropriately translated *Satan-Meshiah*—this Antichrist will unite two strong ethnic groups that reside in Russia, as well as a powerful third ally, a Germanic group of people, more probably the nation of Germany itself. These three distinctly different groups of people will yield to the leadership of the Antichrist, all at approximately the same time. How this man will accomplish this feat, I can't tell you, but when the time comes, he will. After he gains control of this group, his first order of business will be to make some sort of peace treaty with Israel for seven years."

"Do the Scriptures specifically predict that he will make a treaty with Israel?" Anatoly asked, thinking of the plans Nikolai Bulgakov had revealed.

"Yes, that's what the title of the book, *The Covenant with Death*, is referring to. Your prophet Daniel gives us that information. You see, Anatoly, Israel is the key to everything that Antichrist does. *For him to truly gain control of the whole world, every Jew must receive this man as their Messiah—what you call Messiya—or die! From the beginning, God has always had a special relationship with the children of Israel. Therefore, a relationship to Israel must be the number one priority of this false Messiya—the Antichrist!* Whoever this man is, you can bet he will make overtures to key Jewish individuals who can help him achieve his objectives, long before he makes his false covenant with Israel. In fact, it is my personal belief that this man will probably be the one responsible for obtaining permission for Israel to rebuild your temple again, on its original site on the Temple Mount in Jerusalem."

"Why would you think that?"

"For two reasons, both of them selfish from Antichrist's viewpoint. First, by achieving this impossible dream, he will cement his favor with Israel. And second, when he eventually breaks his treaty with Israel—at the midpoint of the seven-year treaty period—and takes control of the world, both the *Brith Hadasha* and your *Tanach* teach that he will rule from the Holy of Holies. That means someone is going to have to come up with a plan to get the temple rebuilt, without starting a holy war with the Arabs. He's the most plausible candidate!"

Anatoly shifted in his seat. "This sounds so impossible. A billion Arabs would explode if you touched their sacred Dome of the Rock, which sits right on the spot where Israel would like to rebuild the temple! Look at what has happened in the past, when archaeologists simply tried to excavate beneath the Temple Mount in general!"

"How Antichrist will accomplish that feat is only conjecture. Perhaps Russia's longstanding relationship with the Arabs will be exploited to accomplish the impossible for Israel, once the treaty has been signed. I only know for sure that the temple will be rebuilt, and that it must be rebuilt before the midpoint of the seven-year treaty this man will make with Israel."

"Okay. So what comes next?"

"After this man makes his peace treaty with Israel, seven other nations will join with the original three. Interestingly, the majority of these ten nations that will initially come under the leadership of this man, will be the same nations that have historically been the arch enemies of Israel! Yet the nation of Israel will enjoy genuine peace and safety under his leadership, along with their former enemies! How's that for irony? If I was making this up, I certainly would come up with a better choice of allies! But to continue, in the meantime, the rest of the world will suffer terrible wars, famines, and plagues— unlike anything the world has ever known."

"That sounds a lot like what is happening today—the wars and famines and plagues, I mean."

"The worldwide problems that will occur after the covenant is signed will be far worse than anything we know today," said Mike. "This is only a foreshadow of what the real thing will be like. But as I said before, Israel and the ten nations who pledge their allegiance to Antichrist will not be affected."

Anatoly was fascinated by what he was hearing, just as he had been intrigued by what he had read on the Internet. Because of Mike's precise outlining of events and when they would occur in relationship to the seven-year treaty he kept referring to, Anatoly was beginning to see the big picture.

"Now follow carefully what I am going to tell you next, Anatoly," said Mike. "This is important! The Antichrist will use this worldwide crisis during the first half of the covenant period to prepare the world for what will follow, when the covenant is broken. As the rest of the world becomes more and more engulfed in the awful problems that occur during this time, the peace and prosperity enjoyed by the nations under Antichrist's rule will become all the more evident to the rest of the world, which is suffering so. Finally, when things hit rock bottom—which will occur at the midpoint of the seven-year treaty period—he will offer the world a deal they can't refuse! Those nations that want the same peace and prosperity his nations have enjoyed for the past three and a half years, can do so by submitting to his absolute lordship and leadership."

"And?"

"And, believe it or not, the entire world will be sucked in by this man's promises. In reality, they won't have any other real choice. Either take what this man offers or die of starvation or war. So, they will choose to follow the Antichrist, lock, stock, and barrel!"

"And that's when he sets up his headquarters in the new temple, right?" Anatoly asked, seeing more clearly how the pieces fit together.

"Exactly! Precisely at the midpoint of the seven-year treaty period. There, in the holiest part of the temple of the true God of Israel, this impostor will desecrate everything the Temple of God represents." Mike leaned forward intensely, as though he did not want Anatoly to miss a single word he was saying. "From there, Anatoly, the Antichrist will publicly join forces with Satan and demand that the entire world worship him. The only ones who will oppose him will be some of your Jewish brothers and sisters—remembering, no doubt, how Hitler enticed your people before the slaughter back in World War II—and genuine Christians like Marlee and me. That's when the real trouble begins for Israel." Mike pounded his right fist on his knee. "Everything—all the promises he's made to Israel before this time—everything has been to gain Israel's confidence before the kill! 'Like a lamb being prepared for the slaughter'! All who refuse his leadership will systematically be caught, persecuted, and killed! At least those he is able to find!"

Anatoly sat like a statue, stunned by what he was hearing.

"You're telling me that this Antichrist will be against you Christians as well as us Jews in Israel? We're all in the same mess with this guy?"

"Yes," Mike confirmed quietly, "that's what the Scriptures teach. Primarily it will only be Jews and genuine Christians who don't buy into this guy's song and dance routine. To the rest of the world, his demands will pose no problem because of what he gives them in return—food, peace, and prosperity. That will look pretty good to the world after three and a half years of famine and war. But those who see him for what he really is, a false God and an impostor, will die rather than submit to either his leadership or his lordship. Many of your people and mine will die because they will refuse to yield to this diabolical man."

"Mike, one thing bothers me about all of this. How can one man, in this day and age, ever expect to rule the whole world?"

"He will do it through the direct power of Satan—which all the world will see and applaud—and through demonic control—literally. This is one more reason why it is so crucial for us to be prepared for this time before it happens." Mike paused to emphasize his point. "Only those who know in advance how he will control the world will have any chance at all of escaping the wrath of this man, once he's actually taken over the rule of the world. Like I said, what he offers will look pretty good after years of war and famine. But, believe me, this man's peace agenda is no more than a ruse to rule the world under the power and authority of Satan!"

"Too much, Mike. You're blowing me away with all of this. Practically speaking, though, how can he pull off peace and plenty in the face of worldwide war and famine? It seems a difficult promise to live up to — one that may get him in the front door but could get him thrown out the back door if he can't produce!"

"The Scriptures are not precise on this point, other than the fact that he will live up to all the promises he makes to the world, for a while, at least. But I've pondered the same question for many years, and I believe the other nations will come into line, primarily by the demonic control he will have over the nations, but also, being more practical, because of the vast military capability Germany will bring into the equation. Their advances in technological warfare have always been second to none, and Antichrist will not hesitate to use his military might to ensure the peace he has promised."

"So much for bringing the wars to an end. How do you suppose he'll solve the famine problem?"

"Once again I can only make some conjectures. In my opinion the most logical way he could accomplish this would be to stockpile food before the famines begin. Other than a handful of Christians who take prophecy seriously, no one really knows the famines are coming except Antichrist and his inner circle. Which, of course, is another thing in his favor. *This man is capable of knowing some of the things that will occur in the future, allowing him to make the necessary moves in advance, assuring his success.*"

"You know that for a fact?" Anatoly asked, remembering a similar conversation when the same question was raised, only days ago.

"Absolutely. This man knows exactly what he's doing and why, well in advance. *Obviously he doesn't know everything or he would never take God on to begin with! But what he does know will give him a distinct advantage over the rest of the world.* My guess is, he will stockpile grain and whatever else he can while there is an abundance in the world, in anticipation of the famine he knows will soon follow. If the people worship Antichrist, they will have food to eat. If they don't, they will die, either at the hands of his followers or by starvation."

"So, he controls the world through military might and through the people's stomachs, right?"

"In part, yes, but primarily through the demonic forces that he will use to control the entire world. They will demand instant obedience from every man, woman, and child—and those who do not obey, will die instantly. His control of the entire world will be so thorough that only the genuine Christian and the serious Jew will ever dare oppose him. *Those who do escape his wrath, will do so only because, having been forewarned, they go into hiding before they are caught.* But most Jews and Christians will die because they are not prepared for what is coming. When they finally realize the trouble they're in, it will be too late."

The two men sat without speaking for a few moments. Anatoly noticed that Marlee's knitting needles were still in her lap and she was resting her forehead in her hand, her eyes closed, as though the enormity of it all made it beyond her comprehension. Her genuine grief over what she believed would someday happen did not go unnoticed by Anatoly.

"Mike, I need you to explain something else to me. You seem to differentiate between Christians and genuine Christians or believers. What's the difference?"

"Anatoly, the word 'Christian' has come to mean very little. Orthodox, Catholic, or Protestant—it doesn't matter. Some say they are Christians because they or their relatives, sometime in the past, went to a Christian church. But most of them don't attend church, except perhaps on Easter and Christmas. You know that's the case with the Orthodox, even here in Russia. On the other hand, many of those who do go to church have never trusted the Iesus of the New Testament with their very lives." Mike was careful to use the Russian name for Jesus—Iesus—when speaking with Anatoly. "Oh, if they're in a jam, they may suddenly decide to pray. But that is not a genuine, true Christian. Do you understand the difference?"

"I think so. You're saying that many Christians simply pay lip service to a faith, but genuine Christians embrace it from the heart."

"That's it. From what my Jewish friends have told me, Judaism has the same problem. Many may say that they're faithful to their Jewish religion because they go to synagogue once or twice a year. But in reality, how many of them really live out their Judaism in faith and practice?"

Anatoly felt the heat of embarrassment. "You have just described me, Mike!"

"Well, it's the same in Christianity. A genuine Christian—what is referred to as a believer—is the one who puts his trust in Iesus, seeking His forgiveness and serving Him alone, 24 hours a day, 365 days a year, and lives his life according to God's Word, the Bible. The rest who call themselves Christian are, in reality, self-deluded. In fact, Christ teaches that these 'look-alike' Christians will fall away from—reject—their superficial religion when the day comes that they must face the persecution of Antichrist. Do you see the difference? The genuine Christians will die for what they believe because it's a part of their very being. The others will capitulate to the enemy because their faith was never real to begin with. Does that make sense, Anatoly?"

"I think so. If I follow you correctly, the genuine Christians refuse to go to the dance with this Antichrist guy, but the rest of the so-called Christians get sucked in, like the rest of the world, right?"

"Right. You're seeing the big picture better than I could have ever imagined."

"Okay, good. Then let me ask you another obvious question: If the Scriptures teach that this Antichrist is coming, why don't your genuine Christians do something about it while they can? Why will so many die instead?"

"Let me ask you a question, Anatoly. Why will so many Jews die at this man's hands when your own prophet Isaiah so clearly warns your people about this 'covenant with death' they will make with the Antichrist? Remember, two out of three Jews will be dead before this is over!"

"Two out of three!" Anatoly repeated. "That number never meant anything to me until I read it on the Internet. Can that possibly be true?"

"That's what your prophet Zechariah said, Anatoly. That's the number he gives."

Anatoly just shook his head, face in his hands, staring at the floor. Finally, he spoke. "I still don't understand why so many Jews and Christians will be unprepared if the Scriptures clearly warn about what this Antichrist is going to do."

"Because many genuine Christians—like so many religious Jews—although serious about their faith, allegorize or simply disregard any literal understanding of prophecy."

"Why?"

"Well, for one thing, they probably don't like what the Scriptures say if they accept them at face value."

"What do you mean?"

"Many Christians have been taught that these things will only happen to the Jews, not to them. For this reason, they honestly believe they will be whisked away to safety before all this trouble begins. They speak of sudden departure from Earth—what is referred to as the Rapture in Christian circles—but the Scriptures never give them this false hope. *In fact, quite the opposite!*"

"So this Rapture will not happen?"

"Oh, there will be a Rapture all right! But it won't happen until *after* Antichrist has made his pact with Israel, until *after* he has revealed himself as the impostor he is. The teachings of Iesus make that absolutely clear. He taught His disciples that God will 'cut short' the persecution by Antichrist of those who oppose him—His 'elect' He calls them—when He gives His sign in the sun, moon, and stars for all the world to see. This sign will announce to the world that Iesus has come to rescue—or rapture—all genuine Christians who have somehow survived Antichrist's persecution. This sign will also announce the beginning of God's destruction of the wicked followers of Antichrist who remain on Earth, after the genuine Christians—Jews and Gentiles—have been raptured away."

"Well, how convenient for you and all your Christian friends that are rescued," Anatoly said with a touch of sarcasm in his voice. "But what happens to those Jews who aren't Christian, who also refuse to follow this Antichrist guy?"

"Anatoly, I know this is confusing, hearing it for the first time, but bear with me a little longer. Some Jews do trust in Iesus as their Messiya. This is the heart of the article you were doing on Messianic Judaism. *These will be rescued—raptured—along with the rest of the Christians who are genuine believers.* But in addition, approximately a third of Israel, although not Christian in any sense of the word, will nevertheless refuse to follow the Antichrist. They will become the arm of God in His retaliation against Antichrist and his armies, but not until after the sign is given in the sun, moon, and stars, not until after the genuine Christians—like I said, Jews and Gentiles alike—are raptured. Your prophet Zechariah had a lot to say about what your people—with God's help—will do to Antichrist and his armies when they finally rise up and retaliate against him! It's pretty gruesome reading."

Anatoly leaned back as he struggled to keep up with what Teasdale was saying. As a reporter, he had interviewed many people, but this was unlike anything he'd ever done. "Mike," he said finally, "I don't like what I'm hearing. If I understand you correctly, the genuine believers are taken care of, but because most Jews who reject Antichrist aren't Christians, they get left behind. This is what's going to happen? Have I got it right?"

"That's the gist of it, Anatoly. That's the bad news. It isn't a pretty picture, *but it's what is going to happen to those who refuse to accept Iesus as Messiya before God displays His sign in the sun, moon, and stars.*" He paused for a second. "But that's not the end of the story. You also need to know what the Scriptures say is going to happen to this small group of Jews that survive the persecution of Antichrist and take up the fight against him, after the true believers are raptured. This is the good news!"

"After listening to all this, I'd like to hear something good."

"God told the prophet Daniel that when the seven-year covenant period is complete, Iesus will return to Earth itself for the first time since He left it, over two thousand years ago. But this time when He comes, He is coming expressly for the salvation of these Jewish survivors we've been talking about. And in the day that He does, your prophets teach that the entire nation of Israel that survives the Holocaust of Antichrist—the one out of three—will receive Iesus as their Messiya."

"It will never happen!" Anatoly exploded.

"Believe it, Anatoly! Your *Tanach* says your Messiya— Iesus—*will physically return to Earth for the salvation of Israel.*" Mike opened his Bible to the Old Testament. "Look what it says in chapter 3 of Habakkuk, and here again in chapter 12 of Zechariah: 'They will look on Me whom they have pierced; and they will mourn.'"

"This is mind-boggling!" Anatoly just kept staring at the two passages that Mike was showing him. Yes, he had to admit that it did say that Messiya would come to Earth to trample the nations in His wrath, after which He would save His people; and yes, it did say that when Israel looked on the one they had pierced—an obvious reference to the crucifixion of Iesus—the spirit of grace would be poured out on all the inhabitants of Jerusalem. The prophets of his people had proclaimed this. But, like the rest of what he had learned tonight, could he really believe it as fact?

Anatoly couldn't absorb any more, but he still needed the answer to one last question to close the loop. "And what happens to Antichrist? What do our prophets say about him?"

"After the salvation of Israel, Iesus and His armies will go to battle with Antichrist and his armies in one final battle called the Battle of Armageddon. At that time, Antichrist and his henchman—his closest associate whom the Scriptures call the second beast—will be cast alive into a lake of fire that burns forever, away from God for eternity."

Mike smiled and he seemed to be seeing something Anatoly couldn't. "The believers who were raptured will live with Iesus in a place called the New Jerusalem. This New Jerusalem will hover in the air over a new, elevated Mount Zion that will rise up above every other mountain in the world.

"But most important, Anatoly, Iesus will rule the world from a new temple that He will build for Himself, on the very top of Mount Zion. The Kingdom of Heaven will become the Kingdom of God on Earth, *and the inhabitants of His Kingdom will be your people*, the one-out-of-three who, for the first time since Abraham, will truly be the people of God. *For the first time since creation, Israel will genuinely be at peace.*"

Anatoly was tired, his mind about to short-circuit. But he still had one more question nagging him. "Mike, what if Antichrist wins?"

Mike smiled. "That's a very good question, one that should be asked. Your prophet Isaiah quotes Almighty God as saying, 'Truly, I have spoken; truly I will bring it to pass. I have planned it, surely I will do it.' No more, no less. If God says it, He does it. The end is never in doubt. Think of the prophecies that have already been fulfilled. Daniel predicted the Diaspora of Israel, which began in A.D. 70; Ezekiel predicted the restoration of Israel, which happened in 1948, to name just two. Isn't it reasonable to believe the prophets are right about Antichrist as well?"

Mike picked up a Russian Bible and a Russian translation of *The Covenant with Death*.

"I want you to have these, Anatoly," he said. "Read the Bible. Study it. Compare what the book says with the Bible. I've given you an overview. Now you must complete the rest of your research. And if you have any questions, please call me. We have a phone now." Mike wrote the number on a slip of paper and handed it to him.

"You are not going to do my thinking for me?" Anatoly asked with a smile.

"No. You have to decide for yourself."

SEVEN

Anatoly opened the door to his flat and stamped his feet to knock off the slush before he entered. As he hung his coat in the closet, his first thought was to put the books in one of his bookcases and head for bed. He set down the book, but the Bible Mike had given him seemed unusually heavy. He looked at the textured leather cover and admired the gold lettering.

Almost before he realized what he was doing, he had settled into his comfortable reading chair and switched on the floor lamp next to it. He knew that sleep would not come until he began sorting some of these things out for himself, so he opened the Bible and turned to the first book.

"In the beginning God created the heavens and the earth. And the earth was formless and void, and darkness was over the surface of the deep; and the Spirit of God was moving over the surface of the waters."

With the care of a reporter and the curiosity of a cat, he read all of Genesis without stopping. It took him four hours to read it with understanding, and by now he was wide awake. His trained mind missed little; even though this was the first time he had ever read the book from beginning to end. His adrenaline had kicked in, as it did when he was working all night on an *Isvestia* deadline. Sleep never came when his mind was racing.

He had never read the *Torah*—the first five books of the *Tanach*—to say nothing of the entire *Tanach*. He knew some of the basic stories, although that was always what he had thought them to be—stories. But what had started out as curiosity had now taken on a new meaning. What he had just read had become more than a mere story. It was the history of his people, the foundations of mankind, and it carried the ring of truth that demanded further investigation.

The warm glow of the lamp seemed to be a safe haven from a surrounding sea of darkness. He set the Bible on the table next to his chair and went to the kitchen to boil a pot of water for coffee. He checked his watch. It was three o'clock in the morning. He drummed his fingers on the countertop as he waited impatiently. It was going to be a long night.

The gray of dawn crept into the flat so gradually Anatoly barely noticed it. He thought about going to the window but knew the view wasn't worth it—row after row of buildings exactly like his, as if they had been dropped from some Soviet cookie cutter, now dusted with a thin coating of snow that had fallen since midnight.

He finished Leviticus, marked his place with a used envelope, and got up to stretch. He was especially taken aback by the 26th chapter, with the blessings promised to Israel for obedience and the curses promised for disobedience. The disobedience part paralleled what he knew of Jewish history, only he had never known how clearly his forefathers had been warned in advance. He went into the bathroom and washed his face. He straightened up from the sink and peered into the mirror, expecting to see a haggard image. Surprisingly, other than bloodshot eyes, he looked as invigorated as he felt. He didn't bother shaving, but showered and changed into a ragged sweatshirt and jeans.

In the kitchen, he made a mug—a gift from Sonya—of instant coffee and took it back to the living room. After reading most of the book of Numbers, he noticed he was hungry. He glanced at his watch. He was late for work, but his boss was flexible as long as the work got done.

Not wanting to break his train of thought, convinced that getting the answers to his burning questions was far more important than the article he was working on—after all, now, thanks to Mike's explanation, he already knew what a Messianic Jew was—he called in and begged for a few days out of the office. "I need to do more research on a story," he told his boss. "Potentially a really big story!" That was the understatement of the year. They were also the magic words that got his boss to grant the request. "Take whatever time you need," he offered. "We'll survive without you."

He put the phone down and looked over at the Bible lying on the footstool. *Is that book really the actual Word of God?* he wondered. He rubbed the back of his neck as he stood there thoughtfully. Then he fixed himself some breakfast and another mug of coffee, and returned to his chair and his quest.

It took Anatoly a little over a week, eighteen hours a day, to read the entire Bible from Genesis to Revelation with a somewhat decent understanding. He was grateful for a good mind that could assimilate a lot of data, all at one time. It had proven to be a real asset in his job as a reporter, and it would prove to be a real asset again as he struggled to understand the Scriptures. He often had to read certain sections several times to make sense of them, but the study notes at the beginning of each book and at the bottom of the pages helped immensely. Many of the stories he remembered from his religious training as a boy, although now that he began to see them in their proper context, they held a whole new meaning for him.

He had considered stopping when he reached the New Testament but decided he needed to see it through, all the way to the end. When he finished, he had to agree that Mike was right. The *Brith Hadasha* was a culmination of the *Tanach*. The final book, Revelation, in particular, haunted him. So much of it came directly from the *Tanach*!

After going out to get some groceries and some fresh air, he spent the next few days reviewing *The Covenant with Death*, looking up all the biblical references given in its text. Mike had spoken truthfully. The foundation for all of the positions the book took originated in the writings of the Jewish prophets of the *Tanach*.

But as uncomfortable as the endtime prophecies made him, these were not what bothered him the most. The first four books of the New Testament told the amazing story of the obscure Teacher from Nazareth. What had this man done to deserve the most hideous form of execution known to the Roman world? This man had helped the poor, healed the sick, fed the starving, and put some self-righteous religious leaders to shame. Anatoly had to admit that he loved some of the honest exchanges Iesus had with the Pharisees and the blunt language He used. Anatoly knew how self-righteous and corrupt religious powermongers could be. That was the heart of the issue. Now that he had come to understand the other side of the story, he was far more sympathetic with Iesus than he was with those religious leaders who'd had such an ax to grind and had done it so brutally.

Anatoly knew how to distort reporting to prove a point, and he had initially approached the resurrection of Iesus with the attitude that such tricks must have been employed by His followers. But after reading the accounts of the event and its aftermath, he had second thoughts. Over five hundred eyewitnesses reported seeing Iesus alive after many people, including Roman soldiers, had seen Him dead and buried. The soldiers themselves faced death if indeed the body of Iesus was stolen by His followers during their watch. But it didn't happen, and for that reason, a corpse had never been found. Rather, many of His followers, cowards before the crucifixion, became leaders, choosing death rather than deny Iesus' resurrection.

Anatoly glanced at his watch. It was past midnight. He picked up a slip of paper from the table beside him and dialed the number written on it.

After three rings, a groggy voice on the other end answered. "Hello."

"Mike? This is Anatoly."

There was a slight pause, then recognition. "Yes, Anatoly!"

"Forgive me for calling so late, but I had to talk to you."

"That's all right." Mike cleared his husky throat a couple times. "We thought you might call sooner, but then figured you were probably away on assignment." He didn't wait for a reply. "Anyway, now that I'm awake, I'm glad you called. How can I help?"

"I have read the Bible you gave me."

"Good. What parts have you read?"

"All of it."

"All of it?"

"Yes," he said. "I've hardly left my flat since I was with you two weeks ago. After reading the Bible from cover to cover, and checking the references in *The Covenant with Death*, I've become absolutely convinced that what the Jewish prophets said has direct relevance to what is happening in Russia today. There is a lot we have to talk about, but that is not why I'm calling."

"Go on."

"It's about the books in your New Testament, especially the first four. I know the difference between fiction and reality when I read it—those things written about Iesus could not be made up. There were too many eyewitnesses, many of whom chose to die rather than deny what they had heard and seen. *A man will die for truth, but never for something he knows is false!* Iesus was the living fulfillment of everything the *Tanach* said about Israel's Messiya. Even how and why He died. Mike, why would He die for the very people He knew would reject Him . . . crucify Him?"

"When God began His work in my life, Anatoly, I asked the same question. What do you think it means?"

"I think it means that Iesus had a far greater capacity to love and forgive than I could ever have. Only God could love and forgive someone like that. Iesus must be our Messiya, the one the *Tanach* foretold. He must be the Son of God, as He claimed."

"You're right. But what does this mean to you personally?"

"I don't know," Anatoly said. "I think that is what I am calling you about."

"I can see you do understand, Anatoly. When the claim of Iesus confronts a man, he must make a decision, one way or the other. You are right—Iesus is your Messiya. But whether you receive Him as your Messiya or not is a decision only you can make. Since you have read the Bible, you know what happens if you receive Him, and you know what happens if you reject Him. You have to do one or the other, and it has to be in this lifetime. There are no second chances."

Anatoly closed his eyes as he thought about Mike's words

and the truth confronting him. He wasn't concerned about what others might think, although a decision like this would distance him from friends and relatives. The real problem was, in his heart he had already come to believe that Iesus was exactly who He claimed to be, God in the flesh, and yet he was totally unworthy of God's love and forgiveness. How could Iesus love him that much, to give His life for someone so unworthy? He had lived his whole life without God. He had grown up hating Iesus! How could God forgive him now?

"Anatoly?"

"I'm still here," he said. "This is difficult for me."

"I know it is. But the question will not go away. I say to you the same thing Moses said to the Israelites in chapter 30 of Deuteronomy: 'I call heaven and earth to witness against you today, that I have set before you life and death, the blessing and the curse. So choose life in order that you may live.' "

Again the line went silent. Anatoly waited for Mike to say something more but he didn't. "Mike, you haven't gone to sleep on me, have you?"

"No, Anatoly, I'm letting God's Spirit do what I could never do—convince you of truth and what your response must be!"

"I want to choose life, Mike. I am willing to follow Iesus the rest of my life. I want His values to be my values. His life was like a single point of light in a pitch-black room. But I'm so imperfect, Mike. Someone like me could never deserve someone like Him. I've rejected Him my whole life. How could He possibly love me?"

"Anatoly, the apostle Paul did worse. He persecuted—and perhaps even killed—genuine believers until Iesus stopped him on the road to Damascus. Later he wrote to the believers at Ephesus, telling them that they, like himself, before they became Christians, had been spiritually dead in their sins—active participants in all manner of wickedness. Then he said to these very same men, 'For by grace, you have been saved, through faith, and that not of yourselves, it is a gift of God, not as a result of works that no one should boast.' " Mike continued, "Grace is God's unmerited favor, Anatoly. We don't deserve it, but He gives it to those who call on the name of

Iesus. In the letter to the church at Rome, Paul said, 'Whoever will call upon the name of the Lord will be saved.' He was quoting your prophet Joel, Anatoly. But Iesus Himself said it best: 'For God so loved the world, that He gave His only begotten Son that whosoever believeth in Him shall not perish but have everlasting life.' That Son is Iesus, Anatoly, and the life He gives is eternal life!"

Silence stretched out over the line between the two men.

"I understand what you are saying. I have to believe that Iesus is Messiya, that He is the Son of God. I have to believe that He died to save us—to save me."

"That's not all," said Mike. "The Scriptures say we must repent of our sin and hate it for what it is. *Without repentance there can be no salvation.* Those whom God saves will be given the desire to turn from the self-centered ways of their past and put their complete trust and confidence in Iesus for the future. His death is the only sacrifice that can cover our sin before a holy God." He paused briefly. "In other words, Anatoly, it takes more than head knowledge. It takes repentance for your old ways and commitment to the only way—God's way. The Scriptures tell us that Satan believes in Iesus and trembles, but he certainly does not stand right before Almighty God.

"In fact, Satan's rebellion against God is what *The Covenant with Death* is all about! Saving faith results in faithfulness. *You can't work for salvation, Anatoly, but when you are saved, your salvation will be one that works.* Do you see the difference? Do you remember when we talked about the difference between Christians in general and genuine or true Christians or believers? That's what I'm talking about now."

"Yes, I do, and it's all beginning to make more sense. I know I'm a sinner, Mike. I believe that Iesus is my Messiya, my God, and my Savior, and I want to follow Him the rest of my life. I want to be a real believer!"

Anatoly heard a muffled voice in the background. "Is that Marlee?" he asked. "What's she saying?"

"Marlee has been praying for you while we talked. She was asking God to give you the understanding necessary to become His child."

"Tell Marlee 'thank you.' I need all the help I can get. I know I'm a sinner, and I hate my sin. I want to entrust my life to Iesus from this day forward, but I still don't know how to do it."

"You've just done it, my friend—when you looked at your sin the way God looks at your sin, and when you acknowledged Iesus as your Lord and Savior and, by faith, entrusted your life to Him. As of this moment, the very Spirit of God now bears witness with your spirit, that you are now a true child of God. He will guide your ways from this day forward. To say the very least, you are a new person, Anatoly. Old things have all passed away. From here on out, all things will become new for you. You have been spiritually reborn, Anatoly—what Iesus calls being 'born again' in the third chapter of the Gospel of John."

Anatoly could hear Marlee's voice again in the background.

"Marlee wants to know if you can come over tomorrow evening—I mean, tonight. I forgot what time it is. We would like to celebrate with you."

"Yes. I would like that very much."

"Good. How about seven o'clock?"

"That would be fine," he said. "Oh, and Mike, one more thing."

"What's that?"

"Thank you."

"Thank Him. This is His doing. I'm only the messenger."

Eight

Less than a week after Anatoly celebrated his new birth with the Teasdales, he invited Yacov Petrov to his flat. Anatoly had returned to the office for a few hours each day, spending all the rest of his time with Mike, immersing himself in what Scripture taught concerning Israel, in particular, what would happen during the last days. His boss had continued to be more than understanding. In fact, *Isvestia* had even asked him to consider making a major move. A promotion, can you believe it? he congratulated himself. They had offered him a correspondent post in Tel Aviv. Coincidence? With what Anatoly knew now, he doubted it. Would he go? He didn't think he really had a choice. Not because of pressure *Isvestia* put on him, but because of his new commitment to Iesus, to go wherever He wanted him to go, no matter how difficult the choice might seem on the surface. Mike had spent hours with him, helping him discern between his own desires and the clear will of God. There was no question what he should do, although the part of him that so needed the approval of Sonya didn't like the final decision.

He was ready to take the next step and tell his best friends what had happened to him. He wanted them to know everything—about his confidence in Iesus as Messiya and his suspicions about Bulgakov. He decided to start with Yacov. One on one was better than two against one! Of the two, Yacov would be the one more prone to carefully consider what he had to say. He was less attached to Bulgakov. When the time was right, he would talk to Sonya.

Yacov punched the elevator button, but nothing happened. He sighed in irritation and started up the littered stairs to Anatoly's fifth-floor flat. He was looking forward to the evening. He was also anxious. Something in Anatoly's voice worried Yacov. It was also unusual for Anatoly to invite him to come alone, without Sonya. Normally Anatoly looked for any excuse to be with Sonya, but for several weeks he had not called her or even come to their flat, something he customarily did on almost a daily basis when Sonya was around. When Yacov tried to reach him at *Isvestia*, he'd been told that Anatoly was out of the office for a couple weeks. At his flat, he got only the hollow voice on the answering machine.

Maybe he has a new girlfriend and doesn't know how to tell Sonya, Yacov thought. Well, whatever it was, tonight he would get some answers.

He was breathing hard by the time he reached Anatoly's door. At his knock, Anatoly opened the door. "Come in, Yacov. Sorry about the elevator."

In the living room, Yacov's concerns took an unexpected twist. A middle-aged couple sat on the narrow couch over by the single window in the room. The man's thick blond hair with a trace of gray gave him an air of dignity, and his blue eyes behind his wire-rimmed glasses seemed to miss nothing. The woman had the kind of beauty and complexion that aged well, and her smile was warm and welcoming. Despite their air of friendship, something was up and he had the feeling he wasn't going to like it, whatever it was.

"Yacov, I want you to meet my new American friends, Mike and Marlee Teasdale. They are living here in Moscow." As Anatoly introduced them, they both stood.

Yacov looked at his friend questioningly. What was he up to?

The Americans shook his hand and greeted him in heavily accented Russian. Then they sat back down on the couch while Yacov took one of the two chairs on the other side of the small coffee table.

Anatoly brought a tray of fruit, cups, jam, and a pot of tea from the kitchen. He spilled as he began pouring tea into the first cup, excused himself, and went to fetch a cloth. Yacov could see that his friend was tense, which only added to his own apprehension over what the evening might bring.

On returning, Anatoly mopped up the spill, poured the rest of the tea, and handed them each a cup in turn. He started the jam around, enjoying the reaction of Mike and Marlee who weren't familiar with their Russian custom of using jam instead of sugar for sweetening the tea. He took the last cup himself and sat down in the other chair.

"Yacov, there's something you need to know. Sonya too," he began nervously, "but I wanted to talk to you first."

Here it comes, Yacov thought to himself.

"I've asked the Teasdales to be here because they are focal to everything that has happened to me in the past three weeks. When I've finished explaining, Mike may be able to answer some of your questions better than I."

"What is wrong?" Yacov asked with growing alarm, sensing Anatoly's urgency.

"Yacov, before I begin, I must ask you for complete secrecy."

"What is this?" Yacov replied with a halfhearted smile. "Russia is different now. I may work for the Federal Security Bureau, but we aren't the KGB anymore. Anyway, since when do best friends reveal one another's secrets?"

"You will understand when I tell you."

"Okay, so tell me," Yacov answered impatiently.

"It's complicated, and, to tell the truth, it will be as hard for me to explain as it will be for you to believe, once you've heard."

"I'm not going anywhere. I have all night."

Anatoly looked at the Teasdales. "We may need it," he said, and Mike nodded.

There is no easy way to say this, he thought, other than to drop my bomb and run for cover, so, here goes nothing! "Yacov, I am convinced that Nikolai Bulgakov has set us up — you and Sonya in particular, but me too." He hurried on before Yacov could interrupt. "And not just us. He is setting Israel up for the kill!"

Yacov slammed his cup down, practically breaking the saucer. "This is not something we need to discuss in front of these strangers, is it?" His voice was rising in anger.

"It is! You will understand when I explain."

"Then by all means, explain."

"Do you remember, about a month ago, I was talking with you about an article my boss asked me to do on Messianic Judaism?"

Yacov nodded, embarrassed and angry with his friend, more so because of having to talk in front of these strangers than because of what he was saying.

"While doing some of my research on the Internet, I stumbled on a book called *The Covenant with Death*. The home page and the title caught my attention and, before I knew what was happening, I was skimming the overview of the book. I had no reason to, as it wasn't directly relevant to my story. But curiosity is the ingredient that drives all surfers on, you know that. However, I quickly realized that what I was reading was possibly the one big wave that comes along only once in a lifetime, if at all. And you know as well as I, if that wave comes, you must ride it out to the end."

In spite of his anger, Yacov had to smile. He nodded his head in agreement, remembering how he had described to Anatoly the surfing he had done in the Mediterranean when he lived in Israel, liking the parallel he was making to surfing the Internet. "So tell me," Yacov asked, calming down enough to enter back into the discussion, "what does your big wave have to do with you, me, and Sonya? And, more important, what does it have to do with Nikolai?"

The Covenant with Death was written years ago. In fact, the author is no longer living. It is a compilation of prophecies, largely taken from the *Tanach*. Basically the book describes a scenario in which Israel will make a covenant with a Gentile leader, seeking protection from her enemies. In reality though, she will actually be signing her own death warrant, setting herself up for a time of persecution that will make Hitler's Holocaust pale in comparison."

"So," Yacov interrupted, "I ask you again: What's that got to do with Nikolai Bulgakov?"

"Be patient, I'm coming to that. This Gentile leader will seemingly spring out of nowhere, making his world debut when he suddenly comes to power in Russia. The book calls this guy the Antichrist."

"Antichrist?"

"Actually, that's a *Brith Hadasha* description. Our prophets simply call him 'the Beast'! In Hebrew, he's called *Satan-Meshiah*! Nice name, huh?" said Anatoly. "Anyhow, the *Tanach* says he will have tremendous charisma, and eventually he will represent himself to the world as the protector of Israel."

"This is going somewhere?"

"Yes. Here's the punch line. This Gentile leader, who seemingly comes out of nowhere, first gets his international recognition when he unites the different ethnic groups in Russia—the Russian Orthodox in the west and the Muslim peoples in the east—and then, out of the blue, brings Germany under his control, all at the same time. And, as if that isn't enough, his first order of business after pulling off his little coup in Russia, will be to make a peace treaty with Israel, under the guise of protecting her from her Arab neighbors." Anatoly paused, looking directly at Yacov. "Sound familiar, old buddy?"

Yacov was speechless. He had tried to cut Anatoly off, but the words just wouldn't come. He couldn't believe his friend was actually discussing privileged information, here in front of total strangers. Again, his initial alarm flashed back to anger. He was finally able to get the words out of his mouth by switching to rapid Russian, hoping the Americans could not understand what he was saying if he spoke fast enough.

"Are you crazy? What are you doing? Why don't you just read these people the minutes of our confidential meeting with Nikolai?" He was almost shouting.

"I've just repeated exactly what the book says, Yacov! It has nothing to do with disclosing secrets we were told at the meeting we had with Bulgakov!" Anatoly fired back in Russian. "The book was written years before we ever heard of Bulgakov. Like you, I'm overwhelmed by the similarity of what the book says and what we heard Bulgakov say with his own mouth. Listen to me! The book goes on to say that Israel will enter into a covenant with this man, thinking he will secure peace for their nation. But, Yacov, that's not what frightens me. Listen to me! In reality, our own prophets say that this man is really setting Israel up for the slaughter! We're being duped! Our prophet Daniel says it will be the worst persecution Israel has ever known since the beginning of time! Did you hear me? *The worst persecution since the beginning of time!* And Isaiah called this so-called peace treaty a *'covenant with death.'* That was almost three thousand years ago! Yacov, how could this book, written so many years ago, foretell so accurately what we heard in a meeting two months ago? We were told that these things were known by no one other than those closest to Bulgakov, yet these specific details were foretold by our own prophets thousands of years ago — only Bulgakov failed to mention *why* he is doing all these wonderful things for our people!"

"Right now, I don't care what some book says — or the *Tanach*, for that matter. What you must have obviously discussed with these people could jeopardize our careers, our very lives, if what you have said ever becomes known outside this room! If Nikolai ever finds out . . ."

"I didn't have a choice! If this book is true, we are talking about the worst Holocaust ever against our own Jewish people. And, what's worse, the three of us are involved in helping make it happen!" He paused. "Did you hear what I just said?" Anatoly shouted at his friend. "You, me, Sonya — all three of us could be helping this man set up our own people for the kill! What do you think I've been doing these past weeks, Yacov? I wasn't on vacation, I can tell you that. I have checked every detail of this book against the *Tanach*. I checked it all for myself, Yacov. I took nobody's word for it. This book is not the nonsensical babbling of some strange religious cult leader. It is based on the writings of *our own prophets*, written thousands of years ago! How could they possibly predict what we see happening before our very own eyes? If you have a gripe, it's with our prophets, not me. I had no choice but to check it out for myself!"

"I don't know what to say," Yacov replied, calming down as

his friend's words began to sink in. "Obviously you believe what you are saying. But why have you told these Americans? Why?"

Mike shifted uneasily, knowing the two men could not speak freely because of his and Marlee's presence. "Anatoly, we don't want to cause any trouble," he said in his heavily accented Russian. "We will leave."

"No," said Anatoly, switching to English. "Please stay. I need you here. Yacov will soon see that you're no threat."

He turned back to his friend, continuing to speak in English. "Yacov, if my work has taught me anything, it has taught me not to believe in coincidences. So to answer your question, 'Why?', when I sent an e-mail to the address on that Internet home page and found out Mike was in Moscow, we got together so I could get some answers. Yacov, you can trust Mike and Marlee. I've spent many hours with them over the past three weeks and I would put my life in their hands without a moment's hesitation."

"You already have," Yacov mumbled under his breath.

"Anatoly has told us nothing about his work or yours, Yacov," Mike explained. "We don't know the details of what prompted him to be so concerned, other than in very general terms."

"All right," Yacov agreed, reassured for the moment. "I'm listening."

"Yacov, this isn't something I made up," Anatoly continued. "I'm amazed at how much the Scriptures have to say about the endtimes and the Antichrist. Our prophets wrote about it, and the Jewish writers of the *Brith Hadasha* predicted the same scenario, filling in more detail, and Iesus talked specifically to His disciples about this man and his persecution of our people. In doing so, He quoted directly from our prophet Daniel to make His case against Antichrist. Nothing that is said in the *Brith Hadasha* contradicts our prophets in the *Tanach*."

"We are Jews," Yacov reminded Anatoly. "The teachings of Iesus are not for us."

Mike cleared his throat. "Iesus was also a Jew, and . . ."

Interrupting what Mike was about to say, Anatoly hurried

on. "But there's something else I have to tell you, Yacov. Something important that you and Sonya must understand." Anatoly paused, choosing his words carefully. "The Iesus of the *Brith Hadasha* is truly the Messiya of Israel, foretold in our *Tanach*. He fulfilled everything our prophets predicted concerning His lineage, His birth, His life, His death— everything! Because I now realize this, I have become a Messianic Jew."

As his friend's words slowly began to sink in, Yacov felt his anger rising again. "So, are you three here to convert me, to overthrow the state, or both?" he snapped. "Iesus, our Messiya? Nikolai, the Antichrist? I can't believe this, Anatoly!"

"Yacov! Please listen to me. Please do what I did. Read the Bible and *The Covenant with Death* before you decide on anything. I only ask you to do what I did before I made up my mind. Check the passages from our *Tanach* and the *Brith Hadasha*. If I'm wrong, it will only have cost you a little time. But if I'm right, we could all be headed for unbelievable disaster—and what's more, we will be partly to blame for the massacre of millions of our people! Solomon, the wisest man who ever lived, said that the man who gives an answer before he hears both sides of an issue is a fool. Don't be a fool, Yacov. At least check it out before you decide."

"You said we *could* be headed for disaster. I thought you were sure."

"No, I have to admit that I am not positive that Bulgakov is the Antichrist," Anatoly answered. "What I do know—at least from what I've been told—is that his strategy for world dominion parallels, exactly, what our prophets foretold this Antichrist will do in the last days. Only the motivation and ending are different! But I'm not privy to the details of his plans. You are. You will know sooner than I will, especially if you know what to look for. All I know is that when we see a leader do the things Bulgakov says he is going to do, we're in real trouble. And when this same man makes a treaty with Israel, the clock begins running. From then on, we have less than three and a half years to do something about it. Look, Mike knows this far better than I do. He can show you what our prophets wrote, what our Scriptures teach. That's why I wanted him here tonight."

Yacov's mind and emotions were a swirling mass of confused feelings pulling him in opposite directions. *Anatoly, a Messianic Jew? Nikolai, this Antichrist predicted by our own prophets thousands of years ago? Sonya and I, part of a plot to destroy Israel?* Finally he shook his head and blurted out, "We live in a different age than when the Scriptures were written. We have science now. We don't need fairy tales to help us through life anymore. You of all people should know this, Anatoly."

A look passed between Mike and Marlee, and they both got up from the couch.

"We've enjoyed meeting you, Yacov," said Mike. "I know you are upset, and for this I am sorry. We came to help out, but it's obvious our being here is making you uncomfortable. We can talk later if the time ever comes that you have questions about what you've heard here tonight. But it is important for you to understand that we care about you and about Israel more than you can possibly know." He turned to Anatoly. "We can see ourselves out. Just speak the truth, Anatoly. The rest is in God's hands."

Mike shook hands with both men, and Marlee gave Anatoly a quick hug, then turned to give Yacov a warm handshake. Then they gathered up their coats and boots, bid both men "Shalom," and left.

As soon as the door closed behind them, Yacov turned to his friend. "Have you told anyone else about this?" he asked harshly.

"No, so you can quit beating on me now," Anatoly replied.

Yacov sat quietly for several moments, thinking about all that had transpired in the past hour or so. Anatoly said nothing.

When Yacov finally spoke again, the anger was gone and the good friend had returned. "Because of my trust and respect for you, I cannot simply disregard what you're saying, Anatoly. But this is too much, too quickly. I need time to absorb it all."

Anatoly smiled. "Believe me, I understand. I've had the same feelings you are experiencing right now—more than once, in fact. But, Yacov, I am afraid that everything I suspect may be true!" he said. "All I'm asking is that you give it serious thought and examine the evidence before you make up your mind."

"I'll think about it," Yacov said. "But I'm not going to say anything to Sonya for now, and I hope you won't either."

"I won't," said Anatoly, then snapped his fingers. "Oh, I almost forgot. There's something else I wanted to tell you—and Sonya. *Isvestia* has an opening for a correspondent in Tel Aviv, and they've asked me to take the job."

"Are you going to?"

"I don't think I have any choice in the matter, especially in view of what's happened to me in the past few weeks." He paused. "I don't like the thought of leaving you and Sonya after we've just gotten back together again. I'll really miss you both."

"Especially Sonya, right?" Yacov said, a grin finally spreading across his face.

"Yes, especially Sonya," Anatoly admitted. "But you, too, Yacov. Friendships like ours—friendships that may stretch and strain but don't break, even when separated by time and distance—are rare. You are my friend, Yacov, even if you do think I'm crazy."

"I don't think you're crazy. Maybe nuts, but not crazy!" Yacov quipped, smiling for only the second time since he had arrived. "I've always respected your mind and how you make decisions. This stuff has just been too much, too bizarre for me to absorb, at least in one evening. Like you, I need time to think."

By the end of December, Anatoly had wrapped up his affairs in Moscow and was ready to make his move to Israel. He didn't want to leave. He loved his homeland and he was certain that he was in love with Sonya. Friendship could stretch across time and space without breaking, but he wasn't sure that applied to the relationship between a man and a woman. He didn't want to leave her and risk losing her. Yet he knew he had to take the job in Israel. Being given such an opportunity at this time could not be mere coincidence. He was convinced that the hand of God was in it.

He and Yacov had talked no more about Bulgakov, but Yacov had agreed that Anatoly should tell Sonya about his spiritual decision. Nothing else. She was shocked when he told her he had received Iesus as his Messiya. But it was his decision to move to Israel that had devastated her.

As Sonya finished preparing the cheese and fruit tray for their guests, she felt the walls of her tiny kitchen closing in on her. This was Anatoly's last night in Moscow. He was leaving. She still couldn't believe it, although the gathering tonight was a farewell party for him. During the years she was away in Israel, Anatoly had always held a special place in her heart. She had dated a few men casually, but was never attracted to any of them and kept them all at arm's length. Upon their return to Moscow, she had been secretly thrilled to see that she was not alone in her feelings. While neither she nor Anatoly had ever voiced any of this, it was there, unstated yet real. How could she bear to part with him now?

She wiped her hands on a dish towel and listened to the sound of voices coming from the living room. At Anatoly's request, she had invited some Americans he had met recently. Sonya was puzzled by Anatoly's new friendship with these people, but the Teasdales seemed friendly as they joined in with their heavily-accented Russian. Tonight, Yacov, usually the life of any party, was strangely subdued. She could hear him saying something to Papa, who had also joined the group. Propped up in a chair, he smiled at the guests and occasionally said a word or two.

Anatoly's decision to take the job in Israel had overshadowed his announcement that he had become a Messianic Jew. As surprising as his conversion was, Sonya wasn't particularly bothered by it. She wasn't a hypocrite. Judaism as a religion meant little to her, so what Anatoly believed wasn't an issue. However, she feared that his religious beliefs would drive a wedge between them. She couldn't understand why all these things were happening. *Now that I have finally come* home to him, why would Anatoly suddenly decide to leave me and go to Israel? she wondered. During all the years she had lived in Jerusalem, he had refused to leave Moscow, even for a visit. Somehow, she knew, the Teasdales were involved in the decisions Anatoly was making. *What kind of religious hold do these Americans have on Anatoly? Doesn't he know that Christianity is a Gentile religion? Doesn't he realize how far away Israel really is? Doesn't he know that I am . . .*

She didn't allow herself to finish that thought as she carried the food tray into the living room and set it down on the coffee table.

"This looks delicious," said Anatoly as he helped himself to delicate Russian tortes she had bought for the occasion. The others murmured their agreement as the tray passed from hand to hand.

"Thank you," she said. She settled once more into her place at one end of the sofa and picked up her own plate. "In a way, I envy you, Anatoly," she said, then glanced quickly at Papa to see if he took this as resentment of their decision to return home. He was asleep.

"Marlee, what did you think of Israel when you visited there?" Anatoly asked, breaking the silent, emotional pull that gripped Sonya and himself like a magnetic force field.

"It's a beautiful country. We loved it there," said Marlee. "The amazing thing to me is the variety of terrain and climate in such a small area. You have seashore, mountains, desert, and the lowest point on Earth."

"Wait till you see Tel Aviv," Mike added. "That's the first stop for most tourists, and it's what a Texan would call 'wild and woolly.' "

"Not exactly a favorite of the Orthodox Jew," Yacov chipped in.

"It does present them some problems, yes. Will you actually be living in Tel Aviv or just working there?" asked Mike.

"I haven't decided. I would like to live in Jerusalem, but then I would have to commute to Tel Aviv."

"A lot of people do that," Yacov said.

"And it's well worth it," Sonya interjected. "That's where Yacov and I lived. There's no comparison between Jerusalem and Tel Aviv. And if you want to go to the beach, Jerusalem's not that far away. In Israel, nothing is far away."

"It is far from Russia," Anatoly said with a tone of resignation.

Sonya knew Anatoly's words had been intended only for her, and after that she found it hard to maintain any sort of cheerful front. The words "far away" echoed in her mind and heart as Yacov poured more coffee and she brought out their farewell gift.

"This is from the three of us," Sonya said as she handed the package to Anatoly.

Anatoly unwrapped a small black-lacquer music box with "SHALOM" printed in gold letters on the top. When he lifted the lid, the tiny instrument played "Hatikvah," the national anthem of Israel. "This should breeze me right through customs," he observed. "Thank you."

Anatoly then gave each of his friends a package. Sonya's was a bottle of White Diamonds, a hard-to-get, imported American perfume that, as he told her, "has a special scent I can pick out in a crowd." Yacov unwrapped his package to find Anatoly's Bible. When he thumbed through the pages, he was surprised to see many passages underlined with different colored markers, reminding him of the way Anatoly tackled every research project he undertook.

"I can't take this, Anatoly. It has all your notes in it."

"I want you to have it. It has become my most precious possession, and I hope it will be for you, also. Maybe it will help you better understand why I am doing what I am doing." He paused briefly, then repeated, "I want you to have it. I can buy another one."

"This may come in handy, then," Mike said as he handed a package to Anatoly. Inside was a study Bible with his name printed in gold on the leather cover.

"How did you know?" Anatoly asked.

"We didn't. We just wanted to give you an interlinear Russian Bible—one with the original languages alongside the Russian translation. It has wide margins for all your notes, and it even has an abbreviated concordance in the back! Please, accept it with our very best wishes."

As Anatoly flipped through the pages, he came to a note

inserted between the pages. He opened it and read: "To our dear friend Anatoly. All our love and best wishes for your new job in Israel. The Parousia Foundation in Jerusalem eagerly awaits your arrival. You will find the director, General Eitan Shachar, very knowledgeable and helpful. God's grace and wisdom go with you. Love, Mike and Marlee." A plain white business card for the foundation was clipped to the note. Only the address was printed on the card.

"Thank you," Anatoly said quietly, his eyes beginning to brim. "I will cherish this."

Marlee turned to Sonya and Yacov as she handed each of them a package. "And these are for our hosts," she said with a smile. Looking at Sonya, she continued. "Anatoly always speaks so warmly of you, and now we see why. This is just a small token to thank you for your hospitality."

Sonya's package contained a silver pin handmade by Indians in San Antonio, Texas. Yacov's gift was a hand-tooled western belt with a large silver buckle that reminded Sonya of a hub cap. It fit Yacov's 36-inch waist perfectly.

As the evening drew to a close, Sonya longed to be alone with Anatoly, but knew she would not have the chance. The Teasdales were taking Anatoly to the airport tomorrow morning because she and Yacov had prior commitments with Nikolai that they could not change. She clasped the perfume he had given her, wondering how long it would be before she saw him again.

NINE

Thank you for meeting me," Yacov said, his breath steaming in the cold January air. He clapped his hands together, grateful for the warm woolen gloves.

"You are welcome," Mike replied. "I'm glad Anatoly left you my telephone number." He looked across the broad expanse of Red Square at St. Basil's Cathedral. Its varicolored onion domes, each topped by a cross, stood out in sharp relief in the floodlights across the street from the Kremlin. "It's beautiful at night, isn't it?"

"Yes, it is." Yacov paused, wondering where to begin. "I realize that I asked you to meet me, but I have to tell you that I feel uncomfortable about it. I am a Federal Security Bureau agent and a government official. Anatoly shared some highly sensitive information with you and Marlee. Even in today's Russia, such actions could have grave repercussions."

"None of what Anatoly told us has ever gone any further," said Mike. "Even the man I put him in touch with, in Jerusalem, was given no specifics."

Yacov nodded. "I believe you. But I wish Anatoly had not told you."

"Is that what you wanted to see me about?"

"No," said Yacov. "But it is related." He paused a second, then continued. "I had planned to forget all about this Antichrist stuff once we got Anatoly packed off to Israel, but I can't. I looked up your web page a couple of weeks ago and started browsing through *The Covenant with Death*. To tell you the truth, I was looking for holes in Anatoly's arguments. But it didn't work out that way. I can't get it out of my mind. Yet, at the same time, I refuse to believe that Sonya and I could be mixed up in what this book is talking about."

"What if the book is true?" Mike asked. "Why don't you do what Anatoly did? Read the Scriptures and decide for yourself."

"One thing at a time," Yacov said, his frustration showing. "If that book is right and a certain public figure does rise up in Russia and fulfill these predictions, then you genuinely believe that two-thirds of all the Jews living in Israel will be killed by this guy?"

Mike glanced at the Kremlin. "When this man, whoever he is, is able to pull together the diverse peoples now living in Russia, and then get Germany to yield to his leadership, you'd better believe it! One of the ultimate goals of this man will be to wipe out any and all in Israel who refuse to go along with his programs. Your own prophets tell us how many that will be!"

"You mean two out of three?"

"Yes, I mean two out of three! Give me a break, Yacov. If I were to make up something that had even a small chance of happening, would I suggest an agreement among Russia, Germany and Israel? Never!" He paused. "But if you know something like this is really in the works, then timing becomes crucial. When this man we call Antichrist starts making overtures about entering into a peace treaty with Israel, everything in that book will happen, and it will happen quickly, exactly as stated. Count on it!"

Yacov jammed his gloved hands into his pockets and regarded the American closely as he pondered what to do next. "I will read the Bible Anatoly gave me," he said finally.

"Good," said Mike. "Anatoly marked up his Bible well, and his notes will help you." He brought a brown paper package out from under his arm and handed it to Yacov. "Here. I thought you might like to have your own copy of *The Covenant with Death*—in Russian. If you have any questions, call me."

"Thank you." He paused. "I have been rude to you, and I'm sorry. I guess I so disliked the message that I figured shooting the messenger would make it all go away. Please forgive me."

"I understand," Mike said. "Don't give it another thought. And remember, you can call me any time."

Yacov turned to go, then remembered something and stopped. "I don't want Sonya to know about any of this yet. Anatoly's departure was a real blow to her. She doesn't need the added strain of hearing these suspicions about her boss. If I think there is truth to all this, I'll know when the time is right to tell her. If not me, Anatoly will. She trusts Anatoly, completely."

"That is up to you, Yacov, but don't underestimate Sonya."

"I must insist. I've always felt that looking out for my baby sister was one of the primary responsibilities I had in life. Therefore, I ask you to let me be the judge of what to tell her, and when. I asked the same of Anatoly that I ask now of you."

"You have my word, Yacov."

Using free time where he could find it, and staying up late at night, Yacov took over a month to read the book Mike had given him, comparing each prediction in the book with the Bible Anatoly had given him. He told his sister he was working on a special project, but gave her no explanation as to what it concerned. Whether she believed him or not, he did not know, but she didn't question him. She knew her brother as well as her brother knew her. If he was doing something she should know about, he would tell her when the time was right and vice versa. In Israel, she had been the one privy to certain highly sensitive, classified research. She understood. She would wait.

Mike patiently answered Yacov's many phone calls, usually late at night and sometimes in the early morning hours. He tried to call when Sonya was out or otherwise occupied, shielding her from his growing concerns.

In mid-February, shortly after he finished his reading and research, Yacov phoned Mike and asked to meet with him in a park near the American's flat. Within hours, the two were seated on a secluded bench under the bare branches of a cottonwood tree that reminded Mike of their home back in Texas.

"This is serious," was the first thing out of Yacov's mouth.

"Yes, it is."

"It may be worse than you suppose."

"How is that?"

Yacov paused before answering. "What Anatoly told you was only the tip of the iceberg. There's a lot he did not know. He was in only one meeting with Bulgakov. But what I tell you now can go no further, Mike. And under no circumstances is Sonya to know. When the time is right, I'll tell her. Until then, it's got to stay between us."

"But if it's as bad as you think, shouldn't you tell her something?"

"No. As long as she doesn't know, she's safe. Trust me on this."

"Okay," Mike said reluctantly. "What have you found?"

"It would be more accurate to ask what I *haven't* found," said Yacov.

"What do you mean?

"What I mean is, you could make a good case for there being no such person as Nikolai Bulgakov. And apparently it doesn't pay to be too curious about him. Working with computers and being familiar with FSB's database, I had no trouble breaking the codes to gain access to sensitive files. All that code encryption training really came in handy. Once I had the passwords, I had access to a lot of information, but I've had to be extremely discreet. Too many questions in the wrong areas can alert the wrong someone. If they know or even suspect you're in their system, there are ways of tracking the invader backwards, back into his own system, blowing the cover of the hacker."

"What do you mean, about there being no such person?" Mike asked, still focused on Yacov's initial statement.

"Well, that may be an overstatement, but judge for yourself. Nikolai's parents, according to the official biography, were Vasily and Tatyana Bulgakov. Both are dead, and neither had any living relatives at the time of Nikolai's birth.

"Supposedly he was born and raised in Smolensk. At eighteen, he entered Moscow State University, where he got his degree. He majored in political science, minored in world history. His grades were good, and after graduation he began to make his way into public and political life.

"If you follow his history backward, everything is authentic until you reach the point where he went to college. By that I mean you can track his progress and accomplishments through sources besides his official biography. Before college, however, the records don't look right—they're too perfect, too uniform, if you know what I mean, like they've all been prepared by the same person. Also, I can't find anyone who can verify these documents or the facts they contain. But even more ominous is the fact that, without exception, everyone who supposedly signed these papers is dead. That includes doctors, teachers, principals, librarians, Party bosses. Not one person from Bulgakov's early years is still alive today. They died from heart attacks, accidents, and even suicide."

Mike listened intently to every word. "This is horrible," he said.

"It gets worse. About a year ago, a writer, thinking he was hitching his wagon to a rising star, started working on a biography of Bulgakov. He did little to cover his snooping, and several months later, when the man took a trip to St. Petersburg, the plane he was on crashed, killing everyone on board. About three months after that, a TV journalist was doing research for a documentary on Bulgakov, and she, too, made the mistake of looking back into his early life. Someone broke into her Moscow flat and murdered her. The police never found the killer. But the interesting thing is this: in both cases, all the data they had collected on Bulgakov disappeared."

"Are the authorities pursuing these cases?"

"I think you know the answer to that, Mike. Both cases are officially closed." Yacov paused, looking around to make sure they were still alone. "What do you make of it?"

"Based on everything you and Anatoly have told me, I'm convinced that Bulgakov is the man we fear . . . the man your prophets warned about. I am also convinced that it won't be long before he will begin to make his move to gain control of this country. To do that, his highest priority must be the elimination of your president, Vladimir Katanov."

Yacov winced. "He is already discussing this. What I don't know is when or how. What's more—as Anatoly may have already told you—he told us that he is already holding secret talks with the Germans. In fact, they have been going on for some time now."

"No. Anatoly didn't tell me that much. Germany, yes, Secret talks, no." Yacov turned on the bench so that he was squarely facing the American, his left arm draped over the back. "Mike, I am almost convinced that all you say is true, but I cannot afford to be wrong. How can I be sure, beyond any reasonable doubt, that Bulgakov is really the Beast that the Scriptures are talking about?"

"What more do you want?"

"I have to be positive. Both Sonya and I hoped Bulgakov would be a friend to the Jews and to Israel, and that is exactly what he appears to be. I don't want to be guilty of condemning a man who is really our friend. I must be absolutely certain!"

"Given what the Scriptures say, isn't that the way you would expect him to act?"

"I guess. But isn't there even a small chance that he could be sincere—that he is genuinely concerned about Israel, and all this is really no more than coincidence? Perhaps Bulgakov does have a love for Israel, does have connections with Germany, and the prophetic words of our prophets refer to another man at another time, if indeed they are true. I know the odds are against it, but what I'm asking is this: If I want to know for sure, how would I go about finding out?"

"It may be foolish to try, Yacov. You have already taken some big chances."

"But I have to know beyond a doubt. Too much is at stake, for me, for Sonya, for Israel."

Mike rubbed his forehead with his hand as he thought for a few moments. "Okay. Ask him about something prophecy predicts Antichrist will do. Something he will need to prepare for, before the fact, yet something that would be foreign to his thinking under normal circumstances."

"Thanks a lot. Any other suggestions?"

"I'm serious, Yacov. We've got to come up with something that Bulgakov hasn't discussed with his staff yet." Mike stopped abruptly, putting his right hand to his forehead. Yacov said nothing, not wanting to disturb Mike's train of thought.

"I've got it! Ask him whether he thinks Israel should have the right to rebuild the temple on the Temple Mount."

"That's pretty important, isn't it?" Yacov said, trying to recall the things he had read about the temple in *The Covenant with Death*.

"You'd better believe it," said Mike. "Crucial, in fact, to the real Antichrist. The temple must be rebuilt before Antichrist can begin his world rule, because the Scriptures teach that the Holy of Holies in the new temple will become his base of operations when that time comes. If Bulgakov really is the Antichrist, he has to be aware of this."

"In all the conversations and meetings I've been in with him, he's never mentioned a new temple," said Yacov. "In fact, if he had mentioned something about the rebuilding of the temple on its original site on the Temple Mount, the rest of us would have thought it really strange. It's not what you call a hot topic of conversation among the Gentiles here in Russia!"

"In addition," Mike added, "in terms of the political situation today in Israel and the Muslim control of this holy site, the very idea of rebuilding the temple on the Dome of the Rock is preposterous. So Bulgakov, if he is the Antichrist, must have some sort of plan to see that this gets accomplished. The trick will be to find out what he knows! If nothing, then perhaps you are right. But if he knows . . ."

"Then that gives me the confirmation I need," Yacov finished the thought. "Thanks, Mike. That's just what I needed." He started to stand up.

"Before you go, I have to ask you something else, Yacov. Can you take a moment longer?"

"Yes, of course," he said, sitting down again on the bench.

"When Anatoly read the first four books of the *Brith Hadasha*, he came to realize that Iesus truly is Israel's Messiya and Savior. Have you given any thought to this, my friend?"

"I am beginning to understand what happened to Anatoly, but I am not ready yet to make the decision that he made."

"Perhaps you could talk to Anatoly again," Mike suggested.

"Not yet. I have to make up my own mind, like he did."

"I understand," said Mike. "In the meantime, Yacov, please be very careful! I believe you are in great danger. You said it yourself. Everyone who has tried to learn more about this man has died, suddenly and unexpectedly. And anyone who gets in the real Antichrist's way is going to be obliterated, unless you see it coming. You have already been poking around. If Bulgakov really is the Antichrist and he finds out what you're doing, he'll try to silence you like he did the others. So please be careful."

"I will. I promise," said Yacov.

"But, more important, my friend, do something about your relationship with Iesus before it's too late. Read the Gospel of John in the *Brith Hadasha*. Then decide for yourself whether Iesus is Israel's Messiya!"

"I will. Tonight." Their eyes met as the two men stood and shook hands, then Yacov turned toward the entrance to the park.

Mike Teasdale prayed silently as he watched the young man walk away, asking that Yacov might find the two things he still needed to know. He knew that his young friend's very life depended on it.

TEN

Nikolai Bulgakov looked around at his personal advisors, zeroing in on the one he wanted. "Sonya, how do you evaluate our position with the Russian people since I became prime minister?"

"On the surface, there doesn't appear to be much change," she began, straightening the papers in front of her. "The polls say you would be elected president if an election were held tomorrow, although Katanov has actually gained about five points in popularity since your active 'politicking' has come to a halt. Our research tells us the people are more satisfied with the president now that you are his prime minister. Still, there is quite a bit of unrest, as the government has done nothing directly about the problems you once preached so ardently against in your rallies." A quiet murmur of agreement swept around the conference table at one end of Bulgakov's office.

Sonya waited for silence before continuing. "As we are all well aware, the president continues to struggle to keep Assam under control. Without much success, I may add. The Muslims do not trust Katanov, and their emotions run deep. The reality is, we could have another breakaway republic on our hands very soon." She paused. "But something else is happening that has me worried."

"What is it?" Bulgakov asked.

"Katanov has been meeting secretly with his former prime minister, Aleksandr Pavlichenko. Those on the inside say that Katanov still sees you as his political adversary and Pavlichenko as his confidant. Putting you in the prime minister's slot is their way of putting you on hold, neutralizing your popularity and keeping you under their control. But he reads the polls as well as we do. He knows full well that you are still the people's choice for president."

"So what do you think he plans to do about it?"

"I don't know. But I think we should be prepared for something that discredits you while making him look good. Setting you up according to his timetable, and then getting rid of you—permanently. With his popularity increasing, he may think this is the time to make a move."

"Would he try something as desperate as an assassination?" Bulgakov asked with deceptive quietness, hoping to prompt one of his advisors to pose the possibility he wanted them to address.

"He is thinking about this, I assure you," Sonya said.

"Perhaps this is why he is meeting secretly with Pavlichenko," another added.

"This brings up a practical question for us to consider," said Sergei, picking up where his master had left off. "Should we not consider making the first move—how do they say in the West, 'the best defense is a good offense'—for the good of Russia? Should we not consider means of giving the people the man they want—Nikolai—by removing, by force if necessary, the man they don't want—Katanov? Is the climate right for such a change?"

A shocked hush fell over those seated around the conference table. Nikolai looked intently around the circle, from face to face. Even if they agreed with Sergei's comment—and it was obvious that most of them did—they were all aware that this kind of talk could get them executed, if it were ever to leave the room.

Nikolai had always been able to read the faces of those he was addressing, an ability that enabled him to hold them under his spell. Clearly those at the table were completely committed to him—with the possible exception of one. He had seen it before, that strange look in Yacov Petrov's eyes. What was bothering him? He had been working long hours lately. Perhaps the strain was beginning to show?

Nikolai glanced at his watch. Time to break up this meeting.

He had accomplished what he had set out to do. Get the idea on the table. Get the initial shock of Sergei's suggestion behind them and then, at a later meeting, begin to work out a solution without emotion. Whatever he finally chose to do, he must have the support of those seated around the table this morning. "It's almost noontime and I have another commitment that needs attention before lunch. We will reconvene at two o'clock this afternoon. In the meantime, Sergei's question will give you something to think about."

Yacov stayed seated as the other members of Nikolai's staff left the room. He was still shaken by the boldness of Sergei's suggestion. Thanks to his discussions with Mike and Anatoly, he knew too much not to know what Nikolai wanted. He was also afraid his expression had betrayed his thoughts. Still, he had come this far. He must now pin this thing down, once and for all.

As the footsteps of the others drifted down the hall, Nikolai shuffled his papers together and looked questioningly at the younger man seated in front of him. "Something is bothering you, Yacov. What is it?" he asked, probing his thoughts.

Yacov hesitated briefly, knowing he was about to cross a point from which there could be no return. "I was wondering, Nikolai. Are you really considering staging a coup, rather than waiting for the state of emergency to be lifted and new elections?"

"I think you know the answer to that," said Nikolai. "Either we move ahead or fail. When opportunity comes, we must strike quickly. We never initiate, but if given the right opportunity, we must be ready to retaliate. To retaliate effectively, we must be well prepared in advance. There is no question that Vladimir Katanov has similar plans for me, you can be sure of that. And when he makes his move, we will take advantage of his cowardly plot and work it to our benefit." He paused. "He will start it, but I will finish it." The intense blue-gray eyes bored into Yacov's. "But I must have the complete loyalty of my staff . . . *your* loyalty, Yacov, if we, together, are to accomplish the great things that our country desperately needs."

"You know my loyalty, Nikolai," Yacov responded, trying to sound enthusiastic. "Katanov may oppose your — our — ideology, but still I can't see him risking all the power he already has to eliminate someone who works *under* his authority."

"He will try to kill me, Yacov. He has to," said Nikolai. "He knows he cannot control me, so he must eliminate me, once and for all. It has always been his plan. All we will do is protect ourselves when he tries, removing any future threat to us in the process. Besides, what we want to do is both for the good of Russia and the good of Israel. We must never forget why we do the things we do, however painful it may seem at the moment. If Katanov destroys me, your dreams for the Jews in Russia and the nation of Israel will die with me." Nikolai shoved his papers into his briefcase and snapped the locks shut. "We are dealing with a man who is not only anti-Semitic, but a terrorist at heart, Yacov. You, of all people, should understand how we must deal with terrorists."

Yacov felt sweat breaking out on his forehead. "I well remember the terrorism during my time in Israel," he admitted. "Frankly, the presence of the Arabs there has always bothered me — especially their monopoly of the Temple Mount in the very heart of Jerusalem."

Finally the real issue was on the table. The next step was to gather the courage to ask the critical question. I must be discreet, yet direct enough to measure Nikolai's thoughts accurately, Yacov cautioned himself.

"Speaking of the Temple Mount . . . Nikolai, you often speak of your love for Israel and your desire to see her at peace," said Yacov. "Do you think that the day will come when you can use your influence with the Arabs to make it possible for Israel to rebuild the temple on the Temple Mount?"

Nikolai responded without a moment's hesitation. "I think the Jews are entitled to rebuild their temple, right where it belongs on the Temple Mount. After all, your people have more historical right to that site than the Arabs do! It is, perhaps, the most important, singular symbol of your people and their rich, ancient religious heritage. Long before we ever met, I had decided to help Israel have their dream. When the day comes that the world is told of our mutual allegiance to one another . . ."

"But how will it be possible," Yacov interrupted, "given

the present state of affairs with the Arab nations that surround Israel?"

"I have already formulated a plan on how to accomplish this for your people. But first, Yacov, I must become president so that I am in a position to make it happen," Nikolai continued, rising to the challenge of promoting his agenda. "But if Katanov takes me out of the picture, none of this will happen. Do you understand, Yacov, that what we do with Katanov has direct bearing on what I can do for your people in Israel?"

Yacov could hardly believe what he was hearing. Still, while he had Nikolai's attention, he had to probe for more. "I'm curious about how you propose to restore the temple without declaring war on a billion Arabs?!"

"Most people don't know it, but the site of the original temple is *not* where the Dome of the Rock sits."

"What do you mean?" Yacov asked in genuine astonishment.

"Simply put, without ever touching the Muslims' holy place, Israel can rebuild the temple on its original site," Nikolai continued, enjoying the fact that he knew so much more about something his Jewish associate here knew so little about.

"But why do you say that the temple site is not where the Dome of the Rock stands?" Yacov persisted.

"Archaeologists have found the foundations of Herod's temple under the Dome of the Tablets, about a hundred meters northwest of the Dome of the Rock. Thus, there is no reason why Jews and Muslims cannot share the Mount. I will use my influence with the Arab nations to make Israel's dream come true, without offending the Muslims. In fact, Assam and I have already discussed this matter, and he will back me up when the time comes." He stopped and pierced Yacov with a steely gaze. "Now I ask you, will Katanov do that for your people? Can I help your people if I am dead? Do you understand what I am saying, Yacov? It comes down to kill or be killed!"

Yacov nodded, trying not to show the fear he felt as he realized fully, for the first time, that Nikolai and Antichrist were one and the same—that the man he and Sonya were helping in his quest to dominate the world was the very same one who would someday slaughter every Jew alive who refused to bow to his lordship or leadership. He knew he had already asked too many questions. He needed to talk to Anatoly.

The prime minister's eyes narrowed, sensing a distance in Yacov he didn't like. "Why all the questions, Yacov? Don't you trust me?"

"Of course I do," he lied. "How could I not, after what you have told me?"

Nikolai gestured impatiently with his hand. "Then what is the problem?" he demanded in a harsh voice Yacov had never heard before.

Yacov answered carefully. "I guess it's still hard for me to accept that the end sometimes justifies the means."

Nikolai seemed to accept the simplicity of Yacov's concern at face value, an understanding tone quickly returning to his voice. "Sometimes we have no choice. Nothing good comes without a price tag," he said. "Don't you see the vision I have for Russia—for the entire world? Can't you understand the vital role you and Sonya play in this?"

"Yes, I understand." I understand all right, thought Yacov. I understand exactly why you wanted Sonya and me on your staff—to help you destroy our people!

"Good, good," said Nikolai, rubbing his hands together. "Yacov, I have a thought."

"What is that?"

"You look tired. You have been working very hard lately. I notice these things, you know. I think you need a break. When you are rested, you will have a different outlook on what we must do to accomplish our goals." Nikolai's smile didn't reach his eyes. "Take a two-week vacation—starting now. Rest up. Recharge your batteries. What do you say to that—a couple of weeks away from this tedious government bureaucracy?"

"Sounds wonderful," Yacov could answer with honest enthusiasm, knowing he could use the time to plan what his next steps should be. "I would appreciate a break. Thank you."

"You don't have to thank me," said Nikolai. He bridged the gap that separated them and gripped Yacov's shoulders with both hands, as though about to award the kiss of merit. "You and Sonya are important to me, Yacov. Take time to think this through. Focus on the result—not on what we have to do to get it." The mesmerizing gaze met his. "Now, you'd better get to lunch before the others eat it all."

Sonya knew something was wrong. Although she would never question him in public, Yacov also knew she would show no mercy once they got home. They got off at their Metro stop and made their way to the flat in silence. The first question came when the door closed behind the nurse who took care of their father during the day.

"What were you and Nikolai talking about today?"

Yacov pocketed his keys and walked into the kitchen for a glass of water. "Why do you ask?" he said after taking a sip.

"I noticed the look on your face during the meeting this morning. Then you stayed behind when we left for lunch. And you were distracted the rest of the day."

"Why didn't you just stay behind and spy on us?" The hurt look on Sonya's face made him regret the words as soon as he said them.

"I'm sorry, Yacov, I don't like to see you in a mood like this. Is there anything I can do to help?"

"No. And I'm sorry I snapped at you. I think I'm just worn out. Nikolai has given me a couple of weeks off. Maybe it will help me get my head back together."

"A vacation will do you good. You've really been preoccupied lately, and I know you've been staying up till all hours." She smiled slightly as she added, "And I haven't been spying; it's hard not to notice in a flat as tiny as this."

"I know," he said.

"But why do I get the feeling that all of this has something to do with Antoly's American friends?"

Yacov refused to lie to her, so he said nothing.

Sonya sighed. "Do you want anything special for dinner?" she asked, changing the subject.

"Don't fix anything for me. I'll get a snack later if I get hungry."

"Yacov . . ."

"Please, Sonya. There's nothing you can do. I just have to think some things through for myself."

With that, she turned and went into the kitchen. She knew the conversation was over, at least for the time being. When Yacov was ready, he would tell her everything. He always did.

After checking on his father, who was sleeping, Yacov went into his room, changed into jeans and his favorite sweater, and sat down at his desk. It was time to make contact with Anatoly—to let him know what was happening and what he had learned about Bulgakov. He attached the phone line to his laptop computer and clicked on the icon to dial his Internet service provider. Seconds later he ran the macro to key his ID and password, logging him into the service's computer. He then started his mail program and keyed in his message, encrypting it the way he and Anatoly had agreed on before he left for Tel Aviv.

A.—

Sorry for the delay in answering your last e-mail, but I have to admit I didn't want to contact you until I worked through some things for myself. After a tough day, I have come to some conclusions you need to know about.

First of all, you and M. were right! Which means I made a jerk of myself the evening you tried to explain all of this to me. Please, my dearest friend, forgive me!

In the last month I have become a student of prophecy—to say nothing of Jewish history—thanks to the Bible you gave me and a lot of midnight oil on my part. I especially thank you for your notes. It made my work easier. M. has been very patient, answering my endless questions.

Second, your suspicions about B. are correct. Today he was talking openly about erasing K. I don't know how, but I think we will soon have a new boss who, for reasons known only to himself, is openly committed to making some sort of treaty with I. once he gets the power to do so. I've become absolutely convinced that his motive for hiring S. and me was not for the good of I., but rather, for her ultimate destruction!

M. and I decided on a way to test B.—to discover something that he normally wouldn't know about, unless our suspicions were right. Get this: B. not only favors the rebuilding of the T., he knows exactly where it will be built! What's more, he's already had discussions with A.—our neighbor to the east—concerning how it can be done and how it can be sold to I.'s cousins—you know, Ishmael's relatives. I hope you're impressed with my newly acquired biblical knowledge!

But there is more. Doing a little computer research of my own by probing some old databases, I've discovered that B. seems to have a false history prior to age 18. His early documents are clearly forged. What's more, everyone who has snooped around into his past has mysteriously died! No exceptions!

I now believe that the Beast Daniel prophesied about will be on the loose before long. We must do all we can while there is still time. Watch your e-mail. I will keep you informed on whatever I find out.

One request I ask of you as my best friend. I know you and S. talk frequently via e-mail. Do not—I repeat—*do not* tell her about this. It would be far too dangerous for her to know about our suspicions at this time. She is safe as long as she does not know. B. trusts her. I can see why B. hand-picked the two of us, but it's S. and her contacts he really wants. They work closely together. If she should ever suspect what we know, she wouldn't be able to hide it. B. would pick up on it immediately. I want to get her out of here when the time is right, but until then, the less she knows the safer she is. Is there any way you might help? Like marrying her? Sorry, I shouldn't joke about it.

B. has ordered me to take two weeks off. "To think things out," he said. I don't think he liked some of the questions I was asking. I don't need two weeks to figure out what's going on, but it will give me time to sort through my options.

For the first time in my life, I am genuinely frightened. Take care, my friend! And if anything happens to me, take care of S. and Papa. I entrust them both to you.
Y.—

Yacov entered Anatoly's Internet address and sent the message. He started to exit the mail program when he realized that he had forgotten to tell Anatoly the primary reason he was e-mailing him. In his desire to bring Anatoly up to date on Bulgakov, it had completely slipped his mind. How could he ever forget something so important?

He tapped out the information and sent the second message. When he finished, Yacov logged off, turned off the computer, and disconnected the phone cord.

He leaned back in his chair, staring at the dark screen, wondering what Anatoly would do when he got the messages.

Fifteen hundred miles away, Anatoly was making his first trip to Jerusalem. Settling into his new apartment in Tel Aviv—an apartment leased for him before his arrival—and into his new job at the Tel Aviv bureau had gone smoothly. He loved being in Israel but sorely missed his friends back in Moscow. Now, having successfully completed several minor assignments that needed immediate attention, he had time to pursue the real reason he had come to Israel. To do that meant he needed to go to Jerusalem.

Touching down on Israeli soil for the first time had been a moving experience, something he had not expected. He had never been a religious Jew, and his experiences as a reporter had tended to make him a bit cynical. So when his plane landed at Ben-Gurion Airport, he was surprised by his own involuntary response—his eyes filled with tears and his throat tightened with emotion. But that was nothing compared to this, seeing Jerusalem for the first time.

He left Tel Aviv, driving the used four-wheel-drive Jeep he had purchased shortly after his arrival. At first, the motorway east, across the coastal plain, looked like any other busy multilane highway. But as he saw signs for places he had just read about in the Scriptures and felt the pull of the engine climbing the steep ascent of the Judean Mountains, thousands of years of Jewish history tugged against his inner being. He found himself trying to remember some of the Psalms of Ascent he had recently read, songs his ancestors had chanted and prayed as they made their way up to Jerusalem for their feasts and sacrifices.

Finally, at the top of the mountain ridge, he saw God's holy city spread out before him. He pulled over to the side of the road for a few minutes, consuming the sight that lay before him.

Later, after feasting himself on the visual delights of Jerusalem for half a day, he followed Mike's directions and finally found the Parousia Foundation. He remembered Mike's explanation to him that last evening together. *Parousia* was a Greek noun—he wanted Anatoly to be sure to know it was a noun, not a verb—that meant "coming." It was the word the writers of the New Testament had used when referring to the second coming of Jesus, when Christ would come as a lion. Few in Israel had any idea what the word meant, but to those who did, it was the perfect embodiment of all the advance efforts of the foundation, looking forward to that great day of Christ's return. A two-story stone building off Derekh Shekhem near the American Colony Hotel in East Jerusalem, outside the Old City, housed the organization with the anonymity they desired.

"Can I help you, sir?" the receptionist asked with an American accent, stopping her keying at the computer. Her hands remained on the keyboard as she waited.

"I'm not sure," he replied in his accented English. "I am Anatoly Altshuler with *Isvestia*. Is this the Parousia Foundation?"

"What is your business?"

"I would like to see General Eitan Shachar."

"Mr. Shachar," she corrected. "Do you have an appointment?"

"No, I don't, but Mike Teasdale recommended that I come here."

Her hands came off the keys. "I see," she said. "Excuse me for a moment."

Within minutes, the woman returned and led him up

stone steps to the second floor and down the long hall to the door at the end. She knocked before opening the door. "Eitan, this is Anatoly Altshuler," she said, "the gentleman Mike Teasdale told us to expect. Mr. Altshuler, this is Mr. Shachar." As soon as she had made the introduction, the receptionist left, closing the door behind her.

The tall, middle-aged man stood and stepped around the large desk. "Welcome, Anatoly," he said, offering a lean, tanned hand and a wide smile. "I've been expecting you. Please sit down."

Anatoly settled into one of the comfortable leather chairs while the general perched on the edge of the desk.

"Thank you for seeing me without an appointment, general."

"Ah. I see you speak Hebrew. Beautifully, I may add. Please, call me Eitan."

"Thank you. Hebrew came very naturally to me. I studied it at the university and my grandparents spoke it all the time when I was a child." Changing the subject, he continued. "I understood that you were in the IDF."

"For over twenty years. But I'm just a civilian now." Eitan paused briefly. "So Mike told you to come and see me?"

"Yes. But I wasn't sure I was going to get past the sentry downstairs."

Eitan laughed. "Telling her you work for *Isvestia* threw her a bit! As you will soon realize, we try to remain very low-profile," he said. "Actually, I've been expecting your call for about a month. Mike has given me a general idea of what's going on in Russia, but told me you would have to fill in the details."

"Then he must have told you of Nikolai Bulgakov and his plans?"

"In part," Eitan said, standing up and walking toward the sun-filled window behind the desk, "but I didn't know who until just this moment. I'd like you to fill me in with whatever specifics you can tell me. As you will come to see, it's critical information that affects all we are trying to do here at the foundation."

Anatoly instinctively knew he could trust the man who stood before him. In addition, it helped to know that Mike said he could be trusted implicitly. It took him about an hour to brief the general on all the information he had. As Anatoly spoke, he carefully watched the tall man who moved with the grace of a jungle cat. His bald head and lean, handsome features reminded Anatoly of Yul Brynner, an actor he had seen in an old American movie on television.

When he had finished, Eitan stood for a moment with his back against the window frame, then sat down in the chair behind the desk.

"Obviously, your Nikolai Bulgakov becomes our major focal point," said Eitan. "Now then, let me give you a quick rundown on what we're all about. From the time the Satan-Meshiah — or the Antichrist — signs the seven-year treaty with Israel until he sets up his one-world government, there will be three and a half years. *Internally, we refer to the second half of the treaty period as Holocaust II. We call this time Holocaust II, because of the senseless brutality he will bring against those who refuse to bow down to him when this time comes.* Which brings me to the reason the Parousia Foundation exists today: Our primary mission is to locate and set up places of refuge for the Jews who will listen to us, for the Jews who will flee the cities in Israel before it is too late."

Anatoly nodded as Eitan continued.

"Therefore, we must be prepared for two separate times of exodus. The *first exodus* will come when Satan-Meshiah makes his covenant with Israel. Those Jews who see this covenant for what it is — 'the covenant with death' that Isaiah prophesied — will make an orderly exodus during the first half of the seven-year treaty. The Scriptures have already told us generally where this first group will go, which makes our job easier."

"The area of Petra, in southern Jordan," Anatoly said, proud to show some working knowledge of the topic being discussed.

"Exactly. You've done your homework. Scripture tells us that about 150,000 men and their families will flee to southern Jordan, so I figure we need to prepare for at least 350,000 people. Therefore, the Petra area is our number one priority. We have already done substantial planning, waiting for the day when we knew for sure that the right man was making the right moves in Russia. To execute our plans prior to knowing for sure, would be meaningless. Now that we know for sure, we need to execute the planning we have put into this site, immediately."

Anatoly nodded, listening intently to every word. Mike was right. Eitan was a strong, organized and decisive leader.

"Along with all this, we must also be prepared for a *second exodus*, one that will occur three and a half years after the covenant is signed, when Satan-Meshiah announces his world rule from the temple, initiating Holocaust II. This is our second priority but we won't activate it until our first priority, Petra, has been properly set up and is running. For this, we must find, prepare and secure many smaller camps of refuge in isolated areas here in Israel, each capable of hiding anywhere from a couple hundred to a couple thousand people. The sites must be capable of hiding and sustaining these people for at least three and a half years, until D-Day."

"D-Day?"

"*D-Day. That's our internal code name for Deliverance Day.*"

"And by Deliverance Day, you mean what?" asked Anatoly.

"*D-Day is when Yeshua will personally return to Earth for the salvation of every Jew who has yet to put his trust in Yeshua, but, nevertheless, refuses to worship Satan-Meshiah and survives Holocaust II,*" Eitan explained. "Those are the ones we will be finding places of refuge for when we begin to execute our second priority."

"And if my mentor, Mike, taught me correctly, D-Day, as you so appropriately call it, will occur just after the completion of the seven-year treaty period, right?"

"Right again," said Eitan, liking the way Anatoly immediately grasped the big picture. "Three and a half years after Holocaust II begins."

"And tell me again, how does the second exodus differ from the first?"

"The second exodus refers to those Jews who escape *after* Holocaust II begins. These will be the ones who won't realize how bad this man really is until he reveals his true intentions as the Satan-Meshiah. Even then, it will be too late for most of them. Two-thirds of them won't survive his wrath!"

Anatoly buried his head in his hands for a moment. The very thought of two out of three Jews dying at the hands of this monster was almost too much for him to comprehend.

Regaining control of his emotions, Anatoly summed up what he understood Eitan to be saying. "So, we use Petra for the first exodus; and then, after Holocaust II begins, these other isolated camps will be used for the second exodus, right?" Eitan nodded. "But tell me . . . why can't the second exodus get down to Petra, too, if it's already set up?"

"It won't be possible," said Eitan, shaking his head. "When Satan-Meshiah declares his true intentions, God will supernaturally seal off Petra—this first place of refuge—to protect those in hiding there. The book of Revelation tells us that Satan-Meshiah will know about this hiding place. He will try to flood them out, but he will fail. They will be safe there during Holocaust II because Satan-Meshiah and his armies won't be able to get in. But that also means that the second exodus won't be able to get in either. Even if that weren't the case, I don't think the Petra area can hold many more than the 350,000 we're planning on now."

"Okay. So what is your thinking on sites for this second exodus?"

"The second group will be under extreme pressure. Frightened. Fleeing for their lives. So we'll need smaller camps, scattered throughout the country. We need to be able to get them to these camps as quickly as possible. It's kind of the good news–bad news scenario. Because they don't take the hint until Holocaust II begins, we have a little more time to prepare places of refuge for them. But because they wait until Holocaust II is actually in progress, most of them won't make it. I estimate that we need to be prepared for at least another hundred thousand or so, once Petra is sealed off permanently."

"That's all? Only a hundred thousand escape during the second exodus?" Anatoly asked.

"Remember, Anatoly, two-thirds of those who wait too long will die. This number, of course, includes the ones who take the mark of Antichrist—they're dead, though they stand, once the wrath of God retaliates against Satan-Meshiah and his followers. Only those who reject this diabolical counterfeit and are able to flee before they're killed become our responsibility."

"But only a hundred thousand?" Anatoly continued to press.

"Well, perhaps that is on the low side, but that's all we realistically can handle, the best we can tell. But remember, Isaiah tells us that some Jews will flee to Egypt, while others will end up in northern Iran or Iraq, probably in the Kurdistan area—the Scriptures don't tell us how or where, only that some will find safe havens in those areas. We have people looking into potential sites in both localities, but working in these areas is far tougher than the work we are doing in Petra. Here in Israel, though, we think a hundred thousand is the number we need to plan for."

"We have some kind of job to do!" Anatoly exclaimed.

"I'm glad to hear that 'we.'" Eitan smiled briefly, then sobered as he continued. "The bottom line is that we need to start work on the Petra site immediately, now that there is a good chance that Bulgakov is our man."

"Isn't Petra a major tourist site?" asked Anatoly. "Won't the Jordanians object to us turning it into a city of refuge? No doubt it will be deserted once the wars and famines begin to plague every nation in the world, but I am assuming there is much we need to do before then."

Eitan smiled once more. "Did you know the Parousia Foundation sponsors archaeological digs? We have an agreement with the Jordanian government to excavate and restore Petra's vast system of cisterns and aqueducts. All done at our expense, of course—which is why they let us do it. But what they don't know is that while we're doing this restoration, which is actually for the benefit of the first exodus, we will also be hiding supply caches in the out-of-the-way caves in remote locations my people have already identified in the area. The planning and preparation work has been completed. Now we have to go out there and do it."

Anatoly shook his head, mostly in amazement at the planning and forethought that had already gone into this operation. "That will take a lot of resources," he observed.

"I assure you, we have everything we need. Friends, especially in America, are supporting us, in prayer and financially."

As the man spoke, Anatoly knew he was listening to a leader worthy of his respect, to General Shachar, not Eitan Shachar. And he knew the answer before the question was even asked.

"Anatoly, will you join us? We need you. We need a man to make our Petra plans a reality, and you come highly recommended. Your job with *Isvestia* can provide you with excellent cover, allowing you to do things we can't." Eitan paused briefly. "But in asking this of you, I must also warn you. If you do this, you will be putting everything, including your life, on the line. There are no guarantees outside of the promises of Scripture. Think it over carefully."

Anatoly slid forward, sitting on the edge of his chair. "There's no need to think it over. I came to Israel because of what I believe the Antichrist—Satan-Meshiah, as you call him—is going to do to our people, and because I am now a believer like you and the Teasdales. Count me in. When do I start?"

In an uncustomary show of emotion, Eitan jumped up from his chair and came around the desk to clasp Anatoly's hand, pulling him into a brief embrace.

"I can't tell you how much this pleases me, Anatoly." Eitan stepped back a few paces. "We start tomorrow, right here, at 8:00 A.M. sharp, if you can work it out with *Isvestia*. We'll bring you up to date on all the specifics of what we're doing and line up your immediate agenda."

"Don't worry about *Isvestia*. I'm the senior man here in Israel, of a total staff of two . . . including me! My time is my own." Eitan walked Anatoly to the door, where the two men shook hands once more and bid each other "Shalom."

Moments later, as Anatoly stepped out of the building into the bright Jerusalem sunshine, he knew he was stepping out into the pathway God had chosen for him.

ELEVEN

"We have a problem," Bulgakov began. He played with a gold pen as he watched Sergei Lomonosov's reaction.

"What is it?"

"Yacov Petrov. He is suspicious."

"Of what?"

"I'm not sure yet, but he's poking around where he has no business."

Lomonosov exhaled loudly and frowned. "Not another one! What can he know that could hurt us? He only has access to what you tell him. He certainly can't be a mole for Katanov, being Jewish and all."

"He has been acting strangely. It became obvious to me at our briefing yesterday. I talked with him at some length after the meeting and things didn't feel right, so I did some checking. Our friends in the Federal Security Bureau tell me that there have been discreet computer inquiries into databases dealing with my past. What he obviously doesn't know is that my personal files are protected three ways; the first two obvious but complicated, applicable to all the databases we have at the agency. The third is impossible to detect and is applicable only to my personal database. He made it through the first two which, in itself, is quite amazing, but the last one nailed him without his even knowing. We not only know when my files are accessed, but from where the intrusion originates. In the past month, our tracer system shows that four or five entries have been made. They were cleverly done by someone who knew what he was doing. Any possible link to

Yacov was carefully concealed, but once our computer nerds knew which direction to look, the rest was relatively easy. They tracked the entries right back to his terminal."

"How in the world did he get the passwords?"

"Don't ask me how, but remember, that *is* his training, his expertise. Somehow he was able to figure them out. As we speak, they're being changed, but that doesn't undo the damage that may have already been done."

"I don't like the sound of that. What do you suggest we do?"

"He must be silenced," said Bulgakov coldly. "Carefully, like the others."

"What about his sister? Does she know?"

"What can she know? What can Yacov really know? It's not what's in the files that can damage us. It's what the files don't tell you. There's no way Yacov could possibly put it all together. But he's snooping, and you never know what he might stumble onto, like that stupid reporter did several years ago."

"But that still doesn't answer my question. What do we do about Sonya?"

"Whatever he's up to, I'm certain that Sonya is not a part of it. Knowing how Yacov protects his little sister, he would keep the lid on what he might suspect until he was certain. He hasn't had enough time to check these things out. If he had been snooping around some of the other sources, we would have heard something by now. No, if she knew, she would not be able to hide it from me—which is fortunate, because we need her contacts with Israeli intelligence to accomplish what I have in mind for Israel."

"We can get someone else."

"No, we can't unless we absolutely have to. With everything moving so quickly now, we don't have time to cultivate someone new for this strategic position. Sonya was perfect when we chose her, and everything she has done since she joined my staff has proven we made the right choice. If you recall, Yacov was the price we paid to get Sonya. Now, Yacov has outlived his usefulness."

"So how are you going to handle him?"

"I've come up with a simple plan that will accomplish two goals for the price of one. Yacov Petrov must be eliminated in such a way that Katanov takes the blame. If it is handled right, it will make Sonya hate him even more and cement her commitment to me and my cause. I need that strong commitment from her now that things are beginning to happen. She plays a critical role in our plan for the Jews!"

"So, how do we accomplish all that?"

"You must handle this personally, Sergei. Nobody can know, not even those on my personal advisory staff. Sonya must have no doubts that this is the work of Vladimir Katanov. So it must have the look of a professional killing with political overtones. I'll take it from there."

"When?"

"Right away, tomorrow morning, shortly after 8:30. Sonya is always here by 8:00. I've given Yacov time off, so he should still be at home that early in the day. Kill him and the father. If that day nurse is there, get rid of her, too. Leave no witnesses. When Sonya comes running to me, I will do the rest."

Sergei frowned. "How can you be so sure?"

"She has nowhere else to turn. She believes in me and what I am doing for her people. With Yacov and her father dead, and her reporter friend now living in Israel, I am the only one left that she truly trusts. She has no one else. Wait and see. I can read people. That's why we must deal with Yacov before he talks to Sonya."

The doorbell rang. Yacov scowled as he looked up from his laptop. He needed this time alone to tie up a few loose ends so he could leave for St. Petersburg the next morning. He was anxious to get out of Moscow for a few days. He needed to talk directly with Anatoly, and it would be safer to phone him from St. Petersburg. After the two e-mail messages he had sent yesterday, they had a lot to talk about.

He glanced at his watch. Eight-thirty. Who could it be this early in the morning? He had told the nurse not to come today. He wanted to spend time with his father before he left.

The doorbell rang again.

Probably someone who can't find the flat they're looking for. On the outside, they all look alike. Must be important if they're willing to climb six flights of stairs this early in the morning!

He walked to the door and grabbed the handle. He started to turn it when he thought about Mike's words to him. "Please be careful!" An icy chill raced up his spine.

"Who is it?" he asked cautiously.

There was no answer. Something was wrong.

Yacov stood back from the door, looking frantically for a weapon. He remembered the butcher knife Sonya had left out on the kitchen countertop.

As he dashed for the kitchen, something smashed against the lock and the door gave way. Yacov almost fell as he slid into the kitchen. He heard a dull thud as a bullet dug into the far wall of the living room. He grabbed the knife and fell to the floor behind the table that served as an island between the kitchen and the living room.

He tried to listen for the killer's approach but could hear nothing over his own labored breathing. He peered around the small table with its neat checkered tablecloth, expecting to see the intruder leap into the room. Something shiny flashed into the kitchen. Yacov's eyes followed involuntarily as it crashed against the wall beneath the cabinets. It was one of the smashed doorknobs.

Yacov heard a sound above him and looked up.

Sergei Lomonosov was leaning over the kitchen table, pointing a gun with a long, black silencer directly at his head. Yacov rolled over on his back and slung the knife. The blade harmlessly brushed Lomonosov's coat before bouncing off the wall behind him.

Sergei sighted the silenced 9mm Makarov between eyes that now looked at him with recognition, fear, and disgust.

The silencer plopped once, and a tiny black circle appeared in the center of Yacov Petrov's forehead. An ugly red spray drenched the floor and cabinet behind him.

Lomonosov cautiously approached Yacov. He lay silently on the kitchen floor, his blank eyes staring up at the ceiling, but seeing nothing. Sergei kicked the body over with his foot, sighted again for the two back-of-the-head shots, the trademark of a political assassination, and pulled the trigger twice. The body jumped but Yacov was already dead.

"What's going on in there?" called a weak voice from a room off to one side of the living room. "Yacov?"

Lomonosov turned and walked toward the sound. The old man was in bed, trying to raise himself with his arms.

"Who are you?" he demanded. "Where is Yacov?"

Lomonosov slowly elevated the gun as the old man stared at him in horror. The assassin squeezed off the head shot, and Vitali Petrov fell back against his pillow for the last time. The two back-of-the-head shots that followed were right on target.

Lomonosov hurried to the door and peered out cautiously. The corridor was deserted. He left the flat, closing the broken door behind him.

At the entrance to the Metro, he deposited coins in the pay phone and punched in the number. When the recording began, he punched in the eight-digit security code number. The phone began to ring.

"Yes?" said the voice on the other end.

"It's done."

The line went dead.

Sonya Petrov's worries carried her through the rush-hour sardine-can ride in the Metro. Tomorrow Yacov would be on his way to St. Petersburg. She would miss him, but she knew he needed the rest. For the past month he had been going at high speed, into the early hours of the morning. She knew her brother well. The look on his face after his meeting yesterday with Nikolai and his mood last night told her something was radically wrong. Did it have anything to do with his work for Nikolai, or did it have something to do with Nikolai himself? She wished she knew. Why was he suddenly so secretive? Was it some confidential project he was doing for Nikolai, or did it have something to do with the Americans? Maybe he would be ready to discuss it with her when he returned from St. Petersburg. Maybe he would discuss it with her tonight.

The six flights of stairs seemed like ten, tonight. She was both tired and worried. She was only a few feet away from their flat when she saw the splintered door. Her whole body began to shake. Slowly, she pushed the door open. She stepped into the room. Nothing was disturbed, but the smell of blood and death filled the silence.

She moved a few steps farther and saw the arm stretched out on the floor beside the kitchen table.

"Yacov!" she screamed.

She rushed into the kitchen and fell to her knees beside her dead brother. The blood drenching the floor beneath him was thick and almost black. She became hysterical, screaming out, again and again. Get a hold of yourself, she tried to tell herself. After a moment, her anguish turned into tears, her hysteria into the groans of the sorrowful. She could feel the stickiness on her hands as she rolled him over and cradled his head in her lap. For several moments she sat there sobbing, caressing his hair, rocking slowly back and forth.

Suddenly, the deafening silence got through to her, screaming out that something else was also terribly wrong. It hit her like a thunderbolt. She knew immediately what it meant.

She stumbled to her feet and ran to her father's room, already dreading what she knew she would find.

"Oh, Papa," she moaned as she fell to her knees beside his bed, clasping his lifeless, cold hand.

Time stood still as she knelt there. Then, slowly, the fog of disbelief began to rise. She had to pull herself together. Death was no stranger to her, not even violent death. But this was different. This was personal. She needed help, now.

Numbly, she picked up the phone and dialed Nikolai's personal telephone number.

Sonya crossed the Oriental carpet covering the floor of the hotel room and parted the heavy brocade draperies at the window. Below her, the evening traffic rushed past in the darkness. As soon as she told him what had happened, Nikolai had insisted that she move here, to one of the guest suites reserved for visiting dignitaries and government guests, just blocks from the Kremlin. His staff would take care of everything, he said, even the funeral arrangements for her father and Yacov. He had also promised to do everything in his power to find out who had done this terrible thing, and why.

Across the street, the lights of the Bolshoi blurred as tears filled her eyes. She hadn't eaten in almost twelve hours and found it almost impossible to think clearly. The shock of the reality of all that had happened began to set in. Why would anyone kill Yacov? Papa?

She debated a moment, then went to the phone on the faux-antique desk. She flipped through her appointment planner. She found it difficult to even find his name. Finally, she found Anatoly's number for his Tel Aviv office. She knew he was a night owl and preferred this time to do his writing. She picked up the phone and gave the number and her name to the operator. A few minutes later, she was connected with Anatoly's voice mail. He was not there, probably out grabbing a late-night snack. She left a message to call her as soon as possible. Then she lay down on the bed, staring at the ceiling.

She was still in the same spot an hour later when the phone rang.

"Sonya, is that you?" Anatoly's voice sounded surprisingly close and comfortingly familiar.

"Yes," she said. "I'm glad I could reach you so quickly." She began to cry, softly.

"I'm in Jerusalem," he said. "I just called the office to check in and got your message." He paused. "Is something the matter?"

"Yacov and Papa are dead," she said, her voice hoarse and without emotion. "Someone broke into our flat this morning and murdered them."

The line was quiet for a few moments, giving Sonya time to cry out some of the emotion that welled up from deep within her heart. "Sonya, why?" was all he could finally manage to say, overwhelmed by the loss of his best friend.

"I have no idea. The door was smashed in, but nothing was taken." She started crying again, remembering the cruel way their lives had ended.

"Sonya, are you all right? Did they hurt you?"

She wiped her eyes with the back of her hand. "No. I came

home from work tonight and found them. They didn't have a chance, Anatoly. Yacov was on the kitchen floor, and Papa was still in bed. Both of them had been shot once in the forehead and twice in the back of the head. What does that mean, Anatoly?" she sobbed.

"Twice in the back of the head, in addition to a shot in the forehead?" Anatoly repeated slowly. "Any of those shots would have killed them instantly. Why?"

"I don't know. When I found them they were both face down, so the two shots in the back of the head came after they were already dead," Sonya barely whispered.

"It has to be a professional hit. A couple years ago, I did several stories on political figures that were assassinated with two back-of-the-head shots. I remember that this style of execution was a trademark slaying that conveyed a warning, Sonya. But Yacov was not directly tied into the political arena."

"I know. That's what I don't understand. Why?"

The first thing that crossed Anatoly's mind was that Yacov had come too close to the truth. Mike had e-mailed him about Yacov's decision to test Bulgakov, but hadn't given him any details. He'd heard nothing from either of them since, although he hadn't been able to check his Internet site yet today.

With Yacov dead, his promise not to tell Sonya about Bulgakov seemed worthless. But since he did not know how secure her end of the line was, he did not dare voice his concerns. He needed to talk with her personally, not over the phone.

"Anatoly, are you still there?"

"I'm here, Sonya," he said. "But I wish I were there with you. I'd try to get a flight yet tonight, but we had a major terrorist attack at Ben-Gurion yesterday. All flights out of the country have been canceled."

"Don't come, Anatoly. Everything's been taken care of, and the funeral will be tomorrow or the next day. You'd never make it in time, even if you could."

"Sonya, I am so sorry I can't be there with you," he said, holding back the tears that had begun to well up in his eyes. "This may not be the time to say this, with all you're dealing with, but I wish you would return to Israel as soon as possible.

You belong here, and there is nothing to keep you in Russia any longer." He paused. "Sonya, I love you."

She could not manage a reply. She knew he was emotional, could sense his tears in his voice. It seemed she had waited a lifetime to hear him say those words, but now that she had, she had nothing left to give in return.

"Will you call me tomorrow after the funeral?" Anatoly added, breaking the awkward silence.

"Yes."

"And think about what I said, Sonya."

"I will," she said through her tears. "I love you, too, Anatoly. Good-bye."

She hung up, threw herself on the bed, and sobbed.

Anatoly hung up the phone. In his frustration, sorrow, and loneliness, he did something he had never done before, regretting it the moment he did it. He grabbed the closest thing—his laptop computer—and threw it, smashing it against the opposite wall in the small room he used for an office at the Parousia Foundation.

Nikolai motioned Sonya toward a chair at his round conference table. "Can I get you anything?" he asked as he sat down beside her.

She shook her head. "Nothing, thank you."

"How are you?"

"I don't know," she said. "Numb, I suppose. I couldn't sleep last night. I just kept thinking about Yacov and Papa."

"Yes, I know. You must deal with your loss and let us worry about the details."

"What about the arrangements?"

"Sergei has taken care of everything. Your father and brother are both entitled to a state funeral and burial in Novodevichy Cemetery. They have earned the right by their loyalty to their country," he said. "That will take place at ten o'clock tomorrow morning."

"Thank you, Nikolai," she said. "I can't tell you how grateful I am for all your help."

"And Sergei has found you a flat nearer the Kremlin. All your things will be packed up and moved there by this afternoon. The phone should be in by then also. If it is unsuitable, please let me know. Your new flat has a security system. The building has only one entrance—with an electric door and a twenty-four-hour guard." He paused for a moment. "And I think it would be best to tell no one where you are."

"I don't know what to say."

He smiled at her. "Say nothing. I do what I can, but I know it cannot make up for your loss."

She nodded.

"Sonya, there is something else I have to tell you. I could put it off, but I think you would want to know now."

"What is it?"

Nikolai sighed. "I have discovered why Yacov and your father were murdered. I had a call only an hour ago from a highly placed friend of our cause. President Katanov ordered your brother's assassination. Your father was killed so there would be no witnesses."

"But why kill Yacov?" she pleaded. "What has he ever done to Katanov? He's not in politics."

"Yacov did nothing wrong. He became the expendable pawn of a high-level game of chess. His death—and your father's—was simply a move to strike at me, I am sorry to say. No more, no less. It was Katanov's warning for me to back off and go along with his program. Killing Yacov in the manner he did was intended to convey a message to me and me alone. If he had eliminated me directly, all fingers would immediately point at him. Because of my popularity, he would never have survived the consequences. But killing Yacov, a member of my personal staff, accomplishes the same thing, from his point of view, without the public repercussions. He knew I'd get the message and he was right! I'm sure if you had been at home, you would have been killed also."

"But why focus on us?" she cried. "If Katanov was going to all the trouble of eliminating an insider, someone like Sergei is even closer to you than we are, and certainly would have set you back more."

"I can't answer that. Who knows? Perhaps he focused on you because you are Jewish. You know his deep-seated hatred for your people. That's why I think you may still be in danger."

He rubbed his forehead pensively. "You know, Sonya, perhaps I should back away from this whole political scene before anyone else important to me is killed."

"Never!" she shouted. "You must *never* back off! Your plans for Russia and Israel are too important. To quit now would mean that my brother and father died in vain." Her face flushed with rage. "I will kill Katanov myself!"

"Easy, Sonya," Nikolai soothed. "I give you my promise. We will dispense with Katanov when the time is right. We always knew this might be necessary. Now there is even more reason."

"I *must* be a part of whatever you decide to do! This man has murdered my family. Even if I die in the process, I must be part of Katanov's demise!"

"You will be, Sonya. I'm counting on you."

TWELVE

Bulgakov glanced up from his desk as Sonya Petrov entered his office. Her athletic frame was thinner and her face was lined with her grief. With her family gone, her work had become her life. He assumed an expression of gravity and concern, but his heart was racing in anticipation. The opportunity he had waited for had finally arrived. All he needed to do now was present the facts to this woman, in just the right way, lead the conversation in the direction he wanted and she would do the rest.

"Care for some tea?" he asked, when she was seated across from him.

She shook her head. "Is something the matter, Nikolai?" she asked. "You look troubled."

He hesitated for a moment. "Yes, I think there is. I need your advice." He pulled a stapled document from a folder and handed it across the desk to her. "No one has seen this except Sergei."

Sonya scanned the pages rapidly. It was an agenda and a logistics plan issued from the president to his prime minister. "I don't like the sound of this, Nikolai."

"What do you think it means?"

"Katanov is calling a policy-planning session with you, his most feared rival, and Assam, the Tatarstan Muslim leader from Kazan, who trusts Katanov even less than you do? Both of you, at the same time? At his *dacha*? That gives him complete control of those he fears most, as well as absolute privacy! It stinks from the word go, Nikolai!"

He failed to tell her that he had been the one who had convinced Katanov that inviting Assam to his *dacha* might go a long way in establishing better relationships; that meeting with Assam, under the guise of a planning session, might be just the right touch to bring Assam to the table on other issues in a more friendly state of mind. "What do you think he's up to?" Bulgakov asked, leading the conversation.

"I think the most recent polls have pushed him over the edge. Your popularity continues to soar. You have not taken the back seat he expected when he had Yacov and Papa killed last month. If he can't get to you through me, he must take his chances and take you out the only other way he knows. I think he is setting up the perfect opportunity to eliminate his two strongest detractors in one swift blow."

"You sense public opinion is that strong?"

"Absolutely."

"And you genuinely believe this policy-planning session is no more than a cover?"

"What else? Since when do we have policy-planning sessions at his *dacha*, to say nothing of including Assam? Think about it," Sonya exclaimed, "the three of you with Katanov, in private, on his turf and on his terms! Never! All it takes is one little accident and all his competition—and worries—vanish. His only challenge is to make it look enough like an accident that the public will buy it."

"Well, you're the intelligence and covert operations expert. That's why I trust your judgment on matters like this," said Bulgakov. "What can we do about it?"

"Turn it to our advantage," she said briskly, scanning the logistics plan again. "This says we all travel by presidential jet to the Black Sea. Then three military helicopters will transport the three leaders and their personal staffs to Katanov's *dacha*, separately." She glanced up at Nikolai.

"So?" he asked.

"So, that's standard protocol. It's what follows that I don't like. It says here that Katanov plans to remain at his *dacha* for several days *after* the planning session is finished. You and Assam are to travel back to the airfield—*together in one helicopter*—where the presidential jet will pick everyone up and return you to Moscow. The logistics plan specifically instructs that the rest of us go on the other chopper. I don't like it! Standard protocol would put you two on different flights, like when we first arrive at the *dacha,* just in case something unexpected should occur. Yet Katanov is specifically instructing that the two of you fly together in one chopper, while your staff travels separately in the second. That's his best opportunity to strike. A simple accident, and he eliminates both his problems at once. Two separate accidents would be a little hard for even the gullible public to swallow!"

"Is there a way we can turn his little plan to our advantage?" Nikolai queried, now turning the conversation in the direction he had intended from the beginning.

Sonya thought for a moment, then shrugged. "I need time to think about this."

Bulgakov nodded. "Whatever it takes," he said. "Use whatever resources you need, and don't forget, for your eyes only."

"I will remember, Nikolai." Her eyes glinted with vengeance. *I promise you—I will never forget,* she thought.

So far, everything had gone off without a hitch. When they'd landed at the military base, the storm had not yet arrived, but the clouds were low and menacing, as though echoing the sinister plans racing through several minds. The president had ushered both Nikolai and Assam onto separate helicopters while Katanov had taken his own private chopper to the dacha. As expected, the trip was uneventful; everyone had arrived at the president's dacha before the winter storm hit.

By nightfall, the wind was whistling off the Black Sea and heavy snow began muffling everything in a white mantle, making the scene around the dinner table almost cozy as white-coated waiters ladled potato soup, rich with cream and sherry, into the large flat soup bowls. Sonya stayed alert through the six courses, ignoring the wine and vodka. Bulgakov, sitting aloof and almost militaristic in his well-tailored dark suit, never touched the alcohol either, nor did the Muslim Assam. If Katanov had planned to get rid of them that way, he'd have a difficult time. Dinner went without incident. Afterward, Katanov excused himself, leaving the others to small talk and relaxation. A few moments later, after she was sure that Katanov would not return, Sonya quietly got up and left the room.

The snow swirled and the wind howled as the March storm increased in intensity. Bundled in layers of thermalwear and polar fleece, Sonya watched from the shelter of the bushes outside the dacha. She glanced up at the sudden noise. Vladimir Katanov was at the door of the veranda, right on schedule. She sighed in relief. Her research was right. She had counted on that. She was grateful that his habit was so well known, even outside his inner circle of friends. First supper, then a steam bath, no matter what the weather was or who the guests were.

Sonya glanced toward the sea. She could barely see the roof of the *banya* that sat halfway between the *dacha* and the beach, but she knew it was there. Earlier, right after Katanov had excused himself, she had hid herself outside the *banya*, waiting patiently for the attendants to leave after taking in the clean towels and vodka, and starting the fire to build the steam. When they left, she slipped, unnoticed, into the *banya* with her own supplies. She moved quickly. What she needed to do took only a moment. She then returned to the *dacha* and found a hiding place with a full view of the veranda. Her research emphasized that Katanov's routine was like clockwork. He would always leave the *dacha* by the back door on the veranda, cross the veranda, and then take the stone pathway down to the *banya*. The falling snow gave the poorly lit veranda an eerie, almost unreal look, but there was still enough light to see anyone who entered or left the building. Visibility was poor and the snow covered her tracks, adequately concealing her presence in the surrounding darkness. As the guards patrolled only the perimeter of the presidential compound, Sonya had been able to move about, almost at will, inside the compound.

Through the glass in the dim light that illuminated the back door, she could see Katanov struggling to button his coat. He had been drinking heavily all evening and his movements showed it. He opened the veranda door. She could hear the wind whistle around the door, trying to fill the warmth beyond it. She wrapped her own scarf more securely around her face and waited.

Pinpoint ice particles stung his cheeks as Vladimir trudged toward the banya. Already the path his attendants had shoveled was drifting over the tops of his shoes. Perhaps he should have insisted one of them attend him, but tonight he wanted to be alone. Steam and vodka would help him relax.

He pushed through the door into the overheated, luxuriously fitted dressing room. A white vapor seeped under the door leading into the steam room. He took off his coat and hung it on one of the pegs above the bench.

A bottle of his favorite vodka and an empty glass were sitting on a tray at the end of the bench. He poured a glass and downed the contents in two gulps. *Nothing like vodka to fight the cold*, he thought, as he slumped down on the seat and removed his shoes. That done, he shrugged out of his shirt and undershirt, then stood to remove the rest of his clothing.

Draped in a towel, he grabbed the bottle and glass and walked through the door into a wall of steam and felt his way forward until he found the bench. He poured another drink and set the bottle down beside him.

Sonya's heart raced as she opened the door into the steam bath. She had left her boots outside in the dressing room. Leather and steam didn't mix well. By now the lethal dose of digitalis capsules should have dissolved in the vodka. Once ingested, that much digitalis should only take minutes to take effect. Katanov was so drunk he wouldn't know what had hit him in time to call for help. Even if he did, there was no phone in the banya. By now the poison should have done its lethal work.

As she entered the far room, the steam enveloped her, taking away her breath for a moment. The air was a thick fog, impossible for her eyesight to penetrate. She felt her way, shuffling one step at a time, trying to remember where the bench was that she had tripped over in the dark, thirty minutes earlier.

Her leg bumped into something heavy and still in front of her. Her eyes strained to see through the steam. She could barely see the outline of a big man. Katanov! She leaned down cautiously and held her breath, listening. Now she could see him clearly. Katanov was still breathing! The naked man was sprawled on the bench, his back against the wall, his arms clutching his chest. She gagged as the smell of his body odor rose into her nostrils. Suddenly, his eyes opened!

"What is going on?" he roared drunkenly.

Instinctively Sonya reached for the power panel on the wall, just to her left. Her commando training had taught her that life depended on remembering the smallest details. The location of the power panel was one of those "small details" on her check list. The lights went off with a loud click and, with them, all the fans and pumps. The wind outside, muted before, seemed to howl with renewed fury as it tore around the *banya*.

Sonya backed away.

"Where are you, woman? Looking for a real man instead of that wimpy Bulgakov you work for?"

Katanov's intentions were obvious. His large frame—made grotesque by his outsized belly—must have slowed the effect of the poison. Would it kill him or only make him sick? He was on his feet groping for her! She edged toward where she thought the door was. Now the sound of Katanov's labored breathing seemed to come from everywhere. He made clumsy padding noises as he groped around for her in the dark. Sonya cried out as her shins hit an unseen bench. Unable to catch her balance, she tumbled over the obstruction and landed heavily on the floor.

She rolled to the side as she heard Katanov rushing toward the noise. He kicked her right foot as he stumbled past. Sonya jumped to her feet and took a couple of steps, then stopped as she tried to hear over the pounding of her heart. She slid carefully over the floor as her stockinged-feet felt for obstacles.

She heard a creaking noise and felt a cold draft sweep through the steam room, then a muted thump as the outside door hit its stop. She crept toward the sound, holding out her hands in the darkened room.

She had gone about 3 meters when her left hand brushed against something wet and hairy. An unseen hand lashed out, grabbed her wrist and pulled her forward. Katanov's other arm encircled her and pulled her into a bear hug, his hands tearing at her clothes.

"Get away from me, you murderer! I hate you. I didn't come down here to make love to you, I came down here to see you die," Sonya screamed out at the animal that was now clawing at her. She brought her knee up, but he turned and blocked the blow. The smell of his body odor gagged her as she struggled against his slippery body. She tried to twist away as his right hand encircled her throat and started squeezing. A strangled cry escaped as she tried to break his grip. Only the training she had received in the IDF, back in her commando days, could save her from the death grip of this angry, drunken animal that now had hold of her.

She threw her right leg around the back of his left leg, and then threw her weight directly into him. Suddenly they were falling backward. Katanov's hand left her throat as he reached back to break his fall. They landed heavily on the floor with Sonya on top. She levered herself up and brought her right hand around, hitting him in the throat with the edge of her flattened hand. He cried out in pain and released his grip. She rolled free and scrambled to her feet. She heard him lash out in the darkness, cursing, mumbling things about her ancestry, about what he was going to do to her when he caught her!

Sonya glanced quickly about. There seemed to be a faint glow about 10 meters away. The cold draft coming from the open door pointed her in the direction she should go. She rushed across the floor, hoping she would not trip. She reached the door and peered out. The heavy snowfall was like a curtain.

She heard a curse and the sound of bare feet stumbling across the floor behind her. Sonya jumped out into a drift, crying out as the snow sucked the heat out of her stockinged feet and legs. The wind tore at her exposed skin. She started running toward the shadowy outline of a fir tree she thought marked the direction of the *dacha*, then glanced back.

For a moment, a black shape hulked in the door of the

banya. Then Katanov stumbled out and moved toward her, faster than she thought he could move. She ducked under the low branches of the tree, brushing them. They dumped their load of snow on her.

Sonya expected Katanov to come rushing around the tree at any moment. She tried to listen for sounds, but it was impossible with the shrieking of the wind. She felt a deceptive numbness stealing over her. It seemed almost warm, inviting her to lie on the ground. She shook her head, knowing this meant certain death.

Sonya turned in a full circle. She picked the direction that seemed a little lighter than the others, hoping it was the lights from the *dacha*. She had no feeling in her feet as she struggled through the drifts. She heard a sound behind her and saw a dark form crash through an evergreen hedge less than a meter away.

Sonya dashed for a towering spruce whose snow-laden branches touched the ground. She heard the thudding of feet close behind her as she dove for the skirt of branches. She ducked under the lowest branches and started wiggling into the aromatic, dark shelter. A hand grabbed her left ankle when she was almost inside. She kicked with her free foot and broke his hold. She felt her way through the blackness toward the other side of the tree, oblivious to the cones that bit into her numbed flesh. She reached a branch with prickly needles and pushed it up a little. All she could see was dim gray light that seemed to come from everywhere. She started crawling out.

Sonya was halfway out when Katanov lumbered around the tree. He grabbed her arms and jerked her upright. Then his powerful hands circled her throat and started choking her. She tried to break his grip, but this time she knew she couldn't. Her vision went black. She felt her mind drifting into the gray tendrils of unconsciousness.

Somewhere on the edge of blackness she thought she heard a sound. She fell heavily into a drift. Something was grabbing at her. She tried to pull away.

"Sonya, can you hear me?"

She tried to focus her eyes. Someone was standing over her, but she could not see who it was.

"It's me! Sergei! You have to get up! Here, let me help you."

Sonya struggled to her feet as he pulled her up. She wobbled as she tried to get her balance. At her feet was a black shape. A whimper escaped from her throat.

"He's dead," Sergei assured her. "Come with me. We have to get back inside!"

He half-dragged her up the deeply drifted slope to the entrance on the veranda, where he held the door open and then helped her to a chair on the dimly lit porch, pulling a heavy quilt over her.

"Is it done?" whispered a man's voice in the background.

Sonya looked up in shock, then relaxed as she recognized Bulgakov.

"Yes Nikolai," was all she managed to reply.

"Sergei," Bulgakov ordered, "take the body back to the steam bath immediately. We have little time. The body must be moved before someone finds it. The snowstorm will cover the tracks. Then go to General Losev! Now hurry!"

"Don't forget my boots," Sonya added. "I took them off in the dressing room."

Turning to Sonya, Bulgakov asked again, "You are sure he is dead?"

"How would I know? Sergei affirmed it!" she snapped with such force that the prime minister stepped back. What have I done? she asked herself. But as quickly as the thought raced through her mind, she remembered. She remembered what had happened to Papa and Yacov, the political statement that had been communicated by the two needless shots to the back of the head! For the first time since that terrible day, she relaxed and enjoyed her brief moment of revenge.

Outside, Sergei grabbed Katanov's body under the armpits and hauled it toward the *banya*. He worked quickly. He had one last stop to make before his meeting with General Losev, one that only he and his master knew about: the old A-frame where the helicopters were hangared. The building, because of its location *inside* the presidential compound, was left unguarded. He entered quickly and quietly, using his penlight to show him where he wanted to go. He checked the aircraft numbers carefully against Katanov's logistics plan. There could be no mistake. He made a small adjustment to the engine of the helicopter. Moments later, he was on his way back to the *dacha*.

Sergei stepped quickly up the broad staircase to the second floor and turned right toward the wing opposite the president's suite. He stopped outside a small room with an open door. The two men inside had their coats off, exposing shoulder holsters. They were drinking coffee and watching a small TV on the counter. As Sergei entered, one of them turned around with a guilty expression on his face.

"I must see General Losev at once," he ordered.

"But . . ."

"At once!" Sergei thundered. "Do as I say, or you will live to regret it!"

One of the guards hurriedly put on his coat and led Sergei to the door at the end of the hall.

"Announce me, you idiot! I have state business to discuss with the general."

The man gulped and opened the door. "General Losev, excuse me."

General Boris Losev looked up from his bed. "What is it?" he demanded as he put down his book.

"Sergei Lomonosov to see you, sir. He says it is urgent."

"I did not say it was urgent, you numbskull, I said it was state business. Now get out. And make sure the general and I are not disturbed. Is that perfectly clear?"

As the man nodded and closed the door, Sergei turned back to the general. Somehow, in this setting, the general looked strangely powerless: in bed in his blue-striped pajamas.

"What state business do you have to discuss with me at this time of night?" snapped Losev, trying to overcome his obvious disadvantage.

"I regret that it is my duty to inform you that Vladimir Katanov is dead," Sergei said stiffly. "Prime Minister Nikolai Bulgakov has now assumed the presidency. You will, of course, want to notify the proper authorities, immediately. The transfer of power must go smoothly and quickly."

"What did you say?" Losev exploded, sitting straight up in bed.

"I said, 'I regret that it is my du . . .' "

"I know what you said." He waved the words away. "How did it happen?"

"He died of a heart attack while taking his steam bath," said Sergei. "A sad business."

"And what is it you said about Nikolai Bulgakov?" the general shouted, getting out of bed and reaching for his robe.

"Nikolai Bulgakov has assumed the presidency," Sergei answered matter-of-factly. "You are to see that the transfer of power goes smoothly."

"You realize, I am sure, that my duties require me to protect the president and to prosecute all threats against the state. Who becomes the next president is not ours to decide."

"I beg to remind the general that Nikolai Bulgakov is the prime minister, and he succeeds to the presidency until proper elections can be held—which, because of the state of emergency, cannot be held at this present time."

"And may I remind you that succession of power is not that simple, Mr. Lomonosov. First I must conduct an investigation."

"Oh, then I am to assume that it is the general's wish to go into the history books as the one who brought Russia into civil war? Or, perhaps, to be remembered as the general who was in bed while his president was dying, a hundred meters away? Have you seen the polls recently, or do you have a problem reading anything more difficult than that cheap paperback I see lying on your bed?" Sergei responded pointedly. "Is the general really that anxious to become infamous, after a lifetime of devoted service to his country?"

"I do not respond well to threats."

"General, you have the power to make the transition go quickly and smoothly at this time of crisis. You should jump at the opportunity, if not for the man who will become president anyway, with or without your help, then for Mother Russia herself. Nikolai Bulgakov will be elected, and he will remember who his friends are." Sergei paused to let his words sink in. "Do you hear what I am saying, General? In the long run, what you do today will make little difference to the outcome. But what you do today *will* determine how you will be viewed by the *rodina* and its new president in the future. If you delay the process, there will only be one loser, and I am looking at him!"

After a moment of painful silence, Sergei continued. "I repeat: we do not forget our friends. Katanov is dead. Why not back the logical successor? It can be smooth and pleasant. And you have both the people and the law on your side."

Sergei waited as Losev thought this over.

"What did you say happened to the president?"

"It appears he has suffered a heart attack while taking his steam bath."

General Losev again weighed Sergei's words, filtering their meaning through the sieve of his own career. Slowly he accepted the only real option available to him. "As chief of security, I will take care of all the details," he said. "Please assure President Bulgakov that I am at his service and that things will go . . . how did you say? . . . 'pleasantly and smoothly.' I will take care of matters as soon as I am appropriately dressed."

Bulgakov stood as the Kazan leader entered the small *dacha* library that until last night had belonged to Vladimir Katanov. The two men shook hands, and Bulgakov led the way to two burgundy leather wingback chairs at one side of the room.

"Please accept my regrets concerning President Katanov's sudden death and the great burden this puts on your shoulders."

"Thank you, Assam. I must confide in you and then ask a favor of you."

The man appeared surprised by the new president's statement, even as he responded politely with a bow of his head. "Of course."

"There is no easy way to tell you this," said Bulgakov, shaking his head sadly. "Katanov had planned to kill both of us during this visit. It was to be a helicopter accident on our return to the airport. The aircraft you and I were instructed to fly in tomorrow carries the evidence of this man's conspiracy against us!"

Assam's large dark eyes opened wide. "It would seem I owe you for much more than the friendship we have shared, indeed, for my life," he said quietly. "What is it that you ask of me?"

"We have talked together, many times already, about what I hope to do for you and your people if this moment ever occurred. Well, that moment has come. That moment is now. I am here, my dear friend, to tell you that the promises I make, I keep! I want to end the unfair treatment of your Muslim people, but I need your help in doing it. I say this as one political leader to another." Bulgakov watched the man closely as he digested what he had just heard.

"You are a man of many surprises, I think. It seems that you have saved my life. Now you tell me you genuinely do want to help my people?"

Bulgakov nodded. "Yes, exactly as we have agreed in the past. I want my aides to meet with yours, as soon as possible, to work out such things as repairs to infrastructure, equal access to higher education and medical facilities, state jobs, and anything else that's been unfairly withheld from your people. These inequities will be corrected."

"And what do you want from me?"

"I want a truly united Russia, and I need you and your loyalty to me to accomplish these things. We will have the Russian Orthodox in the west and your Muslim people in the east, all working together to form a New United Empire. After the *rodina* sees that we are truly united in our commitment to all people of our great nation, I will make one more announcement that will astound the world."

Assam's eyes narrowed. "And what would that be?"

"At the proper time, my friend. For now, trust me." Bulgakov played to the Muslim leader's look of concern. "Very shortly, when you see a powerful country join our New United Empire, you will understand that, at that moment, we become a powerful nation without equal, second to none in the world!" His hypnotic gaze did not waver as he waited for Assam's reply. When it came, Bulgakov's thin lips tightened in a smile.

"I give you my loyalty. I look forward to working with you, Mr. President."

Three days after the coup, Moscow was shivering through another winter storm. Though it was close to the end of March, spring seemed far away. But cold weather meant nothing to the new Russian president as he looked out over a vast courtyard in the Kremlin. Soon even the weather, along with everything else, would be used to his advantage. The "discovery" that the helicopter designated to fly Assam and himself back to the military base had been sabotaged, firmly cemented his relationship with the Muslim leader, as well as the nation to their new leader. It also provided the justification Sonya had needed beyond simply avenging the deaths of her father and brother.

He turned from the window and surveyed his surroundings with satisfaction. The transition to the president's office had been as simple as moving his belongings 20 meters down the hall. His new office was four times the size of his old one, yet it had a simplicity and elegance that he appreciated. He wanted no distractions around him.

He looked toward his desk, where Sergei had just finished barking orders into the phone.

"The secure line is ready."

Bulgakov crossed the room and took the phone, staying on his feet, his shoulders squared, his spine stiff. "Chancellor Otterbein, is that you?"

"Yes, President Bulgakov. I hear that our plans are progressing nicely."

"Things could not be better. We are all set here. Assam and his people are completely behind us," he said. "Finally, our long wait is over."

"Yes," replied the German chancellor. "Over forty years since that day in Bonn. I see no reason to delay any longer, do you?"

"None at all. So, we do it at noon tomorrow, Moscow time?"

"Very good."

Bulgakov hung up the phone and gave an excited stamp with his right foot. "It has begun!" he shouted, striking the air with his fist.

"We have waited a long time," Sergei echoed.

"Yes!" said Bulgakov. "Now, contact all the grain-exporting countries, immediately. Take advantage of the huge surpluses that the farming nations have enjoyed these past few years. Prices are low, so offer them a price they can't refuse, even if it's a premium. Contract for as much as they will give us, with immediate delivery. Take advantage of any liberal-minded assistance they offer. It makes them all feel so good to help a poor struggling country like ours, especially after the unfortunate death of our hard-line president and his replacement by the more democratic-minded prime minister." The last comment had that familiar ring of sarcasm Bulgakov was known to have.

"If they only knew," Sergei said, smiling to himself.

"Next, I want the military buildup plan finalized. Chancellor Otterbein is already gearing up Germany's industrial plant." He paused. "Keep it low-key, Sergei, but make sure it gets done — exactly as planned."

Bulgakov glanced at the planner on his laptop computer. He used the track ball to page forward a day.

"The world will remember this day forever."

News director Yuri Kagan led his VIP guests to the small set with the Russian flag in the background. The president took his place behind the podium and waited while lights were adjusted and cameras positioned. Assam stood at his right hand. Kagan nodded when everything was set and moved to one side, behind camera one.

Bulgakov's heart beat faster as the wall clock's second hand swept toward twelve. Directly in front of him, the camera's red light flashed on and he saw his image appear on the monitor alongside Chancellor Gerhardt Otterbein's.

The media had jumped at the chance to air this joint statement by the German chancellor and the Russian president, to be delivered at the same time on split-screen. The unusual presence of Assam at Bulgakov's right hand assured the world, without words, that the Muslim leader approved of everything that was happening on the screen before them. The telecast was interrupting daytime television and would be carried live on every network. CNN was carrying it worldwide.

"Good afternoon, Chancellor Otterbein."

"Good afternoon to you, President Bulgakov."

Six sets of captions appeared on the bottom of the monitor, simultaneously translating the speech into German, Russian, Arabic, Spanish, Chinese, and English.

"Are you ready for the announcement?" asked Bulgakov. He did not have to force his smile of triumph.

"Yes." The German chancellor waved toward a map beside him, where Germany and Russia appeared in blue, a golden arch stretching between them. "People of the world. President Bulgakov and I are proud to announce the joining of Germany and Russia into what will be known from this day forward as the New United Empire, or the NUE. Today our two great nations will unite under one great leader, Nikolai Bulgakov."

The chancellor waved toward the center of the screen.

"Thank you, Chancellor Otterbein, my dear friend," Bulgakov said, stretching out his right arm in a stiff salute. "To Germany!"

"To Russia!" Otterbein echoed.

"To the New United Empire!" said Bulgakov.

Assam raised his arm and saluted, showing total support for what was occurring on live television.

With this prearranged signal, their joint announcement ended and live coverage came to an end. The door was opened to the press who had been watching the monitors in the studio in the next room. They mobbed the podium, and for the next forty-five minutes, the Russian president answered their questions, explaining that this was only the beginning, that he and Chancellor Otterbein, along with Assam, were inviting other nations to join the New United Empire.

The press was finally herded away, off to write their stories, and Bulgakov was ushered to his waiting limousine.

"Everything is going very well," Sergei commented when they were safely inside.

"Yes, it is," Bulgakov said with a smile.

"Do you see any problems in getting the enabling legislation passed in Germany?"

"None whatsoever," laughed Bulgakov. "My good friend,

Gerhardt—pardon me, Chancellor Otterbein—has planned for this day for well over forty years. It is the ultimate win–win arrangement. The economic benefits alone are staggering. Today, peace and prosperity for the New United Empire. To-morrow, the world."

"With you as ruler."

"With me as leader and lord!" he corrected.

THIRTEEN

Sonya had finished washing the few dishes she had used for her evening meal and was going over in her mind all the things she needed to do tomorrow. Even though she had been involved closely with some of Nikolai's plans, she could still hardly believe that the New United Empire was a reality. Everything Nikolai predicted had come true. And soon he would make the treaty with Israel, as he had promised. It was already on the drawing board. In fact, that was the only reason she had decided to stay in Moscow after Nikolai had become president. Her primary role in the new government was liaison between the NUE and certain highly placed officials in Israel. Because of promises she had made to Prime Minister Shefi when she had left Israel to return to Moscow, she had dutifully gone through the proper channels, even though it seemed to take months to do what otherwise should have taken a mere phone call. She knew the right time to officially reestablish her ties with the prime minister would come.

Her mind instantly shifted to Anatoly. She knew he did not understand her reasons, and there was much she could not tell him at the moment. An emergency situation had made it impossible for him to return to Moscow. Although he had suddenly stopped sending e-mail—asking her to do the same—they occasionally talked by phone, but only when he called. He was very mysterious but said he would explain the next time he saw her, in person. In the meantime, he constantly pleaded with her to come back to Israel, but she believed that her return to Russia was her destiny, and that she was playing a critical part in accomplishing genuine peace for Israel; that was her only comfort following the deaths of her brother and father. The work was grueling and the hours long, but the end result would be well worth all the effort. Nikolai's plans for Israel were well under way. As soon as the work was done, she would go home to Israel to be with her Anatoly.

Sonya clung to her hopes, because hope was all she had left in life. When her long days were over, she had nothing to come home to. No Papa. No Yacov.

It was habit, now, to fight the tears when she allowed herself to remember her loss. Even Anatoly seemed to be part of a different universe, at least for the moment. She wished . . .

She looked up in surprise when the doorbell rang. She never had visitors. Pulling the door open, she was even more surprised to see Mike and Marlee Teasdale.

"Please, come in," she said.

"Sonya, how are you doing?" Mike asked as they came through into the flat, his sincerity momentarily touching Sonya's heart.

"We were so sorry to hear about Yacov and your father," said Marlee. "I hope you received our note. We sent it to your old address but it was returned, so we just sent it to the work address Yacov had given us, hoping it would find its way to you."

"I did get it," said Sonya. "I appreciated your kind words. I'm sorry for the extra trouble it caused you."

"It was nothing. Is this an inconvenient time?" asked Marlee.

Sonya shook her head. "No, I am glad to see you. Let me take your coats." She hung their coats on the wooden tree in the small hallway and led them into the living room.

"We apologize for not coming sooner," Mike said. "But we couldn't find you after it happened. Your old flat was empty and no one there knew where you'd gone. Anatoly had given us a telephone number, but every time we called it, the operator refused to put us through."

"I'm sorry. It is because of security. They are worried that the same person who killed Yacov and Papa will come after me," she said. "I gave them a short list of approved names, but truthfully speaking, I just never thought about adding your names. Anyone who wasn't on that list simply didn't get through—although I'm a little surprised the operator didn't at least tell me you called." She paused. "So how did you find me, if you don't mind my asking?"

Mike held up a slip of paper with her address written on it. "Like I said earlier, I knew where you worked but the guards there wouldn't let us in, so we finally resorted to an old CIA trick. We had you followed after work by a cabby! He had to wait three hours for you to show, but when you did, the rest was easy. You'd be surprised what a few rubles can buy these days." He grinned. "Now how's that for being original?"

"Well, congratulations on your detective work! I am glad you were successful," Sonya said with a smile. "Can I offer you some tea? I've also got some wonderful tinned biscuits I found in a shop the other day."

"I wish we could," said Marlee, "but we don't have much time. We're actually on our way to the airport. We're returning to America and have a night flight to Frankfurt to make our connection."

"I thought you were here long-term."

Mike shifted uncomfortably. "Our visas have been revoked. We've been ordered to leave the country immediately."

"What happened?"

"We don't know. The notification came yesterday from the Ministry of Foreign Affairs, with no explanation. The official was polite and respectful, but he made it clear that we had to leave no later than tomorrow."

"This is wrong," Sonya said. "It must be a mistake."

"Please don't be distressed," Mike said. "We believe it is God's will for us to leave. With the events that have happened during the past few weeks, we have important work to do back in America."

Sonya did not understand what he meant but nodded politely, anyway. Then it struck her that she would probably never see these people again. Her eyes filled with unshed tears—not because she was close to these Americans, but because they had been close to the two men she loved so dearly.

One was dead and the other gone. Now the Americans were leaving too.

Mike recognized Yacov's Bible on the coffee table. He picked it up and ran his hands over the cover. "Sonya, please be careful. We don't know each other well, but you have become very special to us because of Anatoly and Yacov."

She nodded as a tear escaped and ran down her cheek.

Mike set the Bible back on the table, then walked over and took Sonya's hands in his. He spoke as quietly as possible, not knowing what ears might be listening. "Sonya, trust no one but Anatoly. No one! You could be the next target of the madman who killed Yacov and your father. You must be careful."

"I appreciate your concern, and I will take care," said Sonya, knowing inwardly that she'd already had her revenge on the "madman" who had killed her brother and father. But these people would never know what really happened, if for no other reason than their own safety.

She was startled when Marlee reached out to hug her warmly, then surprised herself as she gave in to the comforting embrace.

As the door closed behind the Teasdales, Sonya felt as though a chapter in her life was closing with it.

The president of the New United Empire looked up as his chief of staff entered his office.

"It goes well," Sergei said as he crossed the room, a rare smile lifting his thick black brows.

"As we knew it would," said Nikolai. "What's the status?"

"We have long-term grain deals signed with America, Canada, and a whole list of other countries. Shipments have already begun. Huge warehouses are being erected both here and in Germany, and will be ready by the time the grain arrives." He sat down in the chair facing Bulgakov's desk. "The arms buildup is completely on schedule, and the Russian and German militaries will be fully integrated before year's end. That includes all the major German defense contractors as well."

"How do you gauge world reaction?"

Sergei made a face. "The pundits and pollsters haven't a clue, although they 'generally like' the peaceful things they're hearing. The humanitarian fools have bought into the NUE, hook, line, and sinker. The countries selling us grain are making their farmers happy, selling at premium prices the unwanted surpluses that have kept prices low. A few military experts are making noise about what we're doing with the Germans, but that's not totally unexpected. They are basing their wild predictions on what little they're able to find out, which is practically nothing. Germany's security measures are unexcelled!"

"Are you concerned at all?" Nikolai asked.

"Not at all. It's not a problem. They don't have an audience, for the most part, and of course they can't get much information. When questioned, they must admit it is pure conjecture."

"Just keep emphasizing our defensive needs and our desire to help police the world's conflicts," Bulgakov reminded his chief of staff.

Bulgakov leaned back and crossed his arms over his chest. "And what about those Americans?"

"They've left the country," said Sergei. "They saw Sonya briefly before they left, but our ears picked up nothing problematic. It didn't seem worth the trouble to eliminate them. It might have been too much of a coincidence for her to swallow."

"You're right," said Bulgakov. "We must do nothing to make Sonya suspicious. This is when we really need her and her contacts, to say nothing of what she's already done for us! The time to handle the Teasdales and others like them will come soon enough."

PART 2

THE COVENANT
WITH DEATH

Because you have said . . .
"We have made a covenant with death,
And with Sheol we have made a pact.
The overwhelming scourge will not reach us when it passes by,
For we have made falsehood our refuge
and we have concealed ourselves with deception."
Therefore thus says the Lord GOD . . .
"As often as it passes through, it will seize you.
For morning after morning it will pass through,
anytime during the day or night.
And it will be sheer terror to understand what it means."

—Isaiah 28:15, 19

FOURTEEN

Israeli Prime Minister Binyamin Shefi sat immobile at his desk as the IDF's chief of staff brought him up to date on the Syrian invasion of Galilee and the simultaneous Palestinian uprising within Israel's own borders. Lt. Gen. Shimon Weinstein stood at the map and pointed out the organized advances of the Syrian armor columns as opposed to the disorganized Palestinian infantry movements. Weinstein was grateful it wasn't the other way around and stated as much to the group seated in front of him.

"The Syrians have recaptured the high ground of the Golan Heights, and now they have turned the corner and are coming down the west coast of the Kineret—the Sea of Galilee. The advance is slowing and spreading out, but it has not stopped.

"On the other hand, the Palestinian infantry coming up from the Gaza strip is proceeding north in support of the Syrian thrust—a classic pincer operation on the city of Jerusalem. Arab irregulars, armed from secret weapons caches, are providing a spearhead advancing from Gaza and Rafiah, hitting us from behind while we face the Syrian armor in the north. The primary sources of Palestinian men and weapons appear to be Gaza, Rafiah, and Hebron.

"Our armor is engaging the Syrians all along the front. If it weren't for the blasted Palestinians constantly chipping away at us from behind, we would have had the Syrians halted by now. The Palestinians represent little threat by themselves, but they're draining off important armor, artillery, and infantry units we need in our defense and counterattack against Syria. Because our units are already spread thin on both fronts, we find ourselves in serious jeopardy."

"What about air support?" someone asked.

"With most of the fighting occurring on or within our own borders, air superiority has little effect. On their playing field, things would be different." He paused. "Make no mistake—this will be a costly campaign. We can only be grateful that our friendly relations with Jordan have kept them out of our West Bank."

"What does the staff recommend?" asked Shefi.

"This is blatant aggression, Mr. Prime Minister. The quickest way to make the Syrians back off would be to launch a small nuke on Damascus, warning them of what will happen if they don't make a hasty retreat. With them off our back in the north, we could knock out the Palestinian threat in short order."

"There is no nuclear option," Shefi said adamantly, "large or small. The Americans would cut us off entirely if we did. And the Syrians know it, which is why they are making their move and why the Palestinians are so happy to tag along."

"Then I'm afraid we are facing a long, expensive war," said Weinstein. "In the past, we have won because we struck swiftly and decisively, putting an end to the threat in days rather than months. If we can't do that, we've lost our advantage. And if our other Arab neighbors decide to help their brothers, we are in big trouble."

"What do you suggest, General?"

"Our first priority must be to make Syria pull back—to get them out of our territory—by whatever means possible . . ." Weinstein said, then looked at the prime minister, ". . . short of nuclear power, of course. Then we'll mop up the Palestinians."

"What do you project our losses will be?"

"We are still working on that. All I can tell you now is that they will be heavy—very heavy."

"What can we do, Nikolai?" Sonya asked as soon as she entered his office, knowing full well why he had summoned her.

Bulgakov threw a report aside, then crossed his arms and

leaned back in his chair. "I assume you've heard the latest reports, then?"

"The Syrian invasion and the typical Palestinian stab-in-the-back?" she asked. "Yes, our security people called me before breakfast and briefed me. I got over here as soon as I heard."

"You know how I feel about Israel," said Bulgakov. "Thanks to all the work you've done, we are close to opening a dialog with the prime minister on the treaty proposal."

"Yes, I know only too well. But it seems like our diplomats are taking forever just trying to arrange for a meeting," Sonya complained. "If we want to show Israel our good will, isn't there something we can do *today*, before we get around to working out a treaty together, which, at the rate we're going, could be another ten years?" Sonya asked, irritated by all the bureaucratic delay.

"Absolutely," assured Bulgakov. "I've already been thinking that we might be able to turn this invasion to our mutual advantage."

"Our mutual advantage?"

The president paused again, as though considering how to continue. "Sonya, some things we have to do by the book. Other things necessitate short cuts, as you know all too well by now. This is *another* one of those times. Do you have any contacts in military intelligence that can get us quick access to Prime Minister Shefi, without going through all the red tape that's driving us both crazy? Someone who could circumvent the typical months of maneuvering through diplomatic channels?"

Sonya hesitated. No one here knew of her close ties with the Israeli prime minister, and it had been important to keep it that way. She had promised her dear friend that she would not disclose to anyone here in Russia, her professional relationship to Shefi. And yet, with the very future of Israel possibly hanging in the balance, how could she not use this advantage? Her hesitation was fleeting and went unnoticed, even by the president of the NUE.

"As a matter of fact," she said, "I used to personally give the prime minister intelligence briefings, and he often included me in planning sessions." For some reason, she held back the fact that the two of them had been as close as father and daughter.

Nikolai Bulgakov sat straight up, like a man who has suddenly been jolted by an electrical shock. The blue-gray eyes flashed with excitement. "So now you tell me this, Sonya. You should have told me before!"

Sonya was convinced by his act. "I couldn't," she explained. "By the book, remember, and besides, he made me promise not . . ."

Dismissing her explanation with a wave of his hand, he interrupted with a question. "If you made a telephone call, could you get through to him now?"

She didn't need to think about that one. She knew the answer. "Yes. I know he will talk to me."

"There is little time, Sonya. You're right. We can't wait for the diplomats to do all their elaborate dance steps. If we don't act now, the opportunity will be lost—for us and for Israel."

"Just tell me what you want me to do."

"Call Prime Minister Shefi, today, right now. Tell him you speak with my authority, and that I can have Russian troops and equipment on the way to Ben-Gurion within hours—all under his command. If the Arabs are foolish enough to attack our troops, the New United Empire will consider it an act of war. Tell him this is official and we can work out the details later."

"With your permission, sir, I would also like to tell him of our desire to formalize our friendship with Israel, the one our diplomats have been trying to arrange for the past several months. That will put our temporary help into its proper perspective of a long-term deal. Under the circumstances, I can't see going around the block if ducking across the alley accomplishes the same thing in a fraction of the time."

"If given the opportunity, yes, by all means!" Bulgakov almost shouted, as though he had not always known this day would come. "Tell him we want to provide Israel the security they need, not only to put an end to this current fray, but for the future as well. In return, tell him we would like their technical assistance, free trade, and any other help they can give us as we build the NUE."

"Do I make the one contingent on the other?"

"No. Tell him we will provide the help he needs now, regardless. But ask him to consider our help as a good-faith pledge for the future. Think you can do it?" Bulgakov challenged.

She smiled at him. "I will do my best. You know that."

"Yes, I do," he said. "Tell him I have put the troops on standby, and they can be in the air in a matter of hours."

Moments later, Sonya leaned against the wall in the corridor outside the president's door. She took a deep breath and blew it out slowly, steeling herself for her next move. Then she marched to her office and punched the communications number without hesitation.

"This is Sonya Petrov with a priority call from the president's office." She gave the communications operator Prime Minister Shefi's name and private number, being careful to stipulate that her name should be used as the caller, but in the context of official state business for President Bulgakov. She pressed the disconnect button and waited. In a few minutes the phone rang.

"Sonya Petrov," she answered.

"Sonya, how are you?" said Binyamin Shefi's familiar voice, carrying her back immediately to some of the happiest days of her life. "How is my favorite advisor?"

"I'm fine, Binyamin. Thank you for returning my call," she said. "I wish this were just a personal call, but President Bulgakov wanted me to contact you. We are very distressed at what is happening in Israel."

"It is bad, Sonya. Very bad. We should have seen it coming, but somehow their buildup slipped through the cracks of our intelligence. Perhaps had you still been doing my intelligence on the Arab states, this would never have happened. Now that it has, however, we are trying to figure our way out, short of dropping a nuke on Damascus."

"Do you see it coming to that?" Sonya exclaimed.

"Never," he said. "That might win the battle today, but in the long run, it could destroy all I am trying to accomplish for our people."

"So what will you do, if I may be so bold as to ask?"

"Actually, my dear, I am in the middle of a strategic staff meeting right now, trying to decide what course of action is best for us to take. In fact, for that reason I'm going to have to make this call short. As much as I would like to talk with you, I took the call only because I was told you were calling at the direction and authority of President Bulgakov. Is that so?"

"Yes, Binyamin. We thought I had a better chance getting through to you directly, but that which I am offering to Israel comes with his full authority as president of NUE."

"Which is?"

"He is ready to send troops and equipment to Israel, immediately, to help force the Syrians and Palestinians to withdraw. President Bulgakov is also willing to call their heads of state, telling them that if they don't withdraw now, it will be considered an act of war against the New United Empire."

The line was silent.

"Binyamin, do you understand what President Bulgakov is offering?"

"Yes, Sonya, I do," he said. "You may have given us a solution to what, moments ago, seemed an impossible dilemma."

"He is serious in what he offers, and there are no strings attached. If you give the word, our transports will be on their way within hours. They have already been put on alert."

"Sonya, let me put you on hold for a minute," he said. The background noise from Shefi's office ceased as the other end went mute. No more than five minutes later, the phone clicked back on.

"Sonya, we are grateful for the offer, but what concerns us is bringing NUE troops into our land, onto our soil, without our absolute control."

"I know President Bulgakov is a man with a heart for Israel as well as the Jews in Russia. That is the only reason I am still here in Moscow serving him. For our people, Mr. Prime Minister, yours and mine. His motive in offering his help to you during this time of need is solely out of his concern for the security of Israel. For this reason, he asked me to assure you that our troops would be under your direct command at all times during this crisis."

After another long silence, the line again came alive. "Sonya, I don't know your president's motive, but I trust you," said Shefi. "We have few options right now, but the best one with the fewest consequences is to trust your judgment. Many lives, both Arab and Jewish, will be saved. Your judgment has never let us down before. I will need to discuss this with my cabinet, but I am certain that we will accept President Bulgakov's generous offer."

Sonya sighed with relief. "One thing more, Binyamin. The military aid is in no way contingent on this, but President Bulgakov wants you to know that the New United Empire eagerly desires a mutual-aid treaty with Israel. As I'm sure you are aware, our diplomats have been meeting with yours in an attempt to arrange a summit with you. When this current crisis is past, I would like to bypass all the bureaucratic red tape and go over the points with you alone. The president has asked that I advise him on this treaty directly, so the terms you and I come to, he will, in all likelihood, approve."

Binyamin Shefi laughed, in spite of the tenseness of the situation that occupied his thinking. "Sonya, if you have your hand in it, I like it already," he said. "We will certainly talk when the crisis is over." He chuckled proudly. "I just can't believe that my little Sonya is the one who has saved the day. But, then, what should I expect from my ex-commando, special advisor?"

Within an hour of the first transport's landing, a Russian armored battalion of T–80 tanks and BMP–3 armored personnel carriers rumbled north on the coast highway out of Tel Aviv, under the command of an IDF colonel.

Back in Moscow, Nikolai Bulgakov placed several high-level calls to prominent Arab leaders and, after getting their assurances, called a press conference and forcefully stated that any Syrian or Palestinian attack against NUE troops would be considered an act of war. As president, he was personally committing the entire New United Empire to the peace and safety of every Jew in Israel.

While the armored units were still many kilometers from the front lines, the Syrians began their retreat. By morning, Israel's borders had been restored and the Palestinians had dispersed into their own territories. Few Jewish lives had been lost.

As his final act in resolving the emergency, Prime Minister Shefi announced that Israel and the New United Empire would soon sign a seven-year, mutual-assistance treaty, assuring the peace and safety of all Israelis.

Anatoly Altshuler groaned as he flicked off the television. He had been living in a small apartment in the Jewish Quarter of the Old City of Jerusalem since his move from Tel Aviv a few months ago, shortly after his first contact with Eitan Shachar. He found it more convenient to live closer to the Parousia Foundation, since he spent the majority of his time there. He kept in contact with *Isvestia* headquarters by phone.

While part of him was shocked by Shefi's announcement, another part felt almost a weird sense of relief, as if the other shoe had finally dropped. His major concern was Sonya. The recent political upheaval in Russia had precipitated a sudden cessation of all contact between them. He did not dare communicate with her by e-mail. He was provided with a brand new computer by the Parousia Foundation, but he had decided it was too dangerous to contact Sonya by any means that had even a remote chance of being traced back to the foundation by Bulgakov, should he ever suspect the real reason for their existence. In fact, only when there was an emergency did he feel comfortable using the system at *Isvestia* headquarters. The few times they had talked over the phone, Sonya had been exceptionally secretive—as he was with her—as to what preoccupied most of her working hours.

The clock was running. In a little over seven years it would all be over!

He had always wondered what it would take to drive several hundred thousand Jews out of the safety of their homes into the wilderness of Petra. Now he knew. With Russian troops streaming into Israel—supposedly for protection against the Arabs—their worst enemy had already conquered the land without firing a shot, and the government didn't even know it. But some people knew. And these were the ones who would flee before the real trouble began. It was a good thing the Petra site was almost ready, although without the planning, resources, and manpower provided by Eitan Shachar and the Parousia Foundation, it would never have become a reality in such a relatively short period of time.

He glanced at the bright blue patch of October sky visible through the small casement window above his chair. The weather was perfect, ideal for what still needed to be done. But they had to finish up before the winter rains came. And that meant he needed to be out of here, on his way, at the crack of dawn.

He was mentally reviewing what he needed to do before he left, when a knock sounded at the door. He opened it to find a familiar face beaming at him.

"Hi! I'm Yuri Kagan with CNN, here to interview Anatoly Altshuler. Our viewers are dying to see how the world-famous foreign correspondent for *Isvestia* lives. May I call my crew up, Mr. Altshuler? We'll only need three or four hours of your time."

Shocked to see his old journalism colleague here in Jerusalem, Anatoly managed a smile. It had been a long time, but it was decidedly the wrong time.

"You can come in, but leave your crew outside."

Yuri shrugged, at the same time pushing his horn-rimmed glasses up the bridge of his nose. "Just as well. I didn't bring them anyway. Decided to handle this hot story on my own," he joked. "The truth is, I left them back in Tel Aviv. Presumably they're exploring the city's fleshpots by now."

"Come in," said Anatoly, hoping he could politely get rid of his old friend in short order. "What brings you here, Yuri?"

"CNN transferred me down here to cover the Syrian invasion and the Palestinian uprising," he said, his newsman's eyes flickering around the one-room efficiency apartment, recording every detail. "Looks like Nikolai Bulgakov came through in the nick of time. 'Nik' came through in the 'nick' — get it?"

"Very funny."

"Aw, forget it. You never did have a sense of humor. Anyway, the peace-loving Syrians and Palestinians couldn't wait to get back home, so it looks like my trip was for naught, unless I can talk my boss into letting me cover this big peace accord Shefi and Bulgakov are talking about."

"Have you heard any specifics?"

"Other than the few general statements they've released, probably to test the waters, my information is only rumor. But realistically, I think it will happen, don't you?" Yuri seemed to bounce on his toes as he talked, exhibiting his usual nervous energy. Anatoly was always amazed at the intensity that belied the man's curly-haired, youthful, boy-next-door appearance.

"Count on it, Yuri. It will happen, but it will never work. Some Israelis already see the treaty for what it is."

"This guy is running Russia like it has never been run before," Yuri shot back. "Like it should have been run years ago. He gets results. You should thank your God every day for the friendship he's extending to your people here in Israel!"

"*Our* people, Yuri, our people, lest you forget."

"Come on, let's not debate that one again, old buddy. Whatever you want to believe, I'll take that kind of action over a pack of fairy tales any day." He laughed. "I hear that even your old girlfriend, Sonya what's-her-name, is up to her elbows in this treaty business. You should be preaching at her, not me!"

His observation hit Anatoly like a sharp slap in the face. What Yuri concluded, Anatoly had often suspected. But he also knew he could never make Sonya understand unless they could talk face-to-face. Now that he knew what was going on, that the die was cast, it was too late. Yuri was not the type of friend you confided in, and Anatoly's refusal to be baited by him only seemed to egg him on.

"From what I hear, I sometimes wonder which 'ov' is really driving this hot new relationship with Israel—Bulgakov or Petrov. If it were up to me, Israel wouldn't get anything. We Russians have our own troubles, and we solve our own problems. Let the Jews do the same. They won't get the world's respect until they do."

"I know what you think, Yuri. We've been through it too many times already. How can you stand there and deny your ancestry? You may fool the world but you're not fooling me!"

"Aw, forget it," said Yuri, suddenly anxious to change the subject. "I didn't come here to argue with you, especially about my *German lineage*! I came to see how you were. So let's drop it and find something we can agree on, at least for the moment."

Anatoly nodded and motioned toward one of the two chairs in the compact little room he seldom used. "Make yourself comfortable," he said. "I was getting ready to make myself some dinner. Do you want to join me? For a bachelor, I'm not a bad cook."

"Sounds good. I'll take my chances. Which reminds me," said Yuri as Anatoly walked over to the efficiency kitchen, "before you left Moscow, I would have said your bachelor days were numbered," once again trying to bait him on a sensitive issue, this time using a different tack.

There was a long pause as Anatoly stood looking into the cupboard above the stove. "It didn't work out," he said finally.

"Too bad. That Sonya is some fine lady — even if she is one of the guiding lights behind this treaty you hate so much!"

"She's good, and Bulgakov trusts her. Besides, she knows her way around the corridors of decision-making here in Israel. She's the perfect choice to work on something like this. And one thing I know for sure. Whatever she's doing, she thinks it is in the best interest of Israel."

"No question there, even if it's at NUE's expense."

"Please, can we drop it?" Now it was Anatoly's turn to be pressed on an issue he preferred not to talk about. "I'll get off your back about your Jewish ancestry if you agree to get off my back about Sonya! She's my friend, and so was her brother. The whole subject is very painful to me," he said. "Let's find something that doesn't kill the appetite, or the best you'll get from me is a frozen dinner . . . still frozen . . . right between the eyes."

Yuri laughed as he watched his friend put a meal together from a limited choice of cans. During dinner they brought each other up to date by discussing noncontroversial subjects such as their jobs, living conditions in Israel, what was happening in Moscow — everything but the sensitive issues revolving around Russia and Israel. Afterward, as Anatoly rinsed the dishes and stacked them in the sink, Yuri wandered over to look at Anatoly's computer, which was once again sitting on the small table in the tiny living room.

"Still cruising the Internet for stories?" Yuri asked.

"Now you've touched on something that shows just how human I can be when I get mad," Anatoly said, without humor. "As a matter of fact, I haven't used my portable in almost half a year. I was so enraged when I heard about what happened to Sonya's brother, Yacov, I threw my laptop across the room."

"You're joking? How did you survive without it?"

"My temper or my computer?" Anatoly laughed.

"Your computer, of course. Everyone already knows what a mild-mannered guy you are."

"*Isvestia*'s had me online since I got here," Anatoly answered, giving his friend a half-truth. "But Yacov was the primary reason I wanted my personal computer up and running—so we could communicate quickly, easily, and inexpensively. I didn't want to overlap my personal affairs with business. I had just gotten it hooked up when he was killed. So I took the only remaining link between the two of us and did a number on it."

"Whoa, this man really *does* have a temper!"

"I had to send it back to the manufacturer in the States just to get it fixed. In fact, it just came back two days ago," Anatoly continued, ignoring the comment. "My old account and password should be activated by now. Perfect timing, of course, since I'm leaving early in the morning on assignment and I'm not sure when I'll get back. Where I'm going, it won't be of much help. But at least it will be up and running when I return."

"Well, in that case, you've probably got some packing to do so I'll leave you to it. I'm glad I caught you before you left, though."

"By the way, how did you find me?"

"Actually, I bumped into Sonya before I left Moscow, and she gave me your address," said Yuri. "Well, thanks for dinner.

I guess I better head back to Tel Aviv. I've taken a small flat there, near the CNN office."

"You're not returning to Moscow?"

"Not for the moment. Thanks to good old Bulgakov and your Sonya, I'm getting the feeling I may be here a while."

Anatoly's alarm sounded at four-thirty the next morning. He slapped it off, stumbled out of bed, and hurried through his shaving and dressing routine.

As he stood over the sink munching cold cereal and waiting for water to boil on his little two-burner gas stove, he mentally ticked off his "to do" list. Last night, after Yuri left, he'd packed his camping gear and kit bag, although that hadn't taken long. Most of what he needed was already hidden down in Petra, from previous trips. His rent was paid for the next year, so the apartment would be here, waiting, whenever he was able to get back to Jerusalem.

The water came to a boil, and he fixed a cup of instant coffee. He glanced at his watch. Almost five o'clock. He had time to test his Internet hookup while he drank his coffee. He could see what had accumulated in his mailbox the past six months, and try it out by sending Mike and Marlee a quick note before leaving.

Anatoly flipped on his laptop and plugged in the phone cord. When the screen came up, he clicked on the Internet icon. Within a few seconds a window popped up announcing that log-in was in progress. Good. It had taken forever, but at least it was operating again. It also appeared that its memory was still intact.

He clicked on the mail icon and whistled at the number of messages. Suddenly, the individual items registered. There, near the top of the list, were two messages from Yacov! By the date next to them, he knew that they had to have been sent just before Yacov died.

Anatoly clicked on the first one. His eyebrows went up when he saw it was encrypted.

"Password. Password," he muttered to himself. "What's the password?" Oh yes, now he remembered.

After entering the string of eight numbers, the message popped up in a window. He skimmed through the paragraphs rapidly. Stunned, he read it again, this time more slowly.

So, Yacov did know about Bulgakov before he died—and he'd been afraid. Tears came to Anatoly's eyes.

He saved the message and clicked on the second one. The modem clicked, and the Internet window froze. Then a window popped up stating that the connection had failed.

He glanced at his watch again. He couldn't delay any longer. Yacov's second message would have to wait until he returned.

Anatoly drove out of Jerusalem on the Jericho road, following its twists and turns through the Judean Hills as it descended from 820 meters above sea level to 395 meters below sea level in less than an hour. At the Allenby Bridge, near the modern town of Jericho, he crossed the Jordan River. The border guard glanced at his papers and Jordanian visa and wished him a pleasant trip to Petra.

Anatoly turned south at Na'ur and followed the mountainous King's Highway, which twisted and wound its spectacular way down to Petra. He arrived in Wadi Musa early in the afternoon and parked the Jeep at the end of the road.

There, dozens of Bedouin men stood around their camels and horses, eagerly waiting to take visitors through the narrow, winding Wadi as Siq, which led into Petra from the east. Some wore flowing robes, but most had on loose-fitting shirts and trousers. All wore the traditional headdress—a red-and-white checked or a plain white *kuffeyeh* secured with a black *agal* cord.

Anatoly drummed his fingers on the steering wheel. He didn't like camels or horses. He liked transportation with a gear shift and an accelerator. But since he didn't have time to walk the 3 kilometers through the wadi, he got out and headed toward the horses. A Bedouin in scuffed boots, dirty red pants, and a white shirt stepped forward. Anatoly knew the man from previous trips, although he had never been able to pronounce the man's name. As usual, in surprisingly good Hebrew, the man assured Anatoly he would be riding his best horse.

The Bedouin led the way toward the towering mass of red

sandstone that guarded Petra from the outside world. They entered the narrow gorge of the Wadi as Siq and followed the same twisting path of white stones that travelers had used for millennia.

As they rounded the final bend, Anatoly got his first glimpse of the glory of the ancient capital of the Nabateans, "the rose-red city half as old as time." The sight still excited him as much as it had the first time he'd seen it, months ago.

"I love looking at the Treasury," he said. Then, before the Bedouin could correct him, he added, "Hazanat Fara'un." The man nodded.

The huge facade was sharply incised into the red sandstone cliff. It towered over the visitors as they entered the stone-strewn courtyard before it. Monumental columns on two levels framed relief carvings, all cut out of the living rock.

"The grandeur of this place never ceases to amaze me," Anatoly said, twisting around in his saddle.

He dismounted, paid the Bedouin, and thanked him. He watched the man for a moment as he headed off to snag another customer for the return trip to Wadi Musa. Then Anatoly turned and walked halfway up the steps between the two mammoth entrance pillars and looked in at the carved interior. Soon, he knew, the building would be bustling with activity. He stepped back and gazed up at the beautiful detail of the monumental pediment. He wondered if the refugees would appreciate the fine artistry and attention to detail.

By now, he felt like he knew every rock in the entire Petra area. He scanned the desolate landscape, imagining the hordes of refugees that would soon make their dwelling place in the thousands of caves that dotted the mountainous walls. In his mind's eye, he saw the tents that would be sprinkled here and there for those that could not live in the caves, and the huge assembly areas in the valleys between the rosy red mountains that rose up on all sides. He mentally cataloged the sites being prepared for storage and sanitation — everything necessary to sustain three to four hundred thousand people for up to seven years, until D-Day, when Iesus would physically return to Petra and lead them back to His Holy City, Jerusalem. He thought about the completely repaired system of aqueducts and cisterns, now ready for use. This was his real pride and joy. Water was the key to survival, and the refugees would have all that was needed to sustain them here in the wilderness.

The covenant would be signed any day now. Although he knew that Sonya was involved in the treaty that had everyone talking, he refused to believe that she had anything to do with setting up her own people for the slaughter. Both she and her good friend, Prime Minister Shefi, had been lured into the web of the spider. Bulgakov knew precisely what he was doing, and why. Sonya—or the prime minister for that matter—was no match for this diabolical enemy of Israel. Anatoly comforted himself with the fact that even if Sonya had known and not been a part of what was happening between the two nations, it wouldn't have made any difference. Bulgakov would still be in power, and there still would have been a treaty with Israel. The prophets had foretold it.

The whole world was being duped. Soon, however, thousands of Jews would refuse the covenant with the New United Empire and would begin their trek to this wilderness hiding place. Until then, he still had much work to do. As much as he loved Sonya and feared for her, there was no way he could communicate the truth to her at this time. But the right time would come. He knew it in his heart. Yacov's death told him that the Petrovs had been watched closely. Yacov had been right. He had to be patient and choose the right opportunity. For now, Sonya's safety lay in her ignorance.

Anatoly was able to get out of Petra for a day. He had been holed up in the rose-red city for almost three weeks and he needed to bring Eitan up to date on the progress they were making. He made his way to the village of Wadi Musa where a little hole-in-the-wall room, leased by the Parousia Foundation, was always available to him. That evening, the knock at his door indicated that his radio message had been received and understood.

"Come in," he said when he opened the door to a smiling Eitan Shachar. "I was hoping the foundation could spare you for a day."

"It's obvious that the treaty will be signed any day now. I had to know, firsthand, how you were doing."

"We're doing quite well, actually." Anatoly dragged the other rickety wooden chair to the impromptu work table and cleared some of the papers off the Royal Jordanian Geographic Center map of Petra. "Take a look."

Eitan scanned the map, pausing to read some of the neat notes Anatoly had made with different colored pens.

"I admit, I was skeptical about handling 350,000 people at first, but not after I discovered the extent of the Nabatean and Roman water systems," said Anatoly, "and the abundance of caves that literally cover the mountainsides. There's a lot to do, but the work progresses well. As you know, we finished excavating the cisterns and drains and applying fresh concrete to them at least a month ago. Actually, they finished up just before I got down here this last time. The past four or five weeks, your people have finally been bringing in the supplies we'll need, through the back door to the west of Petra. It takes time, but with the supply sites already identified and marked, it's the best way to get supplies in, unnoticed. We're almost finished now."

Eitan glanced up. "Is anyone becoming suspicious?"

"Not that we can tell. They accept archaeologists as the strange creatures they are and don't really pay attention to what they're doing under their canvas shelters. And most of the supply runs are made at night, through the back door. We have never run into any sort of security problems when we come in that way."

"What if some government official should wander back to the site?"

"Everything is well hidden. There are plenty of out-of-the-way sites, and, as I said, that part of the job is almost finished. All we had to do was make sure we were alone, dig a hole in the back of a remote cave, stash the supplies in 200-liter plastic containers, and cover them up. Everything brought in at night is safely hidden away by daybreak. Even if they suspected something, picking the cave that we use to store things in would be like finding a needle in a haystack. The trenching and excavation tools we use to rebuild the water system by day make it a snap for hiding supplies at night."

Anatoly laughed, then continued. "We had some pointed questions from the Jordanians about the trenchers until I explained that they were used to dig out the large cisterns. Told them if they wanted it done by hand, they could be my guest, and handed them a shovel. We've had no trouble since."

"And you think you have enough room to house three, maybe four hundred thousand people?" asked Eitan.

"No problem! We've located literally thousands of caves, niches, tombs, and ruins of every size," Anatoly explained, pointing to different sites on the map in front of them. "Some of them are huge, like this one over here. If we ever run out of room, we can always use the tents. Hopefully, we won't have to do that. If everyone and everything can be hidden away in caves, we can practically disappear from sight in a moment's notice. That's what we're hoping to be able to do."

"How in the world do you remember where everything is, supply sites, which caves are which, and so on?"

"Every area has been selected and marked out on maps like this one," Anatoly explained. "We're as ready as we could ever hope to be. It may look complex on paper, but when the day comes, it will work."

"You've done magnificent work, Anatoly. You've been the perfect person for this project."

"I guess we both need to thank the Teasdales for that," said Anatoly.

"Indeed we do."

FIFTEEN

Holocaust II Minus 42 Months

Yuri Kagan's heart pounded as the adrenaline coursed through his body. Moments before, at Yad Vashem on the Mount of Remembrance in Jerusalem, president of the New United Empire, Nikolai Bulgakov, and Israeli Prime Minister Binyamin Shefi had applied their signatures to a seven-year mutual-assistance treaty. All the networks had carried the historic event live, but CNN, in Yuri's modest opinion, had provided the best coverage of all. The whole world watched in awe as the New United Empire and Israel became partners. Now the successful wrap-up of the CNN broadcast depended on his commentary, which was scheduled to begin approximately a minute after these two world leaders had left the Holocaust Museum.

Yuri risked one more look at the backdrop for his closing wrap-up of this historic moment. It was a barbed-wire fence in front of a life-size black-and-white photograph of Jewish prisoners, lying in narrow, three-tier wooden bunks like cordwood. Their haunting faces stared out at him as though they knew the elaborate steps he had taken to hide his Jewish background and were accusing him personally. In spite of his detachment from that terrible time in history, he shivered and turned back to the camera, wanting to finish what he had come to do and then get out of there.

Cameraman Andrei Denisov already had his eye screwed into the viewfinder. Egor Kaugin, the sound man, gave a nod, and Yuri heard the cue in his earphone. CNN's Kagan, Kaugin, and Denisov were ready to go.

"Only moments ago, the New United Empire and the nation of Israel signed a seven-year treaty, guaranteeing Israel's right to exist," Yuri began. "Prime Minister Shefi hailed the pact as an unprecedented step forward in the quest for worldwide peace. 'Let it begin here,' he said, in a statement that is sure to enter the history books. President Bulgakov went on to explain that this historic event was taking place at Yad Vashem, to signify 'my pledge that the Holocaust of World War II will never happen again to Jews here in Israel or anywhere else in the world.'

"President Bulgakov embraced the Israeli prime minister after the signing, thanking him for the technical assistance Israel was promising the New United Empire. The prime minister, in return, told the world that without President Bulgakov's intervention on their behalf a short month earlier, Israel would not know peace today. His quick and decisive intervention saved many lives, Arab and Jewish. The president responded to the warm words of the prime minister by promising that Israel would never again fear betrayal by the nations of the world, including the Arab nations that surround her.

"Is this the beginning of a millennium of peace?" Yuri asked his unseen television audience. "Most in Israel think so. Surrounding Yad Vashem at this very moment is a crowd estimated at one hundred thousand people, with another million or so people crowded into the streets all over Jerusalem, watching this historic event on large, portable screens, all chanting and waving signs. Jerusalem is caught up in a carnival spirit that has not been seen since Jerusalem and the Wailing Wall were regained by Israel after the Six-Day War in 1967! Regardless of how this treaty affects these two nations in the future, it is safe to say that Israel will be celebrating tonight!

"Now, for reactions in the New United Empire, we transfer you live to Red Square in Moscow." The red light winked off, and Yuri heard the director tell him the feed had shifted. The reporter exhaled loudly as he willed his pulse to slow.

Grand Haven, Michigan

"Friends, your pastor and elders have called this emergency meeting because of what happened two weeks ago in Jerusalem, when the New United Empire signed its seven-year agreement with Israel," Pastor Ken began. "After careful consideration, study, and prayer, there is no doubt in our minds that Nikolai Bulgakov is the Antichrist, and that in just three and a half years, Christians will undergo the worst persecution ever known to mankind since the beginning of time. We have asked an old friend of our congregation, Mike Teasdale, to address us concerning what we need to be doing, in light of what we believe is now beginning to happen. Mike, Marlee, thank you both for coming."

Mike stood up and walked slowly over to the podium. He knew many faces in the congregation. Being there that morning was just like being in his own home church down in Texas. Marlee thought so too. She gave him her special smile as Mike began to speak.

"As many of you already know, for years now, we at Mount Zion Ministries have been trying to prepare believers for the reality of this day. Now that the countdown has actually begun, the situation is critical. Around the world, similar groups of believers are holding meetings, just as we are doing tonight."

Mike looked out across the congregation. He knew they had been taught well; time after time they had been instructed that the church would face persecution at the hands of Antichrist before the heavenly sign would be given in the sun, moon, and stars, heralding the return of Christ. Only then would Christ return: to rescue the faithful and initiate His wrath upon those who remained. Yet their expressions ran the gamut, from grim-faced agreement, to concern and even cynical disbelief. His eyes moved briefly to Marlee's encouraging face in the front row as he continued.

"Tonight, we will only address the big picture. Details will be provided to you in the weeks to follow, but for now, there are certain decisions each of you, as well as your church leadership, must make.

"Those of you who have sat under my teaching when I've spoken here in the past know how I like to use lists. Well, tonight is no exception. There are five things you will need to focus on, immediately. Write them down. Save your questions until I finish.

"First, *don't panic*. You have three and a half years to prepare. That is ample time to do what you need to do.

"Second, if you are to survive Bulgakov's onslaught, you will have to *go into hiding*. Survival teams must be put together immediately. It will be difficult if not impossible for all of you to go to the same place. It would also be unsafe. Therefore, decide who will go into hiding with you. Be sure you really know those you choose—know them well. Christ taught that many so-called Christians will defect to Antichrist rather than face his persecution, therefore you will be trusting those you choose with your life. For this reason, family units are the most secure. Next, add only your closest friends, those you trust completely.

"Once you have determined the members of your survival group, choose the most capable leader. Not the most popular, but the most competent! Don't give leadership to someone who can't handle it! For those who have no group, your church should provide the groups and leadership necessary.

"Third, the first priority of your leader must be to *locate your survival site*. Find the site that best meets the criteria I will give you. Except for those who have a need to know, the location of the site should be kept secret, even from the other members of your survival group. The fewer that know, the safer the site will be when the time comes.

"In choosing a site, your group leaders must consider isolation, climate, water, trees, and southern exposure. If a member of your group already owns a site that should be considered, give the necessary information to your group leader.

"Fourth, you must begin now to *sell off your personal property*. Sell *everything* that cannot be used directly in your survival effort. All of you! Take whatever you can get and give the cash to your group leader. The sooner, the better. Land prices will probably plummet in the next several years because of the terrible world conditions that will soon dominate the first half of the treaty period. But remember, if you sell cheap, it also means that you can buy cheap. What you need now is cash. Cash to purchase those things that are critical to your survival efforts until Christ returns. You should figure that you will need enough supplies for at least another two and a half years after Antichrist breaks his treaty with Israel at the midpoint of the seven-year covenant; therefore add those two and a half years to any time you will spend in hiding before the treaty is broken, and you can quickly calculate the time period you must provide for. Remember, any property you hold on to, other than that which has a direct application to your survival effort, is worthless. Cash is needed to purchase the land and other supplies that will be necessities to your survival efforts.

"Fifth, other than the survival site, *look for several essential items and buy them when you have the necessary funds.* The most important is a one-ton diesel pickup truck with power take-off and generator. Actually, you should buy as many as you can afford and, if you have excess, help the less fortunate groups purchase some of this basic, necessary equipment that they will need to survive. It should not be difficult to find a pickup truck with this equipment. It is pretty standard farm equipment, but critical to your survival effort. It will provide transportation and minimum power to run your survival camp. Purchase 1,500-gallon fiberglass tanks in which to store diesel fuel, 50-gallon plastic drums for food and other survival items, and supplies of staple grains that have a longer shelf life, such as rice, sugar, and flour. Finally, purchase as many MREs as you think you can afford. Do that sooner rather than later, before the famines hit and drive the prices of MREs out of sight. Question?"

"What's an MRE?" asked Pastor Ken.

"Sorry. MRE stands for 'Meals Ready to Eat'—like the military uses—and they can be purchased at most camping or outfitter stores."

Mike paused and looked out across the stunned faces. He suddenly realized that he must have sounded like all those crazy survivalist cults in the past. How could he convince them that, this time, the apocalypse was real?

"I know many of you have not yet absorbed what I have

said, but it is crucial that you do. Your pastor and I will stay as long as necessary after the meeting tonight to answer your questions. In the past, your leadership has encouraged you to go on with life, to wait until the covenant is signed before you begin to prepare for the persecution that is coming. They told you right. But now, the covenant with death has been signed. The countdown has begun. You have a little over three years to get these things lined up before you will need to completely disappear from society. Plenty of time to do what you must do — if you get started tonight!"

Sixteen

Holocaust II Minus 36 Months

Dawn was breaking as the Tupolev 204 transport touched down at Tel Aviv's Ben Gurion International Airport. For all her outward sophistication Sonya was a jumble of emotions on the inside. This was her long-awaited return to her homeland, Israel, and she was making it alone. When she and Yacov had left to care for Papa back in Moscow, she had no idea that only she would live to see the Promised Land again. But she was no longer the same person. Their violent deaths had left her with a stark hollowness in her soul. Avenging their murders had not relieved her inner pain, but had only left her feeling empty, almost subhuman. Her career continued to advance: she was the integral negotiator in the peace agreement between Israel and the NUE and in recognition of such, she had been allowed to return to her homeland as special delegate to the Prime Minister's office. But none of her successes brought her joy. Being back in Israel reminded her of the only love she might have left in the world—Anatoly—and her own agenda may have cost her that, too.

In the past six months she had tried to call him many times, each without success. The *Isvestia* office in Tel Aviv had politely taken her messages, but her calls had never been returned. It's as though he has disappeared off the face of the Earth, she thought. In spite of all her contacts, she had not been able to locate him. Now that she was finally coming back home to Israel, it would be easier to track him down. Still, she could not understand why he had not been in touch with her. Had his feelings for her changed? Did he not want to be found?

Sonya looked across the rows of huge Antonov transports disgorging armored vehicles, military personnel, and materiel. She knew where the units were going better than their commanders did. Although she believed it necessary, she felt with a strange sense of uneasiness at this huge and awesome foreign presence in Israel.

All of this barely had time to register when Russian embassy personnel whisked her around customs and into a waiting limousine. In less than an hour, she was in Jerusalem — oh, how she loved Jerusalem! — where she was taken to a spacious second-story apartment less than a kilometer from the prime minister's Knesset office. Sonya wore a tired smile as she stood at the window and looked out across the city she had missed so much. It was springtime in Jerusalem, and it was good to be home.

She suspected that Prime Minister Shefi had had his hand in her new accommodations. So much had happened in the six months since they had worked together to formalize the treaty, and now she was here to enjoy the fruits of her labor and help implement the agreement. *Israel is secure for the first time ever*, she thought proudly, *and I played a part in making it happen!*

Turning back to take stock of her new living quarters, she spotted a basket of fruit on the table in the dining area. She walked over and opened the card. The welcome gift was from the prime minister, who had simply signed it "Binyamin."

She needed to unpack, but there was something more important she had to do first. In the living room, she picked up the phone and called the *Isvestia* office in Tel Aviv. The receptionist she had spoken to numerous times in the past again informed her that Anatoly Altshuler was still on special assignment and couldn't be reached. From her accent, Sonya knew she was a transplant to Israel, probably from Moscow. Having had enough of this woman's excuses, Sonya switched back to her native tongue and let fly.

"I am Sonya Petrov, special assistant to President Nikolai

Bulgakov. I am in Israel on special assignment, attached to Prime Minister Shefi's office. I am tired of hearing the same broken record every time I try to find out where Anatoly Altshuler is. Now, young woman, you have a choice. Tell me what I want to know, or I assure you I will do everything in my power to see that you are reassigned to Siberia—and that's no joke!"

Apparently Sonya's credentials and intensity made an impact, because after a few moments of silence, the receptionist spilled everything she knew. All the things Sonya had being trying to find out suddenly came gushing forth in a flood of words.

"Mr. Altshuler has been out of touch for months. His salary deposits remain untouched. Headquarters in Moscow is as concerned about his whereabouts as you are. No one knows where he is or what he is working on. Before he left six months ago, he was working on what he called a potentially big story. He said he would be impossible to reach for some time. He still has an apartment in Jerusalem, but all outward signs indicate that it hasn't been used the past six months. The landlord told me he had another six months on his lease, which he prepaid. Rumors were, he was somewhere down in the Negev doing his research. Since the day he left, however, we've had absolutely no contact with him. For all I know, he's dead."

As the woman talked, Sonya gripped the phone until her knuckles were white. At the end, she thanked the woman for the information and left her Jerusalem address and phone number. "If he calls, you must call me immediately!" she said.

When she had hung up, Sonya slumped into the nearest chair. She was shaken by this latest news, but somehow not surprised. The woman had only confirmed a suspicion that was growing inside her.

Holocaust II Minus 32 Months

Binyamin Shefi looked around at his circle of closest advisors until his eyes stopped on Sonya. "Are you sure everything is ready?"

The question was addressed to all, but it was she who

answered. "Yes, Mr. Prime Minister. I talked with President Bulgakov and his chief of staff just last night. The Arab countries have been informed of what we're doing and what will happen to them if they interfere."

Refael Nissim, the Minister of Security, cleared his throat. "That is very kind of President Bulgakov," he said condescendingly. "However, if things go wrong, we are the ones who will be attacked by a billion angry Arabs, not the NUE. As an IDF general, I am, perhaps, just a little more aware of these dangers than you are."

Shefi gave him a smile that made clear who was prime minister. "We appreciate your input, Refael. But it would seem that the forces that pushed the Syrians and Palestinians back where they belong, the same forces that today protect our borders, are also capable of keeping the peace on the Temple Mount, especially in light of the fact that the country they represent has long been a friend of the Arabs. In fact, some still receive aid from NUE."

Refael pursed his lips and glared at Shefi.

The prime minister ignored him as he continued. "The New United Empire's treaty with Jordan also helps. The Jordanian sign-off on our Temple Project has gone a long way toward convincing their Arab neighbors—and ours—that the two holy places can coexist, side by side. That, along with the presence of the NUE troops, assures me that there will be no trouble as long as we leave the Dome of the Rock alone. Do you agree, Sonya?"

"Absolutely," she stated flatly. "Without question."

"The truth is, Bulgakov has done in months what we could never have accomplished on our own. I think we should be grateful." Shefi saw the line of red rising above Refael's collar and turned back to Sonya with a poorly suppressed smile. "We will make the necessary announcement at the press conference following this meeting. At the same time, I will give the executive order attaching a group of NUE troops to our guards presently stationed on the Temple Mount. Once the Arab world realizes that the Dome of the Rock is secure, they will cause no problems. The crisis will be over before it ever begins."

Sonya smiled at him. "Mr. Prime Minister, it would seem we are on the brink of *another* great milestone in history—laying the cornerstone for the Third Temple. Quite an accomplishment."

"Yes," said Shefi proudly. "And an end to Arab domination of the Temple Mount."

After a quiet dinner with the prime minister and his wife celebrating the events of the day, Sonya returned to her spacious apartment, sat down on her sofa, and flipped on the TV with the remote control. Seeing it was already tuned to CNN, she thumbed the volume up as Yuri Kagan began his evening summary of the world's woes.

The first clip showed scenes from the typhoon that had devastated Sri Lanka and southern India. Muddy rivers, kilometers wide, wiped out whole villages, sweeping bloated animals, dead bodies, and swirling debris toward the sea.

Yuri droned on, unaffected by the carnage, as the next segments covered civil wars all over the world: in Pakistan, Zaire, Brazil, Mexico, China, and an invasion of Northern Ireland by the Republic of Ireland. This last segment lasted longer than the others, almost a minute, as a CNN reporter braved the shelling of the Belfast airport. The report ended abruptly when an artillery shell plowed into the terminal.

The studio anchor continued without missing a beat, moving to a segment covering the widespread famines across central and northern Africa, as well as the serious food shortages that now existed in most of the rest of the world. "These are caused," Yuri explained, "by crop failures in North America and Western Europe." What made the current situation even worse was the fact that most of the world's excess grain supplies had been sold to NUE during the previous years' bumper-crop harvests. Only the New United Empire had foreseen the excessive crop failures that were now sweeping the nations that were so accustomed to feeding the world. Only those nations that were part of the New United Empire were unaffected by this current worldwide famine.

Sonya sighed as the newscast continued its weary requiem for the world. She marveled again at Nikolai's wisdom in stockpiling grain for the New United Empire, but she wondered why he wasn't willing to share it with other countries, now that the worldwide need was so great. She knew that the NUE's food stockpiles were huge, capable of feeding the entire world for years if necessary.

Suddenly she remembered something he had said. "Wait until the time is right," he had told his staff. "Then we will use their stomachs to bring about peace for the world!"

"This is Yuri Kagan, CNN News, Jerusalem." Sonya stabbed the off button, hoping it would also silence the growing uneasiness she felt inside. Trying to change her mood, she turned her thoughts to the historic event that would occur on the Temple Mount in less than a week's time.

The Temple Mount guard held back the crowd as the prime minister's entourage edged slowly down the Street of the Chain in the Old City. Blue-and-white Israeli flags waved and the people sang and cheered wildly, pressed together in the late summer heat. As Shefi and his staff got out of their cars near the Gate of the Chain entrance to the Mount, an angry buzz emanated from a small knot of Arabs clustered near the entrance, providing an ominous counterpoint.

Binyamin Shefi smiled as he walked alongside his ecstatic countrymen. Men in prayer shawls and yarmulkes cried as they pushed against the police lines. Observant Jews were there in great numbers to see the laying of the cornerstone of only the second temple to be built on this site since Solomon's temple, circa 950 B.C. No temple had occupied this site since the last one had been destroyed in A.D. 70. Only the ultra-orthodox Hasidim, with their black hats, long black coats, and side curls, were absent. They were still waiting for their Meshiah to usher in the real state of Israel. To Shefi, however, the rebuilding of the temple was a matter of sovereignty rather than religion, since he, like most Israelis, was not religious.

The official group entered the gate, climbed up to the Temple Mount platform, and passed through one of the archways of the Scales. They skirted the magnificent golden-domed mosque, stopping instead at the small Dome of the Tablets about 100 meters to the northwest. There, on either side of a temporary podium, waited two chief rabbis: Ephraim Ben-Yosef for the Sfardic and Aharon Grossberg for the Ashkenazic.

Binyamin took his place behind the podium and shuffled briefly through his notecards, then stuck them in his coat pocket. He glanced at the bouquet of microphones, then looked out at the cameras arrayed before him. The crowd hushed.

"Today, we begin a new era in Jerusalem," he said, his voice echoing across a sea of faces. "We are here to celebrate the commencement of the building of the Third Temple of God by laying its cornerstone here on the Temple Mount. In a short time, our temple, symbol of Israel, will again exist, exactly where Solomon erected the first one, three thousand years ago." He paused dramatically. "I now call on Rabbi Ephraim Ben-Yosef and Rabbi Aharon Grossberg to place the cornerstone."

The huge rectangular stone hung about 2 meters above the ground, suspended by a heavy chain and a massive eyebolt. Rabbi Ben-Yosef looked heavenward for a moment, then picked up the gold-plated trowel. Both rabbis placed their hands on the implement, scraped a dollop of mortar from the pail beside them, and applied it to the underside of the stone. Then they turned and watched as Prime Minister Shefi pressed a button and a motorized hoist lowered the block into position. The crowd cheered as the stone crunched into place.

Andrei Denisov shut off the camera, and Yuri Kagan let his on-camera face fade away. Things have certainly picked up here in Israel since Bulgakov made his deal with the Jews, thought Yuri. This assignment had turned into a hot one. He was glad CNN had ordered him to stay here indefinitely.

Holocaust II Minus 31 Months

"Sonya Petrov!" Yuri shouted at the pretty brunette. "Wait."

Sonya looked down the hall as she closed the office door and smiled at the reporter. "Yuri! How are things at CNN? It was a nice surprise to see you covering the ceremonies on the Temple Mount."

"Thank you," he said. He pushed his horn-rimmed glasses up the bridge of his nose. Behind them, the light in his blue eyes reflected his excitement. "It's great to see you again, Sonya. Seems like a long time since I interviewed you and your brother for that piece when you returned to Russia."

His mention of Yacov pierced Sonya's heart, although he seemed oblivious to the pain his careless words had caused her.

"I've seen some of your reports," she said, a shade less warmly, "so I knew you were here in Israel. How do you like it?"

"With everything that's happening, it's a fantastic assignment," he admitted. "But I was surprised when I heard you were coming back. How long have you been here now, three or four months?"

"Five months this week," she replied. "How about you?"

"They sent me here almost a year ago to cover the Syrian invasion and the Palestinian uprising, but your boy Bulgakov really put the lid on that in a hurry. Remember? That's when I bumped into you back in Moscow and you gave me Anatoly's address. Anyway, so much has happened since—that big mutual-admiration pact between NUE and Israel, the new temple, and all sorts of other mayhem. Never a dull moment. In fact, so much is going on here these days that I've been assigned here permanently—which suits me fine, 'cause I like to eat."

Sonya laughed, warming a bit more to Antoly's old friend. "Well, then, what brings you to the Knesset today?"

"Actually," he said, the impish grin on his face fading, "I came here looking for you, believe it or not. I was wondering if you've heard anything from Anatoly?"

"Nothing," Sonya replied, the now-familiar pain piercing her heart again. "Absolutely nothing—and not because I haven't tried. Nobody seems to know where he is. How about you? Heard anything from him since you've been here in Israel?"

"No, that's been my experience, too," he said. "You know, I think I might have been one of the last people to see him here in Jerusalem. With the address you had given me, I was able to track him down. The night I was at his apartment, he mentioned he was leaving on an extended trip early the next morning. Said something about doing research in the Negev. That was almost a year ago, and I haven't heard from him since."

"I'm afraid something must have gone wrong," said Sonya. "There's no way he'd stay out of touch this long."

Seeing the sadness on her face, Yuri switched gears. "Mind if I ask you another question? Was that a meeting you just came out of?"

"You know better than to ask me that, Yuri."

"Come on. Isn't there something new and exciting you would like to tell your friend from CNN about? A scoop? I can make sure you're an 'unidentified source.' "

Sonya grinned; if nothing else, she appreciated his thoughtfulness in changing the subject. "I know nothing to be 'unidentified' about. How's that for boring?" she asked as she turned to go. "But what about you? Anything new today on your end, hot off the wires?"

"I could suggest that your question is a two-way street—I help you, you help me—but I know it wouldn't do me any good."

"You're right, it wouldn't," she laughed, leaving him standing in the hall.

Holocaust II Minus 30 Months

In the ornate Papal Library on the third floor of the Apostolic Palace, Nikolai Bulgakov and his chief of staff sat stiffly in dark suits. They were waiting for Pope Leo XIV, Bishop of Rome. The large room had a stunning view of St. Peter's Square, the same view as from the papal apartment one floor above.

The two men stood as a door opened and the head of the Roman Catholic Church entered. Neither of them moved to kiss the pontiff's ring.

"We thank you for seeing us on such short notice, Your Holiness," Bulgakov said in English, the language both men spoke and understood.

"I have been looking forward to meeting you," said the

Holy Father, taking his accustomed seat. "A man of peace is rare in this age of war and unrest. Please be seated." He indicated the two chairs that faced his throne.

"My congratulations on your peace initiatives," the pope continued when the two men were seated. "I am encouraged by what I hear. Peace in Russia and Germany, and now peace in Israel. Peace among the Orthodox, the Muslim, and the Jew. And now the rebuilding of the Jewish temple on the Temple Mount. Today, as never before, our world suffers from many problems—wars, famine, disease, horrible natural disasters—and yet those who have aligned with you know a peace they have never known before. My prayer is that your example will encourage all the nations to respect human rights and dignity, and work toward the peace that your bright light shows to the rest of the world."

"We are of one mind, Your Holiness. And that is why we asked to see you."

"In what way may I help?"

"As you have said, the goal of the New United Empire is world peace," said Bulgakov. "Today I would ask that you join with me in proclaiming and providing this peace by urging the nations under your care to cooperate with us. You are the spiritual leader of a vast portion of the world. Think what we could accomplish together!"

The pontiff nodded once, slowly. "That is a request worth considering," he said. "How do you define 'cooperate'?"

"There are countries over which you exert great influence, countries that, like Israel, could be helped by coming under the direct protection of the New United Empire, where they will know true freedom of speech and religion. Countries that need the food and security only we can provide. May I suggest that my chief of staff," he nodded toward Sergei, "meet with your secretariat of state to develop policies of cooperation that would ensure peace and well-being for all Catholic nations."

"War and world poverty concern me greatly, and I know there are many who would benefit from your generosity and leadership," said the pope. He paused for a moment. "Thus far, everything you have told the world that you would do, you have done. If you can truly deliver worldwide peace, then you have not only my cooperation but my blessing as well."

"Thank you, Your Holiness. I only hope that I can live up to your lofty expectations."

"When we have finished here today, my personal secretary will make the necessary arrangements with my secretariat of state, Cardinal Fernandez." The pontiff leaned forward slightly, his long white hands resting lightly on the heavily carved wooden arms of his throne. "Ah, but before you go, however, there is a small request I would make of you."

Nikolai Bulgakov continued smiling. He knew what was coming. Quid pro quo. "Please. Tell me what I can do for you."

"The Temple Mount in Jerusalem. It has always been dear to my heart . . . to the heart of all Christianity," said the pope. "I would count it a great personal favor if the New United Empire would guarantee Roman Catholics access to it." He paused, as though the idea had just come to him. "Perhaps a small plot between the Dome of the Rock and the El-Aqsa Mosque over by the eastern wall could be provided so that we Christians can share in this holy site, along with the Jewish and Muslim people of the world. Call it a trade-off, if you like. I will help you with your request, and you will help me with mine."

Bulgakov smiled and nodded. "Of course, Your Holiness. Let me see what can be done. It took me over a year of negotiations to get permission to build the new temple. This may take a little time too, but I can assure you that I will do all I can, within my power."

Holocaust II Minus 29 Months

Sonya stood among the confusion in Anatoly's Jerusalem apartment, watching as the movers boxed up his belongings and carted them out to the truck. She didn't know whether to be sad, hurt, or scared. Anatoly had simply disappeared off the face of the Earth. Had his landlord not contacted the *Isvestia* office, which fortunately he had listed on his rent form, *before* they reclaimed his apartment thirty days after past rent was due, she would never have had time to remove his belongings before they sold them off for past rent due. When the receptionist at the *Isvestia* office had called and notified her, Sonya had quickly agreed to take care of storing Anatoly's things. The woman wasn't about to argue with this intimidating, high-ranking female from Moscow.

Where is he? she wondered for the millionth time. *How could he disappear without a trace?* She had mentioned his disappearance to Binyamin Shefi, and he had agreed to have his intelligence people look into it for her. But that was months ago, and they had found nothing. She had to assume no news was good news. Was he alive or dead? Was he being held captive somewhere or hiding for some reason? If so, from what, from whom? He had disappeared thirteen months ago, just before the treaty between Israel and the NUE had been signed, and no one had heard a word from him since. Her reason told her he was dead, but her heart was less rational, as hearts often are.

"Does this go?" one of the movers asked. He pointed to a laptop computer sitting on a small table.

Sonya shook her head. "No. I'll take that with me." She flipped the screen down and added the computer to a small pile of personal items she wanted to keep out of storage.

Where are you, Anatoly? Tears filled her eyes as the question echoed in her heart and mind.

SEVENTEEN

Holocaust II Minus 24 Months

He had arrived, coming through the back door less than an hour earlier, just as dawn had begun to awaken the refugee community that dotted the landscape before him. The steady exodus of Jews down to this remote area in Petra had kept Eitan Shachar and his small staff busy every waking hour for the past eighteen months since the treaty had been signed with the New United Empire. This had been his first chance to leave the hectic metropolitan areas of Jerusalem and Tel Aviv since he had last been with Anatoly, over a year and a half ago now, just before the treaty had been signed. Since then, their only contact had been by radio.

Eitan looked down on the plain of Petra from the vantage point of the Urn Tomb. "You've done well, Anatoly. Everything has gone exactly as planned. I will admit, however, that I wondered how we would ever accomplish some of this. But God, in His providence, had it all worked out."

"Yes," Anatoly replied, laughing, "but not always the way we expected."

"True," said Eitan. "But it's been a year and a half now, and it looks like most of those who are coming are here."

Anatoly nodded. "We seem to be down to a trickle—nothing like the first twelve months. The winter rains haven't helped, of course. But with spring just around the corner, it may pick up again," he said. "How are things on the outside?"

"Like a bad dream, friend. Prophecy is being fulfilled

before our very eyes. The New United Empire now has nine members, and the worldwide famines are horrible. It seems that the food shortages have become the single greatest factor in the accelerating hostility among nations the world over—the nations are literally fighting each other for food! There has been nothing like this in the history of the world. Even the United Nations has come to a virtual standstill, crippled by the insurmountable problems of their member nations. Everyone is affected except those nations belonging to the NUE and Israel."

"And those of us here," Anatoly added. "Thanks to our inside information from the Word of God."

"Yes. Thank God for His Word! Without its clear instructions concerning these days, I'm not sure any of us would—or could—survive what's still to come. But it makes me wonder where Bulgakov's inside information is coming from," said Eitan, then quickly added, "I guess we should know the answer to that!" The two men were silent for a few moments, still trying to assimilate the things that were happening all around them.

"Our network tells us that Bulgakov has stockpiled enough food to feed the world for another ten years," Eitan finally said, breaking the moment's silence. "Of course, as we know, only those nations who are aligned with him have access to his vast food supplies."

"There can be no doubt about it now," Anatoly nodded. "He is setting things up for when he establishes his one-world government."

"Precisely as the Scriptures said would happen. Between the wars and the famines, entire countries have been forced to their knees, either fighting their neighbors who have no more food than they have or begging for help from the United Nations, who can't do a thing about it!"

"Have any nations tried to attack the NUE? It's certainly obvious to the others that they have all the food they need."

"No way. No one has had the guts to take them on. With the sophisticated weaponry at their disposal by virtue of their German connection, everyone leaves well enough alone. Not that there's not a lot of complaining about the fact that Bulgakov takes care of his own and doesn't share with the rest of the world."

"Yes, I'll bet there's a lot of that! That's exactly what Bulgakov wants!" said Anatoly. "He knows the UN can't begin to solve this, and that just sets the stage for his grand entry, two years from now. Just think of what's still to come!"

"That's exactly what I'm doing," said Eitan. "And that's why I am going to need you back in Jerusalem, as soon as possible. How much more time do you need before you can leave here?"

"I figure about six more months," Anatoly replied. "And then I need those two replacements you promised me. By that time I think I can safely turn Petra over to them. But first I want to get what will probably be the last serious wave of refugees in and settled. Will that still give us enough time to do what we have to do on the secondary sites, before the second Exodus begins?"

"We've already done a lot of work," Eitan assured him. "We have quite a few general localities sized up, but we don't dare do too much, too soon and risk exposure. Some supplies are already stockpiled in warehouses we can get to in a moment's notice, if necessary."

"So, as soon as your two men arrive, I'm out of here. Probably for good, don't you agree?"

"Yes. The men I'm sending you, David Gur and Gideon Landau, are the best I have, but I'm going to need them first up in Jerusalem, helping us get the last wave of refugees down here to Petra. It's harder now than before, because those concerned about the NUE's pressure in Israel have already holed up someplace else, and they're not always easy to find."

"I know, but if you want me out of here in six months, I need those two down here in six months!"

"No problem, you'll have 'em."

"Did you know anything about this?" Binyamin Shefi asked Sonya, pointing to the television set in his office where an Israeli newscast was repeating what Nikolai Bulgakov had announced only an hour earlier.

"No," Sonya answered, "this is the first I've heard of it."

Being in Israel had taken her out of the loop with Nikolai. Even she had begun to wonder what exactly he was up to. Was this the beginning of the one-world government he had spoken of when she had first joined up with him, almost three years ago?

"Looks like Bulgakov is testing his leadership abilities," said the prime minister, running a hand across his closely cropped silver hair, "because he's building his empire with rebel nations who have never yielded to anyone before! Think about it. In the past eighteen months, Iraq, Iran, Ethiopia, Libya, Ukraine, and Turkey have joined the New United Empire."

"Seems the Vatican has helped open some of the doors—Libya and Ethiopia, in particular," Sonya added.

"And now the latest, Sonya," the prime minister continued, "Syria has joined. Syria! That ragtag bunch of terrorists that tried to put a squeeze on us a little over a year ago! Who's next, the PLO?"

"I suppose if anyone can control those seven bad boys, he can."

He laughed. "You don't suppose he's found a spot remover for leopards, do you?"

"I don't know," she said, unsmiling. "I guess we'll see."

Shefi looked at her closely, then gestured her to one of the chairs in front of his desk. "Sonya, do you feel all right?" he asked.

She almost lied, but she knew he asked because he cared. "No, to be perfectly frank with you, I don't," she said.

"Do you need to see a doctor? I know my personal physician would see you immediately."

Sonya smiled at him, grateful for his concern. "That's very kind, Binyamin. But I'm not sick—at least not physically. I guess it's the world's problems that are getting me down."

"These past months have been strange," he admitted. "Back when we signed the treaty, I never imagined things would turn out the way they have. Good for us. Terrible for the rest of the world, except . . ."

"Except for those allied with NUE," Sonya continued, finishing his sentence. "But I still believe that the treaty has been a wonderful thing. President Bulgakov has lived up to all his promises to the Jews in Russia, and especially to us in Israel."

"Yes," he nodded. "Because of this treaty, we are at peace for the first time ever. Our economy has never been better, and we have had no problem assimilating any of our people, worldwide, who want to immigrate here to Israel. What's more, the temple is being rebuilt and, miracle of miracles, we have had absolutely no trouble from our Arab neighbors. I know we have Bulgakov to thank for all that."

"He has certainly kept his word and done what he promised," Sonya said.

"Yes," said Shefi. "And what's been good for Israel has also been good for the New United Empire. Peace and prosperity. The man is a genius, although I will admit that I don't always understand what he's trying to do or how he does it!" He paused, shaking his head, his face sobering. "But what of the rest? Other than the NUE and us, the world is getting slaughtered by famine and wars. I feel guilty because things are going so well here, and yet Israel is not in a position to share with these hurting nations, what we don't have. If I could, I would. Certainly, if I was in Bulgakov's shoes, I would try to help the starving nations any way I could."

"I guess that's what really bothers me, too," said Sonya quietly. "Members of the New United Empire are the only ones without problems."

"And Israel," the prime minister again reminded her.

"Yes, and Israel," Sonya agreed. "But everywhere else it has been one catastrophe after another. More wars than anyone can count. Famine everywhere. And then there's the natural disasters—hurricanes, typhoons, tidal waves, volcanoes, and earthquakes—like the one in Tokyo just last week. How do you come to grips with an entire metropolitan area being obliterated? Not just damaged, but wiped out. Nothing left standing. Have we heard anything new concerning that?"

"Not a lot. They've had to declare martial law, of course, and have shifted their capital to Osaka because it wasn't damaged as heavily. But from last reports, Tokyo has become the world's largest open grave. They will never know how many people died there—millions, I suppose. They're talking about completely abandoning the city because of the disease that is running rampant over the entire area."

Sonya shivered. "Thank God that hasn't happened here."

"Yes. I suppose so." The prime minister toyed with his pencil. The handsome lines of his face were sober as he looked at her with intent dark eyes. "As terrible as all this is, I sense that your mood may be caused by another reason, closer to home."

"I don't know what you mean," she said, avoiding his eyes.

"Sonya, I may be getting old, but I am not yet blind. It's the young man you told me about, the reporter, that worries you so, am I not correct?"

"Yes," she finally admitted. "I have almost given up on him. He has just disappeared into thin air. I can't find a trace of him after he left his apartment in Jerusalem over a year and a half ago. There just is no trail to follow." She looked up at Shefi with tears in her eyes. "The fact that he hasn't contacted me makes me think he must be dead. But why? Who would want Anatoly dead?"

Binyamin Shefi got up and walked over to the window, tilting the blinds so he could see outside. "Sonya, I don't think he is dead."

"What?" She got up excitedly and hurried to his side, impulsively grasping his left forearm. "Why do you say that?"

He turned to her. "Six months ago I told you I would have our intelligence people try and locate him."

"Yes. And you said they had nothing to report."

"They didn't. But last week a rather strange surveillance report came to my attention. It's so inconclusive that I wasn't sure whether to even share it with you." He looked at her warmly. "But I can tell how much this man means to you, so I'll give you what we have.

"Apparently, there are some in Israel who don't trust our treaty with Bulgakov—which, of course, comes as no surprise. Somebody is always suspicious about something. But they go even further. Our sources say that they are calling it a 'covenant with death,' and they claim that our Jewish prophet, Isaiah, predicted this would happen almost three thousand years ago."

"I know the type. People and their crazy religious ideas!"

"Well, be careful before you say that. You may be stepping on the toes of someone you love. The really odd thing is that most of the people who have been the most vocal about the treaty with Bulgakov have simply vanished—without a trace. Like your friend Anatoly." He paused.

"But that doesn't make Anatoly one of them," Sonya was asking, more than stating.

"Well, you decide. Here's the kicker. My intelligence people think they may be hiding out somewhere down in the Negev." He began to laugh, shaking his head slowly back and forth in disbelief. "Israel has never had it so good! Why go to some hellhole on the backside of the desert when they could be enjoying peace and prosperity like never before, up here in civilization?"

"But what does all this have to do with Anatoly?" Sonya interrupted impatiently.

"Our agents have a blurred photo of the man they believe is setting all this up. The photo is poor and too distant to match with the passport photo in our files, but in general build and age it matches your description of Anatoly," said Shefi. "So, I guess my question to you is this: Is your Anatoly the type who would get mixed up in something like this? Because he's the man you love, I thought it seemed so unlikely."

"I don't know," said Sonya, sobered by what her dear friend had just told her. When she had told Shefi about Anatoly, she had never mentioned the fact that he had become a Messianic Jew. It hadn't seemed relevant at that time. Now she thought about Anatoly's decision, and then shut her eyes against where those thoughts led her. Was this why Anatoly had never pursued the opportunities Bulgakov had offered him? Was this why he had left Moscow so abruptly? Were the Teasdales somehow involved in this?

"Will you let me see the picture?" she asked.

"Of course."

USA TODAY / JERUSALEM—Technion plotting technicians today reported spotting an east–west groove on relief satellite maps. According to informed sources, it could be a fault line running eastward, straight through the heart of the Mount of Olives, possibly ending in what looks like a huge, underground cavern. Additional tests have been scheduled to ascertain the potential effects on this area in case of a major earthquake. Officially, no comment is being made by governmental spokespeople until more data have been obtained.

Holocaust II Minus 21 Months

"I don't know if I feel up to this," Mike said, as he turned their Ford Crown Victoria into the parking lot of the large Baptist church in suburban Dallas, Texas. "I'm so tired of fighting the very people we're trying to help. Sometimes, when I'm really getting beat up, I wonder if it's worth all the pain and ridicule. If this is what they want, then let them have it!"

"Mike, you're tired. There's less than two years until Holocaust II and then there's no more we can do for them. God has sustained us this far. He will help us complete the race. All you can do is what you have been doing: warn the people," said Marlee. "We can't make them do anything about it. Christ said that many genuine Christians will be killed during the days of Holocaust II. Not only the Jews! When He said that, it was given as prophecy, not possibility. Why? Because many won't heed the warning until it is too late. We can't change what's going to happen, Mike. All we can do is what we've been called to, right? The rest is in God's hands."

He sighed. "Right."

Thank God for a wife like Marlee! he thought as they stepped out into the cool spring evening. As he closed the car door, he heard footsteps. He turned to see a tall man in his mid-thirties, meticulously dressed in khaki Dockers, white shirt, and tie with navy sports jacket approaching them.

"Are you the Teasdales?"

"We are."

"I'm Jim Bowen," he said. "Here I'm known simply as Pastor Jim. It's great to meet you face to face." He offered both of them a firm handshake. "Thank you for coming," he said with genuine enthusiasm.

Mike shook his hand. "I know you asked us to come, but do you really understand the message I preach—where I'm coming from?"

A smile spread across the young associate pastor's face, illuminated under the sodium vapor lights now coming on in the soft twilight. "Absolutely. I've read *The Covenant with Death*. Twice, in fact! That's why I wanted you to come."

"I only ask because most churches around here have labeled me some kind of 'endtimes lunatic.' In fact, in the twenty-one months since the treaty between NUE and Israel was signed, I've been bodily thrown out of more churches than I care to remember. Once the people begin to realize what I'm saying . . ."

"You mean about Nikolai Bulgakov being the Antichrist, and that we have precious little time to go into hiding before his persecution hits the church, dead center?"

Mike couldn't help a rueful grin. "I see you do understand, Jim. Now that's a pleasant surprise. And you're right about precious little time. We have less than two years until all hell literally breaks loose on professing Christendom."

"Our people have to hear this. Most of them don't have any idea of the danger we're in. Rennie Flowers, our senior pastor, is clueless. I've had numerous conversations with him about this. I get the same response every time, like a broken record: Bulgakov can't be the Antichrist because the church will be raptured *before* Antichrist signs the treaty with Israel. He says a loving God will *never* permit His people to be tested in this way. And when I point out that the Scriptures specifically say that it is the *elect of God*—His *saints*—that Antichrist specifically goes after, he tells me I need to go back to seminary and learn the difference between the church and Israel! Like I don't know the difference?! But that will soon be irrelevant. I think he's going to have the church board get rid of me."

"That's sad," said Mike. "There isn't one verse in the entire Bible to support the pretrib pipe dream—the idea that the true church will be whisked away—raptured—long before the persecution at the hands of Antichrist ever begins. They persist in burying their heads in the sand, even with everything falling down all around them."

"That's why I wanted you here tonight. He won't listen to me. Maybe he'll listen to you. After all, you are one of the few Christians in the world who has had firsthand contact with people on Bulgakov's staff when you lived in Moscow. You, better than anyone else who calls themselves Christian, have direct insight on what this man's plans are for the world! Pastor Flowers must be made to realize that Christ's warning to His disciples was a warning that His disciples were to pass down to the church: that the rapture of the church *cannot* occur until after Antichrist begins his persecution of those who claim the name of Christ! Plain and simple!"

"Hey, you're preaching to the choir," laughed Mike. "Save your ammo for the congregation. I understand only too well what you are up against—what *we're* up against. Does Pastor Flowers know what I'll be talking about tonight?"

A sheepish expression crossed Pastor Jim's face. "Not exactly," he said. "Tonight is youth night, and on those nights I'm permitted to choose the speaker. He really isn't sure what you're going to speak on. Somehow your reputation hasn't preceded you here but just to be double safe, I haven't made a big deal about who's speaking tonight. I'm afraid he's in for a big surprise. But if I'm going to be thrown out, I want our people to hear the truth before I get axed!"

"Better now than twenty-one months from now!" Mike observed.

"Agreed!"

"Well, from what you've told me, your pastor will probably throw us both out tonight, but thanks for the warning anyway. I'll do my best with whatever time I'm given."

The three of them made their way into the church. Pastor Flowers was nowhere in sight. Jim explained that on youth night the pastor preferred to be just another person in the congregation enjoying the service the young people put on. After a few preliminaries, a hymn, and a brief introduction by Pastor Jim, Mike stepped up on the platform, placed his notes on the podium, and prayed for God to speak through him. Then, after a brief moment of silence as he slowly looked across the faces in the auditorium, he began.

"All around us, the world is suffering unprecedented wars, famines, plagues, and natural disasters. And yet the New United Empire and Israel have been untouched." He paused to let this sink in.

"Have you ever asked yourself, 'Why is this'? As Christians, the first place we should look for answers is in the Bible. And there we find that God told the prophet Daniel that the final seven years of history will begin when a man arises out of nowhere, takes control of certain northern European nations, and then makes a seven-year peace treaty with Israel. In Daniel 7, we see that his power base grows to ten nations before he makes his move to rule the entire world. Daniel 2 tells us that these ten nations will be nations that have always been hostile to Israel!"

Mike heard the beginnings of restlessness coming from the audience. He knew the sound. The rustle of the leaves before the storm. But he had their interest—even Texas was suffering from drought and food shortages—and he needed to say as much as he could before the storm hit, full force.

"Christ Himself instructs us, in both Matthew 24 and Revelation 6, that the world will suffer unprecedented wars, famines, and plagues *before* this man demands the worship of the world, but this is nothing compared to what this man will do to those who choose not to worship him, when his day finally arrives.

"Friends, this is exactly what we are seeing today! Three and a half years from the time the New United Empire signed its treaty with Israel—that's only twenty-one months from now—Nikolai Bulgakov will reveal his true identity as the man the Bible calls the Antichrist, or if you prefer, the Beast. When that time comes, Christians who are unprepared will have to worship him or die."

Now he could hear the faint sounds of thunder in the distance. Keep going, he told himself. You still have a little time left.

"Christ told His disciples in His Olivet Discourse that 'when you see the Abomination of Desolation'—that's the

Antichrist—'which was spoken of through Daniel the prophet, standing in the holy place'—that's the new temple being built in Jerusalem as we speak—'then there will be a great tribulation'—or persecution if you prefer, the original Greek can be translated either way—'such as has not occurred since the beginning of the world until now, nor ever shall. And unless those days had been cut short, no life would have been saved; but *for the sake of the elect* those days shall be cut short.'

"Please listen carefully to me," Mike pleaded. "This man whom Christ calls the Abomination of Desolation will bring a time of persecution and death on the elect of God, unparalleled since the beginning of time! Those are *Christ's* words, not my words. Are you not the elect of God?

"The seven-year treaty with Israel has already been signed, exactly as the Scriptures teach! The New United Empire has grown to ten nations, exactly as the Scriptures teach. The temple is being rebuilt on the Temple Mount, exactly as Scriptures teach. And Nikolai Bulgakov will reveal himself as Antichrist in less than two years. That's what the Scriptures teach! The clock is running. The countdown has begun. If you are wise, you will do as the Lord commanded. Prepare a place to hide while there is still time!"

Suddenly, the crack of thunder shattered the service. Halfway back in the auditorium there was an eruption! A man, finally able to squeeze by the others that sat between him and the aisle, stepped out of the end of one of the rows and rushed down the center aisle, screaming at the top of his lungs as he charged toward the podium.

"*Stop!*" he shouted, his voice echoing in the large sanctuary. "Do I hear you correctly? Are you saying we're in the final seven-year tribulation period right now?"

"That's right," said Mike. He had a feeling that he was about to meet Pastor Rennie Flowers.

"You just sit down and stop frightening my people!" the man yelled as he stumbled up the steps to the platform. He shoved Mike away from the podium. "This is *my* church and I will not allow you to preach heresy from *my* pulpit!

"Bulgakov can't be the Antichrist," he continued, still shouting, "because my church is still here. It hasn't been raptured! The church *will not* go through the persecution of Antichrist. The church is raptured *before* any of the events you describe—including the seven-year treaty—ever begin! The book of Matthew was written for Jews, not Christians, and it has nothing to do with the rapture of the church!"

Having the advantage of the live mike still clipped to his lapel, Mike interrupted the man's tirade. "Pastor Flowers, this is a life-and-death matter—both for you and for those you have agreed to shepherd. Please, listen to me for just one moment longer," he pleaded. "Do you believe in the Great Commission?"

"Of course I do!" snapped the man indignantly. "What does that have to do with the passage you quoted from the Olivet Discourse?"

"Everything," said Mike. "The Great Commission is our Lord's last command, recorded in the book of Matthew. Do you agree?"

Pastor Flowers nodded his head in agreement, again wondering what that had to do with anything.

"Well, then, if the book of Matthew is written for the Jews only, why do we think the Great Commission is for the church?"

The pastor's mouth hung open in disbelief. "Because only the Olivet Discourse is just for Israel, not the whole book of Matthew," he finally managed to get out.

"I agree. And it is in the Great Commission that the disciples are told specifically by Christ to preach *all* He taught them to the new disciples He would give them after He left. I don't think there's any disagreement—at least not from anyone that I know of—that these new disciples He was referring to would be the new converts that would become the church, as a result of the spread of the gospel, world wide. Don't you agree?"

"Yes, but . . ."

"And wasn't the Olivet Discourse specific instruction He taught His disciples?"

"Where does it say that the instruction He gave to His disciples was instruction we are to give to the church?" Pastor Flowers managed to shoot back at his adversary.

Mike pointed to his open Bible. "Right here, in the last verse of the book of Matthew. 'Make disciples of all nations'— those are the marching orders to build the church of Christ— 'teaching them'—these new converts—'to observe *all* that I commanded you.'" He could see that the congregation was amazed at the drama taking place before them. "You certainly have to agree that the Olivet Discourse was the teaching of Christ to His disciples, right?"

"Yes, but . . ."

"And you have to admit that in the Great Commission recorded in the book of Matthew, Christ told His disciples to pass along all of His teaching to them, to the new converts in the church, right?"

"Yes, but . . ."

"And it is in the Olivet Discourse, again recorded in Matthew's Gospel, that Christ teaches His disciples that it will be the *elect* of God who will undergo persecution at the hands of Antichrist before He comes and gathers together the faithful from the four winds. . . . You *do* consider yourself part of the elect of God, don't you, Pastor Flowers?"

"Stop it! I told you to stop!" Flowers was screaming now. He ripped the microphone from Mike's lapel. "Now get out!"

As Mike and Marlee followed Pastor Jim down the center aisle toward the back of the sanctuary, the congregation sat stunned. Then, a rising murmur began rolling through the crowd. Most glared at them, but a few wore concerned expressions.

The organist began playing, and the strains of "Blest Be the Tie That Binds" followed them through the foyer and out into the parking lot.

Mike tried to smile but couldn't. "Why do I always feel like the bad guy when all I'm trying to do is warn those whose very lives depend on hearing what I have to say? I feel so helpless. And the time is so short. You'd think *I* was the Antichrist!"

"I'm sorry," Jim said. "But thank you for having the guts to do it—and thank you for coming. Our people needed to hear the truth, and they heard enough tonight to get the serious ones thinking." He held up a small tape recorder. "I have your message on tape. Hopefully some of our people will want to hear it again and will take heed."

Mike reached into the accordion folder he carried. "Here are some sheets outlining the things you need to do to get prepared for survival. Unfortunately, I never got to this part of the message. I seldom do! If anyone is willing to listen, share this information with them. And if you have any questions, you know how to get in touch with me."

Jim glanced through a few of the paragraphs. "I think it's time for me to get my family to safety." He smiled. "After tonight, I won't be able to stay here." He hugged Mike and Marlee. "The Lord bless you both. Come quickly, Lord Jesus!"

"Where do we go from here?" Marlee asked, once they were in the car and on their way out of the parking lot.

"Wherever God opens the doors. Like you said earlier, there's so little time to get the warning to our brothers and sisters in Christ. Once the persecution begins, it will be too late for most of them if they're not prepared in advance. The Christians who wait until then will die."

"Well, we know that God has called us to this," said Marlee. "So I guess we just keep going and then we either die and look to the resurrection, or we go up in the Rapture when the Lord puts an end to the persecution."

They were both quiet for some time, watching the suburbs give way to the scrub-oak and mesquite countryside.

"It's a nice evening," Marlee said finally.

"What?" Mike asked. Then he looked around at the familiar countryside, silvery and serene under the full winter moon. He smiled at his wife. "Yes, it is."

"You did say He is in control, didn't you?" she laughed.

"You're right." He reached out and squeezed her hand. Their old Ford rumbled into the night.

EIGHTEEN

Holocaust II Minus 18 Months

Anatoly passed Be'er Menuha at a little past six. The sun had set over an hour ago and he was driving slowly, without lights, over the desert road. Peering through the Jeep's windshield with his low-light goggles, he viewed a surrealist glowing green world rather than the inky blackness of moonless nighttime. Traveling in and out of the back door to Petra by night, without headlights, was the only safe route now, even though the mountainous paths that approached Petra from the west were treacherous at night. Only certain four-wheel vehicles, built to handle rough terrain, could make it into Petra from this direction. When the moonlight was insufficient, his night goggles were his only source of light. Tonight was one of those nights.

Suddenly, just ahead, he spotted two figures standing near the side of the road, exactly where he and Eitan had agreed. He had no idea how they had gotten there, but there they were, right on schedule. He pulled up alongside them, removed the night goggles, and got out and walked over to them.

"David Gur and Gideon Landau?" he asked, holding his low-beam flashlight between them so it barely reflected on their faces. Although both men nodded, Anatoly's question was a formality. He recognized them from the pictures Eitan had given him. David was a solid man of average height, with black hair and a full beard. Gideon was short and stocky, balding on top with a fringe of brown hair.

Anatoly knew that Eitan had chosen these men carefully, knowing they would have to provide the leadership for those in Petra until D-Day, the target date everyone in the Parousia Foundation used as a measuring stick, a specific time that would not occur until the end of the seven-year covenant period. Like all the other Jews hiding in Petra, these two did not believe in Yeshua, but they were wholeheartedly committed to everything else that Eitan and the foundation were doing for the Israelis, and they knew that Petra was vital to their survival plans. Besides that, they were good at what they did! And Anatoly knew that the time would soon come when they would realize that Yeshua was indeed their Meshiah. When God gave His sign in the sun, moon, and stars for all the world to see, then they would see Yeshua, coming in the clouds, with great power and glory! Then they would become the firstfruits of Israel, receiving Yeshua as their Meshiah. But, until then . . .

Anatoly clicked off the light. "I'm glad you're here," he said. "Throw your duffels in the back."

David got into the front passenger seat while Gideon climbed into the back, with the bags. With that unspoken arrangement, the pecking order between the two men was made clear to Anatoly. David was the boss.

Anatoly handed each man a pair of night-vision goggles, then shifted the Jeep back into four-wheel drive. He turned back east, driving across the sand and rock of the Negev until he came to the border fence between Israel and Jordan. He got out and opened a pre-cut section of fencing, drove through, then replaced the wire strands.

"What happened to the border guards?" asked Gideon.

"For some reason, they disappeared along with the tourist trade," said Anatoly. "Actually, Bulgakov did us a favor when he made his treaty with Jordan. One of the things he got was their agreement to end tourism along their border with Israel, and without the tourists, they needed fewer border guards. That has isolated Petra all the more."

"Actually," David added, "I would guess there is no tourism

anywhere in the world today, with all the problems the world is facing . . . wars, famines, natural disasters. . . ."

"I'm sure you're right," Anatoly agreed.

For 10 kilometers or so they followed the dry riverbed, Wadi as Siyyagh, until the rising terrain became too steep for the Jeep. "We walk the rest of the way," Anatoly announced.

He hid the vehicle in a wadi, the trees providing natural camouflage. This particular ravine had been used as a parking lot for his people, for months now. From this point on, he warned them that absolute silence had to be maintained until they reached their destination. He led the way over the rocky ground to a small ravine that came down out of the mountainous region just to the east. The ravine provided a hidden pathway that ran into the back door of Petra that the Israelis had used for centuries to illegally enter the remains of the grand old city.

A cool breeze chilled the November night, and as the sandstone cliffs of Petra began rising around them, they could see an occasional flickering oil lamp in the eerie shadows of the magnificent Nabatean architecture carved into the rock. The lights pinpointed the locations of their own perimeter guards, those who provided the security for the camp. They had no guns. Only oil lamps and two-way radios. During the day, they looked like Bedouin dwellers. At night, they watched this approach with owl-like eyes, no movement or shadow escaping their attention. They were expecting Anatoly's return, so he and the men passed by unhindered. The guards then radioed ahead so that those in the camp could expect their arrival.

An hour later they entered the broad rocky bowl that formed the heart of Petra, an alien and menacing landscape in the darkness. Lights from inside the numerous caves that surrounded the valley twinkled in the darkness, and yet all was still. The first thing every new refugee learned was the importance of silence. To Anatoly, the place was familiar and unthreatening, but he noticed the two men looking around nervously as he led them along the length of the Colonnaded Street and up the stone steps to the Urn Tomb. Inside, at a large work table near the entrance, he lit a kerosene lantern. The men removed their goggles, allowing their eyes to adjust to the light.

"Here's your new home," he said.

David and Gideon threw down their bags in relief as Anatoly brought up three camp chairs. All three sat down with audible sighs.

"That's quite a trek," said David.

"Yes," agreed Anatoly. "Remoteness — like silence — is a significant part of our safety factor here."

"And Bulgakov doesn't have a clue," David said.

"No, he doesn't seem to. It's surprising, though," said Anatoly. "God's plan for Petra is written all over the *Tanach*, yet Satan allows Bulgakov to virtually hand it to us."

There was an awkward silence as neither man made any response to Anatoly's reference to spiritual matters. Finally, Gideon broke the silence. "So how safe are we here?"

"Perfectly. This whole area has been abandoned. The Jordanians still use the two main highways farther east on the other side of the mountain range, especially the Desert Highway, but no one comes into Petra anymore."

"How many people do you have here now?" asked Gideon.

"At last count," said Anatoly, "we have close to 340,000 — 144,000 men and their families."

"And what about water and supplies?" David asked.

"All the supply caches are in place and mapped for you. And the water system is repaired and the cisterns are full. All you have to do is settle in." With this, Anatoly stepped over to a niche in the wall and pulled out two huge rolls of maps and planning information. "Everything you need to know is here."

David and Gideon shook their heads in amazement as they looked at the large charts Anatoly spread out on the ground before them. "You've certainly done a spectacular job in organizing and preparing this place. You've made our work easy," David added.

"I've done what I can," said Anatoly. "But I know Eitan has trained you well and that you'll take good care of our people. It's an awesome responsibility. The people here want no part of the NUE, *that* they can agree on, but they don't always agree on how this camp should operate. So, you must run the camp with an iron fist."

"We'll do our best," David promised, Gideon nodding his assent. David's expression sobered and saddened. "The thing that really bothers me is why more of our people don't realize what's going on. The Arab threat never had the potential for disaster that this crisis has—with five hundred thousand foreign troops stationed *inside* our borders."

"I know what you're saying. I can't understand it either," Anatoly said sadly. "It seems so obvious."

Gideon snorted. "It *is* obvious," he said. "They must be blind. If—or, as we believe, *when*—the New United Empire decides to turn on us, Israel will have lost the battle *before* it even begins. You know, in many ways Petra is a modern-day Masada. It's the last safe stronghold the people of Israel have."

Anatoly nodded, rolling up the maps and replacing them in the wall niche. "I need to be in Jerusalem by morning, so I'd better get going. I'm just glad you were finally able to get down here and relieve me. I've left Zvi Kalisher in charge until you got here, and he'll hook up with you in the morning. As for me, I've got to get out of here tonight. There are still many things we must do before the second exodus begins."

"Before you go, may I ask you a personal question?" David said.

"Go ahead, fire away."

"Eitan said you once had direct access to Bulgakov's inner circle. That's pretty heady business. So what made you leave Russia? And, more important, why are you helping us when you could have been on the inside, with him?"

"I may be Russian," said Anatoly, "but first and foremost, I am a Jew. I also believe in the holy Scriptures—both the *Tanach* and the *Brith Hadasha*—and they both tell me that Bulgakov's true intent in making his treaty with Israel is not to protect our people, but to destroy them! Although you won't understand all of this right now, the *Tanach* predicts the coming of this man—the Satan-Meshiah—and his false treaty with Israel, and it identifies Petra as our hiding place. The *Brith Hadasha* tells us how God will defend Petra when the time comes."

"Then you, too, trust in this New Testament—like Eitan?" Gideon asked.

"Yes. Like Eitan, I am a Messianic Jew. I believe the Yeshua of the New Testament is the Meshiah of the *Tanach*. The New Testament simply fulfills the prophecy of the *Tanach*."

Anatoly glanced at his watch. He should be on his way. But he knew that this conversation was far more important than what time he got back to Jerusalem. After being gone for two years, what was another hour or so?

"Eitan has told you what is going to happen here, right?" Anatoly continued.

Gideon and David nodded. Then David said, "He says the real trouble—Holocaust II, he calls it—will begin in less than a year and a half. Do you agree?"

"Absolutely. As you know only too well, Bulgakov signed the treaty with Israel just a little over two years ago, leaving us less than eighteen months before he makes his move against Israel. It's the prophet Daniel that gives us that timeframe. He tells us that the Satan-Meshiah will break his covenant with Israel at the midpoint of the seven-year treaty period. In other words, three and a half years after the treaty is signed. That's when Holocaust II will begin. When that day comes, all hell will literally break loose here on Earth, for both Jews and Christians alike. The Scriptures tell us that he will slaughter every man who will not submit to his absolute leadership and lordship—if he can get his hands on them."

"And what about those he can't get his hands on, like us here in Petra?" David asked, wanting to know if Anatoly saw things the same way Eitan had taught them.

"Believe it or not, the Satan-Meshiah is going to try to drown those of us hiding here in Petra, by flooding us out! That's what the *Brith Hadasha* teaches."

"That's exactly what Eitan said, too, but I still can't believe it," said Gideon. "Flooding? Here in the desert? Why, virtually next to no rain at all will fall here in an entire year! I think the *Brith Hadasha* is a bit confused on its locations!"

"Yes, by flooding, and no, it isn't 'confused on its locations'!" Anatoly replied. "As I'm sure Eitan also told you, when the flood hits, the ground will somehow swallow up the water. There is nothing you will have to do in advance. In fact, the reality is that there is *nothing* we can do in advance other than trust our safety to the God of our forefathers, Avraham, Yitzchak, and Yaakov. But don't kid yourselves; it will happen exactly that way, exactly as foretold in the *Brith Hadasha*! Just make sure everyone stays in camp."

"And what about the others who are not here with us in Petra?" David asked.

"When Bulgakov announces his true intentions to the world from the Temple Mount, the great majority of Jews living in Israel—outside Petra itself—will die. Only those who flee during the second exodus have any chance of survival. The Scriptures tell us there won't be many. It's as simple as that."

"Is this certain?" Gideon asked, bewildered.

"Absolutely!" said Anatoly. "After this initial flood attack, God will supernaturally protect those of you here in Petra for the entire second half of the treaty, right up until D-Day. Has Eitan explained what D-Day refers to?"

"Yes," they answered, almost in unison.

"D-Day stands for Deliverance Day, when we finally get to leave Petra to return to Jerusalem, right after the expiration of the seven-year covenant," Gideon continued.

"Well, that's the general idea. All you need to know for now is this: your safety depends on staying here until then."

"We understand that," David acknowledged. "And we love you and Eitan for risking your lives to help us."

"I guess only time will tell if these things are true or not," added Gideon. "But rest assured, we will do exactly as you have instructed."

"That's all I ask," said Anatoly. He had already stowed his own gear in the Jeep before setting out on the trip to pick them up. All he had to do now was gather up his night goggles and flashlight. As he was doing so, he remembered a crucial event that they needed to know about, one that he hadn't covered yet with them.

He turned and looked at them intently. "There is one last thing you *must* remember, even if you don't have the faith to yet understand why."

"What is it?" asked David.

"Sometime after Bulgakov takes over the world, after God swallows up the floodwaters here, you will see a great sign in the heavens—in the sun, moon, and stars. There will be no mistaking the sign, but it may be several years after Holocaust II begins before you see it. I can't be more specific on timing than that."

"Yes," said David. "Eitan told us about this, too, although I didn't totally understand the significance Eitan placed on it."

"Me neither," agreed Gideon. "So tell us again, what happens then?"

"This is the sign that our prophet Joel said would come, announcing the day when God will begin His destruction of Bulgakov and his followers. More important, however, this will be the precise time when you will see Israel's Meshiah, Yeshua, appearing in the clouds, in power and great glory. In power—for the sake of destroying the Satan-Meshiah, Bulgakov; in glory—so that every eye will see Him appearing, including everyone here in Petra!"

"And if I recall correctly," David began, "Eitan said we will see this all happen, north of here, over Jerusalem, is that right?"

"To begin with, yes," Anatoly answered. "But that's not the end of it for you here in Petra! Although the Scriptures do not tell us precisely how it will happen, they do teach that when Yeshua comes in the clouds—something you will see right after the sign is given in the sun, moon, and stars—then those of you hiding here in Petra—all of you—will come to understand that Yeshua is your Meshiah.

Gideon frowned. "You lost me right where Eitan always lost me. He tried to explain this to us, but it never made sense. All this stuff about Yeshua is hard to believe."

"I understand," said Anatoly. "But remember, our own prophets, especially Joel, teach us about the sign in the sun, moon, and stars that God will display for all the world to see, just before He pours out His wrath upon Satan-Meshiah and his followers. A time they referred to as the Day of the Lord!"

"I know. That much I understand. The Day of the Lord is when our God will destroy our enemies in the last days, once and for all," David added.

"Exactly. And it is our prophet Ezekiel who tells us that all who are hiding here in Petra will someday, while still hiding in the wilderness, bow down before God and believe. And it is our prophet Zechariah who takes it one step further. He says that you will mourn when you see the One whom you have pierced—that's Yeshua, who was crucified two thousand years ago! However, it is the last book of the *Brith Hadasha*, the book of Revelation, that puts everything into perspective for us here in Petra. It teaches that those here in hiding—here in Petra—will become the *firstfruits* of Israel to put their faith and trust in Yeshua as Israel's Meshiah! That's you, and it will happen right after you see the sign our prophet Joel talks about in the sun, moon, and stars!"

"Please forgive me if I don't have your faith," David said respectfully, "but I will believe when I see."

"I know, you don't have to apologize. Until God gives you the eyes to see and the ears to understand, I might as well be talking a foreign language to you. All I ask is this: when you see the floodwaters come and go, remember that all the rest I have told you will happen as well. Wait and see, but don't forget my words."

"If the *Brith Hadasha*'s prediction concerning floodwaters here in the desert becomes a reality, then we will get ready for Yeshua, fair enough?" Gideon said, a twinkle of skepticism in his voice.

"Fair enough," Anatoly replied. He knew these men understood what needed to be done. They had been trained well by Eitan. They just didn't understand the "cause" behind what was soon to happen to them, and the "effect" it would have upon them! But they had listened carefully and, he knew, they would remember. God would do the rest when the time came. *When they see these prophecies begin to happen, then they will know*, he thought. His only regret was that he wouldn't be here when it happened. Suddenly a smile crossed his face.

"What are you smiling about?" Gideon asked.

"It will be well with your souls," Anatoly stated. "Now, I really must leave you. Shalom, my brothers. Until we meet again!"

NINETEEN

Sonya was awakened by the doorbell. She shook her head groggily. She had been up until two o'clock trying to finish a report for the prime minister on the war that had suddenly erupted among Saudi Arabia, Bahrain, and the United Arab Emirates—another oil patch fight between rich Arabs who wanted to be richer. This war wasn't about food. She was certain of this, because she was one of the few who knew that Sergei was secretly selling the Arabs all the food they needed, for huge prices, cash on the barrelhead. It was primarily their cash that financed all the things the NUE was doing today. No, this war was simply over the control of oil. More money for the winner—who already had more than they could handle—and less money for the loser. Finally, exhausted, she had decided to get a few hours' sleep and complete her work in the morning.

The doorbell rang again. She tried to focus on the green numbers glowing from the digital clock beside her bed. Five o'clock! Who in the world would be ringing her doorbell at this hour of the morning? Apprehension gripped her as she pulled on her robe and made her way to the door. Carefully, she opened the door a crack, against the safety chain. A shadowy figure stood in the dimly lit hallway.

"Sonya?" A voice whispered on the other side of the door.

The low voice sounded familiar, but she stared at the haggard, unshaven face for several moments before she recognized him.

"Anatoly!" She threw off the chain and swung the door open.

He motioned her to be quiet.

Inside, he pulled her into his arms. For a few moments she buried her face in his chest and hugged him tightly, then looked up into his face. "Anatoly! I didn't know if you were alive or dead!"

He lovingly cupped her face with his hands, then lowered his lips to hers. When the kiss finally ended, he gathered her into his arms once more, and she began to sob. "Where have you been? . . . Where have you been?"

Gently he turned her toward the couch, and once there, he drew her down beside him, rocking her like a child.

"Where I've been is complicated and very difficult to explain," he said. "But this is the first time I've been in Jerusalem in over two years. A good friend of mine, a retired general from the IDF, told me where I could find you."

"How . . ."

"In a minute," he interrupted gently, "I will tell you everything. But first, I need to know if you are still working for Nikolai Bulgakov."

"Yes," she sniffed, wiping her eyes with the sleeve of her robe. "What has that got to do with where you've been?"

"Everything." He paused as he looked deep into her eyes.

"What are you talking about?"

"Sonya, you are in grave danger." When she started to interrupt, he placed one finger softly against her lips. "Just wait a minute. Let me explain," he said. "I know you believe Bulgakov is our friend, but he isn't. He is the worst thing that has ever happened to the world — especially to Israel."

A dark look clouded her face. "How can you say that?" She sounded defensive. "Do you remember that time you met with him back in Moscow, when he promised us he would stand behind Israel if he ever got the power to do so? Well, he did and he has. When the Syrians and Palestinians attacked, *he* was the only one to come to Israel's aid. And this treaty *he* has made with Israel is the first real security she has ever had since becoming a nation. *He* even made it possible for us to rebuild the temple. *He* has brought us peace and safety for the first time ever!"

"Yes, and *he* is about to betray us," said Anatoly. "*He's* already betrayed you in a most horrible way, although you don't know it."

"He has not!" she flared. "That's ridiculous! I heard there was a possibility that you were working with that radical 'covenant with death' group. I could never let myself believe you would be a part of anything so bizarre! But now I'm beginning to wonder."

"Easy, Sonya," he said. "I have a lot to tell you. But first, I want to know what you have learned about the deaths of Yacov and your father."

"There's not much to tell," she said, her eyes darkening with sadness. "Katanov found out we were helping Nikolai, and he had Yacov and Papa killed, thinking he could make Nikolai back off. You were right. It was a political assassination meant to warn Nikolai what might happen to him. Katanov's goons murdered Yacov and Papa—and would have killed me if I had been there. Nikolai protected me."

"That's all wrong, Sonya."

"How would you know?" she snapped. "You weren't there!"

Anatoly sighed. "I know because I got a message from an unimpeachable source."

"And who would that be?" she demanded.

"Yacov. He told me who killed him before it happened," he said simply, showing none of the emotion that lay just beneath his calm demeanor.

She stared at him in shock. "You can't be serious?"

"Yes I am. I'd show you his message if I still had my computer. Since I don't, you will have to take my word for it. You know I would never lie to you—especially about this."

"I have your computer here," she said. "*Isvestia* notified me when your lease expired, and I put most of your stuff in storage. Because of its value, I brought your computer home with me."

"I think you'd better get it," he said patiently.

She retrieved his laptop from the bedroom closet, and he set it up on the kitchen table, plugged in the power adapter, flipped the switch, and waited while the computer booted up.

"My Internet account is long gone, but I know I saved

Yacov's message," he said, clicking on the e-mail directory. He rapidly scrolled down the list of saved messages until he came to the last two. "That's odd. It shows two messages from Yacov." He thought for a moment, then snapped his fingers. "Wait a minute. They were both encrypted. I read one and had just saved the other when the connection went down. I was in a hurry to get away and never did read the second one."

He clicked on the first message and pushed the laptop toward Sonya.

She looked at the date and shivered, realizing that these were probably the last words her brother had written. The screen blurred as tears welled up in her eyes. By the time she reached the end of Yacov's message, she was sobbing. Anatoly put his arms around her and cradled her head on his shoulder.

"I'm sorry, Sonya," he said softly, stroking her hair gently.

"He knew they were after him."

"Yes he did," Anatoly said softly.

"But what about the other message?" she asked, swiping angrily at her eyes. "Maybe he found out that Nikolai didn't do it," she pleaded, still not able to believe that the man she had trusted was guilty of this terrible thing.

"I don't know what's in it. As I said, when the connection failed, I didn't have time to reopen it." He clicked on the message, typed in the password for the encryption, and Yacov's last words to them flashed onto the screen.

A. —

I forgot to tell you the most important thing in my last message! Tried to call you about it, but you couldn't be reached. I'm leaving town the day after tomorrow. Need to think out carefully what I should do next, so I'm going to St. Petersburg for a few days. I think it will be safer to call you from there, on a public phone, but I want to let you know that one good thing has come out of this mess. I have accepted Iesus as my Messiya! We are truly brothers now, in every way.

Thank you for your patience, for not giving up on me when I was so rude to you. I just didn't understand, then. M. has been an incredible help to me. But what

God really used in my life was the Bible you gave me, with all your notes, especially the parts you underlined just for me!

No matter what happens, please protect S. at all costs. I know how she feels about you. If something happens to me, take good care of her and tell her I love her. But most of all, please tell her about Iesus. I am praying for you both. All my love.

Y.—

Anger and confusion roiled in Sonya's mind as she tried to understand, all the time holding back a flood of more tears. Yacov, a Christian like Anatoly? Nikolai, the Beast of Daniel whose primary motive is the total and complete destruction of the people of Israel? Why would Nikolai murder her brother and father? Was it possible Yacov was wrong? Had she been duped into murdering President Katanov? Into making—how did they refer to it?—a "covenant with death" with her dear friend and mentor, Prime Minister Shefi? Was she just a pawn in some worldwide chess game? How could she have been so mistaken? The questions wouldn't stop, and she felt a pounding pressure in her head.

"Why, Anatoly?" she pleaded. "If this is true, why would Nikolai have done this?"

Anatoly took a deep breath, then said, "Please sit down, Sonya."

After Sonya regained her composure, he began to explain. "It's very complicated, Sonya, but as far as Yacov and your father, it all boils down to this. Thousands of years ago our Jewish prophets foretold everything Nikolai Bulgakov is doing today. It's the last great obstacle Israel will have to undergo before God destroys all of our enemies, once and for all. It's all written in the Scriptures! As Yacov said in his e-mail, your Nikolai Bulgakov is the man our prophets referred to as 'the Beast,' who will arise 'in the last days.' I wanted to tell you when I first realized what was going on, but Yacov made me promise not to. He thought you would be safer if you didn't know. Also, I think he wanted to be sure, himself, before he said anything to you. As you can see by his first e-mail, he was poking around to see for himself if these things were true. They were . . . and Bulgakov obviously found out about it. That's what got them killed — both Yacov and your father."

Sonya frowned. "I knew you two were keeping me in the dark about something. This is what it was?"

"That's right. As I was saying, we know for certain that Bulgakov is the man our prophets referred to as 'the Beast.' Later, the Jewish writers of the *Brith Hadasha* gave him the name 'Antichrist,' or 'Satan-Meshiah'—that's the Hebrew name for him—because he will be Satan's false Messiya who is opposed to the true Messiya of Israel. This Satan-Meshiah is bent upon one thing: destroying the nation of Israel!"

Sonya listened, trying to understand what Anatoly was telling her, trying to find the answers to all the questions swirling about in her mind.

Suddenly restless, Anatoly stood and began to pace as he talked, pausing to punctuate his points. "The Scriptures teach that Antichrist will actually be a dead man—the former leader of one of seven nations that have always been enemies of Israel—who will be brought back to life in order to institute his plan of world control. To do this, he will take over three strong ethnic groups in northern Europe—one a Germanic people! Sound familiar?" He paused a moment for emphasis, before continuing. "After that, he will make a seven-year peace treaty with Israel, passing himself off as Israel's bene-factor or savior, and then, seven more nations—all former enemies of Israel—will join his new coalition. Sound fa-miliar? Begin to see the picture?" he asked kindly. "In reality, the treaty is just a means to set our people up for the kill, which he will initiate at the midpoint of the seven-year treaty. That's just a year and a half from now! My people call this time Holocaust II because it's the only thing that gets people's attention. In reality, the persecution associated with the Holocaust is actually an understatement of what is going to happen!"

"Which is?" Sonya managed to say.

"Which is that three and a half years after the treaty goes

into effect, he will strike out against us, initiating the worst persecution that our people have ever had to suffer. Like I said, the Holocaust of World War II will pale in comparison."

Sonya listened numbly, trying to take in all that he was saying.

"Do you have a copy of the *Tanach*?" Anatoly asked.

"No." She paused. "Wait a minute. I have the Bible you gave Yacov."

She stood up and walked over to the bookcase and returned with the small leather-bound book. Anatoly opened it and skillfully thumbed through its pages. He found the book of the prophet Daniel and turned to chapter 9. "Let's start here," he said, pointing to verse 27. "This is where Daniel says that the prince who is to come—that's the Satan-Meshiah—will make a covenant with Israel for seven years, and then, at the midpoint of that seven-year treaty, he will break his covenant with Israel, desecrate the temple, and demand the worship of the world. Those who refuse, he will kill."

Anatoly turned a couple of pages. "And look here—in chapter 12. Daniel says that when this time occurs, it will be a time of distress the likes of which Israel has never known! Hundreds of years later, in His prophecies, Yeshua pinpoints this same, exact period of time, describing it with the same frightening terminology." He flipped through the Bible until he found Matthew 24, where he pointed to a section he had highlighted in yellow. "See? Yeshua says that when Antichrist breaks his treaty with Israel, there 'will be a great tribulation'—that's Holocaust II—'such as has not occurred since the beginning of the world until now, nor ever shall!' That's why our prophet Isaiah called this covenant with Israel 'the covenant with death.' "

Sonya's thoughts raced as she read the verses Anatoly pointed out to her. *Is this really true?* she wondered. *After all, I was the architect of Bulgakov's covenant with Israel. If Anatoly is right, in less than eighteen months Israel will face another horrific Holocaust—and I am responsible.*

"Show me specifically where it says all this in the *Tanach*."

For the next hour or more, Anatoly led her through each passage, explaining them and showing how they fit together.

When he had finished, Sonya leaned back against the sofa cushions, her head tilted back, her eyes closed. When she spoke, it was obvious that she had been weighing his words thoughtfully.

"You've just described everything Nikolai has told us he plans to do—except, of course, what his real plans are for Israel. I should know. I prepared a lot of it," she said. She sat up and looked at him directly, her eyes swimming with tears. "Anatoly, I meant it for good. You have to believe that. I didn't know. I only wanted the best for our people."

"I know you did," Anatoly said, gathering her into his arms. "And what's done is done. Whether Nikolai had used you or someone else to achieve his diabolical plan, it would have happened, either way. The important thing now is where we go from here."

Sonya wiped her tears on the back of her hand. "I assume this is what you've been doing for the past months, then? Tell me about it."

"Sonya, many Jews have already fled to Petra, from all over Israel, some even from other countries. We have established a safe refuge there, out of Bulgakov's reach. That's what I've been doing up until tonight. It's a great hiding place, if I do say so myself. As of right now, that phase of my work is finished. That's why I'm back here in Jerusalem. But there is still much work that needs to be done here."

"What do you mean?"

"Many will not realize Bulgakov's true intentions until it is too late," he said. "When his reign of terror against Israel begins—Holocaust II—many will try to escape and hide, but most of them won't make it."

"What will happen to them?" Sonya asked in horror, again thinking of the part she had unwittingly played.

"As we saw earlier, the prophet Zechariah says that two-thirds of all Jews living in Israel will be killed when this time comes. Some will die because they can't make it to a safe refuge. Others will die because they choose to worship Bulgakov."

"Even the ones who go along with Nikolai will die? I don't understand."

Anatoly nodded. "Many Jews in Israel will accept Bulgakov as their Meshiah, taking his mark to prove their loyalty to him. But sometime during the second half of the treaty, during Holocaust II, after a specific sign is given in the sun, moon, and stars, the God of our forefathers will destroy the enemies of Israel, once and for all! Over an extended period of time, He will utterly destroy Bulgakov, his armies, and all who worship him, *including those Jews who submit to Bulgakov—the mark on their persons condemning them when that time comes!*"

"So, you're saying that we die if we submit to Bulgakov and we die if we don't." She closed her eyes and shook her head from side to side, as though to shut out the sight of the future. "What have I done, Anatoly?"

"You didn't know, Sonya. With or without you, Bulgakov would have carried out his plans," he said. "God said it would happen, and it has. What is written, is written. What really matters is what you do, now that you know the truth."

"But what choices are there? What can we do? Is there any hope?" The questions tumbled out, one after the other.

"Before Bulgakov breaks his covenant with Israel, you can flee to a safe place. Not all of our people will die. One-third will survive. And those are the ones we must help."

"What can I do?" she asked again.

Anatoly took her hand between his tanned, work-roughened hands. "Sonya, I want you to go to Petra where you'll be safe. That's what Yacov would have wanted too. The area is open now, and you can get in, but it won't stay open for long. Once Holocaust II begins, any access to Petra will become impossible. God has promised that He will seal off the people there, to protect them from Satan-Meshiah when Holocaust II begins."

"I won't do it!" she said. "I won't run and hide. I'm going to fight back. Nikolai used me—no, he did more than use me. He murdered my family, and then he set me up so I would take vengeance on Katanov. He's going to pay, Anatoly!"

Anger dried her tears as she stood up and looked down at Anatoly. "I need to go to Moscow," she said. "I can kill Nikolai *before* any of this happens! I have access to him, and he would never suspect me. I've killed once; I can kill again! I'll even get rid of his henchman, Sergei. When I do, they'll be history and all our problems will be solved." She started toward her desk to get a pen and paper. "What we need to do right now is devise a good reason for me to make the trip."

"Sonya, just a minute," Anatoly said. He stood and went to her, putting his hands on her shoulders. "Listen, I understand how you feel, but it won't work. You won't be able to defeat him. At this point, our Messiya—Iesus—is the *only one* who can defeat Bulgakov. So we have to leave it in His hands and concentrate on what we *can* do: we must focus on saving those who don't make it down to Petra."

Sonya chewed on her lower lip as she absorbed his words. "You're sure of this? You don't think I can get close enough to him to kill him? I bet I can!"

"You may be able to get close to him, but I'm absolutely positive you can't kill him!"

"Okay, then. I don't fully understand, but for now I'll take your word on it. What can I do to help? Rest assured, I'm not going to hide in some stone quarry down in Jordan while all the action is going on up here!"

"Are you sure that's what you want?" asked Anatoly. "This isn't going to be a walk in the park, you know."

She flashed an irritated scowl at him, and he smiled in spite of the grim seriousness of the situation. "All right. All right: Far be it from me to get between a Petrov and her objective!" His quick laughter was immediately wiped away by his next words. "As a matter of fact, there is something you could do. My next job is to establish and equip hideouts for those who escape Holocaust II after Bulgakov makes his true intentions known to the world. When that time comes, Petra will no longer be an option. You could help me locate and secure the best places for these others. And believe me, this does not mean you will be hiding out. Those who use these hideouts will become the people who will eventually take Bulgakov on, nose to nose."

"What do you mean by that?"

"At some point after Holocaust II begins, God is going to give a special sign in the heavens—in the sun, moon, and stars.

You know, the one I referred to earlier. When that happens, the Jews we prepare hideouts for—the one-out-of-three who escape when Holocaust II begins—will lead the counterattack against him."

"I thought the people in Petra would do that."

"No. Remember, I told you that Petra is going to be bottled up in some way. In reality, they're out of the picture until the seven-year treaty is over. Nobody will be able to get into Petra, and nobody will be able to get out. But everybody else will be under constant attack by Satan-Meshiah and his armies. They hide to survive, and they fight after the sign is given in the heavenlies. This will be our time for retaliation, not a moment before. *Only after the sign is given in the sun, moon, and stars.* Then God will honor these particular survivors. He will fight with them, and together they will slaughter the armies of Satan-Meshiah!"

"Then that's where I want to be . . . that's where I *have* to be. You must understand, Anatoly!" she pleaded.

Though he had always admired Sonya's strength and ability, Anatoly was amazed anew by the woman he loved. Despite the emotional and psychological blows she had just taken, she was ready to move forward. And although she had not yet given her heart to Iesus, she was ready to give her mind, her training, and her loyalty to the total destruction of this man who was so intent on destroying Iesus and those who would someday become His followers.

"So," she said, rubbing her hands together briskly, "what do we do now?" It was obvious that Sonya had made up her mind and was ready to go!

"For starters, you are in a strategic position to tell us what's going on in Moscow as well as what Moscow is doing in Israel. You're still an insider. Bulgakov thinks you trust him completely," he said. "So if you can get me information on the NUE border guards in Israel—where they are, what arms they have, their operational orders—it will help us in selecting the wilderness sites for the secret camps."

"That's no problem. What else? Give me something tough to do!"

"You can help us identify potential camp sites and . . ." He stopped and looked at her.

"And what?"

"Well, you want something tough, I'll give you something tough. I want you to get Prime Minister Shefi to help us."

"You mean convince him Bulgakov is Satan-Meshiah? You want me to lose my credibility with him? He'll think I've gone crazy!"

"No, that's not what I meant. I agree. That might be too much of a leap for him at this point, although you never know," he said. "What I was thinking, though, was, what if you were to tell him that these foreign troops worry you, especially since most of the New United Empire nations are longtime enemies of Israel. Do you see where I'm going?"

Sonya's furrowed brow smoothed. "It might work," she said. "I'm sure he will at least listen. He has always listened to my advice. That's why we're in this mess now! Besides, he has some misgivings about Bulgakov already, I think. I've sensed he is becoming nervous about some of the things he sees going on, especially the bad boy nations that have aligned themselves with the NUE. That never made sense to me until tonight. Now the pieces are falling together. In my opinion, Binyamin would be open to any ideas he felt were in the best interests of Israel."

"Okay, I'll get back to you with more on this later this morning, after I see Eitan Shachar."

"Who is he?" she asked.

After he had explained about Eitan and the Parousia Foundation, she asked, "What will you be doing next?"

"I must begin going from synagogue to synagogue, talking to any of the rabbis who will listen to me, telling them to warn their people of what's coming soon. Most of them won't believe me, of course. Our Scriptures tell us that."

"So why do it, then?"

"Because—remember what I showed you in Yacov's Bible?—some will believe real fast when Bulgakov shows his true colors."

"But by then you told me it will be too late."

"Not if they move quickly," he said. "I'm going to ask the rabbis to circle a specific date on their calendar, eighteen months from now, exactly 1260 days from when the covenant was signed. I've already calculated the exact day. I will also leave them instructions on how to get in touch with me when this time comes, should they have any second thoughts! They may think me a 'crackpot' today, but they will have advance notice of this date, and you can bet they'll watch it approaching with increasing interest. If they forget, I'm here to remind them!" Anatoly laughed. "When Bulgakov does make his move, then they will know I was telling the truth. At that point, they will have a very limited window of opportunity. If they move quickly, we can get some of them to safety."

"Isn't that dangerous? What if Bulgakov has spies in the synagogues or in the groups that try to escape?" Sonya asked, already spotting a potential flaw in the plan.

"That's always a risk. But if we do it right, I think we can limit our exposure. We will have rules, with no exceptions. For example, once someone decides to escape to a survival camp we've set up, and they reach the prearranged meeting point, no one will be allowed to turn back. Those who try must be killed. That is the only way to protect the others. Everyone will be warned of this ahead of time."

"Yes," she said slowly, falling back on her commando training. "That should work."

He paused. "There's only one other thing we need to talk about. Then I'm out of here."

"What's that?"

He picked up the Bible again and turned to chapter 12 in the book of Zechariah. "Here," he said. "I want you to read this."

And I will pour out on the house of David and on the inhabitants of Jerusalem, the Spirit of grace and of supplication, so that *they will look on Me whom they have pierced; and they will mourn for Him,* as one mourns for an only son, and they will weep bitterly over Him, like the bitter weeping over a first-born.

"What's this?" Sonya asked suspiciously, looking at the passage that had been highlighted with yellow marker-pen.

"It's what Yacov was talking about in his last e-mail to me. The prophet is talking here about Iesus, Sonya. Iesus is the one who was 'pierced' by our people—'the house of David and the inhabitants of Jerusalem'—when they crucified Him." Anatoly looked directly into her eyes. "More than anything else, I hope you will see Iesus for who He really is—our Messiya and our God. He is the only One who can forgive our sins. He is our only hope, Sonya."

"If there really is a God, He could never forgive me for this terrible thing I have done!"

"Yes, He can and He will, *if* you repent of your sin and entrust your life to Him!"

Her eyes brimmed with tears. "I wish I could but I can't. It goes against all I know," she said.

"In the *Tanach*, the prophet Ezekiel says that if you do survive the seven-year treaty period, you will see Iesus in person and then you will know the truth. *We call that day 'D-Day,' meaning Deliverance Day, when the ones who survive Holocaust II are delivered from their sins and from the clutches of Satan-Meshiah—Bulgakov—by Iesus, both at the same time.* From that day forward, Sonya, the whole house of Israel will truly trust in Yeshua their God."

"Please, Anatoly, no more of this Messiya business. I am not ready for that. I am tired. My mind needs to rest," she said. "I will help you with the camps, and when the time comes, I'll personally rip the heart out of every one of Bulgakov's soldiers! But for now, that's all I am capable of doing. Do you understand?"

He nodded that he did. Anatoly knew it was useless to push the matter any more at this point. He remembered how he, too, couldn't be pushed by Mike, initially, and neither could Yacov. Likewise, Sonya had to be given room to work through these things on her own. He would have to leave her spiritual condition in God's hands and pray that He would soon show her the truth. If she survived another five years, to D-Day, then she would understand everything. That must be his number one priority for Sonya: keep her alive until D-Day. Convince her that Iesus will take care of Bulgakov when the time comes, that there is nothing she can do about him on her own.

He glanced down at his watch. It was after seven. "I've got to go," he said.

Sonya grabbed his arm as he started to stand up. "I'm sorry, Anatoly. I just don't have your faith. Give me time. Please."

He pulled her into his embrace and kissed her. "I love you, Sonya. I wondered if I would ever be able to tell you that again."

"I love you, too," she said, running the back of her hand gently down the side of his face, lingering against the warmth of his skin. "When will I see you again?"

"I'll be out of touch for a week or so, but I'll try to phone you tonight with the information Eitan has already put together on the secret camps. Right now, what I need is sleep. Eitan has arranged a place for me to stay but I don't know where. I'm going to go to his house now. I'll call you when I get an address or a phone number where you can reach me."

"Promise? Promise you're not going to disappear off the face of the Earth again."

"I promise," he laughed, though he knew she was not joking.

That afternoon, Sonya handed Prime Minister Shefi the report she had completed a half hour earlier.

"Ah, the latest on the new oil-patch war," he said as he flipped through the pages. "I'm looking forward to reading this, although I suppose what the Arabs do to each other is not of vital interest anymore."

She nodded as she stood in front of his desk.

"Is something wrong, Sonya? You seem preoccupied—and you look tired."

"Yes," she said hesitantly. "I am worried about something, Binyamin." She paused for a moment, collecting her thoughts. "There is something I would like to ask you. It's very sensitive, and I don't want to be misunderstood."

"What is it? You know you can be honest with me."

"Does it bother you that security within our borders is

being provided by a Russian army more powerful and better-armed than our own IDF?" she asked. "And along with that, does it concern you that most of the New United Empire member nations are long-term enemies of Israel?"

Binyamin Shefi pursed his lips thoughtfully. "President Bulgakov has been our strong supporter — even more than the United States in recent years. You know this better than I."

Sonya smiled. "With respect, sir . . . am I hearing General Shefi or Prime Minister Shefi?"

A wry smile came to the leader's lips. "You have me there, Sonya. As a former general, I have to admit that this outside involvement does bother me, even though we supposedly have some say on what these troops do. You know as well as I that can change in an instant! And I don't trust most of the coalition members either. But Bulgakov has kept his word, right down the line, and he seems to have the NUE members under control."

"That is true," Sonya admitted. "But historically, all treaties fail eventually. Wouldn't it be wise to hedge against a possible betrayal — however remote?"

"What do you have in mind?"

"What if we set up secret hiding places and stockpile supplies and weapons, just in case? Then we at least have a place to regroup and the wherewithal to fight back — if it should ever come to that. Call it an insurance policy, if nothing else."

Sonya watched the prime minister's face. Considering the time he took to think over her suggestion, she knew she had struck a nerve.

"Yes," he said after only a brief moment. "That would be wise. But I also think this conversation should not leave this office." A smile crossed his lips, but his dark eyes were piercingly serious. "Could I prevail on you to prepare a plan — for my eyes only?"

"Yes, *general*," she said. "I'll get on it immediately."

Sonya spent the next week analyzing potential sites for secret camps. Some were locations suggested by Eitan Shachar, Anatoly's friend at the Parousia Foundation, and some she had found herself. Of particular interest was the area that Shachar had dubbed Camp Moses. It was an unusually large, isolated site and strategically located, making it a logical candidate for the control base. And, while it was relatively close to both Jerusalem and Tel Aviv—especially Jerusalem—it was also isolated.

As the days passed, she purposely avoided any phone contact with Bulgakov. Her hatred smoldered as she thought of how he had deceived her. What he had done to her brother and father was constantly in the back of her mind, and what he planned to do to Israel dominated her thinking. He was responsible for her transformation into a murderess. Only three others knew the truth but because of their involvement, their lips, like hers, were sealed in secrecy. But she knew the truth and she would never forget. Yes, Nikolai would pay—if not at her hands, then at the hands of someone else. And if she could not kill him, she would at least make his life miserable until that time came.

On Friday she went home early, exhausted, determined to do nothing except heat up a prepared dinner from her freezer and watch a movie on her VCR. The doorbell rang just as she put the stroganoff in the oven. When she answered it, she found Anatoly standing there, looking as haggard as he had the week before.

"Where have you been?" she asked as he stepped inside and closed the door.

"All over," he said. "I don't even remember the names of some of the little towns I've been in, but I got a lot done."

"You look tired," she said.

"I'm exhausted," he said. "But there's so little time and so much to do."

"Have you had dinner?"

He shook his head.

"I just started to fix something myself," she said. "Sit down and relax."

He collapsed on the couch, closed his eyes, and tilted his head back.

"I'm having stroganoff. Is that okay for you?" she called

from the kitchen, pulling out another frozen dinner. "Or I can fix you something else, if you prefer."

When Anatoly didn't answer, she looked around the kitchen divider. He was already asleep.

She put the second stroganoff in beside hers and took a small poppy-seed cake—*Pereg* cake—from the refrigerator. While she waited for the dinners to heat, she set the table, put together a salad, and heated the water for coffee. When the oven timer went off, she removed the dinners, turned the oven to a low setting, and placed the poppy-seed cake inside to warm.

Back in the living room she sat down on the couch beside Anatoly. Her eyes traced the beloved lines of his face, drinking in the sight of him. How fearful she had been that she would never see him again. How thankful she was that he was alive and here with her. She leaned over and kissed him as she gently shook his shoulder.

"What!" he exclaimed, opening his eyes abruptly.

"Dinner's ready."

"I'm too tired to be hungry."

"No, you're not," she said. "You need to eat. Get moving."

A flicker of a smile crossed his face. "Now that's the Sonya I know and love," he said. He rose to his feet and rubbed the back of his neck wearily.

Seated opposite her at the table, he sniffed appreciatively at the steam rising from his plate. "Smells good," he said. "I guess I am hungry. May I ask God's blessing on this food?"

Sonya nodded and bowed her head as Anatoly thanked God for His provision, His protection, and the love He had given him for her.

Nice touch, sincere was the only sense Sonya could make out of Anatoly's prayer to God.

As they ate, she told him about Shefi's cooperation and her progress in researching potential camp sites. "Eitan's research was invaluable," she said. "Without that, it would have taken me much longer."

When they had finished, she pushed him toward the living room. "Sit down and relax while I get the coffee and dessert."

She cut him a generous slice of warm cake and poured two cups of coffee. "You're still awake?" she asked, surprised, as she set the tray on the low table in front of the sofa.

"I'm not going to waste the precious time we have together," he said, wide awake, having already forgotten his nap before supper. He took a sip of coffee and sighed. "Oh, that tastes good."

"Thank you." She put her cup down. "Anatoly?"

"Yes?"

She laid her fingers on the back of his hand. "It's so wonderful to have you here. Now that I've found you again, I don't want to lose you." She hesitated a moment, then said, "I have a suggestion."

"What's that?"

"I have this huge apartment all to myself. Why don't you move in with me? Then we can really be together."

Anatoly took her hand. "I can't, Sonya," he said. "It would be wrong."

"Why? We love each other, don't we?"

"I love you with all my heart," he said. "But I can't live here with you while we are unmarried. God says it's wrong, and it would be dishonoring to Him and to you."

Sonya pulled her hand from his. "This is exactly why I could never stand the religious fanatics with their shawls and skullcaps. They're always spouting off about what you can and can't do — mostly what you can't do — and blaming God for their own inadequacies."

"Sonya, believe me, I'm not inadequate. But God intends better for us. He intends marriage to be a sacred commitment and a unique relationship — one man, one woman, forever." He paused. "Sex outside of marriage only mocks God and ruins our gift of love to one another. I will love you just as much, whether or not we live together."

It would be so easy to rationalize living together, Anatoly thought later, after he and Sonya had said good-night. With so little time left, why not be together? Yet he knew that even in the midst of what they were facing, God expected His faithfulness, obedience, and purity. Until Sonya came to know Iesus as her personal Messiya, he could not marry her. And until they were married, he could not have her.

He remembered all Iesus had done for him, when he was so unworthy of His love. How could he do less than give Him his all, which included his relationship with Sonya—not because he had to, but because, out of gratitude, he wanted to! The rest would have to wait for God's timing, and that included Sonya, if indeed she was the will of God for his life.

PART 3

HOLOCAUST II

*For then there will be a great tribulation,
such as has not occurred since the beginning
of the world until now,
nor ever shall.
And unless those days had been cut short,
no life would have been saved;
but for the sake of the elect
those days shall be cut short.*

—Matthew 24:21–22

*Now at that time Michael,
the great prince
who stands guard over the sons of your people,
will arise.
And there will be a time of distress
such as never occurred since there was a nation
until that time;
and at that time your people,
everyone who is found written in the book,
will be rescued.*

—Daniel 12:1

TWENTY

Holocaust II Minus 1 Day

Agentle spring rain greeted Nikolai Bulgakov and Sergei
Lomonosov as they emerged from the Ritz-Carlton
Hotel. Both wore dark trench coats and strode confidently
over the red carpet, their mirror-bright shoes gleaming. Ignoring the swarming reporters on either side of the hotel
canopy, they stepped to the waiting limousine, where the liv-
eried doorman held the rear door for the two NUE dignitaries.
When they were safely shut inside, the motorcycle police escort turned on sirens and began guiding the long, black car,
diplomatic flags flapping, into the sea of Manhattan's midmorning traffic.

In the enclosed privacy of the passenger section, Bulgakov
scratched at his neck. "This beard is driving me nuts. I'm glad
I get rid of it today!" He settled back into the seat. "What are
the idiots at the UN up to this morning?"

Sergei flipped on the TV in the panel before them and
turned to the C-Span 3 channel carrying the General Assembly proceedings. They watched the tiny color image as the
limousine fought its way across Manhattan. At one point the
picture cut to live reports covering the wars, plagues, and
famines that continued to overwhelm almost every nation in
the world other than those associated with NUE. Then the
focus returned to Secretary General Mahdi Abdi, the educated Sudanese tribesman from the Shiluk tribe who had finally made his mark in the UN. He was still railing against the

New United Empire for not sharing its bounty with the starving nations.

Bulgakov made a face and jammed the knob, turning the set off.

"Have you ever seen anything more pathetic?" he asked. "They don't have enough decision-making power to figure out where to go for lunch. Except for the New United Empire, the entire world is fighting, starving, or dying of plagues. But instead of solving problems, all Abdi can do is whine because we're feeding our own people instead of giving the rest of the world handouts. Well, today we'll give them what they want."

The motorcycle escort pulled up to the main entrance of the United Nations building and stopped. When the men stepped out of the limousine, two lines of policemen provided a narrow corridor, which the media hounds immediately tried to breach. Bulgakov hurried toward the doors, staring straight ahead, ignoring the questions shouted at him. One short man ducked under a policeman's arm and pointed his camera in Bulgakov's face. "Out of my way!" Bulgakov roared and swept him aside.

Inside, Nikolai Bulgakov threw open the door to the General Assembly Hall and strode, unannounced, down the center aisle toward the wide podium in front of the United Nations seal, his black trench coat flapping as he walked. A surprised hush fell over the vast auditorium as all eyes followed his progress to the front of the assembly hall. The Secretary General watched him come, the harangue of his speech still hanging over the room like a fog hugging the ground on a still day.

Bulgakov mounted the final steps and walked over to the tall, lanky Secretary General. Without saying a word, he glared up at Mahdi Abdi until the taller man turned away and took his seat on the main floor. As Bulgakov stepped behind the podium, the center TV cameraman trained his zoom lens and adjusted the focus, knowing instinctively that what was coming was important.

"Citizens of the world, I listened to your Secretary General on my way over here this morning. He has rightfully assessed the problem. The world is in trouble like never before." Bulgakov paused and glared directly into the camera lens with the red light. "But I ask you, is it the New United Empire that has caused these problems? Are we to blame for the problems of the world because we choose to feed our own people? Why do *our* people have peace and provision while the rest of *you* battle and starve? I will tell you the reason. Everything hinges on leadership. Do you hear me? Leadership!" Bulgakov's voice began to pick up the fervor and intensity that never failed to move audiences. The General Assembly would be no exception.

"Your member nations have suffered greatly over the past three and a half years. They will continue to suffer until you choose a leader who can provide for you, as I have provided for the New United Empire." He paused. "What has Secretary General Abdi accomplished? Wars in the Middle East, Western Europe, and in his own land of Africa! Plagues in the Far East and South America! Famines in every corner of the world, including the best-fed country in the world, the United States of America! Everywhere except my countries!" he shouted, his eyes a blue flame, his fists clenched.

Not a sound, not a murmur stirred the air in the hall. President Bulgakov had their complete attention.

"And now, your Secretary General blames *me* for your problems . . . for *his* problems. He has accused *me* of refusing to help the world." He paused dramatically and pointed his finger at them. "But *you* have chosen the one you will follow, and *he* is the one who has *failed*. Do you hear me? *Failed!*" he thundered, crashing his fist down on the lectern in front of him. "I ask you, can this man solve the problems of the world? A man who blames others for his own ineptness?"

As Bulgakov's gaze swept from one side of the hall to the other, each delegate felt pinned by his piercing stare.

"He is right about one thing, though. I can feed the world—all of it. And I can bring the wars to an end," he said, reaching his crescendo. "Yes, when I am your leader, the leader of the world, you will be able to fill your stomachs during the day and sleep peacefully during the night!"

He waited in silence for the delegates and the television audience to catch up—to understand what he had just said.

Then, hands on his hips, Bulgakov arrogantly scanned the hall once more. "So, what will it be? Death and starvation, or a better way? . . . My way!" he said. "I offer you a glorious future. Join with me and you will live. Fight against me and you all will perish."

Nikolai paused as murmurs rippled through the hall. Elation swelled his heart. Unseen forces swirled about him—a power these puny people could never imagine. Destiny had settled upon him, just as his Prince had promised. The reason for his existence was now unfolding before the world.

"Hear me, delegates!" he thundered. "I speak with the authority of a higher power. Remove your headphones!"

As his words were translated into their various languages, the delegates responded immediately to his command, despite their confusion.

Suddenly, the lights clicked off, engulfing the hall in blackness, except for the penetrating red light on the live TV camera. A blast of arctic air roared down the main aisle and a luminous blue object whirled around the podium—something transparent, yet suggesting form and substance. It left the floor and drifted up toward the domed ceiling high above, increasing in size until it hung like a cloud over the delegates seated below. In the center, a gigantic humanoid head coalesced, black as space, its eyes gleaming an iridescent blue.

"I am the All-Powerful One, ruler of the universe. And this is my son, god of this world," the being rumbled in a bass voice so low it rattled the walls.

The delegates stirred uneasily, huddling in their seats as they looked upward in horror. As they watched, the glowering head disappeared, again plunging the hall into stygian darkness. Then a blue-white orb formed high above the podium, projecting a brilliant cone of light onto Nikolai Bulgakov below. He reached up and slowly peeled off his beard, leaving only the trademark by which he was remembered—a small, dark, toothbrush mustache.

The audience gasped at the sight of the familiar face.

The man removed his trench coat, revealing a Nazi uniform, complete with armband and leather belt with shoulderstrap. The spotlight expanded and tilted back. Behind him, a huge red flag descended, emblazoned with a black swastika over a white circle. Slowly he raised his right arm in that famous salute known by all.

"I am alive!" he shouted. "I am risen from the dead!"

The delegates erupted in wild confusion, but the man on the platform held his salute while he waited for silence. Then he slowly lowered his arm. Only then did the wound become visible. The wound on the right side of his forehead, a wound that could have only meant certain death when it had been sustained.

"In 1945 my last words were 'Wait for the coming man.' Today I have arrived. I have come again. I have come to save the world. By my death, you shall be forgiven. By my life, you shall be delivered. Come unto me, you who are sick and tired, and I will give you rest!" Hitler thundered. "The All-Powerful One has sent me to give you peace and prosperity! Upon his authority, I will rule the world. Upon his authority, I will feed your people."

He stopped speaking. A hush fell across the auditorium. Then he whispered into the microphone. "But never forget this one thing: The All-Powerful One, father of all, has also sent me to cleanse the world of all unrighteousness! To rid the world of rebels who prefer their God to my god, their leaders over my leadership. These are the blemishes of evolution! They must be eliminated! What I failed to accomplish at my first coming, I *will* accomplish this time!"

The audience was speechless. What sort of lies did this man expect them to believe? Was this the only explanation he was able to give for the death of six million Jews, for a war that took tens of millions of lives? What mindless person would ever believe the rantings of this madman? was the question on every face in the auditorium.

"Upon the authority of the All-Powerful One, I claim the lives of those who stand against me!" Hitler cried out, his riveting eyes demanding the attention of the stunned faces that hung on every word. "To the rest of the world, I give you peace and prosperity!"

With that, the number "666" suddenly appeared in an iridescent red, hanging as it were, without support, in space above the Nazi flag for all to see. Slowly it dropped down into position over the center of the swastika. And then, a very strange thing began to happen. Hitler's appearance began to change. The transition was slow, but steady, riveting the UN delegates to their seats. No one spoke, too stunned to speak as they watched his uniform transform into the dress of royalty. A flowing velvet robe, hemmed in gold, flowed to the floor and covered his feet. His face shown brightly, as if reflecting the light of the sun. In his right hand, a scepter of finest gold. On its shaft, the number 666, each number a single jewel; a diamond, a ruby, and a single pearl. About his waist, a golden sash, tied and hanging down his left side. On it was written, *Lord of lords, and King of kings.*

"Behold, this is my son in whom I am well pleased!" the unseen voice rumbled again from high overhead. "Those who bear his mark will live! Those who refuse will die! I present to you, your leader and lord, Adolf Hitler!"

At first, confusion. Then someone clapping, here, there, obviously delegates who represented member nations of the NUE. Then there were several more, as the delegates of other nations joined in the applause. Then a general applause, and then a generation of leaders who had long forgotten the legacy of the Third Reich stood and cheered.

In the midst of the confusion, the Vatican representative, Cardinal Santucci, who had remained seated, now jumped to his feet. "There is only one true God, and His representative is the pope! This man is a fraud. This man is evil, demonic! Do not be deceived, my brothers and sisters!"

Sergei Lomonosov, now dressed in his Nazi uniform, rushed up the steps to his master's side. He snapped his fingers. The huge TV screens, set high on the walls of the assembly hall, flickered to life. As the picture came into focus, it revealed a live shot of the Vatican in the late afternoon light of the setting sun.

"We will see who is more powerful, your God or my master!" shouted Sergei, now Hitler's enforcer, pointing toward the screen above.

No sooner were the words spoken, than the peaceful scene on the screen, high above the auditorium, disappeared in a brilliant white flash. Seconds later, a yellow mushroom cloud formed above a red fireball. As the circular shock wave spread outward from ground zero, the blast swept over the camera, and the screen image disintegrated in electronic confetti.

A deathly silence descended on the auditorium.

"If anyone else opposes my world rule, let him speak now," Hitler boomed.

"Your leader and lord has spoken. Obey, and you live! Disobey, and you die!" shouted Sergei from his master's side. "Everyone—all households, all organizations, all political groups, all churches—has until midnight, tonight, to show their loyalty and commitment to the Fourth Reich and to our glorious leader, Adolf Hitler. All symbols of other allegiances must be destroyed immediately—all banners, flags, and religious ornaments. All Christian crosses and other fetishes! This is not a request. This is an order!" he shouted for all to hear.

Sergei pointed to the Nazi flag behind him. "The swastika represents the Fourth Reich. The number 666 represents your glorious leader and lord, Adolf Hitler. A sacred emblem representing your loyalty to the Fourth Reich and its illustrious leader must be demonstrated in such a way for all to see. Those who do will eat; those who don't will die. You will combine these two symbols together, imprinting the number 666 on the center of the symbol of the Fourth Reich, the swastika!"

With those final words, Sergei turned and hailed his master with the Nazi salute. Hitler returned the salute. Then both men turned and left the podium, the strange blue spotlight tracing their path down the center aisle and out the double doors at the back. They had departed the hall as suddenly as they had entered it, leaving it in total darkness.

Someone found the light switches and flipped them on. There, at the front of the hall, hung the flag of the Fourth Reich with the red "666" centered over the black Nazi cross, evidence of the fact that what they had just witnessed had, indeed, happened.

"There it is," Anatoly exclaimed. "He's made his pronouncement on the very day the prophet Daniel predicted. Yeshua forewarned John that Satan-Meshiah would be a dead man from out of the past—one who had tried to destroy Israel in a previous life. I always thought the Antichrist might be Adolf Hitler, but the idea was so alarming, I kept my thoughts to myself. I knew that whoever he turned out to be, he would be the worst enemy Israel would ever know!"

He and Sonya had been preparing supper together in her apartment, watching the early evening headline news on CNN. Although they had no idea how Bulgakov would do it, they knew that today was the day and that something was going to happen. In anticipation of this critical event, the TV had been on since early morning. Sonya had already sensed it was coming in her not-so-often, less-than-normal, evasive calls from Moscow. And, of course, Anatoly had it figured down to the day. Thus, there was little surprise when the breaking story from the UN General Assembly Hall suddenly flashed on the screen late that afternoon.

"It's official now. We must leave as soon as possible," Sonya said fearfully. "I've already cleaned out my desk at the office so, except for one last thing I still have to do there, I'm ready to go. I should get out of here while I can. It's time to leave for Camp Moses. Tonight."

During the past eighteen months, with the prime minister's blessing and the assistance of Eitan Shachar and his Parousia volunteers, Sonya had selected dozens of hiding places and stockpiled food and arms for survival, much of which, ironically, Shefi had purchased directly from the NUE! Having served in the Shabat, Sonya knew where the Arab terrorists had hidden out at night, before the treaty with the NUE put an end to their surprise attacks. Those sites turned out to be excellent locations for small survival camps. Sonya realized, all too well, that none of this could have been done as efficiently as it had been, without the prime minister's help. He provided the cloak of secrecy and opened channels of supply that would otherwise have been unavailable to the Parousia Foundation. All the while, she carefully kept track of NUE troop locations and their operational orders. It had been more than a full-time job, but, surprisingly, whatever supplies Eitan and his people suggested to Sonya, Prime Minister Shefi quickly agreed to, letting Sonya coordinate the entire operation. In official circles, only she and Binyamin knew what was happening.

Everything was in place and ready to go. Now that Bulgakov had made his announcement to the world, the prelude to Holocaust II, it was time for her to join the others who were already in the field. She had known this day would come. She had argued with Anatoly about it for months. But as of late, the arguing had stopped, to be replaced by an icy silence on the issue. She wanted him to go with her, while he insisted that he still had work to do in other parts of Israel, especially in the large metropolitan areas where most of the people currently resided. In spite of all Anatoly had already accomplished, he argued that once Bulgakov revealed his true intentions to the world, his most important work would just be beginning. Now Anatoly had to get the people out, during this brief window of opportunity, before the brutal fist of Bulgakov killed them all. That was now, today. He promised he would join Sonya at Camp Moses when he could do no more in the metropolitan areas of Israel.

She understood what he must do, but she had lost him once, and she didn't want to lose him again. The thought of separation brought back the all-too-familiar knot in her stomach. The first time she had felt it was after the loss of Yacov and Papa. The second time was when Anatoly had disappeared for almost two years. Now they were about to part again and the feeling was back.

"You're right. It is time to go," Anatoly said. "CNN says Bulgakov—Hitler, whoever—has left New York and is on his way to Jerusalem." He shook his head in wonder. "Does he really believe he can defeat Almighty God?"

By now, Sonya was used to Anatoly's continual references to God, but try as she may, she still could not genuinely share his faith in her heart. She was, however, beginning to understand his Scriptural perspective on the issues. And though she knew beyond a shadow of a doubt that he loved her, she also knew that their differences on who Yeshua was, had kept him from marrying her. Now, they might never see each other again.

"Can't the others take care of things here so you can come with me now to Camp Moses?" she pleaded, one last time.

"Sonya, if I could, I would. But you know I don't have that choice. We've got to get the people out before it's too late. I've been the key contact with many of the synagogues and their rabbis. They would never trust anyone else, especially with what's happened today. When I can get no one else to listen to me, I'll join you at Camp Moses, but not before."

"I know," she said resignedly. "How long do you think that will be? Weeks? Months? Years?"

"I don't know. But now that the volunteers from Petra have arrived to staff the smaller wilderness camps, you have to get out there and help pull things together," he continued. "No one knows all the pieces better than you. You are extremely valuable to this operation, Sonya. This is not the time to let our personal feelings jeopardize the lives of others!"

The knot in her stomach tightened. "But you will be in constant danger!"

He pulled her into his arms. "I know, but we have to trust God. I'm just grateful that we have been together these past months. If He wants us together, He will protect you until the treaty ends—until D-Day." He felt her stiffen. "Sonya?"

"Yes?"

"Whatever else you take, be sure you take Yacov's Bible. Read the passages I marked for him."

"I will take it. But why can't you come with me?" Sonya cried, making one last appeal from the heart, her head already knowing the answer.

"We have discussed this before. I can't go with you now, any more than you could go to Petra eighteen months ago." He looked into her eyes, wondering if he would ever see her again. Tears had begun to run down his cheeks and he wiped them away quickly.

Sonya clutched his hands. "What will happen to us, my love?"

Anatoly sighed. "Well, you can bet Bulgakov will be after both of our hides when he finally realizes what we've been up to," he said, then gripped her tightly. "Sonya, please listen to me carefully—and don't forget what I'm telling you. I don't know what the next three and a half years will bring for either of us. *But regardless of what happens to me, you must promise to do all in your power to stay alive until the end of the treaty period, until D-Day!* If you do, it won't make any difference what happens to me, because after that, we'll be together, forever—I promise you."

"That doesn't make sense to me," she said. "How can we be together, forever, if I survive until D-Day and you don't? I don't get it now any more than when you explained it to me the first time."

"I know you don't," he said. "But someday you will. So promise me, Sonya—stay alive, at all costs! Don't take any stupid chances. *Remember, only Jesus can bring Bulgakov down from his lofty world-rule. You can't do it, no matter how good the opportunity may look to you at the time. Don't be a hero. You will only lose!*"

"Oh, Anatoly, nothing is going to happen to . . ."

"Promise me!" he demanded.

"I promise," she said, not having any idea why she did, other than that the man she loved asked it of her.

"I love you, Sonya," Anatoly whispered. "I always will." He held her tightly in his arms and kissed her. Then he turned and left the apartment.

"I love you too," was all she could manage through her tears.

After a few minutes of wretched introspection, she glanced around her luxurious apartment. She had to shift gears, get her mind on what she had to do. There was little here that would be of any use where she was going. She hurried into the bedroom and changed into khaki shorts, a T-shirt, two layers of socks, and her heavy-duty hiking boots. Then she gathered up her necessary clothing and toilet articles, her pistol and wallet, and packed them in a nylon carryall. Everything else she needed was already waiting for her at Camp Moses.

She had started for the door when she remembered Anatoly's request. Walking back to the bookcase, she picked up Yacov's Bible and shoved it into the top of her bag. Outside the apartment, she inserted the key in the deadbolt lock. She paused for a moment. Then, she pulled out the key, dropped it in her pocket, and walked down the hallway for the last time, leaving the apartment unlocked.

Sonya stepped down from the Egged bus and waited until it pulled away and the others who had gotten off had dispersed. The nonstop rumble of the old vehicle had calmed her emotions, and she was now ready to focus on what had to be done. One phase of her life was over; a new, more dangerous phase had begun. Although she couldn't explain it, her body tingled with the sense of duty and excitement she remembered from her commando days.

She had made a brief stop at Binyamin Shefi's office, where she left him a personal letter, explaining in detail what and why she had done the things she had done. She knew he would be tied up in emergency meetings after Bulgakov's explosive announcement in the UN just hours earlier, his absence working to her advantage. She didn't want to see him. If he saw her, he would want to talk to her, but there were still some things she couldn't tell him. The letter was all she dared risk. She apologized for having kept her real agenda secret from him, but under the circumstances, she hoped he would now understand. After all Shefi had done for her, she wished she could have told him in person, but she also knew that saying goodbye to Binyamin, after her tearful farewell with Anatoly, would be too much for her to handle all in one afternoon. Especially in light of the fact that she might never see her dear friend again.

She looked around the now-deserted bus stop and shivered, but not from the cold. The long shadows of dusk pointed to the east as she pulled out the hand-drawn map showing the way into Camp Moses. It had been almost eighteen months since she had been there, when she personally confirmed the tentative decision the Parousia Foundation had made to use this location as the base site. She had found that their choice of this particular location was perfect, giving her respect for and confidence in the Parousia organization. With its remote, isolated valley walls honey-combed with caves and gigantic caverns invisible to the outside world, it was an ideal choice.

In many ways, she thought, it must be like Petra, only a fraction of the size.

She was now southeast of Jerusalem, on what her little map indicated as a shepherd's footpath. It was located about 100 meters from the bus stop. Without precise directions, she would have never found it. Her memory was vague. She was glad for the map. Without it she would have been lost. Following the meandering path, she headed southeast across rocky hills for another 5 kilometers. After an hour of difficult hiking, she came to the wadi marked on the map. She followed this dry streambed, twisting southeastward about 3 kilometers, until it dead-ended at the north side of a rocky ridge. It was nearly dark by the time she began picking her way up the face of the ridge, to a limestone outcropping about three-quarters of the way up the side. Once there, she could see a narrow crevice in the rock, about 2 meters wide. Sonya cupped her hand around her tiny low-density flashlight and glanced at the map. This was it. She remembered it from the other time she had been here. It had amazed her that such a small crevice could be the entranceway to such a maze of interconnected caverns.

She edged into the crevice and snapped on her flashlight again. After only a few meters, she came to a solid wall of stone. Shining the light to the left of the stone barrier in front of her, she saw a crack about 2 meters high and 4 meters wide, revealing the hidden entrance to the caverns of Camp Moses. She flashed her light into the gloomy void—and then, in the darkness to one side of the entrance, she saw a man not more than 2 meters from where she stood. He was pointing an M-16 directly at her heart.

"Stop! Identify yourself!"

"*Leolam,*" Sonya replied, giving the cry of Masada, 'Never Again!'—'*Leolam Lo!*'

"*Lo!*" the man answered back. He lowered the rifle and broke into a grin. "Welcome," he said. "I am Shimon Kaufman. Eitan told us you were coming, but we still have to be careful. I have been waiting for your arrival. We were notified when you left Jerusalem."

"Thank you," she said, continuing to be amazed at the

intelligence information the Parousia Foundation came up with. "You must be one of the volunteers from Petra. Are you in charge here?"

"No, but I work directly for the person who is."

"There's a lot to do and not much time. Please take me to him."

The man's grin widened. "That may be difficult, since I am talking to her."

Sonya stared at him for a moment, then smiled and shook her head. Well, I see Anatoly has been his usual thorough self — except he didn't tell me.

"Eitan assured us you are the best person for the job," Shimon continued, flipping on his high-density flashlight. "No one here has had the intelligence background or commando experience you have. If we're to survive, we'll need all your expertise."

"Then let's get going," she ordered, looking down the narrow limestone corridor that led to the caverns.

"Have you heard what happened at the UN today?" she asked, as they began their journey into the center of the mountain.

In the light of his flashlight, Sonya could see Shimon nod in disgust. "Eitan radioed us earlier, and we picked it up on satellite," he replied to her, over his shoulder. "It's hard to believe. Israel's acclaimed 'protector,' who says he'll assure peace and prosperity for every Jew, turns out to be a clone of Adolf Hitler!"

"Can you imagine? Hitler, alive again — or so he claims. But even if it is some trick and Bulgakov's only insanely using Hitler as his role model, his intentions are the same."

Shimon nodded. "Everything has happened exactly as Eitan said it would."

He led her through the narrow corridor. Soon it opened up into a large limestone cavern. Off in the distance, Sonya could see lights and hear the quiet hum of engines. They walked toward the light and soon were standing on a rock ledge, high above an even larger cavern. From here they could look down on a well-lit, huge, open area, with stacks of supplies and boxes of weapons around the perimeter.

"As you well know," Shimon began to explain, "all four caverns have been equipped with lighting and ventilation, operating off generators that are kept in a small cave off #3 cavern which we will look at later. I don't think they had been installed the last time you were here. What you're looking at is #2 cavern."

"You're right," Sonya smiled. Thank you, Binyamin Shefi. The generators and most of the supplies down there are your contribution to Camp Moses.

"In addition, underground springs already provide water to two of the caverns, #s 3 and 4, making us totally self-contained," Shimon exclaimed, obviously proud of all the planning and preparation that had gone into Camp Moses.

"I'm impressed," was all Sonya could think of to say.

"When the people arrive," Shimon continued, "#3 cavern will become the village headquarters, #4, operational headquarters, and the one you're looking at, #2, is where all the supplies are kept. Camp Moses is the refuge center for the families of the men who will be trained as fighting men, as well as the command center for all the other wilderness camps. Although we're only a fraction of the size of Petra, we are the largest of the Judean camps, which is ideal because of our proximity to Jerusalem."

"Great! You've done a lot since I was here last. It's one thing to see it on blueprints. It's another to see it in person. I really am impressed!"

"Well, at least it gives you an overview of what goes on inside the mountain. But as you are well aware, we also have access to a hidden valley where we can do our outdoor training exercises.

"There are hundreds of caves on the interior valley walls. We think the vast majority of the refugees can live there as long as the caves are used only for sleeping and the like. The caverns will become the centers for daily living. Eating, training, exercise, meetings, synagogue, day-care, bathroom and shower facilities, all of that is provided for in the caverns, especially equipped to handle each of these particular needs.

"The caverns are connected to the valley through a single

entrance, a large tunnel of sorts about 40 meters long, 5 meters high, and 10 meters wide."

"I remember its size. Have you been able to adequately camouflage the entranceway that opens up to the valley, on the north side of the valley if I recall correctly?"

"From a distance, yes. But up close, no way, the entranceway is just too large to make it disappear. If we have one vulnerable area, that's it! It's great if we want to get our people into the caverns quickly. But it's a 'Catch-22.' If the enemy ever finds that entrance, he can move a lot of men in quickly, and there's not much we can do about it."

"There must be something we can do?"

"Well, we want you to take a look at it and come up with a plan. Part of the military training *must* include the defense of that tunnel entranceway, though God forbid that day should ever come."

"Okay. Then let's go take a look at it."

Sonya carefully followed Shimon down the crude, rock steps, from the rocky ledge above to the cavern floor below. She stashed her nylon carryall beside an unopened crate of powdered milk, still sitting on a wooden skid that was being used to keep the contents of the crate dry. Then Shimon led her through another cavern, #3, to the long tunnel that would take them to the valley at the back of #4. Unlike the caverns behind her, the tunnel was pitch-black. Shimon flicked on his flashlight and told her to follow. "We keep it dark in here because any light might give us away on the outside, especially at nighttime. We're going to be descending to an exit area halfway down to the valley floor, so watch your step."

After several minutes, they stepped out of the tunnel entrance into the middle of the north side of a long, narrow valley. The moon had begun its slow ascent in the east since she had arrived at Camp Moses, and its light now partially lit up the valley that lay before her. From where they stood, Sonya could clearly see that it was still 100 meters or so down to the valley floor.

Long before Sonya had become involved, the Parousia Foundation had chosen this base site because of its size and isolation. She wondered how they had ever found these hidden caverns to begin with. They were perfect for what they needed. Then, there was the valley! Hidden in the Judean Mountains, the valley was almost 2 kilometers long and half a kilometer wide, a natural depression with no exit, except for the tunnel on the north ridge, leading back to the underground caverns. The flicker of lights from a few of the cave openings that surrounded the valley, gave the entire landscape a surreal look. Shimon explained that only candles were allowed in the caves at night. Those already at Camp Moses were preparing to go to bed. In a few days, there would be many more pinpoints of light and the valley would come alive.

As she stood there, watching the moon slowly rise off to her left, seeing the faint flicker of the candlelight, listening to the night sounds, and breathing in the fresh, cool air, Sonya felt the familiar twinge in her stomach. "May *your* God be with you, dear Anatoly," she found herself muttering to the dark sky above.

TWENTY-ONE

The Beginning of Holocaust II

Yuri Kagan felt his pulse quicken as he waited for the cue in his earphone, the rush of the familiar adrenaline high he always experienced just before going on air to a worldwide audience. Andrei already had his camera rolling while Egor monitored the sound equipment. The Kagan, Kaugin, Denisov team was ready to go!

In his ear, Yuri heard the cue from the studio director and suddenly he was appearing live before millions of CNN viewers around the world.

"This is Yuri Kagan, reporting from Tel Aviv. Moments ago, New United Empire troops, already stationed in Israel, began firing upon a crowd that had gathered to protest yesterday's staggering events at the United Nations in New York. To say that Nikolai Bulgakov's claim to be Adolf Hitler has devastated Israel does not begin to describe reactions here."

Yuri turned slightly to indicate the scene in the distance behind him. "Here in Tel Aviv, thousands of people began gathering in the middle of the night and early this morning in Rabin Square across from the city hall.

"In Jerusalem, at this moment, hundreds of thousands of protesters are packing the Western Wall and the Temple Mount, anticipating the arrival of President Bulgakov. We have been told that NUE troops have already been dispatched to restore order there before he arrives.

"We have also had reports from other countries, the United States in particular, indicating worldwide Jewish protest against what they call 'this hideous outrage.' "

Yuri jumped as an AK–74 rattled off death less than a block away. The screams and blare of sirens underscored his report for the viewers.

"Earlier, I spoke with a protester who would not go on camera. He told me that he was an officer in the Israel Defense Forces. He says that people here are afraid of what President Bulgakov's NUE troops, already stationed here in Israel, might do to Israel. Like others we have interviewed, he cited Bulgakov's claim to be Adolf Hitler and their fear that this will be a replay of what Hitler and his Nazi Party did to the Jews back in World War II.

"This is Yuri Kagan, CNN News, reporting live from Tel Aviv."

The moment he heard the director tell him the feed had stopped, Yuri whirled around to watch the action. NUE troops battled into the crowd and chased the protesters in every direction. One soldier swung his AK–47 like a scythe, firing into the crowd. Dozens flopped to the pavement like rag dolls, their blood forming tiny red rivers.

"Back to the office and then to Jerusalem!" Yuri yelled to his crew. "We have to get set up on the Temple Mount before Bulgakov arrives." As they slung their equipment into the van, he added, "Let's just hope some trigger-happy NUE unit doesn't intercept us!"

The new world leader smiled with satisfaction and triumph as he looked out at the array of New United Empire transports lined up at Ben-Gurion International Airport.

"Are my Imperial Guards ready?" he asked Sergei. The two men were alone in the large private office area in the midsection of the Tupolev 204.

"They are, master. As soon as we left the UN, I ordered them mobilized out of our elite Russian and German forces already in Israel. They have secured the airport as well as our motorcade route into Jerusalem. The Old City and the Temple Mount are also completely covered. By tonight, the entire nation will be secured by the NUE border guard already stationed here. There will be no trouble."

As the aircraft braked to a smooth stop, the two men unbuckled their seatbelts and got to their feet. Hitler grabbed his hat from the desk and Sergei opened the door into the forward cabin, where the flight attendant was already unlocking the outer door. Gone were the flowing robes of royalty the world had witnessed the day before at the UN. Today, in their place, he wore the Nazi uniform, a stark reminder that Adolf Hitler was the man in charge.

He settled his narrow-brimmed military hat precisely and stepped out onto the top of the stairway. Below him, two long lines of his honor guard — part of his new Imperial forces, resplendent in black uniforms and tall black leather boots — flanked the bright red carpet. He was admiring the spectacle when a white flutter caught the corner of his eye. He turned and saw the white Israeli flag with the blue star of David flying high above the terminal.

"Before the day is out, all of those come down. Replace them with the flag of the Reich," he ordered Sergei, who was hovering in the doorway behind him.

"Yes, master."

The two men descended the steps and crossed the red carpet to the waiting black Mercedes limousine. Fourth Reich flags waved proudly from each fender. Prime Minister Shefi and ranking Knesset members waited dutifully beside the car, though their faces revealed their true feelings.

"President Bulgakov," Shefi nodded. His eyes drifted toward the Nazi armband and he could not mask his disgust.

"My name is Adolf Hitler." The words cut the air coldly. "From this day forward, you and your people will obey my every command. Do we understand each other?"

Binyamin Shefi stared straight ahead, giving no indication that he had heard the man's words, trying to control the tears that threatened to flood his eyes.

Hitler started for the car, then turned back, coming nose to nose with the Israeli prime minister. "You had relatives who died in Auschwitz, did you not, Binyamin?" He smiled at the look of horror on the man's face, then turned away.

High in the Judean Hills, the Imperial Guard lined the four-lane highway into Jerusalem, ensuring peace and order as Hitler's motorcade swept into the city. By two o'clock, they were at the gate opening onto the Temple Mount, where another red carpet and display of guards awaited the new world leader.

Atop the famous holy site, the crowd, jammed around the Dome of the Rock and the outer court of the new temple, watched in stunned silence as the man they knew as Nikolai Bulgakov raised his arm in the Nazi salute. One step back, at his right hand, Sergei Lomonosov stood holding a rectangular black box, the sun gleaming on its lacquered surface.

The Imperial Guard held back the surging crowd and the media personnel as their leader stood stiff and silent, his blue-gray eyes searching the crowd. Suddenly, he stalked toward the north entrance to the Dome of the Rock, stopping in front of one of the newsmen.

"Yuri Kagan of CNN." It was a statement, not a question.

"Why—why, yes," the man stammered. "You know my name?"

Hitler gripped his left shoulder. "Of course I know your name. Everyone knows the famous Yuri Kagan, world correspondent for CNN. Have you forgotten that I, too, lived in Moscow during the days when you were but a local, insignificant newscaster for CNN? Now I am going to make you world famous!"

Yuri felt himself beginning to blush, pride and excitement racing through his veins.

"First and foremost, you must never forget that you are a German," Hitler continued. "This is a great day for Germany—and a great day for the world."

"Yes, of course," said Yuri, sweat beginning to bead on his forehead.

"Then don't forget it!" Hitler laughed and thumped the newsman on the back. "The Reich needs your support, and I am counting on you, Yuri Kagan."

"Yes! Thank you. Of course!" Yuri stammered, hoping that

Hitler would never guess the truth. "How can I serve you?" he managed to say.

"This great historical day must be carefully documented for all to remember. Cameras and reporters are here in droves, of course, but they will not be given access to where I am going. I have decided that *you* will be given this exclusive. Don't ever forget your heritage. First and foremost, you are German. That is why I am giving you this exclusive coverage. Do it well, and there will be more. Do it badly, and your career ends—today. Do you understand?"

"Absolutely!" Yuri responded again, trying to drown out Anatoly's accusing words that echoed in his mind. *Anatoly is the only one that knows,* he told himself. *He must be made to keep silent!* "You can count on me for anything!"

"Fine. Now, you and your crew, get ready to film. The world *must not* miss any of the great events that are about to occur here."

Egor Kaugin quickly fitted Hitler and Sergei with wireless mikes and adjusted the levels on his audio recorder, while Andrei Denisov checked the lighting, focus, and framing of his camera against the various backdrops. Then, with sound and camera up and running, Hitler turned toward the eastern entrance to the new temple. As he approached, he saw a man, dressed in what appeared to be a robe made out of sackcloth, sitting in what appeared to be a heap of ashes, attempting to block his entrance to the temple.

"Rabbi Ben-Yosef. Get out of here," Hitler sneered.

The old man glared at him. "You have no business at the Temple of the Most High God!"

"Without me, there would be no temple," Hitler hissed back at the defenseless old man. "I alone am the god of this world. And from this day forward, this temple is my dwelling place!"

"This is not your temple, nor are you the God of this world!" the rabbi exploded. "This is the Temple of Almighty God, the God of Avraham, Yitzchak, and Yaakov!" he screamed, not budging an inch.

"Well, then, let us see whose temple this is: the temple of

your God or the temple of the true god of this world, Adolf Hitler!" Hitler snapped his fingers.

Sergei stepped forward, set the black box down next to where he stood, and shouted, "In the name of my master, Adolf Hitler, god of this world, I claim this temple!" He turned to Rabbi Ben-Yosef. "As for you, I give you lightning without clouds." Again, addressing the empty skies above the temple, he continued: "Destroy this self-proclaimed enemy of the great and glorious Fourth Reich! Let him become the firstfruits of all who would oppose the reign of my lord and master!" he commanded.

Lightning out of a cloudless sky flashed, blinding the crowd. When their eyes adjusted, Rabbi Ben-Yosef no longer existed, his ashes now intermingled with the ashes upon which he had been sitting, only seconds earlier. A quiet moaning was all that could be heard from the crowd that had been so belligerent only moments earlier.

"It is time," Hitler said, as if nothing had happened.

Without any hesitation, Hitler passed through the Beautiful Gate, forbidden to all non-Jews, and marched westward across the Women's Court with Sergei at his heels. The black, lacquered box was once again under his arm. The CNN crew struggled to keep up as the two men climbed the semicircular stairs that led to the men's courtyard and, beyond that, to the sanctuary of the Most High God. Inside, he stopped before the curtain that shielded the Holy of Holies. They were now alone. The mob outside, Jewish or Gentile, religious or not, dared not enter this place. Only the television camera and its crew would witness, in person, the events that were soon to change the world.

For the moment, Yuri just tried to keep out of the way, letting the camera speak to the watching world as history unfolded on their television screens. His own on-camera reporting would come later.

Hitler's Enforcer set down the rectangular black box, pointed at the veil, and commanded, "Open!"

A tear started at the bottom hem of the curtain and ran up to the top in a jagged, ugly line. When Sergei tugged the massive pieces aside, the camera floodlights struck the shining, gold-covered Ark of the Covenant, set on a table of pure gold in the center of the Holy of Holies.

Hitler smiled in triumph. The Jews thought they were so clever, keeping this secret for fear of Arab reprisal. Did they really think he did not know of this discovery, secreted away for years in a remote Ethiopian village? With the ark now back in the possession of Israel, again in its proper place in the Holy of Holies, the Jews thought they were invincible, that they had the upper hand on the rest of the world. Today they would learn different.

He nodded to Sergei, who, at the command of his master, knelt and opened the black box. From it he carefully lifted a solid gold scepter with the 666 emblem and swastika embossed on the back side of a glistening silver blade. He placed it in the open hand of his master.

Raising the scepter high, Hitler smashed the blade end down on the ark's golden cover. It pierced the thin gold covering and almost split the lid, the emblem of the Beast now marking the place where the blade had entered the ark.

"So much for Israel's God!" the Satan-Meshiah cried out.

"In the name of the one and only god of this world, Adolf Hitler, and his Prince, the All-Powerful One, ruler of the universe, I dedicate this Holy of Holies," Sergei announced to the television camera. "It is Adolf Hitler who has been raised from the dead! He alone is worthy of your worship. He alone will rule the world from his throne here in his temple. His Reich will last a thousand years. All hail to our glorious lord and leader!"

A dark form suddenly appeared high above the ark and a hollow, booming laugh echoed through the temple. As the Prince of Demons hovered above, a massive force began swirling and whirling around him, gradually fragmenting into millions of smaller, misshapen, evil-looking faces.

"Go!" the All-Powerful One commanded in a low rumble.

The demons streaked out of the Holy of Holies like an endless river of bats. For half an hour they poured out of the temple, high above the ominously silent crowd, winging to their appointed places in every corner of the world, unwit-

tingly invited by the world's naive citizens who had obediently, but blindly, made Reich Emblems. When all had departed, the face of Hitler's Prince vanished as suddenly as it
had appeared.

As Hitler pulled his scepter from the lid of the ark, Sergei
faced directly into the camera. "Citizens of the Fourth Reich,
you stand on the threshold of unparalleled peace and prosperity! In all great societies there must be order for the
common good. To facilitate this, each of you must receive the
mark of Hitler, '666,' on your forehead or the back of your
right hand. In thirty days, you will not be able to buy or sell unless you have complied with this demand," he said. "Bear his
mark, and live. Refuse it, and die!"

Obeying the silent command in Hitler's eyes, Yuri began to
wrap up the scene that had just been televised to the world.
Yuri motioned for Sergei to move closer, to ask him to explain
what they had just observed. What was it they had just witnessed? Sergei's answer was short and to the point.

"What you saw are the servants—spirits—of the All-Powerful
One, the true Prince of this universe. As of now, they indwell
every Reich Emblem in the world. From this moment forward, these spirit-indwelt Emblems will provide the world detection and direction."

"By detection, you mean?" Yuri asked.

"They will detect anyone who refuses to bear the mark of
Adolf Hitler. The rebels they detect must die!"

"And how will these spirits accomplish that?"

"By the hands of the faithful! Detected by the spirits, destroyed by the faithful! Those who kill the rebels will be rewarded by the Reich!"

Yuri was too bewildered to know how to respond to these
murderous threats. Change the subject, quick, he thought.
"And by direction, you mean . . ."

"Simply this," Sergei replied. "What the spirits command,
the people will do. What they order, you will obey. Obey
them, and live! Disobey, and you die! That is all for now. The
interview is over."

Yuri stood there for a moment, speechless. No words were
adequate to wrap up what had just been televised live. He

simply signed off with the old, familiar, "This is Yuri Kagan, CNN News, Jerusalem." Andrei shut off the camera, and the three men hurriedly retrieved the wireless mikes, gathered up their equipment, and fled the temple.

Hitler and Sergei were finally alone. They moved back to the ark, as if drawn by a magnet. Hitler's destiny had finally arrived. He wanted one last look at the Ark of the Covenant before he left the Holy of Holies, remembering how he had coveted this golden box—which he thought of as his religious "good luck charm"—in his former life. Hearing a familiar sound, they looked up and saw the form of the All-Powerful One, with its attendant beings, materializing once again above the ancient relic.

"Your power is in your submission to me alone," the Prince of Darkness rumbled, his sapphire eyes glaring down at them. "It has *never* resided in that pathetic gold box you see in front of you," he said, accurately reading Hitler's thoughts. With that, Hitler's Prince raised his arm and shot forth a lightning bolt. Before their eyes, the wings of the cherubim atop the lid melted in a river of gold. Then flames leaped high, destroying the entire Ark of the Covenant.

"Now, we have one final matter to attend to today. It is time to begin ridding the world of our enemies," cried the voice of doom. "The time has come to make examples of those who have blatantly rejected your°relationship to Israel. I speak of those hiding down in the old city of Petra. They have been permitted, *by me*, to live *until* this day. So that I can demonstrate my power against those who reject your authority. They are the true enemies of the Reich!" The eyes glowed with hatred. "Kill them all! They, like the ignorant rabbi I destroyed earlier, will be the firstfruits of *my wrath*!"

In immediate obedience, Sergei, now the Enforcer of the Fourth Reich, took the scepter from his master and pointed it at the evil faces orbiting in the place where the ark had stood only moments earlier. "Go forth!" the demons were commanded for a second time. "Gather the storm clouds above Petra. Drown every last Jew hiding there!"

At his command, the remaining demons streaked out of the temple, headed toward Petra.

David Gur stood on his favorite lookout point, at the broad entrance to the Urn Tomb. This vantage point, standing over 80 meters above Wadi Musa and the east–west Colonnaded Street, gave him an excellent panorama—a bird's-eye view of Petra, nestled in the rock-bound valley at the base of the rose-red mountains. Below, the camouflaged tents blended into the midafternoon shadows.

As his eye followed the stepped path down to the wadi, David saw Gideon Landau trudging toward him. He already knew why his friend was coming.

"What do you think?" Gideon asked, as soon as he reached the top.

"Well, I don't see any storm clouds, but I think I saw lightning," replied David.

"Not possible," Gideon laughed. "It's been a lot of years since I was in school, but if I recall Science 101, it takes clouds to have lightning . . ."

"And clouds to produce rain. I know, I know!" David continued.

"And without rain, there can be no flooding! So much for Anatoly's flood theory!"

"Well, no one's perfect. So far Anatoly's been right about everything else, so I guess he's due for a mistake." David smirked. "How did he say it? . . . When the flood hits the middle of the desert here, then we will be convinced that the *Brith Hadasha* is trustworthy—and that Yeshua is indeed Israel's Promised One!" He laughed again. "I think not."

"I agree. He should have quit while he was ahead," Gideon chuckled, then immediately sobered, remembering that there was nothing funny about the rest of Anatoly's predictions that had all come true the past two days. "The satellite reports we're getting out of Jerusalem are something to worry about, though. Anatoly was right about Bulgakov."

"Yes, and he had it figured to the exact day as well," David added, watching the reddish light of the afternoon sun wash over the camp below. "We are as ready as we can be for whatever else may come—except of course, Anatoly's flood. What happens after this is out of our hands."

"Everyone has worked hard, but some struggle with the isolation. They know we have no choice, that they must remain in camp where they'll be safe, yet still they're restless. They also know what will happen if they violate the rules and are caught, but I hope it never comes to that."

"Some people never seem to listen," said David. "As painful as it may be, if you deal with disobedience the first time, it sets the tone for everyone else!" He sniffed the air. "Dinner soon." But he noticed his companion wasn't listening.

Gideon suddenly pointed toward the north. "Look! Do you see that?"

The sky was clear and blue, but a small cloud had appeared in the far distance, in the direction of Jerusalem. In spite of his jest, Gideon had continued to scan the heavens for anything unusual. Clouds were not unusual, but this one seemed to be moving south at an incredible speed, directly toward Petra, increasing in size at the same alarming rate.

As the two men watched, it grew larger by the moment, boiling up into an immense black mass, soaring into the stratosphere and spreading out over the desert like a giant tidal wave.

David's heart began to pound with dread and fear. Although the surrounding peaks and deep wadis helped hide them, they also made Petra susceptible to flash flooding. No sooner had this thought crossed his mind than a solid curtain of water began pouring out of the leading edge of the storm. Soon, he knew, if the cloudburst did not stop, a wall of water would come surging down from the hills, submerging all the low areas, flooding the wadis and the entire valley. There was no way to escape it.

As the dark cloud blocked the sun, the people scurried out of the caves into the valley below, huddling together in small groups, looking up toward the sky. Once they realized what was happening, many ran frantically back to their caves, seeking the higher ground that most of the caves afforded, being higher up on the valley walls.

The storm roared through with titanic bolts of lightning and deafening crashes of thunder. Hail bounced off the rocks, and torrential rain poured across the land. The wind threatened to toss David and Gideon off their perch, and both men quickly moved back into the shelter of the tomb.

Angry brown waterfalls raced from the surrounding peaks, dividing and growing into torrents as they went. Suddenly the ground shook under their feet and a large black circle opened near the Colonnaded Street, sucking the water into its depths. Dozens of similar sinkholes appeared throughout the valley and in the ravines leading to the mountains. Then another tremor shook the ground—this one was prolonged and intense—and an ominous rumbling sound rolled over the camp.

"Look!" David shouted, pointing to the west. A wall of rock was surging upward around the city. The ring of hills that surrounded the Petra valley was being thrust upward. In what seemed like moments, the entire valley was completely surrounded by an impenetrable circle of red sandstone mountains, now soaring high above the surrounding hills of southwestern Jordan.

"What's going on? How high would you say that is?" Gideon yelled to David, trying to be heard above the din.

"At least 400 meters above us. It's like we're sitting deep in the crater of a volcano."

Once again, the storm increased in intensity, but the torrents of water continued to pour into the seemingly bottomless sinkholes. Then, just as suddenly as they had begun, the winds abated and the rains slacked off. Finally, the towering black cloud shriveled up and disappeared, its mission complete, the spirits of the All-Powerful One returning to their master.

For more than an hour the raging rivers and waterfalls continued to drain into the holes, as the evening sun—once again visible to those in Petra—dipped below the western mountain wall that surrounded the hideout of the frightened fugitives. Down in the camp once more, David and Gideon surveyed the damage. The people were wet and the mud would be a problem for a while, but not one person had been drowned, the caves in the valley walls were untouched, and, more important, no one expressed a desire to take a stroll outside the ring of mountains that now sealed them inside Petra. They were happy to be safe, on the inside.

In the gathering twilight, David turned to Gideon. "Anatoly was right," he said. "His prediction from the *Brith Hadasha* did come true. And, as a bonus, this storm completely filled our cisterns. He didn't tell us about that!"

"So now what do you think about Yeshua?" Gideon asked.

TWENTY-TWO

Holocaust II — Day 1

Late afternoon sun was casting dark shadows down the rocky slopes outside the eastern walls of Jerusalem when, across the Kidron Valley, three angelic beings hovered above the rows of white tombstones lining the western slope of the Mount of Olives. The giant figures were 4 meters tall and clothed in blinding white robes. Their faces, hands, and feet glowed, and their eyes were strangely opaque in their perfect, humanlike features.

"It is time!" the first angel cried out, and he began to move forward slowly and majestically. When he was directly over the Old City, his message rang out like the roar of thunder.

"Fear God and give Him glory, because the hour of His judgment has come; worship Him who made the heaven and the Earth and sea and springs of waters."

As he continued his circuit across the nations of the world, again and again he cried out for all to hear. The entire world echoed with the power of his voice, and every man, woman, and child on Earth heard his message in their own language.

The second angel followed the first, with the same effect.

"Fallen, fallen is Babylon the great, she who has made all the nations drink of the wine of the passion of her immorality."

The third angel finished the Lord's threefold announcement:

"If anyone worships the Beast and his image, and receives a mark on his forehead or upon his hand, he also will drink of the wine of the wrath of God, which is mixed in full strength in the

cup of His anger; and he will be tormented with fire and brimstone in the presence of the holy angels and in the presence of the Lamb. And the smoke of their torment will go up forever and ever; and they will have no rest day and night, those who worship the Beast or his emblem, and whoever receives the mark of his name."

Slowly, the three creatures, with their angelic message, proclaimed the true Meshiah, Yeshua, Creator of the Universe, to the entire world below, warning every man, woman, and child of the consequences of worshiping the false meshiah, Satan-Meshiah.

Adolf Hitler nodded with approval and satisfaction as his black Mercedes swept past the massive iron gates of his new palace on the summit of Harmon Hanaziv. He was not worried about the strange beings he had just seen ascending from the Mount of Olives, nor their apocalyptic words that they had proclaimed in the heavens. His Prince had warned him that these strange things would occur from time to time. Not to worry as long as he controlled the food, as long as he controlled the finest weaponry produced in the history of mankind, as long as he controlled the minds of the people of the world. What damage could a few sheets, drifting harmlessly in the wind, possibly do to the great Adolf Hitler? he thought with amusement.

His thoughts shifted back to the present, to Prime Minister Shefi. The old fool would not have been so obliging, arranging for the UN to hand this property over to the New United Empire, had he known what would happen today. Nor would he have so quickly agreed when the NUE requested to convert the UN building that had formerly stood on this site into the NUE embassy, in reality the palatial residence for Hitler.

"You have done well, Sergei," Hitler said as the Mercedes pulled to a stop in the curved driveway before the front door. "This place is all you promised."

"Thank you, master," said Sergei, surprised by the rare compliment.

When the guard opened the front door, Hitler returned his

salute and strode directly into the large living room. There a wall of tall windows overlooked the city. He had wanted this property because it provided not only the security he needed for his Lion's Den, but also a spectacular view of the Old City, only 2 kilometers to the northeast.

"Tomorrow, Sergei, I want you to meet with my new chief of staff," he said briskly, without turning from the window. "It is time for General Anayev to expand the cordon around Israel, protecting its borders and ridding the country of every Jew who refuses my mark!"

"But you said they had thirty days . . ."

"Nonsense. Anyone Jewish or caught in a Christian church, they must take the mark, then and there, on the spot, or die! Do you understand me, Sergei? There will be no exceptions!"

Hitler's tone intensified as he continued. "The work my Prince has given me will not be finished until every man, woman, and child carries my mark, not only the Jews here in this land, but Christians as well, wherever they're found."

"Why do you always limit your opposition specifically to those two groups?"

"Because my Prince has assured me only rebellious Jews and deluded Christians will refuse my mark," he sneered, "the rest of the world is mine! First, those who refuse must be eliminated. Then my Prince will kill their leader, the one called Iesus!" He paused, his next words coming in a burst of anguish. "They must all die, Sergei. I cannot fail! . . . I can never go back! Do you hear me? Never. . . . Kill them all. Every last one of them! . . . I can never return to that horrible pit!"

Sergei said nothing. When his master slipped into one of these dark moods, it was best to stay silent. Besides, he knew well what needed to be done. Those rebellious Jews in Petra had already been eliminated. The Reich Emblems would help rid the world of the rest of the treacherous traitors who refused to show allegiance to the Fourth Reich or his illustrious master.

Hitler turned, the cold blue-gray eyes once more acknowledging his Enforcer's presence.

"One more thing, Sergei. Clear out the Bahai Temple in

Haifa. There is only one god of this world—*me*. And only one way to him—*my* way. Level the temple, but leave the gardens and fountains. Then issue the order to build *my* shrine—a shrine to the *only* true god of this world—on that very spot!"

Holocaust II—Day 2

Binyamin Shefi stood on a corner near a shopping mall in the midst of the urban sprawl of Tel Aviv, disguised in shabby clothing. He was enraged at the events of the past two days, and he was frightened for his people. Israel was no longer sovereign, no longer had a prime minister, only a diabolical dictator that many would still serve—if not out of stupidity, then out of fear! He himself would never bow to Bulgakov or Adolf Hitler or whoever he was.

His face bore the lines of defeat. If only my Judith were still alive, Shefi thought. He still felt acute pangs of loneliness, even though his beloved wife had died just over two years ago now. She had always been his best and closest confidante, his advisor in crisis situations. But he was being selfish. He could only be grateful that she had not lived to see this day—and the coming Holocaust, which many had believed would never happen again.

He thought of the letter he had found tucked under the door of his office yesterday morning. Although some things were still hazy, he was beginning to understand what Sonya had been trying to do, without implicating herself or jeopardizing anyone else. He remembered that first phone call from her when she had offered Israel deliverance from the Arab nations that had been consumed with destroying his people. He remembered the exuberance of her voice. How could she have known? Hadn't Bulgakov manipulated her the same way he had manipulated him, to say nothing of how he had manipulated the rest of the world? Shefi loved her like he would have loved his own daughter, had he and Judith been able to have children. He only wished she had told him more when she discovered the truth. Yet he understood why she could not take that risk. She obviously knew she couldn't prevent this day, only prepare for it, which was exactly what she had done.

Although unknowingly at the time, now he knew he had played a part in helping some survive this maniac!

Now he was alone, and there were decisions he must make. Would he stay and fight? Could he survive the Reich Emblems, to say nothing of the armed guard that surrounded Israel? Should he disappear into one of the camps he was indirectly responsible for setting up? He wasn't sure what he should—or could—do. He needed to know more before he could make an intelligent decision. For now, he had to find the secret meeting place Sonya had told him about. Perhaps he would meet her Anatoly, the person he had heard so much about. Perhaps he would finally get answers to the questions that still burned through his mind. Then he would decide what to do next.

It was nearly nine o'clock at night. A large group of Jewish men and women packed the storeroom at the back of the carpentry shop on Levinsky Street in South Tel Aviv. It was the only safe place to meet. Synagogues were out of the question. The crowd was noisy, still worked up over the events that had occurred on the Temple Mount the day before.

As Anatoly, waiting to speak, looked around the audience, he thought he caught a glimpse of a familiar face. The man, dressed in shabby clothing, stood near the back; then, just as quickly, he melted into the darkness that circled the perimeter of the room. Anatoly forgot about the man in the shabby clothes and returned to the crisis at hand. He sighed as he remembered the reception he had gotten from so many of the rabbis he had contacted over the past eighteen months. Now some of them—and their synagogue congregations—were ready to listen; but for many others, it would be too late. Already he was feeling the pressure, hearing reports that the Reich troops had stepped up the hunt for any and all Jews who refused to take Hitler's mark. Although they were given thirty days to comply, as of this morning the Reich troops had begun raiding the synagogues, rounding up Jews and demanding they take the mark—immediately—or die. Time was quickly running out. This would be the eighth such meeting he had spoken at since Bulgakov's announcement from the temple, yesterday afternoon. In spite of that, he knew that thousands would never make it to safety, especially those who lived in the larger towns and cities.

When Rabbi Yoel Stone nodded his head, Anatoly rose and held up both hands to silence the people. It took a couple minutes for them to settle down so he could be heard. Finally, silence.

"My friends, all of us who refuse to serve Bulgakov, this man who calls himself Adolf Hitler, are in grave danger," Anatoly began. "You know this or you wouldn't be here tonight. If you refuse his mark, you will die. Hitler has two sets of rules: one for the world in general, the other for Jews living here in Israel. By now you all know that the thirty-day grace period does not apply to Jews! There is little chance that any of us can escape the demonic Reich Emblems that he uses to identify us. The fanatical followers of this son of Satan—Satan-Meshiah—will murder you on the spot if you are found and identified! Already these demonic Emblems are everywhere, including every public place! You cannot escape them! Your only hope is to flee to the secret camps we have prepared for you in the Judean wilderness. And you must go now—tonight!"

Anatoly paused for a moment, watching the reactions on the faces before him. He saw anger and fear, but he no longer saw cynicism or disbelief.

"We will meet at the beach at Palmahim, near the wrecked ship. You must be there no later than midnight. That's about 20 kilometers south of here, and you have a little more than two hours to get there. Bring a flashlight if you have one. Pack one duffel bag per person and wear comfortable walking shoes. Once you arrive at the checkpoint, there is no going back. I warn you now, those who try will be shot!"

Suddenly, Anatoly heard the front door of the shop crash open and the unmistakable sound of heavy boots stomping through the building. The people looked around fearfully, but no one uttered a word. Anatoly gestured frantically at Rabbi Stone, who was standing, beside the door leading into the storeroom. Immediately understanding the unspoken command, the rabbi flipped off the lights, plunging the room into darkness.

Using the small flashlight he always carried, Anatoly made his way to another door at the side of the room, which led into an alley behind the shop. He held the door, quietly urging the people out into the night, where they quickly disappeared down the alley and into the side streets. The last man stumbled out just as the soldiers began bashing the locked storeroom door with their rifle butts.

Rabbi Stone slammed the door behind them and Anatoly smashed the bare light bulb over the door with his fist, plunging the alley into total darkness. The rabbi ran north, his footsteps echoing off the buildings. Anatoly spun to the south and started toward the side street at the end of the alley. The back door crashed open behind him and he heard the first soldier rush out into the alley.

As he ran along the alley, hoping he would not fall over something in the darkness, a heavy caliber bullet plowed into the brick wall, just inches away from him. He reached the end of the alley, turned left, and sprinted down the poorly lit side street. He made it halfway to the next street before he heard the command to halt.

Anatoly weaved from side to side, the angry spitting of an automatic rifle sounding behind him. Bullets ricocheted off nearby cars and the pavement, but none hit him.

His lungs began to burn as he rounded the corner. He ran halfway down the street and ducked into the first alley. By the time he made it through to the next street, he was completely out of breath. Many of the stores in this district had recently been abandoned, which suited him perfectly. No business, no people. He slowed to a walk and tried to get his racing heart under control. He heard a few random shouts but nothing close. Then he made another turn and finally, after assuring himself he wasn't being followed, began to feel out of danger.

He sighed. In an hour he would be at the checkpoint.

It was one o'clock in the morning. Anatoly watched the guides lead the last of the refugees away toward Camp Moses. Things had gone smoothly, considering how the last meeting had ended only hours ago. Almost everyone who had been at the last meeting, including Rabbi Stone, along with most of those who had attended the other three meetings held earlier in the day, had shown up at the checkpoint. No one, even for a moment, had looked back.

As the last VW transporter disappeared into the night to rendezvous with guides who would lead them to the camps, he suddenly put a name with the face he had seen earlier that evening. The man in the tattered clothes, the phantom who had disappeared, was Prime Minister Shefi! But he was one of the few Jews who failed to show up at the beach, here at Palmahim!

What had Shefi been doing there, and how had he even come to know about the place or the meeting? Had Sonya told him in the letter she had left in his office? Why hadn't he showed up tonight? Had he been the one who had alerted the troops that broke the meeting up? Was he still alive?

Holocaust II — Day 3

The Gothic splendor of the Lutheran Church of the Redeemer was lost on Yuri Kagan as he peered over the parapet of the bell tower. He did not like being in a church, *any* church, even if it was Lutheran, but this high vantage point offered the best view of the Old City, and it was something he enjoyed doing while he waited for the others to arrive from Tel Aviv. He had come to Jerusalem alone, earlier this morning, trying to assess all the things that had occurred the past several days. His eyes lingered on the Temple Mount to the east, where the golden Dome of the Rock and the white stone of the towering new temple glittered in the late morning sun. Now it had become the throneroom of the world's leader, Adolf Hitler! He moved around the tower until he was on the west side, looking toward Tel Aviv. From there he could see the Knesset, the Israel Museum, and Yad Vashem. He remembered the speech Bulgakov gave there, three and a half years ago, promising that his treaty with Israel would prevent the

Holocaust of WWII from ever happening again to the Jews. He wondered . . .

It seemed he was spending more time in Jerusalem than in Tel Aviv, but who would have known what was to happen in Jerusalem when he had decided to take an apartment in Tel Aviv almost four years ago? When Hitler beckoned, he moved! Hitler would make him an international, household name! Whatever he wanted, he would get, no matter what time of the day it was.

He had just glanced at his watch, wondering when his crew would arrive, when he noticed a strange dark cloud forming in the sky above Yad Vashem. Something about it wasn't right. Maybe because there wasn't another cloud in the sky; maybe because it hadn't been there a moment ago. For a moment it reminded him of the cloud that had appeared out of nowhere, two days ago, when he and the rest of his crew were leaving the temple. But this one was different. Instead of moving quickly to the south, this one was moving slowly in his direction. Seconds later, a violent roll of thunder shook the stones under his feet as the black cloud continued its ominous movement toward the Old City.

Yuri hurried to the other side of the tower, his heart pounding with fear as the churning black mass rushed toward the spot where he stood. Yet something, his reporter's instinct perhaps, held him there.

A bolt of lightning now broke out from within the cloud and hit the street below, seconds before the blackness of the cloud enveloped him. A chilling wall of water drenched him, and the shrieking wind threatened to throw him over the parapet. Hail pelted down around him, stinging his exposed skin. Yuri rushed inside, down the tower staircase and out of the church. In the street outside, Andrei and Egor were just pulling up in the van.

"What was that?" Egor yelled, fear evident in his eyes. "I've never seen anything like it!"

"I think it's headed for where we want to be, up on the Temple Mount. Follow me!" Yuri ordered.

By the time the CNN crew worked their vehicles through

the narrow streets that had never been meant for motor traffic, the cloud draped the cobblestone plaza in front of the Wailing Wall on the southwest side of the Temple Mount. They hurriedly grabbed the minimum equipment necessary and lugged it down the steps to the large open plaza by the Wailing Wall. The mass had stopped and had begun to pour down rain and hail. Another lightning bolt lanced out, striking the pavement only 20 meters from where they were setting up. Yuri winced as pulverized rock pelted him. His ears rang from the thunderclap and his nostrils stung with the pungent odor of ozone.

Andrei and Egor had the recording equipment and camera in place and Yuri put on his artificial reporter's face, smiling into the lens like nothing unusual was happening.

"This is Yuri Kagan reporting from the Wailing Wall in the Old City of Jerusalem, where just a short time ago an unusual weather formation appeared, bringing violent thunder, lightning, rain, and hail. You can see it behind me now," he said, as Andrei panned the camera up the Western Wall to the sky above the Temple Mount. Only a few religious Jews, dressed in black religious uniform, were praying at the wall, defying the edicts of Hitler and the effects of Mother Nature, risking their very lives in the process.

"Sudden storms are unusual here in Jerusalem. This appears to be an extremely localized phenomenon. The storm cloud, which only moments earlier was moving at an incredible speed, is now standing motionless over the Wailing Wall, pouring its wrath down on this one isolated area for some unknown reason," Yuri continued, wondering where all this was leading.

Even as he spoke these final words, the rain and lightning ceased abruptly, and two beams of light slanted down from the black cloud, projecting two oblongs of brilliance on the paving stones before the Wailing Wall. As the cloud began to disintegrate, indistinct shapes could be seen moving inside the confines of what, moments earlier, had been a violent storm cloud. Slowly, two human forms took shape—two men with full beards, dressed in heavy, white linen robes. One carried a long wooden rod in his right hand.

The two figures appeared to descend down the shafts of

light until they touched the ground in front of the Wailing Wall, their clothing completely dry, unaffected by the storm cloud from which they had come. As soon as they touched ground, the light beams blinked off and what remained of the storm cloud imploded and disappeared. Endless blue filled the sky once more, and silence.

"My, how the place has changed since I was here last," the one without the wooden rod said to his friend. "I was there when old Nebby tore the first one down, back in '86 . . . 586 B.C., that is!"

"Talk about change," the other responded, "Solomon's first temple hadn't even been built in my day!"

Their conversation was interrupted by the clatter of boots echoing off the walls, as NUE security forces poured out into the plaza, their assault rifles at the ready. From the opposite direction, coming quickly down the stairway that led to the Temple Mount at the south end of the Wailing Wall, Hitler and his Enforcer, surrounded by his Imperial Guard, arrived at exactly the same time.

Yuri glanced at Andrei to make sure he was filming everything. This was going to be more of a story than he had expected.

"Kill these invaders!" Sergei screamed at the top of his lungs, pointing at the two bearded men. The religious Jews, still praying at the Wailing Wall behind the two men, scattered in all directions, thinking that they were the object of Sergei's command. But the two bearded strangers in the long white robes didn't move one centimeter. Rather, appearing bored by all the activity that now surrounded them, they just looked at Hitler and his Enforcer.

"Well, I see some things never change," the one without the rod said as he began to laugh.

"You mean their ugly looks, their bad smell, or just their big mouths?" the second one asked, joining his friend's laughter.

Enraged, Sergei commanded the soldiers to begin firing at the two strange figures. Slugs tore through the square, ricocheting off the pavement and walls. Bright flashes covered the robed figures from head to toe, but they just stood there, unharmed, staring at their attackers and continuing to laugh.

When the last ammo clip had been emptied, another stony silence descended on those standing in front of the Wailing Wall. The laughter stopped and the figure with the wooden staff stepped forward and pointed the rod directly at the guards, like a weapon. Lightning erupted from the end of the rod, striking the center soldier and moving horizontally in both directions to encompass them all. The guards fell to the pavement in a mass of burning flesh.

"Behold, the man of lawlessness . . . the Beast . . . the enemy of the true Promised One of Israel, Yeshua!" the figure cried out, pointing the staff at Hitler. "And his puny prophet!" the other one added, pointing his finger at Sergei. "Do you think you are Elijah?" the first one with the staff asked Sergei, mockingly, turning to wink at the bearded man beside him.

"Who are you?" Hitler demanded.

"The question is, 'Who are you, little man, who gives orders to the prophets of the true God of the universe?' " the figure asked, once again pointing his staff at Hitler. "We are not your subjects. We are Moses and Elijah, and we declare to you and to all who can see us," he continued, now pointing his stick at the CNN cameraman, "the Son of God, Yeshua, the true Meshiah of Israel!"

"How dare you speak to me in this manner!" Hitler exploded. "I alone am god of this world!" He snapped his fingers at his Enforcer. "Show them my power!"

"In the name of Adolf Hitler, the god of this world, let there be darkness," Sergei said, sweeping his right arm over his head.

Immediately, an ominous disc eclipsed the sun. Automatic floodlights began winking on around them, activated by the sudden darkness.

"Child's play!" Moses said with a roar of laughter. "Let me show you what the real God can do!"

He held up his rod, pointing to the heavens.

"In the name of Almighty God and His Son, Yeshua, let there be light!" he commanded.

A brilliant beam of bluish-white light shot into the heavens, exploding the black disc and ending the artificial eclipse instantly. "So much for that pathetic demonstration of power," Moses whispered.

"Rock breaks scissors. White light destroys black disc. End of argument!" Elijah answered, under his breath.

"You'll have to explain that one to me later," Moses said, sounding confused by what his younger friend meant. He was, after all, almost a thousand years older! A different generation altogether.

Turning to face Hitler, the two old men stared defiantly at the self-proclaimed ruler of the world, their demeanor and very presence challenging all that Hitler claimed to be.

"Your power is as impotent as the two of you are," Moses challenged. "You really think you can match the omnipotence of Almighty God? We may be old, but we're certainly not the fools you two are!"

Hitler exploded. "Sergei, kill them! Now!"

"With what?" Sergei despaired.

"Call down the wrath of the All-Powerful One!"

"*You* do it. He's *your* Prince. *You've* got more clout with him than I do," Sergei pleaded.

"In the name of my Prince, the All-Powerful One of the Universe, destroy these two," Hitler screamed, out of control.

Nothing happened. No flashes of light, no thunder, no voices, nothing. The two old men in white just stood there, their eyes never leaving Hitler and his Enforcer. Finally, Elijah spoke. "I've got news for you, little man. It's kind of like the bad news, bad news joke. The bad news: you can't touch either of us until our work on Earth is finished. The other bad news: we can't touch you, either, because Yeshua has reserved that glorious event for Himself!"

"I think that's what you call, 'stale meat'!" Moses added.

"Stalemate, Moses," Elijah corrected. "Stalemate! Now that Aaron isn't doing your talking for you, you've got to get the nuances of the language right!"

"Whatever. Stale meat, stalemate, either way you're dead meat!" Moses replied, lowering the end of his staff, pointing at the stone pavement in front of Hitler and Sergei. A pool of blood formed at their feet, spreading outward until it encircled the dead soldiers that lay on the ground all around them. Then, in the twinkling of an eye, the dead bodies were gone, consumed—nothing left—the way Almighty God dealt with His enemies back in the good old days of the prophets.

"What is this outrage?" Hitler screamed. "What do you think you're doing? I demand an answer!"

"And an answer you will have," Moses replied. "Almighty God holds you personally responsible for the innocent blood that you will shed," he declared.

"A prediction of things to come," Elijah added, turning away from Hitler and his sidekick, who just stood there, looking dumbfounded. The conversation was over.

"Got it?" Yuri managed to mumble.

"Got it!" Andrei and Egor answered, almost in unison.

TWENTY-THREE

Holocaust II — 2 Months

Commerce restrictions became the law thirty days after the world had been ordered to bear the 666 mark of their leader and lord, Adolf Hitler. From that day on, no one could buy or sell anything until the implanted microchips in the forehead or on the back of the right hand had been scanned.

"There is nothing sinister or evil about this, as some subversive groups are claiming," proclaimed mayors, governors, presidents, prime ministers, and other government leaders in every country, as well as announcements on every television channel. "Most of us have been using scanners for decades. This identifying mark is nothing more than a tiny microchip, painlessly implanted under the skin, only visible to the naked eye at close range. It is a simple procedure and it will be done for you, free of charge, at marking centers in any city, state, or federal government office. The entire procedure takes less than ten minutes. It will protect you from thieves or fraud and will make your business transactions quicker and easier than ever before. It also does away with all the extraneous identification pieces we've been complaining about for years. This rolls everything into one simple set of numbers, burned into the microchip. The first part is your personal identification number; the second part is 666, symbolizing your commitment to the leader of the Fourth Reich, Adolf Hitler."

Those who tried to evade the marking system soon discovered that the demon-controlled Reich Emblems, now scattered by the billions throughout the world, were efficient watchdogs. Mobs of so-called Reich Loyalists, eager for the reward money, followed through with on-the-spot executions of those identified by the demonic Reich Emblems.

Meanwhile, every standing army was being transformed into troops of the Fourth Reich. Once mobilized, their security squads swept community after community, searching out those who failed to comply with Hitler's orders. Those without the mark were summarily executed—unless the Reich Loyalists got to them first.

Holocaust II—3 Months

Andrei and Egor looked over at Zahal Square from the sidewalk on Yaffo Street, oblivious to the noise of the bustling traffic.

"You sure we need this last segment?" Egor asked.

"Yes, I'm sure!" snapped Yuri. "There must be no question that the Reich will not tolerate nonconformity. And the last clip must be from Jerusalem." He turned to Andrei. "Show me what we have so far."

The three walked back to the van, where Andrei rewound the tape and tilted the monitor so Yuri could see it.

A shaky picture leapt to the tiny screen. The congregation of Moody Church poured out of the auditorium and onto the near northside streets of Chicago, moving toward the cameraman's position on Lake Shore Drive. The Chicago skyline provided an indifferent backdrop to the organized carnage that was soon to occur at street level. The terrified worshipers, driven out of the sanctuary by the mobs who had broken into the church's historic auditorium, saw that Lake Michigan blocked their only escape route. They knew there was no way out. Triumphant screams erupted from the pursuing mob. Many held up their Reich Emblems, as those without the mark fell prey by the hundreds to the Reich Loyalists. A young soldier in the mob held down the trigger on his AK-47, pulverizing the traitors into bright red swatches. The scythe of death continued around in a circle until the hail of bullets swept across the witnessing camera. The scene ended with a bright flash.

"Nice touch," Yuri commented. "Next time he'll watch where he's standing!"

The next segment picked up in Seoul, Korea. The scene was remarkably the same, except the congregation being rooted out and slaughtered was larger than the one in Chicago, and the cameraman had the good sense to select the roof of a building for his vantage point. Then came a rapid montage of similar shots from London, Berlin, Beijing, Tokyo, Manila, and finally Sydney, Australia.

"Wow!" exclaimed Andrei. "Can't be many of them left."

"It won't be long until they're all gone," Yuri grumbled. "The rebels who resist our leader must pay the price."

Distant shouts drifted through the ancient stone gate below them, punctuated by the rapid rattle of automatic gunfire.

"Get ready!" Yuri shouted, the familiar knot beginning to form in the pit of his stomach.

Andrei jumped out of the van, hoisted the camera to his shoulder, and focused in on the gate. A terrified human torrent erupted from the narrow opening that served as a back door to the synagogue, as men, women, and children stumbled over each other, trying to escape their executioners. Moments later, the gunmen dashed out, their weapons spewing death. Bodies tumbled right and left as the high-velocity slugs tore them into bloody, misshapen rags. One bullet hit the pavement in front of Yuri, kicking up limestone splinters.

"We'd better get behind the van," Andrei shouted.

The CNN reporters took cover as the Reich Loyalists finished their deadly work below. Yuri took the afternoon off, blaming the stomach flu for the nausea that ruined the rest of his day.

Holocaust II—4 Months

The early morning streets of Jaffa were quiet as Anatoly slowly made his way, on foot, down Yefet Street. He was headed for the Archaeological Gardens in the center of the picturesque city just outside Tel Aviv. Above him, the rosy glow of sunrise edged slowly into the cloudless, deep blue vault of heaven. As he walked, he thought about the close call he'd had in Tiberias the afternoon before. Getting men and women out of metropolitan areas had become almost an impossibility. He knew it was dangerous to be in the city, any city, now that the television reports constantly showed his picture to the viewing audience. He had become the top man on Hitler's most-wanted list here in Israel. In addition, it was becoming increasingly difficult to hide from the demonic Reich Emblems, especially in the cities where they were posted on almost every street corner. Probably another week was all the time he had left. Then he would join his Sonya at Camp Moses. He had begun to sweat in the humid morning air that characterized the summer climate along the Mediterranean sea coast this time of year. Nevertheless, he pulled the hood of his light jacket higher, up over his head, trying to hide his face in order to avoid detection. He knew he looked strange, but at this time of the morning there was no one around to notice. All the activity would be several streets away, in the market area of Jaffa, where merchants would be opening their shops and arranging their produce, conducting business as usual.

He prayed silently as he walked. *Heavenly Father, guide me this day in how I can best serve Your Son, Iesus. Thank You for this privilege of serving You. And whatever this day holds for me, I place my complete trust in You.* His thoughts drifted toward the south. *Please watch over Sonya and all those You have entrusted to her. Protect her and bring her to Yourself.*

When he was afraid, he committed his way to Iesus. When he committed his way to Iesus, his fears fled and the peace of God that surpassed all understanding swept over him. He had work to do, but God was in control—the true God of Avraham, Yitzchak, and Yaakov, not the impostor the world had chosen to worship. One day at a time.

This morning he knew where he must be. The e-mail message had taken him completely by surprise. Yuri had reached out to him by the only way he knew, through his computer mailbox. It had taken him two additional days to ascertain that the message from Yuri was genuine. First, he found an out-of-the-way pay phone and left a message on Yuri's voice mail, leaving no name but knowing that Yuri would know who it was, if indeed he was the one responsible for the e-mail contact. He told Yuri's voice mail that he would call again, the next day at the same time. Yuri was to leave a recorded message, in his own voice, explaining what it was he wanted. He would decide what to do after he heard Yuri's voice and message.

Yuri answered, as instructed. One of Sonya's refugee friends had been captured in Jerusalem. He gave no names. Because of her friend's knowledge of Sonya's whereabouts, his life had been spared until he could be forced to talk. The information had been given to Yuri because of his relationship to Hitler. Yuri had been told there might be a story in this one, before it was over. Out of friendship with Anatoly, he had tried to make contact with him. They needed to get together, the sooner the better. It was important. If he agreed, they would meet in the Archaeological Gardens in Jaffa, the next morning at 6:00 A.M. That would be the best time to assure that they would be alone, thinking, of course, of his old friend's safety. Most people would still be in bed at that time in the morning.

Soon Anatoly would be at the gardens. Peering out through the narrow opening of his hood, he spotted one of the demon-controlled Reich Emblems ahead on the next corner. The black cube containing the demonic Emblem was mounted high on top of a streetlight. Humans still had to do their dirty work, though, and thus far the street was empty.

No sooner had the thought crossed his mind, when a man stepped out of his flat several meters ahead, off to Anatoly's right. Overhead, Anatoly caught a fleeting glimpse of something dull-red glowing eerily inside the swastika with the 666 overlay. The Emblem of the Fourth Reich suddenly came alive.

"Stop that man!" the demon inside shrieked. "Kill him! Do not let him escape!"

Thoughts of flight raced through Anatoly's mind, but were quickly replaced by the strong sense of peace he had experienced just moments earlier.

The man he had just seen turned toward Anatoly, the

incision mark from the recent implant still clearly visible on his forehead. "Bow down to the Reich Emblem," he demanded. "Now!"

"It is Yeshua I serve, not your false god," Anatoly answered quietly.

The man pulled a revolver from his belt. "Traitor! Your own words condemn you! You must die!"

"I am prepared," Anatoly said, "but you are not the one to do it." With that, he walked past the man, turned right at the corner, and continued toward the gardens, leaving his accuser standing in the middle of the street, a bewildered look on his face.

Anatoly walked slowly over to the prearranged meeting place, a bench in an isolated corner of the gardens that were located in the heart of the old city of Jaffa. The glow of the early morning sun had begun to bathe the semitropical foliage in cheerful tones, but the beauty of the moment was completely lost on Anatoly. His mind was now on Sonya and the meeting that was soon to take place with his old friend. He reached the bench and sat down. Beachfront Tel Aviv still slumbered in the distance. What was so important that Yuri couldn't tell him on the phone? Was Sonya all right? Had Hitler's assassins been able to ascertain the location of Camp Moses? Could he still trust Yuri, now that he was on the inside, so to speak? So many questions. The only way to get answers was to meet with Yuri, face to face. Footsteps interrupted his thoughts. Anatoly jumped to his feet.

"Thank you for coming, Anatoly," Yuri said as he approached, looking nervous.

"Yuri," he exclaimed. "What's going on? You know it's not safe for me to be here with you," he explained.

"I know," Yuri answered sadly.

"Why do you do it, Anatoly?"

"Do what?"

"Fight reality!" Yuri explained.

"Because he's a fraud, Yuri. You know that. We both know that."

"Anatoly," Yuri said as he motioned his friend to sit, sitting on the other end of the bench, "you've gotten yourself in a lot of trouble."

"Meaning . . . ?"

"Meaning that you have become number one on Hitler's most-wanted list. Meaning that he will do anything to capture and make an example of you! Meaning that whoever turns you in can write his own ticket."

"What does this have to do with Sonya?"

"It has nothing to do with Sonya. It has everything to do with the fact that you are hiding the terrorists who seek to destroy the Reich!"

"What do you mean, terrorists, Yuri? Those I seek to help are not terrorists! They simply refuse to accept or worship this man as Israel's Meshiah. His intent is to destroy our people, not help them! The Jewish men and women in hiding bear arms to protect themselves from the terrorism of your Bulgakov! Of all people, you should understand the difference!"

"I only understand that you are helping the enemies of the Reich escape," Yuri argued, trying to convince himself.

"How many Reich people have our terrorists killed, Yuri? Come on, you're the reporter. You're supposed to know these things!" Anatoly challenged his friend.

Yuri looked away. He knew the truth.

"Well then, if you cannot answer that question, let me ask you another. How many of my people have been killed by Hitler's terrorism? Your own words bear testimony to this fact. I've seen your specials on television. The whole world has!"

"We only kill the rebels and terrorists. The traitors to the Reich."

"And if I am number one on their hit list, does that make me a terrorist, Yuri?"

"Well . . ."

"How many people have I supposedly killed, to get the number one spot, Yuri?"

"Well, I don't know . . ."

"I'll tell you how many. Efes, zero, nada! You hear me, old friend? Not a single one!"

"I don't know that. I am not given those facts."

"Well, now you *do* know. I just gave you the facts."

"You want facts, I'll give you facts!" Yuri spat back. "You and your *kind* are all going to be killed! Why? Because you prefer to be the enemy of the Reich!"

"What do you mean '*kind*,' Yuri? You're talking about Jews! Don't forget, they're your *kind* too!"

"Shut up! I'm German. I'm not a Jew! My ancestors' name was Klagman, not Cohen! We've been over this before!"

"Kagan, Cohen, they're one and the same and you know it!" Anatoly shot back. "You just better make sure your 'golden boy' doesn't find out who you really are! Anyway, what does all this have to do with Sonya? What did you want to tell me about her?"

"As I told you earlier, it has nothing to do with Sonya. I only used her name to get you here today."

"What do you mean, *you only used her name to get me here today*?" Suddenly, an icy chill of fear settled in Anatoly's stomach. It quickly turned to anger as he began to realize what was happening. Yuri had to protect his own backside, no matter what or *who* the cost. Heavy footsteps in the distance confirmed his suspicions. Anatoly looked Yuri in the eyes. Yuri looked the other way. "Why? I thought we were friends?"

"Because . . . because I had no choice," he lied. "They knew we were friends. If I didn't help them find you, I was told that I would lose the right to the exclusive . . ."

"Did you sell your friend to keep your little secret or to keep the exclusive rights to televise a madman? Which is it, Yuri?"

"Listen to yourself, Anatoly. It's your own fault. How can you call our leader and lord a madman?" Yuri asked, skirting the real issue—not wanting to admit it even to himself. "You can't go around saying those things about him without paying a price. It was only a matter of time before you were caught. You've made your bed, now you must . . ."

"The kiss of Judas. Oh Yuri, I'm so sorry for you. Your leader and lord cannot mock the name of Almighty God and His Yeshua and get away with it! Soon you will understand my words, *when the true God of Israel repays wrath with wrath. When the Day of the Lord destroys your 'god of this world,' his followers, and you. Soon, Yuri, very soon. Watch for the sign in the sun, moon, and stars . . .*"

"Anatoly, please understand. I had no choice," Yuri pleaded as a group of four armed men from Hitler's Imperial Guard surrounded Anatoly, handcuffed him, and began to lead him off.

"What are you going to do with him?" Yuri yelled after them.

"Be on the Temple Mount at 3:00 P.M. sharp," one of the men called back over his shoulder. "Command performance. I don't think you'll want to miss it!"

"Remember my words," were the last words Yuri remembered Anatoly saying, "watch for the sign in the sun, moon, and stars!"

Although beaten and bleeding, barely able to walk on his own, Anatoly felt strangely detached and unafraid as the procession moved along the ancient pavement. It slowly made its way to the Temple Mount, having begun at the police station at the Western wall. No matter how hard they had tried, he had endured their torture and refused to give them the information they wanted. He knew his publicity value was far greater than any information they might glean from him. His torturers had been given orders from the top: keep him alive, at all costs. He didn't care what they did to him. His only concern was for Sonya, and at least for now she was still okay. Yuri had simply used her name to bait the trap.

As for Yuri, that was God's business. God was not mocked. He would deal with the poor fool when He was ready! Yuri informed the world at large, but could never see beyond his own little speck of sand in which he was king, the focal point. He just didn't know any better. Soon he would.

Like hundreds of martyrs before him in history, Anatoly did not find this ugly world a hard place to leave. For all intents and purposes, his work in the cities was practically finished. The Parousia Foundation would mop up the few he had missed. He had no fear for his life, only for the spiritual life of Sonya. *Turn her heart toward You, Father. Keep her safe until she sees the face of Your Son, Iesus.*

Hitler and Sergei awaited their arrival on the Temple Mount. When the macabre procession reached the temple, Hitler led them to the altar outside the Holy of Holies, a replica of the place of sacrifice where the priests had slaughtered the sacrificial animals over two thousand years ago.

"Here!" Hitler commanded. "Bring him to me over here!"

"Sonya!" Shimon shouted as he dashed up to her, excited and out of breath. "Come quickly! You've got to see this!"

He led her to the communications center in the back of #1 cavern, pushing through the crowd already there, jostling to see the television set perched on top of a stack of wooden boxes.

"It's a CNN report," Shimon explained. "Yuri Kagan's doing a live report from the Temple Mount. Something really strange is happening there."

"What in the world are you talking about?" said Sonya.

"I think Bulgakov's about to make an example out of someone."

"Quiet!" Sonya demanded. "That's Bulgakov!"

She watched the procession, as it approached the Beautiful Gate. The procession entered the main temple area, and made its way up to the altar that stood before the massive temple doors. She watched as the man she had once believed in and served, walked over to the altar of sacrifice. Two guards followed closely behind him, holding a man between them. As they turned, the camera caught a partial side view of their prisoner. It was only a glimpse, but it was enough.

"Anatoly!" Sonya cried out. What was he doing there? What was Bulgakov going to do? Her heart pounded in fear and her knees threatened to give way. She pushed closer to the screen, even as she wanted to turn away.

The cameraman followed the surrealistic action taking place in front of the towering limestone temple. Sonya watched in disbelief as the all-seeing television eye entered and panned slowly around the courtyard where Anatoly stood, surrounded by Bulgakov's Imperial Guard.

Suddenly, the camera focused in on Bulgakov, waiting beside the altar of sacrifice. At his feet was a large wooden block.

"Here! Bring him to me over here!" he commanded. His strident voice seemed to mock Sonya, as if he knew she was watching.

The two guards forced Anatoly to his knees and pressed his neck onto the wooden block. As they stepped back, Sergei handed Hitler a massive axe handle, topped by a wicked-looking blade that glistened in the afternoon sunlight.

When Bulgakov raised the blade above Anatoly's head, Sonya lost consciousness. She was spared from hearing the solid "thunk" that came from the television's speaker. Those beside her gave a collective gasp.

The scene cut to an anchorman sitting in a newsroom, scores of television monitors at his back. "Why isn't Yuri doing the final segment on this one?" the studio anchorman asked no one in particular. "I thought he was hot to do these wrap-ups that are networked around the world!"

"Beats me. All I know is that he backed out at the last minute. But don't look a gift horse in the mouth. Take advantage of the opportunity," 'no one in particular' answered back.

"Okay, it's his loss." The red light flickered on, telling the anchorman he was live. "For there to be peace and plenty, there must be order," he intoned. "As our leader has told us, all must take the mark. All who refuse are traitors and will die the death we all witnessed a few moments ago. What you have just witnessed today was the beheading of the leader of a huge terrorist group here in Israel, Anatoly Altshuler, the number one man on Hitler's most-wanted list! Our glorious leader, Adolf Hitler, has asked that his execution be televised 'for all the world to see,' as an example of what will happen to the others when they are caught."

Sonya slowly became aware of Shimon asking her if she was all right. She sat up and looked around. She had been taken to a small cave nearby and was attended by Shimon and an older woman whom she did not know. She tried to rise but Shimon placed a heavy hand on her shoulder. "You mustn't get up, you're in shock," he said.

"No . . . no . . . I can't stay," she stuttered, still disoriented.

"Please listen to us, dear," the older woman said compassionately. "Stay until you feel better."

"Feel better?" Sonya looked at the two of them in disbelief. Had they any idea what she had just witnessed? How could they comprehend that the blade that took Anatoly's life, took her soul as well? They did not know of her love for him, of the hope she held for their future together. She would survive. She would kill Nikolai Bulgakov herself. But feel better? Never! Only pacified when her revenge was complete.

"I have to go. Please, you've been very kind but I cannot stay here." She stumbled past them as they stood mutely watching her.

A few minutes later, outside, she took the narrow footpath to the top of the limestone bluff. A gentle wind blew past, ruffling her hair. She pushed the heavy auburn strands behind her ears. Now that she had no time to bother with haircuts, her hair was getting longer, the way she had worn it when she first met Anatoly. Tears streamed down her face, and she sank onto a low boulder and stared out across the valley. She wanted to remember his dear, handsome face, but all she could remember was the hungry roar of the mob that surrounded him during his last moments. She would never forget.

Her heart ached, but it had to vie with her raging mind. Anatoly was dead, brutally murdered by that monster—the man she had trusted . . . the man she had killed for! He had lied to her! And he had killed everyone she loved. Yacov, Papa, and now Anatoly.

She jerked her head up and looked in the direction of Jerusalem, as if somehow she could see the object of her hatred, but all she could see were the mountains in between. *Her mind spun with a hatred for Bulgakov that would drive her until she saw him dead. That man was hers to kill. She alone had the right to take his life. She had been the pawn that set up his presidency in Russia; the pawn that had unwittingly given him control of Israel; and in payment for her services, he had taken those she loved from her. She would find him and kill him. Tear him to bloody pieces. Her mouth filled with the powerful salty taste of her hatred.*

She would have her revenge. She would kill his soldiers, destroy his government, and, in the end, she would kill him too. No matter what it took, she would kill him with her own hands! Revenge was the only emotion with the power to draw out the pain of her loss.

Holocaust II—6 Months

Yuri Kagan tried to relax, without success. Being the official channel through which Adolf Hitler spoke to the world had its demands; but it also set him apart from every other newscaster in the world. He had paid the price for this privilege. Hitler had delivered, as promised. His ancestry had been the secret of only one other man—Anatoly Altschuler. Now it was only his secret and his alone! Israel was where the action was, and he was the one responsible for bringing the news to the world. He had sold his soul to Hitler, but he had reaped the world in the bargain!

Today, however, the broadcast was a command performance. The subject matter made Yuri uneasy, especially after the part he had played in Anatoly's execution.

Sergei Lomonosov had called CNN's Tel Aviv office the day before, to set up the unprecedented event. Hitler wanted to give a live interview and he specifically wanted Yuri to conduct it. Now, as broadcast time approached, the uneasiness he had experienced since that day in the gardens of Jaffa, began again to take its toll on Yuri.

The backdrop was the Lion's Den, Hitler's palatial private residence on the hill overlooking Jerusalem. For the past two hours, CNN technicians had been scrambling, setting up reflectors, stringing wires, and positioning cameras and chairs.

Yuri's head snapped up as he heard the director's voice in his earphone. "We're ready, Yuri. Look to your right."

Turning his head, as ordered, Yuri saw the leader of the world waiting for his cue.

The earpiece cracked again. "He'll walk on as soon as you start talking. Okay, the show's yours," the director continued. "Give me the nod when you're ready. Five seconds later you'll be live."

Yuri exhaled as he felt the adrenaline kick in; then he nodded. Five seconds later he heard, "You're on," and the red light on the center camera winked.

"This is Yuri Kagan, live from the Lion's Den in Jerusalem

with a special report on the state of the Reich. With me today is our glorious leader, Adolf Hitler."

At Yuri's first words, the trim figure had begun striding onto the set, his military uniform immaculate, his shoulders straight. Hitler smiled, his blazing eyes inviting several billion viewers into his home and his confidence. They sat down in the two strategically positioned chairs and faced the cameras. Yuri felt his own interviewer's edge returning.

"*Mein Führer*," he began, automatically reverting to his second language, "could you share with us your vision for the Fourth Reich?"

"It would be my pleasure, *Herr* Kagan. Particularly since I see nothing but peace and prosperity for the Reich for the next thousand years. I think that should take care of any immediate concerns you may have regarding the state of the Reich," he laughed. Then the blue-gray eyes softened purposefully, his face metamorphosed into a look of sad remorse. "There are, of course, a few hard labor contractions associated with giving birth to such a glorious kingdom as the Fourth Reich. But when that's behind us, every citizen of the Reich will enjoy a future far beyond anything they have ever imagined. But we must all pull together to eliminate the enemy that still exists within our ranks."

"You mention 'the enemy that still exists within our ranks,' " said Yuri. "Could you tell our viewers who you are referring to?"

"Of course," said Hitler, hoping his feigned sincerity was moving the listening audience as much as it was this gullible interviewer. "As I'm sure you are aware, Mr. Kagan, there must be order before there can be peace. Unfortunately, this is still not acceptable to a small group of rebels who have been able, thus far, to escape our detection."

As prearranged, the CNN director cut to scenes of men and women being rounded up by Fourth Reich troops, stopping short of the actual extermination. In many cases, the setting was a church or a synagogue. Some clasped forbidden crosses; others wore skullcaps and prayer shawls. All struggled in vain against their captors. None carried the required mark.

"Those who refuse to bear the mark of our great Reich's

leader have sealed their own fate by their own choice. They can blame no one but themselves. They have been given ample opportunity to yield to the common good. Since they refuse, they have been branded as enemies of the Fourth Reich—and for the Reich to remain strong, her enemies must be eliminated! To allow their outright rebellion and deplorable subversive actions to continue threatens the very peace and prosperity I have promised to our faithful citizens."

"I have heard that it is the Christians and the Jews, specifically, that refuse to bear your mark," Yuri stated as he had been told to do, earlier.

Hitler smiled. "Not so, Mr. Kagan. Not so at all. In fact," he boasted, "the majority of Christians have already recanted their misplaced faith in their false Judeo-Christian God, and have vowed their allegiance and loyalty to me, their true leader and lord. That is true also of *many* who are Jewish in lineage. Only the extreme, the incorrigible religious fanatics, have refused to submit. They call themselves 'aliens' to all that we hold to and embrace. In reality, these enemies of the Reich name themselves well—they have become 'aliens' to the good we hope to accomplish for our people. Every society has a few of these remaining, and they must be purged from among us!" He paused briefly, looking straight into the center camera. "But I want all of your listeners to know that *most Jews and Christians have taken the mark, and are now loyal citizens of the Reich*, enjoying the peace and prosperity only the Fourth Reich can give to the faithful."

The director cut to selected propaganda, of abundant harvests and huge stores with jammed shelves, then segued into various shots from around the world, each a compelling vignette of wealth and personal happiness, carefully keeping the struggling masses out of the camera's view. Then the director cut back to the interview.

"Do you remember how things were, Mr. Kagan, just a little over a half a year ago? How so many of your listeners initially feared the Fourth Reich?" Hitler asked. "Well, today all that has changed. The wars are over! You go to bed with your stomachs full! Your children are safe and being well educated. Your elderly are given the medical care they need at no cost!

You have job security as never before. The Fourth Reich has brought peace and prosperity to the entire world!"

The camera shot came in closer and focused on Hitler's face. He turned and looked directly at the billions who were watching this special interview, finishing with a plea: "But you must all help us stamp out the few who remain, those who resist the good that we seek to do for all! *Until they have all been eliminated, the peace and prosperity we enjoy is at risk.* Do you understand me? All the things you enjoy are at risk! They want all this for themselves. Help us eliminate them—today! Help us purge out the misfits that evolution has failed to eliminate! If you know where one of these rebels is hiding, report that location to us, immediately. If you see one who refuses the mark, kill him. As of now, the Reich will double the reward for any who are caught and killed! The peace and prosperity of the Reich must take precedence over all else. Your first loyalty must be to the Fourth Reich and to me. I have spoken. Thank you, Mr. Kagan. That is all."

"This is Yuri Kagan, bringing you a special report from our glorious leader and lord, Adolf Hitler, CNN News, the Lion's Den, Jerusalem. Good night."

Holocaust II—11 Months

Tim Jackson was seventeen and not at all happy with his life. He had never enjoyed living on a farm, away from all the action the big cities offered. He and his mother lived with her parents because there wasn't any other choice—she said. Why couldn't she get a job so they could live in the city? He swept a hand through his unruly blond hair as he tried to get comfortable, propped up in bed.

"Tim, turn that thing down," his mother, Sandra, shouted from the den.

Tim cursed and waved an obscene hand signal toward the den as he got up and walked through discarded clothes to his sound system. He plugged in his headphones and trailed the long cord back to his bed, where he flopped down again.

There, now the old lady can enjoy her soaps, he thought in irritation. She never thought of anyone but herself anyway.

Tim and his mother were alone now. His father had left his mother for someone younger and more exciting. He hadn't even bothered with a divorce. Apparently it was too much trouble. They didn't know where he was, and really didn't care. Tina, Tim's sister, would have been fifteen this coming April. Tim knew she had been on drugs, because he was on them too and had often procured them for both himself and his sister. But unlike him, Tina had not been smart and had overdosed after her last birthday party. Now she was forever fourteen. Perhaps that was why his mother insisted on living in the boondocks.

Tim felt rather than heard the summons. He shivered, and his guts rolled up in a knot. He threw off the headphones and dashed through the hall to the den, the Emblem's call flailing around inside his head. His mother was already kneeling before the Reich Emblem he had made by gluing CD cases into the form of the swastika, over which he had taped three large sixes. The Emblem rested on top of the TV, and behind it hung a small Fourth Reich flag. Tim slid to a stop and knelt.

He had once made the mistake of ignoring the summons. He would never do it again. On that occasion the demon had flayed every nerve ending in his body, reducing him to a screaming, writhing wreck. He had been too embarrassed to tell his mother about it when she returned home.

A red glow sparkled and danced about the black disembodied face that leered out at them from the center of the Reich Emblem. The eyes glowed greenish-white, above a ridged nose punctuated by large nostrils. The lips parted in a sneer. A sulfur dioxide and ozone stench permeated the room.

"You are learning," the demon said. "Your master has a command for you. The Teasdales, who live down the road from you, are traitors. You must kill them. Others will help you."

"But..." Tim began.

He cared nothing for the Teasdales, but he wasn't sure he was up to killing someone. He had never done anything like that before. At this momentary resistance, the demon seized control of his nervous system and shot excruciating signals into his vulnerable brain.

"No!" he screamed in pain. "I'll do it! I'll do it! Please stop!"

The pain ceased, and the voice continued. "If you fail, you will die. Go! Do it now! Others are outside waiting for you." The image winked out with a soft, plopping sound.

Sandra looked at her son. "Can you do it?"

"Yeah, Mom. I can do it. Anyway, I can use the bucks. Now leave me alone."

She didn't frown, she didn't smile. She just turned back to her television program.

Tim grabbed a large knife from the kitchen and stalked out into the front yard. He shivered. He didn't know if his shakes were his reaction to what he had to do, or to the cool evening breeze.

In the distance, he saw a man and a woman slowly shuffling down the gravel road, like two zombies, heading toward the Teasdale home. The man was carrying an ax. He didn't know either of them.

Tim fell in behind them. When they arrived at the farmhouse, the woman mechanically opened the screen door. The man brought the back portion of the ax head down on the handle of the inside door, breaking it open with a reverberating crash. Without having said one word to each other, the three entered, knowing what had to be done.

Mike Teasdale felt the inner urging while he was still a mile from the farmhouse. Whether it was some sense of nearby evil or simply the need for caution, he wasn't sure, but he slowed the car and turned off the headlights, driving the rest of the way by the pale light of a nearly full moon.

It's time for us to flee to Camp Maranatha, he thought. He and several others had built the place of refuge not long after returning home from Russia, naming it after the Christian conference grounds where Marlee and he had met as young adults.

Most of their friends were already at the camp, but Marlee had insisted on staying by his side until their work was done. He had assumed they would be safe here in the country for a little while yet—or as safe as anyone could be with the Antichrist and his demonic armies on the loose. He thought about Sonya, living so close to the Beast's headquarters. Like millions of Americans, he had witnessed the execution of his dear friend and child in Christ, Anatoly Altshuler. But he had lost contact with Sonya over two years ago. Up until Holocaust II had begun, he had kept in touch with Eitan Shachar in Jerusalem, but when the Antichrist broke loose in full force, they had terminated all contact. Prior to that, however, he had learned, through Eitan's encrypted e-mail messages, that Sonya had returned to Israel and that she and Anatoly had been involved in setting up camps for the Jewish refugees. Sadly, Eitan had reported, God had not yet dealt with Sonya's heart. As he often did, Mike offered a prayer for the protection of the Jews in hiding and especially for Sonya's salvation.

He turned into the drive and parked by the dilapidated barn in the back. He shut off the engine, but waited for the cassette tape to finish. It was one he had listened to often, a sermon on 1 Corinthians 13 preached years ago by a dear and godly friend. He turned up the volume as the sermon concluded. "But the greatest of these is love." The familiar words prompted thoughts of what was happening in the church. How could so many who claimed the name of Christ, take the mark of the Beast, he wondered, and then betray those who were determined to remain faithful to their Lord?

But he knew this was exactly what Christ had foretold would happen. This was the great apostasy the Scriptures warned would occur when the whole world was put to the test. Yes, the mark of Antichrist certainly did separate the wheat from the tares, the genuine Christians from the "look-alikes," Christians "in name only."

As Mike ejected the cassette and stowed it in the glove compartment, he looked toward the darkened house. Marlee must have gone to bed. He checked the digital clock on the dash. No wonder. It was past midnight. He got out of the car and walked across the yard, zipping up his light jacket against the cool northwest wind that refused to let spring have her way uncontested. As he reached the steps, he got out his keys and pulled open the screen door.

Suddenly, his blood ran cold. The front door had been

smashed in; the lock hanging by bent screws, its bolt extended and useless. Beyond the threshold, blackness greeted him. He reached for the light switch and flipped it on. Ripped-open sofa cushions littered the floor. The china hutch stood empty, its doors shattered and every dish smashed. Books were scattered everywhere, covers and pages torn.

"Marlee!" Mike screamed.

He charged down the debris-strewn hallway to their bedroom, frantically calling her name. The bedroom door gaped like an open wound, as though someone had taken an ax to it. He reached in and turned on the light, but he could already smell the blood. The harsh overhead light illuminated the gruesome scene and the blood-soaked sheets that partially covered Marlee's body.

He staggered to the bed and groped for her hand, knowing he would find no pulse. Her image shimmered through his tears and his insides twisted into knots. She had obviously died in agony.

Mike bent double and vomited, then began to shake as he sobbed. He had never felt more alone and helpless in his life. His agonizing grief turned to rage, and then to raw hate. What he wanted, more than anything, was revenge—to kill the animals who had done this.

"Oh, God!" he cried out. "Help me! Please, help me. I loved her so!"

He sobbed and prayed the same imploring refrain, over and over again, until peace descended. This life was not the end—he clung to that promise. It was only the prelude to an indescribable life of joy and peace—a life Marlee had now begun. And justice would be measured out by the only One qualified to give it. "*Never seek your own revenge, beloved, but leave room for the wrath of God.*" The words washed over him like a cleansing wave.

Another verse sprang out at him, like a lifeline. "*And if I go and prepare a place for you, I will come again, and receive you to Myself; that where I am, there you may be also.*" He would be with Marlee again soon—when the signs in the heavens announced the coming of Christ. Then he would see his Savior, face to face.

Grabbing a shovel from the garage, he walked out into the backyard and picked a spot under a scraggly oak. When they had first moved here, he had wanted to cut down the ugly tree. But Marlee had insisted on saving it. Anything that had weathered the years and endured, as that tree had, deserved to live, she once said. Great racking sobs engulfed him as he stood beneath the gnarled limbs. Yes, this was the right place.

It took him over two hours to dig a grave in the rocky soil and bury Marlee's body, wrapped in a clean sheet. Then he washed up, changed into clean clothes, and packed his duffel bag.

Before daybreak, he was traveling west across desolate back roads, heading toward the Santiago Mountains and Camp Maranatha, alone.

TWENTY-FOUR

Holocaust II — 24 Months

Hitler looked down at the relief map of Israel spread out before him on the large table in the plotting room in the south wing of the temple, just off the Holy of Holies.

"Sergei!" he barked. "No more excuses! I want them all! No exceptions! Now!" he thundered. "Every Jew here in Israel must bear my mark. Those who don't must be killed! If I can't clean up the mess in my own backyard, how can I expect to see the rest of the world do what I can't do myself? It's been almost two years. That's one year, eleven months too long."

"But, master, you know we are doing all we can," his Enforcer protested. "We've been over this again and again. Every Jew and every Christian that refuses to bear your mark, or give homage to the Reich Emblem has been hunted down and killed. Millions have already been found. Most have recanted and taken your mark, and the rest have been executed! The few that are left are in hiding, but it's only a matter of time. If they show their heads in public, they are immediately identified by the Reich Emblems and killed by the good citizens of the Reich."

"That's not enough!"

"That isn't all we're doing. Your promise of financial rewards for those who give us the location of family or friends in hiding . . . pure genius! We've already paid out billions, so we know the program is a tremendous success. Except for the few pockets of Jews still in hiding here in Israel, and a few Christians that may still be in hiding in your dominant Christian countries—like in North America and a few of the other quasi-Christian nations—we've got them all."

"And here in Israel? Why can't we find the fools hiding right under our noses?"

"Several million have already been caught and executed. Our troops continue to scour the cities and the rural areas, looking for any of the rebels who may still be in hiding."

"What about Petra?" Hitler asked.

"There is no way anything could have survived the tremendous earthquake and flooding that occurred in southern Jordan several years ago. Your Prince assured us that none of those people lived!" assured Sergei. "Since then, we've picked up nothing to indicate any life down there, no radio transmissions, no sign of any activity at all. The reconnaissance flights continue to spot nothing, although the earthquakes changed the terrain significantly and we don't have the overhead visibility of the area we previously had. Either way, though, there are absolutely no signs of life, and realistically, I think it's a waste of time to put any energy into that area, especially in light of the fact that we know of other general areas where they do exist."

"You must understand, Sergei, I will not go back!" shouted Hitler. "If I don't eliminate them *all*, I will go back to the abyss! My Prince has spoken. I must kill *all* the rebels. Then he will kill their Leader. Until then, our job is not complete! Do you understand? The traitors, the Jews, the Christians— they must *all* be killed or I will be sent back to the abyss! You don't know what it's like. I do! I've been down in hell, Sergei— and that is where you will go, too, if we fail. All the world must bear my mark. No exceptions!"

"I understand, my master. We are searching them out— each and every one of them, in every country, as I speak."

"What about that aggressive bunch up north, near the Golan Heights?" Hitler shot back.

"Our troops have engaged them several times. True, the rebels have killed more of ours than we have of theirs, but still that isn't many. They're well armed, well organized, and well hidden—but eventually we'll get them."

"The report said they were Israeli soldiers?"

"The bodies we recovered were wearing IDF uniforms, that's all we know for sure. IDF or not, they know how to fight."

"And what of Sonya Petrov? Any more news of her? She is the one responsible. Find her, and we find the rest!"

Sergei always dreaded his master's questions concerning Sonya. For all intents and purposes, the woman seemed to have disappeared off the face of the Earth. But there was the talk that persisted, that wouldn't go away. It was this continual rumor-mill talk that was driving his master mad. As long as Sonya lived, he had failed, not only in what his Prince had called him to do, but in the eyes of those who knew of his former relationship with her, as well. No matter that the world enjoyed peace and prosperity as never before. Sonya had become the watermark of his success or failure. Rumors persisted of the "commando woman" with a score to settle because the man she loved had been tortured and executed. Sonya had become his master's obsession, and no one had any idea where she was.

"We can't pin her down exactly," he said evasively, "but it can only be a matter of time. Our intelligence sources continue to tell me that she is not with the northern group. In fact, we suspect the Golan fighters may be independent from the southern groups, which is where I suspect we'll find Sonya."

Hitler stamped his foot. "We've been over this before. Find her! I want these guerrilla Jews wiped out and I want Sonya captured and brought to me, alive. I want to make an example of her for all the world to see! Find her and kill the rest!" he screamed.

Sergei took a deep breath. "Then, master, I suggest it's time to collapse our defense perimeter and comb the entire countryside, one meter at a time. The ones hiding in the cities have already been found and killed." He took the pointer and indicated the troop positions. "Given the topography, it will take quite a while, but I don't see any other way of doing it. If the spacing of the dragnet is close enough, no one will be able to slip by unnoticed between the seams. But it will be slow, and it will take every man we have now patrolling the border."

He paused. "Give the order, and we will begin our sweep in toward Jerusalem, flushing everyone out."

Hitler looked at the map for a long time, envisioning his soldiers working their way methodically across the land, killing every unmarked Jew in their path. That should do it, he thought.

"First the children of God, then the Son of God," he snarled. "I will never go back to the abyss!"

Anatoly could see very clearly—which was strange, since he did not have a body. But then neither did the other souls who had the honor of residing under God's altar in heaven, souls who, like himself, had been beheaded for their faithfulness to Iesus, his Yeshua-Meshiah. With his wonderful new vision, he saw his fellow martyrs as clearly as he saw the ruthless carnage taking place on Earth at the hands of Antichrist.

As the familiar, brilliant glow approached, Anatoly looked up into the loving eyes of Yeshua. He had a question he wanted to ask, but before he could speak, one of the other souls voiced what was on everyone's mind concerning the events happening on Earth.

"How much longer, O God, before the Day of Your wrath begins . . . until You give Your sign in the sun, moon, and stars announcing the great Day of the Lord?"

The answer that came was rich with compassion and understanding.

"Soon, My brothers and sisters. Very soon," said the Lord. "I will avenge your blood, as well as the blood of all saints who have died for My Name's sake, for your blood is precious in My sight. But your number is not yet complete. When it is, I will deal with your enemies."

With these words, Iesus turned and pointed to rows of gleaming white robes near the altar.

"Here are your robes," He said. "You will wear these when that time comes. Just a little longer. Until then, wait."

PART 4

THE SIGN IN THE SUN, MOON, AND STARS

And I looked when He broke the sixth seal,
and there was a great earthquake;
and the sun became black as sackcloth made of hair,
and the whole moon became like blood;
and the stars of the sky fell to the earth,
as a fig tree casts its unripe figs when shaken by a great wind.
And the sky was split apart like a scroll when it is rolled up;
and every mountain and island were moved out of their place.
And the kings of the earth
and the great men
and the commanders
and the rich
and the strong
and every slave
and free man,
hid themselves in the caves
and among the rocks of the mountains;
and they said to the mountains and to the rocks,
"Fall on us and hide us from the presence of Him
who sits on the throne,
and from the wrath of the Lamb;
for the great day of their wrath has come;
and who is able to stand?"

—*Revelation 6:12–17*

TWENTY-FIVE

Holocaust II — 24 Months

Yuri looked up at the large monitor as his lead story aired worldwide over CNN. It had been exactly two years since the inception of the Fourth Reich. There were clips from all the major cities, capturing the wild celebration of Camelot Day around the world. Every city sparkled in affluence — gone were the scourge of slums and ghettoes. Long parades snaked down the main arteries, while revelers jammed the sidewalks. Huge banners proclaimed the prosperity that Hitler had brought to a grateful world.

"You did a good job," said Andrei, watching the panoply.

"Thanks," Yuri replied. "Just reporting the facts." He waved toward a shot of thousands of expensive cars parked outside a new plant in Colombo, Sri Lanka. "He's done exactly what he promised from the beginning. Our leader has given us a standard of living beyond our wildest dreams."

Yuri's optimistic report continued for another fifteen minutes.

Holocaust II — 24 to 30 Months, Exact Timing Unknown

Things are finally going smoothly, Hitler thought. Peace and prosperity for the world, and, finally, progress toward the total elimination of the enemy! The dragnet was slowly being drawn in, here in Israel as well as in other countries that still had pockets of resistance, particularly in the southern portions of the United States, as well as a few remote areas of China,

South Korea, Kenya, and Australia. To the best of their intelligence data, that was all that was left, other than several small, isolated groups still undetected here in Israel. Only those who kept out of sight of the Reich Emblems had managed to escape this long. But his armies were implementing the noose-tightening plan worldwide, and his promise of rewards to all who helped locate those in hiding continued to pay big dividends in his relentless search for the few rebels who remained. It was only a matter of time before *all* Jews and Christians who rebelled against him would be found and killed. All except Sonya, he thought. I want her alive. I will take care of her like I took care of Anatoly—personally!

On the plot map in front of them, Sergei was pointing out the progress they were making in Israel. The main thrust of the border guard had collapsed down to the Judean Wilderness, the biggest push being in the Jehoshaphat Valley, a small remote valley south and east of Jerusalem. Because of the difficult terrain in this general area, he said, pockmarked with small caves and caverns, there was a high likelihood that a large contingent of Jews could hole up somewhere in this territory.

Except for isolated skirmishes with the rebels, the rest of the world continued to enjoy peace and prosperity, and things were going to get even better. A steady stream of government officials from the world's nations came to meet regularly with Hitler on the Temple Mount, each one bearing gifts and only praise for their leader and lord, and for all the Fourth Reich was doing for their countries. From here in his temple headquarters, he was truly master of all the world. My Prince must be pleased, he thought to himself.

No sooner had this thought crossed his mind, when a tremor shook the temple. The shock felt as though it came from deep beneath the city.

Sergei dropped the pointer on the map, and the two men hurried to the window to see what was happening. The plotting room, normally well lit by outside light, was rapidly losing its morning brightness as the sun began to dim; yet there wasn't a cloud in the sky to block the rays from the sun. The two men quickly made their way out onto the open platform of the Temple Mount. As they watched, the blazing orb shifted through the spectrum from white to yellow to dull red and finally to black.

Streetlights clicked on as the city was thrown into sudden blackness, the stars making an unexpected, subdued appearance. They twinkled for a moment, then started crisscrossing across the sky, each leaving only a momentary trail of light in its path before disappearing.

The platform on the Temple Mount began to move under their feet. Another tremor . . . and another . . . shook the ground, the shock waves rising to a dangerous peak. All around the city, ancient stonework ground and shattered. The Temple Mount platform rippled like a storm-tossed sea; small chunks of facade fell from the Dome of the Rock and from the new temple, where moments earlier the two men had been working. Power sources were interrupted or destroyed by the violent shaking of the ground. The street lights, which had clicked on only minutes before, now began to fail, drowning large patches of the city in inky blackness. Finally, the lights on the Temple Mount went out, leaving a ghostly afterglow as the bulbs cooled.

Then, just as quickly as it had begun, the quake stopped. Not a breeze stirred. Disembodied voices floated through the air, carried clearly over the dead calm, sounding frightened and alone.

"What is that?" Sergei asked.

A faint red glow tinged the eastern horizon.

"How should I know?" Hitler snapped.

The red shifted to yellow and quickly became a brilliant white wall sweeping over the Earth. The two men cringed, as if the light were pressing them down. The wall flashed overhead and moved toward the western horizon, its wake continuing to shine over the city, providing ample light to replace the sun.

"Look!" Sergei shouted, pointing.

"I'm not blind, fool!" Hitler's anger flared.

A ruby-red pinpoint of light emerged high above Jerusalem. Slowly it became larger until those below could see a man dressed in a blinding white robe, shining with an iridescent glow. He had a golden band about his chest and His being was surrounded by an eerie red glow. He slowly descended from above, in the direction of the Mount of Olives, disappearing momentarily while still high above the summit, then reappearing in the midst of billowing white clouds that were illuminated by His presence.

Suddenly, the stillness was broken by the sound of heralding trumpets—loud, clear, and majestic. Then a voice, unlike anything those on Earth had ever heard, announced: *"Yeshua has come! Judgment Day has arrived! Let the Day of the Lord begin!"*

At this, explosive sounds burst through the air.

"What's that noise?" Sergei yelled out to his master.

"It must be our troops, firing hand missiles at that thing up there! Good for them!" Hitler shouted excitedly. "I want the name of the man who destroys whatever that is. He will be rewarded beyond anything he could ever imagine!"

"That voice said that thing up there is Yeshua," Sergei contradicted, "Iesus, the leader of the rebels!" Sergei shouted, trying to be heard above the noise.

"I don't give a damn who or what it is!" Hitler spat back. "It can't avoid all the missiles we're throwing at it!"

But Sergei shook his head. "Those aren't missiles," he cried, pointing toward the sky.

Hitler ground his teeth in anger and frustration as he began to realize that what he had thought were missiles were actually bodies drifting up into the air, each with an explosive burst, breaking free from the gravity of Earth. They seemed to be coming from the cemeteries, then a few from here, from there, from all over. They became clearly visible under the supernatural light that crossed the heavens from the east to the west, as they sped, in gleaming white robes, toward the ruby red light in the cloud high above the Mount of Olives.

Soon, brilliant rays of light filled the sky, streaking from every compass point on the globe, white highways of resurrected dead and raptured living, all converging on the cloud that stood still over Jerusalem.

"Do you know what's going on?" Sergei asked.

"Yes, you idiot!" snapped Hitler. "I know what's going on."

Mike Teasdale shivered and pulled his jacket tighter against his body. It was almost midnight and the moon was full and glorious, giving the surrounding brush a dreamlike quality. Moments before he had been thinking of Marlee, how she had loved these mountains, especially on cool, moonlit nights. Now he was ready to lie down and sleep, another night without her at his side. *Oh,* he groaned inwardly, *how I miss her—how I wish I could be with her! How will I go on without her?*

His reverie was broken by sounds of someone thrashing through the brush on the perimeter of the camp. Then, in the distance, he heard the barking of dogs. He knew immediately what the sounds meant, but how Hitler's hatchetmen—they called themselves Reich Loyalists—had found their remote camp, he had no idea. The rough trail into the small valley had been thoroughly erased. It had been carefully turned back into its original thick tangle of scrub oak and mesquite. From overhead, their camouflaging had made them virtually invisible.

He sighed. As far as he was concerned, it really didn't matter anymore. He had waited long enough. He was tired, and he was lonely. Still, he needed to think about the others.

The intruders' careless advance carried clearly through the still air, slowly coming closer and closer to where he lay. It was obvious that they knew where they were going, and they didn't care who knew it. As they closed in, he could hear the dogs panting and snarling.

Mike winced as a shotgun suddenly erupted less than 20 yards away, over to his right, at the same time he heard the sound of men approaching directly in front and to the right of him. They were close enough that he could hear the deadly click of a weapon's safety being slid from on to off. He was surrounded.

The gun fired from dead ahead. As it did, he caught a glimpse of a man's sadistic grin, illuminated by the muzzle flash. From then on, everything seemed to happen in slow motion. He rolled onto his back, clutching the center of his chest. . . . His fingers slid into a wet hole the size of his fist. . . .

His heart pumped out his life blood in a gushing stream. . . . He gasped in agony. . . . He was dying. . . . He was going to his Lord. . . .

At that last moment, just before death, Mike felt the Earth begin to shake as the lights began to dim. At first he thought it was death tremors. But he was still conscious. He could hear the yelling around him and the gunfire, as the moon began to disappear, and the stars winked out above him. Then complete silence. Was this some kind of out-of-body experience? He had read about those type of things but never believed in them. Just as quickly as the thought entered his consciousness, he cast it aside. Out-of-head experience, maybe, but not out-of-body. Then he knew. Through dimming eyes, he saw a blazing band of white light sweeping in from the east. It crossed overhead and continued to the western horizon.

Beneath him, the Earth rumbled again and heaved. Above the tumult, he distinctly heard someone call his name, but he could not answer.

A bolt of energy shot through his body, and instantly the grayness of death dropped away. He felt the weightlessness as he began to rise up into the air. He could see again, every detail standing out with breathtaking clarity. He glanced down at his chest. The bloody wound was gone. In its place was a shimmering white robe.

Mike spun about in joy as he realized what was happening. The Rapture had caught him in the moment between life and death. All around him, the other refugees from Camp Maranatha were rising also, their white figures hovering with him, just above the trees.

He looked down at the site where a second before he had been lying in his bedroll, bleeding to death. There, the murderous mob gaped up at them, the savage dogs cowering behind their handlers, tails between their legs.

As the raptured souls in their new, resurrected bodies began to ascend, several of the men below raised their rifles and fired at Mike and the others, emptying their clips. This time, Mike didn't feel a thing. The spent bullets continued their unhindered flight through the darkness, eventually falling to Earth, as whole as when they'd left the barrels of the rifles.

Looking down from the glowing heavens, Mike could see the entire camp now, and the state highway that passed near the secret entrance. In the distance he could soon see San Antonio. And still he climbed.

Brilliant trails of golden fire shot by high overhead, each one traveling east on the highway of light that had emblazoned the Earth only moments ago. The ground was far below now. As he watched, he began to pick up speed. His involuntary path took on a forward motion as he, too, headed toward the east. He had no sensation of speed, but he knew he was traveling faster than any jet.

The coast of North Carolina approached and disappeared beneath him. Beyond, the Atlantic whitecaps sparkled before the trade winds, and almost immediately he was streaking over North Africa and then the blue Mediterranean.

Mike knew his destination, and now he could see the land approaching at incredible speed. No sooner had he glimpsed Tel Aviv to the north, than suddenly Jerusalem loomed into sight.

High above the city hovered a huge white cloud, a ruby-red glow coming from deep inside it with a brilliant white light at its center. Radiant lines converged on the cloud from every point of the compass, so many that they blended into a sea of gold around it.

Mike shot directly over the Temple Mount and then, at undiminished speed, into the cloud above the Mount of Olives.

He had expected to see millions of people packed inside the cloud, but he was alone — except for what appeared to be an angel. This person, dressed in glowing white robes, was radiating the ruby-red presence.

"Welcome, Mike!"

"Where is everyone?" he asked.

"They are being greeted just as you are."

And then, at that moment, Mike's heart swelled with joy, for he realized he was in the presence of his Lord and Savior, Jesus Christ.

"My Lord! How I have longed for this day. I am forever Your servant."

"Give me your hand," He said: "I will take you to the Father."

Then the Son of God gripped Mike's hand and pulled him through the veil and up into heaven.

The worldwide spectacle that had just taken place in the heavens seemed to have gone on for a long time—and none of the detail was lost to those left on Earth, those who could only watch, not participate. But in reality, it had all taken place instantaneously—in the twinkling of an eye.

When it was over, the brilliant white highways girdling the globe rolled up into the splendor over Jerusalem. Then, like a huge ball of fire, the splendor in the clouds hovering above the Mount of Olives shot upward and was gone, depositing an inky blackness over the face of the Earth. It had all happened so quickly. Moments later, most would wonder if it had happened at all! But they would remember the earthquakes, and they would never forget the words: "Judgment Day has arrived!"

Over the next hour or so, the Earth's light sources slowly returned to normal. Only the Earth, scarred by worldwide earthquakes, gave mute testimony to what had just occurred.

Andrei locked down the camera on its tripod and surveyed the scene with a practiced eye. Once again Yuri found himself in the beautiful gardens in relatively untouched Jaffa, beside the Mediterranean. Memories of his last visit here brought back the nauseous feeling he had experienced so often since that day. It was here that Anatoly had warned: Watch for the sign in the sun, moon, and stars . . . the God of Israel will repay wrath with wrath! Was this what Anatoly was warning him about? Had he just witnessed the sign in the sun, moon, and stars? Is this what the thunderous voice referred to when it pronounced to the world that 'Judgment Day has arrived'?"

To the northeast lay Tel Aviv, smoke from fires obscuring the heart of the once-proud city. Many of the high-rise buildings were severely damaged, and some had even collapsed, crushing the stores and shops that lay in their pathway as they tumbled to the ground.

The CNN crew's cell phone chirped. Egor grabbed it, listened for a moment, then handed it to Yuri. The reporter listened, his angry scowl growing deeper by the moment. Finally he snapped the unit shut and threw it down.

"What is it?" Andrei asked.

"Finish the setup! I've been assigned the lead story on the special coverage of this"—he waved his hand toward the distant destruction—"whatever it was that happened. We're live in five minutes. Lucky me. I'm the one who has to put all this into perspective."

"What are you going to do?" Andrei asked.

"I don't know!" Yuri screamed. "Now, move it!"

Five minutes later, Egor gave the nod.

"This is Yuri Kagan, reporting live from Jaffa, Israel. In the distance you can see the city of Tel Aviv, still reeling from the recent earthquake.

"Much has happened in the past few hours. All over the world there have been reports of mysterious lights replacing the sun, things flying through space, major earthquakes, and countless disasters. Mobs are storming the streets in terror. People around the world, from all stations of life—rich, poor, educated, illiterate—are crying out to some unknown God, a higher being that they believe is responsible for the disasters that have ravaged our world. Many are claiming that they heard a voice from heaven warning: 'Judgment Day has arrived!'

"Reports from all over the world indicate that millions have gone into hiding, into any crevice of the land that would offer protection from the falling debris and flying particles associated with the massive destruction that has suddenly devastated the entire world.

"After the peace and tranquility we have all enjoyed in the past few years, the events of the past eight hours have been doubly terrifying.

"In the midst of all this carnage, our illustrious leader, Adolf Hitler, in a press conference several hours ago, assured the world that he will lead us back to recovery and even greater glory in the future. Already steps are being taken to handle this crisis."

"That's it," Egor broke in, cutting off the mike. "No byline today. The studio just cut us off in order to show footage of Hitler's earlier interview with the press."

Andrei switched off the camera. "That was excellent," he said.

"It was garbage!" Yuri grumbled as he tore off his mike. He turned and gazed at the ruined skyline of Tel Aviv. What in the world are we going to do? he wondered, his thoughts returning to the last words of Anatoly, that last day in the gardens of Jaffa.

"What happened?" Gideon Landau asked.

David Gur shook his head, left speechless by what he had just seen.

When the morning light had begun to dim, the two men had hurried to their favorite spot in the stronghold of Petra, the entrance to the Urn Tomb.

They had watched in awe and fear as the sun disappeared. Then the stars had appeared, blazed like comets, and evaporated before their eyes. They clung to each other for balance and support as the Earth began to shake, and the brilliant band of white light streaked across the heavens from east to west, illuminating everything in Petra's rock-bound bowl. In a last burst of glory, golden beams had flashed overhead, coming from every direction, seemingly drawn by a faint ruby-red glow around a pinpoint of white to the northwest, high above the city of Jerusalem.

David tugged at his beard. "Did you hear what I heard?"

"You mean the trumpets?"

"Trumpets, yes. But, more important, the voice?"

"You heard it too? I thought it was my imagination!" said Gideon. " 'Yeshua has come! Judgment Day has arrived! Let the Day of the Lord begin!' What do you make of it?"

"It has to be the sign of the sun, moon, and stars that Anatoly told us about—only I don't remember him telling us about trumpets and voices."

"Or that red glow in the clouds above Jerusalem," Gideon added.

"But it's got to be Him!" said David, awed by the sight taking place in front of him.

"Yeshua?"

"Yeshua!" David looked out across the encampment. Most of the people had come out of the caves and tents, and were now standing in rapt attention, watching the heavens to see what would happen next.

"So what do we do now?" asked Gideon.

David cleared his throat nervously. "We wait! Anatoly told us that when we saw the sign in the heavenlies, we were going to have a Visitor. I think the voice from heaven was telling us that our Visitor is about to arrive. I suggest we get ready."

"You can't be serious?"

"Oh, yes I am! He's been right about everything else, including the flood. I'm not going to bet against him on this one. Are you?"

Gideon hid his chagrin by scuffing his feet. "What do you want me to do?"

"Pass the word to all the leaders—have everyone gather as quickly as they can," David said, pointing to the large assembly area just below where they stood.

"What are you going to tell them once they're assembled?"

"I'm not going to tell them anything. If Anatoly is right, this morning we will have a guest speaker. When He comes, He can tell us whatever is on His mind. Now, let's move," David said, starting to climb down from the tomb.

The heavenly display had vanished back into the morning sunlight, but many still clustered in small groups, talking excitedly about what they had just witnessed. After David and Gideon had given the order to the twelve leaders, the refugees began to gather into twelve large prearranged groups.

Less than half an hour later the two men met again, back at the foot of the tomb.

"Everyone's in place and waiting. What now?" asked Gideon.

"We wait!"

Looking up, David saw a pinpoint of reddish light coming toward them, from directly above, right out of the heavens. Even in broad daylight, the light appeared like a brilliant ruby set against a diamond background. As it came closer, he saw what looked like a man, dressed in iridescent white robes and surrounded by the same rich red glow he had seen earlier, in the clouds above Jerusalem.

A deep silence fell over the assembled refugees as the dazzling figure slowly descended into the center of Petra's fortress, into the very midst of those watching in awe. David and all the others could clearly see red nail prints on the man's hands and feet, the only thing marring the glowing skin. The sight of the nail prints had the effect of a convicting sentence, one that shook every person present, as though each one of them had personally pierced Him through.

Tears began to stream down David's cheeks, and he heard sobs and moaning all around him as, one by one, every man, woman, and child recognized Yeshua of Nazareth, their Meshiah, the Promised One of Israel. Before the figure of their Lord had even touched the ground, everyone had fallen to their knees to worship their King, with sobs of grief and joy.

"Blessed is He who comes in the name of the Lord," said David.

Those around David began repeating the refrain, "Blessed is He who comes in the name of the Lord. . . . Blessed is He who comes in the name of the Lord. . . . Blessed is He . . . ," and others picked it up, until the words rang off the encircling mountain walls, echoing back and forth like thunder.

"Arise," Yeshua commanded, above the din.

All heard and obeyed.

Yeshua held out His arms. "I have chosen you, twelve thousand men from each tribe of Israel. You and your families, this day, are the firstfruits of Israel for Almighty God, the true and only God of Avraham, Yitzchak, and Yaakov. From this moment on, you are My people and I am your God. Soon, your brothers and sisters—those who have also refused to follow this false meshiah—will join you.

"As of this moment, each of you has been sealed with My mark. And by My mark all will know that you are Mine. By My mark, you will be protected from My wrath, soon to fall on everyone bearing the mark of Satan-Meshiah.

"But for now, you must continue to wait and watch," Yeshua said as He started to rise into the air. "The time is short. When the covenant with death has run its course, I will return for you, and together we will claim your Jewish brothers and sisters who are also in hiding. Then they, too, will know that I, Yeshua, am their Meshiah, their God and their King. Wait for Me!"

When He finished speaking, Yeshua ascended high into the heavens until only a red pinpoint of light could be seen. In an instant, it was gone, His last words still ringing in the ears of the 144,000 men and their families, the firstfruits of Israel.

Sonya Petrov and Shimon Kaufman stood on a high limestone outcropping on the south side of the hidden valley, looking toward Jerusalem. At the first tremor, the inhabitants of Camp Moses had rushed out of the caves and caverns, into the valley, to see what was happening. Although the rumbling continued all around, Camp Moses, like Petra, was not affected by the quake. And then it happened: the sun went black, and the stars that appeared in its wake simply disappeared. Everyone gasped in awe as they watched the brilliant band of light sweep across the heavens, from east to west.

When the red glow appeared, followed by the converging golden rays that came from all directions, Sonya had initially thought that Jerusalem was undergoing some sort of missile attack. But then the red glow began to take shape, and the sound of the trumpets and the voice—"Judgment Day has arrived!" That was all she remembered the voice saying. "Judgment Day has arrived!" And then she remembered the words of Anatoly. In that split second, she knew this was the time she had waited for, planned for, trained for. This was the time for revenge!

It had taken over an hour for full daylight to return, but now things were back to normal. Now it all seemed like a dream, but Sonya knew differently.

"It's the sign Anatoly told us about, isn't it?" Shimon asked.

Sonya nodded. "He told us that when we see the sign in the sun, moon, and stars, then . . ."

"Yeshua will return," Shimon finished the sentence for her.

"Judgment Day has arrived!" she corrected, ignoring the part about Yeshua.

"You really think that was Anatoly's Yeshua?" Shimon continued, refusing to let it die.

"I don't know what to think about all this Yeshua stuff," Sonya admitted, having become suspicious of *anyone* who claimed deity as Bulgakov had done. "But one thing I do know for sure: Anatoly said that when we saw the sign in the sun, moon, and stars, Hitler's troops would become our prey—not the other way around, for a change! He told me again and again, this would be our opportunity to strike back, and that's exactly what I heard the voice say: 'Judgment Day has arrived!' This is what we've been waiting for, Shimon—what we've been training for," she said, her expression darkening with determination. "Assemble the troops, load the ammo in the jeeps, and meet me at the outside entrance as soon as possible. It's payback time!"

Shimon hurried off to assemble the 160 IDF-trained soldiers, carefully retrained under Sonya's commando discipline and expertise for this precise moment. They all knew about the sign, that after it was given in the heavenlies, serious work would begin. They knew what they needed to do, and now the time had come to do it!

Sonya cut back across the valley floor, climbed up the narrow stone path leading to the tunnel, and hurried back to the caverns. There, in #4 cavern—dedicated to daytime exercise and training—she walked past the single column of men standing casually but still in rank, up to Shimon. "The jeeps are loaded and ready to go, parked at the bottom of the ridge by the outside entrance," he reported to Sonya.

"This is it!" she said. "Our time has come!"

"We're ready," Shimon said. "I've instructed the sentries." He paused. "Are you sure we have the advantage, Sonya? You know that the Reich outnumbers us, 100 to 1, making the odds against us staggering!"

"Frankly, I don't know what the odds will be, but everything else Anatoly predicted has happened just as he has said, so I'm not going to second-guess him on this one! This is what I've been waiting for! Let's just go out and do it!" She practically ran as she made her way through the caverns to the outside entranceway and down the back side of the northern ridge until she came to the jeeps parked out of sight in the valley below. "Let's go," was all she said as she jumped into the front seat of her jeep and drove off.

The small caravan of military vehicles moved about 10 kilometers to the southwest of Camp Moses. Finally they stopped at an area just behind a ridge that overlooked the east–west Valley of Jehoshaphat. Eitan and Anatoly had both carefully instructed her that their initial counterattack would begin in this specific valley. Nowhere else. For this reason, the valley had been studied carefully, in advance, the terrain and the roads indelibly imprinted on the minds of her men.

Leaving the vehicles parked below, they moved slowly up the back side of the ridge, on foot, until they were directly in the center of the ridge on the north side of the valley. From here they had a commanding view of the valley spread out to the left and right just below them.

An east–west seldom-used dirt road bisected the valley, taking an abrupt turn to the north, between two hills that lay just to the west of where they were positioned. Earlier that morning, one of their scouts had reported a long line of Reich troops entering the valley from the east. Other than camp security, this had been the only area that had been staked out regularly, morning and night, in anticipation of this day. There was no doubt in Sonya's mind what their mission was. Sporadic radio contacts from other camps had alerted her to Hitler's dragnet tactics. Well, today they would find what they were looking for—with a few surprises!

Sonya climbed a limestone boulder and peered over the edge. She brought her binoculars up and scanned the broad valley below. Stone fences divided the rocky ground into irregular plots, some with orchards, others lying fallow. She swept the horizon from east to west, then followed the old dirt road to the east. There she spotted a line of men moving from left to right across the entire valley, approaching the turn where the road bent to the north, several hundred meters to their right, dissecting the ridge behind which they were hidden. They were moving slowly, obviously intending to form a line across the bottom of the valley before an advance line of troops left the road and turned to the north, sweeping up over the northern ridge where they were positioned. Their objective was to find anything or anyone who might be hidden in the caves on the valley walls.

"What can you see?" Shimon asked.

"A long line of Reich troops, crossing the valley from left to right."

"How close are they?"

"They're already in the valley, on both sides of the road, probably 4 to 5 kilometers away. They're forming a line, covering the entire valley from left to right. I figure these must be their advance sweepers. As soon as the line is in place, the sweepers will turn north and begin heading this way, looking for anything that moves. If I'm right, the rest will stay in reserve, back on the road. If something happens to the first wave of sweepers, they'll send the second wave and then the third until they eventually wipe us all out."

"How many of them are there? Can you tell?"

"There must be ten thousand of them down there," she said, motioning Shimon forward and handing him her binoculars.

Shimon's mouth went dry as he saw the massive troop movement below him. "What chance have we got against so many?"

"We can't lose," Sonya replied. Her momentary twinge of doubt was swept away by her confidence in Anatoly. Things were happening exactly as he had said they would.

"Have our men spread out behind the ridge, every 10 meters or so. Make the line 300 meters long. Position the two mortar teams in the center, below where I am, and bring me the Stinger operator," Sonya ordered. "We'll wait until they begin their sweep of the north wall of the valley. We'll let them get about halfway up this ridge before we let them have it."

"What about their reserves? They'll slaughter us even if we get all the sweepers. Too many of them!"

"We'll take them out the best we can, all at the same time. I have a plan."

"That ought to be interesting!" I can hardly wait to see how you pull this one off! he thought.

She could tell Shimon was still worried about the odds.

She was worried, too. But nothing ventured, nothing gained. And with Anatoly gone, what did she have to lose? *I promised you that I would do my best to stay alive, but when you died, all promises died with you. Now, all I want is revenge—for Yacov, for Papa, and for you, Anatoly,* she kept telling herself. She had waited impatiently for this day to come, had planned every move in her head over and over again. She would not lose this opportunity!

"They've turned north, Sonya, beginning their sweep. Now what?" her spotter informed her.

"Everybody take their positions," she ordered.

Shimon spread out the rifle squads, positioned the mortar teams, and then returned with Aaron, the Stinger operator. "We're ready," Shimon said. "How far away are they?"

"At the pace they're going, it will take them about another hour and a half to get here. Tell our people to keep an eye out for their reserve hardware."

"What are you talking about, Sonya?"

"I've seen at least a dozen Hinds and a couple of dozen Hip transports so far, bringing up the rear. They're ready for whatever their lead troops may run into. That's pretty standard," Sonya turned and smiled at Shimon. "Don't fade on me now, old friend. This is what we've been waiting for!"

For the next hour, Sonya watched the approaching Reich troops as they inched their way up the valley wall. She gave instructions to the mortar-squad leader on where she wanted the mortars placed and the priority of targets. He, in turn, instructed his two teams on where to align the mortar tubes.

Sonya turned to Aaron, the Stinger operator. "Are you ready? I'm really counting on you!"

The young man grinned. "Give me a good heat source and I'll splash 'em all over the countryside down there."

She loved his exuberant confidence. She hoped he was half as good as he thought he was. His IDF record said he was.

A half hour later she pointed toward an approaching helicopter. "Okay, this is it! Get ready. Watch that Hind over there," she said to Aaron. "He'll turn north along the road, parallel it as it ascends up the valley wall for a few hundred meters, then turn back to the east, over the heads of the sweepers who are halfway up the ridge. When he takes his turn to the east, you'll have a good profile to shoot at, with an excellent shot at the exhausts. You knock him down, and it rains helicopter on his troops below! Nice effect, huh? But once you fire, we'll have the rest of their choppers on us, almost before you can reload. So be ready!" she ordered.

"No sweat," Aaron replied.

"Shimon, when the Stinger goes, begin the mortar barrage. Forget the sweepers moving up the hill. Our riflemen will deal with them. Concentrate on their reserves that are grouped together in the rear. We'll hit them in all three areas at the same time. In the air, their front lines, and their reserves. We'll have the advantage for the first few minutes, until they figure out what hit them and from where. Then it's going to get 'down and dirty'! So far, it's obvious they don't expect us. If our luck holds, it should come as a complete surprise to them!"

"Right."

As she had predicted, fifteen minutes later the Hind, its fuselage bristling with armament, barreled up toward them like a huge insect, then turned sharply to the left, over the heads of the sweepers that were now only several hundred meters from the north summit.

"Get ready," Sonya ordered.

A moment later, the huge attack helicopter crossed directly in front of them. Aaron brought the Stinger tube up and squinted through the sight. He aimed at the exhaust baffles, and immediately the seeker chirped. Aaron squeezed the trigger, and the RPG hand-rocket-launcher bucked as the missile leapt straight ahead, trailing white smoke. It flew straight for the hot exhaust gases and exploded against the baffles. In an instant, shrapnel sheared off the rotor blades, and the wounded metal creature dropped to the ground, erupting in a ball of flame just in front of the line of troops that were making the sweep northward.

Sonya watched through her binoculars as the line of troops hit the ground. She grabbed her radio. "Now!" she shouted into it.

Both mortar teams fired at the same time. The shells arced

high in the air and came down on either side of the road, close to where the reserves had stopped, waiting for the sweepers to finish their job. It was hard to tell, but Sonya thought she saw over a dozen men go down.

"Direct hit!" Sonya shouted. "Shift targets."

The reserve Reich troops scrambled frantically for protective cover, but they were on open ground and their reconnaissance had been shot down. The total unexpectedness of the attack gave them no time to set up their own counterattack.

Sonya's mortar teams, following her instructions to the letter, continually shifted targets and poured on round after round, with devastating effect. At the same time, the crack rifle marksmen homed in on the sweepers that were now only a hundred meters or so from the summit of the ridge that they controlled.

Two Hip transports roared in from the south, bringing reserve troops up to where the sweepers were now pinned down. Aaron nailed both of them as they were flaring for a landing. Two red balls of flame roared into the air, marking the final resting place of all those on board. "Gotcha!" Aaron muttered each time to himself.

Sonya ran across the ridge, dodging rocks and boulders as she scanned the ground below for troops. An icy chill shot down her spine as she spotted six reserve Hinds now headed straight for their position. She slid to a stop, looking frantically for Aaron. A second later she spotted him. The medic was bandaging his shoulder, where he had apparently been struck by a stray bullet. As she grabbed her radio to call for a backup operator, the metal monsters loomed larger. At any moment their 30 mm guns would start spewing death.

Protecting herself, she instinctively checked to see that her rifle was on semiautomatic and let fly at the enemy overhead. A torrent of hot lead spewed from the mouth of her M–16, never even coming close to the target.

Then, just as the first Hind was about to cross the summit of the ridge where they were hidden, it veered to the side and crashed, bursting into a red and black fireball. Seconds later, the second gunship crashed as well, followed quickly by a third and fourth. Farther away, the last two aircraft fell from the sky and exploded. As they did, dozens of small black mushroom clouds sprang up in the distance.

Sonya brought up her binoculars and scanned the burning wreckage of the nearest helicopter, wondering what had happened. She looked back at where Aaron was still being attended to. No way was he responsible for what was happening in front of her eyes. She waited for the enemy troops to start advancing again, but all she saw and heard were flames and sporadic explosions as rounds cooked off. Nothing moved in the landscape below. The sweepers, the reserves in the rear, the choppers—nothing in the air or on the ground moved!

Shimon crawled up behind her. "What in the world happened?"

"I have no idea. I know *we* didn't shoot them down. It looked like they just crashed."

"All of them? At the same time?"

Sonya turned back toward her troops. "Let's go see. Pass the word to be careful."

Crouching low, Sonya cautiously worked her way down the ridge. Her riflemen stayed in the background, ready to shoot anything that moved. With each step, she expected to see the bushes up ahead erupt in gunfire, but nothing happened.

Off to the left, she saw sunlight reflecting off metal. She dropped prone and crawled forward, her rifle at the ready before her. Nothing moved. After a few more meters she saw that the reflection was coming from a pair of mirrored sunglasses gripped in a motionless hand. She grabbed a rock and threw it to the side of the soldier. He didn't move.

She crawled closer—and stopped. The sickening smell of rotting flesh assailed her nostrils. She choked back the urge to vomit. From her position, she could see chunks of flesh hanging from the blackened hand that still gripped the sunglasses.

Sonya slowly stood and walked to where she could see the soldier's body. What she saw, she had a hard time believing . . . understanding. The corpse, dead for only minutes, was already bloated and reeking. The eyes appeared melted, with dark viscous fluid staining the shrunken cheeks like tears. The mouth yawned open, revealing white teeth rimmed with parchment lips. The tongue drooped over the lower teeth, shredded, and already gathering flies.

Scanning the ground around her and below, still on the road, she saw dead bodies on every side, thousands of them, in the same condition as this one.

"What is this?" asked Shimon, coming up behind her. "I've never seen anything like it."

"Anatoly said it would happen this way, only I didn't believe him."

"What?"

"It's in the *Tanach*. Our prophets predicted our victory and this outcome. They said that our enemies' flesh would rot while they stood. I told you I believed this was our moment, but I never thought it could happen so literally."

Shimon looked down at the corpses. "Apparently it's true. So what do we do now?"

"There's nothing left to do. Anatoly's God already did it for us," she said. "Let's head back to camp. I want to think about this—all of it."

TWENTY-SIX

Heaven was more beautiful than anything Mike Teasdale could ever have imagined. When the Son of God pulled him up into heaven, Mike found himself surrounded by a great multitude of God's children, every one dressed in beautiful white robes, like the one he himself was now wearing. Off in the distance, but clearly visible, he could see the throne of God, glittering like a perfect emerald on a sea of crystal.

He was still looking around in awe and amazement and joy when he felt a tap on his shoulder. He turned and beheld the most beautiful woman he had ever seen.

"Marlee!" he shouted, the moment he saw her. "Oh, my darling Marlee," was all he managed to say before their arms were around one another.

They stood in this embrace until suddenly Mike leaned back a bit and smiled.

"What is it?" Marlee asked.

"I was just thinking about the funeral plots we bought a few years ago. Neither one of us got to use them, did we?" As soon as he had said it, he remembered the agony of burying Marlee's body under the tree in the backyard. "Marlee, I'm so sorry about what happened—that you had to suffer so, that I wasn't there with you when it happened."

"God's grace was more than sufficient for me, darling, even at that terrible moment. Those people meant it for evil, but the Lord permitted it for good. He more than provided for me when that terrible moment came. Besides that, if I hadn't gone then, I would have had to sleep with you in a sleeping bag, outside, with the bugs and all. You know I'm not the out-door type," she added, trying to alleviate his obvious pain at the memory of what had happened. "But now, that's all behind us! Now we will enjoy Him forever, together."

With that thought, they found themselves drawn, like the others around them, toward the shimmering green throne where Almighty God presided, surrounded by four majestic seraphim. Each of the heavenly beings had six wings, and their voices continually resounded across the expanse, echoing the Lord's praises: "Holy, holy, holy, Lord God, the Almighty, who was and who is and who is to come."

Mike had just noticed that the seat at God's right hand was vacant, when a man approached them, beaming a broad smile.

"Yacov!" Mike cried, and Marlee immediately joined in the joyous greeting.

"I didn't recognize you at first, in your new wardrobe," said Yacov. "I suppose you have cowboy boots under your robe?" he added, laughing, while pointing at Mike's feet.

"I put the order in that way, but this is all I got," Mike answered, showing off his leather sandals.

"All this does take getting used to," agreed Marlee.

Yacov hugged both of them. "I want to thank both of you for your faithfulness to God and your kindness toward me," he said. "You brought me the truth, and the truth delivered me from my sin. And because of that, all of this!" he said with heartfelt emotion, his right hand indicating with a sweeping motion all that surrounded him.

"We were only the messengers."

"Hey, have either of you seen Anatoly?" Yacov asked, knowing he had to change the subject before his own emotions got the better of him. "He should be up here, someplace."

"No," they replied, almost in unison.

"I've asked, and no one seems to know where he is," Mike continued, "but if it's what I think, we shouldn't expect to see him, yet."

"Why do you say that . . ." Yacov broke off suddenly, pointing toward the throne. "Look! Jesus has arrived!"

As they watched, the glowing figure each had met in the

clouds over the Mount of Olives sat down at the right hand of Almighty God, His work on Earth finished—at least for now.

A murmur went through the great multitude, and everyone in heaven fell prostrate before the Son of God as a great choir of angels sang His praises.

Although they were toward the back of the great assembly that surrounded the emerald throne, Mike could see every detail with perfect clarity. Time had no meaning, but it seemed like they had barely risen to their feet again, when seven magnificent angelic beings approached the throne. As they watched, God Almighty handed each of the seven a long, gleaming trumpet.

"Look!" said Marlee. "God is giving them the trumpets! You know what that means!"

As the great multitude surrounding the throne began to understand the meaning of what they saw happening before them, a hush fell across all the inhabitants of heaven. There was only silence, as though each was holding his or her breath in anticipation of what was soon to come. Not a sound could be heard for half an hour. Finally, another angel approached the altar before the throne, holding a large golden censer by its chain.

God filled the censer and pointed down to the altar. The flames from the altar ignited the censer, sending thick clouds of aromatic incense upward before Him, along with the prayers of the martyred saints—the souls of those who had been beheaded for the sake of Christ—still occupying their special place beneath the altar of God. After the incense was gone, the angel filled the censer with fire from the altar and hurled it high up into the air. As it burst through time and space, it fell down onto the surface of the Earth below.

Following the flames of fire, downward toward Earth, Mike's eyes were drawn to the glassy pavement beneath his feet. It was made of pure gold, but was completely transparent. And there, far below, was Israel.

"Look!" he said to Marlee and Yacov.

All three gasped at what they saw. Everything, even the smallest detail, was clear. . . .

As the contents of the censer fell to Earth, lightning flashed out of completely clear skies. Everywhere the flames hit, fires burned out of control. Those who witnessed these mighty strokes of God rolled on the ground in pain, hands over their ears in a vain attempt to mute the deafening thunder.

Then, an earthquake rolled over the land, but smaller than the one that had occurred when the heavenly sign had been given earlier in the day.

As the three watched, the scene below their feet faded.

"The angels are about to sound the trumpet judgments of God," Mike said. "The great day of God's wrath is about to begin!"

Finally, the first angel stepped forward, prepared to sound the long, slender trumpet he held in his hands.

The prophet Elijah nodded toward the CNN van as it parked over to one side of the plaza in front of the Wailing Wall. "The one who sends pictures over long distances has arrived," he said. "These people are clever, in a nasty sort of way. Why do they continue to think that they can defy God and get away with it?"

Moses laughed. "This is nothing new to you, my friend Elijah. You experienced the same attitude from those you were called to lead. Their hearts were the same as those around us—dead as a doorbell, I think the expression goes."

"Doornail, Moses. Dead as a doornail," Elijah laughed again, correcting his friend. "How many times do I have to tell you? If you insist on speaking their idioms, you've got to get the slang right."

"Well, who ever heard of a 'doornail'? What is it?" Moses asked his friend, sheepishly.

"The real question is, how do *you* know anything about doorbells!"

"Well, you see—"

"That's not the point, Moses. The expression is, 'dead as a doornail!' You know, I should have listened to Aaron. He warned me about you. Said you couldn't get it right back in his day, so why should I expect anything different now!" Elijah laughed.

"I stand corrected," said Moses. "But to get back to my

point . . . in my day, people thought they could defy God and get away with it. Jews and Gentiles alike! As I recall, even you, Elijah, had a few problems of your own in that regard. In fact, weren't you complaining that the very people you were told to instruct, killed all the prophets—excluding you, of course—and tore down your altars? And, if I remember right, they were even trying to kill you. You thought you were the only faithful one left, am I not correct?"

"That's true," Elijah admitted. "Then God showed me 7,000 faithful. I only missed by 6,999! One of those little miscalculations of life."

Moses watched as the television cameraman struggled to mount his camera on the tripod. "I suppose we should have expected them to come. Open sores do draw flies, you know." He pointed in the direction of the temple. "And the world's foremost sore is up there now."

"You're starting to get the hang of it, Moses. That time you got it right!"

Turning from his friend, Elijah scowled at the newsmen approaching where they stood. "I don't know about you, but I'm looking forward to giving these parasites the news they deserve!"

Moses smiled. "Well, which of us gets to tell them?"

Elijah pondered this. "May I? I have really looked forward to this day."

"Why, of course, brother. You have mastered their language far better than I have."

"Thank you. Then I will speak for both of us!"

Elijah walked over to the spot where Yuri Kagan was preparing to telecast his latest report. The prophet crossed his arms and patiently watched the activity.

Yuri Kagan, waiting for Egor to check the sound level on his mike, glanced suspiciously at the strange old man. The prophet smiled sweetly at him, making him all the more uncomfortable.

"It is curious what you do," said Elijah. "You talk to people in many places over that thing—and they see you also?"

"Yes, that's how television reporting works," Yuri said, making no attempt to hide his irritation.

"Excuse a humble prophet, but would you like to talk to me? I know something about what happened earlier today."

"That's what I'm here for," Yuri answered. Things couldn't get any stranger, he thought, yet somehow he knew these two old geezers were right in the middle of everything going on. Had been since they made their spectacular entrance, how long ago was it now? Almost three years? Over and over, they kept warning that Judgment Day was coming, but the peace and prosperity the Reich was enjoying took most of the steam out of their hot rhetoric. Now, because of the back-to-back earthquakes, the mysterious voice that said something about judgment, and the strange firestorm that struck Jerusalem several hours later, they wanted back into the act. This would be their moment of glory! They obviously wanted to promote these freak occurrences as a fulfillment of their bizarre predictions. What a joke! Oh, well, even if these old guys were just blowing smoke, at least they provided some comic relief and broke the tension after the wild day yesterday. They always were good for a laugh. He waved for Egor to fit the man with a mike.

A few minutes later Yuri heard his cue over his earphone. "Tape is rolling. Five, four, three, two, one. We're live."

"Good afternoon, this is Yuri Kagan, reporting live again from Israel, where yesterday this nation experienced not only two massive earthquakes, but the worst case of widespread freak lightning strikes in recorded history. Seismologists are now saying that the second quake was an aftershock of the first, and scientists are speculating that the lightning strikes were a result of an atmospheric pressure buildup from the first quake."

Yuri paused. "I am here at the Wailing Wall in Jerusalem. I have with me someone who says he can explain what happened here today." He turned to the old man. "Well, sir, what, for God's sake, *did* happen?"

Elijah beamed at him. "Wonderful question. And you have already answered it. It happened, as you say, for God's sake!"

"What is *that* supposed to mean?" Yuri snarled, forgetting his interviewing dispassion.

The old man shrugged, as if it were obvious. "It means God

is in control—not your pathetic little Adolf Hitler, but Almighty God Himself, Creator of the Universe! And now, for God's sake—as you have so correctly stated—He is going to deal with you again."

Yuri scowled at him. "And you still claim to be Elijah, right? The prophet? The man who lived over 1500 years ago?"

"2500 years ago," Elijah corrected, "and if I recall properly, it seems we had this discussion before. And, lest you forget, my friend over there is still Moses, who lived over 3500 years ago!" Elijah said with a serene smile.

"That's preposterous!"

The prophet smiled into the camera. "I know you find it hard to believe, so today I have decided to prove it to you, beyond any shadow of doubt," he stated boldly.

"Oh," Yuri said sarcastically, "so how have you two decided to prove you are Moses and Elijah?" He had begun to laugh. He could genuinely understand why the listeners got such a big kick out of these two guys. They could really be humorous, and he liked to egg them on.

"You are as bullheaded as the rest of the world—who, like you, prefer to believe a lie! The Scriptures tell us that if a prophet's prediction does not come true, he should be stoned to death. So, I will tell you what will happen next. If I am wrong, you can stone my friend Moses here to death. But if it does happen, you know that we have spoken to you, truthfully!"

"Thanks a lot, Elijah. That's what good friends are for!" Moses whispered to his buddy.

"That's barbaric! We don't do things like that anymore," Yuri spat back, completely missing Elijah's humor.

"Oh, no, you do far worse. You kill men, women, and children who choose to worship the one and only true God," Elijah answered, dead serious again.

Before Yuri could object, Elijah held up his hand, and his entire demeanor suddenly changed. He began to speak with an authority that frightened the cynical reporter to the quick.

"You want proof? Today I give you proof! I give you and your listeners something to judge us by," Elijah pronounced, "and then all of you must decide for yourselves whether I speak the truth or speak a lie."

He raised both arms high into the air. In the background, Moses raised his staff in agreement.

"I call the wrath of Almighty God down upon the Earth!" Elijah thundered. "Let the God of Israel repay wrath with wrath! Let the Day of the Lord begin!"

Yuri trembled visibly as he recalled where he had heard those exact words spoken, before.

The first angel put the gleaming trumpet to his lips and blew. Suddenly, the air was filled with hail and fire, mixed with blood.

PART 5

THE DAY OF THE LORD

Near is the great day of the Lord,
Near and coming very quickly;
Listen, the day of the Lord!
In it the warrior cries out bitterly.
A day of wrath is that day,
A day of trouble and distress,
A day of destruction and desolation,
A day of darkness and gloom,
A day of clouds and thick darkness,
A day of trumpet and battle cry,
Against the fortified cities
And the high corner towers.
And I will bring distress on men,
So that they will walk like the blind,
Because they have sinned against the Lord;
And their blood will be poured out like dust,
And their flesh like dung.
Neither their silver nor their gold
Will be able to deliver them
On the day of the Lord's wrath;
And all the Earth will be devoured
In the fire of His jealousy,
For He will make a complete end,
Indeed a terrifying one,
Of all the inhabitants of the Earth.

—Zephaniah 1:14–18

TWENTY-SEVEN

D-Day Minus 12–18 Months, Exact Timing Unknown

Hitler's promise of a peaceful, prosperous, and idyllic Fourth Reich had come to an abrupt halt thirty days earlier when the fire and hail, mixed with blood, began to drench the world, but only in certain areas. In the regions that were hit, the losses were staggering and continued to rise every day, as the fire and hail continued, day after day. Millions of men, women, and children had already died from the flash fires that set their homes afire and scorched the ground around them. The survivors were preoccupied with burying the dead, providing shelter, and cleaning up the charred remains.

But here in Haifa, where Mount Carmel met the Mediterranean, one would never know anything had changed from the former days of peace. That was certainly true on this cool, clear morning, with a gentle breeze blowing in off the sea, as Yuri Kagan and his CNN crew drove into the city. Along the Jaffa Road, the apartments, hotels, office buildings, and private residences scattered on Carmel's lush green slopes, basked under the sun. On the summit of the mountain, the white monolith of the twenty-five-story Eshkol Tower dominated the campus of Haifa University. For all intents and purposes, the hellish nightmare that was devastating much of the world, didn't exist for the residents in this part of Israel.

Despite the serene surroundings, Yuri's mind was still haunted by the memory of Anatoly's last words and his interview with the two strange, old men at the Wailing Wall.

Whatever the real explanation was—he didn't buy the "wrath of God" scenario that the so-called "prophets of the true God" had tried to sell him—his telecast had been indelibly associated with the destruction that followed!

Reich officials were still stonewalling the public, but judging from the accumulated reports of CNN sources around the world—which finally had been reduced to a trickle—a third of the world had been destroyed by the fierce fire and hailstorms. A significant percentage of the world's arable land was now charred and useless, meaning the return of food shortages and eventually famine. Entire cities had been burned to the ground, forcing any survivors out into the countryside.

The good news was that two-thirds of the world had not been touched, and Israel had escaped relatively unscathed. Hopefully the disaster was over. From all indications, that appeared to be the case. Once again, after weathering this latest storm Hitler promised the peace and prosperity of earlier days. Today he would surely boast of his latest accomplishments. Today was his day!

"There's his shrine," said Egor, pointing to the beautifully landscaped lawns, terraced gardens, and picturesque fountains that drew the eye to the magnificent white temple nestled halfway up the mountain slope, sitting where the Baha'i Temple, world center of the Baha'i faith, had once stood.

A marble colonnade circled the structure, focusing attention on the tall, gold-leafed doors and multiple window-slits that began at ground level and continued upward 20 meters, meeting the soaring glass dome that crowned the structure. Thin rays of steel arced upward, supporting graceful panes of curved glass, glinting in the sunlight. A swastika overlaid with the 666 insignia topped the dome.

Egor parked the van and they got out to look around.

"It's really something, isn't it?" said Yuri. "What a location! No wonder Hitler wanted his shrine here."

"That and the view," exclaimed Andrei. He turned slowly, checking every angle. "This would be a good camera position. A few shots from here, maybe one from the port jetty, and certainly a series from different positions going up the slope. What time is the dedication tomorrow?"

"Ten o'clock," said Yuri.

"Okay," said Andrei. "Let's get our establishing and cut-away shots done today, so we can concentrate on shooting the actual ceremony in the morning."

"Sounds good to me," Egor said. "Will we have a full crew tomorrow, Yuri?"

"You bet," said the reporter. "We can't afford to miss a trick on this one, so we'll shoot with three separate crews. Hitler wants this telecast perfect! No glitches. The rest of our equipment, lighting and sound, is already in place. All we'll have to do is check it out and direct the others when they get here. While you check out the sound, Andrei should get the shots he needs today. I'll be going over the details with Sergei for the big event tomorrow."

"In light of all that has happened—is happening," Egor corrected himself, "why do you suppose Hitler wants to go ahead with this dedication?"

Yuri scowled at the soundman. "To show the world he is still in charge, that whatever happens, he is still in control and will provide for his people. Now, I suggest we get to work and stay away from politics," he snapped, and headed back to the van.

"Good luck! I just hope he hasn't invited his two new friends from the Wailing Wall!" mumbled Egor when Yuri was out of earshot.

The following morning brought another perfect summer day. The blue vault of heaven joined with the Mediterranean's turquoise to form a setting for the glittering temple on the green flanks of Mount Carmel. Yuri scanned the coastal roads, looking for signs of Hitler's motorcade.

He felt his heart lurch when he caught sight of the motorcycle phalanx leading the black Mercedes limousines. Even from this distance, Yuri could see the red-and-white flags of the Reich flapping on the left front fender of each vehicle.

"Camera one," Yuri spoke into his hand-held transceiver.

"They're almost to you. Catch 'em when they turn on Allenby Road."

"I have them," came the static-filled reply.

"Two — ready for the turn up the slope."

"We're ready."

A few minutes later camera crew two reported, "They're past us now. Everything looks fine."

As the entourage made a final turn and swept into the drive at the shrine entrance, Andrei followed with his camera while Egor monitored his recorders and the remote microphones. With his guards forming a protective wedge around him, Hitler got out and, with Sergei, slowly worked through the masses of humanity that swelled in upon him from both sides. When they reached the head of the terraces that led down the slope toward the harbor, a little girl in a bright pink dress presented a bouquet of red roses, wrapped in cellophane, to the uniformed world leader. Hitler smiled stiffly and patted her head. At that moment, positioned down the length of the slope, hundreds of other children unfurled a series of huge Fourth Reich flags, holding them horizontal across the terraces, forming a red-and-white path to the sea.

The CNN cameras followed Hitler and Sergei as they slowly made their way past the packed colonnade, through the arched portico, and through the high, arched temple doors outlined in beautiful, hand-cut limestone. The leader looked up at the magnificent dome and the windows, admiring the architecture. He turned all around, examining every rich detail. He smiled at Sergei and nodded his approval. The dedication of his shrine was what the citizens of the Fourth Reich needed to see. After the terrible events of the past month, the battered world needed to see that he, the god of this world, was still in charge, that the peace and prosperity of former days was back!

Hitler went back outside and mounted the podium that stood high on the tiled walkway in front of the main entrance. Hundreds of thousands now swarmed the area surrounding the podium, knowing that their god was about to speak.

Without speaking a word, Hitler engaged his audience with his hypnotic blue-gray eyes, waiting for just the right moment to begin. A hush swept across the audience in expectation of their leader's words. The all-seeing eyes of the television cameras missed nothing.

"Citizens of the Fourth Reich, we are here today to dedicate the Adolf Hitler Shrine, a shining monument to the god of this world that will last for the next thousand years. For the next . . . *thousand . . . years*," he repeated, emphasizing the last two words. "Each of you will know the peace and prosperity that only I can give. Which of you has gone to bed hungry since I have become the leader and lord of the world? Which of you lacks food, jobs, the finer things of life like a home or a car of your own? Which of you has not personally enjoyed the peace and prosperity I promised to each of you almost three years ago?" Hitler roared into the microphone again rising to the challenge as he always did, in a manner worthy of the great orator he was. The world might be reeling from unexplained disasters, but all of those present, transfixed by Hitler's words, had been transferred to another dimension that had no bearing on what was happening in the rest of the world.

"We will not be defeated! We cannot be defeated! Our enemy will not destroy us! Yes, there are those who would rob you of the peace and prosperity I offer. Yeshua, Iesus, Jesus—whatever you call Him—and those who follow Him—in particular those two madmen at the Wailing Wall *who predicted and then caused the terrible events that have temporarily destroyed the peace and prosperity of the Fourth Reich*. Do not forget! These lunatics are the true enemies of the Reich. *They* are responsible for the mayhem that has destroyed the peace and prosperity I have given you! *They* have turned beauty into charred remains! The evidence of what they offer can be seen in every corner of the world! Is that what you want? *They* prefer death and destruction! Is that the God you choose to worship? One who destroys? One who kills at random? One who burns the beauty of our land?"

The mobs around the podium began to chant, raising their arms, their fists striking out at the air in front of them. "No! No! No! No!" Hitler's words were working them into a frenzy, just as he had planned.

"This is the true enemy. This is why we kill those who follow this Man."

The crowd became more emphatic, their chant now changing to "Yes! Yes! Yes! Yes!"

"We must work together. We cannot know true peace and prosperity until all our enemies are dead! Yeshua and His followers must be killed! *Already millions of those who claim the name of Yeshua have been eliminated.* Many by the Reich's faithful, *the rest killed by the very wrath the two Wailing Wall loonies intended for citizens of the Fourth Reich. They are gone, disappeared off the face of the Earth, consumed by the fury of their own making.* What more proof do you need? Is this how a loving God treats His followers? Is this the way Adolf Hitler treats you? Never!"

The crowd had turned into a sea of arms and hands, moving back and forth, chanting, "Never, never, never, never." Their leader and lord waited, letting the frenzy grow until it was about to explode. Then he continued:

"But you must do your part! There are still a few Jews who live, who refuse to acknowledge me as their lord. Jews hiding in Israel, Jews hiding in Egypt, Kurdistan, and in other remote pockets of the world. The rest have been caught and killed. *These alone remain.* They must be sought out and killed, must be made to pay the price for their insurrection against the Reich! *Then my Prince, the All-Powerful One, the god of this universe, will kill their leader, the worst Jew of them all, Yeshua!*"

The crowd had become a mob. "Kill Him, kill Him, kill Him," they chanted.

Hitler raised his hand and waited until the silence returned. "Choose you this day whom you will serve! I offer you peace and prosperity! Yeshua and His two mad witnesses offer you death and destruction! Which shall it be?"

The crowd erupted into a new frenzy of action, screaming and beating the air with their fists. "Hitler. Hitler. Hitler. Hitler." One moment they were crying angry words of vengeance against Yeshua, the next moment cheering the words of Hitler.

"I am your true leader and lord! This Shrine that stands before you bears testimony of my promises to you!" Hitler screamed, maximizing the moment. "I will bring these two madmen at the Wailing Wall, these prophets of Yeshua, to an end!" Hitler waited for the crowd to stop cheering. "Follow me! I offer you peace and . . ."

The first tremor rippled through Haifa so quickly that some were not sure what it was. Then the second hit with a jarring crash. The hissing roar of rock faces grinding together rolled like thunder down Carmel's slopes. Hitler's shrine shook as if in the hands of an angry giant. Scores of windows began to shatter. Inside, furniture skittered and streaked across the broad rotunda. A heavy whump sounded inside the shrine as an explosion broke most of the remaining windows, casting millions of shards of glass onto the mob. They stood there bewildered, watching the shrine of their god blow apart before their very eyes.

As the sky to the east, so clear and blue a moment before, boiled with ominous blackness, Hitler's eyes took on the look of a hunted creature. He turned and fled, with Sergei in his wake.

Yuri and his crew followed the two men as they rushed down the steps of the platform and out onto the walk leading to the drive. People were running in all directions, their eyes wide with panic, searching frantically for someplace to hide. Many were bleeding from the glass splinters that had viciously laid open their exposed skin. Bright Reich flags littered the ground, forgotten and trampled underfoot. The little flower girl in the pink dress looked frantically for her parents, now lost in the crush of the mob that engulfed her.

Another explosion shook the ground, knocking many of the people off their feet.

When Hitler turned toward the source of the explosion, the summit of Mount Carmel, he thought his heart would stop. The gentle, rolling, green mantle was gone, replaced by an ugly black rift lined with angry red streaks of lava. He watched as the newly created crater lobbed glowing chunks high into the air, where they became missiles raining down on the unsuspecting city below.

Lava splashed the glass dome of the shrine, staining the polished surface an ugly red and black. A huge molten chunk hit the dome, bursting through it in a shower of glass. A second direct hit exploded the steel and stone structure upon which the dome sat.

The ground shook again. A split-second later, Hitler shrank back in terror as he watched his shrine explode into nothingness before his eyes. The shrieking wind blew the dust away, revealing a huge pile of rubble.

Yuri Kagan shivered as he saw Hitler's fearful eyes sweep across the scene. *If Hitler was afraid . . .* He couldn't finish the thought. Instead, his mind went back to the last words of Anatoly . . . "The God of Israel will repay wrath with wrath. . . ."

Sergei signaled for the security detail and guided his master into the armor-plated Mercedes. The motorcycle policemen shouted at the people, ordering them to clear the road. It did no good. The officers started their machines and wove through the hysterical crowd, sirens screaming, hitting whoever got in the way.

At the bottom of the hill, they turned left. Flaming chunks of lava crashed down on the road directly in front of them, and the motorcycle police slid helplessly to a molten death. Hitler's driver ground the Mercedes to a stop, just in time. He threw the car into reverse and rammed the vehicle behind them. Then he roared forward again, desperately turning the large car around.

Without waiting for the security cars, he thundered down the road in the opposite direction.

Within a kilometer or two, the driver swerved to avoid another lava strike and plowed the heavy Mercedes into a tree. The airbag deployed, preventing the man from slamming into the steering wheel. In the backseat passenger section, Hitler and Sergei bounced off the glass partition and fell to the floor in a heap.

"Get us out of here!" Hitler screamed.

Sergei crawled to his knees, lowered the glass partition, and shook the driver. The dazed man turned toward him.

"Get moving!" Sergei ordered.

Untangling himself from the airbag, the driver started the car and backed away from the tree. Hail burst through the windshield and the back window. Hitler and Sergei huddled on the floor to avoid the pelting ice chunks.

The driver knew better than to stop, and he dodged the bouncing hail as best he could. The turnoff roads they passed were completely blocked, either by lava or upheaval from the earthquakes. Trees and shrubs burst into flames all around them. A chunk the size of a bus hit off to the side, spraying a layer of molten rock across the road directly in front of the Mercedes. The driver hit the brakes, but it was too late. All four tires blew out as the car slid through the lava, coming to rest just beyond it.

"What do we do now?" Hitler cried in panic.

"Let me see if the cellular still works," Sergei yelled above the noise. "We'll get them to airlift us out of this mess."

As his Enforcer worked the phone, the great leader of the Fourth Reich sat in silence, a prisoner of the fire and hail that continued to beat the body of the car into ruin.

Yuri could not tear his eyes away from the deadly barrage that surrounded him.

"Grab what you have and let's get out of here," Andrei shouted. "Don't worry about the cameras. Just hang on to the tapes."

As the three men dodged through the crowd on their way to the CNN truck parked next to the rubble that had once been Hitler's shrine, an artificial dusk began to darken the entire area. At first, Yuri thought it was volcanic ash, but soon realized that the source of the darkness was a black cloud that had suddenly appeared over the entire Mount Carmel area. It had come from the east instead of coming the normal westerly direction, over the Mediterranean Sea. Off to the right, a line of tall, thin trees crumpled and burst into flames as lava plowed into them, the red flames even more brilliant in the growing darkness. Large hail bounced on the drive as Andrei wrestled the driver's door open and leapt into the van, shoving the camera behind the seat. Yuri clambered into the passenger side while Egor went in through the side door.

The black cloud produced baseball-size hail, which quickly stripped garden plants of blooms and leaves and beat against the trees. Andrei eased the truck forward as the hail intensified. People in the open fell rapidly, the ice chunks knocking them senseless. The few who were spared ducked into whatever shelter they could find, fighting over benches and cringing under fountains. The hail thundered against the top of the van, denting it in and making a deafening racket inside. The passenger side window shattered, followed immediately by the back windows. All the while the hail increased in intensity.

"Get us out of here!" Yuri screamed.

Andrei switched the lights on and stood on the accelerator, fishtailing out onto the road, bouncing over bodies and debris. Suddenly, a red-hot sheet of lava flamed across the road, sealing the exit. Andrei slammed on the brakes, bringing them to a stop 20 meters from the molten rock. He threw the truck into reverse and backed up. Hail broke through the windshield. All the windows were broken now, and huge balls of ice ricocheted off the window openings and into the van, pelting the exposed men. Yuri and Andrei crawled out of their seats and joined Egor in the center of the van.

"How are we going to get out of here?" Andrei demanded, his voice high with fright.

Yuri felt an icy chill race down his spine and settle in the pit of his stomach. He could only shake his head. Wind rocked the truck like a toy and hail threatened to deafen them. All around them, lava rolled down the slopes of Mount Carmel. Smoke rose from burning trees and shrubs. Yuri feared they could not survive. In that fleeting moment of time, his thoughts again turned to Anatoly. . . .

The first angel set his golden horn down and returned to his place beside the others that stood before Almighty God.

Miraculously, Jerusalem, like the Haifa area before this morning, had been left untouched by the chaos that had hit Mount Carmel earlier in the day. The unruly crowd that gathered at the Wailing Wall didn't know whether to be afraid or angry, so they alternated between the two intense emotions.

Moses rapped his staff against the ancient stone paving until the disgruntled buzz diminished and finally stopped. He looked out over the people and waved toward his partner.

"Your prophet Elijah warned you, but you refuse to believe. You build a shrine to the god of this world, and the one and only Almighty God, the true God of this universe — whom you refuse to worship — destroys it with the mere flick of His finger. At this very moment, your invincible leader, your Hitler, is fleeing for his life. Is this little man worthy of your worship?"

A murmur ran through the crowd, but stopped as Moses continued to speak.

"Almighty God is just. His lovingkindness toward those who love Him is everlasting. But He is a God of wrath against His enemies! You are His enemies! You kill His followers! You curse His Son, Yeshua! You worship the created instead of the Creator! You receive what you deserve!"

Anger now erupted from the mob, and they began pressing in toward the two old men, shouting and cursing God, threatening to kill His messengers, wanting to tear them apart, limb from limb. But try as they might, not one person was able to pass through what seemed to be an invisible shield protecting the two prophets. The two of them nonchalantly continued talking quietly with one another, like two old friends enjoying afternoon tea together.

"Should we not call them to repentance?" Elijah asked his friend.

"The time for repentance is past, Elijah. *There are no second chances anymore.* They were warned, but still they took the mark of Satan-Meshiah. They have made their decision, and they will die for it. Remember what our brother Paul was instructed to tell the church of Thessalonica?"

"Yes, I do remember," Elijah answered. "*He told them that when this time came, the people would be deceived by their Satan-Meshiah, and those who weren't, our God would purposefully delude, so that they would not escape His judgment!*"

"That's right. God told Paul that He purposed for these to perish in this way, because they did not respond to the truth while they had a chance. Sad words . . ."

"But true," Elijah finished for him. "It has happened before. God goes so far and then that's it, kaput!" Elijah commented sadly.

"Ka-what?" Moses said in disbelief.

"Kaput," Elijah answered. "That means 'it's done, over, too late!' But I have to admit that fellow Hitler made a stirring speech. I especially liked the part when he said, 'I am in control.' He certainly timed that comment, perfectly!"

"I think it was the statement, 'those two madmen at the Wailing Wall,' that did him in," Moses added, struggling to keep a straight face. "The man really has a certain flair for the dramatic, but it's his timing that's so impeccable. No sooner were the words out of his mouth, than the final volley of God's first trumpet judgment hits him right where it hurts! He sure knows how to put his fist in his mouth!"

"Foot, Moses. His foot in his mouth," Elijah corrected. "You can't beat God's timing. And I wonder how he's going to bail out of this one? You'd think the people would catch on eventually."

"Well, I guess we'll soon find out," said Moses. "Meanwhile, the mob still rages," Moses continued, pointing to the angry crowd that surrounded them, "and this ancient body of mine needs a rest. I wish we'd gotten our resurrection bodies like the others."

"It won't be much longer, friend. When we've finished the job, then we get our new bodies—that's the deal! Now, why don't you dismiss this little gathering? After all, you're the one who got them all worked up to begin with," said Elijah.

"The meeting is over!" Moses announced soberly to the angry mob that was still clamoring to get at them. He lifted his staff, and fire erupted from his mouth. Before their enemies knew what had hit them, they had been reduced to ashes on the paving stones in front of the Wailing Wall.

Then all was quiet, deathly quiet. A gentle breeze out of nowhere stirred, sweeping across the area in front of the two old prophets. Moments later, even the ashes were gone.

With many detours to avoid lava and burning buildings, Yuri and his crew had made their way, on foot, down the side of Mount Carmel to the Jaffa Road. There, they had finally managed to flag down an army truck. Once they explained who they were and why they were in Haifa, the driver had agreed to take them to Tel Aviv.

Along the coastal highway, traveling south, they had passed several sections where fires were still burning. The destruction was not complete, but it was substantial. The area of Haifa hardest hit was, ironically the Adolf Hitler Shrine and the immediate vicinity. In comparison, Tel Aviv looked relatively untouched, most of the earthquake damage that occurred five weeks ago having now been cleaned up.

The driver let them off in front of the CNN bureau office. Yuri and his crew pushed in through the front door and looked for a place to collapse. Ehud Goldberg, the Tel Aviv bureau chief, spotted them immediately from his glassed-in office.

"Get in here, Yuri!" he ordered.

Relieved not to be included, Andrei and Egor headed for the break room, exhausted but happy to be alive.

"Okay, what happened in Haifa?" Goldberg demanded.

Yuri exhaled loudly as he dropped into the chair across from his boss. He closed his eyes as he struggled to form a coherent description of what they had seen.

"Mount Carmel erupted just as the shrine dedication started, raining lava down on everything. At the same time, there was another one of those freak hailstorms with hail the size of baseballs, or larger. Hailstones, mind you—not rain. Tens of thousands at the ceremony were buried by the lava or pulverized by the hail, and who knows how many others were injured. We were lucky. By the time it was over, the Adolf Hitler Shrine was demolished, the landscape was burned up, and many of the houses and buildings were destroyed or burning."

"What about between here and Haifa?"

"Some fires but nothing like what happened at Mount Carmel. I'd estimate that perhaps 50 percent of the greenbelt between here and there, along the coast, is gone. What about the rest of Israel?" Yuri asked.

"It seems that the worst damage was close to the coast. From the reports we're receiving, the farther inland one gets, the less the damage."

"What's going on? Can anybody make sense out of all of this?"

Goldberg played with his pen. "We don't know for sure. Some think it's tied to those two Wailing Wall whackos you interviewed a month ago. Even Hitler alluded to that. You know, if you had treated them with a little more respect, perhaps . . ."

"Thanks a lot. Now it's all my fault! If I recall correctly, they asked *me* to interview *them*, not vice versa."

"I know, but not everybody knows that," Goldberg replied, unsympathetically. "Others blame it on freak weather, natural disasters—like the Buenos Aires and Shanghai earthquakes. Volcanic activity is way up, but it's impossible to blame all that has occurred the past month on volcanic activity alone."

"Well, you could certainly make the volcano argument for what occurred this morning at Mount Carmel," Yuri commented.

"Maybe so, but don't forget, this is the first we've seen here in Israel, other than the earthquakes and that strange firestorm that hit the area between Jerusalem and Tel Aviv five weeks ago! No matter how you choose to look at it, it's hard to simply blame volcano activity for all the strange phenomena that's been taking place all over the world this past month or so."

"Well, we should thank our lucky stars that Jerusalem, like us, has only had minor damage in comparison to what has happened in other countries," Yuri said. "Do the propellerheads have any explanation?"

The bureau chief frowned at his ace reporter. "If you are referring to our scientific advisors, no, but they're working on it. But what about the two crazies over at the Wailing Wall? Could they *really* have anything to do with what's happening?"

"Give me a break, Ehud. You can't be serious."

"Just remember, the first wave of disasters began right after they arrived. We've got it on tape, in case you've forgotten! Hitler ridiculed them, and they responded by calling God's judgment down on him."

"So?" Yuri asked.

"So, then a month ago you give them another televised interview, but this time they don't talk about God's wrath; this time, *they call down* the wrath of God."

"Coincidence," Yuri snapped, "although"—he stopped for a moment before continuing—"right in the middle of Hitler's speech this morning, he called those guys 'madmen' and 'lunatics' and vowed not only to kill them, but also Yeshua whom they worship. Before Hitler could finish his sentence, the eruption hit . . . and you know the rest. Andrei's got most of it on tape, at least the beginning."

"You can't be serious, Yuri!" Goldberg repeated.

"I am, and the more I think about it, I think you're right! Let me put it another way. A month ago these two guys told me that Hitler was a phony and then they called upon their God to prove their point. At that moment, the world suffers what we call 'natural disasters'—unparalleled in history, mind you, with no explanation—and again, this morning, Hitler challenges them and now the Adolf Hitler Shrine no longer exists! You're right, that's no coincidence!"

"That's what I've been trying to tell you," Ehud replied.

"So, what do we do now?"

"We stay on top of them. We're newsmen. That's our job. I'm assigning a reporter to them, twenty-four hours a day, seven days a week from now on!"

"Bit of an overkill, isn't it?"

"No way! If those two have something to say, I want to be there when they say it! Which reminds me, I want you to interview Hitler tomorrow morning—if he'll do it. I think he owes the world an explanation after what happened this morning!"

"Thanks for nothing. I think that's what he was trying to do this morning. Do we know whether he even got through that mess safely, back to the Lion's Den? I'm telling you, Ehud, it was really bad over there."

"He's back in Jerusalem. Apparently, a chopper got him out. But after what happened today, the Chief has some real explaining to do if he wants to keep control of the Indians! If it wasn't for those blasted you-know-whats," he whispered, looking at the winking black box containing the Reich Emblem in the main office area, "the citizens of the Almighty Fourth Reich would probably . . ." He stopped short, realizing he had already said too much. "I'll make contact with Sergei Lomonosov and see what we can set up for tomorrow."

"Just ask him carefully. Remember, I didn't survive the Mount Carmel disaster to be killed by *mein Führer*. As for the rest of your observations, I never heard them!"

TWENTY-EIGHT

Since the sign in the sun, moon, and stars, the fighting had become intense. Sonya continued to rely on Anatoly's predictions. Confusion now reigned in the Fourth Reich ranks. It felt good to attack a confused enemy, too helpless to fight back. The decision to wait and let the enemy come to them was a wise one. Hitler was enraged when he got word of the Jehoshaphat massacre, and unit after unit was sent down into the Judean Hills, looking for the "terrorists" that kept killing his elite troops. Sonya's troops knew the terrain best, here in their own area, and her men smelled blood and liked the smell. When Hitler finally decided he couldn't win on their turf, he stopped sending his troops out to be slaughtered. Now it was Sonya's men that were getting impatient! They cherished their revenge, and did it in the name of all their Jewish brothers and sisters that had been killed over the past several years. But since the steady flow of troops had dwindled to a trickle, her men were putting more and more pressure on her to move from their own territory and to strike at the enemy closer to home. So far she had resisted, but she knew when the right opportunity presented itself, she would have to cave in to their demands. It's what she wanted, as well.

The hidden valley at Camp Moses was deserted. Sonya walked out into the bright sunlight after finishing lunch with the others. Her heart was heavy as she clambered up the familiar slope on the other side of the valley, reaching the southern ridge above the valley. She sat down on a limestone boulder and looked northwest, toward Jerusalem. She thought about the event they had watched on the satellite earlier that morning. Bizarre. How disappointed she had been when she heard that Hitler had made it safely back to Jerusalem. His time would come. She just had to be patient, a quality she knew was not her long suit.

Seeing him again, listening to his self-righteous words only brought back agonizing memories. Although it had been almost two years ago now, she remembered Anatoly's death at the temple as though it were yesterday. Her heart still ached with her love for him. How she missed him. How she needed him.

She hugged her knees as the tears came. The knife of grief stabbed her heart and seemed as if it would slay her. Waves of emotion washed over her, making her feel helpless and alone. She yearned for something to comfort her, knowing that such wishes were futile. She was really alone now. Her family was dead. Anatoly was dead. Even her adopted father-figure, her dear friend Binyamin, had disappeared without a trace, probably executed by Hitler. The tears streamed down her face. She did not bother to wipe them away.

Elijah and Moses stood in front of a small appliance store in the Old City of Jerusalem, not far from the Wailing Wall. When the two old men arrived, everyone else had quickly departed. They had the area to themselves. In the window, a large TV set was tuned to CNN, where they had just watched Yuri Kagan's interview with Adolf Hitler. He had repeated much of what he had said at the dedication of his shrine the morning before, explaining to the masses that the shrine and the summit of Mount Carmel had been blown up by nuclear devices, by terrorist Jews who were still in hiding in Israel. *In particular, a former member of his staff, one Sonya Petrov, was responsible for what had happened.* The person or persons that found and delivered this terrorist, alive, to him, would be rewarded beyond their wildest dreams.

Elijah shook his head. "Now, that's what I call a whitewash job. How can the world take this man seriously?"

"So, what's new? Look at all those who worshiped a hunk of rock they named Baal. You probably figured they had a few screws loose too, didn't you, Elijah?"

"Well, at least in my day they didn't melt down their nose rings and make a golden calf, which they then decided was God, worthy of their worship."

"Earrings, Elijah, earrings. Nose rings came later. I may mess up the slang, old buddy, but at least *my* memory hasn't deserted me! You're right, though. I got the better of them on that one. I made them tear the thing down, grind it into gold powder, put it in their water, and then made them drink it. I admit it was a little dramatic, but it got their attention! You should have tried that on the Baal worshipers!"

"Sort of like the first real mineral water," laughed Elijah.

"What is this mineral water? Did I miss something?"

Elijah smiled. "Never mind. You're doing just fine. You have a charming way of getting your point across—like yesterday when you opened your mouth and destroyed your enemies with fire. Talk about dramatic! Sometime you've got to show me how that one works."

"Just open your mouth and let it fly. That's it," said Moses. "Speaking of opening one's mouth, is it time?"

Elijah sobered as he thought about what would soon follow. The judgment of God was always sobering.

"Yes, friend, the time has come. The next judgment of God is about to happen."

Moses and Elijah turned and started walking back to the Wailing Wall.

"That new television reporter they sent over last night," Elijah said, "let's give him an interview he'll never forget!"

David Wisenhutt clicked on the icon to start his asteroid tracking program. He scanned in the first of three photographic plates he had taken the night before, then waited for the program to compare the plate with the known star field database.

Kitt Peak National Observatory was arguably not the best for the doctoral candidate's research, but it was near his home in Tucson, Arizona. And the 150-inch reflector did a nice job in the clear desert nights.

The multimedia speakers issued a blast of phaser fire, indicating that the program thought it had found something.

"All right, you liar," David grumbled to his machine. "What do you think you've found this time?"

From past experience, the astronomer knew the program was prone to false alarms. In fact, it had located and logged only two new asteroids, both minor, in the five years he had been using it. This was like finding a couple of night-lights you didn't know you had.

The program popped up a star field and indicated its find with a white crosshair. David sucked in his breath as he approximated the object's position based on surrounding stars. It was impossible to tell much about location or size, but he had an uneasy feeling in the pit of his stomach.

After he processed the other two plates, the uneasy feeling turned to acid. The asteroid, hurtling through space, was uncharted, it was huge, and it would come very close to Earth — and possibly collide with it — in sixty days, give or take a few.

D-Day Minus 12 Months

"What's the latest on the asteroid?" Andrei asked as he entered Yuri's office in Tel Aviv.

"Goldberg got the latest a few minutes ago. We aren't broadcasting this, but now they're talking end-of-the-world stuff here! This thing has an average diameter of 165 kilometers. Although the astronomers and tracking folks aren't positive yet, it appears the asteroid may hit the Earth around noon, our time, one week from today. The technoweenies can't agree on where to put the decimal point, but if it hits, the explosion will definitely be beyond anything imaginable — the largest nuke is a wet firecracker by comparison."

"What if it lands in an ocean?"

"It doesn't matter. Then you just add tidal waves to everything else. The experts don't agree on the magnitude, but they all say this is the end of civilization if it hits."

"And what does our magnificent leader say?"

"He's seen the same feeds we have. His position is still that the asteroid will be broken up before it hits us, or else miss us altogether."

"Do you believe that?"

Yuri scowled. "No comment."

"What about the interview our guy did with those Wailing Wall whackos several months ago? The one who thinks he's Elijah said that a star the size of a mountain was going to slam into the Earth. *Not maybe, for sure!* What's more, they made their prediction the *day before* Wisenhutt made his startling discovery! Sounds like the Wisenhutt Asteroid to me."

"Lucky guess. Those guys are always blowing smoke about something extraterrestrial." Even as he said it, Yuri didn't believe it.

"There wasn't anything over the wires before the old codgers hit up on our guy and gave him this scoop," said Andrei.

"I guess that's why Goldberg has someone on these guys twenty-four hours a day," said Yuri. "We never know what they'll say or when, but when they do, it's bad," he finally admitted. "So far, they're batting a thousand!"

The bureau chief stuck his head inside the office. "Good. You're both here. You're going to cover this asteroid thing. I've made arrangements for you to set up on the roof of Eshkol Tower at Haifa University, practically the only place that wasn't hit when the shrine got it. Should be a good vantage point, right up there on top of Mount Carmel."

"Do they know where it will hit yet?" asked Yuri.

"No," said Goldberg. "Too many variables. But the path will take it across Israel, assuming it gets this far. The reports say the impact point will be somewhere between China and the United States, if indeed it even hits the Earth."

"Well, that really narrows it down," said Andrei. "Think we'll have trouble getting through? The roads were pretty well destroyed when the shrine got hit."

"Actually, they told me most of the debris has been removed and the roads are now passable again," Goldberg answered. "But you can't go up there unless you've got the right credentials." He handed Yuri a one-page, official-looking document.

"Thanks for nothing," said Yuri. "Sounds totally thrilling—recording the end of the world, and all." What he really wanted to say was, *If this thing is bringing the world to an end, who's going to be watching?*

"Quite a view," Andrei said nervously, looking west toward the Mediterranean from the top of the twenty-five-story Eshkol Tower. The early morning sun felt warm on his back. Below, to the left and right, less than 2 kilometers away, he could see the huge lava flows that had erupted out of the mountain the last time they had been on Mount Carmel, earlier in the year. The lava was cold and black now, no longer threatening.

"Yes, it is, if you don't look at the remains of what happened here," Yuri replied, wondering if he really wanted to watch what was going to happen next. Then he shrugged. It didn't really matter where he was. It was impossible to hide from a chunk of rock larger than most islands, traveling at almost 21,000 kilometers per hour. He looked at his cameraman and sound technician, the technical parts of the Kagan, Kaugin, and Denisov team that had become so famous.

"You guys, be sure and get all this. With the satellite uplink, some of our viewers might actually see it just before they die." He laughed nervously as he watched their discomfort. He always made jokes when he was scared to death. "Relax! How often do you get to report the end of the world?"

The technician at the uplink transmitter waved to him. Yuri walked over and cupped his ear so he could hear over the breeze whistling across the roof of the tower.

"It's been sighted over Tokyo," the technician said. "It's clearly visible to the naked eye, even in broad daylight, and it's beginning to glow. There's no question anymore. It's definitely going to hit Earth."

"Where?"

"They still aren't sure. But the most likely impact point is close to where we are, give or take 1000 kilometers."

"Here? What happened to China or the US?" Yuri yelled. "How long till it hits?"

"Roughly a half hour," the technician answered as he continued monitoring the uplink. "Might as well wait it out. If we take off now, the question is not whether we can escape getting hit, but whether we get squashed by the front or the back of it."

Yuri looked off into the distance, seeing nothing but his own roiling thoughts. What would his last moment on Earth feel like? Would there be something beyond death?

He chased the thought away. He had known the answer to that for many years. When you died, that was it, in spite of what Anatoly thought! Oh no, not Anatoly again! Can't I ever get him out of my head?! He sighed. Andrei caught his eye.

"This waiting is spooky!" yelled the cameraman.

Yuri nodded, then turned back toward the uplink technician to forestall any further conversation.

The technician watched his dials and continued to make minor adjustments. Yuri marveled that the man could calmly maintain communications with the satellite, when they might have less than half an hour to live. But then, what else was there to do? Might as well play with your toys.

About ten minutes later the technician's eyes grew wide. He motioned to Yuri.

"What is it?"

"It's over China now, but the asteroid is breaking up into pieces."

"How many?"

"Don't know. At least two, because the glowing masses are beginning to spread apart. No, wait! It's more than two, but they can't tell how many."

"That's still a lot of rock. One chunk or half a dozen, the end result will be the same."

"No, that's not true. The odds of getting hit may be greater, but the more it breaks up, the better chance we have of surviving!" The technician took off his headphones. "Get ready! It should be visible on the horizon in a few moments. The chatter on the commlinks is getting bizarre. I can't tell what's happening!"

On cue from Yuri, Andrei tilted his camera up and adjusted the focus on the gyrostabilized telephoto lens.

A glowing object winked into view above the horizon and appeared to climb into the sky like a miniature sun. Other fragments joined it, spreading out to the north and south. The flaming rocks blossomed until they were beyond number.

Most of the chunks continued to climb into the morning sky, on their journey toward the west. But the brightest one didn't. It hung nearly motionless as it increased in size.

"That one's going to hit us!" Yuri shouted.

The asteroid fragment grew until they could clearly see its irregular surface as it tumbled along in the air toward them, trailing its incandescent wake. At first, it looked like the burning rock would hit the university tower, but it drifted slightly to the north, sweeping past about a kilometer away and streaking into the Mediterranean. Several kilometers offshore, the water's surface erupted in a white explosion. An immense geyser shot into the air, mushrooming out like a nuclear explosion.

The shock wave from the asteroid's passing shook the tower, blowing out many of the windows and causing the building to sway like a weed caught in a breeze. The concussion knocked the men off their feet, and Andrei almost dropped his camera.

"Look!" Egor shouted, pointing toward the sea, where a tall circle of blue was advancing on the shore, trailing a white mist. "Tidal wave!"

Andrei got to his feet and steadied the camera once more, focusing on the scene.

The second shock wave caught all of them by surprise. It lifted the camera up and over Andrei's head, even as it threw the men across the rooftop. Yuri cried out in terror, positive he would be blown over the edge of the tower. He slammed into the far wall, the impact knocking the air out of his lungs. Andrei and Egor landed beside him, but the satellite technician tumbled over the edge, his scream almost lost in the shrieking wind. He was dead. Nobody could survive a twenty-five-story fall.

White-hot pain shot up Yuri's right leg, straight into his brain. He moved the limb gingerly. It didn't seem broken. He struggled to his feet and hobbled to the seaward wall.

The tidal wave was much closer now, spreading out to the north and south. From the high vantage point, Yuri watched in horror as the vast wall of water swept into the twin ports of Haifa and Acre, engulfing the ships in the harbor and tumbling over the low-lying business district. It surged up Mount

Carmel, stopping just short of the tower where he and his crew stood transfixed. Then, just as quickly, the water began its retreat, dragging everything with it.

The three men gaped at the devastation left behind as the waters receded. Most of the ships had disappeared. The few still visible were stranded on Mount Carmel's slopes or bobbed upside down in the harbor. What remained of the city of Haifa after the Mount Carmel eruption, which moments ago edged the low-lying land around the bay, was now gone, except for a few buildings that tilted here and there at strange angles.

"What's that?" Andrei asked, pointing toward the breakwater.

A carpet of white was forming outside the harbor and spreading rapidly in all directions. Then a faint red tinge suffused the Mediterranean blue and swiftly changed to deep scarlet. Myriad white objects floated on red waves as the flowing white carpet spread on out to the horizon.

"It's dead fish," Yuri concluded. "And the stuff they're floating in looks like blood. We've got to get back to the truck."

Andrei retrieved the cartridge from the destroyed camera. Yuri led the way down from the roof to the elevator lobby on the top floor. The lights were out, but out of habit, he pressed the down button. Nothing happened. They made their way to the emergency-exit stairwell and down the twenty-five floors, in what seemed to be a deserted hulk of a building.

Out in the parking lot, Yuri unlocked the back door of the four-wheel drive vehicle. "Try the satellite link to Tel Aviv," he said.

Egor raised the telescoping antenna mast and aimed it. He then fired up the transmitter and fine-tuned the antenna alignment. "I've got the transponder loud and clear, but the downlink isn't there."

"It may have been hit by an asteroid chunk."

"What do we do now?" Andrei asked.

"Break out another camera and you and Egor, start taping this mess. I'll try and get through to someone on the portable phone. After you've got your shots, come back and we'll take care of the reporting."

"Where do you want us to start?" Andrei asked.

"On the top of the tower, where else?"

Andrei and Egor craned their necks upward and groaned.

An hour later, Yuri climbed out of the truck when he saw his weary crew push through the doors of the tower and trudge back out into the parking lot.

"Get what we need?" Yuri asked.

"I think so," Andrei replied. "Even up there, the stench is getting unbearable. Did you get someone at the office?"

"It took some doing, but yes. Ehud was in Jerusalem, attending some government liaison meeting. He said the Tel Aviv office was completely wiped out by a piece of the asteroid. It took out a quarter of the city, but the tidal wave never hit Tel Aviv like it did Haifa. It seems that Haifa was more directly in line with the momentum of the large fragment that landed in the Mediterranean. Either way, direct or indirect, everyone in its path is now dead. Goldberg's setting up new offices in West Jerusalem as we speak."

"Don't we already have an office there?"

"Yeah, on Jaffa Road. But it's small. They don't have any extra room."

"Do we know the extent of the damage, and where?" asked Egor.

"Not a lot. Apparently the asteroid broke up and scattered over the entire Earth, but Ehud said that most strikes hit water rather than land. Only a few pieces actually hit cities—parts of London, New York, and Los Angeles, to name the larger ones. Because of the flooding that came when the asteroid hit the water, he's seeing reports that say that much of the world's shipping has been wiped out, and scientists believe all fish life was killed by the concussion. Their latest prognosis is that what the asteroid didn't kill, the blood in the water will. The only good news is that anyone survived at all. If that thing had hit more of the actual landmass, there'd be no one left to talk about it."

"What are we supposed to do now?"

"Goldberg wants us in Jerusalem as quick as we can get there. The news wires are going crazy. To quote our boss: 'It's our job to tell the world what's going on.' " He sighed. "I feel like the cat with the proverbial nine lives. So far we've managed to survive while everyone around us is getting killed. I wonder how much longer our luck can hold?"

The angel took the golden horn from his lips and, like the one before him, silently returned to his place in the line of angels that stood silently before the Throne of God.

Egor finally pulled up to the small office building in West Jerusalem, a little after midnight. It had taken them a full day to travel what would have normally been a two-hour trip. He woke Yuri and Andrei sleeping in the back of the van, and the three trudged inside.

The night receptionist from the old Jaffa Road office recognized Yuri. "Goldberg wants to see you, now." She pointed down the hall to the bureau chief's new office.

Yuri entered without knocking. Ehud looked up from his computer monitor and his paper-strewn desk.

"Where have you guys been? I expected you earlier."

"Nice office, chief," Yuri clipped, ignoring the comment.

"Shut up and sit down! Just tell me what's going on!"

"Which is it, 'shut up' or 'tell me'? You can't have it both ways," Yuri spat back, in no mood for games.

"Sorry, it's been a long, bad day for all of us. Just bring me up-to-date on your end."

"Most of the main roads along the coast have been washed out. The ones that aren't are secondary, farther inland, and are gridlocked with people trying to get away from the coast—on foot, in cars, any way they can. You're lucky we got here at all."

"Okay, okay. Tell me what you got at Haifa."

"Most of the city is at the bottom of the Med. Fish blood and guts as far as the eye can see. And a smell that is simply out of this world! What do you think we got?" Yuri stopped and eyed his boss. "I'm sorry. It's bad out there, and we're all dead tired. We've been going over eighteen hours straight. What's been happening here?"

"Reports are still sketchy, but there was a secondary asteroid hit, about six hours after the first. The scientists are saying this might be more small fragments from the original asteroid, but they don't really know.

"The secondary impacts were mostly in places the first strikes missed. This time the freshwater lakes and rivers were poisoned. Drinking the bad water is causing vomiting, severe cramps, and in many cases death. We're getting reports from places like Honolulu, Tokyo, Bangkok, Calcutta, Saigon—places on the opposite side of the globe from where the original strikes occurred."

D-Day Minus 10 Months

"Does that report make any sense to you, Shimon?" Sonya asked.

According to the radio transmission they had just intercepted, an IDF force, conducting a clandestine operation near Mount Hermon, took advantage of the confusion caused by the asteroid hit and had effectively wiped out thousands of Reich troops on the northeast border of Israel.

"That makes no sense," replied Shimon. "The IDF doesn't exist anymore, and we have no one hiding up there, capable of pulling off something that large. You got any idea who these guys are?"

"No, but I like their style. Sounds like they're giving old Adolf fits. Wish they were closer so we could work together."

"Shall I have one of the northern camps try to contact them?"

"No. It's too risky breaking radio silence right now, with all that's going on. They're on their own, just like the rest of us. And they seem to be doing just fine without our help."

TWENTY-NINE

D-Day Minus 9 Months

In spite of the derogatory nicknames they were often given, people became frightened now at the mention of the two strange men still camped at the Wailing Wall in Jerusalem. Although the two old prophets still continued to hold court daily, testifying to the true God of Avraham, Yitzchak, and Yaakov, it had been almost two months since they had last demonstrated their amazing powers to the world at large.

Occasionally, when harassed by the Imperial Guard or by some inane comment by Hitler, the two old men would openly challenge his authority, daring Hitler's "toy soldiers"— as Moses liked to call them—to do something about it. They delighted in putting on a little display of their own, such as shutting up the skies so that no rain would fall, or turning the drinking water into blood in the Old Quarter of Jerusalem, but nothing as spectacular as the events that occurred when they called on God to pour out His wrath on the entire world. But now, things appeared to be improving worldwide. Thirty days had passed without a major catastrophe, and the world was beginning to breathe a sigh of relief.

Plants had begun poking their green heads above the blackened ruins in the temperate zones. The cleanup of beaches and ports had begun, and the mountains of rotting fish were buried in landfills. Polluted water sources were beginning to cleanse themselves, and the devastated cities were in the planning stages of a rebuilding and reconstruction boom.

Privately, Hitler was starting to regain his composure; publicly, he had regained some of the confidence of the people. The Reich was providing temporary shelter for the homeless in trailers and tent cities until replacement housing could be built. Memories of the recent disasters still haunted the people, but they had bought Hitler's line that the asteroid hit was a freak of nature and they were grateful for the Reich's rapid response to their needs in the aftermath of this terrible disaster. Their leader had proven that, despite all that had happened, he was still in control.

There were indications, however, that all was not well in Israel—rumors still persisted concerning an IDF resistance group in the Golan Heights, and another powerful guerrilla band was rumored to be operating somewhere to the south of Jerusalem. As for the rest of the world, those who had once resisted Hitler's mark were now gone, "killed by the very wrath the two Wailing Wall loonies intended for the citizens of the Fourth Reich," was the official explanation Hitler had used to explain away their disappearance. Now, with them gone, and the natural disasters over and done with, there was relative peace and quiet once again in the Fourth Reich. The Reich Emblems continued to control the people. Those who became unruly or disobedient were swiftly dealt with by the powerful demonic Emblems. The habitants of the world quickly learned that it was less painful obeying than challenging the leadership of Hitler and suffering the consequences—the intense mental anguish the demonic Emblems used to control the disobedient.

Thus, on this bright autumn day, all things appeared to be stable in the Fourth Reich, after months of devastation. Even the two old men at the Wailing Wall seemed to have been silenced, until yesterday, that is. While being interviewed on an international hookup—perfect for their propaganda—they chose to say little, but, instead, released a live eagle which soared up into the heavens, crying out with a loud voice for the entire world to hear, "Woe, woe, woe, to you who dwell on Earth. The worst of God's judgment is still to come!"

"Do you like it?" Elijah asked.

Moses examined the digital watch strapped to his friend's arm. "It's very nice, if you like these gadgets."

"It was so kind of that gentleman to give it to me."

"Give it to you? As I recall, you scared him half to death."

The incident had taken place just after the tidal wave devastated Israel's coast. The prophets had been on a stroll through the Old City, when they inadvertently came upon a resident of Tel Aviv who was fortunate enough to be in Jerusalem on the fateful day the asteroid hit the Earth. He had followed the predictions of the two old men and genuinely believed them to be the source of all the trouble that had plagued the world since their arrival. The man recognized them immediately. Before even one word had been exchanged, he thrust his watch at Elijah and begged the prophets to leave him alone. Then he dashed away.

"*I* scared him?" Elijah asked in disbelief. "I think it was *you* who scared the wits out of him! Do you have any idea what you look like, beard and all, waving that cane around, fire belching from your mouth, destroying everything in its path? I'm sure it's a bit upsetting to the average Joe."

"Joe who? How do you know his name?" Moses asked, puzzled.

"Forget it," said Elijah, turning back to his watch. "Look at this! If I poke this button, it shows a calendar. I think the calendar part may be broken. It gets all confused when calculating the days between the full moons. Sometimes it figures thirty days, sometimes thirty-one, and look at this, look what they've done to take the month we live in today—February I think they call it. They sure mess this one up! See here."

"Oh yeah, look at that. Twenty-eight days! I wonder why twenty-eight days?"

"Beats me. Maybe they do it that way in order to make a year twelve months instead of thirteen."

"Then why not have seven months with thirty days, and five with thirty-one, and make it simple?" Moses asked. "I don't get the twenty-eight-day routine."

"Look at it this way, Moses. You know how cold it is today.

Well, what they did is very clever. They took the three coldest days of this month, February, and added them onto the warmer months in the summer," Elijah joked. "You know, three more warm days in exchange for three cold ones! Is it any wonder why these people get so messed up on time? Other than that, though, it's really a pretty neat gadget. It keeps track of hours perfectly, even though I can't get used to that little beep-beep that occurs every hour or so."

"It is clever. It's probably one of Hitler's little demons trapped inside that thing, trying to get out," Moses laughed. "So, what does your automated sun dial tell you about today?"

"It tells me that today is the day and the time is now. It's 6:00 P.M. sharp, the beginning of the Sabbath, even though Hitler has forbidden its observance. Well, we'll give him something to observe!" Elijah said, his tone becoming serious as he contemplated what was to follow. "The time has come to call forth the next judgment of God. The time has come to summon the beasts from the abyss!"

Moses sighed. "I keep telling these people that our God is not a God to be mocked. He has warned the world, 'Vengeance is mine, I will repay!' And what do they do?" He looked upward, rolling his eyes.

"They throw stones at us, they shoot at us, they try to kill us — just like the old days," sighed Elijah. "They worship the Satan-Meshiah and curse the true God." He paused. "I had hoped this day would not come."

"So did I. But it is written," Moses said. "Time to wake up those reporters over there and give them what they want."

"I'm not sure that's quite the way I'd put it, Moses. It's more like giving them what they don't want. This is one scoop they'll wish they had never heard."

D-Day Minus 8 Months

As he received his command, the angel bowed before the throne of God. Then he turned and sped toward the Earth, appearing as a solitary shooting star to those on the ground. He touched down gently. To the north, the partially rebuilt city of

Babylon slumbered in the early morning hours, no more alert than the capital city of Baghdad farther to the north.

The angel shone like a star. His face, hands, and feet glowed like fire, and his robes gleamed iridescent white.

"Open," he commanded.

A minor tremor shook the ground, followed by a much sharper shock. A deep growling emerged from the Earth as rock surfaces grated against each other, tearing open a chasm that had been sealed ages ago by the order of the Creator. A crack formed on the surface. It expanded rapidly, forming a rocky crater. Soon the angel could look down into the endless depths of the pit, as smoke and fumes began to make their way up from the center of the Earth.

Then, unhindered by the darkness or the distance, he stepped off the edge and drifted slowly downward. Lights flickered below as the widening crack opened channels of lava. Heavy smoke billowed forth, carried aloft with sulfur fumes. Many kilometers farther, as the murky bottom approached, the heavenly creature began seeing demons, confined to the abyss by divine edict. He saw the hope spring up in their evil eyes as he swept past, but their hope was in vain. The angel was not there to release them.

He touched down on a small ledge above a river of lava, which bubbled and popped as it flowed sluggishly along in the core of the Earth. A high stone arch stood next to the fiery stream. It was natural, but the solid rock-plug sealing it was not. The angel pointed toward the ancient portal, and a brilliant blue beam lanced into the plug, shattering it by permission of the Ancient of Days.

The angel watched the dark passage and waited.

Something moved inside. Two eyes peered out. Then the being came into view. It was over 3 meters tall and had dark, leathery skin.

The creature winced when the angel spoke. "Abaddon, you are released—you and your tormentors—to carry out the mission you have been destined to do."

"I do not need your permission, lackey of the Most High!"

The angel nodded. "This is true. You exist by the power

and permission of Almighty God. But you will do exactly as He says. Now, by order of the Lord God, go forth. Seek and sting those who belong to the one who makes desolate—all who bear his mark on their forehead or their right hand—but do not touch anyone else."

"We will attack whom we please," Abaddon defiantly spat back at the angel of God.

Blue-white fire shot down, spraying Abaddon with rock chips. "You will obey! The mere thought of disobedience will be your last thought before total annihilation! Inject your poisonous venom in only those with the 666 mark, but do not kill them. Go! You have five moons to accomplish your task."

Abaddon's evil eyes glinted and glared with hate. His mouth moved, but no sound came out.

"Go!" the angel thundered again.

Abaddon started his ascent, slithering past the angel and continuing up the side of the pit.

Then, a rustling of wings sounded from the darkness out of which Abaddon had been released, and out of the cave emerged gigantic locust-like creatures, nearly 2 meters long, crawling on spindly legs. They had long, black wings, and their bodies gleamed like highly burnished bronze. The crowns of their heads shone as if made of gold. They had humanoid faces with long hair and sharp teeth, but their power was in their long, segmented tails. Each was tipped with a heavy, curving rapier, the end pointed like a needle for the purpose of injecting the poison stored within their tails.

Loud buzzing filled the pit as millions of the flying beasts clogged the passage. They roared upward on ebony wings— up the long shaft that twisted its way to the Earth's surface, past ledges and fractures beyond number. Occasionally one would brush the wall, sending boulders bounding and crashing into the lava below.

When the last creature was gone, the angel ascended from the pit. He scanned the heavens as he watched them fly, now in perfect formation, toward every corner of human habitation.

Then the angel closed the abyss.

———

Adolf Hitler lay on his immense bed on the fourth floor of the Lion's Den. Anna had returned to her own quarters, where she stayed conveniently out of the way when she sensed trouble in the Reich. She was right to sense trouble today. An overwhelming anxiety had dominated Hitler, ever since he had received the call from CNN headquarters concerning the latest Wailing Wall prediction.

He silently cursed the two prophets, frustration welling up inside because he had no power to stop them. Now they had delivered another threat, just when things were beginning to get better. Something about "beasts from the abyss."

How could he sleep? He threw aside the covers and got up. He walked across the Persian rug, onto the cold marble floor, and over to the sliding door leading to the parapet that circled the top floor. He looked toward the east. It was only midnight. Dawn was still hours away.

Outside the window, a shadow flitted past in the darkness, followed by another, and another, accompanied by an angry buzzing sound. The security lights suddenly clicked on outside, flooding the area with light. Hitler jumped back in alarm when he saw the bronze-colored creature perched on the rail of the parapet. It looked like an immense dragonfly until it folded its black wings. Then it took on the appearance of a giant insect with a human-like face and long, almost feminine hair.

The creature peered at him through the bulletproof plastic shield that protected the glass. It seemed to have some sort of intelligence. Hitler trembled at the sight of the sharp white teeth protruding from its mouth. Suddenly, another identical creature landed next to the first, and then another, until there were three of them, just sitting there and looking through the window at him like vultures waiting for their prey to die!

The phone by the bed chirped. Hitler stepped backward toward his bedside table, keeping his eyes on the winged creatures.

"What is it?" he demanded.

"Are you all right?" Sergei asked. "Have you seen what's outside?"

"Yes, I've seen them! I'm not blind!"

"They're all over the grounds!" said Sergei. "I've ordered everyone to stay inside."

"What about the guards?" Before the question had left his lips, a long scream sounded from the grounds below, trailing off in agony.

"What was that?" he demanded.

"One of the guards is down. One of the creatures landed on his back and knocked him over. It looks like it's stinging him with its tail." Hitler heard muffled sounds in the background, then Sergei was back on the phone. "There—the men finally got it off him. The guy's writhing around grabbing his leg. I'm glad they can't get . . ."

A muffled crash sounded below Hitler's balcony window, followed by another piercing scream.

Hitler dropped the telephone receiver on the floor and ran to the door leading to the hallway. But he couldn't leave. Something kept him there, transfixed by the scene outside. One of the insects he had seen earlier on the parapet rail, now hurtled its body at the window. It bounced off the bullet-proof shield and crashed to the floor of the balcony. Immediately, the second creature buzzed across the top of the balcony, depositing an ugly green film, which ran down and covered the plastic shield. A dense white smoke billowed up when the stuff hit the plastic. Then all three creatures came racing forward, crashing through the weakened shield and lighting on the marble bedroom floor. All three faces looked up as they skittered toward him on their spindly legs.

Icy terror shot down his spine and lodged in his stomach. He turned and grabbed the doorknob, but was unable to open the door in time. An angry buzzing sounded behind him, and sharp claws tore through his pajamas. The flying thing tightened its grip with its feet and one claw, while feeling about Hitler's head with the other, looking for something it apparently couldn't find. He felt its mouth moving wetly over his neck, causing a painful burn. Then, white-hot pain seared his brain as the poison-filled rapier stabbed deep, injecting the viscous fluid into his right buttock.

He screamed in agony and fell to the ground. The room became a kaleidoscope whirling about in a dizzy spiral. The agony grew worse, like a searing iron inside him, burning its way to his brain, one nerve ending at a time.

Hitler rolled over onto his back, and another creature leapt onto his chest. The human-like face looked down into his eyes from inches away. The mouth moved, making loud smacking sounds, dripping yellow slime onto his face. The creature tightened its grip. The tail whipped up, then drove down hard. The stinger plunged deep into Hitler's left thigh and pumped in its searing potion. He screamed and passed out. . . .

When he returned to consciousness, he could hear himself screaming. "Get away from me! Get away from me!"

Silence answered him—that and a disgusting smell.

Someone banged on the door. "Everything okay in there?"

"Help me!" he cried. "Help me!"

Sergei burst in, two guards and Hitler's personal valet hovering behind him. "Master—lie still."

"Get them away from me!" Hitler screamed.

"They are gone, my master."

Tears streamed down Hitler's face. "What is going on? This isn't supposed to be happening!"

Sergei told the guards to get out, immediately, not wanting the men to see his master in this helpless state. He got the medical kit from Hitler's bathroom and gave him a shot of morphine. After the injection began to take effect, the valet helped his master bathe, and treated the two puncture wounds with antiseptic spray. The black and purple stings, still oozing yellowish serum, stood out against Hitler's pasty white skin.

Sergei was waiting silently by the window when Hitler came back into the bedroom, wrapped in a long, black silk robe. The broken glass had been swept up and a temporary plastic shield fitted to the inside of the balcony window. The valet bowed and left the two men alone.

The morphine had taken effect quickly, giving Hitler some relief from the pain. Upon Hitler's insistence, Sergei helped his weakened master walk over to the private inner room that remained locked, night and day. He unlocked the door and helped his master inside. Once Hitler was seated on the floor,

Sergei positioned pillows behind him for support, lit the candles, and then left his master alone.

After the door was closed and locked, Hitler cried out in agony: "Answer me, my Prince! What are these things? What is going on? Have I done your bidding only to die in this manner?" He gripped the pillows beside him as he suddenly felt faint, the pain once again surging through his body in spite of the morphine.

Suddenly the room seemed to tilt and groan, as if it strained under some irresistible pressure. The air began to shimmer, and the familiar dark shape began to form above him. Large eyes appeared first, surrounded by swirling blackness. Then came the huge misshapen head with its prominent nose and wide slash of a mouth.

"You have questions, my son?" asked the deep, rumbling voice.

"Is this how a son is rewarded?" Hitler snapped without thinking. "You said nothing about all this—the fire and lava, the hailstones, the asteroids, the meteors, the tidal waves, the oceans turned to blood, the seas turned to poison! You said this would be my kingdom! And now, these terrible insects, like nothing I've ever seen. . . . Now they even dare to attack me! You promised . . ."

A sulfur stench filled the room and the voice thundered. "Are you forgetting to whom you belong and to whom you speak? I am the All-Powerful One, Prince of the power of the air! Do not forget who rules and who is subservient! You have your throne because I have given it to you. You rule my kingdom solely at my pleasure. Do you understand?"

Hitler cringed and nodded. "Yes, my Prince."

"Our Enemy seeks to destroy us—our kingdom and our subjects! You have known this from the start. You have been given the authority to rid the world of those who will not serve you. By *my* power, the Christians are gone, forever. These were not the victims of God's wrath, as you wrongfully state. *These were victims of my wrath*, because you didn't finish the job I sent you to do!" he lied. "They have been sent to the abyss from whence you came," he lied again.

"Yes, All-Powerful One," Hitler repeated dutifully, his

memories of that place of torment making him forget his aching body for the moment.

"Only a few Jews remain, most of which are hiding right under your nose, here in Israel. These are all you have left to kill. Eliminate the Jews still hiding in Israel. Then I will destroy their leader, Iesus—this time, forever. Until they are dead, your rule over Earth is not secure."

"I understand, my Prince. I must find them and kill them. But what about those two at the Wailing Wall? How do I deal with them? I have done everything in my power to kill them. Nothing I do affects them!" Hitler cried out in despair.

"The Jews in hiding are your sole responsibility. The two at the Wall are also mine. When the time comes, I will personally eliminate them. You have my word on that."

"And these gigantic flying insects—how do I fight these terrible things?"

"These creatures will not defeat you. By my power alone," the All-Powerful One lied again, "those attacked *will not* die! They will suffer, but they will not die! Tell that to the world. Give them the hope they need. *By my power alone, they shall live!*"

"Are you sure?" Hitler asked in astonishment.

"I have given you my word. That should be enough! Proclaim it to the world in your own name."

"I will," Hitler promised. In his pain, he wondered if he would live long enough to make the announcement.

"Only one thing should concern you: Find these rebel Jews who refuse to follow you. Find them all and kill them. That is an order, my son! If you fail, all will be lost and you will go back to the abyss!"

"Please, please don't say that again. I will never fail you, my Prince. I will do all that you command me to do. I can never go back. Never! I will find these Jews—all of them—and I will destroy them!"

"See that you do," growled the All-Powerful One. The room shook as the Prince of Lies disappeared with a loud pop.

It was the last thing Hitler remembered before the morphine put him into a deep sleep.

THIRTY

Yuri heard the ringing as he slowly struggled toward consciousness. He opened his eyes and tried to focus on the alarm clock. A little after 1:00 A.M. He cursed and picked up his cellular phone.

"Hello," he croaked.

"I need you in the office ASAP," the voice demanded. Goldberg rarely identified himself. He hung up without waiting for an answer.

"And a cheerful good day to you, too," Yuri grumbled as he folded the phone up, but he knew better than to ignore the summons.

He dressed hurriedly, buttoned up his heavy winter coat to the neck, and grabbed a bagel on his way out of the apartment. A sodium vapor light on the outside of the apartment building provided a small oasis of light in the darkness. A cold wind was coming from the west, a sure sign that winter was far from relinquishing its hold on the mountaintop city of Jerusalem.

He walked across the street to his car, but just as he started to insert the key in the door, a distant buzzing noise broke the nighttime silence. Confused by what he heard, he glanced to his right and saw a dark shape hurdle past a streetlight about a block away. Then a loud chittering sound came from nearby, this time the noise coming from his left. Yuri turned toward it and glimpsed a dark object disappearing into the alley beside the two-story shop on the corner, just down the street from his apartment. The dry clicking noise diminished quickly, followed by what sounded like a scream of agony. Yuri couldn't be sure, but at this time of night he wasn't sticking around to find out!

He jammed his key into the lock, opened the door, jumped in, and hit the power locks. He started the car, flipped on the lights, and raced to the CNN office, pondering what he had just heard and seen, if anything. After all, night shadows and night sounds could play tricks. At the bureau, he parked the car and hurried to Goldberg's office, throwing himself down in the nearest chair.

"The other two famous members of the team are *already* here," said Goldberg, mockingly. "They're in the other room, lapping up coffee and trying to wake up. What took you so long?"

Yuri choked back what he wanted to say. "I got here as fast as I could. What's so all-fired important?"

"We've been getting reports of huge flying insects attacking people."

"What?" Yuri exclaimed, thinking about the strange sounds and shadows outside his apartment building.

"As you very well know, Harvey Rosenburg's been covering those loonies at the Wall for months now. Last night, one of them calmly calls him over and tells him this was about to happen. Precisely. Right down to the ugly faces and stringy long hair on these creatures!"

"You're joking? Why wasn't *I* told?"

"Because the story was so bizarre—'winged beasts from the abyss—wherever that is—with human faces'? Give me a break! We figured it wasn't worth reporting, so we didn't. The only ones we told were the gang up on the hill because we're under orders to inform the Lion's Den of everything those two whackos say. Harvey got it all on tape, though."

"We've been over this before, haven't we? Didn't we decide that maybe they're not so 'whacky'—to use *your* word—after all? Maybe *we're the loonies* because we don't listen to them. Ever think of that?"

The bureau chief gave him that 'who knows' shrug he'd lately reserved for the topic of the Wailing Wall Whackos, and ignored his comment. "Our scanners are picking up weird dispatch calls, and it's even beginning to come in over the wires.

Large, winged creatures are attacking people and stinging them. From the breadth of the reports, it seems to be a world-wide phenomenon. We got word just before you got here that they've even attacked the Lion's Den, but that hasn't been confirmed—although that might explain why the boys up on the hill were so preoccupied."

"They're here in Jerusalem?" Yuri said, thinking again of what he had seen.

Goldberg nodded. "All the reports sound the same. What they describe sounds like a cross between a gigantic dragonfly and a scorpion with a humanoid face. But it's the tail that's deadly. It's a huge syringe dripping with poison, looking for living flesh to bore holes in! Every eyewitness is giving approximately the same story. But we don't have any pictures yet. That's where you come in."

"You want us to tape these bugs?"

Goldberg snorted in exasperation. "No, Yuri, stay here and hold my hand," he said sarcastically. "Of course, I want you to film them! Now grab your 'world-class' crew and get out there! We need pictures of these things."

"From what you've described, I think I may have seen some of them down the street from my apartment. I thought I was hallucinating!" said Yuri. "Should I start there, or do you have a fresher lead?"

"No, they're extremely mobile. Seem to be in one place one moment, and gone the next. Just listen to the scanners. With as many reports as we're getting, it shouldn't take long to get a reliable fix on one. If you're fast and lucky, you'll get there before it takes off and goes somewhere else."

"Yeah, if I'm fast and lucky!" Yuri grumbled to himself as he headed down the hallway. "It's been my lifelong dream to come face-to-face with a giant scorpion who wants to exchange his venom for my blood!"

He found Andrei and Egor in the break room, drinking coffee. He grabbed a cup for himself, and the three of them headed for the parking lot.

As Andrei backed the van out, Yuri began playing with the emergency scanner. One of the bands squawked with a call for a Magen David Adom ambulance to come to the International Convention Center on Zalman Shazar Street.

Andrei glanced at Yuri. "What would anyone be doing in the convention center at this hour?"

He did a U-turn, then made a right down a darkened side street and then left on Zalman Shazar. They swung into the parking lot beside the huge, glass-fronted building at the same time as the ambulance. Andrei parked at the curb, and the three of them grabbed their equipment and ran across the broad front walk and pushed through the glass doors.

Inside, the only light came from a battery-powered emergency light high above the ticket booth. The area was deserted except for a single guard and a man sprawled on the floor in front of the booth. The man was screaming in pain and holding his right leg. His cries of agony echoed across the empty granite floors, filling the darkness. The ambulance attendants cut away the man's pant leg so they could see what was wrong. Andrei flipped on the floodlight on the top of his camera and started taping.

"What happened?" Yuri asked the guard, who stood nearby watching the paramedics.

"I don't know," the young man replied. "When I came on duty, all the lights were off. Then I heard screaming and someone running through the hall. When I got out here, I found him." He pointed to the victim.

"Anyone else in the building?"

"Only a few maintenance men."

"This guy part of the work crew?"

"I assume so. He must have been cleaning the women's washroom. His stuff is still lying where he dropped it, in front of the washroom door when he went for help. Maintenance are the only ones supposed to be in the building, besides me."

The paramedic examining the wound looked around at Andrei. "Hey, shine that light over here so I can see."

Andrei continued taping as he aimed the light on the victim's leg, revealing a huge puncture wound. Blood spurted from the circular opening, along with a thick yellowish fluid.

"What did that?" Yuri asked.

"He must have been stuck with something like a stiletto," the paramedic replied without looking up. He applied a pressure bandage to the wound. "Let's get him on the stretcher," he ordered his assistant.

"Where's the weapon?" Yuri asked.

"Look around for yourself. I'm busy."

"Who did this to you?" Yuri asked the victim as the men strapped him onto the stretcher.

The man struggled against the straps. "Get me out of here!" he screamed.

The paramedics carried the screaming man out through the front doors of the convention center and loaded him into the ambulance, then drove off with its siren wailing.

Andrei turned off the camera and floodlight, throwing the lobby back into semidarkness. The emergency lightbulb was now dim and yellow, its battery obviously in need of replacement. Finally it went out entirely.

"That's wonderful," Yuri griped. "What's with the emergency lights?" he asked the guard.

"They're being upgraded. The electricians have removed all the ones in the display halls and auditoriums."

"Give me a flashlight, Egor. Let's see if we can find out what happened."

The soundman dug around inside his equipment case for a moment until he found a flashlight. The light came on with a click. It was bright, but the narrow beam left most of the lobby in the dark.

Suddenly a dry clicking sound was heard through the glass doors leading into the exhibit hall. It went on for several seconds, then quit.

"What was that?" Egor asked, trying to find another flashlight for himself.

"I don't know," said Yuri. "But I heard something like it when I was coming to work." He turned back to the guard. "You sure we're the only ones in here?"

"As far as I know," the man replied.

Yuri pushed through one of the doors and followed the narrow beam of his flashlight up the right-hand stairs. They heard the chilling sound again as they turned the corner.

"It's coming from the women's restroom," said the guard.

"That's where you said the workman was. Go see what it is—we'll give you a light," said Yuri.

The man shook his head. "*I'm* not going in there!"

Yuri turned to Andrei, his pulse racing. "We've got to check this out. Egor, wait here." The soundman nodded.

Andrei gave Yuri an "after you" gesture, and Yuri walked to the door of the restroom. He pushed it open a little. Inside, it was pitch-black.

"Anyone in here?" he called.

He stepped in, with Andrei behind him, holding the door open. Yuri panned the flashlight beam around the room. Sinks lined one wall underneath a series of mirrors. Against the other wall stood the stalls, reaching almost from floor to ceiling.

The clicking sound started again. It seemed to come from the corner of the room. Yuri leaned down and pointed the light under the narrow gap at the bottom of the last stall.

"See anything?" Andrei whispered.

"Not a thing."

Yuri tiptoed silently across the room and up to the stall. The door hung partly open, but he couldn't see behind it. He took a deep breath and pushed the door open with one hand, standing as far back as he could.

"Nothing there."

Another click. Yuri swung the flashlight around, two stalls to the right. The clicking increased in volume and frequency. He moved over and pushed gingerly on the door, trying to see into the stall. Something gold-colored glinted in the dark recess.

Yuri was starting to swing the flashlight around when something dark and heavy lunged out at him. He screamed in terror and dropped the light. It smashed on the tile floor, plunging the room into blackness. Something heavy landed on his back and almost knocked him over. He shivered under the weight as he felt something skittering over his shoulders.

He backed frantically away from the stall and crashed into the sink behind him. Pain stabbed his lower back as he staggered and almost fell. Whatever had jumped him, fell to the floor with a clatter, its angry buzz deafening in the silence.

Andrei screamed, and Yuri sprinted for the door. He threw it open and dashed down the stairs, out into the darkened convention center.

Egor swung his flashlight toward Yuri.

"Don't point that at me!" Yuri screamed. "I can't see!"

The restroom door crashed open again. Something large scampered over the floor. Yuri caught a brief glimpse of black wings as the thing leapt into the air.

"Where is it?" Yuri demanded. A loud, thrumming buzz passed close to his head. "That thing is fast!"

Egor bolted down the stairs. Yuri tried to keep up with him, but stumbled and fell as the soundman rounded the corner and dashed out through the glass doors into the lobby, taking the only light with him.

Yuri struggled to his feet and spun around. All he could see was the dim outline of the entry doors leading outside. The clicking sound was coming toward him now, growing louder every moment. He ran for the doors. Halfway there, he tumbled over a table and sprawled painfully on the floor. He heard the creature land, somewhere off to the right. Then the infernal clicking approached again. Yuri struggled to his feet and hobbled down the aisle between the display tables, dragging his hand along them for guidance.

Near the doors his hand brushed across something slimy. He heard rather than saw the thing leap upward. The heavy creature landed between Yuri's shoulder blades and the clawed legs dug into his flesh. He reached behind his back and grabbed something hard and round. He pulled hard and the thing clattered to the floor. An angry buzzing sounded at his feet.

Yuri jumped away and ran for the doors. Just before he got there, the thing pounced on his back again, gripping his sides with its feet and feeling his forehead with its front claws. Yuri screamed as the poison dagger jabbed deep into his left thigh. He teetered on the edge of consciousness as the nerve endings in his leg exploded in brain-searing pain. Then darkness mercifully descended on him.

The women's restroom door creaked open and Andrei

limped out. A moment later, he clicked on the TV camera's dazzling flood, panning around the hallway in terror. His leg was on fire where the creature had stabbed him. His pant leg was matted and wet from the oozing poison. He started shuffling toward the stairway when he heard an angry buzz off to the left. He whipped the camera around and saw the leering face just before the creature hit him squarely in the chest. The camera flew out of his hands and smashed on the floor, the light winking out.

Andrei flipped over onto his hands and knees and started scrambling for the stairs. The thing jumped on his back and clutched him securely with its claws. Blue-white pain exploded in Andrei's brain as the dagger stinger stabbed his right thigh, again and again. Within seconds, he too lost consciousness.

D-Day Minus 7 ½ Months

It had started as a game—sort of. After the initial reports on the worldwide volcanic eruptions, Sonya had offered Shimon predictions of what would follow. What he didn't know was that Anatoly had drummed the precise sequence of events into her head, describing each event in detail before she had come to Camp Moses. The predictions were so preposterous, getting Shimon to bet was like getting a child to eat ice cream. So far, Shimon had lost every bet! Anatoly had made her memorize each event, in order, so she knew them, backward and forward. She also had Anatoly's Bible, and each of these events was described in the *Brith Hadasha*, in the book of Revelation. Everything it predicted, was coming true!

After the sign in the sun, moon, and stars, Hitler's troops would become sitting ducks, fair game for her marksmen— exactly what had happened in the Jehoshaphat Valley. That prediction had come from the *Tanach*, the book of Zechariah.

Then there had been the earthquakes, volcanic eruptions, and hailstones, destroying a third of the greenbelts of the world. Next, the asteroid hit, flooding the coasts. Then the oceans turned to blood, heaping dead fish on the beaches, followed by the meteor shower that had poisoned a third of the freshwater sources of the world. Finally the warning to the world from an eagle, flying across every nation: "Woe, woe, woe to you who dwell on Earth."

Each time, Shimon lost his wager with Sonya, although he wasn't really that sorry he was losing, considering who was getting the brunt of these horrible events Sonya kept predicting! But all that had come before wasn't half as outrageous as what Anatoly had told Sonya would come next. This was the one she had really given Anatony a hard time about. Did he really believe there could be such a thing as giant, flying, stinging creatures from a place called "the abyss," with facial features like that of a grotesque woman with long stringy hair? Nevertheless, Sonya called it and Shimon immediately took her up on it, betting her double or nothing.

That had been yesterday. Today was today. Shimon should have known better. The fantastic creatures had arrived!

The newscasters were calling them "the beasts from the abyss," and they were causing damage where it counted most: on the people themselves who bore the mark of Satan-Meshiah!

Hitler was still trying to protect his image, telling the world that no one would die from the painful stings. He would personally guarantee it! *If he is so powerful,* thought Sonya, *why couldn't he keep them from getting stung in the first place?* Besides, Anatoly had told her that it was God who would not permit the people to die, making them suffer instead! What a fraud Bulgakov was—in everything. Oh, how she loathed that man! If only she could put an end to his lies, once and for all . . .

"Hitler's afraid of us, Shimon. His troops are staying clear of our part of the country. They've already lost too many good men down here. If they won't come to us, I think it's time we go to them!"

"Don't you think," Shimon began, interrupting her thoughts and plans, "that it may be too dangerous for us to leave the territory we know so well—where *we* have the advantage—to go into territory we don't know so well, where *they* have the advantage? Why not just wait and let them come to us? We've done fine so far! Let's not do something stupid."

"No way, Shimon. We've waited here long enough and finally we've got the advantage. Let's make the most of it. These insects are all over. If the Reich troops expose themselves, they'll be attacked. The only safe place for Hitler's goons is close to home. The 'locusts from hell' have them handcuffed. Anatoly told me we'll only have this advantage for five months. That doesn't give us a lot of time. It's already been a couple of weeks since they first showed up. Let's take advantage of the opportunity while we have it."

The discussion was over before it ever began. By now, Shimon and the others under her command had learned that whatever chances Sonya took, were chances based on what Anatoly had told her would happen. And so far, she was batting a thousand. Who could argue with those percentages?

She and Shimon handpicked the twenty men who would make up the commando unit. The group included their cocky little Stinger operator, Aaron, the mortar team that had performed so superbly at Jehoshaphat Valley, two Dragon anti-tank teams, and four of her best sharpshooters. Adding Shimon and herself, the unit was just the right size for the maximum mobility the jeeps would provide. She wanted to be able to move in quickly, do what they came to do, and then get out safely.

It had taken the commando unit four hard hours, even by jeep, to cover the distance over the rocky hillsides, westwardly, to the ridge overlooking the main road between Hebron and Jerusalem. The late February weather was cold, but there was no snow on the ground, concealing their movements and making travel over the hardened earth fairly easy. This was the location her reconnaissance team had chosen after weeks of careful surveillance. They had observed a lot of troop movement on this particular road, recently, each day at approximately this time in the afternoon. They left the jeeps in the wadi on the east side of the ridge, and all—except the Dragon units that needed a jeep to transport their missile launchers—proceeded up the ridge on foot.

Sonya signaled for everyone to stay low. She crawled between two boulders and pulled out her binoculars. She smiled as she spotted an armored column on the main road below, moving from Jerusalem, south to Hebron. However, for some strange reason, the convoy wasn't moving. The lead carrier had obviously had an accident, bringing the entire convoy to a halt. She counted at least fifty T-80 tanks. In addition, there were BMP-3 armored personnel carriers for the commanders and rifle squads. The end of the column extended almost back to the bend of the road that headed toward Jerusalem. It was the perfect target for the statement she wanted to make to Bulgakov!

Sonya was wishing she had more fire power when she spotted a shadow with a bronze glint emerging from the top of the stalled lead carrier and disappearing into the trees on the other side of the road. She focused her binoculars on the carrier. It was tilted precariously in the ditch, all its hatches open. Suddenly, two men exited, looking around cautiously.

As Sonya watched, a shining, bronze-colored creature flew out of the grove of leafless trees where the shadow had just disappeared. It landed on top of the carrier. She gasped as she saw the size of the thing—it was almost as large as a man! Even Anatoly's vivid description fell short of the reality. It was a hideous cross between a giant dragonfly and a scorpion, with long black wings folded along its sleek bronze body. Its humanoid face appeared intelligent but infinitely evil.

Without warning, the creature attacked one of the enemy, knocking him to the ground, feeling about his head with one of its claws before chewing on his neck. The man struggled feebly as stringy, yellow saliva flowed around everything the flashing teeth touched. Then the segmented tail arched over the creature's back, stabbed deep right through the man's overcoat, into the soldier's shoulder, pumping the wound with poison. Sonya cringed as she watched the man flail about, trying to dislodge the hideous thing riding on top of him. His screams of pain drifted up to the ridge.

Sonya tore her gaze away and swept the column. At the northern end of the convoy, near the bend in the road, a T-80 tank was teetering at a 45-degree angle, a limestone boulder wedged under its hull, the treads on one side grinding furiously but futilely against the pavement. The driver had obviously not been prepared for the sudden stop up ahead and had wrenched his tank to the left to miss the vehicle in front, stranding him on the boulder. The column was deadlocked: the carrier in front blocking their advance, the tank near the rear blocking all retreat. Sitting ducks!

The gentle breeze carried the rumbling sound of engines and the smell of diesel fuel. Nothing moved. Just then another winged creature flew directly at the other man outside the stalled carrier. He had been frantically trying to rescue his comrade from the first beast when the second struck him, plowing him to the ground, feeling its victim's forehead before stinging him. A third one flew up to the BMP, landed, and climbed into the open hatch behind the turret.

"What's happening?" Shimon asked, crawling up beside Sonya and peering over her shoulder.

"Looks like those things interrupted a redeployment back to Hebron. My guess is the BMP was cruising along with a hatch open for fresh air. One of the beasts got inside and stung the driver, causing the wreck. Since it's the lead vehicle, the commanding officer is undoubtedly inside. So nothing moves until the mess is cleaned up. That's why those guys risked their lives by crawling out. Believe me, if it were anyone other than the CO, they'd still be safely inside that tin can. The rest are staying buttoned up, probably figuring the things will go away if they wait long enough."

He grabbed her arm. "Look! Flying up the ridge!"

Sonya looked over to where Shimon was pointing. Five of the creatures were soaring upward, in a loosely organized cluster, heading directly for them. It was obvious the things had seen them, even though the enemy had not.

"Run!" Aaron shouted.

"Stay where you are!" Sonya countermanded. She heard an M-16 cock nearby. "Hold your fire!" she ordered. "We can't give our position away yet."

Aaron was halfway to his feet. He hesitated, looking down at her. She waved him down. Reluctantly, he returned to the prone position, the fear in his eyes totally obliterating his normal cockiness.

The lead creature landed in front of Sonya. She resisted the impulse to run as she looked into the round, human-like face with its long hair and golden crown. A viscous yellow slime dripped from its mouth parts as the evil eyes looked into hers. The creature peered at her head. Sonya felt her skin crawl as the thing grasped her hands, one at a time, turning them over before rubbing her forehead with its claw. Oh no, it likes me, she said to herself. She sensed the giant insect was disappointed in what it found.

She risked a glance to the side. Four of her men, including Aaron, were getting the same examination. Finally she understood.

"They're looking for the mark!" she exclaimed. "They can't touch us unless we bear Hitler's mark!" she yelled back to the others, beginning to laugh at the irony of the situation. She turned back to her inquisitor. "Get out of here, you ugly scuzoid!" She poked it with the barrel of her M-16. The thing glared at her and waved its stinger menacingly, but backed away. "You can't do anything to us, and you know it!"

The thing buzzed and chittered as if it understood what she was saying. Then, all at the same time, the five creatures took off and turned back toward the stranded line of metal on the road below.

"Happy hunting!" Sonya cried out after them.

Shimon couldn't help but laugh.

"What's so funny?" she demanded.

"What strange allies!"

"Can you believe it? They only attack our enemy. I love it!"

"I wish I was as confident as you," Shimon responded.

Once more Sonya trained her binoculars on the lead personnel carrier. A hatch popped open and a head emerged for a second. One of the creatures flew at it with an angry buzz that carried clearly up the hill. The hatch clanged shut before the creature could reach the human flesh inside the tank.

"Looks like a stalemate," Shimon observed. He scanned the line of tanks. "What do you want to do?"

"Take 'em out. They're sitting there on a silver platter just waiting for us. Use the Dragons on the lead carriers and the trailing tanks. Take them out permanently so the rest of the unit is stalled, indefinitely. Place the anti-tank teams on our flanks, the mortar teams with the sharpshooters in the center.

Wreck as much as we can. The sharpshooters can fire at will, but tell everyone to be careful. They may be demobilized, but they can still shoot back with the cannons on those things. Tell the men to stay behind the ridge when they're not firing!"

Shimon crouched down and ran over to the anti-tank teams. They quickly spread out and set up the launchers. The first team operator located the lead carrier and lined up his optical sight on a point forward, just above the track and immediately behind the first road wheel. Flame shot out of the launcher as the missile leapt from the tube mounted on the back of the Jeep and streaked down the hillside. The operator kept his laser sight fixed on the target, guiding the missile to impact. Fragments of the drive mechanism and fender rocketed skyward as the missile destroyed the left track but failed to penetrate the hull.

"Great shot!" Sonya yelled.

The first team dropped back and waited for the second team to fire. The second missile hit the last tank in the line. It destroyed the track and exploded inside the hull, setting off the stored munitions inside. The turret rocketed into the air above the fireball, tumbling to the ground 100 meters away.

"That takes care of the front and the back," Sonya spoke into her radio. "Now, get back down below the ridge," she ordered.

She quickly scanned the column. All the turrets were grinding around as the gunners sought their tormentors. The lead tank, behind the carriers, trained on the ridge where team #1 had gotten off the first hit. Orange smoke billowed as the gun fired. The high explosive round blew a large crater just below the ridge, showering the immediate area with dirt and rocks.

Sonya slid back and looked to the right. The Dragon team was shaken but unhurt. She radioed for both teams to pull in toward the center where the mortar teams were.

The ridge shook as round after round of high explosives probed in an unsuccessful search for the raiders. After a few minutes the shooting became sporadic and finally stopped.

Exercising her best low crawl, Sonya peeked over the top of the ridge and brought her glasses up. The T-80s were slewed in every direction as they struggled to turn around without ramming each other. The disorder brought a smile to her lips. She glanced toward Dragon team #1, which was again in place.

"Okay, #1. Nail any of the other vehicles that are still moving, especially the tanks," she radioed.

The operator brought up his sight, centering the cross-hairs on the tank's most vulnerable spot. The missile shot out of the tube and roared down on the lurching target. It burst through the hull and exploded inside, setting off the internal rounds. An angry red fireball shot skyward as the turret tumbled in a slow arc, landing on the road.

A high wail sounded below, barely audible above the crackling roar of the burning tanks. Sonya inched up and peered through her binoculars. The hatch on the lead tank was flopped open, but it had provided no escape for those inside. One of the bronze creatures was perched on it, its segmented tail lancing again and again into the interior. Sonya couldn't see what the creature was hitting, but she could hear the results. Then it crawled inside. Two others landed on the tank, folded their black wings, and joined their brother.

The tank lurched and began a ponderous pirouette as the remaining good tread ground against the roadway. On the second circuit, the damaged tank's gun rammed the gun on the tank behind it. The commander's hatch on the trailing tank flew open as the startled man tried to see what had happened. Two of the winged creatures pounced on him the moment he stuck his head out, driving him back inside. In moments, screams drifted upward. One of the men popped halfway out a hatch, only to be dragged screaming back inside. Scores of the creatures pounced on the other tanks, seeking some weakness in the shell, their claws clattering on the tank armor.

"We've got them bottled up!" Sonya shouted. "Set up the mortars!"

For an hour, Sonya's men pounded the column, alternating the mortar and Dragon teams. When the Reich troops tried to escape, they were attacked by the winged creatures. Those who escaped the clutches of the winged beasts were finished off by Sonya's sharpshooters. Finally, nothing moved on the road below. There was only smoke from destroyed tanks, a few burning BMPs, and dead silence.

"Let's head back to base camp, men," Sonya ordered.

The trip back to Camp Moses was without incident. They arrived after the sun had set, but before the twilight had completely faded.

"You know who I want next, don't you?" Sonya asked as she looked toward the purple sky in the east.

Shimon heard, but said nothing.

"Close that door!" Hitler ordered as Sergei entered the second-floor plotting room. "That noise is driving me nuts."

The sound of electric drills and the pounding of hammers came clearly through the closed door as workers continued installing steel shutters over all the windows and doors to keep the winged creatures out of the Lion's Den.

"It can't be helped, master. If you are to be safe, we must do it."

Hitler glared at him. "They're making the Lion's Den my prison. I haven't been to the Temple Mount for weeks now. But that's not what I wanted to see you about," he continued angrily. "What latest attack?"

Sergei knew he had to tread carefully. "The one on the road to Hebron?"

The blue-gray eyes flashed in anger. "Of course, you idiot!"

Sergei took a deep breath. "It has to be those Jews we've been trying to find."

"Of course it's those blasted Jews! But how can they do it?"

Sergei hung his head.

Hitler slammed his fist on the table. "I've got the finest, best-armed military the world has ever seen, and this bunch of ragtag Jews are running all over the country, slaughtering my troops! When are you going to catch them and put an end to all of this? You know what my orders are! We must get these Jews, Sergei. If we don't, I go back, Sergei, back to hell! And if I go, I'm taking you with me, Sergei. Now find them and kill them!"

"We are doing all we . . ."

"Where is their base? How do they know when to attack? How do they get those flying insects to help them destroy the Reich troops? Why don't they attack them too?" Hitler screamed.

Sergei shifted uneasily. He had seen his leader become progressively more irrational the past few weeks, as if he was coming unraveled emotionally. This was not a time for honesty. "These Jews will be dealt with, but we need time to find their home base so that we can take them all out at once. So far they've been lucky. We may not know for sure where they are, but we surely know where they aren't! It's only a matter of time until we find them. When we do, we'll deal with them, once and for all."

For a long time Hitler said nothing. "You know who is behind all this, don't you?" he asked finally. "It can only be one person."

"Yes, I know," Sergei answered, thinking of several candidates that fit the bill.

"Sonya Petrov," Hitler continued. "It has to be her. How many times do I have to ask you to bring her to me?! Next to the two lunatics at the Wailing Wall, she's priority number one! Do you understand, Sergei?" Then he slumped back into his morphine-induced peace.

THIRTY-ONE

D-Day Minus 6 Months

Defense against the flying creatures proved almost impossible, and in the following weeks the insects continued to find a way around all but the most sophisticated barriers. Ordinary citizens in the Reich had little protection. Hitler's promise that no one would die brought little comfort to the millions who suffered the excruciating pain of the poisonous stings. Although the victims soon found that the injuries were not life-threatening, for many, death was preferable to the pain.

At the same time, raids by Jewish guerrillas in Israel were growing bolder, unashamedly using the flying beasts to their advantage. When the beasts weren't a contributing factor, the hand of God provided assistance in a variety of other ways, each time with the same, devastating results. The attacks increased around Jerusalem, but no part of the country was immune.

Hitler was furious. Like the rest of the world, he was experiencing the terrible pain inflicted by the tails of the flying syringes, and long hours of unconsciousness as the side effect of the drugs used to combat the pain. He had become a virtual prisoner of his own palace, terrified of leaving the safe confines of the Lion's Den. He spent long hours by himself, trying to come up with a solution to meet the only demand his Prince was now making of him: Find the rebels in Israel and eliminate them!

He knew that Sonya was at the heart of his troubles. If he could find and kill her, the All-Powerful One would eliminate those two old lunatics still preaching God's wrath at the Wailing Wall. The peace and prosperity the Reich once knew would then be theirs again.

Trying to figure out exactly where the guerrilla camps were located, Hitler spent whatever waking, pain-free hours he had in the plotting room, relocated in the Lion's Den after he sustained his painful injury. Today, finally, he felt a little better. Perhaps the worst of the pain was past. He was studying the relief map of Israel when Sergei entered.

"What's the latest?" Hitler demanded, expecting the worst.

"Our Pac-Ten nations seem to be hit the hardest, and they are understandably nervous," said Sergei. "Except for Gerhardt Otterbein, of course."

"Pac-Ten" had become Sergei's code name for the ten nations and rulers of the now-defunct New United Empire. What remained of the NUE were the original leaders who still wielded considerable political power and responsibilities over the other nations of the world.

"So what do they want me to do, as if I didn't know?"

"They are concerned, master. Actually, 'upset' would be the better word to use. They have requested to meet with you in person."

"They have demanded, you mean."

"They need reassurance. Now that you are feeling better, I think it wise that you meet with them and tell them what you can. It certainly can do you no harm under the present circumstances. After all, they are your representatives to the rest of the world."

"Very well. Set up a meeting, but let's not be fools. The Temple Mount is impossible, and having all of them come to the Lion's Den would draw too much attention. Wherever you decide, keep a lid on it. We can't run the risk of a surprise guerrilla attack if it should leak that they will all be at one place, at the same time."

"May I suggest Ben-Gurion Airport, master? If we use the conference facilities in the deserted hangar, we will lessen security problems, particularly regarding these flying creatures.

It's a place we can easily get in and out of, and a place that even the press doesn't know about. When it's over, the men get back on their planes and fly out and no one's the wiser."

"Set it up, Sergei, but take all precautions. Remember, twelve of us together will be an irresistible target for Sonya if she knows where we are! We need complete secrecy."

"Yes and no. I'm sure Sonya knows about the hangar facilities if she was really that close to the prime minister. It seems, to the best of my memory, Shefi had that facility built. But my aides also tell me that anything less than a nuclear device won't make a dent in that building!"

"Just be sure! We can't afford to make a mistake."

"Yes, master. I'll work out the details and contact the men immediately on their private lines."

Hitler's frown suddenly turned into an unexpected smile. He stamped his right foot in excitement, by far the most enthusiastic thing he had done in the past eight weeks. "Wait a minute, Sergei! Perhaps we can turn this meeting to our advantage, especially if Sonya knows about the hangar!"

"How is that?"

"Sonya always seems to know what we're doing in advance, and I've never known her not to take advantage of any opportunity afforded her. She needs to find out that we're intending to hold a secret meeting. But the information must be leaked in such a manner that she will never suspect that we know that she knows. That way, she will believe she can safely take the offensive, realizing that she may never get another opportunity like this again. Remember, she wants me as badly as I want her! Set the trap. I will be the bait. When her guerrillas come out of hiding to attack me, the trap will be sprung. It will be the last thing she does against the Reich!"

"But if her information is so good, she'll know the meeting's fake and that she's being set up."

"The meeting will not be a fake. You told me yourself that the hangar is impenetrable, so she knows that if she wants a shot at me, she'll have to take it on my way over. The meeting must be real so she'll have no choice but to go for the bait. What we need to do is make her think she can get away with it."

"So how do we do that?"

"Leak the announcement that there will be a summit conference at the Lion's Den and then do an obvious cover-up. The cover-up must sound legit. But Sonya is smart, and she will figure it's a cover-up and that the meeting is still on. She'll also know that the Lion's Den is a ruse. The trick will be to make Sonya not only second guess the phony date for the summit, but also our choice of a meeting place. We need to get her to come up with the conclusion that we are actually meeting at the airfield, and make her think that we don't know that she knows. Her own expertise will deliver her into our hands!"

"And how do you figure we can do that?" Sergei asked, trying to follow his master's logic.

"She's smart enough to know that if the meeting is supposed to be a secret meeting, we will have to keep a low profile traveling to Tel Aviv. We won't have our troops lining the streets or our tanks on every corner. Externally, everything must look normal. The only thing the public will see is a few military vehicles moving from one location to another. They see that every day now, so it would be nothing unusual."

Sergei nodded. "But what will you have accomplished other than setting yourself up?"

"That's exactly what I want her to think. I'll grant you, there is some risk, but the results will be worth it. If we want to force her out into the open, we must do it on our terms and on our schedule. Knowing the route in advance, she's limited at where she can attack us. We wait for her to come to us, to the only logical places along the route where she thinks she can get a good shot at me. Once she shows up, we spring the trap, taking her and her guerrillas out, once and for all."

"You want to risk all this, your life and the lives of your leaders, just to get this guerrilla band of rebels?"

"We have no choice. *I* have no choice!"

Sonya and Shimon stood behind the duty communications technician as he played the videotape for a second time. Sonya thanked the man and she and Shimon retired to her office area in a remote corner of #1 cavern. They sat down in camp chairs and put their feet up on the empty crate that served as her coffee table.

Sonya frowned. "First, CNN announces a summit with Hitler's ten bad boys at the Lion's Den. Something about an international defense effort against these flying bugs from hell. Okay, under the circumstances, that makes sense, don't you agree?"

"Agreed."

She tapped her cheek absent-mindedly. "Then all the other news services pick it up. Which, of course, is what always happens, so that makes sense as well. Right?"

"Right!"

"But then, less than an hour later, CNN releases a bulletin announcing that the summit has been rescheduled for next month, citing schedule conflicts on the part of some of the member nations. Schedule conflicts? While the Reich is getting slaughtered by these flying creatures? When Hitler's bad boys are on the verge of going AWOL? Now, that makes no sense whatsoever. I don't buy it. What do you suppose they're up to?"

"Well, one possibility is that it could mean exactly what they said," Shimon answered. "The summit was scheduled, but they decided to postpone it after the announcement had been made."

"But because of schedule conflicts?" Sonya shot back. "Hitler *is* the schedule. Your first conflict with his schedule will be your last!"

Shimon laughed. "I didn't say I bought it all. No, it wasn't canceled because of schedule conflicts, we both know that. If Hitler wants a summit, there will jolly well be a summit. *Der Führer hat gesprochen!*"

"Hitler isn't stupid. He knows we'll see through the obvious."

"So, you release the summit schedule to CNN, making a point about where it will be held; then for some reason, perhaps security, you decide you don't want people to know about it. So what do you do? You tell the world it's been postponed."

"That's one possibility," Sonya said.

"Okay, but why all the subterfuge?"

"Maybe they're afraid we'll attack his old NUE buddies on their way to the meeting at the Lion's Den."

Shimon frowned. "Or, perhaps it's just the other way around: maybe Hitler wants us to think we can attack them, figuring we'll see through the postponement and think we can get away with it. Which means that they really *want us to know* that the meeting is still on."

"If that's the case," Sonya added, thinking out loud, "then the talk about it being at the Lion's Den should be suspect as well. In my opinion, that's too natural a target. There are much better locations than that to accommodate the rulers of ten separate countries, all converging at the same time on Ben-Gurion Airport. The trip from Ben-Gurion to the Lion's Den is just asking for trouble."

"Ben-Gurion Airport!" Shimon exclaimed. "That's it! That's got to be the real location for the summit. Didn't you tell me about a hangar that Prime Minister Shefi used to use for secret, high-level conferences?"

"Yes. You're right, Shimon." Sonya suddenly sat up. "It's the perfect location. They could fly in and out of Tel Aviv and no one would be the wiser, because they would never have to leave the airport. It's an old hangar on the far side of the airport that's been carefully rebuilt, renovated with all kinds of security and security systems."

"Let me ask you a question," Shimon said. "Suppose Hitler assumes we're smart enough to see through the cover-up. He also knows that you know about the hangar at Ben-Gurion. Do I smell the possibility of a double sting?"

Sonya frowned at her second-in-command. "Let me see if I'm following you correctly. Hitler assumes we will look beyond the postponement and know that the summit is still on. But he also knows that we'll figure out that it's not going to be at the obvious location. Instead of the Lion's Den, it's at the old hangar facilities at Ben-Gurion. Right so far?"

"Perfect. Keep going."

"Okay, so he thinks that we will think we can take him by surprise, because we will think he won't think that we have figured out both where and when it's really going to be. Right?"

"Right . . . I think!" Shimon laughed. "That is exactly what he wants us to think!"

"Wow. This gets confusing! That's why I know we're right on target," said Sonya.

"As far as I can see, there's only one catch," said Shimon. "We can just blow the hangar to smithereens when they're all inside, and Hitler knows that. So it seems pretty risky, if he thinks we'll figure out the real location of their meeting."

"There's no way we could ever take that hangar out with anything we've got," said Sonya. "It may look old on the outside, but the walls are 2 meters thick and are made of solid concrete and steel. Shefi had it built that way to protect against any possible Arab terrorism. I know. I saw the plans. He never took chances. The best we've got wouldn't put a dent in that thing!"

"Okay, that answers that question. Then let's assume this whole double-talk thing is for our sake . . ."

"Knowing that if I take the bait," Sonya interrupted, "he will have the advantage of knowing in advance where we'll be—and when! Of course, that's got to be it! For the first time ever, he'll know exactly where we'll be waiting, and when! There is only one safe route from Jerusalem to Ben-Gurion Airport, and he knows we know he will have to come in that way."

"Agreed."

"All he has to do is travel incognito, in some run-of-the-mill armored vehicle that is seen every day on the streets, keeping his troops in the wings, but out of sight. He knows there's only one or two locations along the highway where we'd have any chance taking him out, so that's where he'll ambush us."

"Why doesn't he come into Ben-Gurion by chopper?"

"Can't risk it. I'm sure he's aware of what we did to his Hinds and Hip Transports down at Jehoshaphat. If we did it once, we can do it again. He'd be a sitting duck."

Shimon nodded. "You want my opinion, Sonya? I think we should forget about it."

"No, we just can't walk away. There has to be an opportunity somewhere in all of this."

"But, Sonya, we can't hit him if it's a trap, and we can't take the hangar out."

"Right. We won't fall for his little trap. Knowing him as I do, that will completely frustrate him." She laughed. "Wait! I've got an idea! What we need to do is what he's trying to do to us! Strike him when and where he least expects it, right?"

"Right, but where is that?" said Shimon, shaking his head, wondering what this enigmatic woman would think of next.

"We'll wait until he gets back to the Lion's Den that night, after the summit, and we'll hit him there. You know, the let-down after the let-down. When we don't take the bait, he'll return home and lick his wounds, never thinking that's when we'll hit him! He will never see it coming! The timing and the location will give us the advantage of complete surprise!"

"I agree, he'll never see it coming," Shimon grumbled, "because it's impossible to hit! Nobody in their right mind would attempt to attack the Lion's Den! That place is covered in a blanket of security. It's impossible to get to without being spotted. Leave it alone!"

"Come on, Shimon, that's the whole idea. We hit him where he thinks we can't, at a time when he will be the most vulnerable because of his failure to trap us. He'll never see it coming until it's too late. Have any of my plans failed yet?"

"No," he admitted grudgingly. "But how do you expect to pull this off? It's impossible!"

"I have an idea."

Late that night Sonya went out to what she called her "thinking place," the limestone bluff on the south ridge, overlooking the hidden valley. It was a long walk, but she thought best when she walked.

Am I doing the right thing? she wondered. Anatoly had said that no one would be able to kill Hitler because the Scriptures foretold that Yeshua would personally deal with him at the Battle of Armageddon. If that was the case, nothing she did could alter the plan of Anatoly's God. But in spite of all the fulfilled predictions, she was not yet ready to accept the Yeshua part of Anatoly's plan. She wanted Hitler dead, and the sooner, the better. If she waited until the Battle of

Armageddon—if there really was going to be such a battle—more Jewish lives would be lost between now and then.

No, if Israel's God was giving her the opportunity to strike at the heart of the problem, she must take it. Besides, if Yeshua was all that Anatoly thought He was, then perhaps she would be the tool that Yeshua would use to kill Bulgakov. No person alive had a better right to kill him. He had deceived her. He had used her to set up her own people. And he had killed everyone she loved. Yeshua, if He really was God, would understand. She had every right, and she was prepared to die if she could destroy the man who destroyed her world.

But Anatoly's words continued to haunt her. *Stay alive, at all costs* he had drummed into her thinking, time and time again. *Don't take stupid chances to get your revenge.* In fact, he had made her promise. Yet, four months later, Hitler had brutally murdered him. She had made that promise when Anatoly was living. Now he was dead, by the hands of the very man she had trusted, the man she had devoted her life to. On Anatoly's behalf, if for no other reason, she must do what she must do. Her promise to him had died almost three years ago, on the day she watched Hitler behead him for all the world to see.

The familiar, silent tears streamed down her face. She wiped them away and got up, knowing that Anatoly was part of the past and the past was over. She had to live for the present. And in that present, all she wanted was one good chance to get even . . . to kill Bulgakov.

The team leaders were quiet as they entered the small side cave off #1 cavern that served as a meeting room. Sonya and Shimon watched from the head of the table as each man tried to get comfortable in the folding metal chairs. Electricity hadn't been provided for side rooms so the flicker of Coleman lanterns was all the light they had. It wasn't great, but it was adequate.

When they were settled, Sonya began. "Friends, as we all know, the Fourth Reich is not going to simply disappear. We all wish it would do just that, but it won't—not until we chop its head off. To do that, we must do something about Bulg . . . Adolf Hitler."

After she had briefed them on her conversation with Shimon, she said, "The only place Hitler is vulnerable is where he lives. It's the only place he will not expect an attack. So that is exactly where we will strike: at the Lion's Den, right after he returns home from the summit at Ben-Gurion!"

The very idea of attacking Hitler in the Lion's Den generated a firestorm of discussion. Sonya waited for it to run its course. Then she rapped on the table to get their attention.

"Gentlemen, this is feasible. First, because the Lion's Den is vulnerable—precisely because no one believes it can be attacked. Second, because we have a great advantage. I was in Israel, attached to Bulgakov's office when his residence was being built, so I know as much about the Lion's Den and its defenses as he does."

She waited for them to digest this, then said, "The defenses at the Lion's Den are designed to defeat expected threats, repelling land forces approaching from any direction. They are not designed to defeat air assaults—especially if they are stealthy."

"For good reason," said a man near the end of the table. "No one besides the Reich can mount air operations of any kind. Just how do you plan to attack by air, Sonya?"

Sonya smiled. "We are quite capable of doing it, as you will see later. We may not have transports, but we are air-mobile."

"Even if we could get troops in by air, it wouldn't take the Reich long to figure out what's happening," argued another man.

Sonya held up her hand. "Before you come to any conclusions, I've asked Shimon to give you the details of the plan we've been working on. Remember, Hitler is the head of the beast! Take him out, and the rest of the Reich will fall."

For the next hour, Shimon outlined their plan. When the presentation concluded, the group sat in stunned silence. Finally, one voice was heard.

"Hang gliders powered by drone engines? Will they be quiet enough?"

"Yes, they're quiet enough to do what we want them to do. They're completely silent at 3 meters' distance."

"You sure this will work?" asked another man.

"I'm sure. The only way into the Lion's Den is from above."

D-Day Minus 5 Months

Hitler sat forward in his chair in his private sitting room on the top floor of the Lion's Den. "More wine, Sergei?" he asked.

His Enforcer nodded and held out his glass. Hitler reached for the bottle and refilled both their glasses, then settled back in his favorite reading chair again. "It's from the Rhine Valley, did you know that?"

"No, I didn't. It's very good."

"Yes, it is."

For a change, Hitler seemed relaxed. His arms rested comfortably on the arms of the chair as he gazed absently into the crackling, hickory-wood fire in the fireplace. In the safety of the Lion's Den, winged insects and Jewish guerrillas seemed no more than a bad dream whose time would soon come to an end.

"Is everything ready for tomorrow?" he asked.

"Very nearly, master. I have toured the sites myself. Most of the route will be heavily patrolled by unmarked cars, which will be obvious to Sonya's trained eye, but not to the general public. Everything must look legitimate or she'll spook."

"Good, good. And where do you think she will strike?"

"We left a few obscure sites where our caravan would be vulnerable. They are not easy to spot, so she will find them. If they were too obvious, she would suspect something was up."

"Good. And when she arrives, then what?"

"The sites have been designed for our advantage. They are ideally located to give her no possible advance warning."

"Have we done everything possible? We can't afford to miss!"

"Completely. We've operated in total secrecy. Only two others know when and where this operation will take place. The rest are on 'standby' until the 'need to know' time arrives, two hours in advance."

"Good, good!"

"Our firepower is capable of taking them out in seconds.

We're going with ground-to-ground missiles, launched directly from the base, and with the best forward observers we have, at the two most probable ambush sites. They set the laser beam on the target, our ground-to-ground missiles will do the rest! Low profile, high impact! They'll never know what hit them."

"But is it possible to bring Sonya to me alive?"

"We've been through this already, master. I don't know how we can. Our number one priority is to get rid of all of these Jews. If we risk our primary objective to keep Sonya alive, we risk failure. Killing her may be the cost of a successful operation."

"Yes, yes, I know." He resigned himself to reality, knowing full well the consequences of an unsuccessful mission. "What else?"

"We've set it up to look like you'll be traveling to the summit meeting in an APC. In reality, it will be used as a decoy. I will ride in it to make it look authentic. One of your aides will be disguised to look like you. No one knows this but you, me, and the aide. If Sonya's guerrillas have eyes on the Lion's Den, or have any way of knowing what's going on inside, they will have no reason to think you aren't in the APC."

"And your arrangements for me?" Hitler asked.

"You are to fly in later, by helicopter, but not until the APC has passed the obvious ambush sites and Sonya has committed herself, one way or the other."

"Very good." Hitler smiled as he took another sip of wine. "It's nice to relax without morphine for a change. I thought those stings would never heal. But I am feeling good at last," he exulted. "And tomorrow night, we celebrate!"

Sergei fumed as he looked out through the periscope of the APC, clattering along the street on its approach to Ben-Gurion Airport. All along the highway, from Jerusalem to Tel Aviv, they had offered the perfect target to Sonya's guerrillas. However, they had passed the logical ambush sites without incident. The waiting had taken a terrible toll on Sergei's nerves, and now it was beginning to look like all the work they had put into this thing had been for nothing. Obviously, Sonya hadn't bought the double sting. She probably wasn't as smart as his master thought, and no doubt was setting up an ambush for the postponement date! Now, that's real irony, he mused. Sergei began to feel sweat break out on his forehead and under his armpits. How would he explain this to his master? What more could they have done? Well, at least the conference would go on. That was what needed his attention now.

When they reached the back entrance to Ben-Gurion Airport, six armed guards waited at the heavy gate. The driver slowed the vehicle to a halt and gave the password to the guard, who walked over to the APC. Moments later, the barrier began rolling to the side, and the APC lurched forward again.

The driver headed straight for a large, deserted-looking hangar on the far side of the airport, using the back service roads. The approach to the concrete and steel building was unobtrusively well guarded. When they were almost upon it, the heavy roll door started up. As soon as it was high enough, the APC rumbled into the building. Inside, the driver shut down the engine as the door closed behind them.

Sergei's ears rang in the sudden silence. Then he heard an angry buzz.

"One of the stinging creatures got in with us!" a guard screamed over the tactical radio.

"Where is it?" Sergei demanded.

"It flew up into the trusswork of the roof. It's dark up there. I can't see him now."

Sergei cursed. "How long will it take you to get rid of it?"

"Could take quite a while, sir. They're hard to catch in a big building like this. They like to perch up in the rafters. Are you wearing armor, sir?"

"No, I am not wearing armor!" Sergei shouted.

"Then I recommend you stay inside until we catch the blasted thing, sir."

"I don't have time for that! Bring some guards to escort me into the inner office. Now!"

"Yes, sir."

Once the guards were in place, Sergei ordered the aide playing Hitler's double to wait in the APC. Then Hitler's

Enforcer huffed with exertion as he hefted his bulk out of the turret. He warily spun his head from side to side, expecting at any moment to see a bronze nightmare hurtling down on him from the dark rafters above. He slid down on the fender and then onto the concrete floor, where he dashed between two lines of guards in body armor.

Sergei was halfway to the inner entrance when the angry buzz sounded. Two guards brought up their AK-47s and fired bursts at the creature. The thing streaked to the side as the assault rifle slugs flashed and whined off the steel, creating a horrible din.

Sergei slid into the narrow entrance and crashed heavily into the far door. A guard swung the heavy outer door shut, sealing him inside the double-lock entrance to the conference area. Sergei stepped up to the inner doorway. The guard inside, looking through the peephole, verified that there were no armored insects in the double-lock entryway. Then he opened the door to the room.

The huge inner chamber was dim and empty of all furnishings except for an area in the very center of the room. There a colorful pavilion had been raised for the conference. Brilliant spotlights, hung from the ceiling high above, made the pavilion glow like an immense Japanese lantern. The Pac-Ten leaders, Hitler's inner circle who had been with him since the beginning of the New United Empire, were seated in soft leather armchairs around a large table, enjoying drinks and small talk. All ten men had arrived within the past forty-five minutes. Hitler, who had arrived by helicopter only moments earlier, sat silently at the head of the table. To his left sat Gerhardt Otterbein from Germany. To his right was an empty chair for his Enforcer.

As Sergei approached the group, he saw the momentary flash of anger in the blue-gray eyes. Hitler knew the mission had failed. Sergei had arrived too soon; there had not been enough time for the trap to be sprung.

"Gentlemen," Hitler said, as soon as Sergei was seated, "we may begin." He glanced to his left. "Chancellor Otterbein, as the senior member of the council, would you please brief us on this meeting's agenda?"

"Of course, my leader. We are a little concerned about recent events and . . ."

"We are more than a *little* concerned!" interrupted General Franco Yonka of Libya. "The Germans may be pleased with the state of the Reich, but I assure you, Libya is not. And I know I speak for others in this room as well."

"And that is precisely why we are here, General," Hitler soothed. "You know I am always open to input from you, my advisors. You also know I always deliver what I promise. You have been, and will continue to be, amply rewarded for your loyalty. But you are not to forget that I am your lord, the one and only leader of the Fourth Reich."

"Forgive me, my leader, if I am not seeing the benefits of your leadership too clearly right now," General Yonka continued, a ring of sarcasm in his voice. "Are the earthquakes or volcanoes one of the benefits, O god of this world? Or the poisoned water supplies? And what about these blasted flying things that maim and cripple with their stings? We can't do anything with these bugs on the loose—our countries are at a complete standstill. We're crippled! And there isn't a man here who hasn't been stung. Where is your peace and prosperity now? If you are sovereign, why do these catastrophes continue?"

An angry murmur of agreement mixed with fear ran around the table.

"Silence, gentlemen!" Hitler flashed back. "Let me remind you all that it was I who brought peace to the world when it was war-riddled. It was I who fed the world when it was starving."

"No one questions that," said President Hakimian of Iran. "But we now have new problems that plague our nations and cause us untold suffering. We are doing all that we can. But how do you control natural disasters?"

"You call these flying syringes, natural disasters?" General Yonka answered, more sarcastically than before.

"They are an anomaly of evolution—the offspring of Jews and Christians. The Reich is doing all they can to provide medication and hospitalization for the wounded, even as we endeavor to rid the world of these monstrosities," Hitler responded with his characteristic spin of the facts.

"Be realistic, Adolf. We are afflicted with a plague of historic proportions. All the hospitals in our country are down. They can't get any of their staffs out of their homes to take care of the sick, for fear of getting stung themselves," Arrogantyz, the president of Syria, added. "Your efforts have not begun to remedy the situation on a worldwide scale."

"Well, we have done what we thought best. Given all this, is there anything you would do differently?" Hitler shot back at him, regaining the familiar fire in his voice. "If so, speak up now! Your criticism is welcome, but only if it is accompanied with solutions. If not, keep your mouth shut!"

The blue-gray eyes flashed around the table, daring anyone to contradict. One by one, they all looked down.

Chancellor Otterbein was the first to look up. "There is truth in what our leader says. Much has been accomplished; now we must rid ourselves of the enemy that brings death and destruction to our people. To this end, we must work together, not fight with each other! That is why we have come here today."

"Well said," someone interjected. "But what do you consider to be the enemy?"

"Our enemy is no more and no less than those two madmen at the Wailing Wall in Jerusalem. They are responsible for what is happening all around us. They speak, and it happens! They are sorcerers of evil!" Hitler answered.

"You really believe it's as simple as that?" Assam, sitting across the table, asked honestly.

"Absolutely. I agree with Adolf. My question to you, my leader, is this," continued Chancellor Otterbein, respectfully. "If these sorcerers can be silenced, then will our troubles end?"

"Well, wait a minute," General Yonka interrupted. "It's not that simple. Those two claim that the death and destruction are a result of Almighty God's judgment on the Earth. They are only His representatives. A better question, in my opinion, is: If indeed *you* are the god of this world and *your Prince*, the All-Powerful One, is the god of the universe—as all-powerful as he must think that he is—then why are you unable to silence them?" General Yonka again challenged, the mockery of his question obvious to all.

Sergei scowled at the Libyan general. "The last man to publicly show disrespect for our leader was the Vatican's representative at the UN, Cardinal Santucci. Would you like to see my power demonstrated on your behalf, to remind you of who is in control and who isn't?"

"If you are so almighty and powerful, my dear Deputy Lomonosov, why don't you deal with those two old men at the Wailing Wall, right under your nose, instead of threatening me?" the general shot back. "God of this world, my . . ."

A blue-white lightning bolt lanced down from above, ripped through the top of the tent pavilion, and struck General Yonka in the chest. Every muscle in the man's body contracted, throwing him away from the table. The leather chair in which he was sitting streaked across the floor until it bounced into the tent wall. His body twitched for a few moments, his eyes round and startled as if they had seen a fantastic vision. The sickening stench of burning flesh drifted through the air, accompanied by a disgusting sizzling sound.

The hole in the tent ceiling spread into a long rip that traveled quickly to the floor. A blast of frigid air blew into the pavilion, inflating it like a balloon and threatening to tear it apart. High overhead, a luminous blue object formed and swirled down until it was just inside the rip in the tent. A large, jet-black head formed within the blue and grew rapidly. The evil eyes gleamed and looked down at the assembled leaders. No one asked what was happening. No one had to.

Then the thin lips of the All-Powerful One parted. "If you have seen my son, you have seen me. I and my son are one. Honor my son, and you honor me. Those who do not, I will destroy. Am I understood?" The deep rumble rattled the entire building.

"Those two who trouble you will be eliminated at the appointed time. I have reserved them for myself. I will personally rob them of life and when I do, you will see it and rejoice, along with the rest of the world. But only I decide when the time is right, not you!"

While the words were still echoing through the air, the massive head disappeared.

Hitler scanned the table, the atmosphere charged with an electricity from what had just occurred before their very eyes.

"You have heard for yourselves," he said. "The Reich is in my hands. You have your answer. This conference is now adjourned."

He stood and waited for the nine world leaders to depart.

"I don't think we'll have need for any more 'conferences,'" Sergei said when he was sure they were alone. "More important, I think the days of our two Wailing Wall lunatics are numbered."

"What went wrong?" Hitler demanded, his mind obsessed with the failed ambush.

"You mean Sonya? I don't know. For some reason, she didn't take the bait. Perhaps she isn't as smart as we thought."

Hitler smashed his fist on the table. "Sonya Petrov is anything but dumb. She was just smarter than you were and sniffed it out before the trap could be sprung. What is it going to take to catch her, Sergei?"

"I do not know, master. But I will not rest until she is found and caught." The two men walked toward the door to the outer hangar. "Shall I instruct them to ready your helicopter?"

Hitler thought for a few moments. "No, Sergei. With Sonya on the loose, I think one helicopter ride today is enough. I'm sure she's figured that angle out as well. She knows this hangar is invincible against her limited firepower, but I wouldn't put it past her to attempt to bring my chopper down with a Stinger. I think it's safer if I go back in the APC. Is it still in the hangar?"

"Yes, master, but . . ."

"But what!"

"One of the stinging creatures got past the guards. I don't know if they've eliminated it yet. Let me check."

Sergei pushed the button on the intercom beside the door and asked the guard outside the double-lock chamber what was happening in the outer part of the hangar. The flying menace was not yet destroyed, the man said.

"I suggest we wait here until they catch the thing," said Sergei.

Hitler glanced at his watch. "I don't intend to spend my evening in this hangar. A freak spring snowstorm is forecast for Jerusalem and I want to get home before the weather hits. Order the guards to protect us."

Sergei gave the necessary orders, and they entered the double-lock entrance to the armored hangar. Before venturing out, Sergei looked through the small porthole of the second door. "The guards are ready. I don't see the creature."

"Perhaps it found its way back outside," Hitler grunted, distracted in angry thought.

Once they were through the door, Sergei and Hitler were shuffled to the vehicle between the two lines of guards, all suited up in body armor. Another guard waited up on top of the APC. He reached down a hand to assist Hitler.

Suddenly, a loud buzzing of wings sounded above them, and a dark shape streaked downward. Hitler watched in horror as the thing headed straight for him. "No!" he shrieked. "Stay away from me!"

The creature landed on his shoulders, looked for the mark on his forehead, and then drove its stinger deep into his right thigh. It then stuck him two more times before the armored guards could pull it away.

Hitler fell to the ground, cursing the God he didn't believe in.

THIRTY-TWO

Sonya looked over the equipment arrayed before her in the secret valley. A chill wind rippled the assembled Rogallo wings, and the heavy overcast sky promised to deliver the freak snowstorm that had been forecast to hit Jerusalem before morning. The snow was unexpected, coming so late in the winter. But after lengthy discussions, it was agreed that instead of being a liability, the weather was a nuisance that would actually serve as additional cover for their approach to the Lion's Den, even though the attack would be at night. Sonya smiled as she viewed the odd assortment of ropes, grenades, short Uzis, assault rifles, rocket-propelled grenades, flares, and C–4 plastic explosives being packed into nylon bags and clipped onto the open, angular aluminum undercarriage of the gliders.

She had gotten wind of the unofficial name the camp had given the twenty-four-person assault team: "Sonya's Air Force." Well, she thought, that's what it is.

The force was divided into two twelve-person teams. One would provide a diversion on the lower northern slopes of Hitler's mountain, while the other attacked the Lion's Den itself. Shimon and Sonya had the responsibility of finding Hitler and taking him out. At first, Sonya had wanted the privilege solely for herself, but military policy and plain common sense eventually ruled and she had agreed that the successful completion of the mission could require both of them.

Sonya shivered as the wind picked up and light rain began to fall. She was happy that it never snowed over the Judean

Hills. Although close in distance, it was not unusual to have a snowstorm in Jerusalem and just rain showers 20 kilometers to the southeast. She glanced down at the luminous dial on her watch. Almost 10:00 P.M. Hitler would have been back in the Lion's Den hours ago, angry at the failure of his trap but feeling secure in his personal fortress.

"We can still call it off," Shimon whispered in her ear so that the others would not misunderstand his concern.

"Not a chance. He thinks he's safe right now and will probably be sound asleep by the time we get there. Look, even the weather is cooperating."

"You might call it cooperation, but when we get over Jerusalem, the snow and wind will make navigation a little tricky."

"Don't you think I can do it?"

Shimon laughed. "Sonya, I think you can do anything you set your mind to." He paused. "I'm just nervous."

She looked at him seriously and lowered her voice. "Me too, Shimon. But we can do this. We must."

She turned to the rest of the assault team and raised her voice. "Okay, it's time. Let's go!" she ordered, and they all picked up the equipment they needed and headed for their hang gliders.

Sonya made sure her short Uzi and its clips were properly stowed in the nylon bags, then checked the compass, altimeter, GPS—Global Positioning System—and crude turn indicator. She pulled her goggles over her eyes and nodded to the two men standing by the wing. They lifted the glider's light aluminum frame, allowing her to clip her harness and settle in the seat that hung down from the transverse bar.

She turned on the ignition and set the throttle. Behind her, a man swung the prop on the drone engine. On the third try, the engine sputtered, caught, and settled into a nearly silent idle. She pushed the short throttle lever forward slightly, causing the glider to surge forward, threatening to somersault. The two men steadying the wing, dug in their heels to hold it back.

Sonya nodded and pushed the throttle all the way forward. The men ran beside her for a few meters until the glider leapt into the air. She felt her heart jump into her throat as the frail-looking craft soared into the blackness. She glanced back. Shimon was taking off right behind her, with the other team members lined up and ready to go.

She climbed several hundred meters, checking her GPS for the heading that would take her directly toward Jerusalem. Then she leveled off below the base of the solid overcast, pulling the throttle back to its cruise position. It was beginning to rain harder, and she knew the cold wind that numbed her cheeks would soon turn the rain to snow. The rain spattered on her goggles, obscuring her view. She cleared the lenses with quick swipes of her gloves.

She started a gentle left turn, watching the compass swing around toward a northwesterly heading, the lead ball at the end of the string moving to the left of the center line drawn on the tiny instrument panel in front of her. She glanced back, hoping that the indistinct shadow behind her was Shimon.

An icy pang of fear sank deep in her stomach as the glider suddenly seemed to tilt on its side. The rain was slowly changing to big, wet snowflakes and visibility was bad. She jerked around to look at her instruments. The altimeter held steady as the compass continued its lazy turn to the left. She rolled out of the turn when the compass read 315 degrees. The turn-indicator ball was exactly where it was supposed to be, but her GPS had blinked out—the only one they had. Her senses said she was in a steep turn in the opposite direction. She started to correct when she remembered what the Israeli Air Force pilot had warned her about: don't trust your feelings—trust your instruments! Ignoring her senses, she continued the turn, her eyes glued to her compass and turn-indicator ball.

She couldn't see the ground, but knew they should be over the hills of Jerusalem in ten to fifteen minutes. Trust your instruments, she reminded herself.

Ten minutes later, Sonya began to see shadowy outlines below her. She shifted her weight back and started a gentle climb, following the rise of the elevation below. The darkness overhead came closer and closer. She began to worry that she might have to fly into it, blocking all visibility of Jerusalem below and dangerously increasing the risk of an accident. She leveled out just under the base of the solid clouds and watched the ground beneath her climb higher and higher. Something had to give, soon.

Then she topped a ridge and saw winking lights in the distance. She knew this had to be the outskirts of Jerusalem. By now she was only several hundred meters above the rising ground, but still flying just below the overcast. The snowfall was increasing.

A growing uneasiness began to steal over her. Their flight path was supposed to go over the old Absorption Center and the Diplomat Hotel, but she did not recognize any of the large buildings before her. She looked down at her watch. According to her calculations, the hotel should definitely be in sight. Still, she had no idea how fast she had been going or how much the head winds might have slowed her progress. She decided to continue on her present course. The others had been instructed to follow her, and not to break formation. The whole operation hinged upon all arriving at the same time. With the only GPS on the fritz, if she got lost, the whole formation was lost.

The snow continued to fall, streaking her goggles and adding to her worries. Her only comfort was knowing that if she had difficulty seeing the ground, anyone on the ground would have difficulty seeing her. What she needed to do now was pick out something below that she recognized.

The estimated time of arrival at the Lion's Den came and went, and still nothing looked familiar. She scanned the ground, from side to side, as the drone engine purred behind her.

Suddenly her heart jumped! Was that something familiar in the distance? Seconds later, she was sure. The southwest corner of the Old City lumbered into view. The Dome of the Rock and the temple dominated the view to the right, while the thin rock spire of the Church of the Redeemer disappeared into the overcast. They had flown to the west of the Lion's Den without even seeing it!

Sonya turned sharply to the right and settled on a southwesterly course. Moments later she saw the railway station.

She glanced backward. To her relief, she saw the long line of silent gliders following in her wake — she had not lost them!

The checkpoints continued to click off as she plotted her way back to the south. Finally, she spotted the base of Harmon HaNaziv with its attractive stone perimeter fence, bristling with hidden, deadly defenses. Above it, perched on the summit of the mountain, was the Lion's Den, its roof reaching to the base of the snow-laden clouds. Sonya's skin crawled as she saw the main entrance guard tower approaching. She hoped the silence of the night, coupled with the snow, gave the guards no reason to look skyward.

As soon as the fence passed beneath her, Sonya began a climbing right turn. She looked back and saw the next eleven gliders following her, while the twelve after that turned silently to the left. She continued coming around until she was heading east, behind and slightly above the twelve gliders assigned to the diversionary attack. They spread out and, one by one, began dropping grenades and antipersonnel mines on the lower, northern slope of Harmon HaNaziv.

Bright flashes erupted around the main gate and guard tower, followed moments later by the loud reports. Sonya smiled as the guards reacted exactly as she had predicted. They fired blindly toward the western approach to the mountain since they heard the noises from that direction. Besides, it was the most likely direction of a ground attack. Concealed by the darkness, the snow, and their silent approach, the miniature bombers continued their spectacular attack as Sonya and her team circled higher and higher.

When they were level with the peak of the mountain, she turned toward the Lion's Den and swept in behind it. Sonya and Shimon peeled off and circled while the other ten gliders headed for the other side. Moments later, brilliant streaks of light lanced toward the ground. The rocket-propelled grenades detonated inside the transformer enclosure, and lights flickered inside the Lion's Den. Flames shot skyward as more of the grenades found their mark and the lights blinked out. The emergency generator started automatically, but the lights stayed off. The transformers had been destroyed.

The assault team switched to grenades and Uzis and began taking out the guards who were now stumbling around in the dark. Suddenly, the snowfall increased, blocking off most of the view. Sonya looked toward Shimon. She could barely see him, even though he was only a few meters away. She hoped he would be able to stay with her.

She turned back to the Lion's Den, now only a dim shape, threatening to disappear at any moment. She took aim at the steeply pitched roof and killed the engine, then banked sharply and shifted her weight to begin flaring the glider. Too soon. The flexible delta wing stalled, giving her a momentary fright, but it mushed through and continued forward.

She hurtled toward the roof faster than she'd intended, and had to bring the nose up suddenly, flaring the glider to a stall, right on the ridge of the peak. She skidded as her feet touched down on the slippery slate surface, lost her balance, and fell backward. The back ends of the aluminum wing poles hit the slate roof with a loud crack, propping her up from behind. Just then, Shimon landed on the peak several meters away.

As Sonya reached for the clip that attached her harness to the glider's frame, one of the wing poles sprang loose and slipped down the icy surface, tilting the glider to the side. Then the other pole popped free, causing the glider to slide backward down the roof, taking her with it. Sonya was vaguely aware of Shimon, struggling to get out of his harness, as she tried vainly to stop skidding. The roof ridge receded farther and farther. She was expecting to tumble backward off the building at any moment when the poles hit something solid. Her momentum carried her up into the air like a pole-vaulter, until she hung below the almost-vertical wing. The wind gusted suddenly, threatening to finish the job. Then, slowly, the wing fell back to the roof.

Sonya landed on the slate with a thump. She tried to still her racing heart as she looked back up at the ridge of the roof. She saw Shimon's green image clearly in her low-light goggles. He threw a line around the chimney and started down toward her. She finished getting out of her harness and thrust her extra clips, the shaped charges of C–4 plastic explosives, and some ropes into the large pockets in her flight suit. She pulled the Uzi sling-strap up over her head, letting the weapon dangle against her right side.

Shimon reached her. "Are you all right?" he asked, his voice high and a bit shaky.

She willed herself not to shout. "Yes. Help me secure my glider."

After he had grabbed her around the waist and pulled her free, she turned back and grasped one of the wing poles. A gust whipped over the roof and caught the wing, picking it up. Sonya held on as Shimon tightened his grip on her. The wind blew harder.

"Let go of the wing, Sonya—I can't hold you!"

She felt his grip around her slipping. Finally she let go. The glider whipped up into the air, spun around, and disappeared into the swirling snow.

"Put your arms around me," Shimon ordered.

"What about my glider?"

"Can't do anything about that. Now grab on!"

She obeyed, and he pulled them hand-over-hand back to the chimney. Sheltered by its bulk, they sat down to catch their breath.

Shimon pointed to his glider, which was securely lashed to a vent pipe a few meters away. "We can both use it to get away."

Sonya shook her head. "Let's not worry about that now. We came to do a job. Let's do it."

Without waiting for a response, she took the line attached to the chimney and threw it down the north side of the roof. Gripping it for safety, she turned and started backing down toward the edge. Shimon followed. When she reached the gutter, she paused a moment, then let herself over the edge and dropped softly down to the parapet outside Hitler's fourth-floor suite. Shimon came down beside her with a heavy thump.

Sonya pulled the C–4 charges out of her pockets and stuck them, in a rectangular pattern, to the bulletproof plastic shield covering the sliding glass door. She inserted the wires in the timer and twisted the dial.

"Get back!" she whispered to Shimon.

They retreated a few meters and dropped to the deck. The charges went off with a loud boom but very little debris. Sonya rushed to the door. It tilted inward now, held by a tiny metal strip. She pushed it, and it fell with a crash. She grabbed her Uzi in her right hand, rounded the corner, and jumped into the room and to the side, aiming at the huge bed in front of her. It was empty. She scanned the room rapidly.

"Nothing here," she said. "Follow me."

Sonya rushed to the door but opened it slowly. The hall was empty and the elevator doors were closed. Shimon followed as she walked quickly but softly to the elevator and looked around the corner. The corridor leading to the emergency stairs was clear as well. They went to the door and listened. There wasn't a sound. Sonya, leaning against the wall, pushed the door open a little, then all the way. She tiptoed to the rail of the stairwell and looked down. It appeared deserted.

She led the way down to the third floor and put her ear to the heavy fire door. Hearing nothing, she pushed it open and stepped through. There were several rooms all along the corridor, but no sign of life. She pointed to her ear, silently asking if Shimon had heard anything.

Shimon nodded and pointed toward a door near the end of the corridor. They tiptoed down the hall and stood on either side of the door. Sonya reached for the handle and pressed it slightly. It was not locked. She pushed down hard, threw the door open, and jumped inside.

A sudden sound to her left whipped Sonya around, her Uzi ready to fire. A woman was sitting on the bed, shivering in fright, the sheets pulled up around her chin. Off to her right, Shimon and she heard the distinct sound of the door leading to her sitting room clicking shut, and then being locked.

Shimon ran to it. It was locked. He stepped back, fired into the lock, then kicked the door in. Sonya rushed to his side.

"Leave him alone," the woman sobbed from the bed, "he's already been hurt once today."

Sonya crouched and rushed through the door. A pistol spat fire from the far right corner, the blast deafening in the confined space. Her low-light goggles kept her from being blinded by the flash, and Sonya saw the muzzle whip toward her. She fell to the floor and rolled. The gun went off again. She saw Bulgakov for an instant; then he seemed to disappear. Beside her, Shimon's Uzi gave a dry click as it jammed. Sonya rolled again. She looked up. This time her quarry was directly in front of her, less than 4 meters away. She brought up her weapon, and pulled the trigger.

The rounds flashed and sparked as they ricocheted off a dark green shadow that hadn't been there, seconds earlier. The eerie green shadow moved and whirled, blocking her shots. She emptied one clip and reached for another.

"Well, Sonya," came a familiar voice, faintly from behind the swirling green mass. "We finally meet again."

The green shadow faded and a brilliant red line of light shot across the room as Hitler switched on his pistol's laser sight. The laser beam ended in a small red dot on Sonya's forehead.

Hitler laughed in triumph, for the first time completely unconscious of the pain that had kept him bedridden since his return from Ben-Gurion Airport. "You know what happens to traitors, don't you, my dear? Yacov found out, and so did Anatoly. And now it's your turn. Are you ready to join them?"

A sudden noise distracted him, and the red dot wavered. Shimon hurtled toward him from the side.

Instinctively Hitler pulled back, slower than normal because of the excruciating pain in his right thigh. He felt a glancing blow to his temple and dropped the heavy pistol.

Hitler cried out in pain and struggled to reach the door to his left that led into the hall. As he pulled the door open and stumbled through, Sonya brought up her Uzi and pulled the trigger. Bullets stitched the wall and ripped through the frame, but her target was gone.

"I missed him!" she shouted.

"Let's get out of here!" yelled Shimon. "He's protected by something we can't penetrate. For now, *we can't touch him but he can kill us*. His goons will be here, any second now!"

"Not yet," she cried out.

"We have no choice. There are too many of them. We don't have a chance if we don't get out now!"

They rushed back through the door to the bedroom. The woman was exactly where they had left her, clutching the sheets tightly around her. Suddenly Sonya recognized her.

"Anna?" she said.

"Sonya!" Shimon shouted. "Come on! We have no more time!"

For a moment, though, Sonya couldn't move. A kaleidoscope of thoughts raced through her mind as she remembered this woman's kindness to Yacov when he was injured in St. Petersburg, and the friendship they had had, before she had returned to Israel.

"How can you be here?" she blurted out. "Don't you know what he's doing?"

Anna's lips barely moved. "I carry his mark. I fear what he would do to me if I ever tried to leave him."

Shimon grabbed Sonya's arm and started pulling her toward the door. "Come on!" She shook him off and ran ahead of him.

She peeked out. "It's clear," she reported.

They dashed into the corridor and ran to the emergency stairs. Sonya put her ear to the door and listened. The sound of clattering boots came clearly through the heavy steel. Sonya inserted a full clip and reached for the doorknob.

"Don't do it," Shimon whispered. "There's too many of them."

"We have no choice."

"Yes, we do. If we can get out a window, we can reach the parapet on the fourth floor."

"We can't . . ." Sonya started to disagree. "No, wait—that might work."

Sonya raced ahead of Shimon, back to Anna's bedroom. Thankfully, the door was still unlocked, and the room beyond was still dark. As they closed the door behind them, they heard the guards burst out of the stairwell down the hall, coming their direction.

"Who is it?" Anna whispered in fright.

"It's Sonya." She and Shimon hurried around and ducked out of sight behind the huge bed. "Anna, our lives are in your hands."

The door opened and the beam of a powerful flashlight poked into the room and darted around.

"Who is it?" Anna asked, her voice quivering with emotion.

"Sergei," came the reply from the hall. "Are you all right, Anna?" He pointed the beam at her face, then moved it away.

"Yes. What do you want?"

"We must search your rooms."

"They've already gone."

Sergei hesitated. "Are you sure, Anna?"

"Positive. I heard shooting and then they ran toward the elevator. I heard the stairway door by the elevator open."

"They've gone up to the fourth floor, looking for the master!" Sergei shouted to the guards that had crowded in behind him. "Quick, before they get away! Check all the rooms between here and the elevator!"

The guards rushed off in the opposite direction from where they had just come, checking each room carefully as they headed for the elevator at the end of the hallway. Sergei pointed the beam of his flashlight in their direction and hurried after them.

"Thank you," Sonya whispered. "Can we get out on your balcony?"

Anna shivered. "Yes. See that heavy bar on the door? Lift that latch on the handle and swing the bar to the right, then pull it open."

"Thank you, Anna," Sonya said again, moving toward the door. "Be sure and lock it after we're gone."

The woman nodded.

Shimon was already swinging the bar over and pulling the heavy armored door open. They stepped out into the blustering snowstorm a second later, and heard Anna thump the heavy locking bolts back into place behind them.

Frigid wind cut through them, stealing their body heat. The snowfall was much heavier now and the flakes were smaller. Sonya looked up at the parapet that ran all the way around the fourth floor.

"Let me boost you up," Shimon whispered urgently. "As soon as you're up, drop a line for me."

She let the Uzi drop to her side as she climbed onto the balcony rail. Shimon grabbed her ankles in his powerful grip and lifted her up, higher and higher. Sonya felt momentary panic as she thought about the three-story drop. She grabbed on to an iron bar with her heavy gloves and pulled herself up and over the top rail, collapsing on the other side.

She got up quickly and looked over the edge. Shimon peered up at her through the snow. She threw a rope over and made it fast around the iron railing. Then Shimon pulled himself up hand-over-hand and landed beside her.

As Sonya coiled the rope and stuffed it back in her pocket, she looked down. Their dark footsteps stood out clearly on the new snow.

"They'll see us for sure," Sonya said.

"Can't be helped. Let's get back around the other side. They'll be up here any moment."

They ran across the deck and skidded around the corner of the building. The clatter of boots came clearly over the moaning wind. Sonya took the short Uzi in her right hand and made sure the clip was full, then looked around the corner. The leading guard was almost on her. She brought the machine pistol around the corner and fired a short burst, point-blank. The man folded up like a wooden soldier. She fired again, dropping the next man, and the other guards hit the deck. Sonya ducked back as they opened up with their AK–74s.

She and Shimon dashed for the far corner of the building. They turned it and stopped. Sonya peeked around, but there was no one in sight yet. The guards were being more cautious now.

"Have you got your grappling hook?" Sonya asked.

"Yes. But they'll nail us before we can get up there."

Sonya said nothing—she knew it was true. She peeked around the corner again. A guard was now partway along the side of the building, in a low crawl, his rifle pointed straight ahead. He squeezed off four quick rounds, striking where Sonya's head had been only a fraction of a second earlier. She dropped down and brought her Uzi around the corner in one smooth movement. She lined up and emptied the rest of the clip. The bullets tore into the man, throwing pieces of his body armor off into the darkness. She ejected the clip and inserted another.

"Sonya!" Shimon shouted. "We're surrounded!"

She drew back and turned around. A dark shadow poked around the far corner. She took quick aim and shot past Shimon, making the shadow disappear.

"Head for the center," ordered Sonya.

They ran down the slick decking, expecting each step to be their last. As they slid to a stop near the center, a guard brought his rifle around the far corner and aimed. Sonya emptied her clip on the man. He slumped to the deck.

"Sonya! There's another one behind you!"

As she turned, she jerked out the spent clip and grabbed her last one. It slipped out of her gloved hand and spun into the swirling snow. The guard brought his rifle up . . . and disappeared in a brilliant white flash. Another explosion sounded behind them. They turned to see smoke billow up from the opposite corner.

"Our team is hitting them with RPGs!" Shimon shouted.

Sonya pointed. "Up on the roof!"

Shimon leaned out against the rail, pulled out his grappling hook, and swung it up and over the roof. The hook skittered up the slates and over the peak. Shimon pulled the nylon line tight. It held. He looked at her and she motioned for him to go first. He started to say something, then gripped the line and pulled himself up.

Shimon was breathing hard by the time he hauled himself over the gutter. He worked his way quickly to the peak and stood on the hook to make sure it didn't slip. Moments later, Sonya's head poked over the roof's edge. He silently urged her to hurry as she clambered up the slick tiles, pulling herself along the rope. When she reached the peak, Shimon pulled the line up and dropped it at their feet.

They looked at his glider, now completely covered with snow. "Think it will start?" he asked.

"If it doesn't, it's been nice knowing you."

They stepped across the roof peak until they were directly above the vent pipe. Shimon eased down and untied the cords holding the hang glider. He braced himself against the pipe as he spread out the wing framing and locked it in place, then picked up the frame and faced down the slope. He clipped himself to the frame and rested the wing poles on the roof behind him.

"Start the engine!" he told her.

Sonya ducked under the billowing wing fabric and ran a hand across the blunt, two-bladed propeller. "Switch on?" she asked.

"Switch on."

She pulled the propeller down, hard. Nothing happened. She did it again. The engine came to life with a quiet, reassuring purr.

"Come around and clip on!" said Shimon. "Hurry—I can't hold this much longer!"

Sonya clipped her harness to the frame and tapped his shoulder, her way of telling him to get going. Shimon reached over and pushed the throttle partway, and they both ran forward a few steps. The Rogallo wing billowed, jerking them into the air. Shimon sat heavily in the swing seat, but Sonya dangled from her harness strap. He reached down, grasped the strap, and hauled her up until she could grab the frame. She pulled herself up and sat in his lap.

They were immediately swallowed up in swirling snow. The glider mushed into a stall and turned to the side. Shimon pushed the throttle to takeoff power. A moment later, they broke out of the snow . . . on a collision course with the Lion's Den!

They both leaned to the side, putting the glider in a steep bank away from the building. The extra weight of a second body severely slowed down the glider's reaction time. Sonya pointed down to a guard who was training his rifle on them. As the glider continued its ponderous turn away, the guard fired three times in rapid succession. Shimon screamed in pain and stiffened. Sonya felt something like a red-hot iron rip through her upper arm.

"I'm hit!" Shimon cried out.

"Me too!" Sonya gasped.

She squeezed the pain into the back of her mind as she looked down at her wound. Her sleeve was bloody, but she could tell she was not bleeding badly. She looked back at Shimon. His wound was through the shoulder and it was bleeding profusely.

"How bad is it?" he asked.

"Let me look," she said, twisting to her left.

With her free hand she ripped the shredded fabric away, revealing a large, ugly wound. She pulled off her left glove and stuffed it into the hole.

"Keep pressure on it. Hold that in place. I'll take the controls."

He nodded and brought his right hand up over to his left shoulder as Sonya grabbed the control stick that was positioned between her legs.

"Okay, press down on it — don't let up!"

Sonya turned forward again and pulled the throttle back to cruise. The compass said they were flying to the southeast, and they had enough altitude to clear anything in the vicinity, if the altimeter was correct. But she had no idea where they were. All she could see was swirling snow, and she knew that by now the snow clouds probably reached all the way to the ground.

She glanced at her watch. Nearly 1:30 A.M. She made a guess at their location and turned more to the south, her best estimate of the heading to Camp Moses.

"You okay?" Sonya asked over her shoulder.

"Yeah," Shimon grunted through clenched teeth. "We on course for home?"

"Yes." At least she hoped they were. She watched her crude instruments, trusting them with their lives. The minutes ticked off as they flew through the blowing snow.

When the estimated amount of time had expired, she pulled the throttle back to idle and started a spiraling turn to the right, descending as slowly as she could. Shimon's head lolled on her shoulder.

"Shimon! Are you still with me?"

There was no response.

She strained her eyes, trying to see through the snow, which was beginning to ease up. Suddenly the snow stopped and it began to rain lightly. They were still several hundred meters in the air, but Sonya had no idea where they were. She only knew they were somewhere southwest of Jerusalem, but that covered a lot of territory. There were no ground lights for reference in this remote Judean wilderness area.

She tried to remember what her IDF instructor had said about search patterns, but her brain wouldn't work. She was still pondering what to do when she saw a flare several kilometers to the east. They had agreed to risk the flares if the rain continued at Camp Moses and their ETA was thirty minutes overdue. One every fifteen minutes would be safe, they decided, under rainy conditions. She moved the control stick to the right and pushed the throttle to maximum power.

A few minutes later, through the rain, she made out the familiar outline of the hidden valley. She pulled the throttle and put the glider into a steep spiraling descent. She lined up on the clearing and tried to flare. Too fast. She tumbled over as soon as her feet touched down. The glider wing collapsed over them.

"Help us out!" she shouted.

THIRTY-THREE

D-Day Minus 4 Months

Sergei peered through the tough plastic face shield in his helmet. It was stifling inside the body armor, but this was the only protection against the monstrous insects. Although relatively lightweight, the jointed armor gave him an awkward, stiff-legged gait as he continued his outdoor circuit of the Lion's Den, checking on the new defensive construction that would prevent another air attack. As an added benefit, it would also provide additional protection from the continued assaults of the flying beasts.

That the bronzed creatures possessed a keen intelligence was beyond question. Even after the most thorough precautions, they still occasionally got past, with agonizing results. They could be manhandled by two or three men in body armor, but only heavy weapons could kill them. Small arms were unable to penetrate their armored exoskeletons. The few that had been killed had not made a dent in their countless number.

Sergei scanned the front of the Lion's Den. Gone were the simple graceful lines of stone; thick protective shutters now covered all the windows and doors. The shutters were a sandwich of bullet-proof plastic and thick, tempered glass imbedded by a steel ribbing, making the Lion's Den virtually impenetrable.

All first-floor doors opened into armored porches. Like airlocks, the inner doors could not be opened until the outer doors were closed, and armored guards were stationed inside the porches to eliminate any creatures that might get through the outer doors. The final touch had been to replace the Mercedes limousines with BMP-3s, although Hitler, like the first time he'd been attacked, had not ventured outside the Lion's Den since the terrible events of a fortnight ago.

Having finished his rounds, Sergei stopped at the front entrance and looked down the mountain slope at the Old City of Jerusalem. He sighed. It had been a long time since his master had been in his temple throneroom. The plague of the winged beasts had continued for almost four months now, and the entire world continued to reel under the siege, with no end in sight.

Fortunately, Sergei thought, the world is blaming the two madmen at the Wailing Wall for this terrible insect plague. The old men continued to proclaim that the beasts from the abyss were God's wrath against a world that had chosen to worship a false god instead of the one and only true God. Thus far, Hitler was at their mercy. Sergei was told he must wait for "the appointed time," when his Prince—as promised—would personally destroy those two who were responsible for all the pain and suffering that had crippled the entire world. In the meantime, Hitler had become even more obsessed about finding Sonya and her guerrilla band!

Sergei heard a muffled, buzzing noise somewhere to the left. He turned his head and saw three of the demonic creatures flying directly at him. The lead one crashed into him, knocking him to the ground. He lay on his back like an upended turtle, staring out at the disturbingly human-like face peering down at him. Then the thing slobbered its foul-smelling yellow slime onto his face shield, blocking Sergei's vision. He heard the other two creatures thump down next to him. They began rocking his body with their powerful claws as their stingers sought a way through the joints of his body armor.

Sergei could hear guards yelling, but the creatures did not leave. The voices grew louder and the sound of heavy footsteps came through the helmet ear baffles. As the armored guards grabbed the creatures and pulled them off, another man helped Sergei up. Once standing again, he stumbled to the outer front door. When it clanged shut behind him, the porch guard pushed the release on the reinforced inner door. Heavy bolts retracted and it swung open with a groan.

Safe inside the palace, Sergei shed his armor, unharmed but shaken. After taking a few moments to gulp a glass of vodka and collect himself, he mounted the stairs to the plotting room on the second floor. He was surprised to find his master there, dressed in uniform. It was the first time Hitler had left his rooms since he had been injured in Tel Aviv . . . since the day of Sonya Petrov's attack on the Lion's Den.

Hitler heard Sergei enter the room, but continued looking through the reinforced windows in disgust. Because of the steel ribbing, he no longer had a clear view of the magnificent vista beyond the mountain. He was frustrated at having been completely out of touch for two weeks, since the day of the Pac-Ten conference.

His frustration turned to uncontrollable anger as he thought about that day, not because of the excruciating pain of the stings he had suffered, or from the failure to lure Sonya and her rebel force into their trap, but because of her outrageous attack on him personally . . . here, in his own home. He had survived, but at the expense of being humiliated in the eyes of everyone who knew what had happened. Nothing was said in his hearing, but he knew what was being said behind his back. His revenge on Sonya was now his only obsession. *This final insult will not go unpunished! I will find her. And when I do, I will kill her—with my own hands!*

He shook his head briefly, as though to clear his mind. Motioning Sergei toward the plotting board, he asked, "What's the latest status on our Reich forces here in Israel?"

"No good news, I'm afraid: Troops outside the metropolitan areas continue to be slaughtered by Sonya's guerrillas, whenever our troops come in contact with them," Sergei reported. "Those who stay within the confines of the cities are safe from guerrilla attack but not from these flying beasts, which show no sign of letting up. Frankly, I'm not sure which is worse!"

"I ordered protection for our troops. What has been done?" Hitler demanded.

"We have armored our vital installations and vehicles, as you ordered. We have also provided lightweight body armor for the men. We have shielded the entrances to all governmental, public, and military buildings, like we've done here at the Lion's Den, so that the blasted things can't get in. Our key people and troops here in Israel are as protected as we can make them. However . . ." Sergei broke off, suddenly afraid to continue down this road, knowing where it would lead.

"What?"

"Things are pretty bad in the rest of the world. Only the wealthy can afford protection from this plague, and even then they are trapped, afraid to come out of their safety zones. As for the rest, they don't stand a chance against the attacks of these flying creatures."

"First things first," said Hitler. "For now, we need to take care of things here. The rest must take care of themselves."

Sergei nodded at the topographical map on the plotting table. "I see you've been plotting the guerrilla attacks," changing the direction of the conversation.

"Yes," said Hitler. "I've marked all the locations of their attacks before the Tel Aviv summit. Now, I need to know where they have hit us since that time."

"There," Sergei pointed, "and over there, and there." He indicated two spots just south of Jerusalem, another just to the east of Hebron, and several more up in the north, in the Golan Heights northeast of the Kineret. "That group in the north troubles me. They take the initiative and their attacks are vicious. They've got to be stopped but every time we try, our units end up getting wiped out."

Hitler nodded. "We'll get them after we deal with Sonya." He took the pointer and stabbed the two attack areas near Jerusalem and the one just east of Hebron.

"What do you make of it?" Sergei asked.

"All these attacks cluster around this area." With a blue marker, Hitler drew a crude circle about 30 kilometers southeast of Jerusalem. "Look how close these latest attacks are to that terrible loss we sustained back when their attacks first began," he said, pointing to the Jehoshaphat Valley about 10 kilometers south and to the west of where he had circled.

Sergei nodded. "I see where you're headed," he said, "and that would also be about the maximum distance those gliders could go in a snowstorm. We studied the crashed gliders we found. Figuring a twenty percent reserve, they had just enough range to reach that far. Putting what we know together, they've got to be in this area right here," Sergei said, pointing to a particularly remote and rugged area made up of valleys and mountains.

"Very well. Tell General Anayev I want him to reconnoiter this area immediately! I think we're getting close." The blue-gray eyes smoldered with his hatred for the woman who represented the one obstacle that could send him back to the pit. "I want Sonya and her stinking brood found and annihilated!"

D-Day Minus 3 Months and 3 Weeks

Sonya listened to the tactical radio chatter in #1 cavern, unconsciously rubbing her arm. She winced at the soreness and looked over at Shimon. It had been just over a month since their raid on the Lion's Den. Her wound was healing, but Shimon's shoulder was still heavily bandaged. They had lost four men in the raid—three at the Lion's Den and one who had apparently gotten lost on the way back. Like the rest of the camp, Sonya mourned those who had died. They were all the family she had left.

She sighed. The mission had been a tactical failure but a strategic success. Although Hitler had eluded them, there was no question that the direct attack on his lair had boosted morale in all the camps. There was also no doubt in her mind that something supernatural had saved Hitler's life. She'd had him right where she wanted him, in her sights at point-blank range, but the strange green shadow that had appeared out of nowhere, shielded him from her bullets. She reluctantly admitted that Anatoly had been right, again. Hitler was being protected until his showdown with Yeshua. Otherwise, he would be dead by now.

Well, she thought, no use dwelling on what might have been. Now there is something new to worry about.

At her nod, the operator switched off the speakers and put his headphones back on. She and Shimon walked back to her office nook, where the topographical map of Israel was spread out on a table.

"What do you make of those radio intercepts?" she asked, looking at the areas she had marked with red pins.

Shimon rubbed his chin. "The number of military convoys in our area is up considerably, mainly small armored units. And overall military activity is definitely increasing just to the north of us."

"Yes, but what does it mean?"

"For one thing, I think they're beginning to cope with those flying creatures. Our reports tell us that they've armored their vital equipment and buildings. And although the body armor their troops are using may be cumbersome, it works. That we know firsthand. Which means they're beginning to get around again. And, for some reason, they suddenly seem to have a great deal of interest in our general location."

"That's what bothers me. For the most part, we've laid pretty low since our attack on the Lion's Den, considering . . ."

"Well, yes and no," Shimon interrupted. "We've laid pretty low, Sonya, but not the rest of our forces. As you know, they've hit them three times since then. You and I just missed all the fun because of your recuperation. But it doesn't take many brains to figure out that where there's smoke, there's fire, and where there are multiple attacks, there must be guerrillas close by. Probably the only mistake they made was hitting them three times in a row in the same general area. But it's hard to get upset at their enthusiasm, or their results!"

"I agree and I can't argue with your logic either. That would account for the number of fly-overs we've had in the last few days." She paused and looked up at him. "We're in danger, Shimon. Every instinct tells me they've got us bracketed. And if that's true, it's only a matter of time."

"Hitler's got a lot of problems—big problems worldwide, especially with those creatures. How high can we really rate on his attention scale?"

Sonya began pacing before the map. "Number one would be my guess—since he wanted us badly enough to set up that elaborate trap in Tel Aviv. And that was *before* we attacked the Lion's Den!"

Shimon shivered. "What do you suggest we do?"

"For now, really lay low, go under cover. Double our exterior guard. Extend our perimeter outside the ridge surrounding the valley, and increase the number of sentries at the tunnel entrance on the valley side. Camouflage the vehicles and go over the emergency perimeter defense we developed. Make sure everyone knows his job. If they find us," she said fiercely, "we'll give them the fight of their lives."

D-Day Minus 3 Months and 2 Weeks

The night was dark and overcast. A warm wind blew in from the southeast. Since the freak snowstorm a month and a half ago, an early summer had settled into Israel. The sentry posted on the north ridge of the valley, just above the main tunnel entrance to the hidden valley, had picked up something strange in his sector, just north and a little west of Camp Moses. He radioed his warning to those on the inside, in #1 cavern, and Sonya and Shimon, although closer to the main entranceway, decided to play it safe and go the long way through the valley exit and then up the north valley wall to where the sentry was posted. Sonya rested her elbows on the top of the ridge and brought up her low-light binoculars. She soon traded them for an infrared-red imaging scope, slowly examining the entire terrain that gradually sloped downward in front of them.

"See anything?" Shimon said softly.

"Not a thing."

He sighed. "Someone's out there. Our scanner picked up something about the same time Hezzy here did."

Sonya looked back at the sentry, now monitoring the tactical radio nets with the portable scanner. "How many?"

"Just that one transmission," Hezzy replied. "Can't be more than one or two."

"Keep listening."

"Where is he?" asked Shimon. "What's he doing?"

"Don't know yet, for sure. All we know is, he's close," said Sonya.

A dark shadow flitted close overhead. Sonya grabbed the light-intensifying binoculars. The stinging creature bounced in her field of view as she struggled to track it. It flew erratically for several moments, then landed behind a large boulder. A faint clicking noise drifted up to them, along with the clatter of disturbed rocks. This continued for a short time, just long enough for the giant insect to realize it couldn't penetrate the body armor the man was wearing. Then the creature took to the air again, looking for a new target, and silence returned.

"Well, it doesn't take a lot of brains to know where our man is now," Hezzy said with a soft chuckle. "He's moved a little to the east of where he was earlier." He gave his binoculars to Shimon and pointed toward a boulder about 100 meters from the ridge. "He's behind that. I'm sure of it."

"Seems likely," Shimon agreed.

"I'll bet on it," Sonya said. "Let's see if our sniper can flush him out."

Shimon crawled back and returned with the sharpshooter. The man cradled his M-16 with its massive low-light scope. Sonya offered him the binoculars, but the man shook his head and switched on his scope. He brought it up and scanned until he found the large rock.

"I see it," he said, taking his eye away from the scope. "Want me to move around where I can get a more direct line of fire and take him out?"

"Yes, but stay below the ridge as long as possible," said Sonya. "You've got a southeast wind and that will amplify any sound you make."

The sniper disappeared into the gloom and began working his way silently to the west, carefully staying below the north ridge. About five minutes later, they heard a single, sharp report. In another five the sniper had crawled back to where they were waiting.

"I serviced the target," he said.

"You sure he's dead?" Sonya asked.

"You can depend on it. Body armor and all!"

The second spy, hidden farther down the slope, watched

quietly, not moving a muscle when he heard the shot. About ten minutes later, he saw the dark shapes above him retreating from the upper rim of the ridge. He waited for several more minutes, then crawled up to where they had just been seen. He scanned the reverse slope with his binoculars. The men on the ridge, seen just moments before, had disappeared into thin air. No sight of them whatsoever. Instead, a large basin he didn't know existed lay directly in front of him, enclosed on every side by the high hills that surrounded it. Lying on his stomach, he scanned the entire basin, slowly and carefully, without making a sound. Occasionally he saw the flickers of candlelight from what appeared to be caves on the walls of the valley. But he heard no sounds, saw no people. The night was still. He knew what he had found. Now if only he could get out of here alive, he also knew he would be a hero!

Hitler looked up from the plotting table as General Mikhail Anayev marched into the room. "And what is the good news you want to tell me, general?" Hitler barked, impatiently.

"I think we have her, *mein Führer!*" said General Anayev with a broad smile, pleased and proud to be the bearer of such good news. He pointed toward an area about 35 kilometers southeast of Jerusalem, in the Judean Hills. "Our intelligence reports suggest that the main base of the Israeli guerrillas is located right here, in a remote valley that isn't indicated on any of our relief maps. It's surrounded by rocky hills. Tough to get to. A perfect location. We've flown over the area several times and haven't spotted anything, but our geologists say the area has to be pockmarked with large caves and caverns. Last night, we sent in two spies. Their snipers got one, but the other watched them go back over the top of the ridge, down into the valley. When he got to the top, they had disappeared — in less than five minutes! So the entrance to their hideout has to be someplace on the inside north wall of the valley."

"Are you sure?" Hitler demanded, trying to conceal his excitement.

"Absolutely. I'll stake my life on it. Our man also saw lights coming from what appeared to be caves in the valley walls."

Hitler knew they had found what they'd been looking for

the moment Anayev pointed to the location of the valley. It was almost in the center of the blue circle Hitler had drawn on the plotting board several weeks earlier. "That has to be Sonya," Hitler agreed, sobering to the task that was now within his grasp. "How many do you think an area like that could hold?"

The general scratched his chin. "If our geologists are right about the caves, they could have a small city under there— perhaps as many as five or ten thousand," he said. "What do you want us to do?"

"I want her on her knees before me, pleading for her life," Hitler ground out the words between his teeth, glaring at the map before him. Then he turned to the general. "Put together a strike force. Use whatever you need, but I want that camp obliterated and I want the world to know it! This time, we know where she is, so I don't want any last-minute screw-ups. You understand me?"

"Yes, my leader. Sergei and I have already anticipated your desire. We have formulated plans for your approval. We suggest that we use twenty thousand ground troops, after an initial search-and-destroy strike by our paratroop unit. With your approval, we'd like to attack sometime by the end of next week. The moon will be full, and that will facilitate our parachute drop. They'll be the focal point of our attack. If they succeed, the operation will succeed."

"But won't they see you coming?"

"It's more important that our men see where they're going. Moonlight will help us do that. Besides, by the time we get inside that valley, we're practically home free. Our reconnaissance tells us their guards are on the outside of the ridge surrounding the valley, so we'll drop the paratroopers on the inside, behind their line of defense. Almost identical to what Sonya did when she attacked the Lion's Den. This time we use her own tactics against her."

General Anayev realized his mistake even before he saw the look on his leader's face. He continued quickly, hoping the good news would cover his blunder. "We'll drop in behind their perimeter troops and attack the entrance into the caverns before they know what's hit them. By the time those on the inside realize what's going on, it will be too late. We'll bottle them up and what the paratroopers miss, the ground troops that surround the valley will mop up. No one will escape."

Hitler's anger disappeared as quickly as it had flared. This plan meant the end of his problems here in Israel. His Prince had promised to take care of the rest. He rubbed his hands together. "I like it," he said. "Next week is not a day too soon for me. Do it!"

"Consider it done, my leader," Anayev promised.

D-Day Minus 3 Months

The build-up began at dusk, darkness becoming the ally of the attackers. Under strict radio silence, the Reich closed all major highways to the south and east of Jerusalem and started transporting the twenty thousand ground troops, by helicopter, to their designated rendezvous points, 10 kilometers or so all around the perimeter of the targeted valley. Encircling the entire valley and storming it from every side would prevent any of the guerrilla rebels from escaping. That was their primary objective. Every operational Hip helicopter in Israel had been commandeered for this major assault operation.

Yuri Kagan and Andrei Denisov, each dressed in full body armor, felt the wind on their faces as they sat near the open door of the Hind attack helicopter. Hitler wanted the entire operation on tape, for the world to see—but not until after its successful completion. Darkness had fallen. The only evidence of the activity below was the movement of thousands of pinpoints of light, giving Yuri and Andrei the feeling that they were watching the eerie ritual of fireflies from high above. Except for the darkness, they had the best seats in the house. Only the tip of the moon was visible, as it began its debut on the eastern horizon.

The pilot came down, slowly circling the deployment area so that Andrei, now hanging outside the open door by two leather straps secured around his waist, could get whatever he could on videotape. At close quarters, the lights began to take shape. With the help of his own floodlights, Andrei taped the long lines of Reich troops, waiting to board Hip transport helicopters below. As soon as each transport was filled, it lifted off and headed south, hugging the rugged terrain as closely as possible. After a few moments, enough time for Andrei to videotape the activity below, the chopper rose above the deployment area and took a position high above the Hip helicopters that were now beginning to move Hitler's 'stormtroopers' to the rendezvous areas to the southeast. The real grunt work would be left to these ground pounders, the stormtroopers who would be positioned in various sites surrounding the target area, waiting for the signal to tighten their living net that surrounded their living prey. By the time they covered the rugged 10-kilometer distance to the target, the paratroopers would have hopefully neutralized the enemy, the stormtroopers mopping up whoever tried to escape or was left hiding in the caves that surrounded the valley floor.

"I'm glad we're not flying in one of those," Yuri said, pointing to the lights of a Hip that they could see below, the erratic movement giving visual evidence of its presence as it twisted its ponderous way through the ravines beneath them. "Are you getting any of this on tape?" he asked for the third time.

Andrei said nothing as he concentrated on following the helicopter with his camera. Finally he acknowledged Yuri's question. "The viewing audience won't see any detail, but they will see the lights and if you do your job right, they can conjure up the rest in their minds!"

Egor Kaugin sat in a corner of the cabin, looking like the world's best-protected hockey player in his plastic armor. He guarded his sound equipment as he waited for Yuri's first on-camera report. He knew that Yuri would do whatever it took. Yuri was the best.

When Andrei had all the shots he needed, Yuri signaled the pilot and the Hind returned to Ben-Gurion Airport. It set down next to one of the large transport planes that would soon take the paratroopers to the target area. At his briefing earlier in the day, Yuri had been told that General Anayev's plan was to use seventy transport planes to drop two thousand well-armed paratroopers directly into the valley, in front of the stormtroopers who would attack on foot. The paratroopers were already milling around nervously, waiting for their turn to go.

Just before midnight, the three newsmen were hustled aboard one of the transport planes that would soon carry its passengers to the target area. As they pushed their way past the combat-loaded paratroopers, Yuri grinned in spite of the situation. He knew the soldiers were not happy about sharing their aircraft with civilians. But they also knew whose orders they were operating under. As soon as one of the crew closed the door, the pilot taxied into position and lifted off.

The transport plane made a gentle turn to the east and followed the Tel Aviv–Jerusalem highway about halfway to Jerusalem. Then the pilot turned to the southeast and began his climb, making large circles to gain the necessary altitude without flying over the target area. When he reached altitude, he flew to a point 10 kilometers north of the target area. There he cut his engines and began to drift south. At 2,000 meters altitude, a crewman pulled the door open and the paratroopers began attaching their ripcords to the static line. When the green light winked on, the men tumbled out, one after the other.

Andrei had been filming the entire time, and as the last paratrooper jumped, he rushed to the side of the door, Yuri directly behind him. Hanging on against the pressure of the wind, they watched the blossoming sea of black rectangles below them, drifting toward a broad valley surrounded by rugged limestone hills.

Five kilometers beyond the target area, the plane's engines came to life again, well out of earshot of the guerrillas that were holed up in the valley walls. It made a large sweeping turn to the west and headed back for Ben-Gurion Airport, its mission complete.

"Hope General Anayev picked the right valley," Egor yelled above the noise. "I'd hate to have to explain to Hitler if we put two thousand men down there and no one's home!"

Sonya could hear the hushed murmur of the children in #3 cavern. They had been told to stay out of #4. Everyone knew something big was up, although nothing had been said officially. They had not been told if this was just another practice run or the real thing. The Camp Moses fighters were packed closely around her as she waited for Shimon to return. Minutes before, she had gotten a disturbing radio report from the perimeter guard on the north side of the valley. She had sent Shimon to check it out and immediately sounded the alarm that everyone in the caves should get to the caverns as quickly as possible. This had been an ongoing drill since the beginning, almost three and a half years ago now. They had practiced it again and again over the past several weeks, ever since they had been alerted to an increasing enemy presence. Tonight, one and all had moved quickly and silently when the alarm was sounded. Within minutes of the first alert, all were safely within the confines of the caverns.

"What's going on?" she demanded when Shimon returned, pushing his way through the men gathered around her in #4 cavern.

"It looks really bad," he gasped, out of breath. "They're dropping hundreds of paratroopers directly into the valley, behind our perimeter guards. Those already down appear to be waiting till the drop is complete. They must be under orders to regroup before they attack."

"Do you think they know where the tunnel is?"

"Your guess is as good as mine. The moonlight doesn't help us. They seem to be gathering along the northern side of the valley, no more than 500 meters from the entrance, so they must know generally where it is. They can't miss it if they start their sweep up the north wall! Hopefully they'll start somewhere else, but from the looks of it, I doubt it."

"What about our perimeter troops?

"The forward observers have picked up Reich troop movement all around the camp, still three, four thousand meters away. Could be as many as ten thousand! I told them to hold their ground. I think we can give them trouble for a little while, especially with all that pest-control armor they've come up with. That's got to slow them down. But realistically, Sonya, I don't see how we have a chance. It's the paratroopers on the inside of the valley that we're going to have a hard time stopping."

"There's always a chance!" Sonya snapped. She turned to the fighting men who surrounded her.

"Men, we must move quickly. Any moment, the enemy will penetrate the tunnel entrance to the caverns. We must be ready with the interior defense we've practiced so often in the past. The only advantage we have is that they can't get to us unless they come through the tunnel over there that leads to the valley," she stated, pointing at the darkened entranceway to the valley in the far corner of #4 cavern. "Now that the families are safely inside the other caverns, we need to narrow the width of the tunnel entrance by pushing those large boulders into the entranceway, on the inside. That will slow them down, initially. When the barriers are in place, turn off the lights in #4, all except the spots on the tunnel entranceway. After that, our sharpshooters will have to do the rest. Hopefully we can pick a lot of them off as they crawl over the boulders, before they get into the caverns themselves. But realistically, we are outmanned and outgunned, and it is only a matter of time until some of them get in, and then it's 'Katie, bar the door.' "

A murmur swept around the circle of men surrounding Sonya.

"I know the odds are overwhelmingly against us. We knew that someday this day would come. So, now it's here. Now we will see what we're really made of. Anatoly said that the God of Israel would fight for us. He has done that, again and again. We face staggering odds—beyond anything we ever anticipated. We call on the God of Israel to fight for us. But if He doesn't, *we* will still fight to the very end. Remember Masada! *We* will never give up! Now go!"

There were no objections, only resolution on their faces as they filed out, silently, in orderly fashion. This was their destiny, and they would fight to the last breath.

"It's the mothers and the children I worry about," Sonya said quietly, to no one in particular. "The children are our future. It is for them that we fight!" Sudden tears brimmed in her eyes, but she knew she did not have time for the sorrow that gripped her heart. She must be strong. Everyone looked to her for courage. All we can do is defend our little camp the best we know how, she thought. *Anything can happen, but not if we give up.*

Despite her brave words, she felt hollow. She knew nothing could save them. She knew she had just sent her men to their deaths. Their families would be next. She knew the attack would be vicious because she knew the man who had ordered it. But she would never give up. She would fight to the death, with or without the God of Israel!

The angel lowered the trumpet from his lips and bowed before the throne. Then he streaked earthward, trailing behind him a broad wake of incandescent vapor. He dropped to the Euphrates River, near the site of the partially built city of Babylon, and held his hands out over the sparkling waters. A line formed across the river and widened rapidly, parting the waters and revealing the muddy bottom. Then the bottom split, opening a twisting shaft that sank deep into the earth's crust.

The angel descended until he came to a broad niche, where four statuelike figures rested on a large stone shelf. The seated figures were covered with a thick coat of dust.

"You are released!" the angel commanded.

Instantly, myriads of tiny cracks formed in the dust as the four creatures moved. They stood and dusted themselves off, then looked questioningly at the angel.

"By the order of Almighty God whom you serve, your hour has come," commanded God's messenger. "Gather your army and ride forth. *Kill a third of all mankind now dwelling upon Earth. Your death march will begin in Israel.* Now, I command you, go forth!"

The four angels descended even lower into the bowels of the Earth. There, in a great cavern, they walked among their rapidly awakening army and horses.

"The time has come. Avengers from hell, mount your horses!" one of the angels commanded.

The horsemen immediately obeyed. Each of their horse-like mounts stood over 3 meters tall, with a head like a lion. The armor of the horsemen, now free of the dust of the ages, glowed a dazzling red with blue-and-yellow trim. Together, horses and horsemen, their appearance was both awesome and frightening.

Then the 200 million mounted troops lined up in formation, their ranks running down into the very heart of the Earth.

"Follow me!" God's messenger announced as he began to ascend toward the heavens.

The angel of God flew up the rock chimney and streaked toward the west, the four angelic generals and their horsemen streaming behind him. They swept over Iraq and Jordan and, finally, Israel, where the angel led them to a certain spot, high in the heavens above. A full moon cast eerie shadows on the valley below, its light revealing small clusters of tiny living things converging like ants for a feast.

"We begin here!" commanded the angel of God, and he released the horde of horsemen.

"How many?" was all the leader of the horsemen asked.

"All of them!" was the angel's reply.

"I want you to go back and organize the family units in #3. Put the children and women in #s1 and 2, and arm everyone who has demonstrated that they can handle a rifle or pistol — man, woman, or child. The ones with the arms should position themselves at the back of #3. This will be the last line of defense," Sonya told Shimon. He started to protest, but she cut him off. "Don't argue with me. If they get through us at the tunnel entrance, you're the last hope for our people here. Now go, Shimon!"

"Yes, Sonya. I will. God be with you."

"And with you, my friend."

She grabbed her M-16 and sprinted through the large cavern toward the entrance to the tunnel.

The caverns were dark, except for the light of the lanterns that the men used to prepare for battle. The electrical lights had all been turned off, except for the spotlights that lit the rock barriers at the entranceway to the tunnel. The last lantern was behind her now, its feeble light cast dancing shadows on the walls ahead. She wondered if she would ever return this way again. Behind her, her men waited, quietly, expectantly, for what would soon be chaos. She got on her hands and knees and crawled forward, around the stone boulders that blocked the entranceway into the caverns, barriers that had been planned years ago for exactly a time like this. Her rifle at the ready, she moved past the stone barriers into the tunnel.

One of the enemy advance guards penetrated the tunnel entrance from the valley side. Unsure of what waited in the darkness ahead, he shot off a round, blindly. Sonya could see the wink of the weapon fire before she heard the report. She hit the ground and fired back as she did, her actions the product of reflex training more than anything else. The enemy's bullet ricocheted from one wall to the other, spraying rock chips onto the tunnel floor. But before the bullet had even come to rest, the paratrooper flew backward to the rocky floor, both hands around his neck, gurgling his dying gasp. Then all was silent again.

A moment later, a dark figure climbed over the boulders behind Sonya. He carefully felt his way over to where he knew she would be.

"How many are there?" she asked when he reached her side, out of breath.

"Too many. Hezzy's got a good view from the top of the ridge and he estimates there may be a thousand, maybe more in the valley," he answered, excitedly. "They're less than 100 meters away, spread out in horizontal lines. Our only chance is right here, picking them off as they try to get around the boulders. While we can, we need to get out of the tunnel!"

"Okay, let's get out of here. I can hear their voices outside. They'll be here any minute."

First, the sound of the enemy's voices grew louder as they echoed through the tunnel they had just discovered. Then the sound of movement, as the advance guard slowly and cautiously made its way through the tunnel, moving slowly upwards toward the partially blocked entranceway to the caverns. Then, in the distance, the erratic sound of frantic gunfire, not just a random burst of gunfire from here, then there, but rather from all over in the darkness outside the tunnel entranceway. And then, only silence.

Outside, the moonlit sky brightened with a reddish glow, like a spectacular sunset. As Hitler's army watched, frozen in amazement, the glow materialized into a heavenly sea of horses and riders, descending to the Earth.

The horsemen fanned out across the valley and the surrounding hills, leaving death in their wake. The galloping steeds, snorting fire, brimstone, and smoke, fiercely rode down *everyone* who bore the mark of Satan-Meshiah. The Reich troops fired their weapons frantically, but were helpless against the oncoming surge of horsemen that glowed as though they had been plucked from a furnace. Not a soul survived. It was over before it even began.

When the glowing cavalry had finished their assignment, they mounted to the skies, circled above the battlefield, and then streaked away toward the north before fanning out in all directions, to the ends of the Earth.

The valley and the hills that surrounded Camp Moses returned to the silence of the night, the moonlight casting its shadows over the thousands of bodies littering the valley floor and the rugged landscape beyond. Slowly, the shaken perimeter guards returned to the camp, wondering what they had just witnessed!

Cautiously, Sonya and her defense-team leader made their way over the protective boulders, through the tunnel, down toward the valley entranceway. He pulled a flashlight out of his pack and gave it to her. She held it out to the side and clicked it on, ready to drop it if anyone fired.

"Come on," she whispered.

The flashlight kept extending their sight until they got close to the entrance. Then she turned it off.

Silvery moonlight streamed in from outside. She edged forward until she could see out. Her nose gave the first indication that something was radically wrong.

Below her, the valley was a silent landscape of horror. Reich troops covered the valley floor, sprawled on the rocky soil, each body bearing a gaping chest wound and exuding the stench of burnt flesh. Overhead the sky was clear, the moon bright. A cold wind blew through the valley. But there wasn't a sign of life anywhere.

"Back inside!" Sonya ordered.

A few minutes later, Sonya and the other defenders made it back through the confused crowd in #3, to Shimon's side.

"What happened?" he asked.

"They're dead," a dazed Sonya said. "All of them. Every last one of them!"

"How?"

She just shook her head.

PART 6

DEATH AND LIFE

Who is this who comes from Edom,
With garments of glowing colors from Bozrah,
This One who is majestic in His apparel,
Marching in the greatness of His strength?
"It is I who speak in righteousness, mighty to save."
Why is Your apparel red,
And Your garments like the one who treads in the wine press?
"I have trodden the wine trough alone,
And from the peoples there was no man with Me.
I also trod them in My anger,
And trampled them in My wrath;
And their lifeblood is sprinkled on My garments,
And I stained all My raiment.
For the day of vengeance was in My heart,
And My year of redemption has come."

—*Isaiah 63:1–4*

THIRTY-FOUR

D-Day Minus 3 Days

Adolf Hitler Stadium was ablaze, illuminated by banks of stadium lights. Built of concrete and Jerusalem limestone, the 400,000-seat structure was one of the most famous symbols of the Fourth Reich. At one end, a huge 35-meter Reich cross and emblem towered above the seats. Red-and-white neon tubes outlined the insignia and the "666," augmented by laser projectors. Powerful searchlights pointed straight upward, forming a semicircular series of blue-white columns around the top of the stadium. Huge, bannerlike Fourth Reich flags, draped lengthwise, filled the intervals between the lights.

Tonight the seats were jammed, and thousands thronged the broad boulevard outside. But the occasion was not one of joy and celebration. Instead, the crowd's mood ranged from sullen to hostile. Five months of crippling pain from insect stings and then another three months of the marauders on horseback had left Hitler's domain decimated. A third of the earth's population had been wiped out by this last onslaught. Only the Reich Emblems kept the populace in check.

They blame me! Hitler thought angrily as he stood in the private tunnel that led to the stage at the end of the stadium opposite the huge emblem of his reign. They blame me, the god of this world, because I have no control of those two lunatics at the Wailing Wall! No one can destroy those two idiots, or stop the plagues they unleash on my people! He had tried everything and, it seemed, every time he did, they just cranked the terror up another notch! He was tired of making excuses for things he didn't understand and couldn't control. Well, after the rally tonight, things would be different. Tonight, for the first time in what seemed to be forever, he had good news to tell the people. His Prince had finally given him his promise. The great event the world had clamored for would occur in less than three days—on the seven-year anniversary of his treaty with Israel! What irony!

Yes, by the time he got through tonight, he would have the people back under his control. The Kagan, Kaugin, and Denisov team would be there to televise this momentous announcement he was planning to make to the world. Finally, the waiting was over.

Hitler marched up the short ramp and onto the stage, Sergei two steps behind him. Two 30-meter-high television screens flickered to life above the top rows on either side of the stadium, magnifying his image for all to see. Another screen was mounted outside the stadium for the benefit of the crowds watching there. There was little applause when his uniformed figure appeared, only an uneasy hush.

"Citizens of the Reich!" His words rolled out of the powerful sound system and seemed to shake the massive stadium. "We have withstood the worst devastation our enemy can throw at us—death and destruction. Yet, we have survived." He paused, letting the words sink in before continuing. "We have survived the dagger of the beast, poisoned water, asteroid strikes, fire and hail, and finally, the fury of these horsemen from hell. You are alive today because of your strength and my leadership—despite all that our enemy has tried to do to destroy us!"

Hitler held his arms straight out as his scream echoed through the stadium.

"Nothing can stop us but we ourselves! Our enemies can maim us, they can kill us, they can blow up our cities and burn down our forests—but they will never control us. Do you hear me? I said *never*!" his voice thundered.

The crowd was hesitant at first, but then exploded into waves of applause and wild cheering. The blue-gray eyes blazed from the giant TV screens as Hitler waited for the excitement to abate.

"Two days from tomorrow, the All-Powerful One will destroy, finally and forever, those two madmen at the Wailing Wall. Those lunatic prophets of Yeshua who are responsible for the terror that has filled our hearts. We have done nothing to deserve their wrath, and yet they try to destroy our world. Why? Because *their* leader is contemptuous and mean, while *your* leader and lord, the god of this world, Adolf . . ."

He stopped abruptly as he saw the half million people packed into the stadium begin to murmur and point to something high above, behind where he stood. Turning, he saw two bright objects silently drift over the top of the stadium entrance. Their path continued to midfield, where they descended slowly to the ground. A new murmur ran through the crowd. It was the two men from the Wall, their robes illuminated by some brilliant but unseen light source. The noisy stadium of moments earlier had become deathly silent.

"What are you doing here?" Hitler demanded, his voice coming across the loud speaker system, loud and clear.

Moses raised his staff and pointed at the leader of the Fourth Reich. "We are here at the command of Yeshua! Jesus of Nazareth! Iesus to you, little man." Though he had no microphone, the prophet's voice resounded clearly for all to hear. "Just as you are here to serve your Prince, whom you mistakenly call the All-Powerful One."

Hitler stamped his foot in anger. "How dare you say these things? I order you to leave, this minute. Get out!" he screamed.

Elijah tugged on Moses' sleeve. "Is he under the impression we are now, somehow, under his control?"

"It would appear so," Moses replied.

"How sad."

"Leave at once!" Hitler screamed again.

"I fear we have upset him," Elijah observed.

"If you do not leave . . ." Hitler fell silent, even though the television screens showed his mouth moving, framed by his purple face.

"There is only one true God, the Almighty Father, and

Yeshua is His Son!" Moses thundered back, interrupting the puny little man now standing speechless on the platform. "*All glory belongs to them and to them alone!*"

He raised his staff and pointed it toward the end of the stadium. The crowd gasped as fire shot out of it, slashing through the two massive I-beams supporting the Fourth Reich insignia. The huge swastika toppled slowly backward until the "666" was upside down. Then it crashed down on the cars and buses parked below, crushing them and raising a billowing cloud of dust.

Moses aimed his staff again and brought it around in a sweeping arc, severing every standard holding a Reich flag. The red-and-white emblems fluttered to the ground like mortally wounded birds. Then the two robed figures slowly rose into the air and drifted away to the south.

"In three days, you die!" Hitler screamed after them. "Both of you! Do you hear me? Three days from today! Remember this day."

The joy of the people exploded into the stillness, sounding their complete agreement with the judgment their leader and lord had just delivered against the two men who, moments earlier, had stood defiantly in the center of the stadium. Hitler raised his arms to quiet the frenzied crowd. Then he leaned over, knowing he was back in control, and whispered into the microphone. He got their immediate attention. "Then you will know who the All-Powerful One is!"

D-Day Minus 1 Day

"Well, finally, the day is come, the time is here," Moses said to Elijah.

They stood on the summit of the Mount of Olives, looking toward the red hint of dawn in the east. A tiny sliver of sun poked above the horizon, sending golden rays over the Judean mountain wilderness in the distance.

"Yes," replied Elijah. "We have accomplished what we were sent to do. Yeshua will do the rest. I only wish we could be here when the big day arrives."

"Well, in a way, we will be. I have to admit, it's the time in between now and then that I'm not looking forward to. But can you imagine the effect it's going to have?"

"It's going to be something! We were promised we'd see the final results, and we will! That in itself makes what we have to go through today, worth it all," Elijah added. "Imagine, after thousands of years, it all comes down to the next four days!"

"I know. Now, let's do what we have to do! If it gets too depressing, just remember what it's going to be like three and a half days from now!"

They walked slowly down the Mount of Olives, across the Kidron Valley, and around to the Dung Gate in the south wall of the Old City. As the two old men made their way through the gate and down into the plaza beside the Wailing Wall, they ignored the crowds that had already begun to assemble there.

An ugly murmur ran through the crowd as Moses and Elijah arrived, but no one was bold enough to confront them. It had been two and a half days since Hitler's bold prediction at the stadium. If something was going to happen, it had to be today. The people had gathered to see their god carry through on his promise.

"I guess they don't want to miss the show," Moses said. He glared at the crowd. "They still refuse to give Almighty God the glory. They are all a proud and stiff-necked people."

"Mankind has always been this way, Moses."

"Yes, my friend. But they forget. God resists the proud . . ."

"But gives grace to the humble," Elijah finished.

A CNN van pulled up and parked. Yuri Kagan got out and pushed his way toward the Wall. Lugging their equipment, his two cohorts followed in his wake.

"The eyes of the world," Moses observed. "No one wants to miss the kill!"

"So it would seem," Elijah agreed. "We require only the little man before it can begin."

The CNN reporter approached them cautiously.

"So, Yuri Kagan, you're still alive, are you? Are you ready to televise your leader's big moment?" Moses asked mockingly.

"Of course he's here to televise the little man. He's here because God's Word says he's got to be here," Elijah added. "He has no choice, even though he doesn't know it!"

"How sad."

"I'm here because I wouldn't miss the show today for all the money in the world," Yuri objected.

"You know, Yuri, first of all, I don't believe you but more to the point, though, you really don't have any other option." Elijah laughed as he saw the confusion written all over the reporter's face. "You're like a helpless puppet on the end of a string."

"You two are nuts! Everyone knows it!" was all Yuri could come up with.

"Check it out, Yuri. It's written in the book of Revelation, chapter 11, verses 7 to 10."

"He doesn't have a clue, does he?" Elijah said.

"No, he doesn't," Moses agreed. "If he was smart, he'd read the rest of the book, too. But I don't think he'd like what he'd find there."

Suddenly a murmur went through the crowd. Hitler and his Enforcer were coming down the stairs from the Temple Mount. The crowd obediently stepped aside, making way for their leader's grand entrance.

"Ah, the glorious beast is even now arriving," Elijah noted.

Boot leather slapped on the stones as Hitler stormed out onto the pavement, a cockiness in his stride. Sergei struggled to keep up. Yuri checked to make sure Andrei was taping.

Hitler stopped abruptly before the two prophets of God. "Today, old men, is my day, your last day on Earth!"

"What if I call down fire from heaven on you, little man, before you have a chance?" Elijah asked, egging Hitler on.

"Can't do that, Elijah. It'd spoil his final claim to fame. Let him have his last hour in the rain," Moses answered.

"You know, Moses, you must have driven Aaron nuts. What would you do without me? It's his last hour in the *sun*, Moses, not the rain," Elijah corrected.

"Where I come from, Elijah, down Egypt way, one prefers the rain, not the sun," Moses quipped back as he turned toward Hitler. "As for you, little man, you have no authority. Your glorious Reich is a wreck!"

"Reich is a wreck. I kinda like the sound of that," Elijah added, admiringly.

"Say what you may, today you both die!" Hitler raged. "Today the world will know that the All-Powerful One that you mock is the true Prince of the Universe, greater than your Almighty God!"

"Oh, really? Where was your Prince when the horsemen from hell visited you? Or the beasts from the abyss? They really got 'under your skin,' didn't they?" Moses laughed.

"Wouldn't you know it! You're finally catching on to the lingo just when we have to go! Don't stop now. You're on a roll," Elijah whispered to his friend Moses.

"Tell me, where was your precious Prince when you needed him? Well? In fact, where is your Prince now? Did he forget the date that Almighty God decreed for him to come?"

Hitler began to open his mouth in protest when. . .

"Silence!" a thunderous voice commanded from above.

The gentle breeze stopped, and a sharp boom sounded somewhere above where they stood. A moment later, a jagged bolt of lightning streaked horizontally through the morning sky; it ran along the top of the Wall and then out over the crowd, where it exploded with a deafening crash. Most of the people fell to the ground as hot sparks rained down on them.

Moses and Elijah looked up at the large ebony creature glaring down on them.

"It is time!" the deep voice of the All-Powerful One rumbled, and an evil grin split his face. His yellow eyes gleamed with pleasure. Scores of evil acolytes swirled about him.

"Well, what do you know?" said Moses. "Look who showed up. Didn't know if you had the courage to come. Then again, this is your finest hour, isn't it? Everything's downhill after today!"

"Silence! No more!" Hitler's Prince rumbled. "You two have plagued me long enough! Now you will die!"

"We die because it is time for us to return to our God," replied Moses. "You are simply providing the transportation from here to our ultimate destination."

"Kill them! Now!" Hitler roared.

"Though you slay us, we will serve the Lord! All glory belongs to the one and only true God, the God of Avraham,

Yitzchak, and Yaakov, and to His Son, Yeshua. We are ready. Almighty God has destined this . . ."

Twin bolts of lightning shot down, striking the two prophets where they stood. They fell to the ancient stone pavement and lay still. Satan caught Hitler's eye. Then, with a loud pop, he was gone.

Hitler stared at the bodies in disbelief. "They're dead," he whispered to Sergei. "They're actually dead. My Prince actually killed them!" He began to laugh, hysterically.

The crowd edged forward cautiously, anxious to see the proof of their leader's promise. When they realized that the two who had dealt them misery for so long were really dead, they began to cheer.

"What shall we do with them?" Sergei asked.

Hitler glanced at Yuri and his crew. "Leave them right there! The whole world must see what happens to those who oppose me!" He smiled at Sergei in relief. "We have much to do. Finally! The source of our misery is dead. The victory will be mine! It is only a matter of time!"

It was late afternoon when the man staggered out of the bar on Me'a She'arim. Emptied of the ultra-orthodox Jews who had once lived there, the neighborhood had become a solid enclave of bars and brothels. The reveler looked up and down the street. He had plenty of company. He remembered the reason for his joy as he looked toward the Old City.

"To the Wall!" he shouted, almost falling over in his enthusiasm.

He made his unsteady way down the street, picking up followers like a drunken Pied Piper. Someone started playing a small accordion, and the people began dancing and singing. They snake-danced their way down to the Damascus Gate and into the Old City, wending their way to the broad plaza before the Western Wall of the Temple Mount. Men were working frantically to erect floodlights over the two bodies still sprawled in front of the Wailing Wall. To the south, on an elevated walk overlooking the plaza, Hitler and Sergei stood watching the mad party below.

The revelers danced past the bloated bodies, as if to reassure themselves that their two great enemies were, in fact, dead. Many threw rocks at the fallen prophets, cheering with every rock thrown that found its mark.

The celebration was carried live on every news service. The party in Jerusalem soon ignited similar carnivals in every city around the world. People crowded the streets in mass orgies. A flood of alcohol and drugs swept the screaming rabble to heights of ecstasy.

Reports of the worldwide festivities came in through Yuri's bureau feed, and he hurried to tell Hitler. The ecstatic leader stamped his foot and beamed at Sergei. "The people are happy," he said. "They believe, Sergei. They believe! Our troubles are behind us. No one doubts who their leader and lord is anymore."

Hitler's valet approached. "Excuse me, my master. Chancellor Otterbein is on the phone." He handed Hitler the tiny portable phone.

Hitler smiled broadly as he greeted his old confidant. "My dear Gerhardt, how are you?"

"Wonderful, my leader." The German chancellor's voice was clear and crisp. "I am watching the party in Jerusalem and wishing I was there with you. However, we have quite a celebration going on here in Berlin, as well. My aides tell me it's the same in Bonn and everywhere else in Germany."

"It's the same all over the world, my friend."

"There is other good news as well. CNN is reporting that the horsemen from hell have disappeared. The deaths of those two old men have brought our troubles to an end, just as you said."

"Our time has finally come, Gerhardt. You and I, we have accomplished much since those beginning days together in Bonn, almost fifty years ago."

"Since your beginning days, not mine. Remember, I am twenty-five years older than you," Gerhardt laughed.

Hitler turned away from Sergei and his valet, careful that no one could hear what he was saying. Not that there was much danger, with all the noise.

"I guess you could say that you knew me when I was only a jawbone." Hitler laughed at his own little joke.

"Yes, we failed the first time, but now things are different. We are going to bring in a millennium of worldwide peace and happiness such as the world has never known. Under your control, of course, Adolf! I am glad I could play a part in it. You have persevered and you have won. Congratulations, my leader."

"Thank you, Gerhardt."

"One last question, my leader. What are your plans for the remaining Israeli guerrillas, if you don't mind a sensitive question during this great time of celebration?"

"After the events of the past few days, I don't think we will have any more problems mopping up the guerrillas here in Israel," Hitler answered, no animosity in his voice for a change.

"Very good, my leader. The new millennium is upon us. *Heil Hitler!*"

Hitler punched off the phone and returned it to his valet.

"One last little thing still to take care of, Sergei," he said, almost without emotion.

THIRTY-FIVE

Deliverance Day—Day 1

David Gur climbed out of his sleeping bag. He usually slept soundly. Now that fall had arrived, cool nights had returned to Petra—a welcome relief from the broiling heat of the past summer. Tonight, however, he lay awake with a sense of nervous anticipation. He walked over to the cave entranceway and looked out. It was still dark.

"What's the matter?" Gideon Landau asked in a hoarse whisper, knowing full well what was keeping his friend awake.

"What time is it?"

Gideon looked down at the fluorescent dial of his watch. "Almost 4:00 A.M."

"I'm going out." David made his way past the other sleepers and grabbed a flashlight. His boots made crunching sounds on the rocky floor.

Gideon left his warm blankets and joined David on the colonnaded street. Together they climbed the steps up to the Urn Tomb, their favorite lookout over the refugee city of Petra. They switched off their small flashlights, letting their night vision return. Below them, the angular ruins of Petra slept under the pale starlight of the early morning hours, but the flickers of lights they saw below told the two leaders that the old city they had borrowed for the past four to five years was beginning to come to life.

David looked up and traced the faint circle of mountains

that protected the city on all sides. "It's been a good home, but I'm glad that today is our last day here."

"I won't miss it one iota," Gideon agreed. "It's been exactly 2,520 days since Israel signed that blasted treaty with Hitler. Finally, the seven-year covenant with death is over!"

"Yes, finally. This is the day we have longed for. Today Yeshua comes to deliver us! I'm ready to go!" David exclaimed.

They both looked toward the east. As they watched, the sky slowly dissolved into gray, and a pure rose color began to caress the eastern mountain rim. Gradually Petra took on form and color, its own rose-red rocks enhanced by the glory of dawn, as slowly the sun peeked above the ridge, shooting golden rays across the deep shadows to the foothills on the other side of the valley.

"Assemble everyone!" David decided suddenly.

Gideon looked around. "What do you see?"

"Do it now! It's going to happen soon, and I don't want anyone to miss it. Get everyone out in the open, on the double! And tell them to bring their backpacks. We're leaving here!"

Gideon took his radio and spoke excitedly into it. The response was immediate. None of the faithful firstfruits of Israel had slept well that night. At the first hint of daybreak, the people were up and ready to go, waiting for the word to assemble. Like their leaders, they had waited for this day with great anticipation. With Gideon's order to assemble, they poured out of their caves and tents, each with a backpack in hand and only one thing on their mind.

In the time it took the two men to descend the steps down to the colonnaded street, the people had already assembled.

Suddenly, a shout arose, several people pointing in the air, toward the east.

A bright light, larger than any star, formed high above the sun and began its long descent toward Petra. As the light drew closer, it took the shape of a human form, robed in the familiar, glowing-white garments they had seen several years earlier, clearly visible despite the distance. It was their Lord, Yeshua, returning for those He had sealed, on the very day He promised them He would return!

David gasped, just as he had done the first time he had seen the crimson stains on the white robes of Yeshua, the nail prints still marring the backs of His hands and the tops of His feet. He touched down in front of David and Gideon, and both men fell on their faces before Him. A hush fell over Petra as the rest of its inhabitants joined their leaders, bowing before their Lord and Savior, the Promised One of Israel.

"Welcome, Almighty God of Israel! We have eagerly awaited this moment," David managed to say without looking up.

"Arise, my children! It is time to go to My Holy City Jerusalem. It is time for your Jewish brothers and sisters to join the family of God."

Yeshua turned and pointed toward the west. The people got to their feet, still speechless in the presence of their Meshiah. Suddenly, an arch of daylight flashed into existence at the base of the mountain, revealing a tunnel that connected Wadi Siyyagh to the refugee city. A loud boom rolled over the valley as air rushed into the gap.

The Son of God strode down the colonnaded street toward the west, His glowing, bloodstained robes flapping in the early morning breeze.

"Come on!" David shouted, grabbing his backpack.

He and Gideon hurried to catch up. The rest of the people fell in behind them, adjusting their backpacks, walking silently, still awed by the presence of Yeshua. Yeshua continued on, out through the tunnel and then toward the Jordanian highway, leading to the Dead Sea. Close to noon, He stopped. As the people gathered around Him, He broke bread and had the leaders distribute it. They sat down on a hillside and ate.

To the north they could see the Dead Sea, shimmering bright blue under the afternoon sky. It drew them onward as they resumed their march. At sunset Yeshua told them to set up camp at the southern end of the salty body of water. Then He passed among His people, comforting and encouraging each one of them, individually.

"Well done, My faithful servants," He said when He came to David and Gideon. "You have led My people well."

"Thank You, Lord."

"May I ask You a question?" David wondered aloud. "I know it is on the mind of every person here."

"Of course."

"When will You destroy this terrible man, Hitler—this Satan-Meshiah?"

"And when will You set up Your kingdom on Earth?" Gideon quickly added.

"Soon, My children. Very soon. *First* comes the harvest of your brethren who have survived, as you have, and *then* the tares are destroyed, David. *After that*, Gideon, the feast. Be patient, My faithful sons. All will be finished, when the moon returns to the position it is in tonight."

The two men looked up at the full moon, shedding its bright light on their camp. . . .

Deliverance Day—Day 2

By the next evening, the men and women of Petra had walked the entire length of the eastern shore of the Dead Sea and they were now camped on the east side of the Jordan River, just south of the Allenby Bridge. Although not impossible, there was no doubt in the minds of the men, women, and children that traveled with Yeshua, that they had been given supernatural strength to travel the 70-kilometer distance up the east side of the Dead Sea. To the west, in the distance, they could see the green palms of Jericho. Each felt growing anticipation for the great event that would occur the next afternoon, when the King of kings would make His triumphal entry, through the Eastern Gate, into the Holy City of Jerusalem. Then the world would know!

Deliverance Day—Day 3

Early the following morning, in the peaceful grayness of approaching dawn, David and Gideon walked along the bank of the river. The camp was already coming to life behind them— every man, woman, and child eagerly preparing for this final day's journey to Jerusalem. Everyone knew that today would be a very special day.

"I wonder what the Reich's border guards are going to do when they see this huge group entering Israel?" said David.

"Today will be very interesting," commented Gideon, in marked understatement.

At the first rays of sunlight, a brilliant white star drifted down from a nearby ridge, just as He had done the previous morning of their journey. Each night He had watched over them from above.

Yeshua alighted before the two men, and they fell at His feet.

"Arise, My brothers. Today we cross the Jordan and go to Jerusalem. *This is the day that the Lord shall come!*"

When the sun was a golden lamp above the eastern horizon, Yeshua led the people forth. Instead of going north to the Allenby Bridge, however, He marched to the bank of the Jordan and held His hands out over the waters. As though held back by two invisible dams, the waters parted, creating a wide path through the river to the far shore. An audible gasp came from His followers as once again they beheld the power of God in their presence. Then Yeshua stepped down the gentle slope and started across the rocky, dry bottom, motioning for them to follow.

Following in the footsteps of their Lord, David and Gideon led the firstfruits of Israel across the Jordan, onto dry ground in Israel—just as Joshua had done thousands of years before.

"Go back to that!" Sonya ordered.

Shimon flipped back to the previous direct satellite channel. It showed a live report from Jericho, where for three days straight, the people had been partying, dancing in the streets, and rejoicing, now that their troubles were finally over. But what had caught Sonya's eye was the sudden, strange behavior of the reporter. He was shouting and pointing to the south, forgetting he was still on the air.

The camera began panning around with a sickening motion as the cameraman tried to capture what the reporter was shouting about. The picture tilted and spun, then focused on the highway that ran east and west, just south of Jericho.

Sonya gasped. A huge crowd of people was marching

westwardly, toward Jerusalem, a man in brilliant white robes leading them. His robes glowed, even in the sunlight.

"We're not sure what's happening here," the reporter said excitedly, "but these people, led by a man dressed in glowing white robes, have just crossed the Jordan River below the Allenby Bridge. Not on the bridge, mind you, but through the river itself!"

Just then the screen was filled with several dozen border police, racing by in their Reich vehicles. Large flatbed trucks followed closely behind, carrying the roadblocks that would be used to stop the oncoming horde. Inevitable confrontation hung heavy in the air.

"That was the border patrol," the reporter continued. "It is obvious to those of us witnessing this strange event that these people have entered the country illegally, directly against the strict mandate of our glorious leader, Adolf Hitler."

The camera focused in on the guards, straining to set out the concrete roadblocks before the great horde arrived. They purposefully built the barricade on a spot where the shoulders of the road dropped off abruptly on either side, making it impossible for the large crowd to pass until the barricade was removed.

"And that is as far as these people will go, until they explain to the border patrol who they are, where they came from, and what they are doing here," said the officious-sounding reporter as the camera recorded the diminishing distance between the two groups. "We have no idea what is being said, but at this very moment, the Reich Guard has detained the leader of the group! As soon as we have more details, you will be the first to know. We will cover it all, live, from beginning to end, until this crisis plays itself out, so stay tuned to this . . ."

Those were the last words heard by the viewing audience. The entire area flashed white. The border guards vanished, along with their vehicles and their roadblocks. The live broadcast had a momentary whiteout. Then the screen took on a confetti look . . . and then nothing. No picture and no sound. The road was completely clear again, except for a fading afterglow.

"What was that?" Shimon asked.

Sonya could only shake her head.

Noticing the expression on her face and then seeing the tears in her eyes, he said, "Sonya! Do you know what's going on?"

She nodded.

"Well, what is it?"

"Anatoly was right," she whispered. "Yeshua is coming to Jerusalem."

"What are you talking about? What's going on?"

"Those are our brothers and sisters from Petra," Sonya replied, crying openly now. Suddenly it all made sense to her. In that momentary flash, it had all come together. Anatoly had told her, repeatedly, that those who survived the seven-year "covenant with death" would see Israel's Promised One—Yeshua—returning to Jerusalem for the rest of His people. There He was, in all His glory. In an instant she realized that Yeshua—Anatoly's Meshiah—was responsible for her survival and protection, now and throughout her entire life. He was coming to save her and destroy the enemies of her people. And in that moment of understanding, Sonya Petrov knew that Yeshua was her God and Meshiah. Like Anatoly, she would love and follow Him forever. She knew what she needed to do. Now!

"Assemble everyone!" she cried out while wiping away her tears. "We're leaving! We're going to meet Israel's Meshiah, our Promised One! Take only what can be carried. We will never return to Camp Moses. We leave in thirty minutes!"

Sonya, with Shimon at her side, led the people out of Camp Moses for the last time and headed north on the dirt pathways that she had come to know so well during the past three and a half years. If they moved quickly enough, they could intercept Yeshua on the road leading to Jerusalem. The few jeeps they had were used to transport the ones that couldn't travel on their own. After a six-hour march across rugged wilderness, they reached the summit of an east–west ridge. It was early in the afternoon. There, below them, they could see an army of people marching toward Jerusalem on the Jericho Road. At the head was the unmistakable figure in glowing white robes.

Although He was still in the distance, the western sun highlighted the red stains on His robe. She began to weep again, silently, to herself.

"Look how many there are!" Shimon said. "There must be over a quarter million people down there."

"Anatoly thought closer to four hundred thousand! Those are the ones he helped down in Petra!" she added proudly.

Although tired and footsore, ten thousand men, women, and children poured down the north side of the ridge, Sonya and Shimon at the head. Sonya found herself laughing as she ran. They will think they are being attacked by Indians, she thought, remembering some of the old American western movies she had seen. Oh well, at least Yeshua knows who we are!

The Man in white halted as they approached. Sonya and those with her stopped, surrounding Him. Some of the children from Camp Moses sat on their fathers' shoulders to get a better view. Others climbed any object that let them see over those in front of them. A hushed silence fell over everyone present. Tears again filled Sonya's eyes when she saw the nail prints in His hands and feet.

She fell at Yeshua's feet and cried, "Lord, please forgive me. Save me, by Your grace. I am a sinner, unworthy of Your mercy. Why did it take something like this for me to finally see that You are my Lord and Savior, the Promised One of Israel?"

Around and behind her, Sonya heard movement, then the low moaning sound, as if mourning a loved one who had just died. Gradually the moaning crescendoed into the cries of sorrow. Turning to see what was happening, Sonya saw that the children had gotten off their fathers' shoulders. Those who had sought higher elevations had climbed down. Every man, woman, and child had fallen prostrate before Yeshua, weeping unashamedly as they looked at the nail prints in His hands and feet. In that divine moment, each was given eyes to see and ears to hear. Every one of them believed and worshiped Yeshua as their Meshiah and Lord.

"Arise, Sonya," He said gently, extending His hand. "Arise, My people. Your sins are forgiven. From this day forth, I will be your God and you will be My people. Follow Me."

David and Gideon puffed and wheezed as they struggled to keep up with Yeshua. They knew that they would have never made it this far without some sort of outside intervention. The past three days had been a long way to travel on foot. The group from Petra hadn't had the physical training that the other people from these remote survival camps were accustomed to, and though their joy and anticipation kept them going, their weary bodies felt the strain of the long journey. Still, the lengthy procession swarmed eagerly along the Jericho Road as it swept over the Mount of Olives and down into the Kidron Valley, where it headed northward, paralleling the eastern wall of the Old City of Jerusalem. As they proceeded, other survivors continually joined the growing multitude that followed Yeshua to Jerusalem. Each time, the new survivors had the same response to Yeshua as those before them. Each time, they experienced the joy of finding other friends they thought were dead. Truly, for each of these men and women, this was Deliverance Day!

Citizens of the Reich watched them come and, seeing the crowd grow larger and larger as they approached, were afraid to interfere. Even the Reich troops kept their distance. They already knew what this figure in the glowing white robes did to those who got in His way. This was Yeshua, the One whom the two old men at the Wailing Wall had served. Now He was here, alive. Fear flamed throughout the city as the people wondered what He would do if He saw the bodies of His prophets, left to rot in front of the Wall.

"That's where we're going," David said, pointing toward the sealed Eastern Gate in the Old City wall, its golden stones rising above them. Beyond the wall, the Temple Mount.

Yeshua stopped when He came abreast of the Eastern Gate.

"Why are we stopping?" Sonya whispered to the others. She and Shimon had been walking with the two leaders from Petra.

A line of soldiers in camouflage uniforms suddenly appeared on the road ahead, having just rounded the northeast corner of the Old City, and now were marching directly toward them in ragged formation. Sonya tensed, expecting another confrontation with Reich troops like the one she had witnessed on the satellite early that morning. But as the group got closer, she realized that the ragtag uniforms they were wearing were the uniforms of the IDF. Now she could see women and children following close behind. Even more confusing, the soldiers in front began cheering as they approached Yeshua!

"That man in front looks familiar," Sonya whispered to Shimon.

Then it hit her.

"He's alive!" she screamed. "It's Prime Minister Shefi! He's alive!"

She wanted to run forward to meet him, but he never even noticed her. He was bowing before Yeshua, face down in the dirt. One after the other, the people in his band did the same. As had happened earlier with those from Camp Moses, they were given the understanding and faith to believe. Sorrow poured out of their mouths as they looked upon Him whom they had crucified. But their hearts rejoiced, now that they were in the protective presence of Yeshua. Like Sonya and the others before them, they too, at that very moment in time, became the true children of the Most High God.

Tears rolled freely down Sonya's face. Oh, what a day this had become! Oh, what a great God Anatoly had introduced her to! Oh, what a wonderful Savior she had—Yeshua, the Promised One!

When Yeshua told those bowed in front of Him to rise, Sonya rushed to Binyamin Shefi. She nearly knocked him off his feet as she threw her arms around him. "You made it!" she cried. "I thought you were dead. I didn't know if you ever found my letter to you. How I wanted to tell you. Please forgive me!"

"Enough, Sonya. I never doubted you, even when things blew apart three and a half years ago. You did what you had to do. I always knew that. And now I understand why. I thought of you often, Sonya, but I never doubted you. I knew you were still alive."

"How?"

"Because I knew there was only one person who could cause Hitler all that trouble in the south."

She laughed, suddenly realizing who these ragtag, former IDF soldiers were. "You were the ones up in the Golan?"

"Of course! I never could stand that hot weather down south where you were," he laughed, his eyes showing the delight he had in seeing his young friend again.

"What an idiot I am! I should have put it together. You guys were fantastic! We knew we had an ally; we just didn't know who you were or how to get in touch with you."

"We didn't dare break radio silence. We knew the Reich had big ears."

"Do something!" Hitler screamed. He whirled away from the open door to the balcony and stomped back into his bedroom.

"There is nothing we can do, master," said Sergei, cowering on the other side of the room.

The power had failed early that morning. Everything electronic and mechanical had shut down. The security guards also reported that some kind of invisible barrier was encircling the mountain. They were completely cut off. Hitler was being held captive in his own Lion's Den. There was nothing he could do but watch from a distance.

"I am the god of this world! This cannot happen to me! This cannot be happening again! *Nie wieder! Nie wieder!*"

"It is time, My children," Yeshua announced, turning toward the Eastern Gate of His Holy City.

Tears filled Sonya's eyes as she watched her Lord climb the steep, rocky slope outside the old stone archway that had been sealed off for centuries. At the top, Muslim graves and an iron fence barred the way to the sealed portal. Yeshua stopped and lifted His arms toward the heavens. In a shimmering flash of white, the barriers disappeared. Then two perfect arches of light formed over the stone seals, silently and smoothly cutting their way through the rock to the other side of the Eastern Gate. The glow lingered for a few moments, and then the blocks of stone, mortared in place since the time of the Crusades, crumbled to the ground.

The great multitude that surrounded Yeshua cheered as He led them up through the Eastern Gate, across the broad Temple Mount, and down to the Wailing Wall. This was truly the triumphal entry of the King of kings! The streets were jammed by the throngs that followed the Man in the white robes. Reaching the Wailing Wall, He walked up to the bodies of Moses and Elijah. The multitude swarmed around Him. Every square meter in front of the Wall was now tightly packed with human bodies. Curious citizens of the Reich stood back in the rear, keeping as far away from the Man in white as they could. Three of them were more bold. They began working their way through the crowds, trying to get close enough to Yeshua, to record for history what this Man intended to do.

Yeshua looked down on the lifeless bodies of His two faithful witnesses. Their sightless eyes looked heavenward. Their blood still stained the ancient paving stones, bearing mute witness to the hatred that had judged them worthy of death.

Yuri and his crew continued to push through the crowd until they finally worked their way to the center of the great multitude. The CNN reporter shivered when he saw—up close for the first time—the Man in the glowing white robes. The Man looked around, and when He saw Yuri, their eyes met and locked. Although no words were spoken out loud, His eyes spoke directly to Yuri's heart. *Why, Yuri, why? You betrayed your friend, your people, you rejected the teaching of your prophets, and now you seek to condemn Me as well!*

Hatred and anger welled up from deep within Yuri. I have done nothing wrong, his head told his heart. You are the Enemy. You are the One who has caused so much trouble, so much grief to my leader and lord, so much death and destruction to the citizens of the Fourth Reich. What are You doing here? Who are all these people with You?

Sonya, standing near Yeshua, gasped when she recognized Yuri. Her memories swept back to what seemed a lifetime ago. How differently their personal wars with God had turned out. Surprisingly, she felt sorry for him. Still, she had nothing to say to him, sensing in him the hatred he had for Yeshua.

Yeshua knelt and laid one hand on Moses, the other on Elijah. "I say to you, arise!"

The two bodies stirred. The bloating shrank. The smell of death dissipated on the fresh breeze. Life filled the dead eyes. Moses and Elijah blinked, then both rose to their feet. The great multitude that jammed around Yeshua, Moses, and Elijah came to life with a thunderous roar, cheering these two godly prophets who had been so willing to lay down their lives that they might live!

Moses bowed. "My Lord."

"My God," Elijah echoed.

"You have done well," said Yeshua. "Look around you. Testimony to your faithful witness stands before you. This is the fruit of your labor. Your people have become My people. Your work here is finished."

Sonya sensed an immense power invading the air around her. The ground shook. Then all was quiet, as if the Earth itself waited for what was to follow. A hush fell over the great multitude that stood before the Wailing Wall. Only the soft whir of Andrei's camera was heard, recording the events unfolding before their eyes.

"Come home!" a Voice out of heaven commanded. Its awesome force instantly drove all those standing before the Wall to their knees. Even Yuri and the rest who carried the mark of Satan-Meshiah were unable to stand at the force of God's command.

Only Yeshua remained standing, along with Moses and Elijah, radiant as they looked upward. "Go now, return to Our Father in heaven," He said quietly to His two faithful prophets. A white cloud formed high above the plaza, and the two witnesses ascended slowly into it. Then the cloud drifted up into the heavens and disappeared.

Sonya had just gotten back on her feet when another minor quake shook the ground beneath her. It was gone as quickly as the first.

He's waiting for something, Sonya thought. No sooner had the thought crossed her mind, than the pavement began to roll like the sea, as a mighty earthquake tore through the portion of the city that surrounded the Wailing Wall. A crushing roar swept down from above as the ancient blocks of stone that made up the Temple Mount ground violently against each other. The three buildings on the Mount remained standing, as if to say that what they represented was far more important than a mere earthquake, but the damage to the once-elegant structures made them unusable. Building after building imploded, disappearing in a cloud of dust. Only the great multitude, standing around the Man clothed in white, seemed unaffected by what was happening all around them, as if protected by some invisible force that radiated from the Man in the center.

In minutes it was over. Only a fine dust hung in the air, and a fresh breeze soon carried it away to the north. The sun shone as brightly as ever in the blue sky above. But beneath it, a tenth of the city of Jerusalem lay in ruins, and seven thousand men and women bearing the mark of the Reich were dead.

The final angel, the seventh, stepped forward, lifted his trumpet, and blew. Then, with great joy, amidst the jubilation of the other six angels, he took his place at the end of the line that stood before Almighty God.

"Come with me!" the Lord commanded.

He led His people up onto the Temple Mount platform. As they went, they sang a psalm of ascent—a psalm sung by their ancestors for thousands of years, looking forward to this precise time in history.

From my distress I called upon the Lord; and the Lord answered me.

All the nations surrounded me, they surrounded me, yes, they surrounded me.

You pushed me violently so that I was falling, but the Lord helped me.

The Lord is my strength and song, He has become my salvation.

This is the day which the Lord has made; let us rejoice and be glad in it!

The Lord is God and He has given us light.

Thou art my God, I extol Thee. Give thanks to the Lord, for He is good,
His lovingkindness is everlasting!"

Atop the Temple Mount, Yeshua led His people around the damaged Dome of the Rock and stopped before the temple.

He tilted His head toward the heavens above. The Voice from heaven sounded again, this time more powerful than before—so powerful that everyone on Earth heard the mighty proclamation of Almighty God:

"As for Me, I have installed My King upon Zion, My holy mountain. Thou art My Son, ask of Me and I surely will give the nations as Thine inheritance, and the very ends of the Earth as Thy possession. The kingdom of this world is now the kingdom of Our God, and of His Meshiah; and He will reign forever and ever!"*

Then the voices of the children of God sang out to Yeshua, praising His name, rejoicing that the kingdom of this world was now the kingdom of their God!

The kingdom of this world is now the kingdom of Our Lord and of His Christ! And He will reign, forever, and ever, and ever and ever and ever!

Again and again they sang, until the words echoed back and forth, off the surrounding hills.

Faintly at first, and then louder by each moment, the sound of harps rang from the heavens above as the elect of God from ages past, now in the bosom of their Heavenly Father, responded to their Jewish brothers and sisters on Earth:

Righteous and true are Thy ways, Thou King of the nations.
Who will not fear, O Lord, and glorify Thy name?
For Thou alone art holy; For all the nations will come and worship before Thee.

Yeshua stood in their midst, praise ringing in His ears from every direction: from Almighty God above, from the elect of all ages, and from the children of Israel now surrounding Him on His holy Mount.

After a moment, He arose from their midst and drifted silently to the summit of the Mount of Olives, just to the east of where His followers stood. A hush settled on those on the

Temple Mount as they watched Yeshua in awe. Then, in a voice heard by all in the city of Jerusalem, He ordered the Mount of Olives: "Open!"

At His command, a dark line ripped up the slope of the Mount of Olives, dividing the mountain in two, directly beneath where He had been standing. As He floated above, a grinding roar escaped from the fissure, and half the mountain moved to the north while the other half slid south. This massive movement created a wide valley, reaching from the Eastern Gate to a large hole in the ground, which could barely be seen in the distance.

Then Yeshua drifted quietly back to the Temple Mount. "Behold the entrance to the city of Azel," He proclaimed to Sonya, David, and Binyamin, pointing to the hole at the other end of the valley. "Take My people there until I call for you."

"Yes, my Lord," said Binyamin.

Sonya started to ask something, but stopped.

Yeshua smiled. "Not yet, Sonya, but soon."

She smiled in return, knowing the Lord had read her innermost thoughts.

And then Yeshua ascended rapidly and disappeared into the clouds above.

Sonya turned to the other two. "This place had better be big," she said as she surveyed the multitude crowded onto the Temple Mount.

"Somehow, I think size won't be a problem. On the other hand, I'll lay you odds there won't be any extra rooms, either," David laughed.

Sonya laughed. "No, I don't bet against sure things."

Binyamin looked around until he found a large piece of broken rock. He climbed up on it and held up his arms. "Children of Israel!" he shouted. "We are going to a place prepared especially for us!"

Then he and Sonya, followed closely by David, Gideon, and Shimon, started toward the Eastern Gate. The sea of Jewish believers parted before them, and then fell in behind them as they led the people out to the place God had prepared.

When they reached their destination, some 3 kilometers

outside the eastern city wall, the leaders peered into the huge hole that disappeared into the bowels of the Earth.

"It looks like an old mining shaft," said David, aiming his flashlight into the cavity.

They could see a gentle limestone path leading downward until it curved out of sight.

"How long will we have to stay in here?" Gideon asked, uneasily.

"Anatoly said it would probably be three or four weeks," replied Sonya.

"Until the next full moon is what Yeshua told me," David added.

"We haven't got that much food, not to mention water," Sonya's detail man worried out loud.

Sonya put her hands on her hips. "Shimon—would our Promised One send us here and not provide for us?"

He thought for a moment. "No, of course not."

She smiled at him. "Give me your flashlight. Binyamin and I will go down first." She looked at him, and then at David and Gideon. "You two stay here and have the rest follow us. Make sure everyone is in before you come down."

Sonya clicked on the light. "Shall we?" she asked Binyamin. He nodded, and the two friends stepped into the huge hole.

The smooth limestone path, leading through what appeared to be natural caverns, was a delight to Sonya's tired feet. The magnificent sights were a delight to her eyes. She knew she was not alone in these feelings. She could hear the "oohs" and "aahs" of those following behind. Graceful stalactites and stalagmites grew toward each other in a profusion of columns and fanlike screens. They stopped to look around, and Sonya turned off the flashlight, confirming her suspicion. A soft white glow suffused the caverns, providing ample light.

When they turned the final corner on the trail, she and Binyamin halted abruptly. They stared in amazement at the city of Azel.

Before them, the ceiling soared several hundred meters overhead, and from where they stood, it had to be at least 5 kilometers to the far side of the cavern that Sonya could faintly see in the distance. There, far beneath the surface of the Earth, was a beautiful city of stone houses—with a separate name written on the door of each—arranged in a geometrical pattern too complex to comprehend. Generous streets linked houses to larger buildings, with attractive parks scattered throughout. A broad river divided the city, winding to a large lake near where they stood. Fish swam in its crystal depths. And in the very center of Azel stood a small mount, capped by a miniature replica of Solomon's Temple.

Sonya smiled at the sweet reminder. Yes, He had indeed met all their needs.

Hours later, David and Gideon joined Sonya and the others.

"Everyone is in," David told the others.

"Good."

"Did you feel a little tremor a while ago?" Gideon asked.

"Yes. What about it?" Sonya asked.

"The Lord has sealed us in here. The entrance is blocked."

PART 7

THE FINAL WRATH
OF GOD

And I saw another sign in heaven,
great and marvelous,
seven angels who had seven plagues,
which are the last,
because in them the wrath of God is finished.

—*Revelation 15:1*

THIRTY-SIX

Yacov heard footsteps approaching on the transparent gold pavement. He turned and saw Mike and Marlee coming toward him.

"How are you?" he asked as Marlee gave him a warm hug.

"I'm still adjusting," said Mike.

"Why? Isn't Heaven what you thought it would be?"

"It's even better," replied Mike, "but it's nothing like I thought."

"Well, my spiritual life on Earth was cut down to the bare minimum—less than three days if I recall properly—so I never had time to think about Heaven," laughed Yacov. "But I don't believe I could have come close to imagining anything like this, it's so unlike anything on Earth. There's so much to learn and do. And the people I've already met! Believe me, they're household names in Jewish circles. And here I am, talking with them like old friends. Does it ever end?"

"It never does," said Marlee. "That's why it's Heaven."

"Excuse me, you're Mike and Marlee Teasdale, aren't you? And I'll bet you're Yacov Petrov."

Standing to one side, quietly listening to their conversation, was a man none of them recognized. "Yes we are," Mike answered, no longer surprised at whom he met in Heaven, but nevertheless wondering who this stranger could be who knew them all by name. "Who are you, may I ask?"

"Well, Mike, we know each other well; it's just that we've never met before, in person. I'm Eitan Shachar," the man answered.

"Eitan," Mike and Marlee exclaimed together. "I knew you were here. I just didn't know where to look," Mike continued. "I didn't have the slightest idea what you looked like. Come on over here," Mike gestured to benches over to one side, "and let's sit down. We've got a lot of questions and you're the man to answer them."

"Tell me about Sonya," was the first question out of Yacov's mouth.

"Well, Yacov, I have wonderful news for you. But before that, let me start at the beginning."

For what seemed to be hours on end, the four friends talked, nonstop, about everything they had been through since Nikolai Bulgakov arose on the scene in Russia. Each of them had a uniquely different perspective; each of them had been a tool in the hand of Almighty God as He accomplished His perfect will on Earth, ending with Deliverance Day, in particular, the salvation of Sonya and the nation of Israel! Tears of joy rolled down the cheeks of each of them, interrupting their discussion again and again.

Eventually, the four friends stood back up and walked across the golden pavement toward the shimmering white Temple of God. It looked like the model Yacov had seen of Solomon's Temple, only it was larger and every detail was perfect. They walked up the long series of steps until they could see through the open doors. Inside, a gold-covered box rested toward the back of the Holy of Holies. Seven mighty angels, clothed in white, stood behind it.

"That's the real Ark of the Covenant," Yacov breathed in awe.

"What do you mean?" Mike asked. His eyes traced the outstretched wings of the cherubim positioned over the top of the golden box.

"That's the original you see in there. The one Moses built in the wilderness was a duplicate of what was already here in Heaven," Yacov explained, happy to teach his friend for a change. "Can you imagine, the ark that Satan destroyed was never the real thing to begin with!"

Suddenly, the seven angels left the Holy of Holies and stood in the temple entrance. One of God's four seraphim silently approached them. Four meters tall, he towered over the seven angels. He had the appearance of a lion, and his six wings were covered with eyes, front and behind. The seraphim gave each of the angels a shallow bowl, and each bowl was filled with God's wrath. Instantly smoke filled the interior of the temple, and brilliant light shone from its entrance.

"The bowl judgments will be the final wrath of God," Eitan simply said to the others. "The time has come."

"The first seven judgments were initiated by trumpets," Yacov began. "Why are the final judgments initiated by bowls?"

"As you can see, the bowls are wide and shallow. Because of this, when their contents are poured out on Earth, the bowls will be emptied immediately. The final judgments of God will occur quickly, one right after the other. Soon, Yacov, it will be all over."

"How soon?" Yacov questioned.

"Twenty-four days from now, the final battle of Armageddon will be fought," Eitan began.

"The final battle between the armies of Satan-Meshiah and the armies of Yeshua," Mike added. "After that, it is over."

"And if Hitler refuses to fight?" Yacov asked.

"He will fight! It is written!" Marlee stated, simply. "He has no choice."

Armageddon Minus 24 Days

While Andrei and Egor headed for the break room, Yuri checked Ehud Goldberg's office. The CNN bureau chief was in, his telephone securely attached to his ear. It sounded like someone was giving him a very hard time. He spotted Yuri and motioned for him to come in.

Yuri sank into the chair wearily. His head still reeled with unanswered questions. He had been awake all night, struggling with what he had witnessed the previous day. Was the Man at the wall, really the Iesus of the New Testament? And where did all those Jews come from? He'd thought they were all dead. And why were they following Iesus? Didn't the Jews hate Him? And what about those two prophets at the Wailing Wall? Had they really been brought back to life?

For hours, he had replayed the tapes, trying to figure out what had happened, looking for something that gave logic to this madness. Had the Jews made some kind of switch? Had they stolen the corpses of Moses and Elijah and replaced them with actors? Impossible! He had been there, seen it with his own eyes! Besides that, those two bodies had been under constant surveillance since the twin bolts of lightning had struck them down four days ago. Would there be more terrible plagues, now that the two were alive again?

So many questions and no answers. It was hard enough to explain the recently formed rift down the center of the Mount of Olives as simply the natural result of a massive earthquake. But how did one explain almost a million Jews disappearing into a hole in the ground, down at the end of it?

Like the rest of the world, Yuri was becoming aware that the Earth had become a battleground for spiritual powers much greater than mankind. Iesus was the one to fear. He had the power to bring dead men back to life. Yuri had seen it with his own eyes. And then that voice from somewhere up above, proclaiming that Yeshua was the Son of Almighty God, King of the Earth, Ruler of the Nations! Hitler now appeared to the nations as puny and insignificant.

"Earth calling Mars," Ehud growled, startling the reporter out of his reverie.

"Sorry, Ehud. I was just thinking about what happened yesterday. What were you saying?"

Ehud frowned at him. "I was saying that you might have thought you did a good piece at the Wailing Wall yesterday, but you've stirred up a hornet's nest in the Lion's Den. Other than report the news, what else did you do that has him so riled up?"

"For some reason, he missed the whole show, so I had the dubious honor of showing him the tapes. That's it. He's furious about what happened. And he's angry because I covered it live for all the world to see, making him look like a fool."

"And?"

"And he thinks we have some kind of deal that says I only

broadcast the good things, never the bad. It seems every time I cover him live—like the dedication of the shrine or his big speech at the stadium—something happens to make Hitler look like an idiot. Then he blames *me* because I'm simply doing my job."

"Like shooting the messenger because you don't like the message?" Ehud asked, smiling for a change.

"Exactly," Yuri agreed.

"Well, whatever his reasons may be, he's made some changes. From now on, he wants everything taped and reviewed before it's aired. That way he can clean up any 'unpleasant' footage."

"Come on, Ehud, he can't do that to us, can he?"

"Oh yes he can, and he just did! If we want to continue to cover him, that's the deal. In fact, Sergei just let me have it right between the eyes! He told me if we didn't like it, there were a thousand others who would give their eyeteeth for the deal he's offering us."

"And you took it?"

"Of course I took it! It's better than nothing!"

Yuri began to rub his right forearm vigorously.

"Something the matter?" Ehud asked.

"My arm itches, like I've been in poison ivy or something."

"Funny, so does mine."

Both men began scratching vigorously as large red blisters began forming on their arms. Yuri and Ehud watched in horror as the swollen areas grew and expanded until they broke, draining a viscous serum over their skin and clothing. Everywhere it spread, it caused more angry red sores.

"What's happening? This stuff reeks!" Ehud screamed in panic. "It smells like decaying flesh!"

Hitler had just called an emergency teleconference with the Pac-Ten heads of state—minus, of course, General Yonka, the Libyan leader who'd been executed at the Tel Aviv hangar. Television monitors brought each man to the table, as though they were all in the same room together. They were united in their reactions to the events that had occurred in Jerusalem the previous day. Each had watched the CNN reports. Over and over again they had heard the pronouncement: Yeshua, King of the Earth, Ruler of the Nations! To a man, they were enraged!

Hitler informed the group that there would be no more live television coverage of any public speech until the Enemy had been confronted and eliminated, once and for all! All agreed. They also agreed that the Enemy was greater than they had ever estimated. Yeshua, Iesus, Jesus, one and the same, but regardless of what He was called, He was the true leader of the opposition! He was obviously alive and well, and He had directly challenged the rule of their leader and lord.

Something must be done, they agreed. Hitler needed to confer with his Prince. The world was in an uproar, and they needed answers. As before, only the demonic Emblems were keeping the people from rioting against the Fourth Reich!

While listening to his confederates, Hitler unconsciously unbuttoned his sleeve and rolled it up. "What is this?" he cried in alarm when he saw an ugly red sore suddenly break out on his forearm and begin to ooze a stinking pus. "Call my doctor!" he screamed. "What's going on now?"

The last thing the horrified Pac-Ten leaders saw was an incoherent Adolf Hitler, sprawled out on the conference table, with Sergei trying frantically to administer some sort of aid. Sergei looked up, realized that the conference call was still connected, and, without a word, slammed the lever on the receiving unit to the off position. A moment later, the nine Pac-Ten leaders came to know, personally, the new torment of their leader and lord!

Sergei rushed out of the room, seeking help. Each step, though, became agony as his thick thighs rubbed against the raw sores that suddenly appeared on the insides of his upper legs. He managed to make it to the military quarters, located just outside the palace entrance, and barged into the doctor's office.

Hitler's physician was writhing on the floor, eruptions clearly visible all over his skin. Sergei cried out in agony and collapsed beside the doctor.

In the meantime, Hitler had managed, barely, to pull himself off the table and take a few feeble steps toward the couch next to the door. Nerve endings shrieked, washing away his vision in an explosion of stars. Nausea and chills swept over him. He bent double, retching on the Persian carpet at his feet. He staggered a few more steps and fell heavily, hitting his head on the marble floor. He was sure something was peeling his skin away and pouring boiling oil over the raw flesh. But his pain was lost in his greater misery. Then he lost consciousness.

From his bed, Hitler looked out the windows without any real interest. Everyone was gone. He was alone. He didn't want anyone around. He itched all over, but he knew better than to scratch the bandages that covered most of his body. His doctor had shot him up with morphine, and though the itching persisted, the pain was gone.

A shadow passed over the door to the parapet—a shadow that grew darker and began to take on substance, until Hitler could see the familiar face and the large body beneath. The All-Powerful One oozed through the closed door and hovered at the foot of the bed.

"You have failed me," Satan rumbled, "again!"

His heart pounding with fear, Hitler began to protest, but his Prince continued before he could get the words out of his mouth.

"You were to kill the Jews and all who refused your mark, were you not?"

"I have! We have executed millions!"

"You did not destroy those hiding in the wilderness!"

"How could I? I would have had her . . . them, if those grotesque horsemen hadn't . . ."

"No excuses! Those Jews should never have been allowed to escape. Now, close to a million of them have become the followers of Iesus. Because of your bungling, this has happened, and the trouble begins again!"

"But . . ."

"Silence! You failed me, and the world will suffer because of your failure. Israel has claimed Yeshua as their Meshiah, and because of that, Yeshua has now been given the authority to rule the world that I had given you—the world you failed to secure when it was under your control."

"But you said you would kill Iesus, like you did the first time. What would happen if . . ."

"I want to hear no more from you. You have failed me! Yeshua has been reunited with His people. You have ruined all my plans. The world will continue to suffer because of your failure."

"You can't blame me for all of this! I did the best I could!" Hitler cried out.

"I will talk with you again."

The worldwide plague afflicted every man, woman, and child except those tucked safely away in the city of Azel. Hospitals and clinics were of no help, since the caregivers themselves had been affected. Reich citizens had to deal with their own ugly, oozing sores in any manner they could. Nothing helped. The sores spread and the excruciating pain drove many into near madness or unconsciousness. Millions died.

The entire world came to a standstill until—after two long, agonizing days—the sores mysteriously began to heal.

Yuri dragged himself into the CNN office around noon on Friday, two days after his sores had initially broken out. He was exhausted, but thankful that the worst was over and that he could walk again without the pain.

Ehud Goldberg was in his office. Yuri wondered if his boss had been there the entire time, suffering but never leaving his post. When Ehud motioned for him, Yuri walked in and sat down carefully.

"Are you over them?" Ehud asked.

Yuri could see the unspoken fear in the man's eyes. "They're beginning to heal. Still painful to the touch, but no new sores. I'd rather die than go through something like that again."

Ehud managed a rueful smile. "I didn't know you could feel that bad without dying."

Yuri nodded and poured himself a fresh cup of coffee.

Ehud Goldberg snorted. "We've just gone back on the air a few hours ago. Most of our people are still out, though—including Andrei and Egor."

"I may be only 50 percent, but I can move around. What do you want me to handle today? Got another horror story you want me to cover—other than Hitler, live?"

"Careful, Yuri. Those Reich Emblems are still within earshot of this place," Ehud warned. "Actually, nothing new has been going on. The whole world has been sidelined by these sores. Everyone. So why don't you take the weekend off? By Sunday you'll be 100 percent, and we'll have Andrei and Egor back. This plague seems to be going away, but my newshound instincts tell me that all hell could break loose again, anytime, and when it does, I want you healthy."

"I think I'll kill two birds with one stone, then," said Yuri. "I've missed the seashore, and I haven't been back to Tel Aviv since it got slammed with that meteorite-shower tidal wave over a year ago," said Yuri. "I'll check it out and get a little R and R at the same time."

"You'll have the beach to yourself." Ehud managed to laugh.

Armageddon Minus 22 Days

Yuri turned right on Herbert Samuel and headed north along what had been Tel Aviv's famed beachfront. He had to give the Reich credit. The only evidence of the disaster was empty lots and deserted highways. All the rubble had been cleared away.

He parked and walked out onto the beach. Ehud was right—there wasn't another person in sight!

The blue Mediterranean lapped the shore with the promise of peace, and Yuri breathed in the tangy salt breeze. He sat down, drew his knees up, and wrapped his arms around them, watching the huge red sun inch slowly down toward the horizon. It had been too long since he'd had time to just sit and relax. "Thank you," he said to no one in particular.

No sooner were the words out of his mouth, than suddenly, the ground beneath him jumped in one sharp shock and the waters before him turned white with froth, as if a huge bomb had exploded. A mist formed, then slowly dissipated. Now what? was the first thought that raced through Yuri's head.

He expected the water to turn blue again, but it didn't. Instead, it roiled pink and then scarlet and finally reddish-black. He gagged as the breeze carried a sticky, putrid stench into his nostrils.

Countless white objects floated to the surface, dotting the ugly red-black water. It took him a moment to identify what they were . . . billions of fish! Small and medium-sized fish. Farther out, a pod of whales broached, blowing white spume that quickly turned to scarlet . . . and finally nothing at all.

Yuri jumped up and dashed for the van, cursing God as he ran.

An hour later, he stormed into the CNN office. It was well past 10:00 P.M., but Ehud was still there. He marched, unannounced, into the bureau chief's office and closed the door.

"I just got back from Tel Aviv," he said. He could see the fear in Ehud's eyes.

"Were you there when . . ."

"When the sea became blood and guts? Yes." Yuri slammed his fist on Ehud's desk. "What in blazes is going on! Is anything coming across the wires?"

Ehud nodded. "It's not just here. It's affected every ocean in the world."

" 'Affect' isn't strong enough. 'Utter ruin' is more like it. I just saw it with my own eyes! Do you realize what this means? All sea life is dead. No more seafood. No more anything on the coast—not for a long, long time. How do we recover from something like this?"

His boss said nothing.

"Ehud, what can the Reich do about this? What are they saying?"

"Nothing yet. Hitler's still holed up in the Lion's Den, getting over the last disaster."

"Why doesn't Jesus just finish us all off and put an end to this misery? What more can happen?"

THIRTY-SEVEN

Hitler pushed through the door to his bedroom, then leaned back on it until the lock clicked shut. His eyes drifted over to the door on the wall opposite his huge bed. He hesitated, then rushed over, pulling the key out as he went. He inserted it, gave a quick twist, and pulled the door open.

Flipping on the light, he stepped inside, shut the door, and pushed the heavy inside bolt into place. He glanced at the pentagram tapestry and the low altar with the black candle resting in the skull of a goat. He knelt, lit the candle, and closed his eyes.

How long he waited before he felt the familiar presence coming, he was not sure. He opened his eyes as his mind pressed toward insanity. The purple glow formed, providing a frame for the black shape struggling for definition. The large misshapen head emerged finally, and the yellow eyes glared down at him. The mouth opened in a sneer.

"We have something more to talk about?" Satan rumbled.

Intense fear surged through Hitler's heart. "My Prince," he began in a quavering voice, "I am nothing. You are everything. The tasks you have given me, I have failed to complete. I have done my best, but my best was not good enough. I have failed. I am at your mercy. I have no more solutions to the problems of the world. I am at my utter end! Only you can do what I have failed to do. I beg of you, give me one more chance!"

"I have been busy. Many plans have been made," said Satan. "I have decided to give you the one last chance you beg for. Fail me this one last time, and I will reclaim your flesh—what's left of it—and return your soul to hell. Do you understand me?"

"Yes, yes, whatever you ask, I will do," Hitler continued to plead.

"Because you failed to kill the children of God, *you* must now kill the Son of God. It is He who challenges your leadership and lordship."

"But I thought *you* would . . ."

"Silence! You beg for my deliverance, and then you argue with me? The All-Powerful One?! I will send you back to the pit this very . . ."

"No, no. Please forgive me. I will do *whatever* you ask of me."

"The next time you argue with me, Adolf, will be the last time!"

"It will never happen again. I promise you that. If it were not for you, I would still be burning in that blasted hellhole. Anything is better than that. Tell me what I must do?"

"It has been arranged. In three weeks—exactly twenty-one days from today—you and your armies will fight Yeshua and His armies. *If you do exactly as I say, you will win.* If you don't, you will lose . . . and you will be sent back to the abyss."

The black shape looked down, waiting.

"Where?" Hitler asked.

"On the plains of Megiddo, north of Jerusalem."

"But how can I win?"

"Only if you do as I tell you. In three weeks it will all be over. Forever!"

Armageddon Minus 20 Days

Hitler heard the sliding door open. Sergei knew where his master would be. Holed up in the Lion's Den, Hitler worked off his frustration by spending long hours in the plotting room. Lately, except when he slept, he spent every waking hour there. Sometimes he fell asleep on the leather sofa in the corner of the room. Now he was occupied with something new. As Sergei entered, Hitler was leaning over the large table in the center of the room. He looked up from the plotting table and glared at Sergei.

"What is it now?" he snapped.

"More trouble, master. First the oceans turned to blood. Now the same thing has happened to all the lakes and rivers. We have no freshwater sources anywhere on Earth."

"Are you sure?"

Sergei nodded. "The reports started coming in a few hours ago. And boiling or distillation doesn't do a thing. The water is undrinkable. It kills anyone who tries to drink it. Millions have either died or are in the process of dying without water! Bottled water is almost impossible to find, and the fruit juices and canned drinks are quickly being depleted. This can't go on much longer!"

Hitler threw down his wooden pointer and stomped on it. In sheer frustration, he grabbed the underside of the plot table and heaved it upward. Markers tumbled to the carpet as the table landed upside down. He kicked the heavy wooden top, crying out as the edge bruised his foot through his leather boot.

Sergei waited for the temper tantrum to run its course, then asked, "What can we do?"

The blue-gray eyes smoldered with hate. "We must prepare for the *final solution*. We must do it now before He kills all of my people. It is the only way we can stop all this."

"What is that solution, master?"

"My Prince has ordered *me* to kill Iesus."

"Iesus? Are you kidding? *You*? We couldn't even kill His two prophets without the help of *your* Prince! How do you propose to accomplish this?" Sergei asked cautiously.

"Shut up and help me pick this thing up. I want to show you something."

Once the table was upright, they spent several minutes replacing the markers. Then Hitler picked up the wooden pointer.

"Our armies are going to fight the armies of Iesus, right here." He tapped the Plain of Megiddo in the Jezreel Valley, on either side of Tel Megiddo, 100 kilometers or so north of Jerusalem.

"I don't understand. What arm . . ." Sergei began, before Hitler cut his question short.

"My Prince has assured me we cannot lose if I do exactly as he says. When this final battle is won, the war will be over. *Forever*, Sergei . . . *forever!*"

"And just where does Iesus get this army we're supposed to defeat?" Sergei finally managed to say.

"I'm assuming he means that bunch over there," Hitler answered, pointing to where the Mount of Olives once stood. "What other followers does He have that could fight for Him?"

"You're referring to that ragtag bunch of Jews? In that hole in the ground? Against us, in the open, one on one? They don't have a chance. They can't have five hundred guerrillas in the whole bunch that know which end of a rifle you look through."

"Well, they've done a pretty good number on us—you—for the past year or so," Hitler spat back.

"Maybe so, but then their guerrillas were armed and they had help from the flying syringes. The one time we had them dead in our sights, the horsemen from hell bailed them out. But now those creatures are history and the Jews in the hole over there have no weapons."

"How do you know that?"

"We checked that out carefully on the tapes CNN gave us."

"All the better," Hitler replied. "Maybe the Reich's elite can finally accomplish what you and your border guard have failed to do for the past three and a half years!"

"You are missing the point I'm afraid, master. You may be able to kill those Jews," said Sergei, "but Iesus? How do we kill Iesus?"

"My Prince killed Him once before, remember? That time he used the Roman soldiers to accomplish his will. This time, the armies of the Reich will accomplish the will of the All-Powerful One. I have his promise on that!"

Sergei stared at the map, shaking his head. *That's what bothers me*, he thought. *Your Prince did kill Him once before and look what good it did!* Finally, he asked, "Do our military leaders have any input on this, on where we fight this critical battle?"

"We don't need the input of my subordinates. My Prince and I have determined that we are to fight the armies of Iesus on the Plains of Megiddo, at a place called 'Har-Magedon.' You and General Anayev will work out the details."

"Har-Magedon? Don't you mean Ar-mageddon— Armageddon—master?"

Hitler slammed the pointer down on the map. "Yes, Armageddon, Har-Magedon, Plains of Megiddo . . . they're all the same thing. Now, listen! Quit interrupting! Iesus may think He's the ruler of the world, but until He defeats my armies, I'm still in control. We will get rid of Him, once and for all!" Hitler began walking around the table, gesturing with his arms. "We must assemble the finest army ever put together, the elite from our best military nations. Gerhardt has assured me he can supply us with state-of-the-art weaponry, unlike anything the world has ever seen. Already, preparations are being made."

"But master—"

"What is it, Sergei?" Hitler snapped, the veins on his neck standing out like ropes. "Don't you think you can beat that— how did you put it, 'ragtag bunch of Jews'—with the Reich's best?"

"Excuse me, master, that's not the issue. *Doesn't the Bible say we lose the Battle of Armageddon?*" Sergei asked timidly.

"Of course it does, you idiot!" Hitler roared. "Who do you think wrote that pack of fairy tales? God Almighty dictated every word of that book! What do you expect Him to say? 'Hey look, guys, we're going to fight the All-Powerful One on the plains of Armageddon and My Son here, Yeshua, is going to lose?' If their Bible ended on that note, it'd kind of shoot a hole in the rest of it, don't you think?"

"Why not just wait for them to come out of that hole in the ground over there, and shoot them one at a time when they come out? Or, better yet, just nuke the hole!"

"We can't. My Prince says Iesus agrees to fight only on the

Plains of Megiddo or Iesus doesn't play. He sets the location, we set the time. Those are the conditions."

"But why do we need to do it His way?"

"*Because Iesus is the key to it all.* It wasn't those two lunatics at the Wall that gave us all the problems. It was Iesus, their Leader. He's been behind all of our failures. As long as He lives, we've got trouble. And because He is not in the hole with the rest of them, we play by His rules if we want Him in the fight!"

"Well . . ."

"Look at it this way, Sergei. Iesus has stuck His neck out, agreeing to fight this one last battle. He's told His followers He would fight it. Because it's in the Bible, it's in writing for the whole world to read. If He backs out now, He's the loser. And if He goes through with it, Iesus and His followers will be slaughtered by the Reich's elite. Either way, He loses, and I win!"

"But how do you know He loses?" Sergei asked, the worried look still on his face.

"Because My Prince has told me He loses, that's why! The only other time he went one on one with Iesus, Iesus ended up on the cross and then dead in the tomb. That's never happened to the All-Powerful One!"

"Maybe so," Sergei continued to argue, "but He's anything but dead now, isn't He?"

"Of course He's alive, stupid!" Hitler raged. "My Prince raised Him from the dead, just as he raised me from the dead. And 'why' you may ask? For one purpose!"

"Which is . . . ?"

"Iesus represents Almighty God; I represent the All-Powerful One. My real purpose on Earth is to lead the armies that will kill Iesus and all His followers at the battle of Armageddon. No more, no less. It has been predestined. It is the only way to end it all, once and for all!" Hitler punched the air victoriously. "No, Sergei, we can't lose. The All-Powerful One has guaranteed it. His power to raise Iesus and me from the dead is living proof that he will win the battle of Armageddon! Now, we have work to do!"

"As you wish, master."

"Get General Anayev working on these plans right away. We will call this Operation Yeshua!"

Sonya stood on the second-floor balcony of the residence that bore her name, overlooking the southern shore of the river running through Azel. She marveled at the perfection of the limestone masonry, each piece fitted without mortar, the joints almost impossible to see. All the buildings shared the same general design and construction: exquisitely fitted stonework, together with structural and decorative cedar, bearing none of the defects associated with the work of men.

She heard the sound of boots coming up the path between the houses. Shimon rounded the corner and smiled up at her.

"Please join me," she invited.

He hurried up the long, graceful outside stairway to the balcony.

"Have you found anything for us to eat?" she asked.

He grinned in embarrassment. "It was as you said. We have everything we could possibly want. Just like our forefathers who wandered the wilderness for forty years."

With shame, Sonya remembered her own doubts. "Our Lord is the Good Shepherd, isn't He?"

"Indeed He is. So now we wait."

Armageddon Minus 18 Days

The little angel arced through deep space on a trajectory that intersected the sun. He was not an archangel or even one of the leading angels. He was just an ordinary little angel, but his Lord had sent him to carry out this special task.

Solar flares shot into space above the turbulent surface of the wondrous glowing body. The angel plunged toward the incandescent surface, shot through the wall of flames, and plowed forward through an arrangement of matter that human scientists could only guess at.

Near the core, he examined the current balance of nuclear processes. Then he altered them in precise accordance with his instructions. He smiled as he saw the reactions increase in violence.

Here he would remain for two days.

"I beg your pardon?" Yuri asked in disbelief, although he had heard Ehud clearly.

"It's a command performance. Hitler wants to talk to us personally—you, me, Andrei, and Egor. No one else!"

"What about?"

"He wouldn't tell me. The orders were to get over there right away. He's sent a car for us. It's outside now."

"He probably wants to tell the world that he's responsible for the freshwater supply that suddenly replaced the bloody seas this morning. How do you think he pulled that one off?" Andrei asked.

"Beats me. Whether he's responsible or not, it saved our lives! If he's smart, he'll take the credit for it. He needs something good to tell the citizens of the Reich!"

"Are we supposed to bring our cameras and sound equipment?" Egor asked.

"Nope. Just us."

"Well, there goes your theory on the water supply. Believe me, if he was the one responsible for cleaning it up, he'd want this interview plastered on every TV screen in the world!" Andrei quipped.

"He needs to do something. Right about now he's taking all the heat for everything! Without those blasted Reich Emblems, he'd be long gone!" Egor added.

"Watch what you're saying," Yuri interrupted, always conscious of the little black box in the corner of the room outside the office they were in. Moments later, the four men piled into the back seats of the stretch Mercedes limousine. The powerful car made a screeching U-turn and roared back to the east, twisting through Jerusalem's confused streets and up the long, curving drive to the Lion's Den. The driver swept in under the broad porte cochere, and attendants opened the doors.

Once inside, Sergei ushered them into Hitler's plotting room. A moment later, the Reichmaster himself entered the room.

"I've asked you to come here because of a very important event I want you to record for history—one that is to occur in less than three weeks," said Hitler. "For now, this is a matter of absolute secrecy. Do you understand me?"

They all nodded in agreement.

"You will be the privileged ones to record this historic event. Through the eyes of your cameras, the world will witness the greatest battle ever fought!"

"A battle, in the Fourth Reich? We have an insurrection someplace?" Ehud asked, secretly surprised it hadn't happened already.

"No insurrection. This battle will be against Iesus and His armies."

"Iesus and what armies?" Yuri asked, startled at the possibility.

"The Jews hiding in that hole over there. The ones who have been terrorizing our troops," Sergei answered.

"You call those armies?" Yuri began to laugh.

"I think it wise for you to listen before you make jokes," Sergei warned.

Ehud gave Yuri that look that said, *Shut up, fast, if you know what's good for you!* "Where will this be?" Yuri asked. "When?"

"Listen!" snapped Hitler, irritated by Yuri's sarcasm. "This operation has been named 'Operation Yeshua.' It will be fought exactly eighteen days from today, on the Plains of Megiddo." He took his pointer and indicated the area on the map in front of him. "It has all been arranged."

"And you think those Jews in the hole over there are still alive? Come on!" Yuri exclaimed, continuing to push his luck to the limit.

"We're not sure. The only thing we know for certain is this: the leader of the rebellion has agreed to fight our leader, Adolf Hitler, and his armies on the Plains of Megiddo in exactly eighteen days!" Sergei explained, patiently.

"The real battle is against Iesus—hence, 'Operation Yeshua,' " Hitler added.

"And what happens if the Jews over there don't show?" Yuri questioned.

"We don't care if they do or don't. If they do, we kill them along with their Leader. If they don't, after we kill their Leader, we blow up the hole and take care of matters that way. Either way, eighteen days from now, Yeshua and His followers are history. First we cut off the head, then we kill the body. Your mission will be to get the entire battle on tape."

"Realistically, what are our chances of losing?" asked a worried Ehud.

"None whatsoever. The All-Powerful One has assured us the victory. After all, how can a handful of Jews with a few peashooters hope to defeat the mightiest forces and the latest weaponry ever assembled on one battlefield? No, there is no doubt whatsoever as to the outcome. And the famous Kagan, Kaugin, and Denisov crew has been chosen to record this greatest and final battle of all battles for posterity."

"But how can you be so sure of yourself?" persisted Yuri. "What you call 'a handful of Jews with a few peashooters' just happen to have managed to survive the best you have — or am I missing something?"

Hitler exploded. "Are you questioning me, Yuri? You were nothing until I gave you special access to me!"

"You know my loyalty to you and the Fourth Reich," Yuri objected. "After all, I betrayed my friend Anatoly for you, for the sake of the Reich!"

"Yes, I remember, and that is why you are here today . . ."

Suddenly a brilliant light burst through the tall windows, momentarily blinding all of them.

"What's happening?" Hitler held up his hand to shield his eyes. He pointed to Sergei. "Go find out."

They all waited in silence until he returned, minutes later, his face ashen.

"Well?" Hitler demanded.

"Something has happened to the sun."

"What do you mean 'happened to the sun'? How can something 'happen' to the sun?"

"The outside temperature is already 130 degrees Fahrenheit, and still climbing. The observatories report a significant increase in the sun's intensity."

"Meaning?"

"Meaning it will soon be unbearable here, and deathly hot in the temperate zones, and. . ."

"Get out!" Hitler thundered, breaking the pointer on the table. It was happening again. Every time he had something of importance to say, Iesus struck back with crippling force. How much more could he endure?

". . . and the people in the deserts, the tropics, and much of the southern hemisphere will die."

"Out!" Hitler screamed. "Get out! All of you! Get out of my sight! I want to be left alone!"

Ehud jumped up like something had bitten him. He hurried out of the room, with Yuri and the others on his heels. Sergei closed the door after them.

Outside, the CNN crew squinted at the abnormal glare and gasped at the heat.

"Take us back to our office," Ehud ordered the driver. "And turn on the air conditioning. It's boiling hot out here."

The driver nodded, started the engine, and put the air on maximum cool.

Yuri felt the vent beside him as he gasped for breath. "This thing isn't working!"

Ehud checked his vent. "Yes, it is. It's going to take a while to cool this down. But, for what it's worth, Hitler may never cool down after today."

"What do you mean?"

"I mean, you just can't speak to Adolf Hitler the way you did today. Are you stupid or something?"

"I was trying to understand, that's all. It wasn't an interview. I was just asking questions so that I know how to handle the story better. What's wrong with that? Can't he ever get over that little-man complex and talk about real issues?"

"Can I ask you a question?" Andrei interrupted, changing directions. "Did you really betray your friend, Anatoly Altshuler?"

"Why do you think we have the inside scoop on everything Hitler does? Because we're nice guys?" Yuri shot back.

"I . . ."

"Anyway," Yuri continued, defending his actions, "Anatoly was to blame. He betrayed the Reich. It's over and done with. I don't want to talk about it anymore."

They lapsed into silence. Just then a muted thud sounded from somewhere in the front of the car. Yuri glanced forward and saw a white mist curling up from under the hood. A few moments later the engine seized, and the Mercedes coasted to a stop.

They stepped out into what seemed like an oven. The driver got out, too, looking at the car and then back at his passengers.

"Don't worry about us," Ehud told him. "We'll get another ride. Do you want to come with us?"

The driver shook his head. "I'll head back to the Lion's Den."

Sweat drenched their clothes as the four men headed westward toward their office. Even with sunglasses, the intense glare made it almost impossible to keep their eyes open for more than a few seconds at a time. The superheated air seared their lungs, and sweat burned their eyes.

The minutes dragged by as they plodded slowly along, knowing they would never get a ride. They had seen only one car moving, and it had been spouting white smoke. All other vehicles were either parked or broken down.

When they finally trudged through the propped-open front door of their office building, they stepped into a dark sauna.

"What's wrong?" Ehud demanded.

"The power's off," the receptionist announced.

"What about the emergency generator?"

"One of the technicians fired it up. But after a few minutes, it quit too. He's tinkering with it, but so far he can't get it to start."

"How hot is it in here?"

"It was 130 degrees the last time we checked."

The back door crashed open, and a technician stumbled in and fell on the floor. "Engine's seized on the generator," the man gasped. "I think it's ruined."

"What do we do?" Yuri asked.

"Wait until night," said Ehud. "When it cools off, we all go home and stay there until this breaks."

Yuri sighed. *If it breaks*, he thought.

Armageddon Minus 16 Days

Two days later, the little angel received his next command. He immediately departed from the sun and set an easy course for the blue orb of Earth. At an altitude of 800 kilometers, he positioned himself directly above Jerusalem.

It was an hour before noon. Slowly the Earth rotated until the sun reached its zenith on that side of the planet. Then the angel swooped down into the highest reaches of the atmosphere and subtly changed the molecular alignments that his Lord had designed so perfectly in the day of its creation.

Hitler scowled as he sat in his boxer shorts, looking toward Jerusalem from inside the heavily tinted sliding glass door in his bedroom. The air-conditioning system had struggled to pull the inside temperature down to 115 degrees. The Lion's Den had already been through three emergency generators and five air-conditioning compressors, and now none of them worked. Like everyone else, Hitler sweltered through the nearly lethal conditions. With all communications shut down, it would be days before the worldwide death toll could be properly assessed.

The light dimmed. Hitler got up and peered outside. At last, relief! he silently wished to himself. There wasn't a cloud in the sky, but the brightness of the sun seemed to be diminishing. Is it over?

The brilliance returned to normal daylight, then darkened rapidly toward what seemed like dusk, bringing with it a coolness that was a welcome relief after the terrible heat they had endured. "Oh no, something is wrong! Now it's going the other way!" Hitler exclaimed to no one. He glanced at his watch. It was high noon. Soon, however, the blackness of deepest space settled on the Earth, with no hint of moon or stars—and an eerie cold settled in.

With the national power grid still down, Jerusalem was inky black. Hitler felt his way along in the darkness, wishing for any kind of light, but there was none. The world had become a black hole. He rammed his right foot into one of the bedposts and cursed the God he didn't believe existed, as red-hot needles of pain shot to his brain. He stumbled backward, trying to keep his balance, and toppled over, falling heavily on his left hip.

"Sergei!" he roared, feeling the chill in his bones.

There was no answer. Panic swept over him.

He curled up in a ball in an attempt to stay warm, and bit on his tongue as wild hallucinations roared through his mind, stimulated by eyes that longed to see but could not. The floor upon which he lay seemed to spin out of control, thrusting him toward the abyss of insanity. It seemed he could hear jeering laughter and horrible cries of pain.

Minutes later, there was a light tapping on his bedroom door. Hitler opened his eyes. The latch clicked, and he heard the door swing open. He instinctively pulled his knees to his chest as he stared into the blackness, craving his sight, craving warmth.

"Master?" Sergei's voice softly drifted out of the darkness.

"Sergei?"

"I am here."

"What is happening? Am I blind? Am I going to freeze to death?"

"No, master. It is completely dark. The world is in blackness."

"Get a flashlight or a candle, anything!"

"We've tried everything. Nothing works."

"What can we do?" It seemed almost a whimper.

Armageddon Minus 14 Days

The angel did not need a watch. At precisely noon, Jerusalem time, exactly two days after the darkness descended, he allowed the atoms to return to their previous alignment. Light returned to the Earth with a suddenness that was temporarily blinding. And with the sunlight, warmth.

Then the angel returned to Heaven.

The returning light did little to cheer Anna Makarova, although it was a relief from the horrible blackness and the cold that went with it. She looked outside her bedroom windows at the Old City of Jerusalem in the distance. The once-beautiful view had been turned into a war zone. She shivered, as though something overpowering was approaching.

She walked up the stairs to the fourth floor, where she found Hitler standing at the parapet. He was looking toward the northeast with a gaze that never wavered. Even from the side, she could see the hate in his magnetic eyes.

"How are you?" she asked softly.

For a moment she thought he had not heard. Then he turned slightly. "I will be better, soon. Soon it will be over . . . after I defeat Iesus and His armies."

Her eyes brimmed with unshed tears, but he did not notice. "When will it be?"

"What?" he asked absently.

"The battle. When will it be?"

"In two weeks. Only fourteen more days. If we can survive fourteen more days, it will all be over."

THIRTY-EIGHT

Armageddon Minus 1 Day

It was midmorning when Hitler and Sergei boarded the Hind helicopter at the Lion's Den and the pilot set course for Tel Megiddo, the high hill overlooking the Plains of Megiddo. Hitler peered out the window as they flew along, his blue-gray eyes shielded by the narrow brim of his Nazi military cap. He smiled to himself triumphantly, knowing that success was finally within his grasp.

Two weeks ago, the plagues that had been occurring one right after the other had come to an abrupt ending. He considered it an interlude, some sort of unwritten truce before the final battle was fought. The calm before the storm.

The Reich had made good use of the time. Division after division of the world's finest trained troops poured into Israel. Those nations who initially objected were soon persuaded by spirit-world messengers sent directly from the All-Powerful One. Now, 250,000 of the world's elite were arrayed on the Plains of Megiddo, along with a massive supply of armor and artillery. General Anayev and his staff had spent the past two days briefing the commanders on their objectives.

In a rare televised briefing a week earlier, Hitler called on the military leaders of the world to meet the greatest challenge of their military careers: "Operation Yeshua" — the final war of all wars. Yeshua was the true Enemy of the Reich; indeed, the Enemy of mankind. What better cause under which to unite every army in the world? Kill Yeshua and the problems of the world would finally be over. The All-Powerful One had guaranteed their victory. The military's contribution to this victory would bring them unprecedented honor and the Earth would finally experience universal, uninterrupted peace.

As before, the citizens of the Reich responded to the dynamic appeal of their leader. Around the world, the people who had survived the onslaught of God's judgment had but one thought in mind. They expressed it in their battle cry: "Kill Him, kill Him, kill Him!" As each day passed with no new disasters, the confidence of the people mirrored the growing confidence of their leader. One and all eagerly looked to Operation Yeshua as the final solution to their problems.

"Soon, Sergei. Very soon," Hitler said, anticipating the moment. He looked down on the broad plain in front of the tel, from the hill where once the ancient city of Megiddo had stood. For centuries this had not only been the site of important ancient cities, but the scene of countless bloody battles. Now it would be the place of his final solution, his Prince's greatest victory.

"Master, are you still planning to address the troops?"

Hitler nodded. "I must. This will be the Reich's finest hour. I can leave nothing to chance. Is everything ready?"

Sergei consulted his notes. "Everything is in place. General Anayev has performed beyond anything you could ever hope or ask."

"And the media coverage?"

"Ehud Goldberg has cooperated well. He's bending over backwards to make up for what happened at the Lion's Den a couple weeks ago."

"Meaning?"

"Meaning he's agreed not to let Yuri Kagan cover your speech to the troops later this morning. When Kagan finds out, he'll go crazy!"

"But I want that speech taped for posterity!"

"Ehud's number two crew will film the speech. That would be Morris, the studio anchorman."

"When do they arrive?"

"Actually, they're already here. The audio part will be

broadcast live, over the radio, but nothing hits the tube until the big battle tomorrow—exactly as you instructed. Yuri and his crew have been given that assignment. They'll arrive later tonight. That way Yuri's mouth can't get him in any more trouble, and we get the spin we want as both crews will record tomorrow's battle, from two different locations."

"Good, good!" Hitler said, nodding and smiling.

The Hind touched down at the base of Tel Megiddo, precisely at 11:00 A.M., as scheduled. Anayev's temporary command post—a tent of considerable size—was 100 meters to the northeast of where the chopper landed. Behind them was a dirt road that ran to the top of the tel, where Hitler and his Enforcer planned to watch the battle the next morning. Two guards saluted as Hitler and Sergei stepped to the ground. Hitler stood there and looked around, reviewing the scene. Tents, armored vehicles, and parading troops covered every available patch of ground.

"This time tomorrow, Sergei, 'the war of all wars' will be history! Our fighting men must know how important this day will be. Now, where do I address the troops?"

Sergei pointed beyond General Anayev's huge tent, to a high reviewing stand that had been prepared especially for Hitler's challenge to his fighting men.

"First you review the honor battalion," said Sergei. "Then the troops will be assembled before the reviewing stand."

"Will they all be able to see me? That's important."

Sergei nodded. "We have set up closed-circuit screens in the field. Everyone will see and hear clearly."

"Perfect," said Hitler.

Yuri stormed into Ehud's office. "I quit!" he shouted, glaring down at the bureau chief. "You can find someone else to report on Operation Yeshua." He started to walk out again, intending to slam the door behind him.

"Hold on a minute!" said Goldberg. "What's your problem?"

Yuri whipped around, his eyes glowing with anger. "Why didn't you assign *me* to cover Hitler's speech? It was dynamite, and I didn't even know about it until I accidentally heard it on the radio! What's going on here? Why didn't somebody tell me about this before now?"

Ehud struggled to control his temper. "Well, if you'll give me a chance, I'll tell you," he said. "Sit down."

The reporter reluctantly dropped into a chair. "Okay, I'm listening," he challenged.

"Thank you," said Ehud. "I had to make a decision, Yuri. Either you got three-quarters of the pie or you got no pie at all. After you mouthed off at your last meeting with Hitler, Sergei told me he didn't want you assigned to Hitler anymore, especially the speeches that follow with live interviews. I told Sergei you were the best when it came to event coverage, so we struck a deal. You get the battle, the event of all events, but Morris and his crew got the speech."

"But, why didn't . . ."

"I didn't tell you about Hitler's address to his troops this morning," Ehud interrupted, "because I didn't want trouble with you until it was over. You already know that arrangements have been made for you and your crew to go up north, later tonight. If you don't like what I've worked out for you, then Morris gets it all. You got a problem with that?"

"What about the future? Is it me or is it Morris?"

"Handle yourself well on this one, and Sergei says he'll see that you . . ."

The first tremor was deceptively gentle, knocking a plaque off the wall in Ehud's office. Then the floor started rolling like waves on the sea. Yuri and Ehud stood up, struggling to stay on their feet, and rushed outside. They made it to the middle of the street just as the ground jumped. In an instant, the CNN office building disappeared in a dense cloud of dust.

Suddenly, a fissure opened in the road about 30 meters away from them. The crack widened and sped off in both directions with a deafening grinding sound.

Yuri cried out in terror, but no one could hear him. He grabbed an unearthed water main and struggled desperately to keep from being thrown down the yawning chasm only meters away.

Yuri looked around frantically, shouting for help, as he kept his death grip on the pipe. At first it seemed that the hills around Jerusalem were swelling up, but then he realized that Mount Zion, on which Jerusalem sat, was actually collapsing. The temple, the Dome of the Rock, El-Aksa Mosque, all three of the great religious symbols that had miraculously survived the onslaught of God's wrath, now began to sway back and forth, the walls beginning to crash down as the Temple Mount began to heave. The rock under his feet shook again, and he watched in horror as the ground under Ehud broke off. Ehud's mouth opened in a scream as he disappeared into the Earth.

The earthquake hit Hitler's palace like a giant's hammer. Anna's bedroom windows blew out, and the furniture slued across the room as if alive. The huge chandelier swayed crazily before crashing down on the bed in a shower of plaster and glass.

Anna staggered toward the open windows. Jerusalem danced and swayed far below, then seemed to shatter apart. Two fissures tore down from the north end of Jerusalem, moving through the Old City. She heard a thunderous roar somewhere to the south. It grew louder and louder as the quake increased in intensity. Anna looked down in horror. The floor was splitting apart like a giant egg.

She tumbled through the fissure, and the Lion's Den collapsed on top of her. In a fraction of a second she crossed the line between the living and the dead.

This third fracture, coming from the south, met the other two at the Temple Mount.

The commander of the space shuttle, *Adolf Hitler III*, looked down from his lofty perch 500 kilometers above the surface of the Earth. The spacecraft floated upside down with the cargo bay doors open and its black belly pointing toward the sun. In three more orbits they were scheduled to begin their descent.

As the crew finished securing all their experiments, the commander watched the approaching coast of Israel. At first he thought his mind was playing tricks on him; the land seemed to be rippling and blurring. Then an icy knife of terror stabbed deep in his stomach as he realized what it was.

"We just lost all communication!" came a voice from behind the flight deck. "Video, voice, data — everything!"

The commander looked down on what no earthbound human could ever imagine. As far as the eye could see, new land was being pushed up, slowly emptying the contents of the Mediterranean into the deserts of North Africa. One more orbit brought the scope of the catastrophe into clearer focus. The great mountain chains of the world heaved under the pressure of an invisible force. Already many islands had disappeared, and the oceans had created new boundaries. The seacoasts were beyond recognition, at least the parts that were not hidden under clouds of dust. The global reforming process continued, obliterating all that had been home to the human race — obliterating their landing strip. Only an area north of Jerusalem seemed untouched by the mayhem below. And then, just as quickly as it had begun, the Earth's crust became still.

Unknown to the commander, a volcanic eruption in China had flung a chunk of lava the size of a house into space several hours earlier. The crew never knew what hit them.

When the Earth stopped moving, Yuri managed to crawl onto solid ground. There was nothing but a gaping hole where Ehud had stood only moments ago. Somehow, Andrei and Egor had survived. They were huddled together 20 meters away, bruised and shaken.

Yuri stumbled through the rubble toward them. "Are you all right?" he asked. Both men stared at him as if he were speaking a foreign language. Yuri shook Andrei. "Andrei! We need to see if our equipment is okay."

Andrei nodded. He turned to the CNN van. It was on its side, but mostly intact. He made his way slowly to the back doors and reached through the broken windows. He opened the latch and forced the lower door open, then crawled inside and started digging into the jumbled mess.

Yuri turned to Egor. "Are you okay?"

The soundman was deathly pale, but he nodded.

Andrei returned with a camera and several spare batteries, which he stuffed in his pockets. "This looks okay. The case is bent, but the camera runs and the optics look fine. I think we're in business."

"Good," Yuri said. He turned to Egor. "See if any of the sound stuff works."

The soundman rummaged around and found a working recorder and several wireless mikes. He put together an equipment bag and rejoined the other two.

Yuri nodded toward the Old City. "Okay, let's go. Get this on tape."

West Jerusalem had been devastated by the earthquake. Mounds of rubble and steaming holes made the going tough. Dead and dying people were everywhere. Those who had survived wandered aimlessly, as if they could no longer make any sense of their world. They all seemed to have only one goal: get out of the city. Streams of survivors moved in any direction that could lead them safely out of what remained of Jerusalem.

The world-famous three-man team reached the Old City and climbed up on the toppled Damascus Gate on the northern wall of the city and looked down on the devastation within. Nothing was standing.

Andrei panned around and brought the camera down. "Got that," he said. "What do you want to do now?"

"I'd like to tape a report from the Temple Mount."

Andrei whistled. "We'll never get through that mess."

Yuri looked off in the distance. "Let's go around to the Eastern Gate. If it hasn't collapsed, it will take us right to where I want to start this piece."

They climbed back down to street level and continued along Sultan Suleiman until they turned the corner of the city wall and came to what remained of the Eastern Gate. It, too, was ruined, but they were able to make their way over the rubble and up onto what was left of the Temple Mount platform. The once-flat surface was a sea of tumbled stone with three large mounds where the temple, the Dome of the Rock, and the El Aqsa Mosque had stood. The Dome's golden roof lay shattered and crushed.

"Let's use that for a backdrop," Yuri said, pointing to a large piece. "Everyone will know what it is."

Andrei picked his spot and waited while Egor fitted Yuri with a mike.

"Let's make this good," Yuri said to his crew. "This will become one of the most famous reports in history."

Andrei nodded and brought the camera up. "I'm taping."

Yuri looked into the lens. "This is Yuri Kagan reporting from what used to be the Temple Mount in Jerusalem. Today this ancient city—along with its religious temples here on the famous Temple Mount—is dead, completely destroyed in a matter of minutes. Whether or not this massive quake was part of an worldwide disaster, we don't know yet. All communications here in Jerusalem are down. The death toll is staggering. Those still living seek safety outside the city, away from the falling buildings that have killed so many of their fellow countrymen.

"I know your thoughts, like mine, are with our leader, Adolf Hitler, who even now, at this very moment, is preparing for Operation Yeshua. He has guaranteed us that, in spite of the difficulties, at this time tomorrow, it will all be over. Whether Hitler or the elite armies of the world that have gathered together for Operation Yeshua have survived this latest disaster, no one knows for sure. We must find comfort in knowing . . ."

Yuri stopped midsentence. Huge gray objects, shaped like oversized watermelons, were streaking down from the skies, accompanied by strange whistling sounds. One landed about 10 meters away and broke into a pile of ice rubble. Then another and another. The barrage increased rapidly, until the heavens were filled with the dark objects, hurtling down from outer space.

For less than a second, Yuri watched one of the huge chunks of ice heading down toward him from the heavens above. It hit him squarely, crushing his body beneath its icy weight. Before they even realized what had happened to their colleague, Andrei and Egor joined him in death.

The supernatural hailstorm was worldwide, covering

the ground with ice chunks weighing at least a hundred pounds each. Other than the military, providentially protected on the Plains of Megiddo for the final showdown with Yeshua the next day, and the children of God tucked safely away in Azel, few people in the world survived this final devastation.

Like those before him, when the last angel had finished pouring out the contents of his bowl upon Earth, he returned to the end of the line with the other angels. Now all seven of them stood quietly before Almighty God.

Hitler was sitting in the temporary command post when he heard the rumble in the distance. He listened for almost an hour, and then the sound quit. Whatever it was, his troops and the valley that lay before him were unaffected. Only the rumble gave evidence that all was not as peaceful in other parts of Israel. Here, at the base of Tel Megiddo, everything remained the same.

"What in blazes is going on now, Sergei?" he asked as his Enforcer came through the door of the tent.

"We don't know. General Anayev reports we've lost all communications with the outside world," said Sergei. "But he does have an interesting theory, master."

"And what's that?"

"Well, do you remember the last quake we had in Jerusalem?"

"Are you referring to the one that split the Mount of Olives in half, or the one that occurred after the Jews went down into that hole?"

"Well, actually, I'm referring to both."

"Make your point."

"If those guerrillas down in that hole are to become the army of Iesus, they've got to come back up out of it, sometime before tomorrow."

"And," said Hitler, already picking up on Anayev's theory, "if it took a quake to close the entrance, it would take another one to open it up."

"Right. We know that the guerrillas can't move around like

Iesus. That's why He and His followers had to come to Jerusalem on foot. We know they have no means of transportation available to them. If they expect to be up here in the morning, they'll have to get started soon. The quake probably reopened the entrance and, after the guerrillas exited, closed it back up again to protect the rest."

"And that would explain why communications are down as well."

"How do you mean?" Sergei asked.

"When Iesus made His grand entrance thirty days ago, He was able to keep me out of the picture by cutting all power and communications to the Lion's Den—isolating us from what was taking place."

"And so He does it again today, thinking to keep us in the dark about the movement of His troops," said Sergei.

"That's the way I see it. Which means His guerrillas are probably on their way up here right now."

"Which means His guerrillas are probably on their way up here right now," Sergei repeated slowly, a word at a time, making his own point.

"Can't do it," Hitler answered, knowing where his Enforcer was headed. "It's Yeshua we want. Like I've said before, cut the head off first, and the rest of the body dies. My Prince says the only place that Yeshua will fight is right here. Anyplace else and all bets are off. We've just got to wait for them to come to us," Hitler said. "Have we picked up any reports of troop movement in the valley, where they're most likely to come?"

"None, master. We're hoping Yuri can fill us in when he gets up here with his crew." Sergei looked at his watch. "He should have been here by now."

"What about Morris? Is he ready to go?" Hitler asked.

"They've got their own equipment and are setting up on the tel behind us."

"Good. I'll take all the coverage I can get. It's going to be something the world will never forget!"

"What if Iesus doesn't show, master?"

Hitler's eyes smoldered with hate. "He'll show. He can't afford to miss it!"

Armageddon Day

Two hours before dawn, Hitler's APC pulled out of camp and drove slowly up a narrow road leading to the top of Tel Megiddo. They would view the battle from this elevated observation point, generally west of where the final battle was to take place. As the vehicle labored upward, they were lost in mists of ground fog until they broke out near the summit. The driver found a flat spot and pulled over. There the three waited silently: General Anayev, keeping his thoughts to himself; Hitler, his eyes glowing with anticipation as he thought about how close he finally was to his goal; Sergei, quietly watching his master. Although Operation Yeshua was a concept that was less than thirty days old, he knew that *this was the day that his master's Prince had looked to, planned for, from the very beginning*. After today, things would be different. After today, no more problems. After today, his master would truly be the lord and leader of the Earth. This, indeed, was the day. Hitler's day!

The army was deployed generally north and east of Tel Megiddo, at the head of the plains that sprawled out below them. Hitler knew from history that many battles had been fought here before. Barak had fought the Canaanites, and Gideon had fought the Midianites. And both men had won. Today he would fight Iesus—and he, too, would win.

"Any sign of the Jewish guerrillas . . . or Yuri and his crew?" Hitler asked.

"None," General Anayev answered.

"Strange," was all Sergei could think of adding.

"Probably still mad because he couldn't cover my speech yesterday. You know the hot little temper Yuri has," Hitler surmised. "At least Goldberg had him backed up with Morris."

As the sun crested the eastern horizon, Hitler opened the door and stepped out. Sergei and General Anayev followed.

"What a grand sight!" Hitler said, surveying his might. "Gentlemen, before you is the most powerful army ever assembled on the face of the Earth."

He shielded his eyes against the brilliant sunrise. Then, as if waiting for Hitler's arrival, a shadow passed over the land, although there wasn't a cloud in the sky. A blinding white cloud blossomed up to the north and grew until it covered the entire horizon. In the center, a pinpoint of glowing red incandescence formed and grew. It was a sight Hitler and those with him had never forgotten since the first time several years earlier.

Hitler gasped as he watched the pinpoint of glowing red begin to take the shape of a being, mounted on the back of a white horse. The Man wore gleaming white robes, dipped in blood. The red glow that surrounded Him seemed to come from His eyes, which burned like fire. On His head He wore a crown. Written on his robes was "KING OF KINGS AND LORD OF LORDS," and behind Him rode the armies of Heaven, clothed in white linen.

Suddenly, Hitler realized that the armies with Iesus weren't the Jewish guerrillas. He stood there speechless, unable to move. These were angelic armies—too many to count—descending slowly in perfect formation, moving toward the ancient Plain of Megiddo.

Yeshua glared down on all those gathered on the plain, His eyes blazing. Hitler tried to turn away, to escape those accusing eyes, but he couldn't. Fear and despair washed over him. All his illusions about overcoming Iesus evaporated. But not even that could dim his defiance. He raised his fist and shook it. No! He would never submit!

Suddenly, a white-hot blast of pure energy shot out of the sky, striking every soldier on the plain in that brief split-second of time. Armored vehicles turned into blazing-hot ovens, and rivers of blood spread across the ground as each mangled body poured out its life.

Hitler and Sergei looked around them. Anayev and the APC driver lay at their feet, their bodies crumpled wads of bloody flesh. Morris and his crew had met the same end.

Before the battle had even begun, it was over. Everyone was dead. Everyone except Hitler and Sergei.

"Sergei!" Hitler screamed.

"Yes, master?" his frightened servant answered.

But before he could cry out further, the son of Satan was gripped by some unseen force, plucked into the air, and propelled forward. The Earth disappeared, replaced by an oppressive darkness. He knew he was traveling at an unthinkable speed toward a destination unfamiliar to him. Not to the abyss this time, but to someplace far worse. He saw the glow in the distance. The glow grew until he could see yellow flames dancing as far as the eye could see. His rapid descent plunged him, like a rag doll, into the yellow flames.

Every nerve ending shot messages of pain to his brain, but he knew that oblivion would not overtake him, would not drop him into some blissful nonexistence. The flames were real. They burned without killing, without the morphia of unconsciousness, without relief of any kind.

He had been thrown into the lake of fire, where he would burn forever.

Sergei was nearby, enduring the same agony. Neither would see or hear the other again, nor any other being created by God. They were alone with their thoughts and their agony for all eternity.

THIRTY-NINE

The Lord looked down on the mound of lifeless rubble that had been Jerusalem. The area looked like a huge pie divided into three jagged pieces. Flames shot into the air from ruptured gas lines and burning rubble.

As He descended to where the Temple Mount platform had been, Mount Zion—the mountain upon which the city of Jerusalem had once stood—began to shake, causing the paving stones littering the peak to grind and heave. It thrust upward, carrying the Lord skyward on a mighty pinnacle of rock. Zion's flanks ripped ponderously through the crumbling platform pavement. Steeper and more regular than any natural mountain, the shaft of Mount Zion continued to climb until it hovered 1,500 meters over the new Judean plains.

He walked slowly around the barren, flat summit. Below Him sprawled the rubble of man's rebellion against his Creator and the ruined remains of Satan's great plan. The Lord stopped when He came to the northeast side of the mountain. He turned around. A thick sheet of purest gold, transparent as glass, formed over the entire summit of the mountain, and a gleaming white throne thrust up in the center, high and facing east. Mighty walls pushed upward, and the monumental roof slid into place, all made of purest, transparent gold. The symmetry and majesty were perfect—columns, doors, windows, and pediments—like nothing ever seen on Earth. It was the final Temple of Almighty God.

Something like thunder sounded over the plain below as

tons of rock cascaded down Mount Zion's wide flanks, leaving smooth, golden stairs in its wake. The Lord smiled and turned back to the east. There, the landslide covering the entrance to Azel parted, revealing the rockbound entrance.

"Sound the shofar!" He commanded.

Then He waited.

A low sound rolled through the city of Azel. The sound swelled in power, and Sonya thrilled to it, even as she wondered what it was. Then she knew. It was the sound of the shofar.

"What was that?" Shimon asked. He looked over the railing of Sonya's balcony, where he, Sonya, and Binyamin had been sitting together.

"That was the ram's horn, Shimon, telling us the time has come," she said.

The three watched as two soldiers came running toward them. "The entrance is open!" the man in the lead shouted. They ran across the stone bridge and up the curving path leading to Sonya's quarters. Below the balcony, they bent over to catch their breath.

"Did you go outside?" Binyamin asked. "Could you see Jerusalem?"

A shadow seemed to pass over the two. The one who had been first, took a deep breath. "There's nothing left — even the hills are leveled, except for one high mountain. Jerusalem is rubble."

Conflicting emotions welled up inside Sonya. She felt momentary loss, but then remembered who the city and people had belonged to. Peace swept over her. She knew Yeshua's war against Satan was over. The battle was over, the war was won, and now there would be genuine peace for the first time ever.

She smiled. "Shimon, go find David and Gideon, then assemble everyone. We're leaving Azel."

"Where will we go?"

"To the new Mount Zion." She looked at her second in command. "Tell everyone to move out as soon as they can. I'm going to the entrance. Come, Binyamin, let's see what it looks like outside."

The two kept up a brisk pace as they followed the smooth, curving trail that led to the surface. Sonya wondered if they would have to climb over rubble at the entrance, but the way was completely clear, with not even a pebble to stumble over.

Outside, they stood at the high, arched entrance to Azel and looked over the valley that had once led to Jerusalem. But it wasn't a valley anymore. The craggy Judean hills were completely gone. Even the two halves of the Mount of Olives had disappeared. In its place stood a single, gigantic mountain—the new Mount Zion!

Sonya could see the sunlight flashing off a magnificent golden temple, high above on the summit of the mountain, as rivers cascaded down the sides, originating from the very heart of the temple itself. Its beauty overwhelmed her, especially when she saw the desolate plain below it.

Shimon, David, and Gideon joined them. "The people are coming," Shimon announced as he looked in amazement at their new world.

"Good," Sonya beamed. "We're going to Mount Zion."

The five leaders stepped out, and the people of Azel flooded through the entrance, fanning out like a living cape. The sound of awe rippled through the crowd as the people caught their first glimpse of Mount Zion and the new temple of the living God.

Then they saw the desolation surrounding it.

Dismembered corpses littered the ground, each emptied of its life blood. Lifeless eyes stared at the survivors as if accusing them even in death. Weapons of war, bent and mangled, barred the way. Tumbled buildings forced more and more detours, the closer they got. Reminders of God's power and grace. Reminders of man's sin. But Sonya never lost sight of their goal—that high and lifted-up mountain and the One who watched them from its summit.

At the base of the mountain, they stopped and looked up. High overhead, a glowing, golden cube was quickly expanding as it slowly descended toward the new Temple of God. Although the object extended over 2,000 kilometers in all directions, completely blocking the sun, there was no shadow. A rich light source beamed down through its translucent, golden walls. Finally the temple on the peak of Mount Zion penetrated the base of the descending cube, and then all movement stopped.

"What is it?" Binyamin whispered.

Sonya remembered what Anatoly had told her. And remembering, tears filled her eyes.

"It's the New Jerusalem," she said.

EPILOGUE

Anatoly was ecstatic. Moments before a glowing angel had ushered all the disembodied souls from under the altar into the throneroom of God, where, at the Lord's command, each had received their resurrection body. Anatoly examined his arms and touched his face as if to reassure himself he had one. Yes, he had a head, and now he had a flesh-and-blood body. It seemed identical to the one Hitler had killed—how long ago?

He smiled as he began to understand. There had been no calendar under the altar, but he knew it had been over three years.

The Lord smiled proudly at His martyrs, those who had given their lives for His sake and for the sake of their countrymen. Each was now arrayed in a gleaming white robe similar to His own.

"My Lord," Anatoly cried out in joy, falling at His feet.

"Arise, Anatoly," Yeshua said. "It is time for you to leave here. I am well pleased with you."

Anatoly shivered with joy. "I wouldn't be here except for Your grace, my Lord. Thank You for allowing me to serve You."

"You have spoken well. And now it is time to begin the next stage in your life."

"I long for Heaven, Lord."

Yeshua laughed. "Do you, Anatoly? Heaven is not what I had in mind."

Anatoly felt momentarily flustered. *Now why was that,*

he pondered. *Don't the saints go to Heaven when they die? Unless . . .*

"Suddenly, My servant Anatoly remembers," Yeshua laughed lovingly. "I still have special tasks on Earth for those who were beheaded by the Antichrist, as you were, Anatoly. I promised My servant Daniel that those who lead My children to righteousness—like you, Anatoly—will shine like the brightness of Heaven in the eyes of My Jewish children. But I wasn't referring to Heaven."

"You mean, I am to . . ." He couldn't finish it.

"Yes, Anatoly. I am restoring you to life on the Earth, where you will live during My thousand-year reign, helping King David rule over My people, Israel. This is not a punishment, Anatoly. *It is a reward given to only a few—only to those martyrs who were beheaded in their efforts to rescue the Jews from the persecution of the Antichrist.* As you might recall, I specifically instructed My servant John in this matter, in the book of My revelation to him."

Anatoly was speechless. He remembered Mike telling him about this, but he had never seen the application to what he had been called to do for his people. He had done what any other Jew, knowing the truth, would have done. And even his efforts—those things he did for the sake of his people—were a gift given him by God. In the end, there was nothing to glory in but the Lord Himself.

Finally he said, "I will serve You in any way that You ask, Lord. But does that mean that I will not see Heaven for another thousand years?"

The Lord saw his disappointment. "I understand, Anatoly. Come. I want to show you something before you return."

Yeshua took him by the hand, and together they dropped down into a soothing white mist. Below, Anatoly saw flashes of blue and glimmers of sunlight reflecting off the surface of what appeared to be an enormous glass cube. Then they broke through the mist, and then through the cube, passing swiftly through the center of it.

Anatoly gasped as they continued downward, through the base of the cube. They stopped their descent when they were at least 1,000 meters beneath its base, hovering over the most desolate landscape he had ever seen. Except for one towering mountain, everything else was a plain of death. Bloody, mangled bodies lay everywhere, victims of the terrible earthquakes that had occurred the day before. Weapons of war were now junk heaps of metal. The smoke from a thousand fires spread out over the ghastly land.

"Where are we, Lord?" Anatoly asked.

"Jerusalem."

"Jerusalem?" Anatoly exclaimed. "What happened?"

"The wrath of God."

Anatoly's eyes traced the golden spiral staircase that arose out of the debris and wound around the towering, transparent-gold mountain. At the summit stood a golden temple. Overhead, impossibly huge, hovered the giant cube he had just passed through, resting on top of Mount Zion, the temple in the center of its base. He could see through the walls, and his eyes traced the exquisite details for a long time.

"Mike told me about this. This is Mount Zion and Your new temple—and that's the New Jerusalem."

"Yes, Anatoly," the Lord confirmed. *"That is where Heaven now resides.* Would you like to see your future home?"

Anatoly beamed at Him. "Yes, Lord. I would like that very much."

They sped upward toward the temple, and passed back through the base of the New Jerusalem, this time more slowly so that Anatoly could look at the surroundings. Directly ahead, he saw the high throne of God, in the very center of the temple at the very apex of Mount Zion, the focal point of everything, in Heaven and on Earth! A rainbow surrounded the emerald throne, and around the throne were twenty-four smaller thrones. Upon these sat twenty-four elders, clothed in white garments, golden crowns on their heads. Before the throne was a sea of glass like crystal. In the center of the sea were four seraphim, full of eyes in front and behind, repeatedly saying, "Holy, Holy, Holy, the Lord God, the Almighty, who was and who is and who is to come!" And standing around the throne he could see a great multitude, from every nation and tribe and people and tongue, palm branches in their hands, crying out with a loud voice, "Salvation to our

God who sits on the throne!" Anatoly knew that's where he'd find his friends!

Brilliant light, God's glory, seemed to come from everywhere, permeating all of the New Jerusalem, as well as illuminating Mount Zion and the Earth below. They hovered briefly above two broad rivers of crystal-clear water that sprang from the throne of God. One river flowed to the east and the other flowed to the south, gushing down Mount Zion to the bottom. On either side of the twin rivers stood majestic trees, their limbs heavy with fruit and leaves to heal the nations.

The Lord brought Anatoly over the high golden throne and down a broad boulevard. Level after level soared above them, without a hint of crowding or disarray, continuing upward as high as the city was wide. Lush forests and magnificent gardens provided pleasant interludes to the perfect architecture.

Anatoly found the buildings surprising. They were private residences. And although no two were alike in design or size, they all fit perfectly into the city's design. He saw many more people, all in magnificent white robes, but it was obvious he would not be meeting them today. Anatoly felt a deep yearning in his heart.

"These here that you see, and those before the throne of God, are His glorified saints," said the Lord. "And what I am soon to show you will be *your future home*."

They soared on up into the air, past level after level of grand houses, until they stopped outside a building with beautiful towers and gleaming windows. Other homes were nearby, and he could see the glowing inhabitants going about their blissful lives, but this building was empty.

"This is your home," the Lord said softly.

Anatoly turned in surprise. "Mine?"

"Yes. I prepared it for you many years ago, right after My ascension the first time I came to Earth. Remember when I said that '*in My Father's house are many mansions. If it were not so I would have told you. I go now to prepare a place for you and if I go and prepare a place for you, I will come again and receive you to Myself, that where I am, there you may be also*'? This is that place, Anatoly. This is where you will come when your time of service is done."

Then Anatoly noticed that the house next to his was also vacant.

The Lord nodded. "Yes. I built that one for someone you will meet shortly."

Sonya! Was He talking about Sonya? Anatoly's heart leapt. What had happened to her? Had she survived? He had to ask. He had to know. "What happened to Sonya, my Lord?"

Yeshua looked at him with deep compassion. "The answer to that must wait, Anatoly."

Then the Lord turned and drew Anatoly up toward the center of the city, where they followed a curving path toward the eastern wall. Homes, gardens, and forests beyond number flashed past. The wide center gate, tiny at first, grew rapidly larger. The walls glowed like immense stained glass windows with twelve bands of translucent material soaring up to the city's apex.

"They look like jewels," Anatoly remarked.

"They are," the Lord confirmed. "Each layer is a single precious jewel. And each gate is a single pearl."

They touched down on the broad highway. Before them stood a huge white gate whose doors stood open. They walked through the high portal and past the mighty angel that guarded it.

Anatoly turned and looked up at the city wall from the outside. The top was lost in the murky atmosphere above the destroyed plain. He walked to the edge and looked down at the incredible destruction below, illuminated by the glory of Almighty God. At first he thought nothing lived on that deathscape. Then he saw movement among the ruins, and he knew it would be the survivors from Petra and elsewhere, waiting for their Lord to repair the damage done by sin.

"Yes, Anatoly," the Lord said. "There is much to do. And now it is time for you to return."

A thought nagged at Anatoly's mind.

The Lord laughed. "Do not be impatient, Anatoly."

Suddenly, Anatoly felt something like a veil surround him, and he could no longer see his Lord. He seemed to be drifting through a translucent, white void. Finally the veil disappeared and he found himself standing next to a crashed and burned-out helicopter.

He looked beyond the destroyed craft and saw Mount Zion as he would see it for the next thousand years. The city of gold shimmered in the eerie light of God's glory. His eyes followed the golden stairs upward as they spiraled around the mountain leading to the summit and to the New Jerusalem where the elect of God from all ages past now resided. And all around him lay the ruins of the earthly Jerusalem.

Then he heard the sound of approaching footsteps, and he edged around the wrecked helicopter. He knew who it was before he could see her face. His pulse hammered, and a sweetness enveloped his heart, so intense that he had no choice but to cry out.

"Sonya!" he shouted. Her mouth flew open in surprise as she looked up and saw him.

"Anatoly!" she cried, and raced toward him.

He wrapped his arms around her, lifted her off the ground, and spun her around. Then he set her down and kissed her over and over. He felt a wetness on his cheek and looked down in surprise. Her tears turned to sobs, and she buried her head in his chest.

"Sonya! What's the matter, my love?"

"Oh, Anatoly. I thought I would never see you again. You have no idea how I've longed for you." The tears of joy continued to stream down her face as she lovingly caressed his neck where the death wound had once been.

He smiled at her and wiped away the tears with his hand. "And you have no idea how hard it was for me, doing what I was doing and all the time worrying about you—wanting to be with you."

She sniffed. "We both had our jobs to do."

"Yes, we did. And we both . . ."

She looked up at him. "What's the matter, sweetheart?"

"You have accepted Yeshua as your Meshiah, haven't you?" he finally realized.

"Yes! Of course I belong to Yeshua. Why else would I be here?!"

Then they smiled as they looked lovingly into each other's

eyes. Through it all, the Lord had been so generous to them. And now they would be together forever.

The two glowing beings slowly ascended the golden wall, watching the desolation drop away below them. Finally they reached the top. But they stood on the edge and continued to look down, as if waiting for something to happen.

"Did you ever imagine such destruction?" the older one asked.

"No," said the other, shaking his head. "Thanks be to God that He will not leave it this way."

"Amen," agreed the elder.

As they watched, black pillars of smoke below them dissipated and the air cleared. The ground appeared to ripple, and the machines of war dissolved and disappeared. Likewise, the tumbled and broken stones of the ancient city of Jerusalem faded away. The surface itself, brown and black only a moment ago, transmuted into a vibrant green, suffused with a brilliant kaleidoscope of reds, blues, and yellows as silky grasses sprang up, accented by wildflowers. In moments all broken edges were gone, replaced by the exquisite harmony of God's garden tapestry. The fouled lakes, rivers, and oceans cleared in an instant, turning to shades of purest blue. In a moment, by divine fiat, it was done.

"The transformation of Earth is finished," the older man commented.

"Indeed it is."

Moses looked up and toward the southeast. "And there is our reminder."

"Yes," Elijah agreed.

Although it was over 150 kilometers away, they could clearly see the heat waves and smoke rising from the burnpits in Edom, containing the corpses of those who had rebelled against God. It would be man's eternal reminder of God's wrath against the enemies of His Son.

Michael, God's archangel, protector of the elect, faced the dense black shape before him. The being was larger than the archangel and roughly humanoid in appearance, but not much different than Michael in form. However, whereas Michael glowed with glory imparted by God, Satan—once called Lucifer, the angel of light—cowered amidst the debris of the ghastly battlefield that was now as dark as his evil heart.

The Kingdom of Earth had become the Kingdom of Almighty God and His Son, Yeshua. The All-Powerful One, the Prince of Darkness, was being evicted from the very land he had ruled for so many millennia. Satan had lost.

It gave Michael great satisfaction to seize his ancient foe and jerk him off the ground. The archangel carried the creature through the air to a point south of where the ancient city of Baghdad had once stood.

There, at Michael's command, the abyss opened its rockbound throat, and captor and captive descended deep into the belly of the Earth.

"By order of the Most High God, you will be held here for a thousand years with the rest of your followers," the archangel commanded, throwing Satan into a dark cavern. "You will remain here until the Most High God assigns you to your place in the Lake of Fire that burns forever and ever."

Then Michael ascended out of the abyss and sealed it shut.

AN IMPORTANT AFTERWORD

One cannot watch the televangelists, peruse the racks of one's local bookstore, or read the morning newspaper and not notice the dates people have set for the end of the world, or not be aware of the surge of Armageddon, Four Horsemen, and other end-of-the-world science-fiction-based movies that have flooded the media as the turn of this century unfolds. All these writers, of course, would have you believe that the world will end in some like manner—if not precisely as they predict—all their information having been gleaned via some sort of special insight or understanding of the most historical of all books, the Bible, both Old and New Testaments, written two to three thousand years ago.

Against this milieu of end-time propaganda, I believe it would be helpful for readers to know certain things about the author of *The Fourth Reich*. I take the entire Bible seriously, genuinely believing that it contains the answers to the end of the world but only if a consistent, face-value understanding of Scriptures is used from Genesis to Revelation. But in addition, I am also an investment banker whose companies have made their mark in securities research, managing billions of dollars for private and institutional investors alike in the stock and bond markets. Having run my own companies successfully for the better part of forty years, I have often stated publicly that I have no desire to besmirch my business reputation by getting caught up in all the end-of-the-world claptrap that is breeding upon the close of this millennium. Nevertheless, I do have something very definite to say about it all.

It is difficult to use one's mind in pursuit of truth by means of exhaustive research practically every day of one's business life and have it then totally shut down on a subject as important a topic as the end of the world, the religious topic of so much current discussion. For this reason, during the past twenty-five years, my hobby has been an in-depth research project on this issue, attempting to harmonize what the Scriptures really do say about the last days by employing the same consistent hermeneutic from beginning to end and using my computer database as a collection point for my research findings. Here is what I have discovered: Both Old and New Testaments parallel one another, both predict a fiery judgment of God at the end of time as we know it. But equally important, both describe much of the end of the age in specific, graphic detail. And both Testaments give consistent testimony to what the world will be like before these last cataclysmic days begin, giving the reader very definite events and signs she or he must watch for as these final days approach. Although a case can be made that the events and signs could occur at almost any time now, nothing in Scripture pegs those times to the end of or the beginning of a new millennium, to say nothing of a specific date sometime in the near future!

Because of my honest attempt to lay out a balanced view of the end times, my scholarly, theological friends insisted that I put my findings into a book, which I did, entitled *The Sign* (of Christ's coming and of the end of the age)—the third updated edition having been published in spring 1999 by Crossway Books in Wheaton, Illinois. I have been pleasantly surprised that since its initial edition in the early 1990s, 150,000 men and women, give or take a few hundred, have read almost six hundred pages of theology on this topic.

However, laymen and laywomen were still being left out— those who go to church regularly but don't have the theological mind-set or training to sort out a book of this size, to say nothing of the fact that six hundred pages of theology does not make the best bedtime reading. Yet because of the proliferation of material in secular and religious media alike, these people too wish to know what the Bible really has to say about the end times and it is for these people that I wrote *The Fourth*

Reich. This novel is obviously built around fictional characters, but it carefully stays true to a very accurate sequence of events, all meticulously given and described in Scripture, including the location of nations and nationalities that will play such an important part in the end-time events when they actually do occur.

Some of what you read will seem very current with the worldwide political events going on today, not because I want to sell books, but because this is what the Scriptures teach. Some of it will sound like futuristic science fiction, and it will be all of that and worse once the biblical signs begin to signal the meltdown of society as we know it presently.

But follow my narrative closely. When you have finished, you will have a good understanding of who the Four Horsemen of the Apocalypse represent, the role of the Antichrist and the mark of the beast, how the last days play out in the form of a one-world government, when the Battle of Armageddon will actually occur, what must happen before this climactic battle can occur, and what the signs will be that God has promised to give before these final days of judgment begin.

—Robert Van Kampen